# FIRE IN

TOM DAVIES, a Welshr
a journalist with the *Wes*
the *Sunday Times*, the
*Observer*, where for three years he was
Pendennis. Now a full-time writer, he has written many successful books, both fiction and non-fiction. He is married and has three children.

*Fire in the Bay* is the second of a quartet of novels covering twentieth-century Wales. The first of the quartet, *One Winter of the Holy Spirit*, is being made into a major feature film. *Black Sunlight*, the last of the sequence, is his widely-acclaimed account of the decline and betrayal of his native mining valleys. He is currently working on the third in the series, *The Dragon's War*, set in Wales in the Second World War.

*Reviews*

## ONE WINTER OF THE HOLY SPIRIT

'The old Welsh blend of poetry and brutality, tenderness and tragedy, flesh and spirit . . . the whole story is permeated by the same sense of raw power.'
MICHAEL SAWARD, *Radio Four*

'Compelling . . . often funny . . . a wonderful ear for the rhythms of Welsh speech.' *Sunday Telegraph*

## BLACK SUNLIGHT

'Captures well the mood of the mining areas during the year-long strike.' *Western Mail*

'Constantly surprises, constantly rewards.'
*Daily Telegraph*

'Heart-stirring and unforgettable.' *She*

*By the same author*

*fiction*

The Electric Harvest
One Winter of The Holy Spirit
Black Sunlight

*travel*

Merlyn the Magician and the Pacific Coast Highway
Stained Glass Hours

*theology*

The Man of Lawlessness

TOM DAVIES

# Fire in the Bay

FONTANA/Collins

First published by William Collins Sons & Co. Ltd, 1989
First issued in Fontana Paperbacks 1990



Printed and bound in Great Britain by
William Collins Sons & Co. Ltd, Glasgow

For my mother and father,
with thanks for all the love – and the city –
they gave me.

# PROLOGUE
# 1899

The Bristol Channel tides were ebbing fast, that Sunday afternoon when it all began. They were the second fastest tides in the world, they said. The paddle steamer the *Taliesin* was pounding towards Cardiff's Pier Head. Twice already that week she had missed the tide. Once she'd had to anchor off Penarth for six hours; the previous Thursday, she'd got her flat bottom stuck on the mud banks of the Cardiff roads. Her passengers had enjoyed a very long, lopsided party until the bar had run out. Sly jokes about the blind skippers and drunken mates of P. & A. Campbell's fleet quickly began to appear in the local newspapers, and letters were starting to come from readers. One recalled the time when one of the steamers had actually run straight into the pier over at Weston-super-Mare, apparently in some spirited effort to knock the thing down rather than moor alongside it. As high tide approached small crowds of gaily dressed females and foppish men would appear at the tops of the docking pontoons, greeting each safe arrival with ironic cheers and waves of their parasols.

The *Taliesin* captain, one Ernest Cartwright, rang down from his bridge and called on the stokers for more speed. Blacker than the hobs of hell the three stokers were, shovelling the coal into those voracious boilers as fast and as hard as they could go. At full speed the steamer could manage an astonishing eighteen knots, the great paddles hammering into the sea and smashing up the water into a huge, drifting wake of white foam over which seagulls glided and drifted. Sometimes those paddles would knock the odd dreaming fish unconscious, sending it floating belly up in the wake.

Just over on the starboard side of the hurrying paddle steamer, the steam packet the *Charlotte*, a twenty-eight-ton wooden craft named after the wife of George III, was wheezing out to sea. Further out again three coal freighters and a grain ship from San Francisco were at anchor out in the Cardiff roads, waiting their turn for a berth in the crowded docks.

Over the road from the Pier Head was the massive Coal Exchange in Mountstuart Square, at the very heart of South Wales's industrial revolution. Even though still waiting for its seventh birthday this grim Victorian heap already looked stately and old beyond its years. Within its walls a ceaseless round of shipowners, brokers, agents and speculators would spend their working hours building up Cardiff as the great coal metropolis of the time. Here, docksmen like Tatem, Cory, Reardon Smith, Radcliffe, Nicholl and Seager pursued the making of wealth with a mercantile ardour, amassing considerable fortunes by renting out their ships to carry anything from timber to coal, bricks and iron, cement and grain to far-flung corners of the world. But today, a Sunday, the great Exchange was still and quiet.

Inside the Exchange plain matting covered the Floor, a huge, echoey area smelling of stale port and wood polish, where the principals of firms wearing top hats and tail coats mixed with the jobbers and their associates in their pinstripe trousers, spats and bowler hats. The Floor was surrounded by a high balcony festooned with advertisements for such as Avonside Locomotives, Metropolitan Life Assurance and the Taff Vale Docks Railway. The insides of the telephone kiosks were covered with green baize.

A stride or two took the visitor to the beginning of Bute Street, the long, fashionable spine of Tiger Bay itself. Elegant and gracious houses stood shoulder to shoulder, marking out the length of the Bay, an area of some five square miles, bounded on the one side by a railway line and the River Taff. The other side was fenced in by the Bristol Channel, the Pier Head Wall and the thrumming acres of the docks themselves.

This afternoon a couple of hundred people were basking in the sunshine, listening to the German musicians playing military airs on a bandstand in fashionable Loudoun Square, about halfway up Bute Street. Blue-uniformed nannies pushed around perambulators with foaming lace hoods, and the odd hansom cab went gliding past. Men in top hats and with silver-topped canes were chatting on a corner as the bright brassy notes went bounding down the pavements.

A horse snorted and pawed at the cobblestones in the far

corner of the square as Mr Parsons, the salt and vinegar man, was busy slicing a corner off a block of salt on his cart. Next to the salt were three brown earthenware jars brimming with the finest vinegar. Mr Parsons's hands were as rough and white as pumice, the side of his index finger stiff with grey callouses.

In the docks themselves thin slivers of mist drifted across the still waters of the Roath Basin where men were busy unloading sacks of grain from the windjammer *The Solomon*. The sacks came flying up out of the holds like departing souls before being winched down onto the quay. Two men were working amidst the crisscrossing rigging on the triple crucifix shapes of the yardarms and a piglet was tethered to the foremast where it snuffled and slept on a small pile of hay in a wooden box. The windjammer creaked and groaned on its moorings, like a very old man unable to believe that he really did have to get out of bed yet again. Her reflected outline stretched out on the dock water . . . ghostly and shimmering in the falling afternoon sun.

Just nearby an Irish butty gang, those imported powerhouses of sweat and muscle, was busy digging out Alexandra Dock to cope with the increasing demands of a coal boom. With flying globs of snot and ceaselessly driving muscles of iron they worked around the clock, every day of the week. First driven here by the Irish potato famine they had sailed here for sixpence a head or even free as ballast. Captains had jammed them in the holds – saving them the trouble of loading up with lime or shingle – and often they would drop them off at nearby beaches. Half-dead from starvation and illness, the migrants made their way to Newtown, a small groaning slum – addicted to Catholicism and Guinness – on the other side of Bute Street and just before the start of the city itself.

Mrs Betty Driscoll stood at her door in Newtown, all sad black eyes and potato muscles as she looked out on the brown and green froth which regularly spilled out of the sewers and over the streets, particularly when the tide was high. Sometimes this froth came up out of the drains slowly, like pus seeping out of an infected cyst, and sometimes it poured out very fast, as if bursting a hole in a high dam, the bubbling waters swirling around the streets.

Mrs Driscoll wiped her large, torn hands on her pinafore

and looked around to see if Dr Cholera was coming down past these mean terraces again. He would come walking, she had been told, with a small spade of ashes to shovel into the mouths of her little ones. She could actually feel her mind going black with the worry of it all, sprinkling her bairns with holy water every morning and night, looking up to see the sun but finding it raining all the while.

So the tide was coming in again and she felt the stones in her belly as she thought of the bothies and cairns of County Cork where starvation danced outside their doors and the tattie fields were stunted and green, all spread out at her feet in the silvery, dripping light of Famine's morning.

At the furthest end of the street the foul-smelling sewage spilled over into the Glamorganshire Ship Canal where it mingled with warm water and other toxic wastes from the nearby ironworks. This mixture created a massive, gaseous smell which returned to attack the beleaguered inhabitants of Newtown. Sometimes this cloud of gas took fire on the surface of the canal and stopped the passing barges, but today it was a long, straight poem of sunshine burnishing water where, as far as the eye could see, barrel-chested, sweating horses were pulling barges piled high with pig-iron and coal. Their very ropes had cut deep teeth into the sides of the stone tunnel and every so often there were brick ramps just below the water line to help the horses get out after they had fallen in. Just below a sign warning against the 'throwing of live or dead animals into the canal or on the company's land' there was a sunken barge in which sticklebacks swam.

The railway bridge at the end of Bute Street marked the end of the Bay and the beginning of the city itself with its huge, confident department stores, pokey Brains pubs and spritely churches. Pigeons fluttered and shuffled in the wooden eaves of the shopping arcades and, just across the road, was the nation's spiritual centre, the rugby stadium of Cardiff Arms Park, deserted and silent today with nothing but old newspapers and the odd, sodden programme scattered over its rising terraces.

But the building which dominated the city sky-line and drew all eyes was Cardiff Castle, an improbable fairyland creation of spikey black Gothic towers, a pencil-shaped clock tower and high stone walls with arrow-slits. Mallards moved around on the reed-choked moat while, inside the walls themselves, peacocks bleated on the hissing lawns around a ruined keep. Every room was a strange creation of symbols: dragons, griffins and other fabulous creatures. Some of the bedroom walls had been painted with gold leaf while one of the huge fireplaces was carved from a single solid block of stone.

This was the home of John Patrick Crichton Stuart, the third Marquess of Bute. Thanks to the shrewd purchase of coal-rich land by the Bute family which was now beginning to spew forth coal, he was already the wealthiest man in the world.

Bute had spent most of his great fortune on the reconstruction of the castle, given long ago to his family as a wedding present. Together with the fashionable medievalist and architect, William Burges – and with not a little help from opium – they had created a modern Camelot out of a pile of damp Norman rubble. They had built towers where there were none, created Islamic and Arab rooms, even installing central heating in the legs of the tables. They had afforested the outside of the castle with vines to make wines, even growing vines on the meal tables so that Milady could pick herself a fresh grape at the end of dinner. They had made smoking rooms out of Italian marble and built a fairy-tale nursery. They had been planning to build a huge Wagnerian chapel on the mound of the keep but then Burges had went and died – damn him. On the eve of a new century's dawning he had gone and wasted away in a cloud of opium, leaving his master with terminal *ennui*.

There had been no fun for Bute after Burges had gone – no fine parties or pissing drunkenly over the battlements. Life had become a long endurance for this king without a kingdom; a ruler with nothing to rule, impotent and racked with pain. The pain was visible in his fine porcelain features, in the tight constrictions of his throat and the hollow, anaemic cheekbones which stiffened as he breathed.

His wife, tired of the damp, draughty castle and even more tired of the vast amounts of money that had been squandered on it, now spent almost all her time on their Scottish estates – she could not stand the Welsh – or in London, for the season. Bute waited for the end of each season with increasing gloom for then his bitch queen would return, to complain yet again about the servants or the damp in her bedroom or the deafening noise of that ghastly clock.

But it was rarely for long, thank God. Within days she was thinking up some excuse to get back to Scotland to shoot grouse, or foist herself on some house party or other in the shires where she could bore *them* to distraction with her daft wig that rarely sat properly on her empty head. He wondered why she ever bothered to come back at all unless it was to keep a weather eye on his will and a pampered future in some gilded and expensive hotel in Deauville or Biarritz. He had been to Biarritz once and hated it. *All* the women there seemed to be wearing ill-fitting wigs and paste jewels.

Well, she would be reading his will perhaps even sooner than she had anticipated. He was suffering – and had been for three months now – from prolonged and mysterious bouts of bleeding from the genitals. Doctors had been called in from Paris and London but they could not even diagnose the complaint, let alone come up with a cure. Humiliatingly he had to wear women's pads to soak up the blood and often they weren't enough to stop him soiling his clothes.

The bleeding stopped and started for no apparent reason. He now could not even put on decent clothes and take his dogs for a walk around the castle grounds without it starting again. Unable to carry on with the excruciating pain of it all, he would suffer the indignity of getting two of his servants to carry him back to his bedroom where he lay on his bed cursing everyone and everything.

Dying – or so he thought – from his mysterious complaint, Bute spent the remainder of his days in the isolation of his rooms, refusing to see even his dock managers, dressed only in antique nightclothes, brooding about what bastards the Welsh were or else studying yet again Burges's plans for that wonderful chapel. The great pity, he now thought, was that they had never managed to begin on that chapel. It would have made an ideal burial place for him, particularly as his wife would never have been seen alive in it, let alone dead. Now his body would undoubtedly have to be sent back to Scotland and his heart cut out and sent to the family crypt in Jerusalem – just as had happened to his father, and just as his wife had once expressed a wish to share. This was the greatest terror for him, for he just could not face the thought of having to spend an eternity with any part of him anywhere near that old bag.

The castle, then, became a home of melancholy and pain, smitten at its heart and with the distress stretching out even to the servants' quarters.

But on this Sunday the atmosphere suddenly changed when a group of the strangest visitors came to the drawbridge. Everyone in the castle had heard their Gregorian chanting from as far as three streets away until they finally came down alongside the moat, still chanting and swaying together as they shouldered some sort of funeral bier. The leading monk was cowled and holding a tall thin cross fashioned out of metal. It was this he used to knock on the castle door with three sharp cracks. Bute, still in his antique nightclothes, rushed down to meet them, barely able to conceal his excitement as the drawbridge was raised. He ran out, greeting and hugging each of them warmly.

A menu, written in Bute's handwriting, had come down ordering a huge and elaborate dinner. Widespread panic ensued. He had demanded oysters and duck pâté, steak and kidney pudding, cold turkey and ices. He also wanted the best claret and kümmel. And for six people! The cook had gone into a straight swoon as soon as she read it but now everyone had been called into the kitchen – even the parlour staff helped to prepare the meal.

Charles Bethell was a butler with clear demarcation lines in his own mind about his work. He was very angry indeed to find himself cutting up the beef for the steak and kidney pie. And, like everyone else, he had his own ideas about who the visitors could be and why they were there. The lord was going to give the castle to those monks, he explained. That's what he was doing. He would do anything to keep it out of the hands of his wife.

But just where oh where had these monks come from? wailed the cook. They were some sort of foul foreigners weren't they? the parlourmaid suggested. Language! cried the butler. But the butler did later confide in the cook that one of them smelled as if he had been sleeping in cow-sty. And filthy! He had never seen such filth.

Even as he waited on the high table in the banqueting hall that evening – with his eyes carefully lowered and his ears stretched wide open – Bethell still could not even guess at what all the merriment was about. Bute, dressed in his proper evening clothes, was the very picture of expansive geniality, clapping his hands and calling for more and more claret for his guests, insisting that their goblets be topped up even when they had drunk but an inch from them.

What Bethell really did not understand was why Bute was treating these holy ruffians with such deference. He had never seen such unlikely guests at the dinner table before. Neither had he seen the fastidious lord treat anyone with such respect. If they really were monks why then did they drink so much? And, unless his eyes really were deceiving him, one of these so-called monks had just slipped one of the goblets inside the pocket of his habit.

As they lit their kümmel Bute even made a short speech, cryptic in the extreme and explaining little. He said that their task had been long and difficult but worthwhile in the end. Most worthwhile. Again and again he had despaired of any success but now it seemed that his search for wandering fires was over. The great and holy secret was now his. He would remain forever in their debt while their payment would be made, as agreed all those years ago, as soon as he could organize it through the banks. Bethell, at the keyhole, wondered what it could all be about.

The great castle clock struck nine sending its loud doleful booms over a city preparing for sleep. Way out on the horizon the glow of the East Moors steelworks was beginning to turn the bottom of the night pink. Moths danced in the phosphorescent maze of lights and broken-necked cranes surrounding the moored ships.

The hurrying waters of the River Taff caught the moonlight, making sparkling minnows of light that dashed and played together, sometimes all joining in a long golden tongue which seemed to be stretching out and actually licking the coal-dust waters until they too vanished, just like the dancing minnows, and there was just this cold loneliness of a river that had already begun to die from the spreading pollution of black coal.

Green orbs of lamplight hung in the air on the Taff Bridge, their pale hissing glows neutralizing the white colour of the bridge itself. Occasionally the bright silvery glow of a carriage lamp passed through the green orbs, almost as if trying to slice them in half.

The great castle stood black and silent, brooding over the city's panoply of shadow and light. Many of the monks were deep in drunken comas and sprawled over the floor and table of the banqueting hall. Just one light was on in the window of the clock tower which, briefly, framed the silhouette of a man holding something up into the air. As he moved away there was a faint distant scream, a cry of pain perhaps – or maybe it was surrender.

Just a mile from where the Taff actually emptied itself into the sea the tide was beginning to flow, its liberating waters coming to the aid of the *Taliesin* paddle steamer which, yet again, had failed to make it to the Pier Head and had just sat, as bright as a swarm of fireflies, waiting for the tide. The passengers, all dressed in their summer clothes, were cold and irritable. To a man they declared that they would never, *ever*, sail on one of P. & A. Campbell's paddle steamers again.

Down in the streets of the Bay all was as safe as backyard lanes as strolling people took the night air, abandoning themselves to the tropical luxury of the evening. Ladies with bustles the size of small camel humps chatted together as they walked through Loudoun Square and, over on the docks themselves, nothing moved except the wind sighing past the crowds of moored ships, stirring only the telegraph wires as it sang songs of lost nights of innocence.

# PART ONE

The tendency of people in the later stages of civilization to gather into towns is an old story. Horace had seen in Rome what we are now witnessing – the fields deserted, the people crowding into cities. He noted the growing degeneracy. He foretold the inevitable consequences.

J. A. FROUDE, *Oceana*, 1886

# CHAPTER ONE
# 1918

Two ragamuffins were skylarking about on the corner of the Custom House Hotel near the top of Bute Street, taking it in turns to taunt the dozen or so prostitutes who were standing about waiting for business. One might joggle his little finger around in the air obscenely or shout rude remarks about how his brother had lost his horse and cart inside one of them the other night, but the girls took no notice. It was all but a small part of the harassment that they were more than used to in their line of work.

Nevertheless, one of the girls, Sophie James, was starting to get highly vexed by the kids' taunts. Soon she was threatening to come over there and box their ears. At this one of the ragamuffins actually pulled his trousers down and waved his little winkle at her. 'I'll chop that thing off with some scissors if you don't watch it,' Sophie snapped.

She turned her back on them finally and glared up the crowded Bute Street with an impressive snort of her nostrils. It was a damp, grey day, when the clouds seemed unable to decide if they were going to rain. Sophie was still fairly new to this game and had not yet learned the art of stony indifference that came so naturally to the other girls. It hurt her feelings to be taunted like that – no matter who or how old they were. When her feelings were hurt, she rarely just cried like normal people. All she ever wanted to do then was eat and eat, with her whole belly crying out for sausage and chips or a small mountain of toad-in-the-hole. When she was happy she did not eat a morsel for days.

Sophie was a tall, fine-boned half-caste with light brown skin and dark, silky hair. In the lightness of her skin she might have been taken for a Welsh girl with a suntan but, in fact, she was mostly of the olive-skinned Somalis and proud of it, with endless legs and a figure which went in and out in all the right places – no matter how much toad-in-the-hole she ate. A mongrel by race and a mongrel by nature she was nevertheless the most strikingly different of the working girls who, themselves, openly acknowledged that she was the pick of the bunch. They were always glad when she was out of the way first, even if her business sense owed little to accepted Coal Exchange practice. They had lost count of the number of times she had done business with some shonny boy from the valleys and *then* discovered that he had no money. Fleas in a fit came more organized than our Sophie, but she was tough and could throw a mean right hook when she was so disposed.

The rest of the girls wheeling around that damp and cheerless afternoon were as varied a collection as you might find in any dockland port. A few wore gaudy floral dresses with big hats – normal, house-proud girls, always keen to clean the brasses. More than a few were impeccably grubby Woodbiners with fleabag hair and rock-bottom prices. Some, like Irish Joan and Big Tit Lu, were simply outrageous, though perhaps none was quite so outrageous as Marie the Stump, so called because she only had one leg but still, mystifyingly, managed to pick up more customers than most.

Their one real speciality was picturesque Cardiff taunts, teasing one another with lines like 'You look as rough as a robber's dog' or 'You've got a face about as beautiful as a ripped dap.'

Sophie began walking up Bute Street a little way, her whole belly crying out for something to eat. She looked at the men's eyes, trying to pick up that tiny flash of contact which told her that they were interested. But they all averted their gaze or else jerked their heads away when they did catch her look. All this damp must have shrivelled up their plonkers, she thought gloomily. Business, for some reason, was always best in the bright sunshine or when it was freezing cold. As soon as the rain came all the girls might just as well have forgotten it and delivered newspapers or sold fish. She noticed that Spanish Mary already seemed to be doing well, brewing home-made beer and selling it from her doorstep in sauce bottles for a penny a pint. Perhaps she should try something like that. Her mouth gave a bored yawn.

And still the crowds kept coming towards her – the mother with a baby in a shawl, the occasional woman off to the city to do her shopping, but mostly blackened coal trimmers, deal runners, ballast workers, deck hands, dry-dock workers – all representing just about every nationality, and seemingly not one of them in need of a good one. She was still young enough in the ways of the street to marvel at the strange and exotic shapes and colours of some of them – even if, again unlike the other girls, she was still quite fussy about who she went with. Those Chinese bastards seemed to have learned some knack for keeping going for hours. Then there were the Irish, so guilt-ridden by the confessional it took them an hour to get a stand, unless they were blind drunk and then they might just as well be doing it with a jam jar full of old liver. Nothing could persuade her to go with one of those little smiling Indians – or one of those Mission Hall workers who came nosing around at least twice a week, pretending they were interested in the girls' welfare but clearly with something else altogether on their minds. She could always see what was in a man's mind just by looking at his eyes. Everything about a man was revealed by that bit between and around his eyes.

Her real problem was that she did not think much of her job and even less of the men who came to her with money in one hand and their bloated worms in the other. Her main disadvantage in her profession was her wicked sense of humour. What she really liked to do was disgust the men after they had dropped their load, complain that her piles had been troubling her lately or that her last abortion had ripped her insides apart and she couldn't even piss properly any more.

Then she sat back, with her legs apart and a broad smile on her face, as she scratched herself vigorously and watched them desperately doing up their pants and running home to their fat, sexless wives, holding them tight and gratefully and saying, well, she may not be a wondrous sex machine but at least she does not have piles and can piss properly.

Two mounted policemen clattered past and waved at her. Those bastards! Nothing would persuade her to go with a policeman either, even though she could tell by their leers that she could easily charge double. The police were always watching the girls, allowing them to work unmolested just inside the Bay but never letting them go into the city itself. You'd think they all had smallpox rather than the odd touch of venereal disease. The girls had been told, in no uncertain terms, that Bute Street Bridge was as far as they could ever operate – if they were ever caught working beyond it then it was the lock-up. But it wasn't as bad as all that. At least here they were also handily close to the waterfront itself, and there was always the chance of the great bonus of picking up a seaman with pockets full of a year's money and little else to spend it on. The trick was not to be around for a few days after they had sobered up.

Sophie was here just to save a little bit of money. As she told the girls, she fully intended to give up the game as soon as she could. They nodded sagely. She yearned for a fine house and at least ten children – even if they came through ten different fathers. The trouble was that when she did have a bit of money, she was the softest touch in the land. She'd lend anyone anything and almost always forget about it. Many of the other girls had to think quite hard about money since most of them had illegitimate children to support. There were many reasons why they were on the game. At the end of the 'war to end all wars' a lot of them had just been thrown out of their old jobs – as munition workers, toymakers, shop assistants or factory girls. But as many of them, like her friend Betty, were simply on the run from drunk or violent husbands. None of the girls had first stood on a street corner by choice. It had been forced on them by some pig man. She had heard talk that the women were going to set up a Society for Distressed Wives to protect them against bad husbands but it was probably just talk. Bay talk.

With her belly still rumbling she walked down past a few grilled shebeens, the Chinese laundry and an organ-grinder with a skinny monkey that looked even more in need of a good meal than she did.

She stopped near St Mark's Church, which was built in the traditional grey Anglican style – lots of wasted space and soaring stained-glass windows – with iron railings all around it and a notice board listing the times of the services. A group of men was busy unloading furniture from a huge horse-drawn van. She absorbed this small scene of huffing and pulling, trying to work out who was what. It must be the new vicar moving in – the demands of the Bay on the last one had literally worn him away – so that woman in the silly little hat must be the luckless new wife in the parish. Sophie felt sorry for her, standing there fussing about her small pedal organ. From time to time she would give anxious glances at the throngs moving up and down the street, as if she was afraid of them. Two young children stood just near the manse door doing nothing in particular; occasionally the lady in the hat would snap at them.

An old man, stooped and nodding with age, came to add his voice to the activity as the furniture men laboured with the longest settee that Sophie had ever seen. She recognized the old man as the church verger, Harold Finch, a bilious little buggar known to all as 'Halfway Harry' on account of his legendary ability to work out deals and compromises to satisfy the arguments of a parish which was almost always on a constant war footing. He was followed out of the house by a tall figure in black. The dog collar on top of the white shirt dripping with sweat told Sophie that he must be the new vicar. And a real man he looked too – she saw, with slight surprise – with a broad, muscled back and a simply huge nose, full of character, and with dark hair going grey at the edges. But, if anything, he was too hairy for her taste. She had always hated hair on the backs of men's hands but she did enjoy the way he was telling the furniture men what to do; controlling the moves with a calm authority that was lost to his wife, now just standing in the background near the children.

As Halfway Harry was struggling with an aspidistra Sophie noticed the two ragamuffins who had been taunting her earlier in the afternoon. They were standing on the corner of the pavement, hands in pockets and just looking. Sophie saw that they had their eyes on a small sewing bag which had unaccountably been left on its own just next to the gutter. Even before the ragamuffins made their move she knew what they were going to do. The clout she landed on the back of one of the urchins' heads was delicious and even more so was the second, but still the little footpad refused to let go of the bag. They were still struggling over it when the vicar came motoring into the fray, grabbing hold of the boy in both arms and lifting him gently into the air where he kicked and flailed about like a landed fish.

'You shouldn't leave your things about like that,' said Sophie, triumphantly holding the bag up in her hand.

'It's just a bag with some old rubbish in it,' the vicar replied as he lowered the still-squirming boy to the ground.

'This is the rubbish,' said Sophie, aiming another clout at the boy. They both watched as he scampered away, his eyes full of tears.

'They're just boys,' said the vicar. His smile broke up his face into a fretwork of appealing lines. He did indeed have a strong, senatorial nose, but had tiny eyes which clearly enjoyed jokes. He also spoke in a rich Welsh accent which sounded almost comic to Sophie's ears. 'I've never locked anything up in my life. If they want it that badly they can have it. The world's just here to pillage after all – particularly if you are a small boy. My name's Nathan. Nathan Thomas.'

'I'm Sophie, Sophie James,' she stammered, her normal aplomb clearly shaken by the stranger.

'I'm very pleased to meet you, Sophie. I'm the new vicar of this –' he looked around him with his smile broadening, '– this lovely new parish of mine.'

'There's nothing lovely about this dump,' said Sophie.

He raised an eyebrow, his smile hardly wavering. He was as tall as her and gave off a really nice burst of warmth. But what was that look around his eyes? 'Come and see us again sometime after we've settled in.'

'Oh, I'm not on your side, you know,' said Sophie, retreating.

He gave a slight shake of his head. 'That doesn't matter. I prefer people who are not on my side. It's the Christians who get me down.'

What kind of vicar was this then? And first names too! Next there'll be vicars who don't believe in God or come demanding half-price rates from the girls. The wife and Halfway Harry were now walking down the pavement towards her. She'd better be gone quick. She'd had a few run-ins with old Halfway before. 'Yes. Well, I'll best be getting along now.' And just as Halfway Harry was asking him if everything was all right, she had gone.

All the fuss had left Sophie feeling quite hungry. She fortified herself with a double egg and chips in the Port Said Café, all the time wondering about the new vicar; of the curious innocence of his words and that enormous conk of his. She wondered if he had any idea at all of what he had to contend with in the area. He had seemed so strong and positive, even if slightly odd for a vicar. She reached for the sauce bottle. People always had such silly ideas about this area, forever saying how wonderful it was but, as far as she was concerned, the place had gone straight to the dogs. She paid up and, a shade reluctantly, went back to her patch.

After a half-hearted offer from a man pushing a handcart piled high with cabbages – she could not quite work out if he was offering to pay her in cabbages – she had more or less despaired of making any money, and had decided to go off for a quiet drink when a man came walking down the pavement towards her. He too was the colour of a coffee bean but even in the darkness she would have recognized that walk and the white silk scarf he always loved to wear. Letting out a great Red Indian whoop she ran towards him with her arms outstretched. 'Rashed, where've you been?' she shouted. 'I thought you were drowned at sea.'

It was Rashed Ali, a renegade Moslem who worked as a master butcher on one of the P. & O. liners sailing out of London. She had not seen him for all of six months and that was just six months too long to wait for the man you loved.

Rashed had a great gift among men. He was always fun to be with even if, when he was in the mood, he would go on about meat all the time. He could actually get quite carried away talking about a leg of pork or what to look for on a side of beef. They had even lived together for a while once – and a heavenly few weeks it had been too until he had been pressured by his brothers in the Mosque to leave her and go away to sea again. Moslems took a very strict line on one of them going out with a lady of the night. But she knew what made Rashed happy and it wasn't Allah either. She knew what kept him coming back to her. Six months was a long time to be at sea surrounded by nothing but those little bum-boys who depressed him so much.

They grabbed one another and did a little mad dance around the pavement, smothering one another's faces with wet kisses. The other girls moved away huffily. They hated one of their own having any sort of romance because it reminded them so vividly of the empty core in their own lives. Even in all the bouncing about she could tell just by the feel of his body that it had indeed been a long time for him too. But she had always insisted that they had a little trip somewhere first; that he did not act like all the others.

Almost without thinking about it – and certainly without discussing it – they both leaped on the next electric tram which took them down Bute Street to the Pier Head. There they joined the queue for the two-hour night cruise on the paddle steamer *Glen Usk*, first crushing down into the bar for some giddy gins as he told her all about his last trip; of how he had actually missed the ship in Aden, flogged half the ship's meat in Mombasa, got into a knife fight in Cape Town – wonderfully funny stories told in his unsmiling deadpan way about all those wonderfully exotic places she so longed to see for herself one day.

Predictably, perhaps, they never once discussed her work. Neither did she ever offer any information on that point. But it was an open secret between them, and if she ever said something that alluded to her profession he would go strangely and worryingly silent for a bit.

Later, and slightly tipsy, they both stood in the windy darkness on the aft deck with his coat draped over her shoulders. It had always been a favourite trip of theirs and she loved to stand in silence, watching the sea sliding beneath the night as those huge paddles pounded around and around, dreaming dreams of foreign lands.

Rashed produced a small bottle of rum from his pockets – perhaps that's what she had felt when they were dancing around – and, somewhere between the Flat Holm and Steep Holm, she could feel the whole of her being glowing with happiness as her heart chimed pleasantly in tune with the night, the sea and him.

A long melancholy foghorn droned through the night as the paddle steamer berthed at the Pier Head, disgorging its small pile of largely drunk, singing passengers. Then the two of them could not get home fast enough, almost ripping one another's clothes off as soon as they got in through the door of her small flat.

There was none of that genteel nonsense about making love with Sophie. When she was with someone she was fond of she dived straight into it – and hammered away at it – as if she had only just invented it half an hour earlier. Even as Rashed lost himself between her thighs she could never understand why it was so good with him; why he seemed to make every part of her soar and sing. One thing she did understand: her work was going to be doubly hard after he had gone. Perhaps, one day, she could get Rashed to marry her . . . perhaps . . . but even ladies of the night can dream, can't they?

# CHAPTER TWO

An incredible variety of traffic flowed ceaselessly up and down Bute Street both night and day; from electric tramcars to horse-drawn trolleys; from hansom cabs to clattering coal carts; from handcarts to bone-shaking bicycles. The passengers were as diverse as the traffic that bore them, a huge, swirling stream of the rich and the poor, representing almost every conceivable profession. Chinese laundrymen in pigtails jostled with ship-brokers in their toppers; meths-soaked derelicts shuffling in the hopeful search of a night in the Spike passed portly businessmen with gold fob watches on their waistcoats and polished round bowlers, hurrying to do business deals. But the broad rump of all this movement was the endless stream of workmen in knotted scarves and with flat caps sitting squarely and defiantly on their heads.

Each morning, at around nine o'clock, this traffic slackened into a desultory dribble; those who were doing it had got there and those who had finished doing it had gone home to bed. Around about this time, over on the other side of the road, the Treorchy train would go puffing down the Taff Vale Railway to its Bute Street terminus, overtaking the horses labouring with their great beer drays piled high with barrels of Brain's bitter. If the winds were right you could usually pick up the distinctive, hoppy smell of the beer long before you could hear the steady and musical clip-clop of metal horseshoes striking the cobbles.

But small clumps of unemployed men always hung around on odd corners, no matter what time of day it was, as stationary as fish swimming against the stream. There was a distinctive line of black grease daubed by their dirty shoulder pads as they leaned against the walls. They were very strange people were these unemployed, without intelligence or morals in the current argot, highly inconvenient people who simply did not exist.

The war to end all wars had meant the death of seven

million men, with the face of the world altered profoundly and for ever. David Lloyd George's 'land fit for heroes' had become a new wasteland of uprooted hopes and mutual distrust; the war which had promised everything had, in the end, handed over little more than a bucket of broken glass. And Wales had escaped none of the ravages of this long fury of sustained murder. Barely a street escaped the grief and tears of the newly-widowed; barely a club did not contain a father whose dreams had fully and finally collapsed.

There had been no singing when so many of the Welsh Regiment and South Wales Borderers had been mown down into the mud by blazing sheets of machine gun fire in Mametz Wood. A howl of grief had gone right through Wales and, with so many dead, it was not a lot of fun being alive either.

In the parlour of St Mark's manse a grandfather clock was whirring and rumbling like an outbreak of wind and indigestion after a hard night on that Hancock's beer. Brass figurines gathered in glittering assembly on the mantelpiece, embroidered sayings from the Bible spoke out from the walls.

In his favourite and well-worn armchair the Rev. Nathan Thomas was stretched out as stiff as an old piece of toast, his legs splayed out and the balls of his feet resting on the carpet as he read the sports pages of the *Western Mail*. Peerless Jim Driscoll – the one-time world boxing champion from nearby Newtown and clearly in need of a bob or two now – was planning a comeback fight from Charles Ledoux, the French Assassin, in the National Sporting Club in London.

It was all very sad, Nathan decided, when a man did not know when to fight and when to retire. The great glories of a man's body fade all too soon. All too quickly a woman's beauty turns into a quagmire of wrinkles. Now Driscoll, arguably the greatest and certainly the most scientific boxer the world had known was trying to recapture his former triumphs. He had been having trouble with an ulcerated stomach and was giving away eleven years to the Frenchman. Ach, it was a shame, such a crying shame.

Not that Nathan's strength showed much sign of disappearing in this, his mid-thirties. Just like his Master – at the same age – he felt at the very peak of his power and strength. You could see that strength in his arms, legs and broad, muscled neck. He felt strong in his very soul too, sent to this, the most difficult incumbency in the land because the Archbishop of

Wales himself had decided that he was the only man for the job. People looked up to him immediately – and not just because he was a tall man with an oversized nose. There was a triumphant shout of virility in his body, often curiously at odds with the poetic emblems of his mind.

He heard the quarrelling sounds of his two boys being readied for their first day at school. 'I hope you two don't think you're going anywhere without giving your dad a kiss,' he bellowed over his lowered newspaper. 'No one gets out of this house without giving me a kiss.'

The two boys, David and Stephen, came into the room. As scrubbed and glowing as a pair of newly-peeled onions they were too, with new baggy flannel trousers just reaching down to their scuffed and grazed knees. Nathan peered at the two of them gravely. He could never quite look at these two little ankle-biters of his without his heart lurching a little.

'So, then, it's a new school and a new time in your lives. We've left the West Wales countryside now and you must remember that this school is going to be very different, very new.'

'Come on, Dad,' interrupted Stephen, the eldest by a year. 'We're going to be late.'

'What you must remember, on this your first day, is that every eye will be on you. You will be judged by the way you act on your first day and you will always be thought of by the way you behave today.'

'D-a-a-d!'

'So I want you to conduct yourselves with the dignity of this great Thomas family,' Nathan continued undeterred, putting his palms together and steepling his fingers. 'I want you to promise me that you will be good and kind. That's all anyone will ever expect from you and, if you can do that, you will be doing very well indeed. Right. So what do you do now?'

He eyed the two of them as Stephen shuffled forward for the mandatory kiss which, at the ripe age of eight, was becoming more and more difficult to give. It was somehow unmanly, but he gave it nonetheless – on the cheek. David, the seven-year-old, did not move.

'What about you then?' Nathan asked David.

'I'm sorry but my lips have run out of kisses,' David said, deadpan.

'What's all this? Are you saying that your lips are on strike or what? You're not getting out of here without a kiss and that's the end to it. So where's this kiss?'

'They've gone, Dad. I lost them in the park. There was all that wet grass and I just lost them. In the grass.'

'Well, you'd better find them again, hadn't you? And be pretty damned quick about it.'

His wife, Elizabeth, came bustling in, untying her apron then hitting the sides of her head with the hams of her hands. 'Come on, you two. You're going to be late.'

'They can't go,' said Nathan, still staring, unsmiling, at David.

'What do you mean they can't go? It's their first day at school. They're going to be late.'

'They know the rules as well as anyone,' Nathan explained. 'Either I get a proper kiss or they're staying right there. David is saying he can't give me a kiss because he's gone and lost them in the grass.'

'Go on. Give your father a kiss.'

David stuck to his guns. 'How can you give something that's been lost?' he asked.

It was a good, reasonable question and the family pondered on it for a few silent seconds.

'How about –' suggested Nathan '– how about you going up to your bedroom, having a look around and seeing if you can find a spare one that you left lying about?'

Now Elizabeth and Stephen were fidgeting about anxiously as David, clearly keen to continue the pantomime, left the parlour and went upstairs. He seemed to have been gone for ages when his thin voice could be heard shouting down the stairs. 'I've found an old one. It's a bit damp but will that do?'

'That'll do for now, then,' Nathan bellowed back, whereupon David returned and, chortling like a drain, climbed onto his father's lap and gave him not an old damp one but three, extremely nice, sloppy ones.

It wasn't quite so difficult getting a kiss out of his wife. She looked at him with her blue eyes wide open, as if asking if they really had a mental case on their hands. 'He's far worse than you,' she said rumpling Nathan's hair. 'One day I can just see the two of you in the looney bin together.'

Nathan went to the door to see the three of them off, still waving as they turned the corner. He was so worried about his wife these days, taking her to the very heart of his prayers. He couldn't remember the last time she had laughed – certainly not since they had come here – and when he had first met her she was laughing all the time. He had found the dockland bewildering enough, but after the ordered and rural calm of an incumbency in Haverfordwest she had taken to this place very badly indeed. It was the strange and alien imagery of the street that she found so hard to come to terms with, he supposed – the Moslems slaughtering their animals on the pavement; the overpowering and strange-smelling mysteries of the Chinese block; the old-timers driven mad by the trenches of the world war, who depressed her to the point of despair.

From the very first moment he had met his wife he had loved only her. He just so enjoyed their conversations, and very little had given him so much pleasure as their long chats together, in front of the hearth, when he would often give his more fanciful notions a good run in the backyard of her commonsense. In a way it was all part of one long conversation which was going to last for the rest of their lives.

But, for the first time in their nine-year-old marriage, he was finding that they were losing their great sense of intimacy and certainly those long exploratory chats were becoming a thing of the past. What is it? What's the matter?

'Oh I just miss the countryside if I'm to be honest. I remember you once spoke of the countryside as a place of mystical certainty and I didn't know what you meant. But I do understand it now. You always knew where you were in the countryside – there was always this continuity which, somehow, supported you. We always did things in a certain way – we washed our faces in the dew in the spring; we sang in the harvest; we fed the chickens; we chaffed the corn.

'Seasons followed one another and we stuck to the old heroes, old families and old customs. Everything was done the way it was done before and I see now that all that continuity made me remarkably happy. All those old customs made us warm. You could walk into almost any house and know exactly what welcome you would get.

'Here, in this place, you don't know anything at all, can hardly even guess what the next minute will bring. It's all clash and bother with strange people wandering into the house and just wandering out again. They don't even say anything, some of them. Just walk in, sit down, drink tea maybe and stroll straight out again. I'm sorry, but I just don't like all this tension and strangeness. It makes me worried about our boys and because of that I can't be what you would like in bed. I'm just lost in all this, you see, Nathan. Lost.'

Such words made him cry. He was very emotional and cried a lot. Some days he would cry if she told him that she had just washed his trousers. But there were real reasons for his tears now and he just did not know what to do about it. His marriage was all that he knew and wanted.

'But I'm not about to leave you, if that's what you're worried about,' she continued. 'I love you. You are my husband and I agreed to marry you for better or for worse. It's just this tension that's eating away at me – and it stops me being what I should be in our bed.'

In our bed, ah yes. It was in our bed that he had taken so much of his strength and released so much of *his* tension. He tried to explain this; how it would help them both if she became as she had been. But she said that she could not; she could only ever do that when she was feeling relaxed and happy. So they were both getting themselves bogged down in opposing trenches and he just could not see what they were going to do about it. So he cried.

He walked inside his church with its twin and distinctive smells of damp and wood polish. Halfway Harry was busy dusting the pews, not that there were many people coming to sit on them on Sundays. That's what had got Elizabeth down the most. There was practically no fellowship in this dark, deserted place of prayer; nothing of their last church, which had given her such support and strength. They had spoken often enough about how they were going to rebuild the body of this church but these were hard times for people of the faith. Many could no longer believe after so many of their loved ones had lost their lives in the war. The Welsh chapel movement was still claiming a membership of 400,000 but the great chapel movements of the valleys had ground to a halt. And just as the chapels and churches had gone silent the voices of the Socialists, Marxists and Syndicalists were swelling in power and stridency.

He knelt at the altar rail of the church for ten minutes, asking Christ to come into his life and the lives of his family. He prayed for his children on their first day at school and asked that God help re-armour his wife's spirit; that, in all this, He show her the true and real meaning of His Son's love.

Then he did what he had done almost every morning of his life: he stood at the lectern and read a chapter of the New Testament in Greek. He also read Shakespeare, Dickens and Thackeray but, best of all, he loved the Bible, entering into those much-loved pages like a child. The Bible was his nursery rhyme and fairy-tale book and, as he wandered the Holy Land again, he spoke in tongues at Pentecost, cried with joy at the manger, kept careful watch at Gethsemane and broke his heart at Calvary. Every sentence in the Bible, he believed, helped to make him new again. The Bible was his eyes and very blood.

Later, he went out into the street to begin his rounds. To rebuild a church in an area you had to get to know the area first and for his early few weeks here he had just gone pottering around, introducing himself to any friendly face and having a chat. But, in truth, he now felt that he knew less about the place than when he had begun. Nothing in this tormented kingdom seemed to come together. Everywhere, there was evidence of feud and insult – even among the splintered races themselves. The traditionally strong Moslems, he had learned, were split right down the middle, with the younger ones in the Bridge Street Mosque claiming that the lovely, white birthday cake building did not face Mecca. The Chinese community was bedevilled by the depredations of the Triads and even the West Indian domino clubs had broken up in acrimony due to inter-island rivalry.

It was a thoroughly confusing world – a story of all God's people at odds with themselves and others – and all Nathan could do was make his presence known, ask the odd question and just listen. He had soon learned that any kind of moral judgements were difficult, if not impossible, here in the Bay. Just what were God's plans for all those addled tramps who hung around the vestry asking for money for food which, he knew, went straight on the booze? He could not even start thinking how he could answer that one.

He decided this morning to go again over to Irish Newtown and, perhaps, make contact with his Catholic counterpart, Father Dennis O'Reilly.

It was outside a small grocer's shop – festooned with enamel signs for such as Van Houten's cocoa, Aladdin metal polish, Colman's starch, Gossage's dry soap and Kardomah tea – that he met, for the first time since the afternoon they had moved in, the woman who had stopped his wife's sewing bag from being stolen. 'Hah,' he exclaimed cheerfully. 'So we meet again. You remember me?'

Sophie had just been standing there, staring distractedly into space, and visibly jumped when he spoke to her. There was the same coldness and distance in her face that he remembered when they had spoken last.

'I remember you well enough.' Her voice had the harsh flat vowels of Cardiff. 'You're the new vicar, aren't you? I remember all right.'

'I never really had a chance to thank you properly for saving my bag. It's not clever to be too trusting around these parts. I've discovered that soon enough.'

'It was nothing.' She seemed distracted and uneasy when he spoke again, now looking him up and down, almost as if asking how the hell he had the cheek to talk to her at all. She had a long, full, olive throat, he noticed, though her mouth was a bit too small to make her really beautiful. It was her large, black eyes, as mysterious as the workings of the Stock Exchange, that were her crowning glory. Yet it was her dress that he found really puzzling; her black skirt was slit right up the side in the style of a Chinese cheongsam. She also wore high heels with silk stockings and a light wool vest which revealed rather more than it concealed.

'I was just walking down by the canal and was sure that I spotted a kingfisher,' he said. 'It was just whipping along the water like some gorgeous blue flash from heaven. Are there kingfishers around these parts?'

Now she looked him up and down again though, this time, her crouching eyebrows seemed to be asking him if he was making fun of her. 'I wouldn't know about that, Vicar. If you saw one I suppose they must be around here. All I know about birds are those scabby seagulls who go shitting everywhere.'

'It's said to be good luck if a seagull shits on you.'

Her eyebrows jumped a good half an inch when he used the swearword. Just what kind of vicar was this anyway?

'I come from the country and you learn to read all kinds of strange signs there. If a dog eats grass it's said to be a sign of bad luck. Then there's the cricket dancing around the hearth which is thought to be worse, but even worse than that, is when the wren sings as loud as thunder.'

'How can a wren sing as loud as thunder?' she asked.

'Have you ever heard a wren? They're only very small but they make more noise than forty seagulls. Really. I'm not pulling your leg. Wrens are the loudest birds in the business and they are also the smallest.'

'Yes, well.' Now she really did have a sudden and urgent appointment elsewhere. 'I've got to be off now,' she said, taking two steps into the road. 'We don't get too much by way of nature studies around here.'

'Come over to the church any time if you need anything,' he called after her, disappointed that she wasn't going to open up at all. 'Any help or anything like that,' he added, fumbling his words a bit. 'That's what we're here for.'

But now she was off faster than a pursued rabbit, slinging her handbag over her shoulder and clattering off up the pavement without once looking back. Ah well. He wasn't ever going to get that one singing in the choir. That was a racing certainty, that was.

Nathan's long, exploratory rambles around Cardiff's nether regions had taken him to Newtown several times before. He had almost suffocated in this strange, grey slum of crouching terraced houses flung around an impressive number of pubs – some nineteen in all. But even if he had walked around it a hundred times he was still sure that he would find the place shocking in the extreme. Disease – pneumonia and malnutrition predominated, shouting its deadly news from every corner. Glimpses into some of the houses had shown stump beds laid out even in the corridors where rows of children slept top 'n' tailed beneath piles of old coats. Every family seemed to have at least a dozen barefoot kids in baggy handmade dungarees who were forever spilling all over the cobbled, horsedung roads, playing whip 'n' tops, gobs or hopscotch.

Everything was a straight fight to survive, the men digging the docks and the women, in their sackcloth pinafores, working the wharves, unloading the potato ships when they were in.

He walked on, noticing that every limestone wall seemed to be flaking, on the point of falling over. But it was the very smell of the place which attacked with all the vivid force of a punch on the nose – a stinking, drifting miasma of drains, disinfectant and boiling fishes' heads. When the sun came out this smell became as thick as soup and when the tides came in, driving back the sewage in the drains, the smell became thicker still, making every breath as potentially lethal as an inhalation of mustard gas.

Nathan had been amused by the stories he had heard of Father O'Reilly. Right in the middle of a sermon, Halfway Harry had told him, the old priest might even descend from the pulpit to bash a noisy child. The father turned out to be as large as his reputation; a bulky, funny man with strange stains and traces of food down the front of his cassock. There was enough grease on his dog collar to fill a chip pan and he chortled a lot. His large, unravelling nose – all burst blood vessels and dry bits of skin – immediately told of a long love affair with the hard stuff. This was soon confirmed when, to celebrate Nathan's visit, he immediately cracked open a bottle of poteen.

'All you really need to work in this area is a calm temper and a fine liver,' he explained, handing over a glass which, to Nathan's untutored nose, seemed more like petrol than moonshine whiskey. 'It also helps if you develop a strong sense of your own inadequacy. You'll hear things which'll make your ears turn to clay, so they will. You'll see things that'll make you sorry you aren't blind. But there comes a time when you see that you understand nothing, just nothing at all. When you accept that you'll start getting along just fine.'

Nathan, a conscientious man, gawped in astonishment as the father picked up his glass and chucked his drink down his throat, his Adam's apple barely moving, now smacking his lips and pouring himself another.

'We were never much affected by the war here. It's always been like the Battle of the Somme. Every time the tide turns it's like another gas attack. All we've ever really had is just one boxing hero in the unlikely shape of Jim Driscoll. Now I've been reading in the paper he says he's going to fight again but, between you and me, his brains have leaked out between his cauliflower ears, so they have. He's only got to see a bottle of beer and he drinks it down, the whole thing. I'm going to have a word with him but it'll be useless. It's the old story – money. He had it but now it's gone.'

The old priest also seemed to need only to see a glass of poteen and he drank it down, the whole thing, pouring himself yet another, dismayed to see that Nathan had left his untouched.

'I take the odd glass,' Nathan said, almost by way of an apology. 'But never in the day. It makes me even sleepier and stupider than I already am.'

Father O'Reilly shrugged incomprehendingly. 'I couldn't do this work without the odd wee dram. In our positions – as you'll soon find out if you haven't found out already – we get blamed for everything from rising violence in the pubs to the rising cost of Guinness. You need whatever fortification you can lay your hands on. I get by with a bit of prayer and a lot of drink. Can't seem to sleep without a good drink. I just lie there thinking of the terrible things they've told me in the Confessional. I can't even tell you what some of them get up to. You don't take the Confession, do you?'

'Only on the rare occasion. I've had a couple of dying people who wanted to get something off their chest. But that's about it.'

'Well, don't start. And if you ever come across a mad little bastard called MacWhirter – Terry MacWhirter – and he's about to pop his clogs, then don't, whatever you do, listen to what he says. Just go and hide in the vestry. This man could stare anyone down with his beady green eyes, like a snake. Don't you go looking into his eyes, and hold your hand over his mouth in case he tries to tell you anything. Do not, on any account, listen. Just let him go in silence.'

Nathan leaned forward, intrigued. 'What's he done then?'

'I can't tell you. The things this man has done are not fit for human ears.'

'Go on. Give us a clue.'

'I might tell you one day. But not just now. If he ever turns up at your church, just lock the doors and hide 'til he's gone.'

Fortified by another glass Father O'Reilly explained that the Irish had always been the social lepers in Cardiff. They were first brought here to dig the docks at knockdown rates, which got them shunned by the Welsh particularly after the Irish became dockers. 'We were that desperate we undercut everyone. The Welsh dock labourers were paid threepence a ton for unloading goods and two and a half pence for wheeling off ballast. We offered to do it for a penny and a halfpenny. When the Welsh offered to take a cut we offered to do it for a farthing.

'The press were always against us, right from the off. They said our work was the roughest, that it required the least skill. But the Welsh have always had it in for us. As far back as 1413 there was a Welsh statute ordering all – how did it go now? – ordering all Irishmen and Irish clerks and beggars called chamberdekyns to be voided out of the realm. Then there was some trouble with one of our navvies who was supposed to have murdered a Welshman. Riots, they had then. The Welsh came and dumped three waggons full of stones outside my house here. I wasn't here then. That would have been Father Millea. Then a mob came and accused the father of harbouring this alleged murderer. He even allowed them to search the house and, when they couldn't find that navvy, they started to attack all Irish homes. Father Millea had to hightail out of town wearing a disguise and then they smashed all the windows of the church.

'Our real trouble has always been to do with the cholera. One year we lost twenty-seven souls in Stanley Street and then the press started calling it, for definite certain, the Irish disease – the disease of famine – blaming our practice of holding wakes over the dead person's naked body. Everyone knows you get cholera from water – that's why I never touch the stuff, never – and we were forever having protest marches up to the City Hall 'til the Lord Mayor himself apologized. The Common House Lodging Act cleared most of that up though, insisting on lime-washing the walls and cutting down on overcrowding. But it's all still a bit of a powerful wee mess. The drains still stink as much as ever an' I still tell them to boil their water.

'We're not too bad with the Welsh these days. It's all the coloureds over in Bute Street that's giving them nervous breakdowns now. The Chinese did a lot of scabbing in the dock strike so they've been getting it. They say the West Indians have been taking all the jobs, though I've yet to meet a West Indian with one. Everything threatens the Welsh which, between you and me, is why I'm very glad to be Irish.'

An hour or so later – his mind swimming with poteen and Father O'Reilly's endless stream of advice – Nathan found himself down among the docks themselves.

This was the one part of the Bay that he loved unreservedly – the glittering acres of water humming with hooters and the alarmed cries of sirens; the sea winds romping in fresh from the Bristol Channel; the clatter of coal falling into vast, echoey holds; the great ocean steamers lying stem-to-stern with windjammers; the waving arms of the sailors working in the circus-like rigging.

He walked along the Roath East Dock, watching one of those new Italian self-loader ships tying up at the quay. In the Exchange they were muttering darkly about a post-war collapse but, just with the evidence of his eyes, all he could see was post-war prosperity. That day some three hundred ships were anchored out on the Cardiff roads, either waiting for their turn to come in or for a friendly wind to take them out. Apart from the Cardiff-registered ships there were also ships belonging to the Norwegian firm of Olsen and Simonsen, some Chinese freighters taking Welsh coal to Shanghai and numerous French sailing vessels manned by crews who all wore wooden clogs.

Almost every ten minutes one of those small pugnacious pilot boats went dashing out of the lock gates, always competing fiercely with one another and prepared to go anywhere for custom, even sailing right down to the mouth of the Channel where they would shadow a potential customer until he was ready to take on a pilot.

Everywhere workmen such as boilermakers, dockers, seamen and riveters were keeping the quays full of noise. There were the floating repair shops; the yawning dredgers; flaring naptha launches and crammed houseboats. The clippers and windjammers were still doing a fair export in bodies as well. You could still sail the 5,000 miles to New York for as little as eight guineas. A voyage to Australia cost eighteen guineas. The ships carrying iron always had spare berths providing that you were not too fussy about where – or with whom – you slept.

Nathan stopped to watch a chicken being chased around the deck of a windjammer by a cook with a cleaver. The chicken kept reversing one way and skidding the other, jumping over coiled ropes with squawks of outrage and a flurry of feathers as the cook continued his pursuit, with others of the crew joining in as the chicken kept racing for its life. Now the luckless bird was hurrying down to the aft deck, chased by no less than six of the crew, all whooping and shouting and seemingly in the mood for a chicken dinner.

He moved on, wishing the chicken well, stopping again to admire the sheer size of one of the great steamers, its deck like a crowded street. He marvelled at the way the deck always looked as clean and scrubbed as a Welsh village doorstep. Strange faces peered out of the portholes. Turbanned porters shouldered luggage up the gangplank. On the upper decks officers in starched white tunics stood amidst the rising and falling bales, shouting orders at toiling Hindustanis in impeccable English accents.

At times like this he so enjoyed the throb and thrust of all God's people – all of them as different and individual as a fingerprint and all pursuing their various strategies for fun or survival. But he was also seeing how so many of them were lonely and given to drunken lawlessness. It was a rare week when the police did not fish some body out of the dock and a rarer night still when there was not some wild and bloody fight after the pubs had closed.

He found a small gate down near the West Bute Dock. It was what he had always liked to do in the countryside: find a small gate to lean on and daydream of ancient groves full of mystic sunlight. You could lean on a gate in so many different ways – you could lean on it with your chin on your hands on the top bar, lean against it with the small of your back, put your foot on the bottom bar and change when a leg got tired, or you could even perch yourself on the thing like some overgrown budgie.

Thoughts seemed to go better when he was leaning on a gate and, just now, his thoughts were about seamen. He decided to lean on it with his chin on his hands and further decided that there was something quite genuinely attractive about the average seaman. From what he had learned about them they seemed to just bounce from bars to beds with a quite alarming ease. They hated writing letters, engineers, ship's food and sailing on Sundays. They loved receiving letters, nude photographs, complaining and consuming enormous quantities of beer. A Valentino with a pound in his pocket, a seaman wants to be loved by everyone but, having said that, he seemed to manage quite well without any coherent philosophy at all.

Nathan needed a philosophic standpoint just to survive. He used the strength of Christianity to protect himself against his many and self-acknowledged weaknesses. His greatest marvel was that Christianity actually worked. But seamen seemed to be able to field everything life threw at them just with their own two strong hands.

Yet there were things he could do for these men and it wasn't just to wave the Bible at them either. God had clearly brought him here for a purpose and might that be, he wondered, to set up a Mission to Seamen? Might he have been brought here to throw out a love-line to all these low, scurrilous vagabonds in their lonely hours? Was it for this that God had been preparing him?

He watched an aeroplane fly overhead. H. G. Wells had said that those aeroplanes were going to ruin the world.

Later he left the docks and walked down through the small streets around James Street, down past Bailey's Dry Dock. A little further on, past the Hamdryad Hospital for Seamen, he found his progress blocked by a small cul-de-sac, Howard Close. He was about to turn back when the house at the top of the walled close caught his eye; a handsome Victorian red-brick mansion surrounded by black iron railings and with all its windows barred or grilled. He moved closer, marvelling at the fine white gables and spikey crockets of the house – a massively confident building reeking of wealth and which had clearly been built to stay there long after the others had all fallen down. Even the thick mahogany door must have cost a fortune. He was wondering who might live in such a place when the door opened.

Two men walked out and stood in the pillared porch, still talking together. One was a bulky man with short hair, an ill-fitting suit and a hideous red birthmark all over the right side of his face. The other man, clearly the owner, was tall and dark with fierce black eyes. He was dressed in an elegant, black topcoat with brass buttons together with a butterfly starched collar and a black silk cravat.

The bulky man with the birthmark looked at his watch and walked away as if in a hurry. The owner himself just stood there for a moment, looking up at the sky as if studying the cloud movements, and now down the short flight of stone steps to where Nathan stood.

'I'm the new vicar in the parish,' he announced pleasantly. 'I'm just calling on people in the area to see if I can offer any assistance.'

The man's abstracted look turned to the harshest of scowls. His eyes were the blackest and most intense that Nathan had ever seen. His shoulders turned as if to go inside, but then they turned back again. 'You are most welcome in this area,' he said in a rich, educated voice with just the trace of a Scottish accent. 'I am sure that you will find plenty to do, but I am not a believer so there is nothing at all that you can do for me.'

Whereupon the man turned on his heels and withdrew into his house leaving Nathan chilled to the pit of his belly. He had always found that one of the great joys of being a dog-collared man was being accepted and welcomed everywhere – whether by believers or unbelievers. He even considered knocking on the door and explaining that his offer of help did not just extend to believers – rather the opposite – but decided against it. There was something about the man's manner and the exactness with which he chose his words which suggested that he knew his mind and would not welcome any further points of amplification.

Later, back at the church, he asked Halfway Harry about the mansion in Howard Close. 'His name is Alexander Hamilton,' Halfway explained. 'He's a rich shipowner and very little is known about him. He speaks to no one and never has any visitors.'

'Well, today he spoke to me *and* he had a visitor.'

'What did he say to you then?'

'He told me to go away. But his visitor looked a bit odd too. He was a huge man with a blotchy red birthmark all down the side of his face.'

'You mean all over the side of his face like some ravaged beetroot? Short, fat sort of man? There's only one man like that hereabouts. He's Victor Watts, the chief police inspector for South Wales. Now what could those two have been doing together?'

When Elizabeth returned home after picking up the children from school Nathan saw immediately that she was in a defeated, sullen mood. How just a few weeks here seemed to have aged her. She went straight out into the kitchen and he could not hear the boys at all as she clattered things about before bringing him a cup of tea. 'Do you realize that ours are the only two white children in that new school?' she asked, banging down the cup on the table in front of him. 'They've got every colour in the rainbow in there – except white.'

He picked up his tea and put it down again. 'So what? Children don't know anything about prejudice. It's we adults that teach them that.'

'Nathan, I am really not in the mood for your pulpit platitudes. *I* am your wife and those are your children. *I* do not teach them prejudice but, in a school full of every colour, with children who mostly speak almost anything but English – let alone Welsh – those two of ours are not going to learn a damn thing. Not a damn thing.'

'It sounds to me as though they'll learn a lot. Learning doesn't just come from books you know.'

'They've even got Moslem prayers,' she said, warming to her theme and ignoring his. 'What good are Moslem prayers going to be for our children? You said it would be a good C. of E. school.'

'Well, it sounds like a very good C. of E. school to me.' He was getting worked up too. 'God works through all the faiths. He uses all the prophets – they're all the same, just different colours, that's all.'

'They are not the same and these children are not the same either. They are all from different countries and with different cultures. They fight with one another. There's factions in every classroom. I do not want our two boys to go to that school and that's final.'

'Hang on a minute, just hang on. When I was in college we used to talk about doing missionary work in Africa. You remember that, do you? We used to dream of it together. *Together*. Are you trying to tell me now that, all along, you really believed that all African children are white and that they line up every morning in the Congo to say their prayers in Welsh?'

'That was all before we had these two. It's these two I think about now – not my student dreams.'

'Your beliefs don't change because you have children. They should become stronger, deeper.'

'Bah! I can't talk to you about anything. Whenever I want a normal discussion about the children's education all you want is to climb into that pulpit of yours. I've got a headache now. I'm going to have a lie-down for an hour. *You* watch the children.'

'Where are they?'

'Probably down the damned Mosque learning damned Moslem prayers.'

'Look, go and have a lie down and I'll bring you a cup of tea shortly. The children will be all right. And you'll be all right.

These are just strange times for us but we'll learn soon how to cope with it all. Nothing ever comes right early on. It just takes time and then everything will be beautiful.'

He gave the two boys their tea and, after an hour or so, took a cup up to Elizabeth who was just lying on their bed and staring up at the ceiling. He could tell immediately that she had lost her foul mood.

'You haven't slept then?'

'I'm not like you. I can't just fall asleep for half an hour then bounce up again as if nothing had happened. I told you. It's this tension. Sometimes I think I'm just going to snap.'

'You want me to get rid of it?'

'You're not on about that again, are you? I swear that if you were a doctor and people came to you with a head cold or a broken leg, you'd always say that there was only one cure.'

'And what would that be, my love?'

'You know. That.'

'Oh *this*, you mean?' He slid his hand down under the bedclothes and was very surprised indeed to find that she had nothing on. She usually wore a few layers of something or other, if only to protect herself from sudden night-time attacks from him if he was having trouble sleeping. This was the best cure he knew for insomnia too.

'Yes, that,' she smiled, slipping her arm up around his neck and pulling his head down for a kiss.

'Well, we could always try a bit of this, then . . . and a little bit of that . . . and we could go for a touch of . . .'

'Are you going to do all this with your dog collar on? I just can't do it with your dog collar on. I'm sorry. Dog collars just make me laugh.'

'I was worried if I stopped to take anything off you might change your mind.'

'Yes, well, just undo that dog collar and get this bit off and that and, oh yes . . . do you know that I'm beginning to feel a bit better already? You can take the rest of your clothes off if you want.'

'I think I'll just stay as I am if you don't mind. I'm all right as long as you're all right.'

And so, with his trousers just down around his knees and his underpants only a little higher and the back of his dog collar having twanged open, people would never have believed that this was the new Anglican minister to St Mark's in Bute Street, one Rev. Nathan Thomas B.A., M.Phil., extremely busy exercising his marital rights while also busy trying to relieve his beautiful wife's tension.

# CHAPTER THREE

A little before ten o'clock on a dim May morning in 1918 some three hundred of the richest men in South Wales, responsible for more than three-quarters of the wealth of the principality, quietly crowded onto the great wooden floor of the Coal Exchange in Cardiff. There were some thirty millionaires among these Carnegies of coal, all fat of gut and broad of bottom, who loved little more than talking about fine wine, plover's eggs and dreams of good butlers who did not have the cheek to ask for any money.

They were always fastidiously dressed in their silk hats and frock coats, even insisting that one of their number should be thrown off the Floor for actually daring to turn up one morning dressed in loud check breeches with leggings, by God. But the man in question continued to do business on the steps of the Exchange for the rest of his life and still wearing loud check breeches.

Not that there was much business going on just at the moment. Normally these shipowners with their messengers and clerks were hurrying about making deals involving anything from the carriage of ballast to Casablanca to taking bagged flour to Fremantle, but this morning they were gathering for a two-minute silence in honour of one of their number, the recently deceased Albert Gurney, the founder and chairman of the Oriel Steam Navigation Company and the second most powerful shipowner in the city.

Some of the biggest names in shipping had come to pay their last respects; huge, colourful characters such as Tatem, Cory, Reardon Smith, Radcliffe, Nicholl and Seager. Just over there was William Tatem – the owner of the ships *Torrington* and

*Wellington.* When the Queen had opened the Alexandra Dock Tatem had strolled up to Her Majesty, with thumbs in a loud checkered waistcoat, said a curt 'How do?' and ambled away again.

Later in the ceremony the first socialist Lord Mayor of Cardiff, Alderman Bill Crossman, had fawned all over her and was knighted on the spot.

Despite his uncouth manners Tatem was later made Lord Glanely but, if anything, this made him even more uncouth. He was perceived by everyone as a jumped-up bastard and they were all doubly disappointed when, the next year, he managed to make £30,654 by winning the Derby.

Just over there was Reardon Smith with cherubic well-fed features and small gold-rimmed spectacles with glass as thick as the bottoms of pop bottles. He owned the largest shipping line in the country, an immense fleet of tramps and steamers, some of which he had lost through U-boat gunfire in the war. And he had grieved over every loss as a mother would over her favourite son.

But this morning these men, with their Alpine bellies and twinkling gold fob watches, were gathering to mourn the loss of a somewhat different kind – the death of a man who had been with them from the beginning, one who had been as responsible as any for building Cardiff into the coal metropolis of the world; one who had fought long and hard against the Bute family when they kept trying to raise the dock rates. Old man Gurney had even once threatened to take all his business to nearby Barry Docks, forcing Bute to relent on a plan to nearly double the rates.

There was a dim murmur on the Floor when Alexander Hamilton walked out to join them. No one cared much for him; some wanted nothing to do with him and moved away accordingly. For his part he wanted even less to do with them, finding this new manly and healthy habit of smoking – which the troops had brought back from the war trenches – offensive and disgusting in the extreme. The Exchange – run as a club on the rules of gentlemen – found it almost impossible to deal with someone like Hamilton, a trader in mystery who always did his transactions through intermediaries. But what was he doing here for Albert Gurney? Some had speculated on their connections but it had only been just that – speculation.

'Gentlemen. A two-minute silence in memory of Mr Albert Gurney.'

Nothing could be heard, except the distant hooters of the ships and the loud ticking of the Exchange clock, as these busy, important men stood to attention for a full two minutes. The silence trawled up to the huge, glass-topped roof and swept around the ornate wooden balconies supported by elegant columns and intricate panels. It moved in the port-smoked breath and beefy faces of these men whose wealth was almost literally incalculable, hidden away in a global network of holding companies and investment trusts.

The Exchange had been refitted recently to become more in keeping with the way that these men perceived themselves. All those crude advertisements had been taken down and replaced by lines of polished Corinthian columns. Carvings were the order of the day, with one of the mining industry (a laurel wreath with a safety lamp and a collier's pick and shovel) and the maritime industry (an oak wreath with the trident of Neptune entwined with a dolphin).

All eyes gradually drifted on to Hamilton who was also standing ramrod erect looking up at the Exchange clock, which was also surrounded by carved Welsh dragons. They knew little about his wealth; few even had any accurate guesses on the scale of his shipping operations, speculating openly that he was far more crooked than all of them put together which would have made him very crooked indeed. His company had not gone public in the coal boom, and there was never any need for him to publish his books or, pain of pains, declare an annual dividend to the shareholders.

When the silence had finished Hamilton walked away from the Floor and stood for a full five minutes reading the news on stock fluctuations and contracts which Big Bertha blew daily down a pipe to the Exchange from the main Post Office in Westgate Street. Big Bertha, a hydraulic engine taken out of an old paddle steamer, blew the news down two miles of tube, the longest copper pipe in the land.

He was clearly interested in the latest on the Oriel Steam Navigation Company – owned by Albert Gurney d'csd. He could be seen taking out a notebook and jotting some figures down with quick, precise movements of his strong hands. Predictably, perhaps, the Oriel stock had fallen by thirty-seven points. The death of any shipowner always caused a mild flutter on the stock market though it had to be said that the death of some shipowners did sometimes send their stock up.

'Oriel hasn't fallen by as much as I thought,' said William Tatem, coming to stand next to him. Tatem stood in awe of no one. Hamilton looked at him with the mildest curiosity.

'It's surprising to me because I always said that company didn't have much to it,' Tatem continued. 'There was no expansion in it. Old Albert didn't believe in expansion but that's the key to healthy shipping these days.'

Hamilton put his notebook back into his topcoat pocket. 'You must excuse me,' he said and left the building without another word.

Hamilton's next call was at Oriel's shipping offices in James Street where he found Gurney's office manager, Lawrence Partington, sitting in his shirt-sleeves in a tiny room with small mountains of dusty papers piled high on the window-sills and seemingly threatening to engulf him at any moment. Many were tied in red legal ribbons.

Partington stood up smartly and put on his jacket. Ignoring him, Hamilton took a chair and sat down in front of him. Partington was a small man of the most sombre rectitude, loyal to the Gurney interests and addicted to Mint Imperials. He was still wearing the black tie of mourning – and would probably be wearing it for some time yet.

'What we need is immediate and drastic surgery,' Hamilton said bluntly and without preamble. Partington nodded assent. 'Everyone in the Exchange is just acting the fool these days, ordering new ships and patting themselves on the back. There is the biggest crash ever coming to this country and we have to be ready for it. What is the present strength of the Oriel fleet?'

Partington looked over at the map of the world dotted with flags in the Oriel's distinctive red-and-white insignia. 'We've got eight tramps working at the moment – mostly coal out and grain home to the River Plate. There's three in dry dock; the two passenger steamers and the windjammer are in the Bay of Biscay.'

'How many disposals?'

'None at present. But we do have orders for three new ships. Mr Gurney began talking about wanting to show confidence in the future.'

'Cancel the orders. Pay any penalties. How many of the tramps are coal-burners?'

'Four.'

'Sell them for anything you can get. Everything in the fleet must be oil-burning by the end of the year. Sell the passenger steamers too. I hear Russia are buying anything these days. Ask around for quotations on those oil-burning bulk carriers with deck cranes. They are the only vessels that will pull Oriel through this.'

Partington made no comment as he wrote down Hamilton's orders impassively. He would be working on their implementation within hours. He took out a Mint Imperial and popped it into his mouth. 'What about the windjammer?'

'We will leave *The Solomon* for the moment. As yet the winds are free and cheap. I hear that Edward came back for his father's funeral. Where is he now?'

'Probably out having a lot of fun somewhere. You know Edward. Can't see him at home trying to console his mother somehow. But she has taken it very badly indeed.'

'Go over to the family home in Penarth tomorrow morning and tell Edward that I want to meet him in the Angel Hotel at noon. Pass my condolences to Mrs Gurney and tell her the company is in safe hands. Send the company books over to my house this afternoon. I want to go through them all.'

Somewhere around twilight later that day – in that dreaming moment which was neither light nor dark, neither bright nor murky – the Bay took on a cloak of cosmetic gorgeousness, dark enough to hide all its crumbling faults and light enough to gaze down the wide thoroughfare of Bute Street where echoes of alien music hung in the air and strange food smells drifted out of open windows.

Already Billy the Lamplighter was well into his evening round, leaving his bicycle propped on a pedal in the gutter as he mounted his ladder, pulling the ring under the grey metal gauze and watching it spurt and sputter into a bright green light. He could do one every two minutes when not stopping to gossip – which he did avidly – now moving onto James Street leaving pools of light in his wake, all hovering, green on black, in the loaming darkness.

But there was one place that Billy never stopped to gossip,

no matter how late he was, and that was at the entrance to Howard Close where, at this twilight time, the port transvestites gathered. Just there Billy was up his ladder faster than a cat chased by a savage dog, pulling the ring and pedalling off fast into the darkening night. For this was the meeting place of the lowest of the low; the truly alienated from all the ships of the world, given D.R.s and beached by storms of hatred until now all that was left to them was to gather here where they could talk – often in mad gibberish – amongst themselves. Even the police avoided this spot.

There was Lia Ling who joked with Abu Sakar. A few minutes later another wandered across the road to join them. A fourth came swaying in with an exaggerated mincing of the hips. Now there was a lot of low whistling as Nazeem walked up the pavement. A few cackled as others patted their hair or pulled at their drawers under their dresses as if they had suddenly become too tight. Another in a long red ball-gown joined them until there were now about fifteen of them, chuckling and preening themselves as they moved around like river weeds in a slight current.

The undoubted leader of this lipsticked throng was Nazeem, whose long black hair was so well groomed and whose movements were so femininely supple that he, alone of the group, was allowed to walk in other parts of the Bay without being driven back to this, their spot. His singular beauty intrigued rather than gave offence. The exquisite bone structure of his jaw was enhanced by his green cat-like eyes and a scar on his cheek so deep that not even face powder covered it.

Never elected as such, the group nevertheless bestowed leadership on him, some even approaching him, saying a few obsequious words before stepping to one side. Some looked to him for advice, which he gave freely, if sometimes pompously. If he ever actually asked any of them a question some of them became so overwhelmed they babbled incoherently in reply and, bored stiff, he just stepped past them. But all the time his wildcat eyes kept looking around him as if he was expecting someone important to arrive. All the time his hands kept playing with a green chiffon scarf. It was almost as if the others saw in Nazeem what they could be if they had some luck and played their cards right. That beauty! Those clothes! And all those men!

Lia Ling muttered a few incoherent sentiments to Nazeem but he just yawned and looked away. Soon he became tired of their company entirely and, with an impatient jerk of his hips, and chiffon scarf trailing behind him, he walked off towards Bute Street.

Just near the bottom of Bute Street men were going to the Mission Hall near the post office where, it being Wednesday, they were hopeful of being entertained by a Go-As-You-Please concert and a small boxing tournament. Further on again the shutters were going up and the lights were going on in the Chinese block, built around a small laundry and restaurant. Precisely what went on inside this block was a deep mystery, even to the most curious, since of all the races the Chinese were the most insular and defensive, openly reviled because it was thought that many had not come from the English colony of Hong Kong – as they always claimed – but from mainland China. Many of them had also earned themselves undying enmity by working the wharves during the 1912 dock strike.

One could only guess at the nature of their business by rare glimpses through open windows; at the statues of Buddha and Taoist deities in small forests of smoking joss sticks on the mantelpieces; at the men in shorts and vests playing noisy games of mahjong in the hallways; at the smells of baking spring rolls and frying seahorses coming out of the kitchens. The Cardiff joke was that no pet was safe to fall dead in the streets without quickly ending up in a Chinese cauldron.

Duw, *everything* those Chinese did was a bastard mystery, *mun*. And none was more mysterious than those old men in their small back yards practising the slow, balletic movements of Ta'i Chi. Pub talk also had it that there were sodding great opium parlours in that same block, but it was only pub talk and was never confirmed by the Chinese themselves.

Certainly these tales of strange doings had seeped out into the ears of every child in the Bay to the degree that, if any of them was luckless enough to be made to take the laundry to them, he always took a friend to keep the door open so that, if they ever did try to grab him to shove him into one of those big cauldrons, he could make a quick run for it.

Pak Chen came and stood at the window of his second floor apartment, clearing his chest and spitting down into the street. In just half an hour it would be his turn to take guard on the corner block where there were never less than eight young men patrolling in the shadows. Like the rest of them Pak Chen was conversant with the ancient arts of Kung Fu and able to wield a rice flail. Like the rest of them he was also fully prepared to defend his family and home using extreme violence if necessary. These were the hardest of times for the Chinese, no matter where they came from or how they got there.

Further on up again and near the Custom House Sophie was out doing her own patrolling and looking for some business. She was not best pleased at the moment, was Sophie, since she had just completed a bit of business which she could well have done without.

She had been standing in a ship chandler's doorway when a man had walked up to her and just stood there breathing heavily. Nothing was said as he shifted his weight from one foot to the other, staring uneasily at her bosom. She stepped towards him and he stiffened, taking a step backwards.

'I've got a nice little bed around the corner,' she offered.

He gazed at the wall behind her as her hands went down playing around with his pneumatic bulge. Now she was cupping it and fondling it and he was swaying slightly like a mesmerized cobra facing a mongoose but, otherwise, making no move nor indeed any sound at all. She took him by the shoulders and tried to pull him back into the darkness of the doorway but he was having none of that either, just holding his ground like he was on sentry duty. She pushed him slightly but he did not seem to want to move away either. So what did he want? His bulge was still bulging nicely.

'I've got a nice little bed around the corner.'

He breathed deeply and mumbled something incoherent. Her first instinct was to tell him to piss off but he was quite nicely dressed and money was money. She unbuttoned his flies and took out his pole, ready, if necessary, to lead him back to her bed like a dog on a lead, when he put his head on her shoulder and mumbled again. Her eyes widened into small brown saucers. He was saying something about money. Hadn't her little darling got any money? No, her little darling didn't have a bean. Didn't have a bean? Not a bloody bean.

She whacked him straight on the cheek with the palm of her hand and her little darling stepped back, biting his lip and crying silently. Hot, sad tears rolled down his cheeks, catching in the green lamplight. He rubbed his eyes with the backs of his hands like a baby in need of sleep. She just stood back and watched him crying like this for up to a minute, and yet his erection was still amazingly erect.

She just did not know what to do – offer him a handkerchief or a good toss – so, in the end, unable to stand all this sadness any more, she put an arm around his neck, eased him back into the darkness of the doorway and took hold of his erect pole to give it a good joggle. Her little darling took ages to come and her wrist was getting quite sore towards the end but, when she did feel the start of that old stammering, spurting fountain, she made a jump for it, and was lucky she did, since there was so much in him he all but whitewashed the green door.

It did the trick though and she could almost see the terror draining out of him when, with a tearful smile, but nothing by way of a polite thank you, her poverty-stricken little darling took off into the night, leaving her rubbing her sore wrist. Free tosses indeed. Ah well, charge a few, give a few away free. The girls always said she was bad for business. Soon the word would get around the Valleys that you could get a free toss down in Bute Street, and where would it all end? It would end in a happier Valleys, wouldn't it? With unemployment up there being what it was the men could do with something to put the smile back on their faces because, as sure as eggs, their wives didn't seem able to do much for them.

She was walking on up towards the Custom House when she heard a loud cry from the girls, since a car had come along to pick one of them up. But this was no ordinary car, she soon saw, but a racey Adler with an open top and a Gabriel bugle. The driver was not too bad either, a young man with sandy hair and a smiling way as he gunned the car slowly along the pavement. He was not good-looking though, she decided. His eyes were set too close together and, just by the way he was teasing the girls, you could tell that he was a hundred-carat bastard.

The girls moved around in the bright flare of his headlamps, smiling voluptuously as they tried to catch his attention, some by banging on the car bonnet or giving him a judicious glimpse of their legs. Even Marie the Stump was trying her luck – though not by showing her stump, Sophie was relieved to see – while a few even tried to open the passenger door. He just laughed and merely gunned his accelerator a little, moving some ten yards down the road.

His engine was ticking over throatily as his headlamps picked up Sophie standing on the edge of the pavement. He edged closer and she stood there looking down at him imperiously, letting her coat fall apart revealing her suspendered stockings and yellow pants. But it was those long olive legs that always got them. He ducked his head down to get a better view before pulling up next to her. 'Well, are you going to get in or are you going to stand there all night?'

Sophie brought her coat together and stepped into the car, sitting down and staring in front of her.

'Do you think you could manage to close the door?' he asked.

'I always thought gentlemen closed doors.'

'Listen, lady, let's be very clear about one thing – I am no gentleman. I can be very rough and twice as nasty. I am upset and I need some fun. Now close that bloody door, will you?'

'Close it yourself.'

He jumped out of the car and walked around the bonnet, closing the door with a hefty thump before getting back in behind the driving wheel again. 'Right. Where are we going?' he asked.

'Depends what you want.'

'What do you think I want?'

'I don't know. Do you want an ice cream or a waltz or a soccer match? I'm no mind-reader. I don't carry a crystal ball around.'

He seemed to be sniffing a lot before he slipped the engine into first gear and accelerated slowly up the road. 'Look, I'm tired and very upset. I've got plenty of money . . . look, I'll be honest with you. I'm so very upset because my father has died . . .'

'Your father has just . . .'

'Yes, two days ago. I've only just come down from London and, just as soon as possible, I'm going back there. But I just can't tell you how badly I need it. I don't want any messing around. No kissing, no holding, no nothing.'

'Just explain to me what you want and I'm sure I can manage it.'

He explained.

'How much money have you got with you?'

He told her.

'Yes, well let's do it.'

She just did not know what to make of it all, she decided, as they both whizzed around the city that night. Here was a young man with obvious intelligence and a public school education;

an attractive man, who could never have been short of offers from women, and all he wanted to do was drive around the city at top speed, stopping every half an hour or so when she was expected to jump out, with him jumping out after her, whereupon he would have her against some railings, against a warehouse wall or even stretched out on a park bench. Yes. *Every* half an hour or so. He was like one of those frogs in the mating season. Fortunately he didn't go on for too long – after some twenty seconds he was finished. She shuddered to think what they taught them in public school these days.

Well, everyone to their own, she decided, as he got her down in the middle of a school playground. He admitted later that it was his old school and it was just his way of saying something to them.

'You're just like some cat who goes pissing around his territory,' she said. 'No, not a cat. A very horny dog. Are you always like this?'

'No, not always. I only seem to like doing it this way about once a year and then I can leave it alone for ages. I can't usually find a woman to do it with. All my girlfriends don't much like it in public.'

'I can't imagine why.'

But it was soon becoming quite clear that all this malarkey was doing him a great deal of good since, miserable as he had been at the beginning of their tryst, he was now acting quite positively chirpy, telling her that his name was Edward Gurney – most unusual for a man to tell her his name, though perhaps it was false – and that, almost as soon as his father's funeral was over, he was going straight back to London.

'You always grieve like this, do you?'

'I've never been much good at mourning. Never seen the point of it.'

They got to the back of the fire station in Westgate Street just after three in the morning and she was beginning to feel very sore indeed, wondering when he was going to run out of steam. 'When are you going to run out of steam?' she asked. 'I'm going to have to go in for a new one if this goes on much longer.'

'Oh, I think I've just about had enough now,' he said cheerfully, pulling up his trousers and checking the time. 'Come on, we'll catch a quick drink and I'll take you home.'

She decided that she liked him a lot. He had so much life

about him and he probably couldn't even spell inhibition. 'I've got a nice little bed, you know. You could try a bit of sleep if you want.'

'Never been much interested in sleep, you know.'

'Really?'

'Really. I've never been much interested in doing things in beds either. The best bit of sex I ever had was dangling off Clifton Suspension Bridge once. All that freedom. All those winds.'

'You wouldn't catch me doing that. I like it in bed, me.' By now she wasn't sure if she liked him or not. The man was clearly as mental as anything.

The next morning Edward Gurney was sitting in the drawing room of the family mansion on the high headland of Penarth, overlooking the Bristol Channel, smoking a cigarette and feeling very sorry for himself indeed.

It was just that he was experiencing such a mixture of emotions and all of them regrettable. He supposed that, mostly, he just felt guilty about being so happy at a time when he should have been feeling sad. But he wasn't feeling the slightest bit sad. That woman he had found the night before had certainly been a whore with a difference. She seemed almost ready to do anything *and* he had forgotten to pay her.

But his main regret was the general pain he was feeling from coming down after taking so much cocaine. His head throbbed at the very thought of those mad hours buzzing around the city doing wild, daft things. He really would have to leave the stuff alone. The trouble was all the sophisticates in London had got their noses buried in the snow just now, sniffing small piles of the stuff which, if nothing else, seemed to give him a semi-permanent erection. There was talk of making it illegal but it had not happened just yet.

Three ships were moving, black on silver, through the early afternoon sea mists. He sucked heavily on his cigarette, still gazing into the middle-distance. There was no fire in the large stone firegrate and it was getting quite chilly. He could always ring for someone to make the fire but he didn't and just sighed again. But that figure of hers was quite awesome and he felt around it yet again in his mind. From another wing of the large grey granite house he could hear his mother playing the piano.

Penarth was a fine spa town, built at the height of Edwardian confidence and ebullience, with its own sea baths, an iron and wood pier and a wide seafront promenade favoured by the arthritic and asthmatic in their bath-chairs. Its rough pebble beach – dotted with limpets and bright lumps of red and white marble – had saved it from going the way of neighbouring Barry Island which, when the sun was high, was overrun by the whole of South Wales with its sand bucket. But, even if Penarth had a beach worthy of a name, the mucky sea would still have been its saviour: sewage pipes emptied directly into the Channel at Penarth and it sat virtually opposite the entrance to Cardiff docks, where the ships discharged unmolested night and day.

More ships swung into view on the Cardiff roads. His father had bought this house so that he could keep an eye on his shipping through his telescope and he was most strict that no Oriel ship should discharge on his doorstep. The soonest they could dump anything was at Lundy Island when the English would have to put up with it. Keep Wales tidy: dump your rubbish in England, his father had told his captains. His father, Edward recalled. Mmm. What a tyrant he had been. Well, he was gone now and all Edward wanted to do was to return to London. *Everyone* was having fun in London and here he was stuck with his grieving mother who seemed only to want to play Bach on the piano all day long. Where others were content to cry into a handkerchief all she seemed to want to do was cry into her damned piano. Such music seemed to console her but it added considerably to the melancholy which kept rolling through the house. It was everywhere . . . in the curtains, the firegrate, even in the servants' quarters.

But that woman had been just so unusual – just so good at it and, quite soon, he had even forgotten that she had been a whore. Not that he had ever been short of girls. What he really wanted was some Fifth Avenue American heiress so that he could fill the bath with cocaine and dive into it whenever he was feeling blue. That stuff again . . . it was going to be the death of him if he didn't watch it.

But he wasn't going to find a woman – American or Welsh – just sitting around here listening to that bloody piano. He tossed his cigarette into the empty grate – an action which he knew would severely vex his mother – before standing up and walking over to the bookshelves. But there was nothing of interest there either. Just books about shipping and yet more books about shipping. Even when he came home at night his father would fuss over his empire until it daily became a larger and larger headache – just too much for his weak heart. All Edward had ever really enjoyed was champagne, cocaine and following the fortunes of slow horses and even slower women.

The only part of the Oriel Steam Navigation Company that Edward had any interest in at all was *The Solomon*, the windjammer, an epic poem of grace and movement, which his father had kept going despite the strictures of his accountants. Even now the ship was sailing back to Cardiff and an uncertain future. He would dearly love to be able to save her – if only to charter her out of Cannes or Nice for the stinking rich. The rest of the fleet could sink straight to the ocean floor as far as he was concerned.

The doorbell was pulled and across the hall he heard the maid's voice announce the arrival of Lawrence Partington. The piano-playing stopped in the music room and Edward went to the door, trying to hear what was being said. He had been very keen on having a discussion with Partington ever since his father had died. Partington – who knew everything about his father's business, who could liquidate the Oriel empire, pull out some ready money and let Edward get on with his chosen career of having a lot of cocaine fun. Yes, Edward was very keen indeed to have a discussion with this Mr Partington.

But his mother and her visitor seemed in no hurry to talk with him. Soon he was gazing out of the drawing room window again, thinking of that whore again. Suddenly the drawing room door opened.

'You remember Mr Partington, of course,' his mother said, her trembling fingers touching the three-decked choker of pearls around her neck. 'There are certain things he wants you to do to save the company so he would like you to go and meet a gentleman in the Angel Hotel later this morning.'

Save the company, mother? *Save* the company? That was not what he had in mind at all. Sink the company, mother, *sink* the whole rotten mess. His eyes looked at his mother and back at Partington, managing to make him look very shifty indeed. His slicked-back brilliantined hair added to his aura of a cornered rat as he tried, but failed, to come up with a few other options. 'Who is this gentleman, then?' He managed to inject a very fair sneer into the word 'gentleman'.

His mother and Partington looked at one another, almost as if they were unable – or was it unwilling? – to answer the question.

'His name is Alexander Hamilton, Mr Edward,' Partington explained finally.

'Never heard of him.'

'Your father and he had a lot of interests in common,' Partington said. 'These interests were – how shall I put it? – delicate, informal, not widely discussed. And neither were they just to do with shipping. This gentleman has a lot of power and immense connections in society.'

Edward's interest visibly brightened at these promises of power and connections. He was very interested in them also. 'But what does this powerful gentleman want from me?'

'He had better explain that himself, Mr Edward. All I can tell you is that the current wave of optimism in the shipping business is soon going to expend itself. Already David Lloyd George has been warning the shipowners that coal is going to turn traitor. The French and the Poles are busy opening up their mines. Mr Hamilton is most anxious that we ready ourselves for the coming slump.'

'But what use can I be? I've always hated commercial shipping. My father was always most bitter on that score.'

'Just go over and talk to this man, Edward,' his mother intervened. 'He did a lot with your father – too much, I always thought – but he is very, very important. Just go and listen to what he has to say.'

The Bay of Biscay was rolling in gently swelling hills as the windjammer *The Solomon* sailed close-hauled to the wind, bringing home her cargo of tea and grain. All of her eighteen sails had been set and trimmed, filling up in a great moving washing line of billowing white segments. Some of the deckhands were hauling on the buntlines while others were up in the creaking yardarms, resetting the sails and freshening the nip. Their hands were gnarled and strong. All carried knives in their belts to cut themselves free if they ever got into any trouble with the miles of rope which hung like rogue spaghetti from every yard and sail.

Just next to the varnished deckhouse a fat black cat was sleeping with head on its paws and one eye open watching for any migratory birds foolish enough to try and take a rest on *The Solomon*. Then the cat would become alarmingly and ferociously awake, pouncing on the exhausted bird and giving it a rest for good. In the mahogany-panelled ward room four officers were playing a quiet game of crib and, down in the galley, a boy was busy peeling his third bucket of potatoes of the morning. Smells of horse manure and frying potatoes came drifting up from one of the hatches.

Further on up the deck a piglet was tied to a hatch doorway and the crew kept making jokes about how much they were going to enjoy eating the poor thing. But these jokes were only made to upset Cookie since he had become unreally fond of the animal, feeding it better food than he gave to the crew and not at all looking forward to putting it in the slicer when they did eventually run out of fresh bacon.

A man sat alone on a box on the prow whittling a doll. His unlikely name was Dai the Murderer; he was always on his own, not so much because of a very murky past, as the fact that he had the most rancid body smell imaginable, which you could pick up, to your extreme discomfort, from as far as ten feet away. The only time the crew didn't mind being near him was when they were working up in the yards reefing the sails. But even then it wasn't entirely pleasant if there were no strong winds around to carry away Dai the Murderer's smell.

In her gleaming white sails and polished wheeldeck; in the sparkling deck and glittering brasses, *The Solomon* revealed all the certain signs of a driven and tough master. The general rule of the sea was that a dirty, rust-bucket of a ship was a happy ship, but the more sparkling she was the more miserable she would be to work and the tougher the master. Captain Abraham Turner was the toughest master of them all, a burly man with a square beard, a notorious slapper-on of sail, who would happily stop you a day's pay if you as much as looked at him in the wrong way. Even now he was filling up the ship's log, checking the chronometer and noticing that the barometer was beginning to run low.

He chewed the end of his pen as he studied the page. The winds were gusting well and giving him speeds of up to sixteen knots. Good winds always put him in a good humour and, on such days, you might even get away with looking at him the wrong way. He understood that it was the winds and not the sea that always controlled the fortunes of this old lime-juicer. It was the good winds which made the yards creak peacefully and became the bearers of health and wealth. Good winds scoured any foul smells out of the cabins and holds, filling the sails and blowing good luck on his bonus. Good winds made him happier than a small baby.

No winds at all made him miserable and, when he became like that, his crew became miserable too. They made no progress when there were no winds, as they languished in the doldrums. Yet even worse than no winds were wild squalling winds which blew hard and stopped sudden, sucking sideways and whirling madcap about the waves. Even after a lifetime at deep sea – in which he had frequently tackled the greybeards and crashing mountains of the Horn – he had never really understood the ways of the winds.

But this morning the winds were good and sunny, actually lifting the prow slightly out of the water, leaving a widening trail of foam in her wake as the bulkheads creaked and groaned, all making steady progress towards Captain Turner's bonus. He looked out through the porthole and smiled at the waves as he listened to the deeply satisfying conversation of good winds in swelling sails. Yes, this great cathedral of canvas was sailing very well just now, uplifted and sustained by the prayers of the good winds of God. But why was that mercury leaking so low into the barometer? He tapped it with his knuckle and squinted at the numerals closely.

Edward drove his car fast down the Penarth toll road and parked it outside the Angel Hotel, a vast many-roomed battleship marooned on the corner of Westgate Street and opposite the Arms Park rugby ground. The hotel was indisputably the finest in the city and Edward felt completely at home as he took the steps three at a time up into the reception hall. Looking up approvingly at the curving marble lines of the chandeliered staircase, he asked the desk clerk for Mr Hamilton, and a bellboy took him into a vast lounge with carpets so thick he had the sensation of losing his shoes in them. Directly in the corner Hamilton was taking tea. He stood up and motioned Edward to sit down.

'Would you like some tea, or perhaps something stronger?'

'No, nothing just now.' Edward eased himself down into the

green leather armchair. He found something about Hamilton quite intimidating and wanted to keep a clear head for what was to come.

'Thank you for coming to see me,' Hamilton said, flicking his fingers and waving a hand, telling the waiter to clear the table. 'I have asked you here because I want you to continue with your father's shipping company.'

'I know nothing about shipping. I know nothing about business at all.'

Hamilton said nothing and just stared at him as if he was content to listen to the expected objections.

'I may be a Gurney but, when it comes to running any business, you have quite the wrong man in me. The mere sight of a balance sheet gives me the most awful headache.'

'I am not asking you to look at any balance sheets,' Hamilton snapped with a slight note of impatience. 'Partington is paid to look after all that. I just need your name and your occasional presence on the Floor of the Exchange. We need a Gurney name to continue the Oriel operations. We are just looking for some family continuity to get us through the coming storm. This country is heading into a very great depression and only the lean and fit are going to survive. Soon Oriel is going to be very lean and very fit.'

'Can't it just be sold and be done with it?'

'No. We need to keep this business going. Your father and myself were engaged in a long-term work, work which is going to need a few more decades of this business.'

'What kind of long-term work would that be?' It was the first of many questions that Edward would like to have had answered until he quickly discovered that it was quite useless asking Hamilton any questions at all.

'I propose keeping the windjammer, which I know you are very fond of. If you come in with us and help the family I might even be able to find a way of deeding you that windjammer.'

'I couldn't run *The Solomon* on my own. Father was always complaining about the wage bill for that. Quite frankly, I would far prefer to sell everything, set mother up in a small house in Penarth and get back to London.'

Hamilton stared at the table, as if studying a chessboard and trying to work out the next move. Edward looked at the board too, almost knowing that, very soon, his defences were going to be in total disarray. A bellboy walked around the lounge holding up a board with the name *COTTERELL* on it. He held it up in front of their table but was promptly waved away.

'Let us say, right from the outset, that if you tried to sell Oriel – or rather, if your mother tried to sell Oriel since, as you know, until she dies, you only have a small share of the company equity – then you would be very lucky to come out without a massive tax liability which would be far in excess of what you would make. I also control a substantial share of the equity.'

But how much did he control? And just what was his connection with his father? What was this long-term business all about?

'Furthermore I know a lot about you, Edward,' Hamilton continued. 'More, perhaps, than you realize.' Edward held his breath and could almost see Hamilton's powerful chess-pieces being moved into attack. 'I know that you have an expensive drug habit and that you have also had difficulties with the police in London.' His black eyes fixed on Edward's and his bushy eyebrows crouched into a frown. 'Did you ever wonder why those charges against you were dropped?'

Edward had long wondered why those charges had been dropped but such matters, he had long believed, were not known in Cardiff. Such was his shock at Hamilton's revelation that he did not even try and bluster his innocence and just gave a slight shake of his head.

'They were dropped because certain people were told to drop them,' Hamilton went on. 'But you, as a Gurney, understand the nature of power and wealth. Our wealth is perhaps not what it used to be, but our power remains extensive. So all I am asking you to do is lend your name and presence to help Oriel survive. And I also want you to use your undoubted skills to do a small job for me.'

'A small job?' Every part of him told him that there would be nothing small about anything that Hamilton had planned for him. He had not even agreed to do the first job, come to that. And what did anyone know about his particular skills? It wasn't something he advertised exactly.

'We will talk about this job again. Just come to my house next Saturday afternoon and we will discuss it. But can I take it that, in principle, you are now prepared to help us?' He paused before adding, as a sort of clinching afterthought, 'You will, of course, receive all the money that even *you* need.'

# CHAPTER FOUR

A strange, clashing music filled Sophie's mind when she woke in her bed in her small terraced house near the Custom House. Sunshine slashed through the curtains and her eyes opened wide, trying to work out what the music was, until she went to the window and looked down at a one-man band stomping the street followed by a small crowd of enchanted children.

In an area swarming with strange characters up to even stranger activities, she had never seen this one before, elbows pumping away at cymbals, feet attached to strings which pounded a bass drum and hands strumming away on a banjo. He was also blowing some sort of tune on a kazoo and she smiled as this one-man wall of noise continued on his way like some Pied Piper of the Bay, his music soon to disappear into the general medley of wailing ships' hooters and the ceaseless drone of docks traffic.

She climbed back into bed and stretched, happy at least that she did not have to service some hungover drunk who, having taken his fill, would then complain long and loud about his empty wallet. But clearly her friend, Betty, with whom she shared this small house, had no such luxury, since she could hear a man's moans and groans coming through the wall – though whether he was moaning out of happiness or pain, Sophie could not tell.

Now the man was shouting with some anger, she heard, and would probably try to bash Betty any second. It was the way with all these men. Sober, remorseful and full of guilt, they would lash out and start demanding refunds. They were such babies. But, if he was foolish enough to try and bash Betty, he would be bashing the wrong girl and no mistake – as more than a few would-be pimps had discovered to their cost. For Betty packed a wallop even deadlier than their local boxing champ,

Jim Driscoll. Come to that, Sophie would not have put money on even the great Driscoll beating our Betty.

They always seemed to pick up such different men from night to night. You could never predict who they would be or how they would behave. One old salt, Twm Shun Conti, never seemed to want to do anything but just sit on the end of the bed and tell you how he had won the last war single-handed. A few came over for the night because their wives had kicked them out. One customs man just liked to dress up as a woman and wander about the bedroom. It was the seamen she liked the best though. They were usually fun and at least brought their own French letters with them. She was intrigued to learn that they often received a free pile of them with their pay.

There was a thump against the wall, a crashing-over of what sounded like a wardrobe, a short silence, a loud tinkle of breaking glass, a longer silence and the same aggrieved voice of the same aggrieved man, still shouting the odds but now out in the street with his clothes being thrown out after him. 'I'll be bloody back, don't you worry about that. I'll be bloody back to get you, you bitch.'

'Well, when you do, bring some bloody money with you.'

Sophie smiled. Our Betty also had a very big mouth to go with her big muscles.

'Sophie,' Betty yelled out. 'These punters are getting worse and worse. I'm off down the Custom House for a drink. You coming?'

'Not just now, love. I'll see you later.'

In truth, Sophie had to do some serious work just now because she was running very low – and only touched her secret tenner in the case of dire emergencies. Of all the strange men she had furnished, who could have been stranger than that Edward Gurney, who had forgotten to give her money, *and she had forgotten to ask*! And after all that effort! Just where had the little snot got all his energy from . . . time after time . . . place after place . . . ? Perhaps he was taking something. He certainly seemed to sniff a lot.

Then she thought of her Rashed and had a choking unhappy feeling in her throat. She could not remember when she had last seen him. She missed him so much she was eating far more than was good for her, and her sense of loss had become that much more intense because she felt sure that now she had lost him for good. She had heard in the gossip that he had become heavily involved in Islamic politics. Rashed into politics? It almost made her laugh out loud.

Only the other night she had spotted a group of Moslems in their distinctive white songkoks, milling around outside the Mosque. The young wanted to get back to a form of Moslem fundamentalism, she had heard. It seemed pretty strange to her that all those healthy young bucks just wanted to get back to the Koran, but there you are. She had walked near the Mosque window, listening to the furore inside when, amidst the babble of many excited Arab voices, she heard the unmistakable voice of Rashed. She recognized it immediately since he was the only man she knew who spoke Arabic in the hard, flat vowels of the Cardiff accent. And there he was, dressed in a body-length sarong and wearing a songkok on his head, haranguing the mob like one of those big-mouthed union leaders at a meeting of coal trimmers.

She had sighed hard and walked away. She had always known that there was a seriousness beneath Rashed's laughter – she had even loved that seriousness – but not *that* serious, for heaven's sake.

It was quite within the bounds of possibility that Sophie was a Moslem herself – or a Catholic or a Hindu – but, in truth, she did not really know. Her father – whom she had never known – had died in a nitrate explosion at sea, and her mother had gone out to buy a box of matches one night, never to return. There was Bay talk that she had drowned herself in the docks, unable to stand the loss of her husband. But, again, it was only Bay talk.

Along with her sister, Sylvie, she had been brought up by her grandfather, Daddy Langlo – who never supplied too many family details since he suffered from a wandering memory, hardly able to remember his own age. They had grown up in Rat Island, down near the Roath Basin and by the time she was ten she had learned things that most women never discovered in a lifetime. She soon knew about the rats on the ships and the men who sailed them – sometimes finding it difficult to tell them apart. She had learned that life gives but it takes away a lot more. She had also learned how to fight and, even more importantly, when to run.

But, strangely in the tough circumstances of her life, she had also learned how to love and, when she pitched herself into that forlorn, helpless state, she stayed in love, remaining unthinkingly loyal and devoted. There had been three affairs of her heart and, while it was Rashed she now loved, she still, at times, missed the other two.

Having no family she had also loved her sister Sylvie but saw almost nothing of her these days. The real trouble was that Sylvie had always been something of a snob and did not understand why Sophie did the work that she did. She was also one of those women keen to adopt white middle-class values and Sophie wanted none of that. Sophie was unfailingly proud of what she was and sorry the two sisters had not managed to get along better. It had been almost a year since she had seen her last.

There was a knock on the house door and Sophie groaned. She did not feel like doing any business at this time in the morning. But sometimes Billy Hywel, the customs officer, liked to come up for half an hour and merely wander around her bedroom in her knickers. It was the easiest quid she ever earned – and he sometimes threw in a few odd things, like bottles of rum or tobacco, that he had impounded from the sailors – so she had better look lively, pulling out a few of her lacy knickers and putting on her dressing gown before going to the top of the stairs.

The front door was ajar, letting drifts of dusty sunshine into the hall, but there was no sight of her perverted customs officer – nor indeed of anything else except a wooden banana box. She went down the stairs and stepped past the box to look out into the street, when she heard some sounds behind her. Thinking it was some sort of animal, she moved to one side and looked down into the box.

The first thing she saw was a small brown hand and, going down on one knee, she pulled back a white lace shawl to find a small baby with almond-brown skin. She caught her breath. It had a thick thatch of black hair and, when its small dark eyes looked up at her, it gurgled and its legs began kicking. Further investigations revealed that 'it' was, in fact, a girl.

With strange emotions running hot and cold inside her chest she picked up the box and took it into the kitchen where she placed it on the table and studied its contents again. It was, she decided then, the most beautiful sight that she had ever seen; almost like a personal gift from Allah himself. The baby gurgled again, cartwheeling her legs around in an energetic spasm of delight. Sophie reached down and picked her up, holding her firmly in her arms and kissing the top of her head.

As she paced around the kitchen holding the baby to herself, her thoughts worked in a circular fashion, trying to sort out the issues. Most of the working girls down here had illegitimate babies – it was the reason why many of them were here in the first place – and even foundling babies were not at all rare. She used French letters, when she could afford them, or the sailors brought them along themselves but, even so, there was a lot of luck in it. Most of the girls went in for a very hit-and-miss approach – usually just cotton wool packed up the vagina and frequent douches of carbolic. So many of them continued having babies even though there was never a father around.

Bringing up a baby would be no large problem but what, if any, were her rights? Could the mother just come along at a later date and demand the return of her baby? Could one of those interfering Mission Hall workers just come along and take her into a home? She did not know, but she did know someone who might. Nathan Thomas, their new vicar.

She wrapped the baby up in the shawl, stuffed her secret tenner into her blouse – she would have to buy babyclothes and food – and walked along towards the Custom House. She had spoken to Nathan a few times now, and after her early wariness, found that she had a friend, even once telling him about her problems with Rashed but quickly discovering that he knew even less about the ways of the Mosque than she did. Nevertheless she found him warm and concerned, never taking a tough line on anything and never once asking her about her work either. She had once mentioned that she had a cleaning job down in the Exchange and left it at that. Apart from his dog collar she found it very difficult to believe that he was a man of God. He was certainly not like some of the holy busybodies that she had come across. Yes, he would know what she must do.

Betty was standing on the corner of the Custom House waiting for some early morning business when Sophie walked up to her, finding it difficult to control an idiotic smile on her lips. 'Hello, Betty love. I've just had a baby.'

Her friend, her lipstick badly smudged and, despite her being in her mid-twenties, crow's feet spawning alarmingly around her eyes, took one look into the shawled bundle and then another at Sophie. 'Where'd you get that, then?'

'Had it this morning after you went out. Lovely, isn't she?'

Betty, still unable to believe her eyes, looked down at the baby again. It was the right colour, sure enough. Two of the other girls came to have a peep, making Sophie pull the baby away from the small bad gales of their beer-soaked breath.

Now Betty was sputtering and blowing like an engine unable to start. 'But Sophie . . . you can't have . . . Sophie . . . you . . . well, I don't know.'

'She was a bit premature, that's all.'

'A bit premature! A bit bloody premature! I've heard mice have babies in a week but you're not a bloody mouse, are you? You didn't even get fat.' Betty took yet another disbelieving look at the baby who was staring up quietly at the gathered heads all around. 'What are you going to call it then?'

Sophie remembered an old aboriginal name that she had long liked. 'Effey. I'm going to call her Effey.'

The two others sighed, putting their heads to one side and looking down at the child. Betty shook her head again. 'I've heard of phantom pregnancies but this beats all, this does. That baby can be nothing but wind.'

They both sat in Nathan's study and he listened gravely as she told him the story of her foundling baby. He leaned across and took the baby from her, now cradling it in his arms and staring down at her black eyes. 'Such innocence,' he said to the baby softly. 'One of the very greatest joys in this life is to hold a new baby – I used to sit holding mine for hours, not that there's much chance of holding the brutes now. I'd say she's about a month old – perhaps more.' He smoothed the head with his hand. 'Their eyes don't focus properly 'til well after a month, you see. And the skull hasn't quite closed yet. But she's well fed. Nice shawl – an expensive shawl, I'd guess. She belongs to some mother, Sophie . . .'

'But . . . but . . .' Her mouth twisted in alarm and tears began welling up in her eyes. Even she could not believe how quickly she had become attached to her Effey.

'Don't worry now, girl,' he said, handing the baby back to her. 'I'm only telling you what you must already know. But you must also remember that the baby was left on your doorstep for a reason. The baby's mother must have picked on you as being a proper and decent woman. This baby has been cared for. You can see the girl has had a lot of love. You can always tell these things. So . . . how are you going to look after her?'

'You think, then, do you, that I can keep her?'

'Why not? This is Tiger Bay after all. This is not Cardiff, nor even Wales. This is an enclosed society struggling to find her soul and her future; a small mixed place trying to discover new rules of living together. New rules are so often better than old rules.'

Sophie loved the way that Nathan never tried to talk down to her; never tried to preach the Bible dogmas. Her sparky street intelligence had soon built up an uncannily accurate picture of a man who was both warm and tender, good and kind; but one who also had an innocence and vulnerability which might, in the end, be his undoing in life in the Bay. Well, one day she might be able to help him on that score. She had learned lots of the tricks of survival – even if he hadn't.

But where had this baby come from? You didn't just go around leaving something as beautiful as this on other people's doorsteps. And why had they picked on her?

Even after just a few hours of holding the baby her desire to keep her was quite overwhelming. Her family had been as nothing – she might as well not have had a family at all – and here was what her heart had longed for all along. She had always said that if she had fallen for one, there would be no abortion in Betty Pryce's around James Street for her. She would have had it.

So now she actually had a baby, and quite the strangest aspect of it all was that she could easily have been this baby's mother since, when she looked at those brown eyes, and when her fingers caressed that soft, olive skin, and when she kissed all that dark silky hair . . . all she saw was a tiny version of herself.

'Nathan, you haven't forgotten, have you, that you were supposed to be meeting our sewing circle this morning?'

Elizabeth had walked into the study, staring at Sophie and then at the baby in her arms. She was another aspect of Nathan's life that Sophie worried about. If he was an innocent abroad in the Bay then she was a positive liability. When Sophie's perceptive eyes looked at Elizabeth's face all she could see was one thing – colour prejudice. There was an awful lot of prejudice in the Bay – not the least amongst the coloureds themselves – but when your position obliged you to deal with everyone *and* you were prejudiced, that spelled a lot of trouble.

'Ah, the great sewing circle of four old ladies,' said Nathan, stretching his arms wide with mock joy as if he had been waiting for this date all his life. 'Yes, dear, I'll be there. Elizabeth, have you met Sophie, one of our parishioners?'

The two women nodded at one another.

'There's a beautiful baby you have there,' said Elizabeth without moving any closer. 'Does he sleep well at night?'

'He's a she, actually.'

'Oh yes. I'm sorry. Mothers are most particular about that, aren't they?' There were sounds of busy footsteps in the corridor outside and Elizabeth turned, seeing Halfway Harry and a policeman standing in the study doorway. 'Ah, some more visitors,' she said. 'Isn't life in a busy manse just such a wonderful thing?'

'Vicar, we need you over in the Alexandra Dock,' said Halfway without apology or preamble. 'There's some mischief with a shipful of West Indians and they are asking to speak to the local church leader.'

'And what am I expected to do with a shipful of West Indians?' Nathan inquired, slightly taken aback.

'You could always bring them here,' said Elizabeth, adding a small cough before she left the study.

'Yes, I suppose I could.'

'Better get there fast,' said Halfway, defusing the frostiness. 'They've even called in the Army. There could be a lot of trouble if something isn't done quickly.'

Nathan put on his jacket. 'Remind me which one is Alexandra Dock,' he said, busy with the buttons.

'It's the one just over the road,' said Sophie. 'Come on, I'll go with you.'

The small group crossed busy Bute Street and hurried down to the No. 3 quay in the Alexandra Dock. They found the *Caropic*, a tramp cargo registered in Cardiff, berthed there with twenty or more policemen alongside her on the quay. Even as they headed towards the gangway they heard the trill of bicycle bells and the 7th (Cyclists) Battalion of the Welsh Regiment came turning into the docks and pedalling towards them. They parked their bicycles quickly and ran smartly to attention. All held rifles. A sergeant major barked orders as the soldiers lined up two-deep behind the policemen, fixing bayonets whose silver blades glinted ferociously in the morning sun.

Nathan watched the soldiers and then looked up at the ship's rails, chilled to the pit of his belly. All along the rails he could see hundreds of black faces staring down at him. Clumps of tiny children were hanging from the derricks. Black faces gazed watchfully out of the portholes, there were figures crowded around the tops of the gangplanks and some actually on the bridge itself. Thin wisps of smoke from the idling engine curled up out of the funnel, occasionally turning into a thundering belch.

Yet what Nathan found so eerie about the whole crowded scene was its total silence. There were the usual dock noises – the gabbling gulls and the ship's hooters – but here were some five hundred people soundlessly confronting one another as the sun tried to blowtorch a hole through the cloudless blue sky. It was certainly the closest that he had seen to something out of the Old Testament. Even as he looked along the crowded deck, he thought of the Israelites of old, wandering lost in the deserts, following the great stone of water and waiting to be returned to the Promised Land.

An old man with silvery grey hair was sitting on the aft deck, huge black hands dangling between his knees as his rheumy red eyes stared squarely into the face of another defeat. On his wrists were the clear scars of slave shackles. Some old mamas were fanning themselves with their hands. The young men were standing, arms folded in grim-faced groups. Other younger women had babies in cotton shawls tied to their backs. Sophie looked down at her own baby, asleep in her arms. 'You'd better get up there,' she told Nathan. 'Go and give someone a good kick.'

'Men wearing dog collars don't go around giving people a good kick,' he pointed out amiably.

'Well, at least you now know what it's like to be black and have the spit of nine men on your tail,' she said softly. 'Look at all those women with their babies. They've crossed the world and this is all we can do for them.'

'What do you suggest I do for them?'

'Oh I don't know. Just get them off that old tub, that's all. We can always throw them a party or something.'

'What kind of party would that be?'

'I don't know. Why are you asking me these things?'

'Well you're a darkey as well, aren't you?'

'I'm not a darkey. I'm a sort of browney but, if you really want to know, I haven't a clue what I am.'

A few late-arriving Army cyclists came clattering onto the quay as Nathan strode through the blue line of policemen. 'Who's in charge here?' he shouted at a group of men standing, fingers poking the air and voices rising in angry decibels, at the bottom of the gangplank.

'Who wants to know?'

'I'm the vicar at St Mark's over the way. I've been sent for.'

One of the group broke away and came to talk to Nathan. Even before he held out his huge shovel of a hand Nathan knew him by the blotchy red birthmark which covered most of his face.

'Victor Watts,' he introduced himself. 'For my sins – which are many – I'm the chief police inspector in the area.'

Nathan took his hand away as quickly as he decently could. There was something about the man which troubled him. Apart from his birthmark he also had a strangely-shaped head with virtually no forehead. Also his jawbone was so large it might have been a Neanderthal club.

But his manner was affable enough as he briskly explained the situation. There was a total of four hundred and ten West Indians on board the *Caropic*; many had been brought over as ballast from Barbados. Each of them, he added, had paid about three guineas a head. With the food and conditions being so poor, there had been much illness on the voyage; an old man had died when they were two weeks out. The captain had been told by the customs people in Cardiff to sail away again but, so far, he had refused. The shipowner himself, Arthur Tatem, had been called for, even the Lord Mayor. But the West Indians had insisted that they would only speak with the local church leader.

'Of course I'll talk to them,' Nathan cried. 'Even though I'm sure we're not members of the same church.'

'Most of them, I gather, are Pentecostalists or Church of God or something,' said Watts. 'But I don't see what all the fuss is about myself. The West Indies are British after all. What's a few hundred more?'

Nathan followed Watts through the police line and approached the group at the gangplank. The portly Arthur Tatem himself was explaining, in between puffs of his cigar, that no laws had been broken. He was merely a businessman doing any lawful business that came his way. The port authorities disagreed violently.

'Come off it, Arthur,' one of them protested. 'There may have been cholera on board so they'll have to go into quarantine whatever happens. None of them has got an address. They haven't got a job between them. They can't spill into a small city like this. There'll be murder.'

'Well, what are you saying?' Tatem asked, examining his cigar as if looking for cracks. 'Are you telling me I should tell my skipper to go out and dump the lot in the sea? They're getting off here, I say. This ship sails next Tuesday for Curaçao and Curaçao is a long way from the West Indies – even if there was room for them in all the coal, which there isn't.'

The argument was cut dead by an unexpected sound. All heads looked up. There, on the foredeck, they saw a young, muscular black stripped to the waist, the sun gleaming on his brass trumpet, as he played what sounded to Nathan like some old West Indian spiritual. It was an eerily beautiful rendition, the full, sorrowing notes echoing out over the morning dock, telling of the islands which they had left behind and the stormclouds into which they had sailed.

As the gusting solo continued, it was supported by a murmuring groundswell of voices from the deck, humming gently and becoming louder and louder until the very air was alive with the music of weeping, breaking hearts. The massed voices began duelling with the trumpet, rising up to its sonorous sweetness and falling away again, the words telling of their certainty that the sweet Lord Jesus would one day come and rescue them from their pain and take them up to new life.

The effect of the hymn on Nathan was devastating and his eyesight became blurred with tears. As a young man in West Wales he had been first called into the service of God by the great Revival meetings when, in packed chapels and churches, astonishing preachers like Christmas Evans and Evan Roberts had first orchestrated the sorrows and glories of his Welsh tribe. It was that marvellous and marvelling poetry of men beholding the Cross of Shame that had become the love and lifespring of his life. It was those hymns which had first captured and imprisoned his spirit. Yet, with the same churches and chapels now beginning to fall silent, here it was again – the perfect, wonderful sound of a lost people, come to the end of a long voyage and putting their faith and trust in the God of Abraham.

The spiritual did not affect his heart alone. Almost everyone on that quay fell under its spellbinding thrall. The waterguard officers and the police studied their shoes in shuffling embarrassment. Tatem quietly rocked back and forth on the balls of his feet and conducted it with his cigar. The soldiers, who were only part-time volunteers, lowered their bayoneted rifles.

The hymn continued in a series of eddies and crescendos until it finally came to an end. An awesome silence fell on the dock. It was Nathan who stepped forward and spoke first.

'Ladies and gentlemen and children of the West Indies! I have come to offer the friendship and fellowship of the people of Wales,' he shouted up at the ship. 'I have come here to tell you that we are all sorry that you, who are under British protection, have had such a poor welcome from the people here. But I want to assure you now that these people do not represent the whole of Wales and that we are all one and equal in the eyes and arms of God.'

A breeze ruffled Sophie's skirt and she felt so *proud* that she knew him, cradling her baby tight as his clear, resonant words echoed around the tall, silent cranes, amplified by the amphitheatre of the ships moored all around. She admired anyone with the confidence to address a crowd of complete strangers like this – it was a trait, she thought, which always marked a man apart. He seemed to care about so much, making meaning out of his calling by just being what he was – a caring, great man.

Nathan paused and stood staring up at his audience, knowing that he had created an opening for these trapped voyagers. He recalled Sophie's – doubtless ironic – idea that they should throw a party, and half-looked back to see if she was still there.

'I gather that you have no homes to go to but, as of now, your home is St Mark's Church over the road. You will be under the protection of my church until such time as we can find you proper accommodation and work. I suggest you pack your luggage quietly and form up on the dockside here. You will be fed and your sick will be taken care of. We Welsh are about to show you the real meaning of love and hospitality.'

Some began to file below deck to collect their belongings. But, even as the barking sergeant major ordered his men to get back on their bicycles and return to base, many of those on the ship remained standing, unable to believe that the invitation was genuine.

'Well, what are you all waiting for?' Nathan bellowed. 'They'll be filling this ship with coal in half an hour. You don't want to get as black as coal now, do you?'

It was just the right remark to defuse the uncertainty. The vast gathering slowly began to file below decks. Soon the first of them came down the gangplank, some carrying huge bundles balanced on their heads.

Tatem walked over to Nathan. 'You did well,' he murmured. 'If you need money or help you'll find me over in the Exchange.'

'God is good,' Nathan replied cheerfully. 'We'll manage just fine.'

By mid-afternoon the exhausted Barbadians had settled down in the church. Many were asleep on the pews, some with their bare feet sticking up into the air, others making small family encampments in the corners and around the pillars. One baby was fast asleep in the grey stone christening font.

From the very moment the first of them had walked in, the demands on Nathan had multiplied in a dizzying spiral. Official and unofficial bodies had ricocheted in and out of the vestry. Danny Moses had come down from Loudoun Square and said that he would be happy to take in any Bermudians, but there were none, so he had left again. The Lord Mayor turned up only to be sent away and asked to come back again tomorrow. A reporter from the *Western Mail* cornered Nathan and told him that he had heard that some of them were dying of cholera or even worse.

*Six* ambulances arrived from the Royal Infirmary only to find, disappointingly, that none of them was terminally sick – from cholera, bubonic plague, leprosy or anything else – even if a lot of them had quickly developed sneezing head colds after contact with the fresh Channel winds. Many of them were shivering in their thin cotton clothes.

Halfway Harry – in between moving the precious relics from the altar and being told by Nathan to move them back again – was now worrying what was going to happen to all his lovingly polished tiles. 'But we should be able to find a new home for them in a day or two, wouldn't you think?'

Nathan did not know quite what to think, though his spirits lifted when he spotted Sophie, with about eight of her friends, bringing piles of old woollen clothes into the church and handing them around. Her friends were strange, gaudy girls too, he saw, with a fondness for thick lipstick and bright, flowered dresses. The few bits of language that he caught were pretty ripe as well. They were probably prostitutes, he guessed. He was becoming gripped by the thought that Sophie was a prostitute too, but had decided to say nothing.

He heard Sophie ask one old woman what they liked eating. 'Nothing too fancy, ma'am. Fried yams and toasted plantain we like. But best of all we like coconut pie.'

'We could probably get you some fish and chips. You'd eat that, would you?'

His two boys, David and Stephen, were having a wonderful time with the new visitors, standing around and watching with quiet absorption. One of the men showed Stephen his conjuring tricks, making a lighted cigarette disappear into his mouth, chewing on it, giving a little belch and making it reappear again. Nathan was struck by the free and easy way with children that all the Barbadians had.

He spotted the young trumpeter sitting near the altar. 'Hello, I'm Nathan Thomas,' he said. 'I admired the way you played that hymn on the boat.'

'Obadiah Brown,' he said, holding out his hand. 'Entertainer, calypso singer and the best jazz trumpeter in the whole of the West Indies. Just call me Obe.'

Nathan took an immediate liking to this intelligent young man who chuckled a lot, often smoothing the sides of his cheeks with the tips of his long fingers. He had big lips, swollen even bigger by his constant trumpet-playing, and an enormous conk with nostrils so cavernous he might even have played his trumpet with them as well. He explained that he had asked for an English churchman because most of Barbados was under some form of English church or other. Sometimes Barbados was even called Little England. 'All our laws are English an' cricket is our way of life,' he added. 'Ah was born with a cricket ball in mah hand.'

But these days, he murmured darkly, there was almost no employment in Bridgetown. The worldwide collapse of sugar prices had seen to that. There seemed almost nothing for anyone to do, so when the chance of some cheap berths came along, every damned one who could walk found the money from somewhere and made one big stampede to the harbour. More were left behind than got on. Few even knew where Cardiff was. Some thought that it was the name of a dock in London. The trip was pretty damn awful with a lot being seasick over one another. He burst out laughing. 'Boss, have you ever seen a black man go green?' he asked.

Nathan was marvelling at the way Obe and his countrymen never seemed to let their circumstances get them down for long when his attention was caught by some screeching noises and into the church, to his considerable surprise, came Elizabeth pushing a trolley with a big silver tea urn on it. Behind her came three more trolleys, all pushed by smiling, burly women from the sewing circle. 'I just thought we'd better feed them,' Elizabeth explained when he walked over to her. 'I can't think what the Bishop would have said if we'd allowed them all to starve right here.'

'No. Neither can I. All we've got to eat here is a tin of stale communion wafers.'

His spirits rose a good ten points as the Barbadians hauled themselves up to queue in front of the food trolleys and, with a bright smile, he manned the tea urn as Elizabeth and the others passed around plates of cold sausage rolls, pickled onions and slices of cheese.

Their guests were clearly hungry enough to eat almost anything and, later, Sophie and her friends came clattering in with trays piled high with steaming fish and chips. They had also acquired five large bowls of jellied eels, and the church was filled with tantalizing smells.

The Barbadians swooped on the hot food with alacrity and glee, the event becoming an almost celebratory feast as they forked it all down. Elizabeth drew her husband to one side. 'Just what are all those foul women doing in here?' she hissed.

He was taken aback. This was not the time for personal bickering. 'That's just Sophie and a few of her friends helping us out,' he explained. 'They're just trying to help, that's all.'

'But they're all prostitutes, Nathan. Every single one of those women is on the game.'

'Ah well, everyone's got to make a living somehow. Maybe we're putting together a decent church after all.'

'A church it may be but decent, never. You'll be having all

those whores in your bed next. Is that what you call a decent church?'

'At least it will mean that there's something going on in our bed,' he muttered softly; a hurtful jibe which he instantly regretted since the wound was visible and the blood real. She stared down at the trolley in front of her, so upset that she was unable to speak. She knew – as well as he – that the passion had been short-lived and the marriage bed had gone cold again. Just then, with a most fortunate sense of timing, their two boys went chasing past. 'I'm not having those two running around in all this,' she said, dashing off to round up her children, leaving Nathan in a pall of black gloom. After so much that had been promising, his marriage seemed to be sinking into a rut in which he was unable to do anything right at all.

In desperation, and perhaps under the influence of Father O'Reilly, Nathan had even been taking the odd drink to enable him to relax in the evenings and that little habit had driven Elizabeth to quite unexpected heights of fury. 'Look, Nathan. I have decided to try and work here with you. I understand that this is a difficult parish and I am worried about the boys. I also know we have little money and that my home is never going to be my own. I can take all that, but one thing I will never compromise on is the health of my husband. I will never tolerate you drinking alcohol. Every glass you take you become half the man you were.'

But he didn't stop drinking; just started taking the odd one in secret.

Even as she and the girls were busy handing out the fish and chips – there were no takers for the jellied eels – Sophie had kept an eye locked on the small conflict between Nathan and his wife. She understood and genuinely regretted spoiling Elizabeth's big moment. She had also picked up on the dark looks that Elizabeth kept shafting in her direction, guessing that Elizabeth had almost certainly told him what any woman could work out in ten seconds – that she was in the business of the streets.

Sophie was worried busybody tongues would get to work on him and it would all spell yet more trouble for the troubled Nathan. He had so many strengths but they underpinned so many weaknesses. Even with all his education he knew so little about anything important. She so wished that she could help him in some way; that he would take her into his confidence. She knew a trick or two for reviving shaky marriages but, for the moment, all she could do was wander over to him and offer a saucer of jellied eels.

'I'm not hungry,' he said, still behaving like a ball with very little bounce. 'And even if I was I wouldn't eat that.'

'Funny that. This lot can't stand them either.' She plopped a glutinous lump into her mouth. 'Me, I just love jellied eels.'

But, with Nathan, the black dogs rarely kept yapping for long, and that night in the summer of 1918, in St Mark's Church, Bute Street, Cardiff, a service took place that Nathan would remember until the day he died. It was a high essay in hope and consolation; an electric charge of pure spirituality which he had long prayed he would see again in the Church whose work he believed in so fervently.

It had all begun quietly enough, if indeed it could have been described as having begun at all. It just sort of started happening when one old woman sang a plantation song of slavers and suffering, in the mellow resigned tones whose secret is only properly known by the very old. Obe picked up his trumpet and played around with the melody when, without warning or apparent rehearsal, others began waking in the pews and joining in with some force. Obe then played a haunting version of *That Old Rugged Cross* which, just as seamlessly, moved into yet another plantation song. By now the whole event was working up a full head of steam with the rhythms becoming wilder and springier with lots of body-swaying and hand-clapping.

As the singing continued all the candles were lit on the altar with figures circling around in the smoky stammering darkness. Some stood at the altar holding their arms apart while others kneeled in prayer as they sang songs celebrating the manumission of slaves; songs bemoaning the hurricanes and volcanoes which had put their beloved islands to fire and the sword.

Yet in between the minor-key, sorrowful hymns – so beloved of the Welsh – there were also outbreaks of carnival happiness with eruptions of clattering tambourines and strange exotic images curling in the church rafters – the light and shadow of the banana plantations, the huge white feathers of the sugarcane in full flower, the sun on the sands of the Caribbean shores. Spattered through all this was the lilting, subversive humour of calypso, the protests against the slavers' whips, the exuberant jazz riffs of New Orleans and Harlem . . .

Nathan just sat in the rear pew, sometimes clapping and sometimes humming, but always marvelling at the rich and eclectic culture of these island people. They seemed to have absorbed almost anything that had wandered the face of the earth, with their worship as diffuse as their culture, embracing almost everything from Pentecostalism to Shango and Shouter, with even a touch of voodoo.

But most marvellous of all was Obe's jazz trumpet which ran through everything in a glittering vein of pure gold.

As the evening progressed others from the street came crowding in to join the celebrations until the air was as thick and humid as any Caribbean evening. Nathan spotted Sophie carrying her baby in a shawl West-Indian-style. She wrinkled up her nose and waved at him. He waved back but did not invite her over. So she really was one of those whores, he thought, with something deep and dark lurching inside him. So she really was . . . but no . . . no . . . His fingernails cut into the hams of his hands, then, quite soon, he was lost again on Caribbean shores, with a young girl singing a calypso to the joys of lazing in the shade of a palm tree.

But, beneath it all, there was only one theme for these people, carolling and at ease at the feet of God. And that was peace at last, peace at last. After a long, tough voyage, peace at last. Their people had been delivered.

The service rolled on for close on five hours in all, and when it finally fizzled out in the small hours, almost as incoherently as it had begun, everyone seemed complete and whole, satisfied that they had honoured God who, in his turn, had honoured them too.

Nathan put his arms above his head and stretched until he was as rigid as a plank but, even after this, his longest day, he did not feel at all tired. The only dark shadow on his sun was that his wife and children had not been there by his side to experience the joy also.

# CHAPTER FIVE

It was just gone seven o'clock in the morning near the Bailey Dry Dock. A wan sun was inching up the back of a pale sky as two respectably-dressed men – unusual in such a setting at such time – came into view. Partington grabbed Edward by the elbow. 'We'd better go the other way, Mr Edward,' he muttered.

Edward followed his companion's pointing finger. Amidst shouts and curses a pack of some twenty or thirty labourers was brawling on the cobbles by the dock entrance. It was the biggest and most ferocious fight that Edward had seen in his life. Two spitting, snarling men went rolling over and over, clawing at one another in the middle of the road. Only an oncoming tram – bearing an advertisement for Bovril: *It's better than influenza* – made them break it up and return to the heaving mêlée around the dock gate.

'It happens all too often, I'm afraid,' explained Partington, sucking on his regular Mint Imperial as they both watched the continuing maul. 'Some of them are Somalis and the others are Chamari tribesmen. Both try to get here first to pick up a tally for a day's work. The fighting between them gets so vicious that no one else bothers to try and get work in this dock. It's almost a tribal ritual now. A little like a morning tea-break.'

'The shipowners let it carry on?'

'Not all of them, but some don't do much to discourage it. It's a bit of good sport, they say. I've known some of them come down and throw out the tallies themselves. This is a very odd corner of the world, Mr Edward.'

'We used to fight over our hampers in school, but never like that. And over the opportunity to do a hard day's work too!' He gave a mock shudder before Partington steered him towards a side alley.

Four policemen began circling the fighting mob but made no effort to control or contain them. Some of the warring dockers, clutching their precious tallies, had passed through the dock gates. But outside, if anything, the fighting had become even more intense: one tall Chamari was whirling a huge plank in the air as if he was intent on beheading someone.

They continued down the alley to the Coal Exchange, Edward glancing back in case the fighting rolled towards them. 'It'll break up in a minute,' Partington said. 'It rarely lasts for more than ten minutes and, apart from the odd cut or black eye, few really get injured.Most of them are made of granite or something even tougher.'

Partington was certainly a courteous, amusing and efficient guide to this odd corner of the world, as Edward was quick to learn when he was introduced to the mysteries of the Floor of the Exchange, where the lords of commerce mingled with the various brokers and their minions, all busy discussing types of cargo, where it could be transported and the costs of hiring vessels. Porters continually called out the names of members who were wanted outside. Office boys scuttled over the Floor as if their very lives depended on the next deal.

Everywhere Edward turned he heard the music of money, the hum of men working to make the greatest possible profit for themselves, who were all intimately connected with other men with money, in almost every part of the world.

The same groups of principals and associates stood behind the same pillars or walked the same parts of the Floor, fixing deals with the cheapest man or inviting offers for a charter, then, as often as not, making a quick profit by discounting the same deal with another broker behind another pillar on another part of the Floor. There were the buying and selling brokers – men who knew every ship on the market and what it cost – engaged with bargaining shipowners, anxious to expand or, in Partington's case, contract their fleets. A small huddle of brokers was anxiously studying the shipping news, trying to learn about a ship that had been caught in a gale and working out what sort of profit they might expect to make out of her salvage. As far as Edward could see unbelievable amounts of money were also salvaged in the process.

Partington knew and pointed out most of them by name, warning Edward that many of them might look dim but were, in fact, as sharp as blades, as you soon found out to your cost. He pointed at two brokers standing together, talking mysteriously and gazing into one another's optics. 'Those two have spent the whole of their lives trying to cut one another up, but

I doubt if they have made so much as one lump of coal out of one another. When it comes to plucking a chicken they do it like gentlemen but, oh, so thoroughly. All those people rob you in style. They've all basically got the minds of thieves and the accent of the public school. That's all you need to do well on the Floor. Oh yes, and a good head for Canary wine. Mr Hamilton thinks you are going to do very well here after you've learned the ropes.'

'I'm not at all sure I like this Mr Hamilton. Could you tell me something about him? Exactly what did he have to do with my father?'

'You really must ask him about those things for yourself, Mr Edward, but I must warn you that the one thing he does not like is questions of any description. Just remember that he enjoys a lot of power and a lot of money – an awful lot of money, Mr Edward – some of which will certainly come your way as long as you learn not to ask any questions.'

'But was he in partnership with my father?'

'Questions again, Mr Edward. The great advantage of not asking any questions is that you do not then get answers that you might not like.'

'Exactly what are you saying?'

'What I am saying just at the moment, Mr Edward, is that you always have to keep the most careful eye on coal here since that is the chief marker of them all, often influencing commodities like wheat or barley, which have no relation to it. When coal is brisk the chartering of everything is brisk. When coal is stagnant the rates of everything fall.'

But it also soon became clear that there were great risks in the mere buying and selling of coal since coal prices could go through long periods of depression for no apparent reason at all, then enjoy short periods of very high prices, again for no apparent reason. Somewhere in the middle of all this someone was making a great deal of money, Edward decided, and he wanted it to be him.

'The only real rule you must follow in all the doings of the Floor, Mr Edward, is to always take a cash profit. Taking a cash profit is the only justification at all for being here. You can make a million pounds on paper but you can always lose it again just as quickly. Take the cash and bank it. That's the only way to beat this system. Remember. A fiver in cash is worth a million on paper. Follow that and everything else will look after itself.'

They watched the to-ings and fro-ings on the Floor silently for a while, then Partington took Edward to meet Big Bertha, the great pipe which blew down news of arrivals of vessels, notices of freight wanted and lists of homeward-bound ships. He also took Edward on a tour of the notice boards, which detailed market fluctuations in the Stock Exchange, any political or general news which might have a bearing on shipping, together with European Bourse prices and the latest prices on the various Welsh coal mines.

For Edward, all this was a bit like finding an old and well-loved heirloom which had been lost for years. Even though he could still only see the outlines of the Exchange through Partington's knowledgeable eyes, he knew that he would master the detail soon enough. After all, he was a thief with a public school accent. And he had a good head for Canary wine.

He was even more interested to learn that everything on the Floor was done on a handshake without a single binding document. These men may well have been as sharp as blades but he knew that he could be sharper than anyone and, where there was trust, that could be quickly abused too.

Culley's restaurant, in the basement of the Exchange, also exercised a strong fascination. Apart from giving a wonderful plaice meal for 3s. 6d. they also specialized in sauté kidneys or roast saddle of lamb. But there was also a load of pot-bellied men sitting around those tables feeding their fat faces, who, between them, must have one rich and, preferably, single daughter whom he could marry for heaps of money. He had never once in his short, erratic life even so much as briefly entertained any thoughts of love.

He was further delighted to learn that you could always get Albert Sims, the hall porter, to put a bet on a horse for you. Yes, this Exchange had the most agreeable smell of money and the prospect of a lush and laundered future.

It was twilight, getting on for dark when Sophie was walking down Bute Street trying to trawl up a bit of trade. She crossed the road and stopped still when the door of the Adelphi pub cracked open and a man in a French matelot uniform bulleted out of it, tottering across the pavement and collapsing, with arms akimbo, on the street's tramlines. He stood up, took a few swaying steps, stumbled forwards, went down on one knee and, gratefully, hung onto a stationary lamppost where he vomited once, twice, three times . . . long rancid splashes of beer and bits of spaghetti, which a passing dog found attractive since he started lapping it up and was so clearly enjoying it that another passing dog joined in and what started as a free meal ended up in a snarling bloody fight between the two dogs, rolling over and over in what they had hoped to eat.

The sailor hauled himself onto the other side of the lamppost, away from the fighting dogs, before lurching sideways again. Sophie turned back the way she had come, her nose wrinkling up in disgust. Give seamen a few drinks and they never seemed to know how to behave but, heyho, here were a few of the burly officers of the French Naval Patrol and that sailor was going to sober up far sooner than he had hoped.

The night was crowded enough, but not with anything by way of custom, she was disappointed to see. A few of the newcomer Barbadians greeted her before going on their way. A man from the Mosque nodded. Another called out to her from the other side of the road. She had always enjoyed the intense friendliness of the Bay; something to do with the poverty here, she supposed. If a woman made a stew for herself she also made one for her neighbour. If a child had no food at home he would get a plate of chips over the road. Doors were always left open or on the latch. The money for the insurance man was left on the windowsill. Poverty never meant dishonesty in the Bay.

The Naval Patrol men frogmarched the drunk sailor past her, their hands keeping his head well down in case he found any more beer and spaghetti that he wanted to throw up. This was the usual way of getting a drunk back to the ship though there were other methods for those too drunk to walk and too heavy to carry. Some were taken back to their ships on handcarts and she had seen more than a few, unable to stand and singing saucy songs, being taken back in a wheelbarrow.

She stood on the edge of the kerb, the headlamps of the passing cars dancing in her eyes like a miniature firework display. She had a way of making her lips pout too, not that it was doing her too much good at the moment.

She was still worried about her Effey; still asking herself where the baby had come from and if she might soon be taken away again. But at least the girl was well looked-after while she was out at work, left with Mrs Phyllis Jones, a cheerful, beefy child-minder in Angelina Street, who also looked after all the other prostitutes' children in the area.

The doorway of Mrs Jones's house was a busy railway terminus of babies being dropped off for as long as the girls wanted and taken away again. Mrs Jones was not too fussy about being paid, either, only too happy when her small terraced house was throbbing with squalls of gurgling kids who, in an odd sort of way, all looked after one another. It has to be said that the children liked the house too, more often than not laughing their little heads off when they were taken in there and crying their little eyes out when they were taken away again.

And it was not just the prostitutes who relied on Mrs Jones. She took in seamen's allotments (those keys to the Bay economy) and cashed advance notes. She arranged for money to be sent regularly to distant relatives, such as arthritic mothers stranded on top of rain-swept Welsh mountains, or Woolworth girls putting together the doings to set up a house when Wandering Billy finally decided to call it a day and get that shore job he had been talking about ever since he first signed on at the age of fourteen. Mrs Jones would also give a seaman a straight loan, too, while he was waiting for a berth, perhaps, and never, ever asked for it back either. She always knew that it would be repaid, perhaps a year later, when he got his next advance note – in full and at just a modest five per cent interest.

But the standard and unvarying payment for her vital social services was the providing of – and listening to – gossip. When any mother came in through the door to pick up her baby, Mrs Jones made the ritual cup of tea, when it was expected for them to sit there for ten minutes, exchanging the news about anything at all.

A car with its hood down pulled up in front of Sophie and she immediately recognized that young snot who did the strangest things hanging off Clifton Suspension Bridge. 'Oh it's you again. You owe me a lot of money, you do.'

'Get in.'

'Not likely. I'm not falling for that one again. You're like some frog on a gallon of Spanish fly you are. Too much for me. Just give me my money. I'll settle for a tenner.'

'Get in and I'll give it to you. I might even give you two if you give that mouth of yours a rest.'

They were smiling throughout the banter and she got in, even closing her own door, before they roared off up Bute Street, accelerating through the Civic Centre and up North Road. 'Don't you worry now. I'm not in one of my moods tonight. It's just that I like a little sniff of cocaine now and then. That's what it does for you.'

'Really. Well, I'll be staying off that stuff, I can tell you now. I don't need any of that to keep me going. Where are we off to anyway?'

'Just a ride.'

Well, at least they weren't going to Clifton Suspension Bridge. The wind lifted her hair and she had a feeling of a lot of air rushing around everywhere as he gunned the car again. She had taken her shoes off and put her feet on the dashboard, showing him a lot of leg. She was not at all sure what to make of this impulsive young snot, who clearly thought so much of himself. He was actually being quite nice now, but he wasn't all that likeable. She had to be very careful in all this. He may well be an impulsive young snot but he probably did not have too many communicable diseases; he was not likely to vomit beer and bits of spaghetti over her bedroom floor *and* he clearly had a lot of money. As she had suddenly become a mother, with widely enlarged responsibilities, she now needed as much money as she could lay her hands on.

'I don't know about cocaine, but if you want to try something really interesting, I've got a fresh lump of opium back at my place,' she offered. 'Opium is something different again. It makes you slow and dreamy. You lose all sense of time and body. I like that a lot. It's much better in a bed too – rather than dancing around the city *or* your old school yard come to that. I've never heard of anything so daft.'

He braked at the entrance to a muddy lane as some lowing cows walked in front of them. It was an immense star-spangled night, the air thick with the smell of dung. Over in the bottom of a distant valley there were the dotted lights of the Glamorganshire Ship Canal.

'I thought *I'd* tried everything, but never opium. It's that good is it? Why didn't you tell me before we drove out here? We're going to have to drive all the way back again now.'

'There's no rush is there? But first things first. Before we dive into that opium I want to be paid for it now. *And* I want paying for the last time. So hand over.'

The following Saturday was warm and still, with small summer storms shivering against one another over the Bay. Lightning darted silently. Thunder rumbled softly, but there was no sign of rain.

Come the twilight the air was still motionless and humid. Billy the Lamplighter did his work, coming to the entrance to Howard Close and ignoring the transvestites as he shinned up his ladder and made off as fast as he could. The transvestites swam in and out of the green pool of light like ghostly, gaudy fish. They circled one another, sometimes breaking away and disappearing into the loaming shadows. Bright cackles of laughter erupted amidst short, incoherent sentences.

Edward's brisk walk broke into faltering, hesitant steps when he approached them. They stopped circling one another, coming together in a shooting gallery of circus clowns as they admired his black polished shoes, his brown, worsted suit, his white starched collar, bamboo walking cane and lavender leather gloves. They might have come from a different planet and he waved his bamboo cane imperiously for them to step aside. They made a parting in their ranks, still silently leering at him as he stepped through, one cautious eye still on them. Partington had warned him never to stop walking: any sign of fear and they might jostle you or pull at your clothes. 'But only if you look uncertain or weak, Mr Edward. Those mad, bad bum-boys never go near you if you look certain or strong. They never go within ten yards of Mr Hamilton.'

Hamilton's house loomed large as Edward approached and he coolly appraised the high, black iron railings, the barred windows, the locks and catches. The solid mahogany door had a dead-bolt on it, he noticed, as he pushed the huge brass doorbell. It would be very difficult indeed to get into this house uninvited.

A white-gloved manservant answered the door, bowing low and inviting Edward into the oak-panelled hallway. Oil paintings of country scenes hung on the wall. There were six doors leading off the hallway and, after taking his walking cane, the manservant led Edward into the drawing room where he poured him a sherry. 'Mr Hamilton will be with you in a moment or two,' he intoned gravely.

Edward had seen the great casinos of the South of France, even the palaces of minor European royalty, so he immediately recognized the smell of power and money. A small coal fire flickered in the stone grate; a huge circular oak table in the centre held a spectacular silver candelabra; an equally spectacular crystal chandelier hung from the ceiling. But, even if these were commonplace in the homes of the rich, it was the ancient Welsh weaponry dotted around the walls that were the real items of interest – old arrowheads with shafts fletched with peacock feathers, crossbow quarrels with armour-piercing heads, daggers and crude iron swords, early pikeman's breastplates and, right at the end of the room, two full sets of armour with close-helmets and hinged visors. On the opposite wall, next to the suits of armour, was a sort of altarpiece with a huge six-foot iron sword resting on it.

Sherry in hand, Edward walked around inspecting the pieces, hardly able even to guess what they might bring if he got them into the right hands. Even the books on the bookshelf were unfamiliar to him – works on the Holy Crusades and the Knights Templar; a selection of seventeenth-century poetry . . . Carew, Lovelace, Suckling, Herbert. The *Selected Writings of Jules Laforgue*, Frazer's *Golden Bough*, Defoe's *Journal of the Plague Year*, *Night Thoughts* by Edward Young. Such an odd collection by an extremely odd man. A slim volume caught his fancy and he put down his sherry before he picked it out. It was called *The Dead before Dead* and the author was A. E. Hamilton. He opened the cover and saw that it had been published in 1872 in, as far as he could see, a private edition.

'That would be of no interest to you,' said Hamilton, who had walked into the room so quietly that even Edward's attentive ears had not heard him. 'The poetry is very bad,' he added, taking the book out of Edward's hand and placing it back in position on the shelf. 'I wrote it when I was young. The poetry is very poor indeed, very derivative, as I remember.'

Hamilton beckoned Edward to take his drink and sit at the oak table, heavily polished with beeswax. He glanced up from his drink at Hamilton who was just looking at him intently with his deep, black eyes.

'People say the most strange things about you,' Edward said when it was clear that, for the moment, Hamilton was not about to say anything. 'They wonder who you are and what you do.'

'What people say about me has no interest for me at all,' Hamilton replied flatly, laying his palm on the table and smoothing it, as if examining if it had been polished properly. 'I hope and try always to live in the isolation of myself, which is why I am a believer in absolute formality in all matters. It was only the Victorians who ever really understood that formality is the key to the proper life of a gentleman. In this Edwardian age everyone wants to get their nose into everything that does not concern them, which is why we are sliding fast into the present morass.'

He stopped speaking for a moment, regathering his thoughts. He looked around him, now continuing in a brisk, business-like manner, almost as if there were many items on the agenda which he wanted to deal with in half an hour flat. 'I gather that you have already learned something about that Exchange of ours and that you are willing and enthusiastic. Although you know little about me I know a lot about you and have followed your career with some interest. Those charges against you in London were dropped because of my extensive influence – both down here and up there.'

Edward swallowed hard but said nothing. Offhand, he could not remember when he had last met a man who had gone so directly to the point. Some might have seen it as rude, uncouth. But it was that very directness which inspired respect and even confidence. He used words with the utmost precision and in tones with a suppressed melody about them. He did not converse so much as make statements, with one thought moving to the next with a cold, chopping logic.

'I have made arrangements that you take over your father's membership on the Floor and, while I do not want you to make any dealings as such for a while, what I *do* want is for you to listen to Partington, to be with him throughout his work and find out everything about this business of shipping. It is important to a lot of people that the Gurney name and the Oriel business continue in a fit enough state. Only the fittest will survive the coming depression.'

Edward tried to frame a few question marks with his eyebrows and Hamilton began examining the table again. 'In return for your good endeavours I have asked Partington to pay you ninety guineas a week on top of any expenses. There will be an added bonus payable to you soon also: we really cannot keep the windjammer going for too long now. A refit is long overdue; it would be prohibitively costly. Since the opening of the Suez Canal it has become an expensive luxury. Even coal is going to become an expensive luxury and we must move into oil. When the time is right, the Oriel line will deed you the windjammer, with which you can do anything you think fit.'

As Hamilton carefully laid his hand on the table Edward could see that there was almost no point in making any comment or complaint. There was certainly no future in asking any questions since they would merely result in no answers. All this had been well thought out and presented in an almost unrefuseable package. In the present shaky state of his finances he had been well and truly hooked. He also wanted that windjammer almost more than anything.

'Now, please do not worry about my position or motives – let them worry about themselves,' Hamilton continued. 'All I am asking is that you address your abilities to making Oriel shipping viable and oil-based. I also want you to wait and watch for the right time since, again for reasons I cannot just now divulge, we must subvert and destroy the remaining Bute interests in this borough. Let us just say that the honour and memory of your father demand that.'

Edward's insides stiffened a little at the mention of his father. His work was clearly central to the mystery that was beginning to surround him so thickly. Had he known about his aborted jewel theft in London? Had old man Gurney – the very pillar of South Wales respectability – been instrumental also in getting those charges dropped? He could not contain his curiosity. 'Can I just ask about your partnership with my father?'

'You can ask by all means but I will not answer. You may well learn the whole truth one day. You have your faults but you also have a shrewd brain, which brings me to that small job I said I wanted done.'

Yes, that small job. But just how small is small? With this man, Edward decided, it could easily be murder.

'It is very small indeed,' said Hamilton, as if reading Edward's worried thoughts. 'But it will require a little organization and you will not be able to do it alone. All I want you to do is break into Cardiff Castle and steal something for me.'

'Oh *that* small,' said Edward, trying to make a joke of it and feeling quite wretched. 'I'll do it on my way home.'

But such lunges at humour were clearly lost on Hamilton who, with a suddenness that made Edward quite uneasy, leaped out of his chair and began pacing about the room. He put Edward in mind of a lion hungrily and impatiently waiting for feeding time. Lightning still flickered occasionally outside, sending stammers of bright electricity flashing through the barred windows.

'You will have heard much about the Bute family, Edward, but indulge me for a few moments while I try and tell you a little more. You will know that your father spent much of his working life in fighting with them over dock rates and berthing rights. The Butes were monumentally greedy and their dynasty built Cardiff's docks and made it into the greatest port in the world. They owned the Dowlais ironworks, the world's largest, and first put the sinkers down for Rhondda coal – also said to be the finest steam coal in the world, but already going the way of the dodo.

'The Butes, Edward, became the richest and hence the most powerful family on earth. Money flowed into their vaults in unstoppable rivers. They were the lords of coal; the landlords of the whole of Cardiff – everything they could see from those castle ramparts of theirs they either already owned, acquired or plundered. The fool now resident in the castle is the fourth Marquess of Bute, but it is his father – the third Marquess – that I want to tell you about.'

He walked to the furthest corner of the room and unlocked a cabinet, taking out some rolled-up drawings, putting them on the table in front of Edward but making no attempt to unroll them. He paced around the room again as Edward's eyes followed his every move, noting that he put the cabinet key into his waistcoat fob pocket.

'Not to labour the point too heavily the third Marquess was quite demented. He suffered from colossal *folie de grandeur*, was almost always ill with some ailment or another and squandered a great deal of the family fortune rebuilding that castle into a cross between a Grimms' fairy story and the *Arabian Nights*. His capriciousness knew no bounds. When he built Castell Coch in Caerphilly, in the style of a medieval castle, the view of the brickworks on the other side of the valley so upset him that, when he could not buy the works, he just abandoned the castle and never went back there again. A Catholic, by late conversion, he was fascinated by monasteries and saints, was forever babbling the strangest nonsense about liturgy and the cosmos, always travelling the world buying allegorical jewellery and religious icons. His great love was Palestine, where any urchin with a bit of wood could sell it to him saying it was part of the True Cross. He even gave the Pope a cross and bought his wife – whom he hated – a crown of rubies.'

Edward's interest stirred thickly at the mention of a crown of rubies. He would have loved to have got his hands on a crown of rubies, though quite how he would fence such an object he could not think.

'But he also acquired one object which I hope you can help me to acquire. Let us say, that if you can do this small job, I will give you £50,000 in cash or gilts, or put it in any Swiss bank account that you care to nominate. Shall I go on?'

Edward nodded.

Hamilton walked to the other side of the room. 'There is a huge market in authenticated medieval reliquaries, and what you see here is but a small collection of weaponry from the Middle Ages. When the depression comes money is going to collapse and so, for years now, your father and I invested heavily in objects like this. Some of these thirteenth-century arrowheads are already priceless. These quarrels are sixteenth-century and even that pikeman's breastplate could already bring four thousand pounds. This sword . . .'

He lifted up the sword from the altarpiece and Edward's elbow rose slightly as he wondered if this queer cove might even be going to attack him with it. 'This is a fifteenth-century, two-handed sword, carried by the Knights of St John. Something like this would have been used in the Crusades by the Knights Templar, but this one was probably only ever used for ceremonial purposes. It was thought to symbolize strength, nobility and righteous causes. You will notice how it resembles the Cross.'

He replaced the sword on the altarpiece carefully and returned to sit at the table, smoothing its polished surface with his hand again. 'The third Marquess of Bute managed to get a chalice which I very much want for my collection. It might be worth nothing and yet it might be priceless.' He examined his palm but did not look at Edward. 'In old Welsh myth it was said to be the dish that fed the Sea-god Bran, the son of Llyr. That apart, we have good reasons for believing that it is one of the oldest drinking vessels in Wales; that it would be a valuable part of the collection that your father and I were building. We had common cause. We needed to be the custodians of the nation's most truly valuable objects.'

Edward hated all the frequent references to his father, but he quite loved the idea of something being so priceless that he was being offered £50,000 to go in and get it. This cup clearly had to be worth a very great deal indeed, even if he was also certain that Hamilton was lying. A man like Hamilton could surely have no interest in the history of the nation – and the Welsh nation at that. He still could not quite work out where Hamilton came from, but he was never Welsh. He had thought he might be Scottish but he was now beginning to doubt that.

'Our best information is that this chalice is still in Cardiff Castle, hidden inside a statue, part of the newel gate on the stairway. We also know that the third Bute so revered this chalice that it still contains his heart. His will directed that his heart should be cut out of his body and buried in the Mount of Olives. In fact, he ordered his servant to cut it out secretly. It is still in the chalice since the poor fool really believed that it would bring him some kind of immortality. Are you still with me?'

'Yes. Well, somewhere or other.'

'The fourth Marquess lives in the castle but he hates the Welsh even more than his father and is rarely there. He spends most of his time in the family estate in Scotland and the family is selling off parcels of land everywhere to pay off their debts. Security in the castle is very tight but I have a good contact inside – an old family retainer called Charles Bethell – who can take you around on some of the small, exclusive tours that are allowed occasionally for important people and family friends. Such a tour will give you the layout of the castle but, even better than that, I have discovered an easy way inside.'

He unrolled one of the drawings on the table and spread it out in front of Edward. 'The second Marquess was a typical Victorian inasmuch as he was very enthusiastic about sewage. All the Victorians ever worried about was their empire and new sewage systems. At one time the second Bute called in Sir Joseph Bazalgette, the great London engineer who built the Thames Embankment, to come and sort out the bowel movements of the castle. They even had tunnelling machines on the job and it was an amazing piece of engineering.

'That other plan is of the castle itself, but this is the map of the underground sewage system which was never, in fact, completed, probably because the third Bute always had his mind on more metaphysical matters. This map, Edward, is your route straight into that castle.'

Well, straight into the bowels anyway, Edward thought grimly as he turned the map towards him.

'You can see from this that it is a complicated series of waterways and tunnels – Bazalgette loved complication above all else – but the main tunnel, once you get in past the iron sluice gates, leads directly to the bottom of the clock tower. That's the main entry, there. There's a lot of muck down those tunnels, and I hope you are not afraid of rats, but it is safe enough – both in and out.'

Even as this singular story had unfolded there had never been any real doubt in Edward's mind that he would do the job. He had done some modest burglary in the past, so a damp fairyland castle was probably, in any terms, quite an easy proposition. But, even as he pored over the diagrams of underground tunnels and waterways of Bazalgette's grand plan, he knew another thing with equal certainty. He knew that Hamilton really was lying. You might go to all this trouble and spend £50,000 for a crown of rubies, but not for an ancient chalice – even if it had been the drinking cup of some old Sea-god and contained the wizened heart of a man who had once been the richest man in the world.

There were still shivers of lightning but no signs of rain when Hamilton saw Edward to the door and continued to stand in the doorway, framed by a bright orb of yellow light, as he watched Edward stride down through the murmuring transvestites. Edward had fallen into a black, vexed mood; he felt that he was being manipulated and deceived but could not even start thinking his way through it. He glared at the circus clowns, half hoping that one of them would try and bother him. Hamilton was not the only one interested in weaponry. Edward's bamboo cane was also a swordstick, as any of them would quickly find out to their painful cost.

One strange, green-eyed man just smiled but made no move as his hands played with a green chiffon scarf.

Down by the Exchange Edward found his parked car, accelerated down Bute Street and slowed near the Custom House. There should be someone here who could help him in his present mood, but that Somali bitch was nowhere around, he quickly saw, accelerating again and lucky enough to miss a few of the girls who had walked too near. He had really enjoyed their little opium session the other night and would have liked to have enjoyed another tonight, but he just could not bring himself to go and knock on her door. It would have been quite unbearable to have found her with one of her customers. She was just too good for all that and he wondered why she did it at all.

Hamilton was still standing in the doorway of his house as Nazeem walked uncertainly across the cobblestones of the Close towards him, his hands still threading and re-threading his chiffon scarf. Hamilton remained motionless and just stared as Nazeem edged closer to the centre of the Close but, just when the transvestite was about to bound up the steps, Hamilton closed the door with a bang and turned off the outside house lights. With a mock flounce and a laugh Nazeem returned to his friends.

# CHAPTER SIX

About six dice schools were in progress on the corner of Sophia Street and Angelina Street – the air alive with noisy supplications and curses – when Sophie hurried past one of the police lookouts on her way to leave Effey at the child minder's.

'Sophie, I'm not sure how to tell you this but I'm going to have to tell you anyway,' Phyllis Jones said when Sophie had put the baby on the floor with the rest of them. 'I've just heard that your sister, Sylvie, has died.'

'You're joking are you?' Sophie asked, the sluicegates of alarm and grief opening up inside her, and knowing full well that she was not.

'I've told you, I've only just heard. She died in the Infirmary. From a heart attack, I heard. About three or four weeks ago. An' they've buried her too.'

'How could they do that? Without me knowing. How could they?'

'They just did it. You know them. They can do anything. Go and have a drink, Sophie, love. Leave the baby here an' go an' have a good drink.'

Sophie did go and have a good drink and another one, not at all sure what she did over the next three or four hours, so chokingly unhappy and grief-stricken that it was as if someone had pulled out her insides. She was surprised as much as anything at how grief-stricken she was, particularly as they had not seen one another for – how long? – a year, maybe two. Perhaps you only really knew how much you loved someone when they were dead and gone. It needed that for you to know.

The whole day was so chaotic and out of control. She remembered walking down by the canal and just standing on the edge with an almost uncontrollable urge to throw herself in, until she thought of Effey. She also remembered sitting in The Fountain pub and burbling so much that the landlord finally put her out for being drunk and disorderly. She even went into the docks themselves, finally going over to Rat Island, to the house where she had grown up with Sylvie, and just standing outside the door, crying copiously into her sodden handkerchief.

Oh, it didn't have to end like this, did it? She saw herself and Sylvie going off into town, a cold chip sandwich wrapped in some newspaper and carrying a bottle of water, to have a picnic. She saw them both playing on the floating logs in Dumballs Road or else going off to scrump apples with the Jones kids in the great backyards of Cathedral Road. They had walked to Penarth to pick up the lumps of red marble on the beach then walked all the way back again, throwing most of them away when they became too heavy. *Everything* had been so blissfully happy. They had just laughed and laughed all the time. Two sisters never had so much.

And now they were just not going to see one another ever again. Ever? Ever! Ever.

She was so red-eyed with crying that she had the physical sensation that her eyes were going to wash themselves away as she went back through the docks. And she still owed her that two pounds also. There was no chance she was going to be able to repay that now. She had wanted to, as well. It really stuck right inside her when she had thought that her sister was looking on her as a scrounger. But she had helped Sylvie out too. She had given her money when she wanted to go to London for the weekend and never once asked for it back.

The very worst part of it was that they had left one another as bad friends, she found herself explaining – in between sobs, silences and tears – to Nathan in his study in St Mark's. There they were, two sisters, with no other family anywhere else in the world, and they had left one another as bad friends. 'It may sound silly, Nathan, but if only I'd kissed her last week I wouldn't be feeling half as bad as I am now. Just one kiss would have made all the difference. Just one.' She sat there sniffing for a while when her tone changed. 'But she was always so snobby – always so high-and-mighty. You wouldn't believe how high-and-mighty that one could get. Never liked me being a whore, always looked down her nose at me. Said it was the lowest of the low. The lowest of the low!'

Nathan raised his chin a shade, keeping both hands clamped on his knees but making no comment on what she had just confirmed for the first time. Not that it seemed to matter; it was important for her to talk just now, to try and find the words to lance the grief.

'I didn't mind her being a snob, but she really objected to me being on the game. Objected! You'd think I'd asked her to go into partnership with me! But what had always upset her was she thought I was better-looking than her. That's what upset her – all the boys always went for me. But, you know, I wasn't better-looking than her. I wasn't. It was her high-and-mighty ways that scared off the boys. *That*'s what it was.

'Oh I feel so sad. I just want to lie in some dark corner and make a loud noise for a long time. Why didn't anyone tell me, that's what I want to know? I could have taken some flowers to the funeral. But they just did it. You know them. They can do anything. You're a man of God, Nathan. What's all this about? Why does God allow these things? All these rotten people in the world and He's got to take away my only sister.'

'I couldn't even start giving you the answer to that one. Life is always a mystery and all I've ever known for sure is that God renews it in mysterious ways. The flame of love is always passed on. Just look at the past few weeks. You've lost your only sister and gained a baby. Nothing could be more mysterious or beautiful. That's renewal of the highest order. Life always renews itself. We hand on things to one another – that's all I know for certain.'

'They wouldn't take Effey from me, would they? I couldn't stand that.'

'No. But I've been thinking about that baby of yours. You must get the child christened. No, I'm not doing my religious business now. You must get the child christened and I'll become the godfather. It'll help with the authorities, you see. If there are any problems they will be most impressed by your concern for the child's spiritual, as well as physical, welfare. It *will* help.'

Just then Sophie experienced something that she was quite ashamed of. Despite her red-eyed sadness and howling misery at losing her sister, she felt a surge in her loins and became quite wet between her legs, crossing and uncrossing them quickly, hoping that he would not pick up that, had he felt like a quick one, he could have got two quick ones, right there on his study floor. Oh she was disgusting, all right. She knew that.

But, perhaps fortunately, the subject changed and soon they were talking about Sylvie again. Within half an hour she felt a good deal better than when she had first come sobbing to him, immensely encouraged that a man of his standing and learning had also offered to become godfather to her child. She had never been quite sure about all this religious business but had to grant that he had a most forceful way of expressing himself. He was a real man in a real world, as he demonstrated yet again when he fished out a bottle of something interesting from behind a row of books, pouring two stiff ones.

'A present from my Catholic counterpart over in Newtown,' he explained, holding up the poteen bottle. 'There's none of that teetotal nonsense with any of them over there. He says he can only listen to Confession when he's half cut . . . You wouldn't know a Terry MacWhirter, would you?'

'If he's one of the MacWhirters over in James Street . . . yes, I do.'

'Well this Terry MacWhirter has committed some terrible sin and I'd just love to know what it is.'

Just then the study door opened and Elizabeth put her head inside, first looking at Sophie and then at her husband, now looking at what he was holding in his hand and then at what she was holding in hers. 'I'm just off down to the shops to get some margarine,' she said, closing the door again.

'I'm sorry,' said Sophie.

'Nothing to be sorry about,' he replied, throwing his drink down in one gulp. 'It's me that's going to be sorry. Yes, I suppose we, all of us, must wonder what the hell is going on sometimes. We are not getting on at all well just now and I'm becoming very worried about it.'

'Would it be better if I didn't come here, perhaps?'

'It's nothing to do with you. It's more to do with everything. She just doesn't like disorder, people running around everywhere, all that kind of thing . . .'

'I can see she's not very keen on me.'

'Nonsense. It's me she's not keen on. The dreaded drink, I'm afraid. It just helps me to relax. Here, let's have another sniff and then you'll have to be off.'

The next morning he sat at the breakfast table, listening and talking to his boys, but, at the same time, watching his wife. Had he been a gambling man he would have wagered a million pounds that this would never have happened to them. But it had, it had. And here it was.

Buoyed by a belief that he was a first-class cleric, who had the protection of a first-class family, he was now staring with outright disbelief at the breakdown of their marriage. It had been tested and found wanting. There had never been any pressure on it in the countryside, he now understood, but here in the Bay, there had been pressure aplenty and the hard nut had duly cracked, almost with the first tap.

He still cared for her – cared very much – but was not at all sure what he could do about it. Ask for another incumbency? Resign? He didn't want to do that since he still believed that this was the right parish for him, that here he could achieve some real pioneering work for the Church. But, perhaps in such a situation he should sacrifice his ambition – and the Church's – and just do anything, anything at all, to save his family. These two boys here, laughing and busy trying to stuff bits of bread into one another's ears, were clearly more important than him and his Churchy dreams.

'There's no school today and we haven't had much time with one another so I thought we might all go to Barry Island or something,' he offered.

A chorus of happy agreement from the boys but no reply from Elizabeth, busy buttering some bread.

'Elizabeth, we can't get through any of this if we don't talk to one another. Our language is all we've got left to us. Let's have it all out – find where we're going wrong.'

She slapped the butter knife down onto the table. 'Yes, that would be very nice, wouldn't it? A day at the seaside with all your whores. You could give them all a bucket and spade. Teach them how to build sandcastles.'

'I wasn't talking of taking anyone with us. Just the four of us – off away somewhere for a day, to have a talk.'

'You mean you could bear to be parted from all your whores for the day? How would you manage?'

'You're being silly now. And we don't have to talk about this in front of the boys, do we?'

'*You* were just telling me that language is all we've got left. Perhaps I should do it all through hand signals?'

She had come to look so old since they had moved here, he saw, and it was quite alarming when he came to look closer. The lines of age and worry had begun to appear in that wide and innocent beauty. That full, generous mouth had already begun to stiffen and harden before its time. Oh, Elizabeth, girl, what are we doing with our lives? 'Come and talk in my study,' he said.

'No. We're not talking in your study, not talking in Barry Island, nor anywhere else. There is just nothing at all to talk about.'

He had to work quite hard to stop himself being sick as she charged out of the room. He didn't think that she would leave him and the boys – her sense of duty and loyalty was too strong for that – but the alternative was almost as appalling; the two of them just living here together and slowly bleeding to death. 'You'd better go and wash your faces,' he told the boys still sitting there, silently waiting on his word. 'We'll go to Barry Island tomorrow perhaps. But don't worry about any of this. It's just Mummy and Daddy having an argument. It's just the way some parents say they love one another. That's all.'

He went down to his study, finding that Halfway had left a couple of letters on his desk. One was a gas bill and the other was a typed letter from Gerald Hastings, the Bishop of Llandaff.

'*It has been drawn to my attention,*' the Bishop said, '*that some two hundred people of West Indian origin are still living in St Mark's Church. While it has always been the duty of the Church and its servants to be the Vicar of Christ on Earth it is emphatically not the proper function of a church building to act as a hostel for the homeless. Further reports have been brought to my attention that the said West Indians were conducting services of crude Pentecostalism – speaking in tongues and voodoo-type dancing to the accompaniment of jazz. These services have no place in the modern Church and must cease forthwith.'*

Geraldus.

But Nathan's beleaguered heart brightened a little when he read the handwritten P.S., which suggested that he was not in as much hot water as he had at first thought. 'When we next meet can you explain to me what is jazz?' the Bishop had scrawled in purple ink.

Jazz is the funny noise that gets into ageing bishops' heads through too much incense and chanting, Nathan thought, as he re-read the letter. Jazz is what dusty cathedrals like Llandaff need to brighten the place up. He turned the letter upside down but that did not help much either.

What the letter did not do was suggest what Nathan might do with his new jazz-loving residents; a suggestion which he would have welcomed most warmly because he did not know what to do with them either. He walked into the vestry, just standing there and looking at them, many still asleep, and others sitting around in chattering groups. They were getting bored and fractious too, wanting somewhere to live and be themselves. Some had ventured into the city but returned quickly, finding the populace hostile and sarcastic. Many had drifted away to other, friendlier, ports. But the rump that remained could find nothing at all and was becoming increasingly isolated.

Despite frequent calls on the council and even the Salvation Army, they could not – or would not – help him. Nathan Thomas alone was the West Indian benefactor. He had found them and he could house them.

The Barbadian plight was a never-ending marvel to those who lived outside the Bay. Curious and unfriendly groups often gathered outside St Mark's just to jeer at them. This really sickened Nathan and he would often go out into the street to remonstrate with his critics but this only infuriated them even more. They called him 'nigger-lover' or even worse. Savage editorials appeared in local newspapers. He tried to rationalize all this hostility by telling himself that this was a time of rising unemployment and, while the politicians were still trying and failing to find an answer to joblessness, the simple-minded found it easy to blame the jobless West Indians. Everyone, he reasoned, needed a scapegoat for the country's problems and, after the Irish and Chinese, it was now the West Indians' turn to be blamed for the next deep conspiracy to drag the country to her knees.

Warm and sensitive to a fault, the Barbadians could not understand this reception. They would often speak in loud, embittered tones about finding a ship to return home. But the trumpeter, young Obadiah Brown, was emerging as a useful leader, encouraging the older men in particular to go out into the city and look for work. A few had even been given vague promises and told to come back again next week, but many were falling at the first jump – because of the blackness of their skin.

On top of all this Halfway Harry was now making alarming noises about resigning as verger. Also, such congregation as he had inherited from the previous incumbent had already left. Virtually his only help with the Barbadians was coming from three faithful parishioners and Sophie and the girls.

It was getting that he just wanted to cry all the time. How much worse could it all get? he wondered. How much worse?

He chatted briefly with a few of them before returning to his study for a quiet hour of prayer and Bible reading. But even this was not helping much and he was staring blankly at the sun, incandescent in the window pane, when the door opened with a resounding crack. He did not need to look up to know who it was, nor did he have to look to know that her face was etched with thunder.

'Nathan, I'm sending the boys back to my mother's immediately. Immediately, do you hear?'

These startling words actually made his heart butterfly in fright. He squinted hard at the sunshine window. She couldn't do that, could she? She just *would*n't, would she? 'What's the matter now?'

'The matter now is that I was just out in the yard and found that young West Indian girl – Patricia, isn't it? – the silly one with a stammer – lifting up her skirt and showing our boys what she'd got.'

'What she hadn't got, you mean?'

'Nathan, this is no time for your silly jokes. I am not going to put up with that. I am *not* going to put up with that. Those two are going back to my mother until we can sort them out a proper school with some proper friends.'

'A posh school with some posh friends, you mean?'

'No. That's not what I mean. I mean a proper school where they can learn something useful. They've learned nothing at all in that school. Not a thing. And their language and manners have become foul in the extreme.'

Given the heat of the moment he was very surprised to see that she did have a point. Sometimes, when she got her rag out, she had just wept and mixed up her thoughts. But there was no mix-up in her mind just now. Her arguments were lucid and strong because she had thought them through. Her words were hard and sharp because she believed that she was right. Perhaps she was.

'I accept that I am your wife and I must stay at your side for better or for worse,' she continued. 'But not at the cost of our two boys. That cost is far too high. Nothing is worth that cost.'

'But my place is here, *our* place is here. It was always the duty of the Church to be in the front line. We always understood that nothing would be easy about working in the front line . . .'

'We, Nathan, *we*. But there is nothing in the Gospels saying that we should sacrifice our children on this front line of yours. They are going back to my mother's until we can sort . . .'

A loud knock on the study door interrupted Elizabeth's future plans. It was Halfway Harry. 'Vicar, all the local prostitutes have been rounded up,' he said, slightly breathless. 'The police have taken them all in, the whole lot.'

'Well, thank God for that!' Elizabeth exclaimed.

Nathan shot her a withering glare. He would never leap to hasty judgements, unlike the woman he had married. If it hadn't been for the 'girls', those West Indians would have been in an even greater plight. Halfway just stood there, staring at the floor unhappily.

'Is there anything else, Harry?' Nathan asked.

'There is. They all want you to go down to the police station to help them get bail.'

'Oh, doesn't that just beat everything?' Elizabeth shouted. 'Doesn't that win a prize for just about everything going? Go on, Nathan, hurry down there and save all your whores. Perhaps they've got a drink for you. You could all have a big party in the cells. You could become godfather to all their bastard children.' He hadn't told her about his promise on that front.

'I'll be going down there,' he said evenly as Halfway

disappeared. 'I'll be there helping my flock while others run away and cry because they don't like the colour of other people's skins.'

'Oh don't give me that . . .'

'While others think so much of themselves they cannot think of anyone else – who are so poor and mean in spirit they can only think of their own narrow, selfish interests – who want to hide their children in dull schools in case they hear a swearword or see up a girl's skirt. Yes, yes, yes. I am going to be there with them today and tomorrow and the day after that. I am going to help all those whores because they once helped us. And if you want to run away, then run. But do not expect me to do the same. I live and work here. And here, with these people, I am going to stay.'

The cells of Cardiff police station had not been the scene of so much noise since the far-off day when a travelling circus and its animals had once been pulled in for trying to set up business on the sacred lawn in front of the hallowed City Hall.

That morning, the order had gone out to arrest every working prostitute in the city. At the appointed hour, six police wagons had moved out in a joint operation with the plainclothes men. They had managed to pull in almost all of the working girls and a few who unfortunately just happened to be standing around in the street at the time.

Sophie had been with Betty, looking up and down Bute Street for any approaching business, when the boys in blue had called. Sophie had, as usual, been talking about *her* Effey who had been left with Mrs Jones in Angelina Street. Quite frankly, her friend Betty was quite fed up with all this incessant chatter about the girl, but in the event, they both stopped talking, about Effey and everything else, when they saw two police wagons edging out of a side street with their engines growling throatily. Another one came and pulled up directly on the other side of the road.

'Betty, girl, hitch up your skirt and make a dash for it,' called Sophie.

But before they could make a move they were both grabbed by four burly men and propelled towards the back of the police wagon. Betty cried out as she allowed herself to be wafted along but Sophie was a spitting, clawing wildcat, kicking and scratching before receiving a sharp punch in the mouth. 'I'll get you for that,' she spat at the sergeant who'd hit her, in between gobbets of blood.

Other girls were bundled in after them, some half-dressed and others dressed not at all. The police had even broken down the doors of known brothels, hauling the girls out, even Marie the Stump. 'I was just 'aving a quiet sleep when 'e just charged the bloody door down, din' 'e? Came in so fast 'e fell on me bed. I woke up an' said that he must be really desperate for it but 'e should knock the next time. They didn't even want to let me put on my wooden leg so I 'ad to just grab it on the way out.'

'I wish I'd had a wooden leg or a surgical boot or something,' Sophie sighed with real feeling. 'I'd let those bastards have it.'

'You can always borrow mine, dearie. See, it unstraps there. I've brained a few men with this, I can tell you.'

They all fell to studying the straps on Marie's wooden leg when the door was opened again and in sailed Gaynor Evans, also screaming with outrage. ''E'd finished, 'e 'ad, an' 'e 'adn't even paid me. "Just lemme pick up me money", I says, but they wouldn't 'ave it, would they?'

By now, Sophie's mouth was swelling painfully and she touched it delicately with her fingertips. Two more girls were bundled in, one actually spitting in the policeman's face before he managed to lock the door. Sophie liked that. It was always right to show some spirit with those bluebottle bastards. They respected *that* well enough.

She held her belly tight and worried that Effey might miss her if she was kept away for too long. But the girl was in good hands there. She wondered if she could get word to Nathan so that he could come and help them. The girls had, after all, been so much help to him. She had never known them to work together like that before. It was not like them, somehow. But they had taken to Nathan quickly enough. He had something special about him. The girls had quickly seen that he was a big man. She found that she thought about him a lot – and always with affection. Rashed rarely wandered through her thoughts at all.

After they had been driven to the police station behind the Law Courts they were escorted to their cells. Sophie held the bars and looked out. She had never realized that there were so many girls working in the city, but there they were, all rounded up and corralled, shrieking and wailing louder than anything that had ever been heard in the halls of Bedlam. There might have been three hundred of them, ranging from loud-mouthed, lipsticked viragos bellowing their outrage through their ostrich feathers, to pale young madonnas, quietly tearful after the most recent – strictly temporary – loss of their virginity. The very old ones accepted such round-ups with a quiet and dignified grace, though. Such abuses were but part of the job, they told themselves with a quiet pride; they were the price they had to pay for their popularity with men.

A sergeant pounded his desk with a truncheon. 'All right, you lot. Shut your racket, now. You've all been brought in here for a purpose.'

Ironic jeers and cries of 'Sod off' and 'We don't do business with bastard coppers.'

The truncheon pummelled the desk again. 'All right, all right. Inspector Watts – whom I believe you all know – is going to speak to you.'

Inspector Watts was greeted by even more spirited jeers and boos. They knew that blotchy-faced bastard well enough. 'Now then, ladies,' he said, one hand in pocket and the other holding a thick white document. 'We've brought you all in 'cos there have been complaints.'

'What sort of complaints, beetroot face? There's never been no complaints about my fanny.'

'That's not what I heard,' said someone else.

'Listen now, ladies,' Watts continued when the heckling had died down. 'What I have in my hand here is a report by the Public Health Society. Heard of them, have you? No, I shouldn't think you had or you wouldn't be in here now. Well, some men from this Public Health Society have made a study of the Valleys, and this here is the result of their labours. It says . . . it says here somewhere . . . that there has been a sharp rise in venereal disease in the Valleys . . .'

More comic 'Ooohs' and wide-eyed 'Get aways'.

'And more to the point, those same men from the Public Health Society have blamed all this on you ladies working the streets here in Cardiff.'

Sophie joined in the subsequent gale of horrified boos and cries of dissent. The bloody nerve of these people. Next they'd be blaming us for all those deaths on the Somme. 'How do they know it was us?' Sophie called out.

'They know it's you and can even prove it,' Watts continued when the noise had abated. 'They have found that the numbers of reported cases in the Valleys always go up immediately after a rugby international in Cardiff. Why those shonny boys always celebrate the country's wins by sticking their dicks into you lot . . .'

'Hey, hey. Language, Inspector Watts. We are *ladies*, you know.'

'Yes, I'm sorry,' he smirked. 'Well, that's what's been happening, so, on orders from above, I've had to bring you all in for a medical examination and a few jabs.'

Moans of dire pain and widespread dismay. 'Not all of us?'

'Yes, every single one of you. And can't you use more of those johnnies? There was old Mr Condom spent his life perfecting them and you all charge around as if he had never existed.'

'Rubbers are expensive, Mr Watts, and we are only working girls,' shouted Marie the Stump. 'And our clients don't like them either. They say it's like chewing a sweet with the wrapper still on. They all like it bareback, Mr Watts. You can't put rubber between yourself and life. We're always keen to give value for money.'

'Well, I don't consider that giving out clap is value for money,' Watts snapped back. 'So you can make it hard for yourselves or easy. You'll all be getting a medical examination and you'll all be getting jabs – whether you've got the clap or not. Do I make myself clear?'

It was late in the afternoon when Nathan came striding grimly out of the police station, closely followed by Sophie, who was limping and faltering just behind him. Occasionally she caught up with him and linked her arm in his but he shook it away and walked on again. Now they were walking along past the moat outside the castle wall, and spread out behind them, almost as far as the eye could see, was a thin straggle of faltering, weeping whores, all stopping now and then to rub their very sore buttocks.

Nathan had simply gone into the station with a solicitor and demanded their release. But the police had given in quite happily since, by then, almost all of them had been examined and duly jabbed with vast quantities of bismuth.

'Nathan, it was the biggest needle I've ever seen. They put one in my right buttock and then picked up another for my left. You could even see the needle glint. Bigger than a cucumber it was, honest to God. Stop going so fast, will you? You can see I can't walk proper.'

She tried to grab his arm but he shook it away again. 'Woman, I can't go walking around the city arm in arm with you, now, can I?'

'Why not? What's wrong with me?'

'Because I'm a man of the cloth and people will talk.'

'Since when did you worry about talk? Oh, just let me hold onto your arm, will you? My mouth is swollen where that bobby punched me an' I tell you, those needles were as big as umbrellas. They must have pumped half a gallon of that stuff into my poor little botty.'

'I suppose it's better than spreading clap all over the Valleys.'

'I've never had the clap.' She snorted at the very thought of it, touching the side of her mouth again. 'No Valley boyo has ever got inside me – particularly after one of those rugby internationals. Don't look at me like that. None of them ever got it in 'cos they were too damned drunk. We just takes them 'round the corner and plays around with them, you know . . .'

'I know what?'

'You know, we give them a good joggle, with your wrist like.'

'A good joggle, with your wrist like?' He stopped walking and screwed up his nose in disbelief, raising his hands into the air as if about to conduct an orchestra, only to let them fall again. 'A good joggle with your wrist like?' he repeated, as if this strange, repulsive item was the very last left on the menu. 'That might even be the most disgusting thing I've ever heard. And you do that to those poor Valley boys?' He lurched over the road as if he was going to be sick and she lurched after him.

'They're not so poor. Don't believe all that in the papers about them being poor. Those Valley boys have got stacks of money.'

Just near St John's Church, they were still talking animatedly as they passed a capsized coal handcart whose axle had broken, spilling the coal in a small avalanche over the pavement. The reflections of the trams drifted, silent and huge, across the crowded shop windows and through the lines of expressionless dummies. A lone mouthorganist was playing a tune in St Mary's shopping arcade, his music curiously amplified by the arcade's wooden acoustics, picking it up and turning it over like an autumnal leaf bouncing lazily on a light breeze.

Sophie just could not understand Nathan's mood. He had come to bail the girls out and here he was acting worse than those bluebottle bastards who had pulled them in. He wasn't even speaking to her properly, just snapping and digging all the time. But he was getting into a difficult position; she could see that clearly enough. His bosses weren't going to be very pleased with all these whores and Barbadians he had around. Particularly if they all had the clap.

'How are your two boys getting on?' she asked, deciding on a change of tack. He always liked to talk about his little boys. In many ways he was a little boy himself.

'I don't want to talk about them.'

'What do you want to talk about, then?'

'You don't *have* to talk all the time, do you? Just because you're walking together it doesn't mean that you can't enjoy some silence, does it?'

'I thought we were friends.'

'Well, we *are*, aren't we?'

'Friends should talk to one another, then. They should tell one another what's wrong and maybe they could sort it out.'

'Yes, well, I'm sorry. Sorry, yes.' He shook his head and sighed, stuffing his hands down into his pockets, his mood changing abruptly. 'It's Elizabeth. She's fed up with everything and wants to send the children back to West Wales.'

'What, exactly, is she fed up with?'

'You name it. She's fed up with the West Indians in the church. Fed up with "all those whores" – as she calls them. Fed up with me. Fed up with you. And she'll get even more fed up if she sees your arm in mine. So take it out, will you? Things are not going well, Sophie. They are not going at all well. I've got the Bishop after me. There's going to be a race riot on the church doorstep any day now.'

Sophie put her face in front of his, catching him directly in the eyes, and she laughed. Laughed! He asked her what the hell she was laughing at. He didn't see anything at all to laugh at.

'It's one thing all we Somalis learned. We learned it from when we were no higher than a cow's knee. You've got to laugh when you feel like crying. It's a great African secret, that is, so don't go telling anyone about it. Go on. Well, try a little snigger, then.'

'Oh I can't think of much to snigger about. The real trouble is that I can't seem to see what's happening to me. Bad things are moving around me and I can't seem to read the signs. You could always do that in the countryside but not here in the city. In the countryside you could work things out by the way the cattle were lying in the fields; by the way the smoke curled the wrong way; by the way the swallows flew too low and distant trees were too clear. The city doesn't give you a warning about anything – it all just happens with a bang in the city.'

It was odd, he thought then, how easily and freely he could talk to Sophie; he never seemed to have to patronize or talk down to her. In many ways she seemed to understand him better than his own wife.

'Perhaps you'd better go back to the countryside, then,' she suggested. 'Perhaps it would be better for your wife and the boys.'

'Perhaps. But I really want to be a part of this world. In ways I can't explain, I'm sure that history is now being made in the Bay. Look at it.' They both stopped and gazed down the high, wide thoroughfare of Bute Street. 'There's not a street like that in the whole world. It's full of tension and clash, full of every colour and idea. We're going to learn a lot from how the races get on here. In some ways the Bay will become a blueprint for the future of the world.'

'Oh, I don't think about all that,' she said after a while. 'I don't see things so broadly. If I were you, I'd be more worried about my family than the whole world. Perhaps you'd better go back to the countryside. I'm not at all sure how you'd manage without your boys. I've seen how happy you get when you're near them. And I'm not at all sure this *is* the right place for them to grow up. Perhaps your wife is right.'

Nathan actually managed a bit of a smile, but it wasn't so much at what she'd said. It was at what his Bishop would have said had he known that a limping whore was counselling him on the state of his rocky marriage.

They were approaching St Mark's when a brown monkey with a bright red arse dashed across Bute Street chased by a gang of kids. The monkey turned this way and that, followed by the kids who turned this way and that until, it seemed, they had him cornered in the mouth of an empty workshop. Then, unwisely, one of the kids made a grab for him, only to let go after the monkey gave him a sharp bite on his hand. The chase then continued along the dock wall until the monkey shinned up a lamppost and just sat there looking at his pursuers, who jumped up and down throwing stones and tin cans at him, but otherwise, were not quite sure how to continue the hunt since none of them was prepared to make a grab for him again.

'Well, you wouldn't get that in the countryside,' said Sophie.

'That is true. All you can be sure of seeing in the Welsh countryside is an awful lot of rain.'

Meanwhile, just near the Central Library, young Obadiah Brown came and stood in front of Tubby Aitken's fruit stall on Hayes Island, about a hundred yards down from the library entrance.

He just stood there admiring the vivid piles of oranges and buckled shapes of the bananas. There were glistening grapes and velvet peaches; spiky pineapples and whole piles of yellow lemons. The stall's exotic look and drifting smells reminded Obe painfully of his lost island home when – as long as the Boss Man wasn't looking – he could just wander down to the banana plantations and pick as many as he could eat. Oh, how he longed to feel the fat curve of those bananas in his palms again.

But there was another calculation working in his mind. One of the young lads in the church had been suffering from shingles and a doctor had said that he needed to have oranges to put him right again. Oranges were the key to all health, the doctor had said, but the trouble was that they didn't have the money to buy such precious things.

'Come on now, boy,' Tubby Aitken said, picking up a box of grapes and loading them onto his cart. 'We're closing now, so shift yourself out of here.'

'Let me help you, boss,' offered Obe.

'Not on your big black life, boy. Now, hop it.'

There had been no plan, no premeditation, not even any past form, but just at that moment, for a variety of complex reasons of which the sick boy was the main one, Obe picked up a half-full box of oranges and began legging it back to his dockland home, leaving a scattering trail of bouncing, rolling oranges behind him.

Tubby Aitken could never have run – not even if his very life had depended on it let alone half a box of oranges – but he did shout an alarm, sending two youths from the nearby butcher's shop in pursuit of his vanishing goods. Obe could easily have outpaced these two but, just near the corner of Caroline Street, his luck ran out. There was a crowd of some sixteen ex-servicemen, still in their khaki uniforms, standing around the corner, all waiting for the pub to open.

The two butcher lads were shouting 'Stop thief. Stop thief', and immediately the soldiers dashed across the road to form a line to block Obe's chosen path home. Obe wheeled and wheeled again, now stopping with his warm breath pluming against the coldness of the darkening evening, as his big black eyes looked around for a way through. There was only one thought in his mind – absurd though he knew it was – his sole thought was that all he wanted to do was to get these oranges home for the shingled lad in St Mark's.

He ran one way, reversed sharply in the other, pirouetted around and, with a jink which had the Army boys blinking in amazement, accelerated straight through their khaki line, untouched by any of them and still with the box of oranges in his hands.

Now he seemed to have half the city chasing after him, all whooping like Red Indians, as he kept running for the relative safety of Bute Street. Obe had never seen so many people after his black hide, now ducking behind two parked cars and looking up to find that another small group of whites was even now cutting off his approach to Bute Street. A gallon of adrenalin surged through his body and his long black legs became like pistons as he hurdled over some low iron railings and headed towards the Glamorganshire Canal. All around him bodies were running and shouting to one another. Then a knifegrinder, hearing all the commotion and spotting its cause, left his work and jumped out in front of their quarry, brandishing the biggest knife that Obe had ever seen.

Obe ran out into the middle of the road and turned, deciding to run back to Bute Street anyway. Just for now it was home. It may not have been much of a home, but it was the only home he knew. He saw that he was going to have to run through a mass of some thirty men to make it. Oh, Lordy. With his head well down and still clutching his crate – in which there were now but six oranges left – he charged straight into them, knocking a few aside, and scaring quite a few more, until an outstretched leg sent him sailing into the air with a small, orange shower of fruit falling all around him. He landed with a sharp crack on his side and everyone rushed in to lay about him.

Obe had been beaten up before – many, many times before – and ancient plantation habits told him to curl up into a tight ball, stretching his arm over the back of his head and putting the other hand over his groin. The plantations had taught his fathers and forefathers that, in this way, you gave them the smallest possible targets to hurt you; that, given the inevitability of a beating, this was the only way of cutting the odds on a nasty death. And, as those Army boots went thudding and crunching into his body, he even heard himself jabbering those same old plantation words: 'No, boss, no, boss. I didn't mean it, boss.'

But even if he really didn't mean it this was a painful and most savage beating. Shoe caps cracked into his teeth, a stick broke three of his ribs and his right leg was shattered in several places. Someone grabbed his wrist and, holding it down on the road, smashed into his hand with an iron bar. He could actually feel all the bones in his fingers breaking and splintering like cold ice under hot water. He actually saw an orange, as huge as a coconut, rolling a few inches away from his eyes. And, just then, mercifully, he lost consciousness and fell into a deep darkness in which there was no sound and no pain except for the distant echo of his own voice shouting, 'No, boss, no, boss. Ah didn't mean it, boss.'

That Wednesday night, thick purple clouds came scudding in over the Bay, chasing one another around and rolling silently into each other before breaking apart again. The full tide and a stiff breeze brought the stink of sewage onto the streets, where small, white, sullen mobs were roaming about ceaselessly. Occasionally the very darkness erupted with the discord of shattering glass. On the edges of Newtown a few deserted houses had been set alight. Barefoot children, drawn by the eternal fascination of fire, stood watching as the milky-red flames crackled and bit into the old rafters. The pungent smoke drifted in waves out towards the better parts of the city.

Old Charles Boden walked out into the porch of St Mark's, standing well back in the shadows as yet another white mob went marauding down Bute Street. His old bloodshot eyes had seen all this before, of course. His old nose had smelled anger like this many times. This was white man's anger; this was his honky way of taking it out on others when things were not going right for himself. And at such times there had never been quite so much fun as whippin' some black arse. Just as they had now done to Obe for stealing a few oranges. Old Charlie had seen bodies smashed up like Obe's before. He had even seen white men chop off black thieves' fingers and give them out as souvenirs.

'It's damn hard being a little nigger boy,' he had told Obe when they had finally brought him back from the Hamadryad Hospital, his whole body swathed in plaster and bandages. 'It's always been damned hard. That's why we're so good at the blues. There's none better than us whipped niggers at the blues.' He moved closer to Obe and whispered a question directly into his ear. 'But tell me one thing, boy. Why did little Rastus try to steal those honky oranges?'

Obe's bandaged head shook, his words barely audible. 'Because they wus there, Charlie. They wus just sitting there all pretty an' I wanted a few for little Joey.'

'Because of little Joey? Because they were sitting there? Is that what you're going to tell them in court? Because they were sitting there, just looking all pretty?'

The bandages shook again. 'It was all for Joey. The thing is, I hate oranges. I've always hated oranges. It's bananas I've always loved.'

'That's stupid, little Rastus. That's what I call really stupid.'

More bricks and bottles clattered down Bute Street and Charlie moved deeper into the covering shadows. Everyone in the Bay was moving deeper into the covering shadows that night. All the shutters had gone up in the Chinese block with not even the look-out men now daring to hang out on the corners. The Moslems had taken to carrying their shoes into the Mosque after a gang had come across them and hurled them over distant rooftops. Even the proud Somalis – never ones to turn away from danger – were staying indoors. Yes, there was a great anger roaming those bad streets.

Old Charlie could never remember his own people being so uneasy either. None of them had any patience and they were all complaining about this and that, at loose ends, fighting with themselves. One of them had even suggested that they boil a cauldron of tar; an ancient ritual for getting rid of the plague. There was none of the Creole songs and, now that Obe had been given a stiff battering, there would be very little jazz either. It would be a long time before Obe would play his trumpet again. If he would ever play . . .

Even their minister, Mr Nathan, who had given them the sanctuary of his church, was having his own problems, they said. The islanders had all watched late that afternoon as his wife and children had climbed into a furniture wagon, clearly going off somewhere for a long time. Both the children had been crying and so upset they wouldn't even wave goodbye to the black children with whom they had become such good friends. Old Charlie blamed the mother for all that. She was just stuck-up white trash, that's all. But the minister had taken it very hard when he had come back to find them all gone. No one had seen him all night – even Sophie had not been able to get in there. He had not even come out to see how Obe was. Now, there was a white boy chewing on the black man's blues.

A lot of low whistling broke through the air as a small group of white youths went running around behind the church. More whistling followed as others went hurrying around the back of the Chinese block. But all this activity was something and nothing; a mindless force rolling about the streets in cartwheels of angry and indecisive strife, looking for something to roll over – but never quite sure what.

There were two distant explosions and another derelict house went up in flames, burnishing the bottom of the night a bright red. The broken-necked silhouettes of the dockland cranes stood, black on crimson, in the manner of huge roosting waders. Ship's hooters sounded distantly and mysteriously like rumours of war.

Old Charlie had seen something like this fiery canvas once before, back in his island home. It was the reflected glow of boiling lava in the throat of the volcano. This hazy heat had also turned the nights *and* the mornings red, and kept on turning the nights and mornings red for weeks to come, giving the whole mountain a giant, fiery crown. The volcano had boiled with thin puffs of smoke and tiny tremors had shaken the earth. Fissures had widened and steamed. Frightened snakes and centipedes had come running down the slopes looking for shelter in the town. Sulphur had ridden on the wind, making the eyes water. There had been short showers of pumice and electric spurts of flame.

The volcano had retained its crown of fire for almost three weeks, when one bright morning, it erupted, pouring blood and death all over the sugarcane fields.

How long now, oh Lord?

# CHAPTER SEVEN

The red wooden door opened and a flunkey in a powdered wig, gold-brocaded jacket, white leggings and black polished shoes addressed the small party waiting at the top of the castle battlements. 'Welcome to the home of the Bute family,' he announced, staring expressionlessly ahead of him. 'Please take off your shoes. Slippers will be provided. Please have ready your personal letters of invitation from the estate manager. Lord Bute sends his apologies for such formalities but there are items which are literally priceless in this castle.'

The door closed leaving Edward and Partington staring at one another. 'The Butes might not be the global power they once were, Mr Edward, but that sense of family grandeur will always be the same,' said Partington. 'The Butes grew up in an age of deference and feudalism. And here we are in the twentieth century, still taking our shoes off for them. Better do as he says, Mr Edward.'

There were three others in the party – two who dressed like city financiers and an excited churchman who beamed at everyone before taking out his notebook and jotting down items of interest. 'It's always difficult thinking of something to say on Sunday mornings,' he told Edward and Partington, but the pair merely nodded and walked away from him, feeling slightly foolish in their stockinged feet, each holding out their shoes like a couple of newly-caught fish.

A morning of showers had just cleared up, leaving a bright sun pinned to the top of a clear blue sky. The city itself seemed dazzlingly bright, with the streets and houses looking like brand-new gifts laid at the feet of this nobleman's castle. Over to one side was the rugby stadium and the soccer ground, together with the rolling acres of the castle grounds and the hurrying River Taff. On the other were the towering Portland shapes of the Civic Centre, the huge department stores and arcades, all throbbing with the vitality of a great coal metropolis at the very height of its wealth and confidence.

'I've always been very fond of Lord Bute's little town,' said Partington, shielding his eyes from the sun's glare to look at the thin silvery ribbon of the Bristol Channel. 'Such a fine centre, I've always thought. Probably the finest in the world. But it was such a pity that all this was owned by just one man. As far as you can see, everything was reduced to an appendage of the Bute dynasty. Everyone was expected to share the castle viewpoint. They even evicted farmers to create those castle grounds. What Bute wasn't chairman of he was trustee of. Look, there's Sophia Gardens, Ninian Park, the Arms Park – all named after Bute family titles. Bute wives had streets named after them – even Bute agents had their own avenues. A lot of streets were named after Bute estates in Scotland. Your father hated this whole empire with a rare passion. Those damned dictators in the turrets, he liked to call them.'

'But what exactly did my father have against the Butes? Was it money or was it personal?'

Partington waved his hand over the great sparkling kingdom at their feet. 'Mr Gurney hated the privileges of being born in the right bed, the corruption of what he saw as inherited wealth. He hated seeing all that Welsh money being pumped away to the Bute estates in Scotland. But, yes, there was something personal between him and the Butes. He used to urge me to contest every clause in every contract with the Bute estate. They were the first masters of the one-sided contract, he used to say. There's little I don't know about punitive leases, reverted mineral royalties and agreements which stretch in perpetuity. The old Butes were crooks, Mr Edward, and your father knew it better than most. This whole empire was built on extensive land frauds.'

'And Hamilton? How does he fit into all this?'

These were clearly questions to which he was never going to

have a satisfactory answer. Edward watched as Partington put another Mint Imperial into his mouth; he always did this when he needed some time to think and not to talk.

'You'll find out in your own time, Mr Edward. All I can tell you is that Mr Hamilton and Mr Gurney were both engaged in the same work and shared broadly similar ideals. I am just satisfied to be their unquestioning servant.'

'And what do you make of this cup – this thing – that Hamilton wants me to steal?'

'I don't like the word "steal", Mr Edward. I'm led to understand that it's a very old and sacred drinking vessel which Mr Hamilton sees as being of the utmost value. I am told that it might be a Roman drinking cup once used by the Emperor Nero. It might even be the same one that Nero was drinking from when he shouted "Let Rome burn".'

Edward frowned, clearly remembering that this version directly contradicted the one that Hamilton had given him. 'You don't believe that, do you?'

'I'm not saying I believe it, Mr Edward. I'm just saying what I've been told.'

Partington never seemed flushed or embarrassed, even when he was being asked questions to which he did not want to give answers. Edward could see why his father and Hamilton seemed to trust him so implicitly. Partington combined the rare abilities of being able to think for himself and doing as he was told. Edward had collaborated with some rum types in his past enterprises but was more than confident that this small formal man, with his old-world manners and dedicated loyalties, was more than a perfect accomplice to have in the same foxhole. But he clearly did know more than he was letting on.

When the flunkey finally allowed the party inside the building, carefully examining their invitations and handing out the slippers, he took them on a short, ungenerous tour, low on information and high on the undying glory that was the Bute family. 'The third Marquess had a marvellous taste for art and archaeology and, happily, the means to indulge them,' he pontificated. They went into Bute's Batchelor Room in the clock tower. Down below, the mouths of goldfish rose to feed among the lilies on the moat. Peacocks pecked around and displayed their tails on the grassy banks of the keep.

'Note these beautiful cupboards made from Spanish walnut. The third Marquess had forests in Spain and his workmen used the wood from there. See how beautifully balanced the drawers are. The jars of tobacco are kept in here and the cigars are kept in these hidden drawers. This wine container can hold up to forty bottles which were made in Bute's private vineyard.'

Edward and Partington did not speak to one another throughout the tour, though they did exchange glances from time to time. Despite Hamilton's assurance that gaining entry was no problem Edward could see nothing but difficulty. Some of the doors had three bolts and two deadlocks, while the windows had tricky brass latches with small mullioned panes set in lead diamonds, which would be almost impossible to break through.

'We now go up one hundred and one steps – we do it in two stages so it's not too bad – to the Batchelor bedroom with its theme of the making and acquisition of jewels. Note the gold leaf on the ceiling. All this was extracted from the family gold mines in Dolgellau. Every object and ornament here was made from a different mineral on Lord Bute's many estates. See that mouse there – William Burges's trademark. He loved them and they are dotted all over the castle. Notice how the chimney pieces depict the pleasures of the season, particularly of lovemaking.'

Some of the pleasures seemed decidedly erotic, Edward noted as he looked closer. He visibly cheered up just then, thinking of Sophie and her endless limbs, though the churchman pointedly stopped making notes at this stage. Edward thought of what he would like to have done to Sophie on that bejewelled bed. How he would make even that fine gold ceiling turn red with embarrassment at what he would do to her and how!

They went to the Bute Tower with its second suite of rooms and astonishing stained-glass windows. One bore an inscription in Greek: 'Entertain Angels Unawares'. One set of rooms led into another, and swirling, ornate murals of the Seven Deadly Sins merged in Edward's mind with the Seven Churches of the Book of Revelation.

'This is the fairytale nursery created for a fairytale castle. The dolls' house and the crib, the beds and walls, all created and decorated out of such tales as *The Sleeping Beauty*,

*Cinderella* and *Little Boy Blue*. But there are no children living here now. The master prefers them to be schooled in Scotland.'

Edward continued his count of the locks, discreetly pointing out one door which had no less than four bolts on it. Just how were they going to get through them all? In a quiet moment he asked Partington if they would be able to get that manservant Bethell to leave a few windows off the latch.

'He'll do whatever he can, Mr Edward.'

'And doors?'

'Security is not part of Mr Bethell's job. Doors might be difficult, however.'

Edward's anxiety was by now making his heart pound quite hard. His palms were becoming sweaty and he was wondering what he was doing in this preposterous building. He was half sorry that he had not taken a small sniff of snow before coming here. Snow always calmed him down, making him strong and wondrously inviolable.

After leaving the Arab and Chaucer Rooms in the Beauchamp Tower they came to the Fleche Tower, which the flunkey described as his master's favourite. Here they stepped down a spiralling stone staircase – which had been carved out of an eighteen-foot-thick stone wall – until they came to the newel post, a seated stone lion with a visor and a dragon on his head. So, inside this half-gargoyle, half-mythic beast was a mysterious cup which might have been used by Nero and which now contained the heart of the man who had been the richest man in the world.

At last! This was what they had been waiting for. Edward simply stared at it, his belly sucking in on itself. He put out his hand and stroked the base of the plinth. It felt surprisingly cold to the touch. It must be a good foot thick, he reasoned to himself. We're going to need pulleys to move that. He waited until the others had moved away before putting his shoulder against it to give it a tentative shove. Pulleys *and* a lot of muscle power, he silently added. Partington looked at him inquiringly and Edward shook his head.

Towards the end of the tour they came to the great banqueting hall, the largest room in the castle. Edward marvelled at the minstrel gallery, an oak hammer-beam roof and a blaze of heraldic shields. The guide's voice droned on. 'This is a table of tooled leather where Burges put central heating in the legs so that that room, at least, is never cold.

This is the third Marquess's family tree – he spoke nineteen different languages, including Aramaic though, oddly enough, not a word of Welsh.'

The flunkey marched swiftly across the hall and stood by the firegrate. 'Here at the back of the firegrate is a real curiosity – a priesthole which connects with three miles of sewers beneath the city. The second Marquess had a private sewer dug after the cholera scare of 1851 but did not have it finished, largely because he fell out with the engineer over the growing expense. He had what was left connected with the rest of the system.'

Edward looked over to the door to the newel gate, mentally measuring the distance from the priesthole leading down to the sewers. They would need a dynamite man to get that grille off but then there was only one door to break through. Only one! And then the prize would be theirs!

'We're going to need at least five men on this job,' he told Partington as they crossed the castle drawbridge together. 'I don't expect you'd want to come in on it yourself so we'll need at least three for scaffolding and pulleys. Also, a dynamite man for the grille – we could never cut through that. But just where are we going to find them?'

'We'll find them, Mr Edward. There's some three thousand Irish in Newtown and the IRA have long been sending their men there whenever it gets too hot back home. There's bound to be a dynamite man in there somewhere.'

Nathan was surprised and appalled at how much and how quickly he came to miss his wife and children after their departure for West Wales. Elizabeth had promised that she would come back one day but it was those two little urchins of his that he yearned for so much. The loss of them was almost like having his insides torn out. He could feel himself going through periods of isolation and madness, catching himself staring at his eyes in his shaving mirror, asking himself what was happening to him and why. His verbal ebullience had left him and he spent long hours in his study, facing the flaking wall, unable even to console himself with reading his beloved psalms, whose life-giving sonority now seemed to ring hollow.

*'Therefore we will not fear though the earth be removed, and though the mountains be carried into the midst of the sea.*

*Though the waves thereof roar and be troubled, though the mountains shake with the swelling thereof . . .'*

Yet, with the removal of his earth, he was beginning to fear greatly. When the waves had roared, he felt lost and frightened. The mountains had shaken and he was shaking too, wondering why God had abandoned him in the time of his destruction.

He knew, with all the conviction that had once been the very engine of his life, that he needed the full armour of his faith to contend with the problems of his ill-assorted parish – problems which seemed to increase with the arrival of every ship. Only that morning a small party of East European Jews had been dropped off in the West Basin – all hungry, shivering and clutching tickets to New York. New York! The captain of the steam packet had assured them that this was indeed New York, and that all the skyscrapers were just up the top of Bute Street. Then the packet had sailed on the next tide. The waterguard officers eventually contacted Nathan who, in his turn, had contacted the synagogue in Cathedral Road who, to their credit, had come quickly to their abandoned Jewish brethren.

After the Barbadian incident many people thought of Nathan as the saviour of the parish. He laughed bitterly, knowing that he had neither the talent nor the strength for that mammoth, impossible task. The Bay was continuing to boil almost nightly, holding up a curious and accurate reflection to Nathan's growing sense of breakdown. The disjointed violence in the streets found echoes and resonances in the crumbling patterns of his mind. He was getting frequent headaches, unable to think anything through to the end. He needed a plan of action but could think of nothing.

On top of all this the swelling crowds of angry whites were still gathering threateningly at the top of Bute Street each afternoon. Many of the racial groups were still quarrelling openly amongst themselves. Grudges were being settled with the odd knifing. The Moslems were still embroiled in a row about the positioning of their Mosque and any Bay boy found by the police wandering outside his area was swiftly picked up and dumped back in the dockland where, he was told, he belonged.

It might have been bearable if it hadn't been as hot, the summer boiling everything in sight. That Thursday was so hot that Albert, a local coal horse for nineteen years, finally gave up and died on the corner of Angelina Street. He was just coming to the end of his round, sweating and snorting miserably while pulling the coal cart around the corner when a massive heart attack exploded in his chest and, as silently as a passing angel, his legs splayed out and his head sank down, every limb giving way as he collapsed onto the hot tarmac in a very dead heap, his tongue hanging out of the side of his mouth, the flies buzzing around the puddles of frothing piss that were already eddying around his tail; a sad and undignified epitaph for a great horse.

The extremely upset coalman even came to see Nathan to ask if the horse could have a Christian burial and there was a right old fuss when he was told that he could not.

Nathan did not want to leave all this and neither did he want to stay. He wrote long, soul-searching letters to his wife but, as yet, had received no reply, reinforcing his sense of isolation. '*Dear Elizabeth,*' he wrote to her one afternoon, '*as usual I miss you and the boys desperately, keeping you closely in my prayers. Certainly we need all the prayer support we can get at the moment and I would ask you to remind the congregation of St Bart's to pray for me also.*

'*I've never known a place where so many are at each other's throats and I just wish there was something I could do about it. We seem to be just standing here waiting for someone to light the match to the powder keg. It's become quite, quite dangerous to live here . . . if only there was something I could do . . .*'

His pen was poised in mid-air, for a moment, when he had a flash of an idea and he wrote it down. '*It has just occurred to me that perhaps we should try to organize some sort of Mardi Gras in which all the separate groups could come together in a spirit of joint celebration. Each group has its own culture and skills which could be brought together for a day of happiness and fellowship. The West Indians could play jazz, the Chinese demonstrate martial arts, the Italians put on some opera . . . all that kind of thing.*'

Almost immediately he had finished the letter he went over to see Father O'Reilly in Newtown. The ubiquitous bottle of poteen appeared but, even as they discussed the merits of the new idea, Father O'Reilly listed such a long series of objections and likely problems Nathan soon began to see that it would be almost impossible to get the idea off the ground.

It was all very well. Father O'Reilly thought, but in the current climate, it was far too soon. Single groups could scarcely make a single contribution since they would never be able to agree what it would be. The Somalis were on a permanent war footing with the Ethiopians in some sort of skirmish that had lasted all of a thousand years. The Chinese were still too afraid to come out onto the streets since they would doubtless get a good cuffing from everyone for what they did in the dock strike. Even now, most of the Italian community was planning to move out into ice cream parlours in the Valleys. More to the point, he did not see his own Catholic community being too keen to join in either. 'You know my people, Nathan. There's no bigger racist than your working class Catholic. They have one Church, one marriage and one closed mind. Any smell of intermarriage or anything to reduce the potato purity of their blood and they immediately start worrying about that burning place. It's all tribalism and we're as bad as any of them. Everything you see going on around this place is all down to tribalism.

'We had a wake here yesterday. You ever seen anything more tribal than a wake? They were there, all of them, for this man, a workman who was in and out of death for years – the very divil for living, but then he just went and died. So they gave him a big wake and I've never seen my people so happy as when they've all got their arms around one another an' are crying into their drink.' Father O'Reilly sighed and refilled their glasses. 'The only real thing which is going to help this area is time. Oh sure it's a tip-top idea to have this Mardi Gras of yours but these people need to get used to one another. They need to stop thinking about colour at all. Here, throw another of these down your neck. Drink is the best thing I know to cure you of the despair of tribalism.'

Heavy showers of rain went gusting and rolling around the twilight streets, underlining Nathan's sense of dejection when he returned to St Mark's. Despite his encircling gloom he had tried to break out and counterattack with a bright idea which had merely gone the way of all the other bright ideas around here – straight down the plughole. The idealist meets the blazing cannons of reality.

The rain was picking furiously now, sheeting against the rooftops and sending the litter and rotten fruit swirling down the gutters. The rain had driven all the people off the streets too. Right now the Bay looked almost pleasant, almost clean, almost at peace with its own volatile heart. The suspended glow of the lamplight had turned silvery green, the light refracting in the raindrops to make great ghostly ships which had sailed down from other planets and were now moored in long perfect lines all along Bute Street and over the dockland itself.

But it wasn't quite as bad as it might have been since his sessions with Father O'Reilly had given Nathan his first ever taste for alcohol. And he had found that he quite liked it. His sense of despair eased and lifted a little when he had a drink. The world was so much easier to look at and confront . . . But there was nothing quite like rain dribbling down the back of your neck to sober you up. Nathan found himself quite steady and clear-eyed when he reached St Mark's. Inside the air was warm and damp, making breathing as difficult as chewing nougat. He stopped inside the door watching Sophie, graceful in every move, setting up the tea-urn and putting out plates of biscuits for afternoon tea. Already the Barbadians–whose numbers had now been whittled down to about fifty (largely because three of the families had gone to Swansea) – were queuing up quietly next to the trestles. Nathan had long noticed how good they were at queuing; they were patient and rarely vexed even if the queue turned out to be a wait for nothing.

Sometimes he watched them sitting around the church and marvelled at how relaxed they could be doing nothing. He only had to sit down for a few minutes at the most and he would be looking around for something to do. But these people seemed to do nothing with almost no effort at all and he wished he knew the secret. Successful idling was, after all, a very fine art. He walked among them and his imagination framed them in their West Indian setting, chattering together on coconut beaches or lazing on a hammock in a patch of shade. It was, of course, ridiculous rushing around in the heat of the West Indies, though it was so hot and stuffy in the Bay now it was not very clever rushing around here either.

But it was Sophie who caught his attention again. He gazed at her, standing there laughing and brushing a lock of dark hair out of her eyes, with her baby, Effey, whom she now carried in a shawl African-style on her back, looking around with those black saucer eyes full of innocence. Sophie's work may have prevented her from winning the sewing circle award for the best mother in the Bay, but much of the time Effey slept, often she laughed and, as far as Nathan could see, the girl never cried. Sophie used all her natural intelligence and grace in being a mother. She really wouldn't have minded a hundred babies, Nathan heard her say, at the same time as she caught one of the Barbadians taking too many biscuits and forced him to put a few back with a playful smack on his wrist. Then, when she thought no one was looking, she slipped a couple more into the old man's pockets.

Although she was something of a renegade herself, Nathan had, through her, come to know a lot about the Somalis and their desert ways. They were a nomadic people from the Horn of Africa, defiant and as strong as oaks, brilliant at survival and loyalty – all learned by their ancestors from the unforgiving harshness of the desert, the long monsoons, the shadow of drought and the continual wars with their neighbours. He had heard tales of women having to stand in a field for up to eight hours acting as scarecrows, just waving their hands up and down to frighten away the birds. He had also been told that it was the practice to stitch up a young girl's vagina before marriage to ensure her virginity. Not that, as Sophie would add, they managed to do that with her. She was, in all things, her own woman.

His imagination began working again and he saw her, baby on her erect back and water bottle on her head, walking through some dusty African township where flies buzzed around sleeping dogs and the heat was merciless. He would be out in the fields with the cattle and, come sundown, he would go home to her magnificent body, in their mud hut, alone with just a hundred babies crawling everywhere.

'You've been drinking,' Sophie said, coming over and giving him a playful nudge with her elbow and shattering his African daydreams. 'And you never used to drink at all, did you? Look at the bloodshot in your eyes. I bet I know where you've been to. Those Catholic priests are terrors for the falling-down stuff, you know. Absolute terrors.'

'So what else is new around here?' he smirked, dismissing her accusation with a shrug of his shoulders. 'How's young Obe doing today?'

'Young Obe is not too well, Nathan, and he's got worse since you saw him last. He was complaining about pains in his hands so they took him back down to the hospital. We're all worried stiff he won't be able to play his horn again.'

'He could use his other hand, couldn't he?'

'It's both hands, Nathan. They bashed in both of his hands. Why didn't they just burn him at the stake and be done with it?'

'Well, the chapel-loving citizens of Cardiff have done that once or twice before now.'

'If I got *my* hands on them . . .' She held up her bunched fists and Nathan had no doubt at all that she really would have done something very nasty to all of them. The Somalis were good at war – they'd had a thousand years of practice with the Ethiopians after all. 'Just five minutes that's all . . .' But her threats trailed away and there was that smile again. 'You're wet through. Come on. I've been doing some cooking and put something in the oven for you.'

'Sophie, I'm just not hungry.'

'That doesn't matter, does it?' she said, grabbing him by the wrist. 'You're still going to eat it. We don't want our vicar fading away now, do we?'

She set a huge meal of boiled beef, carrots and pease pudding in front of him on his dining table and, with upturned knife and fork in either hand, he surveyed it dismally.

'I'm going to give the baby a bath and, when I get back, I want every bit of that gobbled up.' At the door she turned again with Effey now looking at him as well. 'And don't forget to say Grace.'

'Grace,' said Nathan, prodding the thick slivers of meat around and wondering quite where to start excavating this steaming mountain of food. He did manage to eat about half of it and, hearing that she was still in the bathroom, he quickly scraped the rest out into the backyard where the local cats would see it off in no time. Such ploys were but part of his Welsh way; he never liked to give offence, particularly after someone had gone to such trouble. The local cats did very well out of this Welsh *politesse* too.

He had picked up a newspaper, when he realized that she seemed to have been gone an awful long time just to wash a small baby. Newspaper still in hand he walked down the corridor, stopping just before the bathroom door. With the help of a mirror, he could see her sitting naked in the bath playing with Effey.

Strange, troubling emotions came pouring hot through his veins as he stood there watching them both gurgling and laughing together. Perhaps it was the alcoholic subversion of

Father O'Reilly's poteen and perhaps it was something else again, but he could feel his mouth going as dry as sawdust, and some fat worm turning over and crawling around the pit of his belly. He knew all too well what this was about. This was the very first sin of them all, that's what this was about.

He shifted his position slightly to get a better view of her lovely olive body. Oddly enough it was not her foam-flecked bosom that he found so exciting – nor indeed the faintly visible heart of her pubic hair. Rather it was her magnificent shoulder bones, lean and angular, which braced and relaxed as she lifted the gurgling baby up and down. In their loving unity and trusting understanding no one would ever guess that they were not mother and daughter, even the shades of their skin were similar.

She caught a glimpse of his enraptured face in the mirror but pretended that she had not seen him as she continued playing with the baby, now flicking water onto the little girl's back. 'Nathan, come and hold the baby will you?' she called out in a voice loud enough to reach into the dining room. 'Just hold her while I get out of the bath.'

The loudness of her voice startled him but, after hesitating for a suitable length of time, he dropped his newspaper and walked into the bathroom which was as boiling hot as his flushing cheeks. His chest seemed tight with asthma, his heart thumping like a steam hammer. Also his hands were trembling so much he thought, for one terrifying moment, that he was going to drop the baby when she was held out to him.

But the soft touch of the child's dripping wet skin reassured him and he felt calm and overwhelmingly loving as he moved his arms around for a better purchase and looked down at her, careful to avert his gaze from Sophie's body. He brought the child close to his chest when, without warning, he began to cry.

Sophie hurriedly wrapped herself in a towel and held her hands out to take the baby but he made no move to release her.

'I miss my two boys something terrible, Sophie,' he said, the tears still pouring down his cheeks. 'I don't know. I just don't know about anything. I sometimes think I won't be able to carry on.'

'It'll work out, Nathan. You know you've got a friend in me. And Effey. Look at her. She loves you too.'

'I've always loved babies. One of the greatest pleasures of

my calling has been to hold a baby at the christening font. All God's greatest secrets and most amazing joys lie in these little ones.'

She put her hands on his shoulders and their foreheads touched as they both looked down at Effey, her short legs kicking out in spasms of pleasure at all this attention. 'We're both your friends,' Sophie repeated softly. 'Just treat us as family. We'll support you.'

'I couldn't, girl,' he said, stepping back and handing the baby to her. 'The old prophet said that a man with two women loses his soul. I'm still married and I want my wife and children back.'

'I wasn't saying anything, Nathan. I wasn't saying nothing. Just let's be friends.'

'In some ways you're lucky, Sophie. You don't seem to need anything. I need God, and there's one thing you should understand about the Welsh. It's called guilt and it runs deeper in us than our very blood.'

She laughed at all these strange words. Some people got themselves into a pickle about so little. 'Well, in that case, let's have a cup of tea then. You won't feel guilty about that, will you?'

For the next few nights Edward and Partington toured the forty-two cafés, seamen's lodging houses and some dozen pubs which had sprung up in and around Bute Street. The cafés in particular were rough and seedy, like beer shebeens, where gin was distilled in the back yards and everything was carefully embroidered with filth. The watery beer was served in chipped cups and the gin drunk straight out of the bottle. When anything was broken it was merely swept under the bare wooden tables with a foot.

A few had fans to blow the smells straight out through the windows but mostly they were thick with the stagnant smells of oil, coal dust or urine. The later it got the more likely there was to be trouble, and once, when they were in Morty's, Edward and Partington actually saw a burly Arab being hurled through a window. To their amazement the Arab jumped straight back through the shattered hole and head-butted his assailant. 'Find out who he is,' Edward told Partington. 'We could do with someone like that.'

The bouncing Arab turned out to have the unlikely Welsh name of Owen. Or, as he was known to all in the Bay, Owen the Bastard.

Many of these shebeens were merely gambling clubs where men played poker, dice or seven-and-eleven craps, ganging up on any strangers who made a double hundred. Edward had always taken a lively interest in gambling and was often invited to join in the games. But he always refused, knowing that he would immediately be marked as a double hundred and they would all work with one another until he had lost the very shoes off his feet.

Despite the smartness of the two men's appearance even the most incoherent, dribbling drunks rarely bothered them, largely because Partington's pinstripe suit and bowler suggested that he might be a policeman – or something worse. Also, Edward could hold himself with a confidence and compact meanness which said, very clearly, that in a spot of fisticuffs he could handle himself very well indeed. Edward was rather short, and one of the golden rules of any dockland bar was never to pick on the smallest. Just like aroused Jack Russell dogs, the smallest could also be the most deadly.

They rarely had a drink when they went into such bars; instead they merely stood around looking or waiting for someone to react. Had Edward not gone missing when Lord Kitchener was telling him that his country needed him then Edward would have made a fine officer. He had a natural intelligence in assessing men just by looking at them and then, perhaps, listening to a few of their words. He could tell what a man was like just by the way he walked across the bar to buy a beer; by the way he drank that beer and the way he mingled with his drinking friends. And from just those observations in those seedy bars he did nothing at all and merely nodded at Partington, indicating that they should go elsewhere.

The real problem with most of these men, for Edward's purposes, was that a lot of them had been injured in the war. They might have lost their hearing after being blasted by trench mortars in Gallipoli or else been blinded by flying shrapnel in some muddy trench near Vimy Bridge. More than a few had jagged scars across their faces after a ferocious entanglement with barbed wire while others might even have lost an arm or a leg. Even worse they might bore you into insensibility with tales of what it was like in the trenches. If anyone told him again what it was like when a mortar bomb came screaming overhead he was going to scream himself.

The worst of these men gathered outside the Salvation Army hostels in the mornings for their farthing breakfasts; broken, shivering reeds who shuffled around in patches of green grease all over the pavement.

What Edward looked for was a sparkle in the eyes, some glint of devilry or personality. But almost everywhere he looked there were dead, defeated eyes which spoke all too vividly of the death and destruction in those trenches. You would never have guessed that they had won the war, though, in an odd sort of way, Edward decided that many of them would be quite happy to fight again; certainly the khaki idiots who were taunting the blacks at the top of Bute Street – and were now being daily dispersed by the police – seemed only too happy to start a second world war.

Yet, just from keeping their ears open and making the odd discreet inquiry, they had picked up one good lead. Edward had, at first, thought it was another bit of Bay folklore but it turned out that there was a well-known pimp and hard case in the area, one Therence Towney, who had a gang which gloried in the nickname of The Forty Thieves. The word was that they were largely ex-servicemen and three-time losers who were now operating a variety of activities from burglary to protection rackets – even charging bookmakers for supplies of chalk, sponges and buckets of water. You paid up – or got cut up, it was said. Towney, the word was, operated out of the South Star Club near the Pier Head.

When they called at the South Star they found a murky, pokey dive with sawdust and odd bits of food and streamers scattered over the floor, the remnants of some party. A huddle of redundant prostitutes was sitting around a table in one corner, while in the other some old man was busy coughing his lungs out into a spitoon. A sign said: 'No credit Mondays and all through Mondays'. Another said: 'No starched shirts'.

Towney himself turned out to be a most unlikely Ali Baba figure, thin, with disjointed nervous movements and starey eyes with so many grey rings around his green pupils he might have been a pigeon. He wore a shabby suit, which might have seen service in the Boer War, while his fingers played incessantly with some Arab worry beads which, irritatingly, he cracked and rattled continuously as he spoke. Edward decided he would have the greatest difficulty cutting up a potato let alone a wayward bookie.

'You men want a little job done, I hear,' Towney said without preamble. 'What is it?'

'We don't want to talk about that just at the moment,' said Partington. 'We just need two, perhaps three, strong men who need some good money and are prepared to take a slight risk.'

The beads rattled again. 'What sort of risk would we be talking about?'

'We don't want to talk about that just now,' Partington repeated.

Towney jerked away from them, walking back into the darkness of the club, his beads still cracking. 'I can find you men,' he explained, when he returned, stretching out his hands, as if offering some amazing bargain on the cheap. 'I can find you all the men you need – a dozen, two dozen – but I've got to know what they're going to do and, more to the point, what's in it for me.'

'You don't need to know anything,' said Edward, taking the worry beads out of Towney's hands and slipping them into the pocket of his Boer War jacket. 'All you need to know is that they will get thirty pounds each for one night's work. If you get us the right men, you will also get a hundred pounds. But only if.'

'Well, that's different, innit?' Towney said without hesitation. 'That is very different, that is. Just meet me in the Hotel de Boilermaker on the Marl next Sunday afternoon.'

'Hotel de Boilermaker?' Edward queried.

'It's a Sunday open-air drinking club in the Marl park,' Partington explained. 'It's also called the Hotel de Donkeyman. They get in barrels of beer there on Sunday afternoons to get around the Sunday Closing Act. Just an illegal booze-up really.'

'Beer *and* pitch-and-toss,' Towney amplified. 'I don't suppose I could have that money now, could I?'

'When we've got our men,' said Edward. 'And I mean good men, not war cripples likely to lose their nerve.'

That Sunday afternoon it was a dull, smouldering day with some eighty customers of the Hotel de Boilermaker gathering around five barrels of beer stacked up on trestles in the middle of the Marl. Two coins were being flipped in the odd gambling groups with cries of 'I'll head a tanner' or 'I'll head a pound.' On the outlying reaches of the park ragged urchins were posted to warn of any unwanted incursions by the police. The gambling was as illegal as the drinking.

Towney, Partington and Edward were standing some twenty yards from the main group as Towney gave a rundown on the men. 'A lot of these are my boys and, quite honestly, most of them are as thick as planks, but depending on what you want them for, I've got a few good ones here.'

He paused, as if hoping that Edward would explain his purpose. But when he did not, he continued. 'Just on the corner of that group is a Malt who is brilliant with a knife. And when I say brilliant I mean just brilliant. He'll take on anyone and they'll be stuck before they've even seen the knife.'

'We don't need a knife.'

'You don't need a knife. It would save me a lot of trouble if you told me what you did need. Right. Next to the Malt is a Greek captain. George Crocodoulous or something. No one can say his name so we just call him The Greek. Now Greeks are so green they could get lost in a lettuce, but that one has the heart of a lion. And he's stronger than any six men I know.'

'Anyone there know dynamite?'

'Dynamite? The stuff that goes bang, you mean? No, I don't think so. Old Titch Wilson – the one carrying those two pints – now he used to be the best burglar in Wales and he's been inside . . .'

'He's too old,' Edward interrupted snappily. 'Now look. I want young ice men. You know what I mean by that? Athletic men with nerves of steel.'

Towney shook his head. 'A lot of these have been shot up in the trenches an' they shakes like jellies. Most of them need at least three pints to calm their nerves enough to get out of the door.'

'I don't want drunks either.'

'But . . . ah yes, see that one sitting on his own at the far end of the bank? He's the boy for you, and he's skint. Hard as nails that one. As hard as nails. They call him Slogger. He was a sapper in the war, but spent most of his time in the glasshouse painting coal. He's one of the Dacey boys. They're all hard, them. An' none of them 'ave got any nerves at all.'

They discussed a few more likely candidates then Edward

turned to Partington and asked him what he thought. The inevitable Mint Imperial preceeded the reply. 'Well, I must say, Mr Edward, I'm very glad that I'm not going on this little job with you, but I'd say the Greek gentleman and perhaps the Maltese. We've already got that Arab gentleman, so as a sort of reserve we could try that Slogger Dacey boy. But I do like the idea of brothers who will work together, so what about another Dacey?'

Both faces turned towards Towney. 'They're inside. All the Dacey boys are inside.'

'In that case,' Partington continued confidentially with a swallow, 'I suggest we take these three. As we've got the Arab, we are still short of someone who knows dynamite so I'm afraid we'll have to try the Irish in Newtown, after all.'

But Towney had overheard. 'Talking of the Irish in Newtown, I've got the man,' he said. 'But, as he's not one of my people, it'll cost you an extra fifty. In advance. Then I'll give you an address.'

'You know, Mr Edward, I've never understood the arguments against capitalism,' Partington mused out loud. 'Money oils every transaction – straight and crooked alike. It is the only possible motive for doing anything, providing you do it in cash and put it in your pocket. Mr Towney understands that clearly enough, so you'll get your fifty, Mr Towney, but first tell us exactly what this most expensive man is capable of.'

# CHAPTER EIGHT

By Tuesday a scorching summer had taken up residence in the city. The very streets sweated and groaned. There were few shoppers in Queen Street; so many had headed for the seaside that five trains were blocked up waiting to get into Barry Island station. Lazy windmills of sunshine came rolling in over the glittering, still Channel. Even in the docks themselves, all most of the dockers were interested in was finding some shady corner in which to have a quiet game of cards.

Except for the usual trickle of handcarts going about

handcart business there was almost no traffic in Bute Street. Cats basked on hot corrugated roofs. In No. 14 a multicoloured parrot sat on its perch in a hall muttering language so obscene it would have made a bosun blush.

Sophie had stood around for an hour on the corner of Custom House before giving up along with the rest of the city. 'Contraceptive weather, this,' she murmured, picking up Effey in Angelina Street and taking her home. For the rest of the afternoon they played together in the small backyard of her house. At this time the yard always had the eye of the sun and she liked to sit next to the zinc bath letting Effey wriggle around on her blanket.

She tickled the baby's toes and sighed, looking up at the brick wall. She was not a happy girl these days but neither was she terribly unhappy. She was certainly not stuffing herself with as much food as usual.

Nathan had become predictably distant after the encounter in the bathroom. A man like that would always spend part of his time having bad thoughts and the rest of the time worrying about them, she guessed. A man like that would never know real happiness because the key to that elusive state was always love and someone like him would never let go enough to abandon himself to that. Nathan would always be worrying about what was right; that was always the trouble with religious people.

Her elbow on her knee, her chin resting on her hand, she sighed again. With her other hand she reached out and tickled Effey's fat brown belly. She wasn't having much luck at all with love, she reflected ruefully. Occasionally she still saw her Rashed – and still, just at the thought of him, her whole belly lurched as if punched – but he was too deep into Moslem politics now. He, as well as Nathan, behaved as if he'd just committed a triple murder when he saw her. What was the matter with these men? She reckoned he would rather cross over the other side of the street than walk past her, the dope. At least they could have stayed friends. More than anything she regretted the loss of this friendship but, in the circumstances, she did see how it could be one thing or the other. It was that religious thing again.

But Rashed would sometimes stand and look when she was out in the street with Effey. He had a certain torment about him and, no sooner had she spotted him, than he was gone again. She often wondered if he thought that the baby was his. Now that would be fun, wouldn't it? Moslem activist with bastard baby. That would give them something to talk about after prayers in the Mosque.

The only man she saw with any kind of regularity was that young snot Edward Gurney, who paid so well that, at least, she did not have to worry too much if business did go slack. There was no love between them, of course, just a lot of sex which could get very high-powered if he had had his nose into that cocaine again. At times he would go on for so long she was fully intending to charge him double for 'a snow job' but, just recently, he had been giving her the odd sniff and, somewhere deep in all the whizzing, she found that she quite liked it herself.

But Edward was also talking to her more these days, answering a few more of her inquisitive questions and she fancied she was enjoying herself more too. A rich regular was what every business girl dreamed of, so she always made herself available to Edward and always did what he asked. He was no longer so rough with her either and she was wondering if he was becoming a little more keen on her than he would have liked.

It would never lead to anything of course. While a man like Nathan would always be imprisoned by his conscience, a man like Edward would always be imprisoned by his class. She would never be seen out in public with Edward. She was just his whore. She accepted that cheerfully enough, even if there were sides to him that she was coming to like. He seemed to have a lot of nerve and he was clearly up to something very interesting but she didn't know what. She'd heard, through the gossip, that he'd been going around picking up some of the biggest villains in the Bay for some job. She wouldn't have got on the same train as that Owen the Bastard let alone done a job with him. And that Slogger Dacey had no more sense than a sack of nails.

Meanwhile the other man for whom she'd had a special fondness was in prison. Hardly waiting for his recovery in hospital, young Obadiah Brown had been taken before the Cardiff Police Court where the magistrate had given him the maximum of six months for stealing a box of oranges, the property of William Aitken of Hayes Bridge Island. Nathan had gone down and spoken on Obe's behalf but the magistrate had been most insistent that an example had to be set for the other immigrants – 'They must learn that they cannot just go and steal fruit whenever they need it – as they probably do back in their own homes' – then he had handed out the staggering six months' sentence with a further recommendation that he be whipped by the cat-o'-nine-tails.

Poor old Obe. It was all just because he was black, Sophie was convinced. All this colour hatred seemed to be everywhere and she never knew where it was all going to end. Even the dole office gave less than the standard twenty-nine shillings to coloured families since, they argued, coloured people lived communally and therefore needed less.

Obe's imprisonment had been doubly frustrating, since he had been teaching Sophie to sing songs. Obe had always loved all the new jazz sounds that were coming out of New Orleans and had taught her the saucy words of *All the Boys Like The Way I Ride*. Obe had said that she had a great jazz voice, whatever that was – she had always thought her husky voice sounded more like a rope under a door. But she ought to do something with it, he had insisted. Not that she could do much with it now that he was locked up in the pokey.

She fed Effey with some tinned 'goldfish' – or salmon as they otherwise called it – which had fallen off the back of a boat. Everyone in the area loathed goldfish heartily – there was clearly an unwanted mountain of salmon somewhere – but Effey could never get enough of it down her. For herself, Sophie would never touch the foul stuff and wished something more interesting, like a chicken or a leg of lamb, would fall off the back of those boats. But no. It was just goldfish, goldfish, goldfish.

At least she had Effey now. Her baby, even if she still asked herself about six times a day where the girl had come from. The only thing she knew with any certainty was that Effey was not going away again. She was here, with her, to stay.

In certain ways the baby had transformed Sophie, making her more mellow and even a little more responsible. She actively enjoyed the fact that she now had to think of someone else; she had to care for someone else. It stopped her brooding too much about herself; about these ill-assorted men who kept wandering in and out of her life – confusing her feelings, giving her the blues. Ah yes, the blues. Obe had been telling her about the great Bessie Smith and she had become very interested indeed in that woman. Sophie knew a lot about the blues too.

The castle clock was chiming six times when old Charlie Boden walked past feeling pretty damned pleased with himself. He had gone with his young nephew Joey up to the weir in Llandaff and fished out six large mullet which now hung on his line and would soon be simmering in the kitchen at St Mark's.

Dusk was thickening slightly and the last of the city shoppers were leaving the arcades to catch their trams back to the suburbs. Charlie was walking down into St John's Square, where an old man was playing *Comrades in Arms* on a mouth organ, when a small group of black youths went running past. They were just passing the market when a group of white youths came running out from behind the graveyard railings and pounced on them, starting a rolling, flailing maul which surged around and around like two rugby packs fighting for the ball.

Charlie took Joey by the hand, uncertain which way to move to get away from the running scuffles, when one of the black boys took out a huge razor. He held out his weapon in front of him, sticking the air again and again. 'Come on then, let's see what you honkys are made of,' he taunted the white boys.

For a moment there was a stunned silence. Then there was a yell and the white pack surged forward again. Someone's boot kicked the razor high into the air and more whites, many in khaki uniforms, came running out of the side streets. Soon a plate-glass window of a department store had shattered. Every corner had come alive with shouts, screams and the continual blowing of policemen's whistles.

Charlie turned and turned again, dropping his fish and holding Joey's hand tight. His old black face was almost white with fear. He decided that it would be safest, just for now, to get back into the city itself. He knew then that there would be blood on the walls that night. He knew then that the volcano had finally blown.

Elizabeth Thomas had got off the 6.05 train from Haverfordwest at the Cardiff General Station and decided to walk the short distance down to St Mark's. She could not remember feeling quite so good, quite so pleased with herself. She had settled the boys down into a good pre-prep school in Pembroke and, after extended periods of prayer, now believed that God was telling her to return to her husband. She believed that He had scolded her for her weakness and that He was also giving her the strength to carry on with their marriage and work. So here she was, going back to where she belonged, her husband's side, and determined that she was going to make a good job of it this time.

She was even enjoying looking at the city around her, basking in all this sultry heat, and her heart lifted yet again when she heard what she imagined were the sounds of carnival coming from the top of Bute Street. But, as she soon discovered, it was not the cheerful noise of carnival that she was hearing but the rather more deadly sounds of riot.

She walked closer and saw a tram pull up and a load of Australian soldiers jumping down. She looked the other way and saw a line of screaming white youths spreading across the top of Bute Street, clearly intent on blocking the path of a group of blacks who had been running down past Hayes Island, trying to get back to the safety of the Bay.

And then she saw something she would never, ever forget. She saw a young black being punched and spinning around and around, before he pulled out a revolver from the inside of his jacket and began firing at his assailants. Elizabeth dropped her bag and held up her hands as if about to cover her eyes but, instead, just stood there, frozen, wondering if she really was seeing all this or if it was just some terrible dream. The black with the gun now shot one of the soldiers in the hand. The bullet hit the soldier with such force it turned him right around and he just stood there looking at his hand, amazed, since there was a small entry hole in the back of his hand but, when he turned it over, there was a huge jagged hole in his palm where the bullet had exited. Small fountains of blood poured over the ham of his hand and into the arm of his uniform.

Now the gunman let off another shot, felling a man in white decorator's overalls. The next shot felled a woman passer-by who, shopping bag in hand, had just been standing there gawping at all the commotion. The next shot ricocheted off a wall and hit a brewery horse which later had to be destroyed.

Yet more people were running down past Elizabeth towards the action and the blacks were all literally trying to kick their way through the white cordon. Completely overcome by shock and fear Elizabeth just about managed to get her legs moving again – back in the direction of the railway station.

Sophie had been walking alone up towards Custom House to pick up some early evening business when she heard all the baying and screaming. She frowned and walked a little way up Bute Street to investigate when she saw about four blacks running down the centre of the tramlines followed by a huge gang of angry whites. Suddenly one of the black boys was bowled over by a serrated German bayonet hurled straight into his back. Another of the fleeing blacks, whom Sophie recognized as that Royston Boyce from Loudoun Square, pulled the bayonet out of the back of his friend and ran back screaming towards his pursuers, who retreated judiciously before the flashing weapon. When the bayoneted man had been half dragged and half carried back to the Bay, Royston dropped the bayonet and made a run for it.

It was not like Sophie to be afraid of anything but, nevertheless, she decided to move out of the way as those storming waves of men came breaking towards her. She crossed over into a lane on the other, quieter, side of the street and was lucky she did, since what happened next sickened her to her nerve ends and, had she been nearer, she might have done something very silly.

Three of the young blacks ran into 250 Bute Street and the white mob went screaming in after them, smashing down the front door and roaring up the hallway. Window after window was punched out by chairs or ornaments which sailed down into the street and smashed into thousands of pieces. The white mob continued to swell, all shouting for 'the blood of those darkeys' as one of the black youths came sailing out of the shattered door, landing at the feet of the mob who proceeded to give him a good kicking. Then another was thrown out, and another, *and another* – all receiving the same fearsome kicking and beating by the mob.

Several times Sophie dashed out of the mouth of the side street, intent on intervening, and several times her commonsense caught hold of her and brought her back again. There was nothing at all she could do in the face of such furious mindlessness and, in the end, she concluded that the best she could do was to run down to St Mark's and warn Nathan about what was up.

The din that swept along the streets was a strange, baying roar of discord. People looked out of their windows, alarmed by its urgent immediacy. Fifteen feet below the surface of Bute Street, a group of men dressed in waterproof corporation overalls paused as they moved around in the bowels of the city. In the damp, dark sewers, lit only by two large coal-oil lamps and the small carbide lamps tied around the waists of the six sewermen, the noise seemed to echo and boom mysteriously. But there were the strangest noises in the dripping tunnels too – rushings, gurglings and hammerings – and, when they were satisfied that the outside noises represented no threat to them, they moved on.

The sewers were not high enough to walk in erect so they walked with a stoop, their lamps throwing hunched shadows onto the slimy brickwork all around them. These shadows lurched forward and raced away; they approached the men again slowly and even loomed right over their own heads in silent menace before disappearing again. It was very difficult for the eyes to become accustomed to this constant dance of light and shadow; even more difficult to get accustomed to the foul, turbid smells that seeped out of the yawning mouths of these city sewers.

But the group was silent and resolute. They emerged onto a new level and came across a giant brick weir. Just above it water was hissing down through a giant manhole. Lit by their lamps these chambers seemed like hidden, holy shrines where underground pilgrims might have journeyed in medieval times for deep reasons of faith.

But there was plenty of life in these sewers. A couple of frogs watched them from behind the moving curtain of the weir's waterfall. Small black eels wriggled in the brown sludge that was a foot thick beneath their feet. On occasion their lamps caught the fiery red eyes of a rat, angry at this intrusion into his domain.

But it was the continual shunts of noise in these tunnels that were the most curious. Every sound seemed to be amplified a dozen times by this underground shrine. So a sudden *whoosh* might sound like the tail-end of a hurricane. The pained iron screeching of the city trams sounded as if something serious was about to break before the roof fell in. The distant screams and crashes of riot seemed to be so near they could be actually happening inside their own heads. The drips could sound like hammer blows. Even their own body sounds were unusually loud – their muffled coughs, their occasional words to one another, the very beating of their tense hearts . . .

Edward was leading an exploratory trip through the sewers to see if, complete with their equipment, they could in fact make it to the grille in the castle's banqueting hall. But there must be other obstructions, they had already decided, since their lordships would never have put on a banquet, with rancid smells like this drifting up to the dining table.

But his small gang was moving together well enough, Edward had been both pleased and relieved to see. Despite their individual toughness they were not quarrelling. Nor, more to the point, did anyone lose their nerve when they saw a rat. He had seen strong men freeze in terror at the mere sight of a rat's tail. Many servicemen were said to be more terrified of the rats in the trenches than they were of the Kaiser's guns. But there were other, more potent dangers down here, which he had not told them about. In sudden downpours of rain these tunnels could flood; in certain circumstances pockets of deadly gas would build up from a century of the city's excreta.

If anything, the four of them – Slogger Dacey, the Malt, the Greek and Owen the Bastard – seemed to be enjoying their underground journey. It was only their new dynamite man, Gerry McGilligut, an old Sinn Feiner in whose whereabouts the British army and police were keenly interested, who might cause some difficulties. Though he clearly knew the difference between a big bang and a small bang when he heard it, the drink had long undermined his nerves. His fingers flapped so much he did not look capable of holding a cup of tea steady let alone a few sticks of sweating gelignite. Not that he was carrying them now, fortunately. They had agreed to go down first to see what had to be blown before they went to buy the stuff from a compliant colliery manager in Merthyr.

They had travelled another five hundred yards when they came out onto yet another great weir, the junction of some five intercepting sewers from different parts of the city.

Another huge pool hissed softly some six feet below them, the beginning of a series of storm drains in the event of floods. The weir itself was surrounded by a series of pillars and buttresses and Edward took his party off into the huge hole on its left where, he knew – if Hamilton's diagrams were correct – they would locate Sir Joseph Bazalgette's strange and unused creation.

Here the brickwork did indeed become newer. There was less dripping damp and the foul sewer smells lessened considerably. It seemed to be too clean even for the rats and frogs. They walked on another two hundred yards and now, Edward decided, they were directly under the castle walls, perhaps a further hundred yards from their goal. He looked behind him and saw that Slogger Dacey had disappeared from the group. Where the hell was he? Perhaps the stupid fool had decided that he'd had enough of all this and gone home to bed. Apart from his being thicker than all these bricks put together he would be no great loss, Edward thought. He had foreseen that one or two would drop out and, if necessary, he could do the job with three men (and just the smallest sniff of snow).

No, Dacey would be no great loss, but the one he really missed was Partington; not for his muscle power but for his calm commonsensical advice. Partington had the gift of seeing directly into the heart of any problem, and had the gravest of misgivings about their new dynamite man. But, nevertheless, he had simply announced that, at his age, he was not up to such a venture and refused to join them.

Another level brought another chamber. Here they came across a miniature Cornish beam engine with its two brass pistons – one for sucking in the sewage and the other for pumping it out again. It seemed so very odd to find this nearly new piece of machinery abandoned in an underground chamber. By some strange trick of chemistry the brass still seemed perfectly new and gleaming.

'That would bring a few shillings in scrap for definite certain,' said Gerry, holding up his lamp to it. 'We could pull that apart fast enough.'

'But what about this door?' Edward asked, swinging his lamp around and spotting the obstacle that they had long thought would be there. 'That's what we want pulled apart.'

They crowded around the old oak door while the Malt took out a large chisel, jamming it directly under the rusty iron hinges and, with a quick series of jerking rips, pulled the door off backwards. 'Had to do this once or twice when my wife locked me out,' he said with comic modesty as the others patted him on the back. 'I never believed in doors.'

Edward went through the broken door, holding his lamp in his teeth as he climbed up the iron steps of a vertical tunnel. This went up for almost twenty feet before his lamp picked out the black geometric shapes of the grille in the distance. 'Send up Gerry,' he called down to the men below.

Sighing and muttering all the while the old Sinn Feiner inched up the vertical steps and spent an age examining the grille. His trembling fingers touched every joint, occasionally he tapped it with his knuckles. 'Dynamite is no good for that,' he announced, after taking another age to climb back down to the waiting group. 'Apart from anything else it would bring the whole tunnel down on our heads. But that iron is even older than my old bones. A couple of hacksaws could take that off in half an hour. Oh, to be sure certain. Half an hour at the most.'

On their return journey they had passed one of the weirs, when the lights of their lamps seemed to pick up some great monster splashing around and washing himself in the next weir. It rose from the water making loud snorting noises before diving back into it again.

Edward crept forward slowly, only to discover that it was Slogger Dacey, who had lost one of his shoes in the weir and was not going to leave until he found it. 'They were new, they were. My Mam only bought them last week,' he shouted across to them before he dived again into the foul-smelling cesspit.

They left Slogger to find his new shoe and had got into the final tunnel when they heard a terrific bang which echoed and re-echoed down through the sewers, searing their ears. Then there was another and another. The hurrying sounds of many running feet chattered down through the dark tunnels, followed by distant screams and shrill whistles. They heard the sounds of galloping horses too. It all rather sounded like a strange new re-creation of the Battle of the Somme; the murderous symphony of a world at war.

They stopped still, uncertain whether to go back into the labyrinth of drains and find another way out. Again it was Edward who climbed up to the manhole where they had come in, shifting the huge iron plate to one side and bringing his head up into Bute Street. He could scarcely believe it. They had gone down that manhole on a hot, deserted afternoon and had come up into a night of riot and anarchy.

Houses seemed to be going up in flames; whinnying police horses were galloping up and down the street and battling groups were running in every direction. There was another huge bang and the white gas of a phosphorus bomb went billowing over the road making people run out of their houses holding sheets and handkerchieves to their mouths. Edward's head turned and turned again as he surveyed the terrible scene.

They would have to find another way out of the sewers. The whole of the Bay was on fire.

The old women in the Chinese block huddled together and howled in purest fear as violence kept driving into the streets like giant charges of lightning. The old women had seen – and remembered – all this nonsense before. They had crossed the world to escape it and here it was again.

Down in the laundry itself a grim-faced Pak Chen stood with the other men, all silent and wondering what to do next. They could go out there onto the street and face all those destructive white waves or else they could just sit tight and hope that it would all pass away. The trouble was that, unless they made some active defence of their property, it might get fired, along with the other houses. It was a fine decision and no one quite wanted to make it – least of all Pak Chen. But they *were* all armed to the teeth. They had meat cleavers and rice flails and were masters of Kung Fu.

More windows were smashed and more houses put to the torch. Another gas bomb exploded and a man ran past the block wearing a gas mask. Finally Pak Chen nodded to his colleagues. 'We'll just have to protect the pavement,' he said to them in Hokkien. 'There is no choice.'

They slipped out of the laundry door, standing shoulder to shoulder along the pavement, waiting for anyone to take their chances, when they might have every bone in their head broken with a rice flail or their chests smashed in with kicks of unbelievable power. Two men with the backs off their shirts ran towards them, only to run straight off again. Another gas bomb went off and more police horses went galloping down into the violence-fouled night. Pak Chen nipped down to the corner, and saw that the Moslems were also out on the streets, surrounding and protecting their Mosque.

Barriers had also gone up in Loudoun Square to protect the West Indian ghetto but, in all the hysterical excitement, that did not prevent them from fighting among themselves. A few took the opportunity to work off an old score against the owner of the local shebeen, smashing the windows and making off with the stock. One white gang went pouring after a small fleeing figure only to find that it was an eight-year-old girl in her nightgown who had lost her mother in all the hullabaloo. A Moslem was brought down on the tramlines and actually held there before an oncoming tram which spotted them and braked in time.

The tearing, racing sounds of riot filled every corner. Flickering flames leapt high into the night. Hadji Mahomet, a Somali holy man, of No. 1 Homfray Street, had to escape via his back drainpipe when a baying crowd gathered outside his door. He watched from a safe distance, chanting prayers to Allah as his house was wrecked; first his front door kicked in and then his furniture hauled out into the street and set on fire.

Another gang raced towards the Chinese block, and Pak Chen stepped out on the road in front of them, whirling and rattling his rice flail around his head and shoulders in the old manner, supposed to inspire terror in the enemy. But, just then, something even more terrifying happened: there was a sharp bang and Pak Chen's hands dropped his rice flail and flew up to clutch his forehead. He then sank slowly down onto his knees, as if settling down into a bowed position of prayer. The whole of his body fell forward, and there he remained with his hands actually resting on the road, the back of his head shot away and the blood pouring out in hot red bubbles over his fingers. Even the most skilled practitioners of the martial arts have no defence against the bullet.

The other Chinese immediately ran back inside the laundry and closed the door, when the sniper struck again, bringing down a passing policeman with a shot in the leg. It was impossible to see where the gunman was – he could have been almost anywhere, from the tops of the high houses all along Bute Street to the dark forests of warehouses and cranes in the docks themselves. This mysterious murderer, who was to claim a further two victims later that night, was never caught.

In the main front room, on the second floor of his house in Howard Close, Hamilton stood at the window looking out over the exploding bonfire nightscape. Chief Inspector Victor Watts was sitting on a high leather armchair next to the firegrate, holding a glass of dry sherry. Partington was standing at the table pouring one for himself.

Hamilton's lips were almost close to a smile as the orange flames flickered in his black eyes. The whole of the night was full of the most vivid colours of violence and destruction –even the clouds, radiant with moonlight, looked menacing as the winds shunted them high across the fiery skies. There was another explosion and he half closed his eyes, lifting his head back slightly, as if listening to a well-loved aria.

'You are to be congratulated, Victor,' he said finally. 'I call this a definite success, an unmitigated success. To think that we managed to start this with just one small group of louts. But it proves one thing; all this commotion shows that the fires of racial passion were always there. We just provided the added petrol, that's all. The fires were there.' He prodded his forefinger out into the night. 'But these are just the very smallest beginnings. We will need a lot more racial disorder than this. It will only be out of the flames of such disorder that we will ever be able to start purifying this great race of ours. And, you know, the real beauty of a riot is that everyone gets blamed for it. Even the innocent get blamed for racial disorder, particularly if they are black.'

Watts walked across the room to stand next to Hamilton, the city's flames almost making his ruddy birthmark come alive.

'Our party is making great progress in Germany and we expect to gain power within the next few years,' Hamilton continued. 'We still have a very long way to go but we have got the beginnings right. Bloodshed and anarchy are the necessary forerunners of our great political movement since they create so much anxiety and tension people long for the hand of firm government. And none will be firmer than ours when we take power. Yes, prolonged bloodshed is the very first act of a great bout of purification which will, in its turn, lead to the creation of the philosopher king. I find almost nothing more exciting than the notion of the philosopher king.'

He left the window and went over to Partington who was quietly communing with his glass of sherry. 'The real trouble with Partington here is that all he ever worries about is money.

There is nothing at all mysterious about his motives. It all comes down to money. That's why I have to pay him so much. But he is worth almost every penny.'

'You're too kind, Mr Hamilton.'

'But do tell me, Mr Partington. Did young Gurney and those brigands go down the sewers this afternoon?'

'They did.' Partington nodded at his sherry. 'They went down about four o'clock. We were watching them from the clock tower on the Pier Head building.'

'I am most anxious that they do not make any plans of their own. Young Gurney is a very smart operator. If he senses that there might be some real money to be made elsewhere with that cup he might get ideas of his own. The Party are very excited about the cup; they have been pursuing it almost for ever. It is most important to their plans and ideals.'

'We'll keep a weather eye on him, don't worry about that,' said Watts. 'There's a man called Towney who runs a gang of thieves in the South Star Club. They're pretty awful thieves if you ask me – never got away with anything that I know about. But Towney is in my pocket and he'll keep me posted on what's going on.'

'He is reliable, is he, this Towney?'

'I wouldn't exactly call him reliable, no. He's just a small-time chiseller who is too terrified of going back into prison to double-cross me.'

Hamilton strode back to the window. 'Good. All I really fear is any freelance behaviour. Warn the Kabulukam that we may need them sooner than we thought. Just make sure that they're around since, if Mr Edward Gurney makes the smallest amount of difficulty after he acquires that cup, I want him killed.'

With occasional lulls the rioting continued well into the night. By then the Irish – perhaps with strong, tribal memories of other, older attacks – had set up a barbed-wire barricade across the entrance to Newtown. They had Very lights too and, at times, it looked like a fragment from some old war nightmare as they stood three-deep, carrying poles and knives, in tattered greatcoats and frayed jackets, ready and waiting to repel any incursions into their territory.

Throughout it all Nathan had decided to stay in his church with the Barbadians since, all the long night through, it had been subject to repeated stoning attacks. Many of the small panes of the stained-glass windows had shattered and someone had hurled a pot of white paint over the door. 'Nigger-lovers' had been daubed on the church wall. It was useless even to step out of the door. Whom would you talk to? Who was fighting whom? And about what? He had gone out into the porch once, and, catching a stone on his shoulder, turned around and gone back in again.

Such Barbadians as were left were all huddling together for comfort near the altar, a tangled heap of shivering bodies and limbs, all as if they had been washed up and left on a beach by a storm and all asking themselves much the same question. Just why had they left their sunshine islands to journey to this city of hatred?

The noises in the street were tremendous.

'Jess like a volcano eruptin',' old Charlie Boden told Nathan. 'I saw all this a'comin', Mr Nathan. Yes, sir. There wus everything but centipedes and snakes out in those streets over the pas' few weeks.'

For herself, Sophie had been very quiet since coming to the church, staying with some old ladies and trying to calm them with a lot of warm tea and some of her old stories. But even she started to get worried when they heard more gunfire from that sniper. Her eyebrows shot up and many of the Barbadians muttered cries of fear.

Nathan asked God for advice and again was given the same verse from the Psalms. There was a rolling roar and another window shattered as he stood at the lectern and opened his Bible. He cleared his throat with a cough.

'"*Therefore we will not fear though the earth be removed and though the mountains be carried into the midst of the sea. Though the waves thereof roar and be troubled, though the mountains shake with the swelling thereof.*"

'What the Psalmist is trying to tell us is something about the nature of courage when love has failed,' he said. 'We have gathered here in a city of fear and violence and the Psalmist is telling us to be strong and beautiful in our courage. We are reminded often enough that Our Lord was both faithful and courageous right until the painful end of his short life, and this building here is the very house of God and, as long as you are here, then so too you will be under His divine protection. So you too must be courageous and strong.'

He ignored the heavy irony of the breaking of yet more windows before lifting his voice and feeling that certain quickening of the blood that he sometimes had as a prelude to a burst of the mystic Welsh *hwyl*. 'What we are seeing here tonight is the continuing heartbreak of this beloved country of Wales. We lost a lot of our young and beautiful gods in faraway places like Gallipoli, and now that war abroad has come home here to our very doorsteps. This is the way of violence and hatred. It is the very method of the devil who even now may be taking a great delight in what is happening in these evil streets. But I want you to know that the Welsh know and love the things of God too; that Wales can be both strong and weak, but there are times when she lets her eyes turn away from the sun. So tonight, take on the full armour of faith and know that this nation will again find its faith and love too; that she will look again to the sun; that she will cherish her families again – all her families, regardless of their colour. And that's the trouble just now, isn't it? In you, Mother Wales has been given new members of the family, but she is not quite sure how to handle them. But she will, my people, she will.'

His eyes caught Sophie's and he just looked at her for a few moments when, embarrassed, she turned her head away and began fussing over a baby. Outside there came a few isolated cries.

It was just then that he felt a rising of the *hwyl*, that Welsh roller-coaster of oratory which has thrilled the minds of generations of chapel-goers; the musical gift of tongues which first gave rise to the Pentecostal Church. He could feel all that poetry swimming in him as he took his thoughts to their climax.

'The Welsh go through terrible periods of sleep and despair. They can be so very weak when they actually want to be strong. So remember my words about your new homeland, and what I want you to do now is just to sing for this lovely, tearstained land of ours. I want you to sing with the same spirit of love and celebration that we all had here on the night you arrived. Sing in the certain knowledge that God knows and cares about you just as he knows and cares about every other living creature on this war-torn planet. And sing in the equally certain knowledge that Mother Wales will, one day, very soon, take you in her arms and bathe you all in the tears of her grief, love and profoundest regret.'

He took the lead in the singing, and the hymn rose and echoed out into the blood-splashed, riot-exhausted streets. An organ joined in the harmonies and swelled the sound with a raw beauty, filling every corner of the lovely, tearstained land.

We are the new children of Mother Wales, the hymn said, and – come flame, flood and bullet – here, in her arms, we want to stay.

# CHAPTER NINE

Soon after dawn Sophie picked up Effey from the child minder's and hurried back to her own house. Bute Street was almost deserted. Flies buzzed around the dried blood on the pavement outside the Chinese block; there were chalk marks where Pak Chen had fallen. The smell of phosphorus hung in the air as death-dealing wisps of smoke drifted up out of the charred houses. Faces appeared behind the net curtains, though most people were still afraid to come out of doors. Posses of police, drafted from every area, stood around discreetly at corners, in readiness for any fresh trouble. An American patrol car – seconded from a visiting warship – swept up and down the streets ceaselessly.

She found it so strange seeing such inactivity in one of the busiest thoroughfares in the land. Every shop was closed, every door bolted. The door of her own house though had typically been left open and she scuttled up the stairs to find that Betty, again typically, had clearly slept through it all. An empty bottle lay next to her bed and she was still fully clothed.

'Can't you lock this damned door at all?' she blustered so loudly it made Effey jump. Betty, thick with hangover, opened her eyes and asked what she was making all the fuss about.

'Half the place has gone up in flames – that's what all the fuss is about.'

'Oh is that all?' she groaned, her eyes closing again. 'Pity the *whole* place didn't go up in flames if you ask me. I've never hated anything so much.'

Sophie, scarcely believing such indifference was possible, went down the stairs again and put Effey in her playpen. Then she went into the kitchen and fried everything – including some three-day-old rissoles – that she could find in the larder. Perhaps she should take to the bottle like Betty instead of the frying pan, she thought moodily. At least you could face the world with the hard stuff inside you.

Later that morning the newspaper was delivered. It bore a long account of the rioting. They had not yet had a full reckoning of numbers of dead and injured but the Royal Infirmary was reporting up to fifty people in the casualty department, with one policeman needing his leg amputated. So far the police had confiscated three revolvers, a pile of razors, countless bludgeons and a length of wire with a brass plate on either end. Whatever could anyone do with something like that? Up to twenty men were due to be charged, though, curiously, there was no mention of the sniper. The newspaper also carried an editorial calling for all the black rioters to be returned to their homelands forthwith.

Her fry-up did little to relieve her gloom. In the unlikely event of receiving some early-morning clients, she went upstairs to tidy her bedroom. She busied herself among the wicker chairs, Arab carpets pinned to the walls and cushions scattered all over her bed. Behind an Islamic ornament on the mantelpiece she found an old, but still lively, lump of opium left over from her days with Rashed. She had always liked to make love smoking that – everything was languid and dreamy – not so fast and desperate as Edward on his cocaine. She'd better get him on that again, come to think of it; slow him up a bit.

She was washing down the door when Nathan's face came to her mind. She had so loved and enjoyed his words the night before but knew that they were just, well, words. She could see that he was achingly unhappy but there was so very little that she could do about it. A man like that needed the support of a strong woman and his wife had given him precious little of that. Her own Somali spirit could have kept him in place, she thought defiantly. The Somalis knew all about fighting to win but, as it was, he was so alone; just another good man drowning.

When she had finished cleaning she picked up Effey and stood at the doorway, finding warmth in the morning sun as she gazed out on the still-deserted streets. It was strange not to see eyes peering over at her – all those eyes seeing who was coming in and out. Those prying, puritanical Welsh who, if they didn't like anything, attacked and burned it. The arms of Mother Wales indeed! The good kick of her old Welsh surgical boot more like!

A hobnail-booted urchin was kicking a ball around until he was called back in by his mother and given a clip across the ear which sent him flying down the hallway. The mother then went out and picked up the ball before running back to the house herself. Don't forget the ball, dearie! That was the Welsh for you. Batter the kid but save the ball. Sophie kissed Effey on the top of her head and walked back inside her house.

There had been odd comings and goings all morning at St Mark's. If it wasn't the police it was the workers from the Mission Hall or newspaper reporters. Nathan was beginning to feel quite beleaguered and never more so than when, just after noon, a black Daimler drew up and out stepped the red-cassocked figure of Gerald Hastings, the Bishop of Llandaff.

'I've just popped over to see if I can be of any assistance,' he told an astonished Nathan. 'We hear you've been having some fun and games down here.'

'I wouldn't exactly call them fun and games,' Nathan replied.

'No, I don't suppose you would. The wrong choice of words, completely wrong. But let's have a quiet conversation anyway. We must be sure that you have all the help that you need.' He put his arm around Nathan as they walked towards the manse. 'Tell me. How are your wife and children managing in these unfortunate times?'

'Fortunately, *they* are managing quite well. They've been away on holiday.'

'On holiday! Well, thank the Lord for that. Thank the Lord. And your verger, Harry? How is he faring?'

'He's on holiday too. They certainly know how to pick their holidays around here.'

They both sat together in Nathan's study as the bishop continued with his little politenesses. Nathan wondered if these ecclesiastical bigwigs were fed little politenesses for breakfast. You could not imagine someone like him farting or belching or cursing. Everything had been woodsmoked by prayer and the public school, from his carefully modulated voice to his tidy grey hair and his enormous glittering gold ring. Nathan had often wondered why he had gone into the elaborate Church of Wales rather than the simple, old-fashioned Chapel. Bishops like these could kill you with their High Church airs and graces.

'Perhaps, Nathan, you could give me a small account of your troubles? Just a small account,' the Bishop said, relaxing back in his chair.

Nathan began to tell His Grace something of the problems of running a parish in the Bay. The Bishop let him talk in his own way, only occasionally asking for extra items of elucidation or information. But, even as Nathan spoke, he could smell something in the air, particularly when the Bishop asked about the church finances. He had dealt with bishops before. They rarely spoke what was on their minds but, when they arrived at a decision about anything, they spoke with all the authority of a steel-sprung trapdoor. Everything was then irrevocable. That's why they had become bishops. But, just for the moment, he did not seem in any particular hurry to announce any decision at all, merely fiddling with his ring and saying that, yes, everything really did need the most careful prayer and consideration. And then the trapdoor was sprung.

'I seem to remember,' he said, leaning forward in a carefully abstracted pose. 'I seem to remember writing to you and outlining that the church here could not be used for the homeless.' He stopped speaking, leaving his words dangling in the air like a worm waiting for the fish.

'There was just nowhere for them to go. I couldn't throw them out into the street, after all.'

'But it seems to me that you made the church vulnerable by continuing to have them here. It then became an object of attack, you see, and another aspect of the polarization of the community.'

Nathan could actually see himself rising to take the worm. 'But the Church is a defender of the poor and homeless regardless of their colour. It *is* the community.'

'Yes, that is true. That is certainly true. But *regardless of colour*, Nathan. By doing what you did you made that colour black. The Church does indeed minister to all colours but, you see, there were also complaints by the white members of the Church that they could no longer worship here.'

At which point Nathan took the worm. 'The white members of this church were just a bunch of blundering old ladies who wanted to run the place as a cosy sewing circle. I know they were upset but their loss was no loss at all. I want a real church, a vigorous church which testifies to the Resurrection; not some sort of godly whist drive.'

The Biship visibly winced at his blasphemous choice of words and now began studying his ring carefully. 'We chose you for this difficult parish, Nathan, because it was agreed by everyone that you were the right man for the job.'

'Are you saying now that you made a mistake?'

'No, not at all. I still believe that you are the right man for the job, but the job has become somewhat different to what we thought it would be in the beginning. I know that you have had difficulties with your family here. I know that Halfway Harry has had his difficulties working here. I am also becoming increasingly worried about your future and safety here. You did your Christian duty in taking in our Barbadian brethren but, as I said earlier, the Church cannot be seen to be a part of the polarization of racial attitudes. It must always be seen as neutral – as part of the greater body of the Church.'

The Bishop's intelligence service was clearly more efficient than Nathan had thought possible, and he wondered who the rat in the pack was. 'Just what are you trying to say, Bishop?'

'What I am trying to say, Nathan, is that we are giving the most careful prayer and thought – the most careful prayer and thought – to suspending the work of St Mark's until the air becomes clearer. It might be some weeks – a few months at the most.'

'You can't do that,' blustered Nathan, knowing full well that the Bishop could do anything he wanted. 'You can't just throw these people into the docks, just because they have become inconvenient to the sewing circle.'

'No. You are quite right. But my secretary has made some inquiries and we think that we have found the Barbadians a proper home.'

'A proper home! Where?'

'The Church has some farmlands in mid-Wales. There are some empty buildings too.'

'Farmlands in mid-Wales!' He repeated it as if the Bishop was handing out life sentences on Alcatraz. 'What are they going to grow on these farmlands in mid-Wales? Sugar cane?' The incredulity in his voice was rising.

'They can grow anything they want, Nathan. *Can* you grow sugar cane in mid-Wales?'

'You need sunshine to grow sugar cane, Bishop. All they ever get in mid-Wales is rain and yet more rain. The one abiding sound of mid-Wales is the sound of falling rain. These people need sunshine. They'll die of damp and arthritis up there.'

'Now you are just being silly, Nathan,' said the Bishop, rising suddenly from his chair as if someone had lit a fire underneath his holy behind. 'That is being very silly indeed.'

The machinery of business and its lubricating oil, money, is always sensitive to any hints of anarchy or civil commotion – as Edward and Partington quickly discovered when they visited the Floor of the Exchange that day. It was almost as if, within seconds of those phosphorus bombs being thrown, Cardiff was well on the way to losing her crown. The brokers were still conducting their daily discourse on empty holds and cargoes to fill them, but now they were paying almost anything to re-route the incoming cargoes to the nearby ports of Barry, Newport or Swansea. No one wanted to use the great Bute docks. Nervous bankers, fearful that the restless natives might even burn down the Exchange, were making the first telephone calls to foreclose on weak or suspect accounts.

Even just strolling around the Floor Edward could see that these normally cool men had lost their nerve, striking any sort of deal which would keep their precious cargoes away from Cardiff. It was time for a little stock sleight-of-hand. Edward announced that he had three 'fully empty' ships which could sail that day and was immediately offered three loads of Welsh coal at almost half-price. In no time at all these 'fully loaded' ships of Welsh coal became three incoming ships of imported French coal which could be taken to Swansea and which Edward then sold on the Exchange telegraph, on the full discount premium, making him a shilling a ton profit or around £50,000 in hard cash.

Such deals began moving at a dizzying pace. Within half an hour – on the cool advice of Partington – Edward had made another £30,000. They both knew that there was an economic storm coming and that Oriel would need a strong, cash-rich arm to weather it. And now, providing that you had the clear nerve of a poker player, was the time to make the cash. The word went around the Floor that Edward was buying any 'full loaded' ships coming into Cardiff. But no sooner had the deal been struck with one broker, than they became 'fully empty' to another broker who wanted to move his cargo quickly out of Riot City.

Somewhere out in the tidal surges of the Bristol Channel there was an Armada of invisible ships with invisible cargoes which were mysteriously flying from one hold to the next and then, just as mysteriously, flying back again.

None of these buyings and sellings were exactly illegal. But it was a trick they could only do once and, by the time the lumbering Exchange committee had made its ponderous deliberations, the monies would all be safely in the Oriel account. Then it would doubtless just be a committee warning made by members jealous that they had not been able to think of the same stroke themselves.

In the space of three hours Edward had done more to put Oriel on a solvent footing than his father had done in a lifetime of honest dealing. His father had never quite understood the mind of a thief. And this gentleman's club of the Exchange had not yet understood that they were dealing with an accomplished thief either.

Not that Edward or Partington had any real reason to feel regretful about their renegade dealings. They had long planned their little coup for when the moment seemed right. They had long decided that the dealers had it coming to them, particularly those representing the Bute interests who had always taken commissions on gross earnings rather than gross profits. Then, together with the exorbitant Bute docking fees, it was not difficult to see why so many of the smaller shippers were stumbling towards bankruptcy.

It was also very much a part of the strategy that Hamilton had urged on them. Edward and Partington had together taken an axe and swung it at the Bute tree beneath which nothing could grow.

Partington had been particularly valuable in advising how a

deal might be best gilded or left alone. He seemed to come alive when he was working out figures. Edward liked him a lot and, when the Floor closed, they both went back to the Oriel office where they shared a quiet, celebratory glass of sherry.

The afternoon came, hot and humid. Now an even greater outburst was building up on the horizon. Small electric storms shivered together. Darts of lightning flashed and trembled. There was a shower of rain which made the air go chilly but, no sooner had the rain stopped than the air became warmer and thicker than treacle again.

With no business for any of the girls – it was not just the business of the Coal Exchange that was sensitive to outbreaks of anarchy and disorder – Sophie dropped Effey off at her minder's and walked up to St Mark's to find a group of Barbadians being loaded up onto a wagon. 'We're going to a new home, Miss Sophie,' one of the mothers explained.

'What new home is that?'

'Some farm a long way away. Mr Nathan told us we'll just love it.'

When Sophie went into the church she was alarmed to see that it was virtually empty. Those she had seen were the last to leave: there were just piles of dirty plates left on the food trestles. She hurried along the corridor leading down to the manse and found Nathan sitting alone in his living room. One look at his red, rheumy eyes and at the half-full bottle on the table told its own story.

'So what's all this then?' she asked, waving a hand in the general direction of the bottle.

'What's all this?' He held the bottle up in the air. 'This is a bottle of poteen, sent over by Father O'Reilly to cheer me up. It works too. I am now completely happy. I now understand why he drinks so much.'

'I'd send it back if I was you. I've never seen you so unhappy.'

'What have I got to be happy about?' he asked, putting the bottle back down on the table and looking up at her. 'Eh? Just what? I've had a note from my wife Elizabeth saying that she's never coming back here. She is very sorry but she *can't* come back here. Just can't face it, she says. Then my bishop goes and closes down this church. And for most of yesterday they were all trying to kill one another in the street. I'm sorry, Sophie. I'm very, very sorry but I don't really see how I could be any unhappier.'

She was still standing on the same spot as she had been when she first came into the room, hands on hips, unsure how to play it. 'So where's mine then?' she snapped.

'Where's your what?'

'My drink. Father O'Reilly send over another bottle, did he?'

'He might.'

'What do you mean, he might? Did he or didn't he? I feel like a drink too. I've never seen anyone as happy as you and I want to get like that also.'

'Have a small drop of this. Not too much. That's it.'

The offered drop was the tiniest that had ever got into a glass and she held it up to the light to see if, in fact, it was there at all. All this happiness wasn't doing much for his generosity, that was for certain. 'Do you think you could possibly add another drop to this drop?' she wondered.

Muttering to himself he took the glass off her and added another, larger splash. Not exactly a large splash, Sophie saw as she sat down at the table with him but, as they say, better than a poke in the eye with a sharp stick.

'I'm not up to any of this,' he said after taking a long sniff and looking at nothing in particular. 'I just can't do it, Sophie. It's getting like I'm not even sure if I can get out of bed successfully. It's true. I open my eyes and almost start panicking at the thought of sticking my legs out from beneath the sheets. I'm even terrified when I'm asleep. I dream of arid deserts and large black birds.'

'What's all this about the church closing?'

'That's what he said. Old Fancypants came here in his Daimler and said he was closing the place down like some old knacker's yard. Phut! Just like that. Closed for the summer holidays. It's the shame and failure of it that I can't take. I come from a country village. All that matters to you there is your good name.'

'Poor, poor Nathan.' She reached out and took his hand in hers, holding it tight and lifting it up and down slowly on the table. He put his other hand on them too and, perhaps because it was the first gesture of sympathy and comfort that he had received in a long time, it made him cry.

'Do you know, this is the first time we have ever touched one another?' he said after two slippery processions of tears had carried on down his cheeks. 'God knows I've wanted to often enough. There's been moments when I've been crying inside just to reach out and hold you in my arms. Do you find that shocking? Me a man of the Church and all that.'

She shook her head and picked up his hand, kissing it warmly. 'There's not a man alive who could shock me,' she said, looking him in the eye and then back down at their entwined hands. It was terribly sad for her to see him like this, she decided. She felt like crying also. He was like some dinosaur out of his time who, with every step, was only managing to get himself more stuck in the mud. She would do almost anything to make him happy; drown him in a great sea of pleasure. But pleasure would only make him sad too. She knew how the Welsh were.

'But I've known that my want of you – no, my love for you – is only something of my imagination,' he went on. 'And I use the word "love" advisedly. This is not really drunk talk either. I really do think that I have come to love you – just from what you did and said. Just from being the way that you are. You were tremendous with the Barbadian people we took in here, and my wife – hah! my *wife* – all she did was run away.'

'People are different, Nathan. Women are different. She would have stayed and helped if she could have. She just wasn't strong enough, that's all. You shouldn't blame her for that.'

'Yes, I know that. I accept that. That's why I'm going to have to leave you – a woman I have come to love – and go back to her – a woman who, well, I have just lost interest in. I could never imagine hating her. That's for sure. She never really inspired much emotion in me at all, but she's my wife and the mother of my two boys, so I must be with her. It's all quite as simple as that.'

Now Sophie was silent, turning his hands over and over as if examining to see if he had washed them properly. She didn't like his line of thought at all. If you loved someone you wanted to stay with them. It was all quite as simple as that. 'You'll be going away then, will you?' she asked.

'Yes. I won't be able to stay here anyway – even if I wanted to. Particularly if the church is closing down. I'll just go and stay with Elizabeth for a while, and she'll relax when we're both out of this place.'

'And what about me?'

'Sorry?'

'What about me, Nathan? Me. You say you came to love me and now you're standing up and walking away. I'm not like this table, you know. I've got feelings too.'

'I'm sorry, Sophie, my angel. It could never have worked between us. It was just an absurd dream of mine, that's all. Just the way someone falls in love with a music hall star. *That*'s all it was, Sophie. Perhaps I shouldn't have said anything.'

'No, perhaps you shouldn't. Ah well, at least we've got the drink left to us. *Did* that Father O'Reilly send over another bottle of poteen or not?'

'He did as it happens. To be awful truthful, as he might have put it, he sent over three.'

'Three! Well, where are they?'

# CHAPTER TEN

That night they raided the castle, and those small electric storms were still shivering in the sky. The same darts of lightning forked over the city skyline and the odd showers kept cooling the air. In his bedroom in the manse Nathan was lying on his bed smoking opium with Sophie.

Her perspiring naked form hung over him as she held the lump of smoking opium with tweezers, telling him to breathe in through his nose as the white smoke curled slowly and lazily, then rushed up his nostrils. He spluttered and coughed. His eyes opened wide and closed again. His hand moved across her buttocks, brushed up against the side of her silky leg before his mind drifted away again, kneaded and stretched and squeezed by the drug's elastic powers.

She felt parts of her tensing again. Her body may have been exhausted but she was more than ready to go another round or three. Whole torrents seemed to be pouring out from between her legs. She had gorged herself on him but *still* didn't seem to want to stop.

He coughed again, held her thigh tight and drifted away. Drowsy and seductive images wandered in and out of his mind. He was walking green fields, holding a teddy bear and being read nursery rhymes by his mam. The teddy bear's eyes were large, brown and made of glass. Now he and Teddy were sitting together on the banks of the river watching a shoal of fish, whose silver bellies caught the light as they turned and fed in the weeds. The pure river, which had always been his strength and inspiration, forever flowing on and on, forever vibrant and full of joy, bringing all life into its arms and sustaining it faithfully. Yes, it was always the river which brought life, and did so abundantly; the river which fed the outlying fields and overhanging trees; the river which had run through all his childhood hours – juggling light with shadow, running through his early dreaming of a strong faith which would protect him from everything; swirling and pushing through his long quest for meaning, gliding silently and yet with immense power, so central to his childhood; just as now it was flowing through the exploding, shifting landscape of his opium dreaming.

Sophie ran her wet tongue around his neck, working down through his muscled, hairy chest, licking out his navel, sliding down the insides of his legs, chewing and nipping at his flesh with her teeth, stopping for a moment for her hands to brush up and down his thighs before her mouth went down to his feet, first taking his big toe in her mouth then the next and the next, her tongue exploring every cranny and crevice in his foot, running under the balls of his feet, all the while breathing hard as her tongue kept working around and around in hot, wet licks.

His body quivered and trembled as if being touched by live wires as she continued the foot treatment, learned from a Chinese man in another night of long experiment. Not for this wonderful man a quick drunken fumble in a back alley. Instead Nathan would have a night of drugged and exquisite carnal contact – a long bodily siege – whose very memory would always make his spirits sing and dance whenever he thought of it.

They say that when just two people are in bed, there might be four or five people there. Certainly, in the past, when she had entered into carnal contact which was enjoyable rather than just work she had found other men and other beds sweeping through her mind. Almost always Rashed had got into the act but there were others too – oddly and maddeningly a rugby player whose name she had never discovered; an uncouth bullock with an enormous stonk who had paid her one night and then gone on and on until dawn. By the time he had finished she would have happily paid him.

But there were no Rasheds or rugby bullocks here in this bed now, just this great man with a marvellous mind with whom she had entered deep into an almost sacramental communion.

Another flash of lightning lit up the curtains and he could feel huge globules of sweat breaking out both on his forehead and on his groin. The river began flowing before him again and he opened his eyes, looking at his bedside clock set in rosewood, trying to tell the time, when his consciousness dislocated again and a wooden crocodile went hurrying down the river bank, slipping into the water only to turn on its back and sail away on the driving currents. Oh, Sophie, my broken angel, here I am back on the river of my greatest dreams and I am broken too, you and I both, broken on the bank of my childhood.

Outside, the city waited and held her breath. Police in pairs and police on horses were patrolling the Bay, finding watchful groups out on the pavements. Even high up on a horse the police could feel the incredible tension of these gaslit streets and kept their distance, hoping that no one would provide yet another match for the powder keg.

Nothing seemed real in that rumbling, lightning-flashed night. Even a stranger would have seen that the Moslems were carrying bulky objects beneath their sarongs. He would have been able to see the smouldering anger in the West Indians in Loudon Square. The Irish were still maintaining their barricades around Newtown, silent and hostile too, showing the odd glimpse of a shillelagh or emitting a poteen-soaked curse.

The thin white stream of opium smoke curled lazily and rushed again as Edward and his boys waded through the sewers to return to the castle. This time they would enter the castle and seize their prize. The showers that day had made the water levels rise but now the air was less foul and turgid. Nor had they spotted any rats. No one spoke as they shouldered the pulleys and scaffolding along the small brickwork tunnels. Yet every time one of the scaffolding bars hit against the bricks it seemed to make a thin screeching noise like a giant tuning fork, the screeches echoing down through the sewers, turning into a long, dull sound, racked with pain.

They had still not spoken when they came out onto the next weir. Owen the Bastard did try and light a cigarette but Edward snatched it off him and threw it into the flowing waters. They all stood holding up their lamps as they watched the cigarette rush away, giving a horrifying indication of how fast the water was actually flowing. Even the normally calm Edward was feeling edgy; he was picking it up from the others. The real trouble with this job was that they were not to be told what they were going in to get. Villains always liked to know what they were after, but he could not tell them – because he did not quite know himself.

Now Slogger Dacey was taken by a fit of coughing and the Greek cussed quietly when the scaffolding yet again hit the brickwork, sending out that long, awful sound of pain. But Gerry, the old Sinn Feiner, seemed calm enough, Edward was relieved to see, with a huge hacksaw tied around his neck with rope, like some improbable crucifix. Edward thought he saw the long black back of something moving in the waters but he swallowed hard and decided that it could only be yet another shadow.

On the next level, as planned, Edward sent Gerry up to tackle the grille with his hacksaw while the others stood around near the silent Cornish beam engine, waiting for the word that he had got through. He seemed to take an age. As the hacksaw continued rasping, those below crouched down on one knee, listening to the distant noises and staring blankly into the flickering darkness.

Edward thought of his little flat in London, wondering how it was – if it still was, since he had not paid the rent for an age. He remembered his club where he liked to go with his friend Morris for dinner, discussing women and cards with the other young blades over the port and cigars. He thought of the great larks later with a Northern nanny, perhaps or, if he was lucky, a fleshy chorus girl.

He thought of all these things as they crouched listening to the rasping of the hacksaw, and wondered how it had come to pass that, after all that fine life, he had been reduced to scrabbling around in this foul sewer with this bunch of brainless hooligans. He wondered again, for the tenth time that day, what his oh-so-proper father had been up to when Edward had always thought that he was just some brainless old man, worried about his ships and an old empire, long since fallen to pieces, shot apart by the Kaiser's guns.

In his work room at the top of his house Hamilton was sitting at a desk, working by the light of a single oil lamp. Small moths danced around it in some darting rapture as he studied the diagram of a long altarpiece which he had taken down from the wall. He measured its length with a ruler, jotting it down on a scrap of paper before re-measuring it. He made a few more calculations on paper before carefully rubbing out and re-drawing the sign of the cross. The long strong fingers of his left hand held the diagram in place as he drew the cross with quill and ink. Occasionally he stopped work to compare what he was drawing with another diagram in a book which was propped up against others on his desk. The quest for accuracy was absolute. He, the lonely god of the darkness, still had not got the positioning of the cross exactly right, so he scratched it out again. Another light shower of rain stuttered on the roof but he took no notice; throughout his work his concentration was complete.

He pushed his elbows out and straightened his back to gain some brief physical relief. Another flash of lightning slashed over the walls, dancing on his face and even arresting the moths in their dance for a second. After a few more minutes of work Hamilton put down his quill and looked out over the silvery mud banks leading down to the still sea. Cormorants called out in thin, long cries. A brisk wind seemed to be picking up and moaning soft against the window pane. He reacted to all this strange tropical weather with the calm imperturbability of a gardener surveying a dying flowerbed in the autumn. Very little ever impinged on the strange, mystical scaffolding of his medieval soul.

He picked up the diagram and took it over to his workbench where, with patient care, he had been carving a huge mahogany altarpiece. There was an ominous roll of thunder. A single bead of sweat rolled down his cheek and the hopeful new Fisher King wiped it away with the tips of his fingers. He stopped again and walked over to the other side of the room, looking down on the curiously empty Howard Close. Two mounted policemen clattered past but then there was that empty silence again. The lamplight picked up but one moving object below: a green chiffon scarf being threaded and rethreaded through the same set of disembodied hands.

Sophie came working back up Nathan's leg, taking his boiling manhood into her mouth. Now her whole body was aching for him to be inside her, everything burrowing and clawing deep inside her like a great pain of hunger. But she would put up with any pain and work the night through to achieve a fitting and proper end to this. Nothing in sexual pleasure came without the deepest pain, she believed. Everything lay in the wanting and the aching. Her tongue went around and around and she could feel him getting fantastically bigger, even though, by the relaxed movements of his hands, she knew that he was not quite ready.

Her head moved up and down and she could feel him touching her very tonsils. Some lovely juices were coming out of him too and she could feel them trickling around her tongue and through her teeth. Now her bosom was aching with that hunger as well and she rubbed it feverishly across his thighs, almost as if trying to rub away the ache.

Nathan had been wandering his river bank again when his eyes opened wide and he saw a fantastic vision. He saw a great bird circling above an ancient blasted heath. After flying around and around she alighted on a tree where all her young were lying dead in the nest. When the great bird settled on them and found her young lifeless she stabbed at her breast with her beak until her own blood was spurting out everywhere. As soon as the warm blood touched them, the young came to the life while the mother bird slumped among them dying. The offspring were being reborn in the blood of the parent bird.

The summer lightning sent mazey tramways of light down the flowing black waters of the River Taff and peacocks cried out in the battlement darkness as the raiders crept silently through the severed grille. Thick shadows settled across the lawns around the keep and Edward's eyes caught the Greek's as they heard that distant groan of pain deep in the sewers again. But, by now, Edward was really at home, nerveless and strong, as he stood waiting for the rest of them to come through, looking around at this strange, stone fortress.

The banqueting hall seemed so huge and empty, echoey, with bare wooden floors and the brilliant gilt images of the suspended coats of arms . . . the harps and guitars, the bronze Madonna. A quick recce established that they did not need to break through the door to the newel post, as they had planned. They need only go up the stairs and come back down through the Fleche Tower.

Painted faces looked down on them as they shouldered their scaffolding along the stone corridors. With every flashing tremble in the night the carved mice seemed to move around on the walls. A wooden crocodile watched a plump baby. Children's nursery rhymes jingled in the spiral stone stairs. Musical boxes chimed with well-loved tunes in the empty nursery. The long-lashed eyes of rosy-cheeked dolls clicked open.

There was the harsh crackle of a struck match and Sophie lit the lump of opium in her tweezers again, waving it beneath the nostrils of Nathan's pale, drugged face before taking a long sniff herself. Now she moved his arms away and climbed over him, bringing her body down on his and lowering herself onto him, letting him enter slowly. She lifted her head and looked down at him with a smile. He had been making so many odd sounds but now he was just sighing happily. She felt so *tender* towards him – so completely and utterly tender – moving her buttocks around in small slow circles.

He could feel himself rising out of his reverie and his pelvis jerked up hard, taking a few silky stabs before settling back on his beloved river, enjoying the sunshine on the water, when its quietly flowing currents began racing and rushing with tremendous surges. His eyes opened a little in fright and the rivers of her black hair fell back over his face as she leaned her head forward and kissed him, first on the nose and then on the cheeks.

But the storm on the river was coming – it was, it was. The

mercury was trying to leak out of the very bottom of the barometer and Captain Abraham Turner could see vast black thunderheads rolling towards *The Solomon*, driving wild, bad winds before them. He cupped his hands and called out to the men to trim all sails and take in the spanker but, by now, the winds were so high they actually blew away his commands and he had to rush down onto the deck himself, even cuffing a few of the deckhands and screaming at them to get up into the yards. But it was too late – it was, it was.

The winds were beginning to scream in the ratlines as the ship and the very sea seemed to be boiling. A huge meteor came whistling out of the skies, narrowly missing the mizzen before being swallowed up by the heaving waves. By now Captain Turner had got more men up into the yards, when rain began pouring down in blinding sluices. Even as the sailors were frantically trying to pull in the sails it was hopeless, since the wind and rain were already busy tearing them to rags, making them fly out and flap with the dull boom of guns. The windjammer rolled one way and pitched in the other as she struggled up the sides of the mountainous waves, now sliding down the other side and crashing down onto her bows so hard that even the deckhands could feel their bellies being shaken right up into their throats. Those guns in the torn sails kept booming.

Great walls of screaming foam collapsed around the masts as two seamen fought like tigers to control the bucking wheel, their arms aching terribly as they struggled to pull the wheel spokes one way and another. Everywhere there was the smell of burning ropes. Mouths shouted orders and warnings but they were swept away by the howling winds. The galley echoed with the bright, brittle sounds of things breaking. The very bulkheads screamed out with furious laments as if all the furies had just been ordered in there for all eternity.

There usually seemed to be a brief second of quiet at that moment when the ship was actually reaching the top of a huge wave; it was almost a holding of the breath, with just the distant screaming of winds in the rigging when, with a long dive, the bowsprit plunged down again into the howling waves as the seamen continued to fight for control of the rogue wheel.

The winds blew the very tops off the waves, breaking them up into hissing bursts of stinging saltwater. The loud breaking noises of cracking stanchions came from deep within the hull.

Then the anchor line broke and there was the terrific whip-crack of a loose iron chain snapping around trying to smash something up. With this the ship felt lighter and seemed to romp around the waves more, Captain Turner thought. It was probably not true but that's how it *felt*. The ship scampered up the back of another wave – there was that silence, that holding of the breath – and then that lurching, groaning slide down into hell again.

The men were still trying to take down the topsail but it wouldn't come, much of it breaking away from its yard and flying wide of the ship; more like a flag than a bastard sail, Captain Turner thought, as he screamed uselessly at the men who were working some thirty feet above his head, still trying to pull in buntlines that just did not want to come in.

More oilskinned men went slipping and sliding over the deck, trying to help Dai the Murderer who was fighting with a romping halyard which had become fouled in the ratlines. The ship rolled and Dai the Murderer rolled with it; the ship came back and was blown again before its arc was complete so that Dai went sailing out into the waves, screaming almost as loudly as the winds before he was seen no more.

Just then the worst possible thing happened since, deep in the hold, the cargo moved, making the whole ship list badly. Another whinnying meteor went speeding overhead. Captain Turner, veteran of the Horn and the 1868 great tea races, a man so tough he always carried a derringer in the unlikely event of any of his men harbouring mutinous thoughts – had never seen anything like it in all his lime-juicing days.

With all the sails gone he ordered all spare hands to the bilge pumps and lashed himself to the bridge, holding onto the tilting rail as he continued screaming unheard orders into the teeth of the storms revolving all around them.

Lightning zigzagged the length of the sky followed by a high flash of fire which struck and toppled the main mast. Captain Turner shouted at his deckhands to chop off the weather rigging, but even as they tried to make their way across the listing deck another huge wave washed a few over the side. By now the whole deck was a tangle of wreckage and loose, flying blocks. Wooden pulley blocks cracked together in loud staccato hammer blows. Even the brass compasses were being torn from their fittings and Captain Turner shouted his loudest and most bitter curse at God for piling so much fury on his old windjammer. But, like his other orders, that too went unheard.

By now the castle raiders had managed to set up the scaffolding around the newel post. Ropes had been tightened and the pulleys ratcheted until everything had gone taut. Edward circled the engineering, his hands pulling at the joints until he was satisfied that the structure was stable. 'Right,' he said, raising a finger. 'We'll take it very slow and just see how it comes.'

Hamilton blew the dust off his chisels before carefully putting them back into the rack and leaving his work room, descending the stairs to his wash room. He was sweaty and dirty now, quickly stepping out of his shirt and trousers and leaving them on the floor before standing before the washbasin, soaping himself down and cleaning himself off with a flannel. He tied a towel around his waist, crossing the landing, when lightning slit the sky again, making the tropical fish in the ornamental tank dart forward as if menaced. But the alarm was short-lived. A bright blue fish, which had been swimming around pulling a streamer of dung behind it, dived down, letting the streamer float upwards to the surface.

Hamilton's powerful frame padded silently down the stairs. He opened the door of his chapel, right down in the basement of his house, and walked in to stand in front of the altar. Now a rumble of thunder shook the clerestory windows as he just stood there looking at the ornamental cross. There were brass altar rails, one oak pew and, just at the rear of the room, a large wooden chair with the words THIS CHAIR IS GALAHAD'S carved on it. He heard a soft cough and turned to see Nazeem framed in the doorway.

Hamilton stood motionless, barely breathing, as he watched Nazeem pulling his chiffon scarf through one hand and another, twisting it around his wrist and running it through his fingers. Another massive shiver of electricity followed as Hamilton tugged at his bath towel, letting it fall silently down around his ankles.

Nazeem smiled and, with a subdued whimper of joy, came walking down the chapel aisle until he was so close to Hamilton he could feel his breath on his painted face. He kneeled down and pulled his scarf around Hamilton's ankle. Then the other ankle, his calves, his knees . . . he brought his head forward and rubbed his cheek up and down the side of Hamilton's hard, muscular legs, gradually standing up until they were almost nose to nose, and Nazeem ran his scarf around and around the taller man's shoulders. Nazeem's eyes quizzed him humorously as if asking if the ship owner was enjoying their little game.

Hamilton's black eyes remained unrelentingly cold. One of Nazeem's arms reached up around his back and over his shoulder. Hips were pressed into groin as another arm travelled around his waist. The night's continuing spasmodic luminosity danced again in Nazeem's made-up face. The cheeks with their light film of rouge; the lips a deep shade of smudged red. It was a circus face, a floating image in a drug withdrawal nightmare.

Nazeem pushed his face forward and grazed his cheek up and down the side of Hamilton's chin. Hamilton's head lowered slightly and then the two men kissed.

'No, don't do that, just don't.' Nathan's head rose up, eyes wide with astonishment when it fell back on the pillow again, his hand shielding his eyes from the glare of the sun as that great bird circled around the blasted heath. Small, fabulous creatures with horns came bounding down the high grass banks to stop and look. From somewhere deep in the jungle came the triumphant bugle call of an elephant. A group of chattering monkeys went leaping from vine to vine. Then there was just Sophie's face close to his again, hair falling everywhere, just like those dark tangled vines.

The opium was lit again and both their noses came close to the drifting smoke, he smiling dreamily as Sophie sucked some into her mouth and brought it close to his face, blowing a thin fast stream up Nathan's nostrils. He too took some into his mouth and blew it up her nose, his whole erect manhood still skewered right up into her. They were as one, as if clamped together by a giant vice.

The plinth creaked and rumbled and finally inched higher as The Malt and Slogger Dacey kept ratcheting the pulley blocks.

The visored lion tilted a little but it was coming up cleanly enough, with thin slivers of light glimmering around the stone base. A dark cup stood there in the filtering, running lights. When the ratcheting had stopped, everyone moved closer to look at it.

No one seemed inclined to reach out and touch it. Their wide dark eyes gazed at the cup which was more like a large goblet and made from some sort of metal. It seemed to radiate some sort of ineffable calm, capturing even their ragged souls. Thin patterns of light were still trickling back and forth, creating an elusive, brilliant ingathering of images which meant different things to different eyes. 'I've never seen anything so beautiful,' said Gerry. 'That's what I call really beautiful.'

'Where does the light come from?' asked Owen the Bastard.

'Must be some sort of lamp, I s'pose. My auntie tole me about some sort of mystery light she 'ad once.'

'Do you need gas for it, do you?'

'Search me.'

Slogger wiped his nose with the back of his hand as Edward's eyes squinted into the lights, now touching the cup with his finger to see if it was fixed to the stone base or, in some way, alarmed. It moved to his touch and there were no bells either, so he held it with thumb and forefinger by the brim and made it lean to one side, his mouth drying up, as a powerful fragrance came swirling up out of the cup; a fragrance so strong that it seemed to all but transfix the men who neither came near nor moved away.

'What's that smell?'

'Some kind of perfume.'

Edward looked at the others before sliding his hand down to the base of the cup. He tilted it a little further. 'Jesus,' he muttered with a faint tremble, breaking into a sweat. A human heart was lying at the bottom of the cup. But this was no ordinary heart. It was still beating, with three rivulets of blood trickling steadily out of it. Even as he stood there, holding the cup in the same position, the blood kept flowing, and now it was almost as if the heart was starting to float on the rising red sea. There was that fragrance again and, when Edward looked up, he saw that all his boys were running up the stairs, with the exception of the old Sinn Feiner who was down on his knees mumbling lines from the Rosary. 'Hail Mary full of grace for the Lord is with ye,' he was gabbling. 'Blessed art thou amongst women and blessed is the fruit of thy womb Jesus Christ.'

Edward looked down at the gabbling Irishman and back at the cup which was now quite empty. He was sure that it had changed its shape too. 'Come on, Gerry,' he snapped, placing the cup inside his shoulder bag. 'There's no time now for any of that nonsense. Let's get the hell out of here.'

He grabbed Gerry by the arm, pulling him up and half dragging and half kicking him up the stairs, only once turning back to look at the plinth which, surrounded by the scaffolding and still holding up the lion's head on a rope, looked exactly like a hanged man on the gallows. 'Holy Mary Mother of God, pray for us sinners now and at the time of our death,' Gerry continued muttering, his old hands still fluttering upwards in prayer as Edward dragged him along the stone corridor down to the banqueting hall. 'Blessed art . . .'

As they hurried along the stone corridor to the Fleche Tower there was that terrifying graveyard cry of pain from the sewers again and the stricken windjammer was listing on her side, preparing to have herself torn apart by the pounding seas. What was left of the wrecked masts was now dipping into the sea. All the yards had been stripped of their sails and rigging. Captain Turner was still lashed to the bridge rail but had now given up all thoughts of orders or even curses. He had just *accepted* whatever was to come and just bowed his sou'-westered head beneath the thick, driving rain.

The deckhands at the wheel had long given up trying to control it, taking the captain's lead and lashing themselves to the bridge also. The wheel spun one way and another like a crazed whipped top as they tried to lash themselves tighter in this hurricane-scoured night, those angry waves still piling up with unbelievable height and ferocity.

The ship seemed to sink a further six feet into the water. The terror-stricken deckhands had given up working the bilge pumps and were clinging to anything that was fixed to something else. Yet more foaming walls of water came crashing over them, hissing around their frozen bodies, sucking back away again, with a great draining wheeze, before yet another wall fell on them, colder and yet more destructive than the one before.

Every soul on *The Solomon* knew that the hull was going to

break up at any second – they had been prepared all their seagoing lives for this moment and, as they thought their last thoughts, a few remembered that they had always been told by the old salts that, when plunged into the sea and drowning was inevitable, they should not hold their breath but swallow the water since that would hasten their ends.

Captain Turner looked up for the last time when he saw – or at least thought he saw – that the frothing seas had broken *into fire*. Everywhere huge, hungry columns of flame were marching down on the sinking ship, turning from white to crimson and crackling with flying sparks. Even faced by the very gates of hell the old captain felt his first moment of peace and calm, thinking of his wife crocheting by the log fire and bowing to the inevitable, as he prepared himself finally to meet his Maker.

As they came out onto the next level in the sewer the leading four stopped dead in their tracks, out of breath and almost exhausted. A forest of lights crisscrossed one another. They blinked and could not see who was holding them. But they soon found out.

'This is the police. Do not make a sound. We are all armed. Just put down your lamps and come out quietly.'

Now Nathan had mounted Sophie to begin taking her home, quietly beating up and down between her long legs with growing power. For hours, days, even weeks . . . it felt as if they had been sharing the mansions of their bodies, stirring together in the same visions and glories, not even thinking that they should draw the long communion to a close. He held her head in his arms, taking long deep intakes of breath; the sprinter at the start, ventilating in preparation for the long final run home.

He had never experienced a night like it, his spirits boiling hot and then becoming freezing cold, his mind seeing things and wandering in dreams that it had never been in before. Together they had found something which had shaken his life to its very depths. Even then he knew that he would emerge from it all totally changed. Moments of savage fury had mingled with bouts of the most exquisite tenderness.

In between the scattered dreams and the transactions of pleasure there had been moments of anxiety – fleeting images of his wife and children, or else hearing the words of the prophet declaring that a man with two women always loses his soul. But then their bodies had moved with a new power again and the prophet's warning words had been lost, had been lost in a hot storming sea of physical ecstasy. He took another deep breath and drove his hips hard down into her.

Edward had just managed to half kick Gerry down through the grille when he looked around the castle, noticing lights being switched on. When Gerry was safely down he ran across the banqueting hall to look out of the mullioned windows. Something had gone wrong somewhere. He held his shoulder bag tightly and pulled himself into the thick shadows behind the curtain. He looked down into the darkened courtyard which had come alive with policemen's whistles and barking dogs. His old animal cunning told him to stop quite still and do nothing as more and more lights came bobbing into the courtyard.

He heard footsteps coming rushing towards him from the direction of the Fleche Tower. He retreated deeper into the shadows just as two policemen ran across the banqueting hall. As the excitement and the light of bullseye lanterns probed the hall, he became cooler and more thoughtful. There was only one way. If he could make it down to the first weir in the sewer he might be able to get out through the other tunnel leading to the west side of the city. Even if he couldn't get out that way he could at least lie low in some dark corner until the police had given up. In any chase the fox always ran straight for a deep hole in the earth, did he not?

For five, ten minutes maybe, he kept behind the curtain. When he dared peek out there was no sign of any police in the banqueting hall. He ran silently across the floor and wormed down through the grille. The tunnel leading down to the first weir was suspiciously and ominously quiet as he inched out to the edge of the waterfall pool. He stayed in the darkness for a full two minutes, telling himself to keep calm, keep cool, which was always the thief's ace in the hole on any job, no matter how big or small. He took a chance on shining his lamp around the weir, only spotting a frog slithering through the brown slime. It stopped still in the unexpected spotlight and croaked at him.

There were no signs of old Gerry and neither were there any sounds in the tunnel. Edward turned off his lamp and edged down into it, listening for anything which, given the tunnel's acoustics, would be amplified for miles. It was painfully slow making his way through the damp darkness and, although he still could not hear anything, he saw some torchlight flickering on the waters of the next weir. He knew he wouldn't win any prizes for guessing who were holding those torches. Instinctively he turned back to the waterfall weir which he waded through to get to the next tunnel.

This was, if anything, lower than the others, but he could move quite freely, stopping only to take off his shoes which had become so waterlogged they were beginning to squeak like excited mice. He had gone a further two hundred yards when – hell's teeth – he saw some more police lamps coming towards him. He backtracked quickly to the first weir. Now he had no other option but to hide behind the moving curtain of the waterfall.

With so much water raining down on him he had to breathe through his clenched teeth but at least he was well concealed as three policemen in waders went sploshing about in front of him. He could even have reached out and touched them. They were obviously uneasy about working in this kingdom of rats and shadows, grumbling frequently and loudly. Edward enjoyed the idea of being some underground monster, grabbing one of them by the ankle and pulling him down into the dark, smelly drink.

'Better get out now, lads,' one of them said when they decided that further search was pointless. 'We've got four of them, so they're going to flood the place to make sure of the other two.'

Edward's heart stopped beating. If they had got four of them what had happened to that old bastard Gerry? With general rumblings of relief the police whistled for the others, now splashing away into the echoing darkness. For maybe a minute Edward remained frozen behind the waterfall, then there was a foaming roar and he could actually feel the water rising fast around his legs. He turned and turned again. They couldn't catch him so they had decided to drown him.

The water continued to rise so fast he had no other option

but to get back into the castle. In a mad, sodden scramble he reached the ladder beneath the grille. Yet, even with the odds stacked so highly against him, he was still feeling surprisingly light and fit, confident that he could outwit these brainless coppers any day. Just before he stepped on the first rung he went down on his knees and opened his bag to look at the cup which seemed, well, like any other cup. There was still that strange perfume about it though. All this fuss had merely confirmed that the cup was very valuable indeed and, if he could get out of here, he was going to make some real money out of it. If . . .

Dripping wet and with his lamp no longer working he scurried across the banqueting hall, finding that the whole castle was alive with lights and activity. He bounded up the stairs and feather-stepped across the minstrel gallery, careful that his bare feet did not slip on the polished floors. He ran out onto the battlements but stopped when he saw another two policemen at the far end. There really was nothing for it now except one big gamble. Far better to die than rot away in some prison cell. They would probably throw him into Cardiff prison too and he had heard more than enough about that infernal place. Oh well, shit or bust.

He leaped onto the castle ramparts, lowering himself off the other side and reaching out for the autumn vines which were clawing all over the castle walls.

In that strange tropical night he might have been some huge ape stumbling through thick jungle. Black on grey, he came crashing down the castle wall, with the vines falling away each time as he reached out for another clump, his hands cutting on the wires as he kept moving, leaping out and grabbing another breaking handful until the momentum of his fall had become such that he could only push himself out with his feet, twisting and turning, with his arms and legs moving around slowly, as he fell some thirty feet into the deep still waters of the moat.

He landed with a loud splash, quickly swimming to the bank and hauling himself up. Barely waiting to recover his breath, he scrambled down into the castle grounds, finding deep cover just behind the animal wall where stone tigers and lions crouched atop each parapet. As he edged along the wall there were some more whistles and he heard the low thunder of police horses. Great black shapes were snorting and pounding back and forth through the trees but, if anything, the fox became sharper as the hunt got hotter, diving into some low eucalyptus trees as yet more horses came careering across the lawns. The stone animals seemed to move and snarl as more torch beams swept over them. Thunder rumbled again.

He was in a dreadful mess, covered in mud and with his hands cut into ribbons. His feet had been badly gashed and he had twisted his shoulder. But, all that apart, he was still feeling surprisingly confident. He couldn't understand it; he wondered if his continuing luck and strength had something to do with what he had in his shoulder bag.

The searching horses continued quartering back and forth across the grounds and around the stumpy ruins of the old nunnery as he ran from bush to bush, finally making it to the comparative safety of the swollen River Taff, flinging himself into the cold, coal-black waters, wading across the slippery pebbles and then stumbling face-forward into it, coming up for air and gasping for breath until the glazed torrents picked him firmly in their arms and began carrying him off towards the docks and the sea.

He had made it. Even as he floated away he gave a silent laugh and threw a clenched fist up into the night in triumph.

# CHAPTER ELEVEN

The revolving storms and waves of fire lifted as suddenly as they had come, leaving *The Solomon* a ruined rubble of a ship with no sails or rigging and the mizzen swept away. Her only recognizable feature was the fine lines of her hull drifting in the calm, glacial sea. The mercury was high in the barometer.

Exhausted deckhands moved around, hardly knowing where to start on the repairs. There was precious little left to put right. With the compasses gone, all the sails swept away and the wheel useless, they could not even steer the battered windjammer. Now she was just drifting in the soft, whispering zephyrs, like some giant resting after a titanic struggle with an army of other giants. The sun was beginning to rise over the horizon and up into a ravishingly blue sky.

Most of the navigational instruments had been smashed by the storm. Until the stars came out they had no real idea where they were, or how far they had been blown off-course. They just had to wait and watch for the black smoke of a passing steamer, or listen out for the sounds of breaking surf or the cry of sea birds, telling them that land was nearby.

Captain Turner guessed that they were somewhere near the Scillies and Land's End. They would surely be picked up as salvage soon. Every captain would gladly give his left arm rather than have his ship towed in as salvage, and he was no exception. He might lose his captaincy and would certainly lose his bonus. But, in the circumstances, he was calm enough, thankful that they had been delivered after sailing in through the very gates of hell.

Five men had been swept away in the storm and, the bosun had just reported, the ship's cat had been lost too. Captain Turner did not believe that, since he was fairly certain that the animal, which had six toes on each paw and had been given to him for luck by another captain in Shanghai, was pretty indestructible. The scabby, malformed thing would be around somewhere, having hidden herself in the hold or a corner of the galley, doubtless emerging again when she wanted some food.

Normally a master who ruled with a rod of iron and a stream of barbed commands, he had nothing to say as he walked around the deck inspecting the damage. He could see that his men were too tired to do anything useful – even if he could find anything useful for them to do after the bilges had been pumped. There was not a shred of rigging left, so he let them alone. Watched by the men, who were puzzled by his silence, he walked back to his cabin where, out of a lifetime's habit, he first tapped the barometer, then lit his churchwarden and put his feet up on the desk. The blue clouds of smoke curled around his great black beard as he enjoyed the utter calm of the morning. Even the lack of good winds failed to disturb his serenity. This morning, he prayed he would spend the rest of his earthly life becalmed in the doldrums. His sea days were done and so too were the days of the windjammers.

That storm was certainly something, wasn't it? He had seen his crew going down with smallpox and sobbing with pain, their skins turning to raw jelly and smelling like rotting carcasses. More than fifty had got it on one trip and four had died. There had been outbreaks of dysentery and yellow fever, not to mention one drunken night on the dogwatch when his own second mate had been murdered. He had faced spear-carrying savages on the guano run out to Tierra Del Fuego, and even sailed into a sky blackened by locusts off the coast of Africa. But, for pure ferocity and destruction, there had been nothing like that storm.

A school of dolphins broke the glittering, still sea, leaping in silvery, grey-backed curves before diving back again. The cook brought the captain a plate of his favourite – plum duff swimming in yellow custard, placing it on his desk.

'Thought you'd like a bit of this, Skipper,' Cook said quietly.

'I can always eat plum duff, Cook. Always. How are things in the galley?'

'We'll sort it out somehow, Skipper. That there is about the only plate left in one piece.'

'Make sure to give the men a double ration of rum, if you can get at the cask. Don't forget mine either.'

Just then the two men heard some mewling. They turned to see a fat, six-toed cat wandering around the cabin floor and crying out hungrily.

'You're having none of this,' said the captain throwing his arms around his plum duff protectively. 'So be away and out of it!'

The streets of the Bay, rinsed clean after a night of showers, were as clear and silent as that wakening moment after a nightmare. Already the sun was making everything look burnished and new, from the sparrow-coloured Shipping Exchange to the white Mosque and the low, squat corrugated sheds of Bailey's dry dock. A stooped old hermit had taken up residence in a shed behind the white Norwegian church. How he had got in there and what he was doing no one knew, or asked.

The flat chimes of the castle clock went bounding down Bute Street, but disappeared somewhere in the middle, as doors and windows were opened to let in the morning. Three piles of dirty laundry had been left outside the Chinese block and a lone Brains beer dray cart came clattering out of Newtown. Coal barges were gliding slowly down the brilliantly varnished

Glamorganshire Canal, two of the burly drovers sitting together and kicking their heels as they shared a pile of cold chip sandwiches. Their roped horses ambled slowly along the towpath, stopping just before the lock gate with their tails flicking away the morning flies.

Golden leaves were falling off the trees next to the towpath, some fluttering down onto the still surface of the canal where they floated, half-curled and motionless, until they were disturbed and pushed aside by the passing coal barges. Then the leaves were slowly sucked into the barges' wakes, whirling around and around, sailing right up to their blunt aft ends like a fleet of wizened, brown coracles clamouring to be let aboard along with the coal.

Nathan pushed right down into Sophie again, feeling everything inside as taut as a wound-up spring. And then, finally, with a soft whimper and a long bodily shudder, the spring snapped. With a hot surge of energy which seemed to be connected to some terminal deep in the earth's core, he let it all go and his seed came racing and galloping out of him in a jerking, burning series of discharges.

Fantastic relief flooded every part of him. As he gasped for breath the sounds of the morning whispered against the window. Just for a moment all his anxieties and guilt evaporated like snowflakes in the sunshine. He kissed her on the lips, fully and gratefully, then laid his head on her shoulder, immediately falling into a deep sleep.

She cradled him in her arms for a while, now rolling him over and kissing him on the cheek and ear before getting up. She smiled as she looked down at him curled up on the bed, with his hairy arms and legs relaxed, hand lying under the side of his face, child-like in his slumber. She was feeling quite drained herself, her eyes puffy and parts of her mind blown away by the seductive opium, but happy and satisfied nevertheless. She poured some water into the basin, splashing her perspiring face with quick scoops of her hands, smiling to herself in the mirror then splashing on some more. She could never, she was sure, move first thing in the morning without the feel of cold water on her face.

When she had finished washing herself she went over to him again, pulling the sheet up over his body, tidying his clothes and folding them up on a chair. He looked so contented sleeping on his hand, his lips whiffling a little and knees moving around to get one leg lying on top of the other. He was certainly going to be gloomier than a raped baboon when he awoke and she had no intention of being around for that. She had seen enough men come to her hungrily and sweetly, before slinking out of her bed, dressing without a word and leaving, blackly depressed by the mysterious appetites which had brought them to her in the first place. She knew men well enough and guessed that, if anything, in the remorse stakes he would be the worst of the lot.

She had to pick up Effey anyway. After dressing quickly, she closed the bedroom door quietly behind her, walking down to the back door where she had the extreme bad luck to bump into Halfway Harry, just returned from his holidays and now, bucket in hand, about to clean the church.

It was difficult to tell who was the more embarrassed – Harry coughing and looking down into his bucket or Sophie, flushing up and wondering what, if anything, she should say. Unwisely, perhaps, she said nothing at all – her wits dulled by the excesses of the night – except to mumble a soft 'Hello, Harry' before stepping out into the back lane, where she just stood in a flat panic wondering what on earth she *should* have said. But there was not much to say, was there? She could hardly have said that she had been there waiting for a tram or wanting to borrow a cup of sugar. Harry would have worked it out quickly enough, no matter what lies had come tumbling out of her mouth. But the sheer sunny cheerfulness of the morning soon subverted her worries and she was so looking forward to holding Effey again that she strode down the sunny lane without a care in the world.

Babies were crawling around the floor of Mrs Jones's house in Angelina Street and Effey's fingers kept trying to work their way into Sophie's mouth as Mrs Jones brought her up to date on the aftermath of the rioting. There hadn't been much trouble the night before, though Sam Shields had had too much to drink again and fell through a plate-glass window in James Street. In the Police Court Mahomed Abouki had got six months' hard labour for hitting a policeman with a stick, and John Marsden got only a month for kicking a policeman and *he*'d been in court sixty-one times previously.

They were still stopping strangers going into Newtown, Mrs

Jones had heard, but there was still a big fuss about Jim Driscoll doing his come-back fight. Now his wife wasn't sleeping with him. What did he want to fight again for? Three of the girls had been taken into the pokey by the police last night and Doris Manning – that's her new kid over there – played hell because they gave her faggots and peas, an' Doris hates faggots and peas. Threw them all against the wall of her cell, she did, so I s'pose she'll get a bit on top of her fine for that.

Sophie continued playing with Effey, listening as politely as she could – her mind beginning to fret about Harry and those tell-tale lumps of opium she had left on the bedroom floor – when Mrs Jones made a remark which made her blood run quite cold.

'There was some trouble in your 'ouse last night I 'eard, Sophie.'

'Some trouble?' Sophie asked vaguely, rising to her feet and cradling her baby tightly.

'Wasn't there some sort of fight?' Mrs Jones persisted, her eyes widening with a wondering innocence, clearly angling for further detail. 'Some screams an' that, I 'eard. I dunno. That's just what I 'eard. It was prob'bly nothing.'

'I wasn't there last night. I was out all night. Why didn't you tell me before?'

Mrs Jones shrugged her shoulders. 'I was waiting for you to tell me. It was prob'bly nothing. That Margaret on the corner said there was a lot of screaming an' thumping.'

With alarm bells ringing Sophie took Effey over to the playpen and put her down in it with two others. 'I'll leave her for a bit, Mrs Jones. Better go and have a look-see. It's probably Betty fighting with one of those shonny boys from the Valleys again. I just don't know where the daft cow dredges them up from.'

She ran down past Custom House like her back was on fire, until she had reached her own front door, left open, as usual, for the whole world and his dog to walk in. 'Betty,' she called out going into the hallway and stopping still to recover her breath, her arm resting against the flaking plaster. 'Betty? Are you all right, Betty?'

The house was eerily quiet. There appeared to be mud on the passage carpet, she noticed. Then she heard some low moaning coming from the kitchen. She opened the door slowly only to find that it was stuck. She pushed it again – something was lying against it. She put her shoulder to the door and eased it open, spotting a *bare muddied foot*. Now she really pushed hard at it, worming through it sideways, to find a man lying on the floor, his head lying in a pool of dried blood. He moaned again, one of his hands fluttering to touch the gash on the back of his head. His clothes were so dirty and ragged they would have been rejected by any self-respecting dosser and there were even more cuts on his legs and feet. Just what had Betty found here? Sophie wondered, her Somali bad temper rising. Well, she was out on her ear after this. That was for certain that was.

'Come on, you,' she said, reaching down with both hands and pulling him roughly away from the door. 'You'd better get back to the mud flats, you had.'

She rolled him over and then let out a tiny yell. It was Edward Gurney, now sitting up, alternately touching the back of his head with his hands and then examining them. He looked up at her and down at his hands again.

'What's happened to you then?' she asked.

He groaned and shook his head, stuffing the hams of his hands into his eyes and rubbing them around.

'Betty. Where's Betty? Is she all right?'

He groaned again, trying to straighten his back and almost toppling sideways.

'I'm going up to her bedroom.'

'No. Don't. Just don't.'

'Why not?'

'Because . . .' He seemed to be trying to shake the concussion out of his brain. 'Because she's dead. Some men got her . . . and, when I came in, they got me too.'

Sophie took the stairs three at a time, opening the door to Betty's bedroom on a sight that made her reel back as if punched in the belly. She was sick all over the floor. Her friend's naked and bloodied figure was spreadeagled all over the bed like some animal carcass on a slaughter slab. Her legs were splayed at ungainly angles as if broken at the knees, her glassy eyes bulging in horror and her knickers were stuffed into her mouth.

Even as she vomited again Sophie's crying eyes looked back at that bed, small fiery stars exploding everywhere as she took in the frozen, broken body, the torn curtains and the dried fountains of blood on the walls. Almost all the muscles in her face were twitching as she backed onto the landing, turning away from the bedroom, shivering and crying into her cupped hands. 'Betty, love, Betty, love. Oh Betty, baby.'

She might have been shivering there for a full minute when Edward, more or less recovered, came up and took her by the elbow, trying to lead her back down the stairs. 'Leave me alone,' she said, jerking her arm away. 'Just leave me alone. Oh, Betty, baby. Oh, Betty, girl.' The bloodied carcass scorched into her mind again and she retched once more though there was nothing left inside her.

'Sophie, you may be in a lot of danger.' Edward was almost calm and rational, talking softly but urgently. 'There were three of them and they may have been after you.'

'Me! Why me? I haven't done nothing.'

'Just come down, will you? We have to talk because I've got to get away quickly.' She kept turning away from him and he kept moving in front of her. 'You must listen to me, Sophie. You may be in a lot of danger. Just come down.'

He finally managed to get her downstairs into the kitchen and settled her in an armchair. She was already red-eyed with weeping. Thin streaks of vomit straggled in her hair as he kneeled in front of her. Her body was still shivering with shock waves but, somehow, many of his words managed to get through to her.

'I was on the run from the police, Sophie. I had nowhere to hide so I came here to get out of the way. I had to jump into the river to lose them, which is why I'm in such a mess. I came in through the backyard and there was a terrific fight going on upstairs. I thought they were attacking *you*.'

'*They*? Who are *they*?'

'I just don't know. There were three of them, I think, but it was dark. I could see they were attacking your friend, who fought like a wildcat. I did what I could but, in the scuffle, I was shoved down the stairs. I tried to get out into the backyard but one of them got me with something just there. I don't . . .'

He stood up abruptly, with his eyes darting back and forth, pacing around the room, looking under the table and behind the curtains. 'I had a bag – a shoulder-bag.' He went out into the hallway and into the living room, pushing furniture aside, almost incoherent with anger when he came back into the kitchen and went out into the backyard. 'Those bastards,' he spat continually. 'Those thieving bastards.'

Sophie began to watch him carefully. He was in an almost murderous rage, his fists clenching and unclenching as he strode back into the hallway again. He looked completely insane in his torn rags, with the muddied blood clotted in his hair. She wondered if his account of events had been the truth, and began worrying that he might turn on her. Her eyes looked on the rack next to the sink where she kept a long carving knife. It would take her about three steps to get it, she decided, her head clearing rapidly.

Just then his rage passed into a sort of sorrowing resignation and he sat down at the table, studying his torn arms. 'Sophie, I don't know exactly what or whom I'm up against. Whoever they are they have a great deal of power and money. I have to get out of this city fast. You must leave here too. I did a job last night but I was set up. I managed to get away but they came here for me too.'

'Why here? I haven't done nothing.'

He seemed to take an age studying his arms again, turning them over and over. 'They weren't after you. It was me they wanted. They must have known I've been coming here to see you from time to time and *guessed* – just guessed that I'd run here.'

'But why hurt Betty? She never did any harm to anyone. Betty never hurt a fly. It's so unfair.'

He began fingering his head wound again. 'I don't know. Just can't think. Nothing makes any sense. Nothing. But there's something valuable they wanted at any cost. It was in the shoulder bag.'

'But who are they?'

'Sophie, you really must go straight to the police and report your friend's murder. Forget you've seen me. I'll get out the way I came in. Tell them where you were last night and just clear this up.'

Her whole body stiffened with a new anxiety and her shoulders rose when he said that. She could never, ever tell anyone where she had been last night.

'I've got to get away somewhere and get matters sorted out,' Edward continued. 'I need to rest up. Need to think things out. You'd better get away too. Is there anywhere you can go?'

'Not me. I'm a Somali,' she snorted impressively, recovering some of her old spirit. 'We Somalis never run from anyone. Never.'

He eyed her, nodding his head slightly as if to acknowledge her nation's warrior ways. 'I'll send you some money when I get settled and . . .'

'I don't want your money either,' she interrupted, the irony of the remark lost on her since money had been the very basis of their dealings with one another.

'I'll send you some money anyway. Are there any old clothes I could use?' He rummaged in his pocket for some keys, putting them on the table. 'I don't suppose you drive? My car is down by the Exchange. I won't be able to get to it now. Find someone who can drive and get it put away somewhere safe in the city. I may be away for a long time, but I will be back. Tell anyone who asks that I will be back, and I'm going to play holy, bloody havoc.'

Now it was her turn to acknowledge his spirit with a nod. He was a strange young man, impressive in so many ways. The toughness of his words was all the more real because he never raised his cultured voice. Like her, he was a fighter. But never a cold-blooded murderer. A man like Edward would never kill someone like Betty. She always had good instincts about things like that. 'You'll find some old clothes in the cupboard in the front room,' she said evenly. 'They were here when we moved in. I can't think they'll fit you but there is a pair of trousers you can probably turn up. There's some money under the floorboard too, my little nest egg for a rainy day. I want it back. Do keep in touch, won't you? I also want to get whoever got Betty.'

'Yes, well . . .' He stood up awkwardly, his body quite tired but his spirit undimmed. 'Just go straight to the police first. We'll get those bastards in our own time, Sophie. And just tell anyone who asks – holy bloody havoc.'

By one o'clock that day the sun was boiling the brains out of Newtown, and the small, dishevelled terraces of Little Ireland were sighing in this endless Indian summer. The crowded beer shops were as hot and stuffy as the insides of roasting ovens, the heat blasting in and out of their open front doors along with their thirsty, flat-capped customers. Three women tatie-hokers, sweating and still dirty after the morning shift of working the shovel on the potato wharves, stood on the corner outside the Erin Go Bragh tavern, silently sharing a pint of beer.

A frothing, brown water – not unlike that beer – came oozing up from the drains, showing that the tide had turned, trickling over the rutted and holed roads, shoving against a scattering of rotten vegetables and even carrying some of them for a few inches before dumping them down again.

Small, laughing children playing tag ran helter-skelter through the shifting rubbish, their bare feet slapping into the brown pools. They ran one way and another in a screaming bundle, now stopping to tease and torment Tin Ted, a young man who had lost his sanity and sight amidst whistling shells and howling howitzers. His arms waved around like a demented scarecrow as the children circled him, pulling at the back of his jacket before running away, screaming with mock terror as Tin Ted shouted his incoherent outrage. They called him Tin Ted because, along with two medals, he had also gained a tin nose after his old one had been blown off in those exploding trenches of the war.

In the cool, wood-panelled presbytery of St Stephen's Church, a thoroughly wretched Nathan was sitting in conversation with Father Dennis O'Reilly. Nathan had hurried straight there after awakening hungover in his stained, bed and had not so much bared his soul as poured it all over the floor. He had told the old priest everything, from the loss of his wife and children to the warning from the Bishop and his night of adultery. Nathan had long admired the educated certainties of the Catholic priesthood which came, he guessed, from their long Jesuitical training in the most authoritative church of them all. He also admired the old priest's utter placidity in the face of a daily blizzard of venial and mortal sins; that unshockable wall against which you could throw every weakness and failure. He was not looking for absolution so much as a pair of understanding and experienced ears, which is why, racked by the twin perils of sexual and alcoholic remorse, he had run to Father O'Reilly first.

The inevitable bottle of poteen had risen, as if by invisible strings, out of the old priest's bottom drawer. But, when the two glasses were filled, Nathan found that his hands were shaking so much he could not pick his glass up. Father O'Reilly quietly sipped his, though, courteously listening to this endless catalogue of sin and personal disaster until it seemed to be finished, when he sat back in his chair, arranging his old fingers as if considering a fine theological problem.

'I like you, Nathan,' he said finally in his soft Irish brogue. 'I can see that great flame of Celtic poetry in your heart, but the trouble with these flames is that they sometimes sputter and die. Then they come alive again. You should not judge yourself too harshly about all this. Men do fall into black waters and the birds they do fly upside down. It's in the blood that's rolling through your veins. But a flame like yours will return and it will burn brighter and stronger because of what you have been through.'

He pushed the glass over his desk towards Nathan, who did manage a few sips but spilt most of it over his butterflying hand.

'But it's nothing to be flashing the tackle about. You must remember that you are still a young man. When you first came here, I thought then that you were heading full steam into trouble. You never did learn the first secret of an active ministry, which is to *do nothing*. It is to be inactive. But you kept trying to do things – revolutionary things like taking in all those homeless West Indians, when you should have got someone else to do it. You took in girls off the streets when they were happy on the streets. The key to all success in these matters of the ministry is to drink a little and do nothing; just be around and be seen, but go missing when it all starts to pile up. You must always have a powerful sense of your own inadequacy. Let them find the answers to their own problems – they always do in the end, unless they find someone who'll solve the problems for them. Now, you say you've gone and had sexual intercourse with one of your parishioners. Nothing terribly revolutionary about that, I suppose, but, I needn't tell you that it would have been better if you had done nothing. Sex will always come and smack your ears out. Sex is always best left alone – that's the only way to handle sex.'

'It's slightly worse than just sex, Dennis.'

'Worse than just sex? I don't understand. How could it be worse?'

'This parishioner. She's a prostitute, *and* we were smoking opium.'

O'Reilly's mouth formed a silent 'Oh' and he threw up his hands, almost spilling his poteen. 'Yes, that's worse for sure. You didn't pay her, did you? But tell me, this opium stuff. What's it like to be going with? Does it make you not quite right in the head? I've had talk of it in the Confessional often enough but I've never met anyone intelligent who can explain what it's like.'

'It's odd, strange. You seem to be there and not there. It gives you an endless procession of weird dreams and a hangover you can sell by the pound.'

'And how does it affect the sexual side of things? Any improvements in that department?'

'Hard to tell really. You just go on and on and on, never knowing where you are.'

'Mmm. I thought as much. Yes, well, I think I'll stick to this stuff. Better the devil you know and all that. But, Nathan, seriously, you know about the nature of sin. You, of all people, know that you can confess yourself before God. Offhand, I'm not sure about my right to give someone like you absolution and I would happily and a hundred times forgive you for anything, but this problem of yours is between you and God. It gives Him the greatest pain but He does understand everything and He does forgive everything. That's the great joy of our Christian faith.'

'But I can't seem to find God. I don't know. There's no prayer in my life any more. I can't even seem to read the Bible and that was always my backbone. In some certain way I seem to have turned my back on Him and, when you do that, we are told, He gives you up.'

'Nonsense. Didn't they teach you anything at all in that theological college? Forgiveness is at the very centre of the Gospel. It was for your sins that Jesus died on the cross. He took them all on Himself for us. Which includes me and you. Do you think I haven't committed the most terrible sins?'

'What sins would they be then?' Nathan asked, cheering up a little.

'I'm not telling you.' He refilled his glass, sighing and smiling to himself as if they had been very wonderful sins indeed. 'But I will tell you that they were big mortal ones.'

'Bigger than mine?'

'Look, Nathan, nothing is as it seems. Nothing. It's just our ideas that are so often wrong. I go to wakes here and my people are as happy as pigs in a rut. They sing to everyone else enough to make them barmy. I ask myself, where's the grief? but it's what they've grown up with – what they have been taught by Mother Church – that life is a long sadness from which death is a release and triumph. Your ideas, you see. Your problems may make no sense now, but, one day, God will show you what it was all for. It will be for something, Nathan. It will all be for something.'

A deep silence hung in the presbytery, embroidered slightly by the ticking of an ormolu clock. The afternoon sun was glazing the windows, with the sounds of shrieking children coming from the road outside. Faraway there was the melancholy drone of a ship's hooter and, deep inside, Nathan could actually feel a great sorrow decanting through him. He sniffed, giving a tearful smile as he examined the fat gold ring of his priesthood.

'There are times, I think, when God asserts Himself in your life and you feel wonderfully protected and warm,' he said, still looking down at his ring. 'But then come the times when He seems to let you go and you are adrift and lost in some sort of storm that you don't understand. Somehow you feel that He is testing you out. I have known the practice and presence of God and would say, unhesitatingly, that the day I was ordained was the happiest day of my life. I kept thinking that I was just going to die of happiness and it continued well into my first ministry; every new day was a marvellous personal gift and my cup was overflowing. But then . . . I moved here and, you know, Dennis, I felt both that God was testing me and that I was under constant and unceasing attack. Everything I touched went wrong; everyone I loved left me and it just came apart in my fingers . . . until today, now, here. I know now that I failed the whole test. I don't know where to turn and reach out for the face of God any more. I just don't know. I see what you are saying about time bringing its own meanings, but for the moment I feel so lost and alone and wanting. I was attacked, perhaps by the devil, and found completely wanting. So I want to leave it all alone . . . and be . . . be . . .'

'Be what?'

'Be nothing. Be nothing at all. Just wake up and wait for the night to come. Just wake up and look forward to going to sleep again. That's all. All these things I've been telling you about. They've gone through me like fire and I look down into myself and see this charred, smoking shell. I was tested and found wanting. There were no defences, and now I know that I've lost my calling because I never had a proper and holy one in the first place. I am no use to anyone. I have to leave the Church.'

# CHAPTER TWELVE

'I just cannot believe my ears,' said Hamilton, with a calm but barely controlled fury. 'They were not supposed to kill *her*. They were just supposed to get that cup for me. You have half the police force in the county at your disposal and you let young Gurney get away! All that careful planning and he just vanishes. He must be around here somewhere, and I want to know where. I want to know because I want that cup. More than anything I want that cup.'

Hamilton was staring out of his window at the Bristol Channel sinuous with sunshine. Two paddle steamers were crossing past one another, the one going out jam-packed with holidaymakers and the other coming in empty. The burly Inspector Watts felt distinctly uncomfortable sitting there, flicking his shirt cuffs as if for the want of something to do. Partington was standing behind Watts, only the jaws of his tidy, formal face moving slightly as they worked over a mint.

'We have a full meeting of the Party in two weeks' time and, as I stand here now, I just do not know how I am going to explain all this,' Hamilton continued without turning around. 'The times are right, everything was gelling well, and now this foul-up.' He turned around and thumped his fist down on the desk in an uncharacteristic display of anger. 'It just could not have gone more wrong even if we had planned it that way.'

'We've got every available man out looking for him,' Watts said hesitatingly. 'But I needn't tell you that we are hampered on a number of fronts.'

'Hampered? By what, exactly?'

'Well, we have to be careful to keep everything quiet. You've always insisted that there should be no publicity about the castle business, so we've had to tread very softly in what we say to our men before they go out on their inquiries. As you'll also know there've been endless commotions in Bute Street following the riots so we've been fully stretched on a number of fronts. I've got five of my best men working through the lodging houses but, with so many ships coming in and out, the landladies barely know who are in their own rooms.'

'What about the five men you picked up? Do they know anything?'

'Four. We only got four, I'm afraid. We missed the Irishman as well. The pair of them seemed to just vanish into thin air. One of my men thought he'd spotted the Irishman escaping into the river.'

'Into the river? How did he get there?'

'I've not a clue, Mr Hamilton. Not a single clue. I've got a nark in Newtown but he hasn't come up with anything yet. As for the other four we've got behind bars, they haven't got half a brain between them. They weren't told what they were going in for and didn't know what it was when they saw it. They can't even spell their own names and, by the time we finished with Owen the Bastard – as he's called – he wouldn't have been able to write it even if he knew how.'

'Young Mr Edward didn't even tell them *his* name,' Partington amplified. 'He was most careful on that front. But he did have a car, an Adler, which he left near Mountstuart Square. You should keep an eye on that because he was awfully fond of that car and will certainly return for it.'

'I'll put a man on that,' said Watts. 'But what do you want me to do with those blockheads I've got locked up?'

'Do? What do you mean *do*?' Hamilton inquired.

'I'll have to charge them with something or they'll be getting some fancy-pants solicitor down there crying about their rights. They may be brainless but there isn't a villain in Cardiff who doesn't know how to scream out for a solicitor. In fact that's all they usually start screaming for as soon as you lay a hand on them.'

'Let them go,' Hamilton snapped irritably. 'Let them go, providing they say nothing about this to anyone. And promise them that they will be locked up for a very long time indeed unless they tell us where young Gurney is. Better still, promise them a lot of money if they find him.'

'Talking of which . . .' said Watts, his fingers tightening his tie-knot and squirming his neck around as if trying to stretch it.

Hamilton looked at him hard, bad temper still smouldering in his eyes, before taking out a fat brown envelope and flinging it on top of the desk. 'You have hardly earned it,' he grumbled as

Watts picked it up. 'But leave us now. I want to talk to Partington alone.'

'We'll find Mr Gurney, don't worry, Mr Hamilton,' said Watts putting the envelope into his inside pocket. 'We may not find him today but we'll get him within the week.'

'Just make sure that you do.'

When Watts had left, Hamilton sat at his desk and shuffled some papers around. 'Partington, I am so very tired of dealing with bungling amateurs,' he said finally. 'We just seem to be pouring money away everywhere and to so little effect. I have been looking at these new figures of yours for Oriel. Edward Gurney was the best man we have ever had on the Floor. There is liquidity in almost every arm of the business. He was such a natural, and was most valuable where he was. We should have sent someone else into that cursed castle but I just could not think of anyone else who would have been able to do it.'

'May I remind you, Mr Hamilton, that we knew what we were doing and that the strategy was always short-term. The strategy was always that he would spend a few years inside so we could divest him of his inherited rights. If he'd had any long-term prospects on the Floor he just could not have done what he'd done. The company liquidity figures are very good just now but, in the long term, they wouldn't have improved a lot. He was getting a very bad reputation and there were a lot of brokers and dealers who were saying that they wouldn't do business with him again.'

'A lot have said that about me but, given the smell of money, those brigands will do a deal with anyone. However . . .' He shuffled his papers together into a neat bundle, took them and put them in his safe. Here his tone changed and he put his hands down into his trouser pockets, lowering his head and voice as he spoke. 'Partington, I want you to go up to London and spend some time there since, I am certain, that is where young Edward has gone. We have some important police contacts there too so I will telephone a few of them to ensure that they will be of assistance should you need it. We know about Edward's Belgravia flat and his clubs, so you can start there. Try and contact him and do a deal with him. He might trust you. Insist that you knew nothing about the police set-up and offer him anything. Tell him I can manage a thousand pounds a week if he will come back and run what is after all his business. Remind him of his windjammer and . . .'

'Bad news about the windjammer, Mr Hamilton. I haven't had the right moment to talk to you about that but it's been badly smashed up in a storm off Land's End. We've had a cable from an agent in Penzance saying that it's almost a total wreck. The Penzance people are towing it in to claim salvage.'

Hamilton blew a thin stream of exasperation through his teeth. 'Well it is clear you had better not talk about the windjammer then. But promise him almost anything at all as long as he will come back here and bring that cup with him.'

'I'll go to London as you ask, Mr Hamilton, but I must say that I wouldn't be surprised if Mr Edward was still somewhere in the area.'

'In the area? How? Why?'

'I didn't say anything in front of Mr Watts since it may well be nothing, but I found these two white feathers on your doorstep when I was waiting to come in.'

'White feathers? What are you talking about? This is not Haiti, Partington. We are not in voodoo land now.'

'Ah, not voodoo, Mr Hamilton. These feathers are – how can I put it? – symbolic. Mr Edward told me about white feathers like these. During the war, in London, young ladies would wander the streets handing them out to any young man who looked fit enough to fight. Mr Edward was always getting them and he was fearfully sick of it. They mean that you are a coward. These feathers are an invitation to fight.'

'A man with a taste for symbols.' Hamilton all but sprang across the room, pacing up and down, hands and arms moving around in a sudden fury of restlessness. 'I'm coming to admire that young Gurney more and more. He should be with us, on our side, and I made a grave error trying to put him away. A very grave error. If you find him and all else fails to induce him to return, tell him I will fight him anywhere and at any time. Just tell him that. Tell him that the winner will take all.'

The cell door closed with a shuddering clank. As she heard the rattling keys being turned a wave of sadness came over Sophie. She gazed about her: the window bars sliced up the single shaft of pale daylight and the cell was insufferably hot.

A sign said, 'No Spitting'. She lay down on the bed and quickly sat up again: the stained mattress reeked of urine. Instead she sat on a chair at a wooden table just next to the door, humming sorrowfully to herself.

Her progress to this cell had been swift and bewildering. She had reported her friend's murder to the police station in Bute Street and, within minutes, they were swarming all over the house, taking measurements and photographs, asking her about this and that. Questions, questions, questions. She had never thought that a group of stupid policemen could come up with so many questions. Then *another* group had arrived with yet more questions. It was rapidly becoming clear that she was under some suspicion since there was one obvious question which she would not answer. Where and with whom had she spent the night?

She had got drunk, she said, and had gone to do some business with a man, which was all she could remember. Her memory quite failed her on where she had got drunk, what the exact nature of the business was and, most crucially, the identity of the man. 'I was drunk. You don't remember anything when you get drunk, do you?' she pleaded over and over again.

An invitation to go back to the police station had followed. There, in the interview room, they started all over again, asking much the same sorts of questions. She kept pleading a ravaged memory but, the more she persisted, the more they persisted too. At one point she came dangerously close to hitting out with her fists.

Then they left her to her own devices for half an hour. Eventually a huge man who seemed practically to fill the room came in, introducing himself as Detective Brigg. She had seen him wandering the streets before but had never guessed he was a policeman. He had a somewhat softer approach than the others, even apologizing for holding her like this.

'I've got a baby girl, you know. I can't leave her with her child minder for ever. She never stops crying when I'm not around.'

But, quite soon, Detective Brigg introduced the main reason for all those questions. 'Put quite simply, Miss James, we've found some men's clothes in the bin in your backyard. How do you explain them?'

'I don't know. I'm a woman, in case you hadn't noticed. I wear women's clothes.'

'We've also found a patch of blood in your kitchen which we are reasonably sure is not your friend's.'

'So?'

'So there was a man in the house.'

'I know there was a man in the house. You're not thinking that Betty killed herself, are you? For the tenth time, I came home and found her dead.'

'And you were with . . . ?'

'I've told you. I've forgotten. You have to drink a lot in my business. You can't face them sober.'

'So you've forgotten who you were with, what you did and where you did it?'

'Yes.'

'So how do you explain this bunch of car keys which we found under the draining board in your kitchen?'

She stared as he pulled the keys out of his pocket and placed them on the table in front of her. 'Never seen them before in my life,' she announced after a long sniff.

'We think we know the owner of these keys and we want to talk to him most urgently.'

'Well, go and talk to him then.'

'But, you see, Miss James, we don't know where he is. We are hoping that you know.'

'Don't know what you're talking about. Look. I've had enough of all this. I've got a terrible headache and just want to go and pick up my baby.'

'Where is the man you were with last night?'

'I've told you, I can't remember anything about last night.'

The detective left the room and she could hear muttering noises coming down the corridor. She could not make out what was being said but knew that she had not heard the last of it all. Not by a long chalk. Finally the same detective came back again saying that they had decided to lock her in a cell for as long as it took for her to find her memory again.

'Well, that's going to take a very long time indeed,' she snorted.

So now she was sitting at the table of an airless cell with a sign warning her not to spit and humming sorrowfully to herself. She could, of course, remember all too clearly whom she had been with the night before and wondered how he was getting on. Probably wrestling with his own remorse and in an even worse state than her, she guessed. Poor Nathan. If ever a man was born to suffer it was he.

Another hour passed. When she was beginning to think that they had forgotten her entirely the door slammed open again. In came Old Blotch-Face himself, Inspector Watts, who was acting in such an agitated manner – working his huge shoulders around as if they had become uncomfortable weights and lifting his fat hand as if swatting invisible flies – she was even becoming wary that he was going to give her a swipe as well.

'Don't you lay a finger on me,' she warned him with such authority it suggested that *he* was *her* prisoner. 'I'm a Somali with lots of Somali friends. You lay a finger on me and you'll be very sorry indeed.'

'Sophie, there is . . .'

'Miss James, to you.'

'Sophie, there's no reason why you can't walk out of here right now. All we want is to find the owner of those car keys. He was in your house last night. Tell us where he is and you can walk out now.'

'Don't know who you're talking about.'

'Who were you with last night? Was it Edward Gurney?'

'Who? I've told you once and I'm telling . . .'

'You haven't told me anything yet, Sophie. Tell me where you were.'

'I've forgotten.'

He just stood glaring at her for a few moments with, she fancied, the one side of his birthmarked face as ruddy as the other. 'Can you write?' he asked finally.

'Course I can write.'

'I'll give you a pencil and some paper then. Just sit here and write down everything you can remember about last night. Write down anything at all. If I'm satisfied you've made your best effort you can go. I want every single detail that you can remember.'

'As you please.'

Her visiting party left again and she gazed at the ominously white sheet of ruled paper. An eyeball in the peephole of the cell door was watching her so she licked the pencil lead and wrote: 'I cam home to my hose and found my frend deado.' She re-read her report and crossed the letter o off the end of deado. She was never much at spelling.

The eyeball continued watching her as she put down the pencil and folded her arms, humming again and looking around. They seemed in no hurry to come in to read her report so she picked up the pencil and began inscribing the verse of a song which began working around in her mind:

You cam into my life alone
And left it agan free
But what about me?
Do I stay a prisoner of love?

And warming to her theme:

Wher is the key to my cell?
What is this prison with no wals
I do not want to stay
A prisoner of your love.

It was to be the first of many such verses about love and pain which she was to write and sing; they would one day make her very famous. But Inspector Watts was not at all impressed by the lyric he read, crushing the paper into a ball and throwing it onto the floor. 'You've gone and done it now,' he told her and stormed out.

She was left alone for a long time. Still unable to face the foul mattress, she lay her head on her arms on the table, falling into a light sleep with troubled dreams, until she was awakened again by the sound of rattling keys. She glimpsed the legs of two men standing in front of her and groaned, closing her eyes again.

'Sophie, I've only just heard you were in here. I came over to see you straightaway.'

She smiled and felt something bright lift inside her drowsiness. It was Nathan whose hand rumpled the top of her hair.

Inspector Watts left and locked the door as Nathan walked over to the other side of the cell, sitting on the side of the bed. He had huge black circles of sleeplessness around his eyes and his hands were none too steady, either, she noticed. But his voice was quite startlingly firm and purposeful.

'I came and asked to see you as soon as I learned about this whole shocking business,' he said in a brisk, almost formal tone which she did not like at all. 'Inspector Watts has told me the circumstances of your being here; I gather you are not being at all helpful and I want to say right now that you must tell them everything. My position doesn't matter a fig in all this.'

'Of course your position is important, Nathan. Don't worry about me being locked up. I can do this standing on my head. They'll let me go soon enough when they see I've got nothing to say.'

'Inspector Watts had told me that there's a man they want to talk to urgently – an Edward Gurney. He says that Gurney may be the one who murdered Betty and they want to catch him fast. They think that you're shielding him for some reason. Well, are you?'

Her eyes wandered to the closed peephole and then to the cracked tiled wall. Every part of the police station seemed surprisingly quiet and still. 'It seems a funny place to put up a No Spitting sign,' she said absently.

'Sophie, this is a deadly serious situation and it's called murder. Do you know this Gurney?'

She took a deep breath, not liking to tell him, of all people, any lies. 'Edward Gurney? Never heard of him. Watts asked about him but I've never heard of him. Look, Nathan, you know where I was last night. I went home and found Betty dead. That's all there is to it really.'

'Well, if you're not going to tell them, I will. It doesn't matter, Sophie. My position is not important – it is most unimportant. I salute your loyalty, Sophie, but it really would be best if you told the police everything.'

'You can tell them what you like but I'm telling them nothing. I don't owe the police anything and they have no right – no rights – to know that I spent the night with you last night.'

'But the man who murdered Betty may murder again. You want him behind bars, don't you?'

She could feel something invisible yet tortuous struggling inside her chest like thick jealousy. That was the real trouble with lies – they just led to yet more lies. She knew that Edward had not murdered Betty but even to say that would be an admission that she did, in fact, know him. She smoothed out the crumpled sheet of paper and handed it to him.

He read the paper, puzzled. 'What's this, then?' he asked,

holding the paper up into the air with thumb and forefinger as if it was a rotten fish.

'It's a song I've just written. Obe and me always used to talk about songs so I've just written one. I'm going to call it *Prisoner of Love*. Do you like it?'

'Marvellous. That's marvellous. Sophie, this is very, very important. I've found out things about myself and my faith last night in bed with you. No, I'm not blaming you for anything. Nothing at all. It's just that I've decided to leave the Church. I've just realized that I'm not right for it.'

'Don't, Nathan. Just don't do this.'

'I'd decided to do it quite soon after I woke – even went to speak to Father O'Reilly over in Newtown about it.'

She closed her eyes. For a second or two her mind swam. Then she felt a stab of pain as her eyes erupted with weeping. She had guessed that he would suffer from a bout of remorse, but had never foreseen that it would have been quite as bad as this. She had only wanted to comfort him and not to wreck his life. She had only wanted to show him things that he should have known about. You become stronger when you know such things – or so she had always thought. She'd clearly been very wrong on that one. 'Don't, Nathan.' She shook her head, her eyes still swimming with tears. 'You are so right for what you are doing. Don't do this.'

She stood up and walked over to him, going down on her knees, trying to put her head on his lap. But he caught her by the wrists, led her back to her chair and sat her down again.

'There is another factor, Sophie,' he hissed, his face close to hers. 'And please do not think that it is your fault, but Halfway Harry has reported everything to the Bishop. He told me so this afternoon so, you see, I have to jump before I'm pushed. Being defrocked is a terrible process.'

'That little bastard . . .'

'But what it does mean, Sophie, is that you don't have to protect me. Nothing matters any more – except that you get safely home and out of all this.'

Sometimes she found his goodness so overwhelming and, with his every word, she kept crying more and more helplessly. Everything had now become too much, all out of control. 'I didn't mean any of this, Nathan. I didn't want any of this. All I ever wanted was to show you some real happiness.'

'None of this is your fault, Sophie.'

'Of course it's my fault. Whose other fault could it be? If I'd kept myself out of your bed none of this would ever have happened. Betty might even still be alive.'

'Nonsense. But what's done is done, so all I want you to do is tell the police the truth and we can both leave here. Now, do you know anything at all about this man?'

'Nothing. Nothing at all.'

'The police say they've found his car keys in your house. Do you know anything about them?'

'Nothing. Nothing at all.'

'How did they get there?'

'Nathan, I wouldn't lie to you. I just don't know. I've never seen those keys before.'

A long silence followed, broken only by her sniffing and sighing. She wiped her nose with her sticky hands for a while, her body still reeling with the unbelievable sadness of his decision to leave his work. She had never had much truck with the Church as such, but he just seemed so right for it. 'Are you going to leave the Bay now?' she asked finally. 'Where is going to be home for you now? I couldn't bear not seeing you again. I just couldn't.'

'As of this moment I just don't know where I'll be going.'

'Come and live with me, Nathan. I'll give up my work – I've always hated it anyway – and we could do something together. You and me could just walk out of here and find something to do. We could do some proper social work or something. There's so many people who need help.'

'No. I will be going away for some time. I need time to think. I . . . oh, I don't know what I'll do.'

'I love you, Nathan. I just want you to know that. Once a girl like me gives her love she never takes it away again. It's there – a given thing – for ever.'

'Yes, well . . .' He stood up, embarrassed, shoving his hands into his pockets and looking down at the floor. 'Just tell the police the truth about everything. That's all. Just tell them everything.'

With a metallic crash the cell door opened and Inspector Watts stood framed in the doorway, almost as if unwilling to walk inside. 'I'm not sure how to say this, Vicar,' he said, dusting his bulky hands together and looking behind him. 'But I've been sitting out here in the corridor listening to everything that you've said to one another. We seem to have the full story now. I suggest you take your whore home to bed.'

It was the sixteenth round and the old boxer blinked hard, wondering what had happened to him. Nothing seemed to want to move. He sent frantic messages to his legs but they did not respond. He tried to lift his fists but they were complete deadweights. He feinted with his right which only served to play the twinkling pains of a renegade ulcer. He feinted with his left but the blow would barely have knocked the skin off a rice pudding.

His opponent was circling him with his arms down, keeping a wary eye on the old boxer, but also looking at the referee, wondering when he was going to stop this massacre. The old boxer had drawn on every punch in his extravagant arsenal – thundering body blows, head-snapping rights to the mouth, close-to jabs, uppercuts to the chin – but his opponent just seemed to shrug them off, and still he kept coming forward. The only way he could have stopped him would have been by breaking both his legs with a hammer. They had said the old boxer was too old – they had *all* said that he was too old – and now he was feeling it. He was feeling every year, hour and minute of it. Old age, oh aye, the end of the line.

The ring lights were burning deep into his eyes. His breath was coming in short, painful wheezes. He could not even hear the roar of the crowd since they were not roaring any longer; they were silent and watchful, knowing that they were witnessing the passing of an era, that nothing would be quite the same again, that a great king was about to pass on the crown.

The old boxer tried to engage his opponent again but he could do little more than try to grab hold of him; try and smother yet another murderous assault. His opponent just shrugged him off and looked appealingly at the referee again.

Thus, on October 20, 1919, at 8.20 p.m., in the National Sporting Club in London, a bloodstained towel was thrown into the air and landed in the middle of the ring. The king had indeed abdicated and an era had passed. Charles Ledoux, the Little Assassin, had won, and Peerless Jim Driscoll – who first learned to box in the streets of Newtown and went on to become the finest boxer of all time – had come to the end of an illustrious career.

# PART TWO

'One leak will sink a ship and one sin will destroy a sinner.'

JOHN BUNYAN

# CHAPTER THIRTEEN
# 1930

Light drifts of snow went swirling around the valley slopes in shapeless spinning tops. The harsh winter winds cut into Obadiah Brown and his mates as they trudged the four miles to the pithead for the start of the morning shift.

They said nothing as their bodies leaned forward into the face of the winds, carrying their tins of snap and jacks of water under their arms as they kept shuffling onwards like some vanquished Napoleonic army retreating from the Russian front. Obe found the going all the more difficult since he wore two pairs of flannel pyjamas under his working clothes. He also had an ex-army greatcoat, several sizes too big, and a black woollen balaclava helmet. The boys on the shift called him Obe Fortycoats but, even with more layers than a large onion, his whole body shivered and his fine teeth audibly chattered under the balaclava.

Just below them, nestled at the base of the slope, sat the curving, snowcapped terraces of Trethomas: a lost, small village in a lost, small valley in South Wales where Obe had made his home. He did not find it so bad in the summer but his black body shrank with pain in the winter. Even after eight years of trudging the four miles to the pit – and a further six to the face – he had never come close to getting used to these freezing valley winds, which presented him with a bad cough, running nose and a head cold almost the day winter settled in. Then he was pursued by dreams of endless Barbadian sunshine and cooling coconut juice. Barely an hour went by without him thinking of his island home and in weather like this he thought about it all the time.

Those six months in Cardiff prison had shattered his self-esteem. Unable to look anyone in the eye when he came out, he had used his discharge money to take a bus up to the valleys where, he had heard, there was still work to be had down the coal mines. With just his trumpet and a bundle of clothes, he had come to this small, lost village, to work and find himself again.

The work was the hardest and most dangerous ever; a punishing fight against cracked coal seams which disappeared into stone; one day sloshing about in two feet of water because the deputies had turned off the pumps 'as an economy measure' and the next hardly able to see his black hand in front of his black face because of the billowing gales of black dust which swept in from every direction. Jagged stone ripped at his bare back as they tackled coal seams sixteen inches high. There was the constant threat of methane gas or a breaking rope which would send the loaded drams careering down slopes, smashing the arms and shearing off the legs of anyone not lucky enough to find a refuge hole in time.

But doing this work was far better than doing no work at all. On an increasing number of days now, the men were just being sent home either because the face had flooded again or because there was simply no demand for coal. There were no telephones to inform the men before they left home, not to bother to turn up to work. And so, on such days, they just turned around and trudged straight back home again.

Obadiah Brown, alias Obe Fortycoats – the only black man in a white Welsh village – was readily accepted into the community almost as soon as he had arrived and he had been grateful for that. Trethomas was a loving, honest place, attentive at times of accident and death; its people knew a man who had lost his way when they saw one. It did not take them five minutes to work out that he was even poorer than they were and Obe soon learned that they loved to make a joke out of everything. So he joked a lot too, often in an exaggerated West Indian patois which made them roar with laughter.

'Ah've bin doing some figgurin',' he would shout accompanied by a lot of comic chortling. 'Ah've bin doing some figgurin' an Ah've decided that Ah'm far better off than you white boys 'cos Ah'm the only one who doesn't have to wash at the end of the shift.'

The freezing winds continued to cut into them as they shuffled up to the office to clock on. But everything was eerily and suspiciously quiet. The aerial ropeway which carried the slag in iron buckets out to the tip was still and the flame which burned off the excess gas was out. Men were standing in silent groups in different parts of the yard. Obe decided that it looked like yet another lay-off. He walked over to the night-shift boys, their washed eyes but white sockets in their coal-black faces. Snow settled in tiny drifts on their flat oily caps. It was their lacklustre eyes that Obe could never quite get used to; they never seemed to sparkle at all, always the dull colour of the mine they slaved and died in.

'There's been word Powell Duffryn's closed the pit, Obe Fortycoats,' one said to him. 'You might as well go home to Barbados and starve there in the warmth. We're waiting for the manager now.'

Obe merely nodded, just jumping up and down again and clamping his arms to his body. Other men came up the pit road, surging silently out of the drifting snow mists, black on white, to swell the waiting groups. It was their silence that was strangest as they stood around, all shivering in the savage, siren music of the Depression. One of them turned away, coughing up a lump of black sputum which dribbled and stretched until it splattered on the thin film of snow like a huge alien leech.

Obe spent most of his free time reading in the Miners' Institute. He had long seen this, and all those other pit closures, coming. Only last year the Wall Street Crash had wiped out most of the savings in America, putting a quarter of the work force out of a job. Thousands of men were sleeping out in the streets. The Crash caused a worldwide slump in trade, throwing nearly three million out of work in Britain and five million in Germany.

The Liberals had watched the coat-tails of their power disappear around the corner; Baldwin could find no solutions, so now the first Labour prime minister, Ramsey Macdonald, was tackling the unemployment figures, and they had got worse. The South Wales valleys in particular had been crucified by unemployment and near-starvation, with more than half of Merthyr's men unemployed and forty per cent out in the Rhondda and Aberdare Valleys alone. Chamberlain had announced that 200,000 miners in South Wales would never work again. The giant Dowlais steelworks had also been closed last year, throwing 12,000 men onto the dole queue in a single day. They used to fire the furnace before the start of the nightshift, setting up a second brilliant sunset all over the valleys and mountains of South Wales. But, that day, yet another Welsh light had gone out for ever.

Obe, who had worked as the Trethomas lodge secretary in the bitter 1926 strike – which had led to a bitter defeat for the miners, who lost everything and took heavy wage cuts – also came to understand, from his studies in the Institute, that the coal industry was being overhauled by gas and electricity. It was becoming difficult for coal to compete, particularly with the big combines like Powell Duffryn buying up all the pits and closing down all but the largest. Oh, how these eight years in that library and lying on his back underground had radicalized his black soul. He was now convinced that what the people needed more than ever was socialist co-operation and not capitalist competition. They needed to organize and unionize themselves. They needed to come together and make themselves strong, since only then would they be able to shake the structures to their very foundations.

Meanwhile, here he was, another redundant man in another redundant pit, shivering in a biting blizzard and with little to look forward to except a journey to the Public Assistance and a visit from the man from the Means Test.

The men may have been standing around for half an hour but, typically, neither the manager nor anyone else came to tell them of their fate. Word went around that the men should pick up their pay and dockets, which were being handed out through a broken window in the office. Obe joined the others in the queue, looking up at the black iron gallows of the mineshaft, over to the foundry and lamp room and then back down at his boots which were still tapdancing about in an effort to keep his feet from freezing up. He just never understood how Powell Duffryn got away with it. No announcements, no expressions of regret, no nothing. Just a few shillings and a docket handed through a broken window. He supposed all history was made up of moments like this; moments of nothing and thoughtless cruelty. Real life rarely had any moments of real drama.

By now his ears were almost screaming with the cold as he waited his turn. He was nearly there, when the office was closed for a while after one of the men, in a satisfying display of mutiny, had reached through the broken window and grabbed the pay clerk by the throat. The others managed to pull him off. 'Strangle the bastard after we've been paid, *mun*,' they snapped at him.

Obe's pay came to four shillings for the two shifts he had

worked that week. There had been stoppages, it was explained gruffly when he queried the meagreness of his pay-off. The men on his shift hadn't yet paid for their oil, chalk and explosives. Obe wondered aloud if he could buy some explosives with what was left of his pay. 'I'd love to blow this bastard pit sky-high,' he said with real feeling. He was getting very Welsh too.

The snow thickened and the wind howled harder as the men trudged back to the village. None of them was making the usual jokes; many of them were walking back singly. Did such grinding poverty lead even to the death of friendship? Obe stopped just by the bridge leading over the river and into the village. A mother of three had flung herself face-down onto those rocks two nights ago. She had ripped most of her face off but her real tragedy had been that she had lived. Another man had thrown himself down the mineshaft that week but he had been lucky enough to die.

Even in the driving snow, groups of men were standing around in the village square, their ulcerous faces with small blue scars staring into the empty winds. A lot of men became very adept at standing around and staring at nothing in particular during those black days; they seemed even to like standing out in the cold. But Obe hated it, and he walked into the warm library in the Institute, peeling off a few layers of clothes before queuing with the others for his turn to read the morning newspaper.

It was in this library that Obe had first learned and absorbed the new socialist gospel of Anatole France, Marx and Engels. The newspapers had been particularly valuable in keeping up with the activities of such as Arthur Horner, A. J. Cook and Aneurin Bevan, the silver-tongued Tredegar miner who had become an M.P. the year before – the youngest coal-miner ever sent to Parliament – and who was to become the most dynamic personality in the history of socialism. Even now Bevan was campaigning to reopen the steel works in Ebbw Vale. Yes, socialism was sweeping the valleys, and just about everywhere the Left were making exciting claims. S. O. Davies, a young Marxist, had been elected as Member for Merthyr.

There was very little compelling political news that day but he did find one item in the entertainment section of the *Echo*, together with a photograph, which he found very interesting indeed. 'One of the newest and most exciting jazz bands now in Cardiff's dockland is the Razzy Dazzy Spasm Band,' the item reported. 'A few leading London agents have been down to look at the band which is attracting huge audiences to the Ship and Pilot public house. The undoubted star of the group is Sophie James, aged 36, of Custom House, whose song *Prisoner of Love* is sung with such feeling that many are comparing her to the great Bessie Smith.'

At first Obe did not recognize her picture, and then remembered that *it was her*! He had always known that there was something special about her voice. It had range and a gravelly sorrow, but it also had one thing that marked it apart from all the others – it just stank of sex.

Obe had kept up with all the developments of jazz; that brawling bastard child of the Depression, listening to broadcasts on the wireless and, whenever possible, getting hold of the odd edition of the *Musical Express* and *Accordion Times* which were aimed at all jazz aficianados. But, in nine years in Trethomas, he had only blown his horn once, one night up inside a deserted mine-working, largely to see if he could still do it. He couldn't. The trumpet needs spirit and he had left most of that behind in the cells of Cardiff prison where they had robbed him of just about everything. He found that he was too sad even to play the blues. There seemed to be nothing wild and young left inside him at all; nothing to call up from deep inside him and pour into his golden horn.

But there was another compelling reason why he had hidden his trumpet away. When you were out of work you could qualify for Public Assistance – not much, but it was slightly better than starving. But, before you qualified, they sent a man around to see if you had any disposable or valuable means – such as furniture, a wireless, ornaments or a trumpet. These then had to be sold or pawned before the family was given two shillings and ninepence a week to keep them alive.

He studied the newspaper photograph again, recognizing a few other faces from that brief dockland stay that he had come here to forget. They all looked so happy and warm and full of, well, fight. He wondered what had happened to that minister Nathan, who, so many years ago, had taken them off that stinking ship and into his church. His eyes ran down the report and found that the band's next venue was at 9.30 p.m. in the Ship and Pilot that night. *Time to go, Obe, baby. Time to be with your people again.* No, it ain't, it ain't. It was time to stay here with these people; to fight with them in the time of their trouble. *Your people, Obe, baby. Your own black people. Time to blow that horn again.*

He put all his tiers of clothes back on but his teeth were soon chattering again as he trudged back to his lodgings down next to the dairy. White winds drove against the boarded-up shop windows in long, sullen whines. It was so cold even the men standing at the corners had gone indoors where anything from the stair banisters to furniture would be chopped up and put on the fire. He stopped in front of the Zion chapel where a group were talking in the vestry, doubtless preparing yet again to set up a soup kitchen to keep the people going. It had been bad enough around here during the strike, Obe recalled but, now that the pit had closed, it was doubtless going to get a lot worse.

Yet more would soon be driven mad by it all – women complaining that potatoes were growing on their backs, grown men starting to dribble and gurgle like babies. Yet more pawnbrokers and talleymen would grow fatter while the mothers starved and their babies were stillborn. Yet more would waste away to nothing from that peculiar Welsh valley malady *Y Dicai* – tuberculosis.

'I must go away today, Mama,' Obe told his landlady after he had taken off his greatcoat. 'I want to go back to my people.'

'These are your people now, Obe.'

The frail lady with tight grey curls stood facing the fire. She could not bring herself to look at him. He walked towards her to put his hands on her shoulders but instead let them fall to his side. She kept looking at a small fire which was smouldering in the black leaded grate. A wooden clotheshorse was standing next to the grate with some of Obe's clothes hanging on it.

'My own people, Mama. My black people. The pit has gone now and I want to go back to my people.'

'I don't want you to go, Obe. You've been like a son to me, you have.'

'I don't want to leave you either, Mama, but I'll keep coming to see you.'

'You'll take your trumpet with you, will you? I mean, you couldn't leave it here safe with me, could you? I'd always know you'd be coming back then.'

'I have to take my trumpet, Mama. I've got to find out if I can still play it. But I will be coming back regular. I promise you, Mama. I was paid well today so I'm going to leave you a few shillings.'

'You keep it, Obe. You'll be needing it. I've got a roof over my head.'

'Mama, I'll be very sad if you don't take it. Obe has never been affected by this Depression 'cos he never had anything to start with.'

And so, that angry winter of 1930, Obadiah Brown, with just his trumpet under his arm and nothing by way of money in his pocket, set out to walk to Cardiff. He followed the winding, snow-blasted valley roads, sometimes stopping in the doorway of a Co-op or a library to shelter from the driving winds. He saw closed mines and deserted chapels as he walked; the men run away to find work in the car works of London and Coventry; the rugby players gone North; many of the young children dead before they had had a chance to grow. He saw whole communities seeming to dissolve in his eyes as effortlessly as the snowflakes. DOWN WITH THE MEANS TEST and COAL NOT DOLE were chalked on school walls while, out on the frozen tips, people were digging and riddling for lumps of coal; pushing the dripping black bags down to the villages on makeshift carts and bogies. But, even as he continued struggling through this savage, cold landscape, Obe felt some faint stirrings of hope. He was going to find his people who had also suffered much. They too knew of food tickets and wooden clogs. Big Bill Broonzy had sung: 'Starvation in my kitchen, rent sign's on my door.'

The streets of the Bay, that night, were so quiet and deserted it was almost as if the word had gone out that the Kaiser's troops, with their pointy helmets, had somehow got themselves organized again and were on their way back to cause some real mayhem. Ice sculptures hung from the walls and eaves, trembling like fiery green moonstones in the glow of the gas lamps. The whole of Bute Street was covered with a glittering sheen of frost, with the trams – usually with just a few passengers inside them – rattling past as if in a great hurry to get back to their warm garages. A horse was hauling a barge along the Glamorganshire Canal, nostrils snorting with plumes of hot breath and flanks smoking as if on fire.

Even the doors and windows of the pubs and shebeens were closed and shuttered. The only heat coming into the street was from the Chinese laundry, where some six tramps were moving around outside the laundry vent, comforting themselves in the dry blasts of warm air. One had small dripping icicles in his tangled beard. A pair of policemen stopped to look at the tramps but said nothing before moving on again. The prostitutes did not stand out in this cold either, keeping to the bars where business was slack, though warm, since being so visibly in the public eye meant that most men would not approach them. Their business only prospered in back alleyways and under the shadows of darkness.

Just near the new glittering white Mosque, which had been erected only two years earlier, a boy and girl were going along the pavement, with him walking ahead of her and waiting until she had caught him up. When she did catch up to him and tried to link her arm in his he walked on again. They passed a patch of waste ground where two cats, their saucer eyes blazing, were facing up to one another and crying that harrowing pain of sexual torture that upsets everyone who hears it. A dustbin lid came whirling out of the darkness, just missing one of the cats who ran away with a venomous hiss. The boy took the girl by the hand and tickled the inside of her palm with the nail of his index finger. She giggled a bit at this naughty suggestion but said nothing.

'Do you know what happens when a pro's daughter gets married aroun' 'ere?' the boy asked.

'No. What happens?'

'The pro gives 'er daughter a 'undred feet of her pitch as a wedding present. That's why there's so many of 'em.'

'Wedding present? I don't get it.'

'Didn't think you would. Got a match, 'ave you?'

She pulled a matchbox out of her coat pocket and handed it to him. He stopped walking for a moment, striking the match and cupping his hands around the flaring flame as he lit his cigarette, which he left dangling in his mouth as he put the matchbox back into his own pocket. They were just passing the railway station when the girl began stepping between the lines around the slabs on the pavement.

'It's a game,' she explained. 'We always plays it when we're kids. If your foot steps on the line you get to get elephant feet. See these letters 'ere. E.L. That stands for elephant feet that do.'

He strode on with his hands thrust down into his pockets as she stepped from one paving slab to the next. Just next to the traffic lights near the dock gate he stopped to wait for her, the cigarette smoke stinging his eyes as she continued spider-legging her way down the pavement, sometimes taking small steps one way and another, now leaping a few feet with her arms windmilling around to stop her falling backwards and stepping onto the taboo lines which would give her those dreaded elephant feet.

'You looks like some grasshopper that's been on the piss,' he said to her when she had caught up with him again.

'Oh that's nice, init?' she replied. 'That's bloody nice that is. A real docks charmer you are, aren't you?'

The glassy acres of the docks themselves were startling and empty parallelograms of water; all those ships of the boom years long since sailed away in search of a boom in another part of the world. The slump in the exports of Welsh steam coal had meant a corresponding slump in the port until, tonight – apart from a sundry rabble of little brigs, schooners and ketches – there were just seven grain ships, two Greek oil tankers, three coal ships and four tramp cargoes, moored in what was once the busiest and largest port in the world. There was also *The Teviot*, a small passenger-cargo boat plying its trade back and forth to Glasgow, but West Bute dock was closed completely.

This port, which once supplied a third of the world's coal and fuelled the Victorian Age of Steam, was now supplying less than three per cent. There was still a flurry of activity here and there – dancing rainbows of golden sparks from the oxyacetylene welders in the Bailey dry dock or the dull pounding of steam hammers in the repair sheds – but whole fields of water were now just given over to the cold winds humming in the telephone wires. West Bute dock, in particular, was as sad as an empty nightclub with the chairs stacked upside down on the tables. Buddleia grew in the gutterings of the warehouses and ghosts of old sea captains met nightly around the capstans on the quays, bragging about their speeds in the tea races or the size of those waves around the Cape.

The economic shunts and crashes of the Depression actually increased the numbers of seamen who made their home in the Bay – from the Chinese, paid off hastily by the East India

Company, to the Greeks, abandoned after sudden business liquidations in Athens, or the Arabs who jumped after bankruptcies in Beirut. The dying docks were becoming the natural home for all men shaken out of their old ships, homes or families. They lived where they could; in the Salvation Army hostel perhaps or on the East Moors foreshore where there were up to two hundred men living in makeshift bunkers next to the sea, all sitting around fires and brewing up tea in butter tins, like some routed army patiently waiting to be shipped home, except that there were no ships to take anyone anywhere in these bad, hard times.

The one place you could go to keep warm was the No. 5 Rowntree warehouse in the Queen Alexandra dock where, even now, several hundred men were all pacing around a large fire. In this graveyard of hopes the only price of admission was that you had something to burn, and the homeless brought park benches, books, boxes – anything wooden at all – which they flung onto the fire that had been burning with a deep, fierce heart for some two weeks now. As the fire blazed the men formed a huge circle and kept walking around it; a shuffling, broken army in battered bowlers, flat caps and clothes tied together with string and pins; ragged oily coats and cardboard shoes falling to bits; some with but one eye; and gnarled, weather-beaten hands – all moving around and around the fire in a long, coughing journey, which was busy journeying nowhere. Acrid smoke drifted out of the warehouse doors and sometimes blazing sparks went spinning up to the rafters. But the Rowntree was one of the first warehouses designed to be totally incombustible. It had been built out of a revolutionary structure of wrought-iron plates and cast-iron circular columns. The floor was brick. So, despite many local complaints, the police turned a blind eye and allowed the men to continue walking around their great fire.

It was the sheer rootlessness of the period that was so striking, with innumerable men – and not a few women – drifting into the area and then drifting out again. One man who was still living around the docks, however, was the tiny hermit, in the same ramshackle shed behind the Norwegian Church. Sometimes you could spot his light through the small frosted window or else you might hear the soft sound of some chanted prayers. With an ankle-length black cloak and a huge cowl which largely concealed his sharp, bird-like face, he went about his mysterious hermit business without talking to – or indeed bothering – anyone. No one was even very sure if he could speak English but, as the Norwegian church had no objections to him occupying their back shed and the Bay was learning to absorb almost everyone in these the toughest of times, the hermit was left alone.

The hermit was out walking that night, muttering holy riddles to himself – or perhaps it was merely some Scandinavian scripture – walking past the Roath Basin dock where, moored in the far corner, was a real maritime curiosity – the mouldering hulk of the windjammer *The Solomon*. She had been lying here for as long as anyone could remember; wrecked, it was thought, in some savage storm off the Scillies about ten years ago. No one was very sure who owned her – even though the mooring fees were paid regularly and on time – but what everyone was sure of was that this great ship – one of the very last of a noble line – would never sail again. The hull was thick with barnacles and moss; what was left of the grey-white rigging had long gone rotten while a slimy fungoid grass was growing on the deck where, by night, rats with fat, pink tails wandered about, sniffing around the broken stump of the mizzen mast or wandering into the fo'c'sle, looking for something interesting to gnaw on.

Below decks it was the same despairing tune of battered and broken bunks in the apprentices' quarters; rusty and jammed bilge pumps; vast cobwebs stretching across the carpenter's shop and bosun's locker. All the brass portholes had turned into a thick purple and green paste, with cockroaches feathering up through the dark bulkheads. The very air hummed with the smell of its own decay punctured only by the sound of ceaseless drips.

But there was life in the old ship yet. In the galley, by the fading light of a hurricane lamp, a man was trying to boil a billy of water. He was having no luck getting the kerosene fire to light, as four or five cats kept moving around and around his legs, brushing their bodies up against him and purring very loudly in the expectation of food. He lit another match and cursed loudly as it broke and burned the tip of his thumb. After another try he gave up and went stumbling back to the ward room where, followed by the cats, he sat in a corner next to a large, circular oak table, now withdrawing into the darkness and muttering evilly to himself. His hand kept sweeping across his face as if he was brushing away a cobweb. One of the cats jumped onto his lap but he lifted it off, putting it gently back down on the deck.

He stared out of the porthole, the pale yellow phosphorus lamp of the quay washing over his sallow features. Only the great curved beak of his nose belonged to the minister who had come to the dockland ten years ago. There was a gaunt, grey tension in his face and he had lost a lot of his hair. He still tried to shave every morning but usually managed to cut himself, leaving his face an untidy tapestry of cuts and unruly patches of stubble. His eyes seemed to have changed the most, sunk deep into the black circles of his sockets, as distant and melancholy as those of a dead man. His hand brushed away another cobweb and he walked across the ward room, stopping to look out of another porthole.

This priest who had read the burial service on society spent a lot of his hours looking out of the portholes watching for any movements on the deserted quay or gazing at the white seagulls circling overhead. As he watched he listened to the ship, his thoughts, his life. He heard the occasional arthritic creak of the bulkheads, the scampering dashes of the cats chasing away any intruding rats, the very soft lapping of the water against the hull if there were any winds. He thought of those he had loved and spent hours carefully constructing lost moments in his mind; he thought of river bank days and crossing fields worrying that his Mam would stop loving him; he remembered paddling in the waves on sunshine beaches, the smell of roast beef on Sundays, the horse and cart taking them on their Whitsun treat . . . But bad things came back to him too – being made to stand with his nose to the wall in the dunce's corner, his dada smacking him for falling into the river, his sexual adventuring between a woman's legs. Yes, all that guilt and shame were still burrowing into the very scaffolding of his heart like a tireless tunnelling worm and then his memory snapped and he became blank, just thinking of nothing; a lonely denizen of the shadows, staring through a porthole at the shapes and emblems of a sort of life which had twisted around and turned in on itself, leaving him with nothing.

There are no patterned steps when you go down; it does not move along on ordered rungs like a successful career. One day he was a minister and the next he was a down-and-out trying to fight off numerous alarmed hands who only wanted to help him up again. He became an aeroplane in an uncontrollable nose spin, first finding a room near the Exchange, then a source of opium from a friendly Chinese waiter. The opium made him pleasantly comatose for almost a fortnight until he was caught one afternoon by the irate landlady and, still pale and drugged, hurled out into the street.

When opium was scarce – or too expensive – he drank meths, denatured alcohol, shoe polish, anything he could lay his hands on. It was Sophie who had found him this ship to live on, since she had some sort of connection with the owners that he did not quite understand. Apart from being a home *The Solomon* was also the base from which he engaged in a variety of quasi-criminal activities and fiddles to finance his drink and drug-taking. He would often be seen doing deals with warehousemen, sometimes carrying a box of something or other back to the windjammer and storing it in the hold. At night, when there were no police around, he could be seen carrying the same boxes to some distant site on the other side of the dock. If the deal went well he might not return for a couple of nights, waking up with a very sore head in some back alley with a group of other men, perhaps – or even on the banks of the River Taff. Then he would make his way home to the ship. It was not much of a home but, even in his misery, he did feel something inside him lift and brighten when he saw her again and was able to walk up that gangplank.

Some men would have quickly died after such long orgies of drink and drugs but he was saved by a number of factors. Many in the Bay watched out for him, remembering what he did for so many so long ago. He also had an iron constitution which enabled him to get through the aftermath of his excesses without too much damage. And Sophie, helped by her daughter Effey, almost always managed to get one meal a day inside him when he was not actually missing. They usually took it in turns to bring him a plate of something, staying with him until he had eaten it and then taking the dirty plate away again. The cats stayed alive largely thanks to the girls' efforts too.

There were even some days when he actually did some work on the ship, telling Sophie that he intended to put it right one day. It was a sort of dream within him that might even, more than anything else, have kept him alive, Sophie thought, and she even encouraged him by bringing tools, nails or odd bits of wood for him to work on some rotten stanchion or bulkhead. These bouts of work did not last long, of course, but at least he was still doing something and, while he was doing that, she still had hope for him.

But today had been a bad day – a do-nothing-at-all day – and while he had not been drinking a great deal because there had not been a great deal to drink he had been suffering very much, yet again entering into distant moments of his memories. For almost all of the day he had been feeling a pain at the back of his head; on the very spot where the bishop had placed his hands during his ordination. Sometimes this pain became quite unbearable and he just sat in the darkness holding his head tightly. At other moments he heard the words of the St Qui, a document read out during Divine Service asking if anyone knew of anything that made him unfit for Holy Orders.

Then he would think of his two children again, remembering how he had once smacked them quite hard for using bad language and then sent them to bed, refusing even to give them anything to eat. They had cried long and loud over that but he had been adamant that they should be punished in a way they would never forget – except that it was he who was now unable to forget.

Yes, it had been a very bad day, sitting there in the damp darkness of his ship, listening to the crumbling music of his loss and guilt. No bright laughter punctuated these days and even his visitors did whatever they had come to do and then left again. On such days he lost all remembrance of God and would often wake up in his bunk in the middle of the night crying.

A gang of men came running up along the quay, their ragged hats and silent gesticulating announcing that they were up to no good. They stood for a few moments looking at *The Solomon*, pointing at the helm and aft deck before moving off as quickly and threateningly as they had arrived. Nathan watched them come and go with quiet interest. He had his own ways of dealing with unwanted visitors. There were too many gangs of men marauding round the streets these days. You could never be too careful. He looked up at a cupboard where he kept an old gun and, for the moment, felt secure.

Sophie stuck her head around the corner of the crowded tap room of the Ship and Pilot and gave a little whoop. The pub was jammed with customers, shoulder to shoulder, a bed of coloured flowers in a storm. They were standing on the chairs and the tables, many still queuing on the stairway trying to get in. A comedian, wearing a tartan kilt with a paintbrush for a sporran and a cardboard soapbox for a hat, was trying to tell a few jokes, but few were listening since they had come from far and wide to enjoy the tremendous noise of the Razzy Dazzy Spasm Jazz Band.

'Mummy, Mummy, is is true that you're a lesbian?' Gruffly: 'Shurrup while I'm shaving.'

But they all laughed at that one, including a seaman who was on the point of downing a pint when the laugh collided with his beer somewhere in his throat and he began to choke. Now a young black, Victor Parker, all sweat and smiles, was working his way through a saucy West Indian calypso. *And I've got me here a big, big banana – Oooooo! Ain't that sweet?* His fingers scrambled through the chords as another black thumped on the piano as if he was determined to break it up. *So where can I put my big, big banana?* Rolling eyes, dirty smiles and more bashing on the piano. *I know where – oh baby I know where.* A pretty young girl in a Salvation Army poke bonnet was squeezing through the crowds selling copies of the *War Cry*.

Sophie loved the electric exuberance of these sessions and rarely suffered from nerves, unlike a few of the black members of the band who went quite white-faced about now and spent most of their time either drinking too much or throwing up in the back yard, or doing a bit of both. Success had come to the band quite fast, with yet more men in expensive suits coming down to see them. Not that she ever worried about anything like that, anxious only to get up there in front of the band and let it all go. She loved the sheer communion of these sessions when the 'funk was a'flying' and they all came together in the heartaches and jubilations of jazz, hot off the griddle. Before that audience she was someone else again; a spirit that soared and was free.

The band had started one night as an impromptu jam session in the lounge of the Quebec pub just near Custom House. Some wandered along on Thursday nights, sat in, and wandered away never to be seen again. A bastard child of a multi-racial society, you could never be too sure what instrument they would bring either – anything from bongos to kazoos – but just now they had settled into something like a traditional jazz group, even if a bit ragged at times and lumbered with a pianist who liked to play a different tune from anyone else. They were a terribly undisciplined bunch with certain members given a lot to showboating, but it did not matter all that much with jazz – the colourful offspring of the grinding greyness of that winter. But the real jewel of the band was Sophie's voice which alternately growled the blues and shouted rebellious defiance. There was something to cheer everyone in this great new sound.

And then, to a huge roar and much foot-stomping, the band trooped onto the stage, carefully set their pints of beer under the chairs and, without much further ado, Sophie moved straight into *Ain't Misbehaving*, hardly able to make herself heard above the drunken throng who were singing along with her. Fats Waller's song was all the more attractive for the way Sophie handled it, hands banging thighs, then fondling her bosom, making it very clear that she was misbehaving all the time. A rousing rendition of *All The Boys Like The Way I Ride* followed with yet more yelling anarchy from the crowd.

But even in all the rowdy excitement she could hear that the band was not pulling along behind her, rather more interested in fighting amongst themselves for the spotlight. And what the pianist was playing she could not even guess – they only kept him because he was the only one who ever turned up regularly. She had lectured this rabble often enough about playing *as a group* but it was hopeless with the pianist on a cloud of his own or the banjo player and the trumpeter trying to grab and hold the solos. If the trumpeter went on too long the banjo player just barged in – if the banjo player started to work up a bit of a pace on his own the trumpeter just leaned on him, blowing straight into his ear. They were just a bunch of kids really who, when not fighting, might be away with the fairies on some new drug they had got off a ship. Just lately the drummer had taken to biting the clarinettist on the ankle – or else the other bit of nonsense was that they were stuffing bread rolls into the mouth of the trombone during the solo.

As it happened, it all added to the fun for the audience, but that was not quite the point, and matters came to a head in the middle of *You Must Not Get So Nasty 'Cos Your Water's On* when the trumpeter actually put down his instrument and thumped the banjo player on the ear.

The audience enjoyed the ensuing fight almost as much as the jazz. Sophie stepped aside as the banjo player upped and whopped the trumpeter, followed by a great clatter and crash of the drums as the trumpeter leaped into the whirling mêlée. The clarinettist began swinging his instrument around like an avenging knobkerrie and then half the front row of the audience dived in for a rolling, laughing maul, with the banjo player rising up out of the fighting sea clutching his precious instrument.

It took a full five minutes for the fighting to die down and Sophie to restore order. 'Well, we hope you all enjoyed our new little number,' she said amidst laughter. 'We've been rehearsing that one for a long time now.' Then turning to the boys, a few nursing cut lips and swollen eyes: 'So, then, are you lot going to calm down now? Are we going to fight all night or are we going to play us some jazz?'

When the drummer had set up his stand they tried again with Sophie singing Old King Bolden's *Barrelhouse Blues*:

> I got de blues,
> But I'm too damned mean to cry!

The trouble was she was still having to drag the band along with her since they were all too busy sulking to play properly. The trumpeter was more worried about his split lip than blowing his horn and the banjo player was strumming along, half a beat behind everyone else, and with all the verve and spirit of someone waiting for a bus in the rain.

Sophie kept turning to them, trying to jostle them along, but it was next to hopeless. She closed her eyes, trying, but failing, to save the set herself. She was even trying to listen to nothing else but her own voice, wanting to carry it all alone when, just at that moment, she heard a trumpet riff so catastrophically beautiful she lost the very words in her mouth. The rowdy audience went silent too and, still with her eyes closed, she sang another verse with the trumpet following her again, lifting her higher and higher. She turned around to nod her appreciation at the trumpeter but he was just sitting there, fingering the cut lip and with an even longer face than usual. So who was this . . . ?

She looked across the room and saw a black man standing in front of a crowd next to the window, holding his trumpet to his chest and with such a broad smile on his face it was as if he had just been presented with a personal lease on the sun. He gave her a little wave with his hand, putting his trumpet back to his lips and blowing a few more barrelhouse riffs.

'*Obe-e-e-e-e*!' Sophie not so much screamed as yelled at the top of her voice. 'Obadiah Brown, you big black rascal. *O-b-e-e-e-e*.'

She jumped off the stage, wading past the crowded tables, her throat choking up and eyes welling with tears. 'Obe-e-e-e.' The crowd took up the cry. 'Obe-e-e-e. Obe-e-e-e-e.' She half-dragged him up onto the stage where, still in his old army greatcoat, he stood with a smile as broad as the Bristol Channel, his fingers still playing with the trumpet taps.

'Thought you could do with a little help, sister,' he smiled at her.

She hugged him close. 'Ladies and gentlemen, this is Obadiah Brown, the greatest trumpet player and musician ever to set foot on these shores. Where he's been we don't know, but now he's back.'

With that Obe hoisted his trumpet into the air and with a curling wail started a set which not so much danced as exploded. If the Razzy Dazzy Spasm Jazz Band lacked a certain discipline before, it now acquired all the authority of a marching band. It hardly mattered that they had never met before since the rest of the musicians – except the regular trumpeter who packed up his horn and took it home – went skating and dancing around the impeccable authority of a great trumpet as they all went charging into a dizzying series of hollers, stomps and barrelhouse. The banjo player took up his mandolin and even the pianist seemed to get the message, chugging along with more or less the same tune as the rest of them.

What was even more exciting than Obe's new spirit of leadership was the way in which he always gave Sophie's voice the space to move, doing nothing to detract from or impede the great glories of her jazz voice. His best asset was that he could listen and he even gave careful and thoughtful brass embroidery to her own *Prisoner of Love*, which nearly did bring the house down, before he led the band straight into some boogie-woogie, the new bad boy of rag. For all the thunderous music in that trumpet no one would ever have guessed that he had spent the last nine years in a dark, dripping Welsh pit. Indeed he might even have been depping for the great Bunk Johnson in some New Orleans whorehouse.

Obe may well have been out of practice but it was soon apparent to everyone that he could take a tune and tackle it with an audacious waywardness, sometimes holding the lyric steady but then, unexpectedly, making it explode into a shower of falling leaves. But, apart from his imaginative freshness and his willingness to take a risk, his real quality was passion. It was the same passion which had made him a socialist; the same passion that made him cry out against poverty; the same passion that made that trumpet of his soar and sing.

That night almost everyone played and sang their brains out in a set of pounding and increasing excitement for almost three hours. The audience were left fulfilled and helplessly happy, all with the same uniform chant: 'Obe-e-e-e-e. Obe-e-e-e-e.'

That which had been lost had been found again. Obadiah Brown had come home to his people in the Bay.

## CHAPTER FOURTEEN

Deep in the scorching coldness of that night Hassan Shier was sitting on a box in his yard in James Street, slaughtering chickens.

It was not a job that he enjoyed; chickens have souls too. But as he was preparing for the Moslem festive meal of Idal-Fir, the feast of fast-breaking, the next morning he was lumbered with having to put some thirty chickens to sleep in the arms of Allah, and that was that. Tomorrow was the day of the new moon and the end of the holiest month in the Moslem year. It was just 1,300 years ago that their prophet Mohammed had received the first revelation of the Koran from the angel Gabriel in a cave.

Hassan humbly apologized to the chickens, was deeply sorry

for this outrage, but there were lots of hungry mouths to be fed and that was about the long and short of it. It was a pity that they had not been pigs or anything with webbed feet since then they would have been safe, but they were chickens of the feast so they had to go straight into the broiling pot. With contrition welling deep inside he repeated the same line from the Koran, thrusting the knife into their squawking necks and tossing them onto a growing pile in front of him. One actually climbed off the pile and danced around the yard, colliding with a bucket before stiffening and keeling over on its side.

Down in the Mosque the male Moslems were gathering for a night of prayer, many coming from different parts of Wales for this great day of celebration. When they walked in they left their shoes at the entrance, discarded their clothes in the changing room, washed every part of themselves and tied on white prayer robes. Inside Rashed Ali was standing in front of Islamic texts and incense-burners, leading the prayers. '*Seven times a day do I praise your righteous judgements.*' A clock chimed as they stretched out on the thick carpets, humbling mind and soul before the Inscrutable and Autocratic Majesty of Allah. Rashed stood upright and faced Mecca again, the palms of his hands raised to the level of his ears. '*Allah is greater than all else.*' Arms were lowered and the right hand placed over the left arm. '*Glory and praise be to thee, oh Allah. Blessed is thy name and exalted is thy majesty.*' The kneeling body bent forward, hands clamped on knees. '*Glory to my Allah, the exalted.*' He kneeled upright, lips muttering, eyes closed.

At the end of the prayers Rashed and some of the Mosque elders retired to the back room where they normally gathered for *Zawya*: periods for private prayer and the settling of disputes. Here Rashed kissed his fingers before unlocking his own private altar, lighting the incense sticks which smouldered over the holy scrolls. Amidst the scrolls was a pewter chalice; a holy relic, he explained to anyone who asked, brought back for him by a leading hadj from Mecca.

'Tomorrow is a great day for us,' Rashed told the five elders. 'Since we came here we have all gone far and will go yet further. Many have set up businesses and now the Saleh family have news of the possibility of a shop in Swansea. They need a thousand pounds to acquire the premises so I suggest we support them out of our funds.'

General murmurs and noddings of assent from the elders.

'They understand, of course, that they must repay with keen rates of interest, and in so doing, we will become yet stronger. Hassan Shier's son also wants to go to Mecca. Hassan is one of our best workers and the son is now of age so I suggest we fund that journey too. The boy has the qualities of his father and could become another great asset for us. We'll soon need a new slaughterman and he could be the right man for that.'

Though still a young man Rashed had acquired the gravity and mind of the wisest *imam*. The sprinkling of grey hairs conferred the air of someone who gave every decision the greatest thought, and indeed he wrestled with all problems with the same shrewd intelligence, always calculating the better interests of the whole of the Moslem community. When he spoke in his carefully measured tones his judgements had a decisive clarity. He was almost never wrong, and elders bowed to his wise head and strong leadership. Even in the stickiest situations he seemed to have a circle of inviolability around himself and his work.

Few had ever really understood how the wild young ship's chef of yore, with his taste for unsavoury habits, had become one of the most powerful men in the Bay, taking control of and uniting the feuding Moslem groups under one *hadith*: Moslem fundamentalist law. He had just emerged, singlehandedly resolving the constant rows about the positioning of the Mosque, raising funds to build a new one and forging a lively and industrious community with a wide range of prospering business interests.

Only recently he had been leading deputations to an uncomprehending city council who had begun complaining about the Moslem practice of slaughtering sheep in the street during their religious holidays. The controversy had been kept going by the magazine *Animal World*, which had written a steaming editorial about this practice, particularly concerned that there were often children present. Then the Cardiff City Health Committee had let out an angry chirp.

But, as usual, Rashed had shown himself to be a born diplomat and negotiator, actually appearing before the Health Committee and explaining that they had been given permission by the police to slaughter in the streets in their traditional manner. He also explained to them the long and complex rules governing Moslem slaughtering methods. The committee had been unable to reach a decision, but there was a renewed row when the International Cultural Forum, U.K. called on the Moslems to use the new humane killers which had just been introduced in the local abattoir.

Again Rashed appeared before the Health Committee to explain how they believed that the old ways were best. He even took along the old Sheikh Zaid Zunan from the University of Cairo – a visitor to Cardiff – who bored the whole committee into insensibility by actually reading out, in Arabic, all the authorities for slaughter in the Koran. An interpreter then related them in English. The nub of their objection to the new humane methods was that they could never use the same equipment on other animals that had been used to kill pigs or anything with webbed feet, since the equipment would be irredeemably tainted. That meeting took four hours and the committee were then even more confused than they were before. Without admitting they'd done so, they climbed down yet again.

For the Moslem leader life was an endless round of resolving one dispute after another, protecting his people's traditions and customs in an alien country. Just lately he had been negotiating with the city undertakers who would not – or could not – see why they should take the trouble to ensure that the body's head faced Mecca when it was laid to rest. Then there was the recurring problem of post mortems, with the city coroner ordering that all bodies so required – be they Mohammedan or lapsed Baptist – should be cut up after death. That was strictly *haram*, forbidden, and Rashed had real difficulty in getting the coroner to see his point of view. But again, he won through in the end, only to face more trouble with employers who tried to sack a Moslem for taking time off to say his prayers . . . and there was that . . . and there was this . . .

'We've been having the usual trouble with someone stealing shoes from outside the Mosque again, Imam,' said one of the elders. 'It's never more than two or three pairs but it's happening every night now. There are a lot of desperately poor people around these days.'

'We'll bring the shoes in for a while,' said Rashed. 'But leave some old shoes out. If they're only taking two or three pairs it might suggest that they actually need them. We can make it a sort of contribution to the community. There are indeed a lot of desperately poor people around.'

Rashed stood up and kissed his fingers again before relocking his private altar. It was time now to return to the Mosque for another round of prayers in preparation for dawn and this their greatest day.

Icy winds were still blowing in off the sea, with the first shift of dock workers already beginning to file past the policemen at the dock entrance. Down on the Pier Head pontoon the stewards were busy loading the crates of beer onto the paddle steamer. The lamplighter was doing his rounds and, down at the tram stop, a lone woman was crying into her handkerchief. Ships' hooters droned but these were the usual morning sounds of the Bay.

An amplified wailing came drifting out of the back of the Mosque, and was answered by a rising chorus of chants. Rashed's voice wailed again, telling them all of the good news from Mecca which had just come via the BBC. *Eide Mombarik.* A month of fasting from sunrise to sunset had come to an end. *Eide Mombarik.*

*From the earth we have come and to the earth we shall return.* As the time of *rakaat* came to an end everyone poured out of the Mosque and into the street where Rashed held up his hands, his dark eyelids closing as the slaughterman straddled the sheep on the pavement, slitting its jugular. Prayers followed the gush of blood, everyone now shaking one another's hand in a spirit of charity and forgiveness. *Eide Mombarik. Eide Mombarik.*

The children in their pretty, coloured ceremonial costumes were all milling round the street, shouting excitedly. Soon it would be the feast of Eid-Ul-Zua – mountains of curried rice and lakes of pop – and later it would be the great lamb dinner but, just for now, Rashed was calling them all around him. When he was sure they were all in line he let out the wildest yodel and began running down Bute Street, his headdress and white robes flowing behind him. All the children went running after him too, waving their arms joyfully and chanting the good news from Mecca.

In the living room of her home in Custom House Obe and Sophie were *still* sitting in front of the firegrate having a long chat. Perhaps it was something to do with the high charge of adrenalin from the jazz concert but it was beginning to sound like a conversation which would never end.

Obe spoke of those dark days in Cardiff prison, even showing her the scars on his back where they had given him the cat-o'-nine-tails. 'The most vicious thing, sister, the most vicious.' Quite the worst part of being in there, he added, was always being hungry, forever rootling through the garbage cans looking for something to eat. When he came out he just didn't know what to do with himself. He was too ashamed to face any of his old friends in the Bay so he just caught a bus up the Valleys and there he stayed, the blackest miner of them all, down the wettest pit of them all.

'I'm still not sure how I managed to play the trumpet like that tonight. That trumpet hasn't been near my lips for close on ten years. I was even thinking I couldn't play any more. Isolation does strange things to a man but, in a way, it made me very strong. It made me more political and now I know things about how to make the working class strong too. There's things going on in the Valleys which would make you die of shame. You've heard of the man from the Means Test, have you? They turn your house inside out to see if you have anything of value which you can sell before they'll give you any money to eat.'

'We've heard of him all right. But he don't bother us down here too much. There's some around here who'd shoot him and then piss all over him. And they know it.'

For herself Sophie explained how her life had changed, largely because she had finally given up her work as a prostitute. 'It clearly wasn't right, particularly with Effey around and, well, I had a good friend who was murdered, so I took that as a sign that I should pack it in.'

It had been very hard at the beginning and they had even refused her National Assistance. She could have insisted but there was a problem over Effey's birth certificate – or rather lack of it – so she dropped her claim. But she had been lucky enough to get a housekeeping job for a rich shipowner living in a large house down near Pier Head. 'His name is Mr Hamilton and he's a strange, strange one, but I hardly ever see him and he does pay me every week. I have him to thank, really, for not having to go back on the game.'

The Razzy Dazzy Spasm Jazz Band had just happened. One

night there had been three instrumentalists in the pub fooling around, the next there were five and, finally, she just stood in the middle of them and began hollering her head off. They were making a little money out of it and she was now considering giving up her cleaning job since the soapy water was playing murder with her hands. The real problem though was that the hat man was pocketing most of the money himself. 'You know, Obe, it's more difficult getting a good hat man than it is a pianist. Every hat man we've ever had has turned out to be a thief. They just don't like passing over the money.'

Nathan was discussed and, perhaps inevitably, Obe asked if they could go and see him.

'I really don't want to take you to see him, Obe. I go as often as I can but you never know what kind of mood he'll be in. Effey gets on better with him than I do. I really came to love him in a sort of way but it hurts me so much when he sometimes won't speak to me. It might be three or four weeks that he won't say a word. Other times he'll be really chatty and friendly.'

'What happened to him?'

'I wish I knew, Obe. It's been a long time now but I really wish I knew. His wife and children had left him. There was some sort of, ah, trouble with his bishop and he seemed to just dive straight into the gutter. Some nights I'd go out looking for him. I found him on park benches in the middle of winter. Once I just stumbled into this drunken bundle of rags in the rain, and it was him. He just seemed to want to die, you know. Lost his faith, his laughter, everything. I managed to get him on that ship in the end – that was just luck, because it belongs to this Hamilton man – and that's about the only place he will stay. I take food over for him but don't know if he ever eats it. There's some cats there he seems to be fond of so I suppose that's something. Every time I go there I expect to find him dead. It makes me happy if he just looks up at me.'

Sophie, of course, knew far more than she was saying about Nathan's decline; she remembered all too clearly that ruinous night of sex and opium. But it had never become public and she chose to try and forget about it or, at the very least, never to talk about it to anyone. In their different ways both she and Nathan were sharing the same burden of guilt. It had ruined him and she sang about hers. She found singing the blues easy and natural whenever she thought of that man on the windjammer. She knew what she'd done all too well.

'Is he political at all?' Obe asked, sensing an opening. 'I've met defeated men come alive in the Valleys with the new socialism. Men like Nathan will always need a cause, something to live for and, with the chapels dying, it's amazing how just ordinary miners change with a belief, some fire in their belly. Young Nye Bevan can give you a glimpse of heaven, Sophie. He's what all the poor people of the world have been dreaming of. He'll be speaking down at the miners' rally in Cardiff soon. You must come with me to hear him.'

'Oh I don't know about any of that, Obe. I don't know anything about that. I understand a lot of things about men and, in a funny way, I thought I understood Nathan. I loved his warmth. He was just so good, so different. But there's nothing there now, Obe. Nothing at all. He's like some great roaring furnace that's been burned out. I'd really do anything for him – anything at all – but I can't think of anything *to* do.'

'You'll keep trying though, will you?'

She got quite tense at the merest suggestion that she might stop trying. 'Don't you think I haven't tried? Don't you think I haven't always tried? I've tried and I'll keep trying. People like me never give up.'

'Don't get like that. I didn't mean anything. Let's just go and see him. There must be something that can be done.'

'Not with him, there isn't. There's nothing at all.'

'We might come up with something. I owe him too. There's a lot of people that owe him.'

'Sometimes it's me I think he blames. He never says anything but he just looks at me and I see all this accusation in his eyes. I don't know. I don't know anything no more. I worry about him all the time. I've even tried staying away from him but just keep going back again. I want him to be well again, Obe. I just want him to be what he was.'

They both sat silently, with Sophie sniffing and staring at the fire in the grate. 'But there's one thing I want to know, Obe,' she said finally. 'You'll stay with us now, will you? You can't be doing more with those pits – you're black enough as it is.' She began struggling for the right words; to make the right sort of offer. 'There's no man in my life – if you know what I mean – so you can stay here if you want. You're just what the band needs, Obe – a good front man who can keep them in line.

They're all wild men, that lot, can't even agree on the time of day. We could do well with you. You will stay with us, won't you?'

'Well, I'll tell you one thing. I don't want to go down that pit again – that's for sure. I need to be with my people. My black people.'

There was a small cough and they both turned to see a young girl standing in the doorway buttoning up her coat. 'I'm going out,' she said quietly.

'Effey, this is Obe,' said Sophie. 'He might be staying with us for a while.'

She nodded at Obe. 'Can I go now?' she asked her mother, putting on a red French beret given to her by a passing Johnny Onion man. For someone so young she had an eye-catching beauty, with long-lashed black eyes and an unusually long throat. If anything, she would grow up to be far more striking than her mother, Obe decided. He had often wondered who the father was but had never asked.

'Can't you say hello to Obe properly? He's a wonderful trumpeter, you know.'

'*M-u-u-m*! I've got to go. See you later.'

'Where are you going?'

'See you later. 'Bye.'

Groups of celebrating white-robed Moslems were still standing on the corner of James Street when Effey went racing past, one hand hanging onto her beret, swerving over the road in front of a tram and tearing down towards the Pier Head. Just three huge clouds were cruising in over the Bristol Channel like a fleet of visiting battleships. Everywhere, bright sunlight glittered in the frost and patches of ice, trying, but not quite managing, to take the chill off the morning.

At the entrance to the docks Effey waited until the policeman was looking into the back of a furniture van before scampering in behind him. She hurried over the lock gate and down past the Norwegian church where she waved at the old hermit before dashing into the Neale and West fish wharf. She went straight into the office, her nose running from all her haste, banging her small fist down on the desk bell.

'Ah, there you are. You're late this morning. I don't know what's the matter with kids these days.' Bill Huish shuffled out of his office and she followed him along the wharf piled high with columns of wicker fish baskets. 'No one comes on time any more. I had two of my customers late this morning. You can't be late for anything when you're in the fish game. They know that but they don't listen, do they? Even an hour can make the difference between what's fresh and what's not. You don't come back for anything that smells, do you? Stands to reason, don't it?'

He continued grumbling to himself as they came down to a long white marble slab, snotty with glutinous globules of fish innards and lopped-off fins, where two men were still busy gutting and filleting. Seagulls hovered and cawed in a hungry rage, hoping, usually in vain, that the men would toss them a head or two. There were plenty of paying customers for Neale and West fish heads.

'We're not catching anything much good these days. I don't know. Either it's crabs or dogs. Look at them all over there. Four boxes of dogs – good for nothing but manure. You'll have to have some of them today.'

'I told you. I told you before,' Effey said firmly. 'They don't like dogfish. They need proper fish – like them there.'

'I can't give you them. They're mullet. They go at sixpence a stone.'

'Mr Huish,' she said, taking him by the hand. 'Just give me six of them and that's all I'll need. You've got plenty. Go on. I'll be your friend for ever then.'

'Don't come here with all that,' he said, pulling his huge large hand out of hers as if it had suddenly become hot. 'I'm not taking any blackmail from you. That was your mother, that was. All big eyes and no do. Here.' He took a sheet of newspaper from under the slab and bent down, grabbing four of the silvery mullet by the bellies and slapping them down on it.

'Six, I said, Mr Huish. I need six.'

'You've got four here.'

'I can see that. I can count. But I need six.'

With groans and bitter recriminations he picked up another two fish and added them to the pile. 'Now go on and git,' he exclaimed. 'I've got a business to run, not a charity. That was always my trouble. Too soft by half. I don't want you coming back, do you hear? This is the last time. Go and find some other old fool to rob. There's no fool like an old fool, is there?'

She took the package, standing up on her toes and beckoning him to come near, as if about to tell him a secret. When his face was close enough she whispered, 'See you tomorrow, Mr Huish,' and planted a kiss on his cheek.

He jerked his head away, rubbing his cheek as if it had become fouled for ever. 'Go on. Go and find someone else to bleed dry,' he shouted at her as she ran back past the Norwegian church. 'Far too soft all my life I've been. What's going to happen to me in the workhouse, eh? I bet I'll get no one taking me fish when I'm in the workhouse.'

The broken hulk of *The Solomon* looked beautiful, even mystical that morning, huddled at her moorings in the corner of the glittering waters of the dock. The slimy, fungoid grass on the deck and the barnacled hull was covered with a thick layer of hoar frost which sparkled in the sun. Patches of the frost had melted but whole areas of the deck twinkled as if dusted with powdered glass. The yardarms were incandescent too and even the dirty glass of the portholes seemed to be blazing with yellow fire, making the ship look like some magical craft which had survived and even triumphed over long voyages to distant shores inhabited by ferocious monsters.

The ship's very strangeness was enhanced by the troop of black cats with huge green eyes which appeared from everywhere when they heard Effey's call from down the quay. They emerged silently, about a dozen of them, black on silver, from behind the broken mizzen and abandoned boxes, bounding up through the hatches and jumping down from the bridge, all moving around on the deck, their watchful eyes locked on the little girl who had come to feed them.

They circled closer around her as she skipped off the gangplank and jumped onto the deck. She bent to smooth one of them and two others bayed at her newspaper package whose very smell kept them circling around her with barely-concealed impatience.

Down in the galley she took a knife and sliced up two of the fish into fat cutlets, just throwing them behind her onto the floor, where each of the cats picked one up and ran off to some safe place where, unmolested by the others, they could eat their fresh, lovely breakfast in peace. The only one who behaved properly was the eldest, with white socks, who waited for the others to be fed before accepting her own bit – always the largest – which she ate on the spot. Effey put the rest of the fish in a locker and went down to the ward room where Nathan was sitting, hands on the circular oak table, looking out of an open porthole.

'I got some good fish for them today,' she said.

'You make too much fuss of those cats,' he replied. 'They're growing fat. It's not good for cats to eat too much. They get lazy and don't chase after the rats. The rats always get cheeky after the cats have been fed. It's as well for cats to be hungry sometimes. Keeps them on their toes.'

Effey unbuttoned her coat and sat next to him, smiling and hunching her shoulders as if in anticipation of some great fun. She always liked it when he talked, but when he said nothing much at all, that was all right too. Sometimes he seemed to be suffering too much to talk but she understood that silence was also a sort of talk; she was just happy to spend some time with her friend. Some days he bought her a Lucky Bag or some treacle toffee and they even went for walks around the dock, often saying nothing. She accepted his moods and did not feel the need to burden him with questions – as other older, more inquisitive people might – content to let him say whatever was on his mind.

'It was a bitter cold night last night,' he went on. 'Probably the coldest night of the year. But I never understand how the ship keeps so warm. I kept having to take off some blankets and still I kept sweating. It's tea that keeps you warm, you know. You drink tea, do you, Effey?'

'Nuh. Can't stand it.'

'You should. It keeps bacteria down too. Everything's all right as long as you keep warm inside. I got hold of a case of tea the other day. Indian tea it was. You can take some of it if you want. It's not easy to get hold of tea, but I've got mates, you know, lots of good mates. They give me tea to keep me warm.'

'Think Mam may be coming to see you today. She's got some new friend with her. He's black. Obe, I think she said his name was.'

'Obe? Obadiah Brown. Some sort of trumpeter, is he?'

'Mmm. She did say something about a trumpet.'

His wandering, abstracted manner changed almost immediately and he half stood up before sitting down again. 'Go home and tell them I'm not receiving visitors today. Tell them that, will you? Tell them I'm too tired for any of that. I don't need any visitors. They all make me so tired.' He pulled his fingertips tightly down his cheeks, his voice getting harsher, more whining. 'That Father O'Reilly keeps coming over here too. How can I get any rest when I keep getting visitors all the time? I've things to do. Important things.'

'We could always go for a walk.'

'Yes, let's go for a walk. No, you just tell them I don't want to see anyone today. Tell them I'm too tired, can't take all this strain. That Father O'Reilly came here yesterday, and do you know what he told me about? History. He likes to give me history lessons and it makes my head hurt something terrible. What do I need to know about history? I thought he'd never shut up, but he had brought some drink over and he just went on and on.'

Effey stood up and walked over to the porthole. 'It's too late for our walk. They're coming now. They're over there by the cranes.'

'How many?'

'Two. I said. Mam and that black man.'

'Let's go out. I can't see them. No, it's too late for that. Tell them I'm asleep. I'm that tired with all these things I've got to do. Why can't people just leave me alone? Why do they want to keep bothering me all the time?'

'I'll tell them you're asleep then.'

'Yes. No. Oh, I don't know.' He dropped his head into his hands, now using his hams to rub around his baldness. 'All their questions. History, questions, words. What do I want to know about history for? I don't want to know about the future, still less the past.'

He heard Sophie's voice calling out his name from above deck. It was almost as if she was shouting out some kind of warning. For a second, Effey thought that he really was going to be sick.

'I'm going to bed. Tell them I'm fast asleep in my bed and I can't be disturbed for anyone.'

He stood up and hurried out of the ward room, disappearing down a hatch, just as Sophie and Obe came in. 'Oh, you're here, are you?' Sophie said looking around her. She was wearing a scarlet cloak and a broad felt hat with a shallow crown. 'Where's his nibs?'

'He said he was tired and had to go to bed.'

'But he sleeps up *here*. That's where he sleeps. There. Just look at it, Obe. Have you ever seen such a mess? And everywhere just stinks of cats' piss.'

'They don't stink, Mam,' Effey objected. 'They're lovely, those cats.'

More cats began padding quietly around them, as if in the hope of another meal. Obe picked one of them up but it squealed and wriggled so he let it fall again.

'Not very friendly either,' Sophie said with clear distaste. 'They're all as daft as brushes these cats. You see that, Obe, they've all got six toes from some kind of inbreeding. The original ship's cat had six toes and now they've all got them. Pretty soon every cat in Wales is going to have six toes.'

Obe stayed standing at the door as she sat down at the table, fanning the smell away with her hand. 'So is he coming in to see us, or what?' she asked Effey.

'I dunno. You know how he gets. He just said he was tired and off he went.'

'But off where?

'I dunno. Off somewhere.'

'You're getting as bad as he is,' she told her daughter with a glare. 'You're not going to go dotty like him, are you?'

'He's not dotty, Mam. I told you. I told you he was just feeling tired.'

'Let's leave him,' said Obe, starting to feel highly uncomfortable, aware perhaps that the daughter understood Nathan better than the mother. 'We can always come back another time.'

'It's too early in the day, Obe,' said Sophie, lifting her hands. 'He's fine when he's got a drink inside him. Some days you just can't shut him up when he's had a drink. Oh, I just don't know anything.' She began to get quite miserable. 'It's like dealing with some delinquent just out of Borstal. I sometimes think that man is going to be the death of me.'

Way down, deep in the bowels of the ship, Nathan was sitting in the darkness of the locker room. Something scuttled past his ankles before disappearing between some duckboards where it landed with a soft splash. But he took no notice, drawing his coat collar up around his neck and shivering a little.

Occasionally there were the creaking sounds of the rotting timbers or the distant drone of some incoming freighter. But most of the time there was just silence and the merciful darkness. This darkness was his closest friend since, deep in its intimate secrecy, he really did feel that he had no future, no past, nor indeed any present. Just behind him rusty irons were fastened on the bulkheads since this was the locker room where wayward scrubbers and swabbers were once clapped in irons and put on bread and water for misbehaving.

Here, in the darkness, he could also listen to the dislocated sounds of his own madness. It might be the pained cry of birds who had lost their young or the prolonged shrieks of people being roasted in a great fire. But, just now, his mind became crowded with images of a busy street and he was running down it, shoving people out of the way, since he had been told that his two boys were around somewhere and they were in danger.

He seemed to be running for a long time but could not find them anywhere, backtracking up the pavement and calling out their names again and again. But he did finally bump into Elizabeth who was crying and, later, Sophie, who offered him a drink. But he refused it with a pious wave of his hand. He did not drink. He was a good father who was just concerned about the safety of his boys.

'Oh no, no, no,' the people in the crowded street all shouted back at him, making him start snivelling. 'You were such a good father you deserted your lovely boys and fell in love with the drink. You left your lovely wife and climbed into bed with a whore. You sinned and gambled with your immortal soul. And you lost.'

# CHAPTER FIFTEEN

Hamilton strolled purposefully into the Exchange in Mountstuart Square where he spent ten minutes studying the shipping news. It was uniformly bad. There were barely a dozen ships due to sail from Cardiff that week and all of them had been declared 'partially empty'. More often than not this phrase meant 'totally empty' but the ships sailed regardless, in the hope of picking up other loads in distant, more prosperous parts.

The Oriel Steam Navigation Company now had five ships berthed in Cardiff, immobile; Hamilton could not see the point of sending them anywhere just on a whim. The coal depots throughout the world, which once formed their stock-in-trade, had turned into monuments now that Poland had begun to swamp the market with cheap coal and all the French mines had fully recovered after being closed down in the war. And the Welsh miners had done themselves no favours by strike after strike, cutting themselves out of what was left of the market. Even when they took a cut in pay – day men dropping from £1 a shift to 8s 9½d – it was useless. As David Lloyd George had warned a long time ago, coal had turned traitor.

Hamilton took out a pair of half-moon spectacles and cleaned them with a handkerchief. Time seemed to have made little difference to his solid, mahogany features – the skin was still darkly smooth, the neck still tightly muscled, the hair still an oily black with not even a hint of grey. He still dressed in formal Victorian clothes as if he had just stepped out of a tailor's window. None of the other shippers bothered much with him either; they were content to wrestle with their own problems. Oriel was one of the few to have survived the slump, due in no small part to Hamilton's foresight in refitting his ships as oil-burners years ago. But trends were moving fast against general freight, too, and it was a time of cautious contracts, keeping all costs to a minimum and, where possible, hiring cheap Asian labour.

Right now – for those who could see it – a new and potentially profitable market was opening up in munitions. Through his German contacts, Hamilton had been told to expand his fleet and keep them in readiness for the new market. What he was looking at closely, that morning in the Exchange, were the lame old lines, tottering on the verge of bankruptcy, which he could strip and absorb into his own line. He took out a notebook and made a few notes. The thin were indeed getting thinner. Only William Tatem's line had somehow managed to stay as fit and lithe as Oriel.

The Tatem line was just right for Hamilton and he had been stalking it for some time, watching its shipping movements, studying its company reports, probing for weaknesses in its solvency, but no such weaknesses had yet become apparent. Tatem did not seem to believe in disposals either and, so far anyway, his ships seemed to be reasonably busy, scraping a living as general tramps around the seaboard of America. Another three of them were on the move again, Hamilton noticed – all carrying cotton out of New Orleans to Australia. He would have to look again at that run. Almost everything William Tatem did he looked at again.

With the exception of three brokers standing near to the door of the coffee shop discussing likely winners at that afternoon's meeting at Newmarket, the Floor was deserted. The towering, polished emptiness of the vaulted room amplified their argumentative chatter – 'Come, come, Willie, you couldn't pick your own nose'. But, that apart, there was just the ticking of the great clock telling of the long hours since the commercial power and glory of South Wales had vanished for ever.

Hamilton was studying Lloyd's List when he heard footsteps behind him. It was Partington, bringing intelligence from the office.

'Just one interesting call, Mr Hamilton,' said the dapper clerk. 'I've had a man on the line this morning. Captain Gustaf Erikson. He's a Swedish gentleman and, or so he says, he's the only man in the world still buying windjammers. He's rung asking if, by any chance, *The Solomon* might be for sale.'

Hamilton looked around cautiously. 'Did he mention a figure?' he asked in a quiet voice.

'I did ask him what he had in mind but he wouldn't come out with it directly. He kept insisting that he'd heard that it was in a very bad condition and that it would cost a lot to make it shipshape.'

'He wants it for nothing?'

'He didn't say as much but I got the impression he had no more than the very smallest pile of pound notes in mind.'

'Not interested,' Hamilton snapped, his eyes watching the clock. 'If he rings again see if you can get a figure out of him but, unless it's a very large sum of money indeed, I am not interested. I am getting so very tired of this gin-and-aspirin age in which everyone is wandering around looking for something for nothing.'

'He did say that he would ring again.'

'See if you can get him to come up with a figure. I'm curious to know what that old hulk might be worth. But first make it clear that we are not interested. That might just polish up his offer. One day, I might even get it restored myself. Also, it might tempt Edward Gurney back. I just cannot understand how someone can disappear so completely.'

Partington said nothing.

'I might even go up myself this time. He has got to be somewhere and London is still the most likely place. You would think he would get in touch with his mother. How can a son be a son and not get in touch with his own mother? A postcard at the very least.'

Partington wondered when his boss had last managed to send a postcard to anyone – let alone his mother. His employer never spoke of his parents. 'Perhaps he knows we'd be on to him then,' he ventured.

'None of it makes any sense. There was only one thing that ever motivated Edward Gurney and that was money. He must know that Oriel is one of the few solvent companies left in the land so why has he not come back to claim it? Why is he not also interested in the ship?' He lifted a manicured finger and tapped a page of Lloyd's List, as if looking for flaws in the paper. 'It can only mean that he is in prison somewhere. Why did we not think of that before?'

'Well, we did.'

'Yes, but not in this country or our people would have found him. He must be languishing in Europe somewhere. Telegraph Schnell in Berlin and try Flambert in Paris. Get them to check on their prison lists.'

'Do you really think it'll come to anything, Mr Hamilton?' There was a slight note of weariness in his voice. 'A man like Mr Edward could be just about anywhere. He's one of life's adventurers, someone who'll turn up when you least expect him.'

'That man has got something I want and I do not like sitting around until *he* decides that *he* is going to turn up. That is extremely bad practice. It means that, when he does come, he will do so on his own pre-planned terms. That man has become an itch I cannot scratch. I will never rest until I have located him.'

'I'll contact Berlin and Paris.'

Hamilton raised his head in a slightly abstracted position. 'You will remember that we have three of the Party coming down tomorrow to talk about the munitions contracts. Have you booked those rooms in the Angel?'

'Three rooms, as you asked.'

'They are taking a lot of interest in South Wales just now, particularly with all that pestiferous communist activity in the Valleys. The Reds organize in public, but we have been doing so much better organizing in private. These are exciting times, Partington. Everywhere there are the shadows of impending conflict, with the whole of the land locked in the politics of the boxing booth. World Jewry is on the rise and I just know that soon we are going to seize the time and enter that period of social purity we have all been dreaming of for so long. Yes, exciting times. And they would become very exciting indeed for us if only we could find young Gurney. A very great deal would become possible then.'

Sophie whipped through the last verse of *I'm Wild About That Thing* and collapsed on a stool. She could have murdered a pint or two of cider. The sweat had made her dress stick to her back and her throat was feeling none too clever either. It would not have been so bad if the room was not so small and smoky and they could let some air in through the windows. But it was so cold outside that the freezing blasts of air threatened to turn them all into icicles. She hoped that they were not going to carry on for much longer. The real trouble was that she could not relax her voice, even when rehearsing. She always had to give those songs all she had. She knew no other way.

The band had been rehearsing for two hours. She heard Obe explaining that, when it came to the middle eight, he wanted them to stay quiet while Sophie sang so that he could play his horn softly and embroider her voice. But the band in general and Errol Martin in particular did not quite see it like that. Errol, the very large Jamaican banjoist who looked as if he had been constructed out of big, black balloons, thought that he should pluck his way through the middle eight and that Obe should stay quiet. So they were locked in argument again with voices rising and forefingers poking the air.

Sophie sighed. The band had undeniably improved since Obe had joined them but he had such a strong personality he always wanted it his way. Yes, his way was often the best; he had such a natural feeling, particularly for the quiet desperation of the blues, but all this incessant niggling was not doing the band much good at all. The arguments upset Obe as well and she noticed that he sometimes got flustered and was unable to play properly. But there was an even deeper problem between Obe and a few of the band which he did not seem able

– or want – to see: they were from separate islands in the West Indies.

'All right, we'll do it your way, then we'll do it my way,' Obe said, his black face going quite taut with anger. 'Than we'll let Sophie decide how she wants it.'

'No, no, no,' Sophie intervened, spotting one deep trench of trouble ahead. 'Let's just do it the way we all want it. We'll just let it fly.'

'You can't just let it fly, sister,' Obe snapped back sharply. 'There's times to fly and times to stay grounded. We need that natural break in the middle. We don't need them all flying around in that part. Perhaps it would be better if you just took it on your own.'

'I don't need none of this,' Errol kept repeating theatrically, taking his banjo from his lap and putting it down on the floor between his feet. 'I don't need none of this.'

'Me neither,' said Peter Paas the pianist, closing his piano with a thump. 'All this bother just gives me a headache.'

Sophie's eyes flashed over the quarrelling group. Only Smokey Joe, the drummer, seemed unaffected by all the tensions, sitting there with his pork-pie hat perched on the back of his head, cigarette dangling from his mouth, content to bang on – or keep quiet – in whatever manner he was told. Despite his name Smokey was the only white member of the group.

'Right then,' said Sophie swivelling around on her stool. 'Let's take it again from the top and I'll just take the middle on my own. Then you'll all come in at the end of the break.'

'But we'll come in soft,' Obe added, his fingers fiddling agitatedly with his taps. 'You see, the whole mood of the song changes here. See, she starts dirty and the words get more soulful after the middle part. You just can't busk it here. The whole song changes.'

'I can't take none of this,' Errol decided, putting his banjo into its case. 'I joined this band for some fun, not to be ordered around by him.'

'Me neither,' said the pianist, picking up his coat. 'I'm off home.'

'Right, we'll break for the day,' said Sophie. 'Let's meet for a couple of hours before the gig tomorrow.'

'Not me,' said Errol walking out. 'Find yourself another banjo.'

Sophie said nothing, still on her stool and staring at the floor as the rest of the group packed up and walked out, their complaints still echoing in the emptiness of the stairwell. 'I need a drink,' she told Obe. 'Take me down to Ma's and we'll have a drink.'

'Just what's the matter with them?' Obe asked her. 'We're trying to do a little soft blues and they think everything is some New Orleans marching song.'

'It's not that, Obe. It's not that.'

'What is it then? Is it me or what?'

'It's not you, Obe. It's your island. It's Barbados. That's what this is all about.' She stared at him hard. Sometimes he could be so sensitive and other times you needed to take a sledgehammer to him. She had better spell it out. 'Errol and Peter are from Jamaica. You're from Barbados. That's what this is all about.'

'I don't get it. We're all black, ain't we?'

'There's been big changes around here since you went away, Obe. How can I put it? Oh, I don't know. It's all so stupid.'

'Just put it any way you can.'

'The Moslems are all united under Rashed Ali and they're doing well. They don't bother with no one. The Chinese have got their laundry and they don't bother no one. The Sikhs have got their own temple outside the Bay and they're settled. The Irish have got their church and will talk to anyone – you know how they are. But there's this problem with the West Indians and it's got worse over the years.'

'What problem's that?'

'Obe, they don't get on with anyone else and they can't even get on with one another. The old ones aren't so bad but the young ones stay grouped around their islands. *You* are from Barbados. *You* are from Jamaica. *You* are from St Kitts . . . see what I mean? They've tried setting up clubs but they've always broken up over this stupidity. I could see it coming a mile off with Errol and Peter an' I just hoped it would go away but it didn't. That's what this is all about.'

Obe closed his eyes and mouthed some silent curse. 'So they don't get on with anyone else and they don't get on with one another?'

'That's it, Obe. That's just it. Errol nor Peter will take anything from you 'cos you're from the wrong island.'

He was silent for a moment, examining his trumpet closely. 'Better I left the band, sister?' he asked quietly. 'Is that what you're trying to tell me?'

'No, no, no.' She jumped up off her stool, putting her hand on his shoulder and squeezing it tight. 'I'm just trying to tell you about the way things are around here. But, you see, we might have to do it another way now. You taught me about jazz, Obe. You were the one who first found this voice inside my mouth. I want us to stay together. I really do. But we might have to start thinking about a new band.'

'A white band?'

'No. Any old colour band. But we can't go having all this island stuff. Aggravation is all right for jazz but there's a point where it gets too much.'

'Colour, colour. Everyone is into it and here my own people are the worst of the lot. I'm going to see those two and have a word with them.'

'It's no use, Obe. It's all gone too far. This West Indian thing just gets worse. They've got nothing to rally their black arses around. I've never been anything much for the Church or any stuff like that but they do keep the races together – and apart. They give them an identity that they can be proud of. There's no real race thing around here any longer. They're not knocking one another around like in the old days an' they keep to themselves. But, you know, the West Indians have got this problem and I don't know what they're going to do about it.'

'Well I'm going to do something about it, sister. Jazz should bring us together. That's what socialism is all about too. Brothers united shoulder to shoulder and fighting the capitalists who are grinding our noses into the dust.'

'I don't know nothing about all that, Obe.'

'Well I do, sister. We'll rally those black arses around something or other. An' I don't want no new band either. Ah want *this* band.'

'Oh come on. Let's go to Ma's and rally our black arses around a drink.'

After his return Obe lost no time in getting out and about trying to make contact with his people. He found them scattered through different parts of the Bay, some making their home in a small terrace near the Greek Orthodox church, others down in James Street next to Little Madrid, while the bulk of them had taken over most of the large but crumbling houses in Loudoun Square.

Obe had no family on his original journey from Barbados and neither had he any particular friends from the old days. But they were all delighted to see him back nonetheless, especially old Charlie Boden, with whom he spent a joyful hour largely reminiscing about life in the sugar cane outside Bridgetown. Old Charlie had confirmed that they were all indeed having a tough time in Cardiff, unable to get work in the Depression and dependent on extremely small handouts from the Public Assistance. But the colour of their skins was a large drawback as well, Charlie added – any colour of any skin if it was not Welsh white. The biggest employer of labour in the city was the council yet they had no black bus conductors, park keepers or even street cleaners. Obe asked if it was true that the West Indians did not get on with one another either.

'It ain't no good, Obe. It ain't no good at all. Whenever two of us do meet there's three points of view. We've gone and got ourselves good and lost in this here city. Good and lost. I hear from American seamen that black folks are doing so much better in North America. They know when to fight and when to run. But here we don't know when to fight nor when to run. We don't seem able to do nothing.'

Such news made Obe feel extremely sad. No one knew better than he that he had got off to a very poor start by being locked up for trying to steal a box of oranges. But at least he had done *something*, which is more than a lot of them had around here – unless you counted pointless quarrelling as doing something. It was some sense of national unity which they lacked, he guessed; a sense of a common identity. All he really knew for certain was that he had to find some way of bringing them together. But what?

He continued his travels, stopping to talk to the prostitutes who were still gathering around the Custom House. Many recognized him from his turbulent stay in St Stephen's ten years earlier. Others already knew of his new residency with the Razzy Dazzy Spasm Jazz Band with Sophie, no longer, alas, out on the corners with them. He remembered a lot of the girls too, hugging, with an especial affection, Marie the Stump who, despite her wooden leg, still seemed to be making a living of sorts, boasting that she had three regular clients all of whom had one leg too.

But there were more than a few of his Barbadian cousins standing out on those corners too, he noticed – a few who had left Barbados as mere girls and one who slipped quickly away pretending not to recognize him. So she had made her long journey full of hope just for this. This!

The Domino Club in Loudoun Square was a grubby, dispirited corrugated-iron shed and many of the younger blacks were busy propping up the walls and doorways with their shoulders, barely moving aside when Obe tried to walk in. The inside was almost as bad as the outside, with tatty, torn curtains punching out most of the daylight and old men sitting around the rickety tables and chairs, just staring into space. He crossed the room, picking up a few of the dominoes scattered on one of the tables. 'Yuh can't do that,' said one of the old-timers. 'There's a game starting in here soon. Which island yuh from anyway?'

'The Island of Mars,' Obe snapped, putting down the dominoes with a sharp bang and shouldering his way out of the door. Just what was going on? Were all those old jokes true? He felt a bright flare of indigestion and a dog came out in front of him, crouching low and growling with a quiet fury. He still remembered that day they had sailed out of Bridgetown to start a new life . . . the sunshine, the drifting smell of cloves, the way hope sang in your very gut and made you stupidly happy.

But, ever since that day, all his brothers and sisters seemed to get progressively more lost; shipwrecked in an alien land, at odds with everyone including themselves. The dog continued to menace him so he lashed out with his foot and was lucky enough to connect with a satisfying thud making the dog yelp with pain.

Just by the Glamorganshire Canal, this cold, bright day, he stopped to watch a group of about twenty women standing on the canal bank throwing bread into the water. Many wore shawls; some had only sackcloth pinafores and others were clearly tinkers. Of different coloured skins, they stood silently gazing at the bread floating on the still glazed water with ravenous seagulls hovering over their heads, their wings squeaking loudly and rhythmically, anxious to get at the bread when the women had left. The picture of the women and the widening circle of bread was so haunting that Obe had to remain standing on the iron bridge, wondering what they were up to. They were throwing yet more bread on the water when he saw that a sobbing woman was talking to a policeman who was taking notes. Obe moved closer to them.

'I was plaiting her hair, you know, same as I did every morning. I was cooking beans on the fire, said to her to come back soon. It was my wee boy who came back, saying she had fallen into the water. Oh my poor gal. I threw meself against the wall. I bashed the backs of my hands with rocks. I went home and swallowed hot ashes from the fire. I drowned on my tears when I see her lovely face. Oh my poor gal. Did you ever have wee ones, officer?

'The women are looking for her now, you see. They are looking for her soul with that bread. I don't want to live any more. Don't want to live. I'm just a wrecked person now – I'd give anything to be lying on the floor of that canal if she could be up here again, playing around with the other babies. I'll be having no more, officer. I'll stab my belly with a knife if I think I'm going to have any more.'

Obe walked on feeling infinitely more sad. It was sometimes useful to learn that suffering was not just the West Indian prerogative. Others were suffering too and showing the same strange responses.

Apart from the thin trickle of traffic going up and down Bute Street – once the busiest street in the land – he decided that the Bay had not changed in any great particular. Pigtailed Chinese were still hurrying in and out of the laundry and, down the warm, steam-heated corridors; there were still sudden, surprising aspects of old men in vests sitting around playing mahjong. The pubs and shebeens were still doing some sort of trade while the boarding houses seemed astonishingly full.

But it was the new Mosque that next caught Obe's inquisitive stare. From the doorway he stood peering down the small corridor into the empty, carpeted prayer room then walked around to the rear where, through a barred window, he saw a man sitting silently in front of a small altar. There was a movement behind him; it was Rashed, who looked him up and down with barely concealed distaste, as if asking what on earth a black West Indian could possibly want in a Moslem mosque.

'My name's Obadiah Brown,' Obe explained, marshalling his broadest smile. 'I've been out of the city for a few years and now I'm just going around saying "Hello" here and there.'

'Ah yes, I remember now. You're some kind of trumpeter, aren't you?' Rashed asked, his iciness melting somewhat. 'Come in. Better take your shoes off. I might be able to find you a cup of tea. You do drink tea, do you?'

'Ah drink anything, me.'

Rashed went out into the kitchen as Obe took a chair, slightly embarrassed by the holes in his stockings and trying to stuff his feet under the seat. But he soon lost his uneasiness as he looked about him, noticing that there was clearly no shortage of money here. The Domino Club this was not. The Arabic carpeting was thick and the curtains were made of green silk. Even the incense seemed to add to the air of expensive opulence. His eye was caught by the magnificent small altar, containing some bright lettered scrolls and a leaden cup. He stared at the cup hard, drawn to it in a curious way because it was so simple, even battered, at odds with the elaborate gold lettering of the surrounding scrolls. There was something about the cup that was, ah, almost sacramental; its simplicity seemed to have a beauty all of its own and, in some forceful but incoherent way, Obe wanted to own it. There was still something of the impulsive thief in him but the real problem was that he was never attracted to anything of value. Images of oranges danced in his mind.

'What sort of cup is that?' Obe asked when Rashed returned with the tea tray.

'They all ask about that. It's nothing much – just a holy relic brought back from Mecca,' Rashed said, putting down the tray and locking up the altar.

'I couldn't hold it, could I?'

'I use it to help my private prayers,' Rashed replied evenly, slipping the key into his pocket. 'We Moslems like relics. You're a Christian, are you, Mr Brown?'

'Sort of, I s'pose. If I'm anything at all I'm a Christian. Back home we were brought up in the Pentecostalist Church.'

'There's something of an affinity between Moslems and Christians,' Rashed explained, pouring a cup of sweet tea into a distressingly tiny cup and handing it to Obe. 'We make much of our differences – too much really – but your Jesus is mentioned thirty-five times in the Koran under a number of names, including that of Messenger of God and the Messiah. The Koran says, "They did not kill him, nor did they crucify him but they thought that they did". I often think about that. If they thought they did it then they clearly did do it. An act of thought is an act of will. Jesus was one of the great, if mortal, prophets – a forerunner of the true son of God Mohammed.'

Obe listened to this tiny sermon with an interested look in his eyes but he had no time for any such religious claptrap. It was still the opium of the masses – be they Christian, Mohammedan or Buddhist. He would have happily signed a decree banishing the lot. He gazed down at the tea – he didn't think much of that either. There was only one real religion and that had just begun moving with great transforming force among the men of the Valleys.

'Have you ever considered becoming a Moslem?' Rashed asked.

'Never.'

'That's a great pity. A very great pity. We are all, after all, African brothers who came here by different circular routes. The West Indians are not doing too well just now, Mr Brown.'

'So I've been seeing. So I've been seeing.'

'Whereas we Moslems have done very well indeed. There's been the light of Allah on our shoulders for some years now. I've often thought that the West Indians could do with some sort of light too. Allah gives much that's good and takes away a lot that is bad.'

'We'll sort out something one day p'raps,' Obe said, trying to suppress a bright burst of laughter. The light of Allah was almost the very last thing that his poor, beleaguered people needed. 'But, tell me, what do you know about those women throwing bread on the waters of the canal?'

'They're doing that again, are they? I'm afraid some of our women have been doing it too and I wish it would stop. It's just witch doctor stuff. I sometimes wonder where it will all end.'

Even as Rashed continued complaining about other such witch doctor habits Obe's mind felt drawn again by that leaden cup and his eyes gazed again at the locked doors of the altar. The daylight was striking on the Arabic gold lettering, making the incomprehensible words shimmer as if in reflected fire. On no evidence, he guessed that the cup was somehow at the heart of Moslem prosperity in the Bay and he wanted it for his own people. Obadiah Brown wanted some of that witch doctor in the cup.

But, even as he examined those locked doors, his mind drifted back all those years to when he had last looked at something – a box of oranges – which he did not own but wanted anyway. He had been overcome with just the same feeling that he was nursing in his chest now and he remembered all too well what had happened after that – a very long time indeed in the pokey. No, Obadiah Brown did not want to eat six months of skelly all over again.

'Exactly where are you staying then?' Rashed asked, holding his tea to his mouth.

'Sophie James, an old friend down near Custom House.'

Rashed's calm and dignified composure seemed to crumble at the mention of her name and he quickly put the cup down, covering up his shakiness with a bout of coughing. 'Yes, I know her. And how is that daughter of hers, Effey?'

'Effey's just fine. A great little kid.'

'You couldn't bring her around to see me some time, could you, Mr Brown?'

'S'pose I could. Don't see it as much of a problem. She flies around the docks all the time. You've probably seen her often enough.'

'Yes, but, you know, I don't get on with Sophie now. We used to be friends, but I'm keenly interested in her daughter. Bring her down for some tea some time, would you? Help me to get to know her.'

'You don't want me to tell Sophie about it, I take it.'

'No, that would be most unfortunate. What's happened has happened but I would very much like to talk to the daughter. I might be of some help to her.'

'Effey isn't the kind of girl who needs much help,' Obe laughed, sensing that perhaps Rashed was looking for another convert. 'That girl will manage whatever she decides to do. She's very like her mother.'

'Well, remember the offer anyway. I really could be a lot of help to that little girl if she'd let me. But I wouldn't want Sophie to know, of course.'

'Of course.'

In the end Obe had practically to run out of the Mosque to escape Rashed's mounting insistence on meeting Effey. He could never remember a man of such dignity losing his composure so fast. When he got home, he asked Sophie about him.

'You've been down there, have you?' she laughed. 'Whatever did you want to do that for?'

'He seemed very keen on getting to know Effey.'

'Ah well, there's a simple reason for that. The Moslem fool thinks that Effey is his.'

'And is she?'

Sophie laughed again. 'No. Effey's mine. There's no man and that's the end of the story. I gave up men years ago. My best friend was murdered by a man and one day I just gave up the game vowing that no man was going to get between my legs ever again. Not even if I was starving. Stupid as it sounds there's only one man I've ever really been interested in and he's gone off his head in that windjammer. That's really stupid, isn't it?'

'That's stupid all right. So, sister, how do you manage for, you know, that?'

'What?'

'You know, that.'

'I'd better tell you 'cos you're going to find out sooner or later. There's nothing regular, but when I get screaming drunk an' need some bodily affection, I find myself a woman.'

'Sister!' Obe was quite shocked.

'It's nothing, Obe. Just some affection, that's all I do it for. It's got that I can't even be near another man particularly if they're getting horny so I find myself a woman. It's only a touch thing, that's all. That's all women do, you know. Gentle and no complications. Men and me are nothing and, while we're on the subject, I don't want Effey seeing that Rashed again neither. Not never, I don't. He's not getting that girl on his prayer mat. You'll make sure of that, won't you, Obe?'

'Rashed is a rich, powerful man, sister. I've met men like him before. They're always plotting, working things out. Men like him usually get their way.'

'Not with me he won't.' It was Sophie's turn to start losing her composure. 'He may be rich and powerful but I've got a rich, powerful punch. If I ever see Effey in that Mosque I'll burn the place down, I will. I'll just burn the bloody place down. So please, Obe, keep the girl away from him, because if he starts trying to convert her, I really don't know what I'll do.'

'Tell me about one thing, sister. He's got some cup in there on his little altar. You heard anything about that?'

'Did he tell you it was brought back from Mecca by some holy man?'

'Something like that.'

'There's been some talk about it an' I remember someone saying he found it on some corporation rubbish heap. He even talks to the thing, but it's just a bit of Moslem voodoo. That's the trouble with any religion, isn't it? It's all just bloody voodoo.'

There was something deep in the spirit of that crumbling ship that Nathan found very comforting, and he rarely ventured out of it, particularly during daylight. He still busied himself with little jobs, still dreamed of putting the ship right himself one day, but such work as he did was just token work. The shelf he had been repairing all day did not look a lot better when he had finished it. But come the night he took some deep swigs from a bottle of denatured alcohol and went up on the deck, hanging back in the shadows, pulling up the collar of his overcoat around his mouth, waiting for the right moment when no one would be watching him or be about to attack him.

It was the roaming desperados of the night that worried him the most, those small roving gangs of men who were always flitting around. But others were waiting for him too, always wanting to follow him, so he had to be doubly sure, welcoming the darkness when he was free to move without too much attention. He never quite escaped their prying eyes, of course – not even in the darkness – but it helped if he kept going fast, gliding from shadow to shadow, doubling back around corners, never following the same route twice.

He could just see the light of his distant neighbour, the hermit living in the shed behind the Norwegian church, who seemed to share his own distaste for any sort of attention. They had never exchanged any words but Nathan felt a brotherly communion with the old man, sympathizing with those rapacious forces which drove men like them out of society in the first place. In many ways they were both out on the margin, clinging by their fingertips, crushed into the same corner by the same sense of shared menace.

The night wind was whining in the warehouse eaves as Nathan finally left the ship, head bent well down, hurrying past the empty dock. He continued walking until he stopped near the Rowntree warehouse where that army of men was shuffling, melancholy black on flaming red, around their enormous fire. Just like a child drawn to a bloody accident he always stopped here; always felt sick with anxiety and fear when he looked at the fire. It struck deep inside him since there was something almost Biblical about it; a startling vision of that burning place where lost souls were lost for ever, journeying through the eternal flames.

He had stood there for some five minutes when, curious to know why they kept moving, he actually joined them, shuffling around and around in that endless circle, watching some drifting away and others joining in. He soon found that their constant movement had much to do with the acrid woodsmoke dancing in the changing gusts of the unpredictable warehouse draughts. Sometimes the smoke swept all over him, stinging his eyes and making him choke, but if he kept moving he was soon in the warm clear air again. When he did stop the others barged into him angrily, since they moved with their heads down – barely looking at where they were going, let alone where they had been. A constant blaze shimmered in his eyes and on his cheeks; the warmth penetrated right into his bones, working up something of a sweat until that woodsmoke engulfed him again. The shuffling anonymity of this human roundabout also had its appeal; no one looked at or spoke to another. Once in a while they took a hand out of their pockets to sweep off an odd spark which had settled on their clothing, already charred and holed by other sparks which had evidently burned unnoticed.

As he left the fiery warehouse a Salvation Army van pulled up to dole out some soup and prayers. He walked on to find that the streets were mercifully empty. Occasionally he took a careful swig from his bottle which, apart from anything else, kept the warm glow in his belly. It was all about warmth these days, he decided. Only that army in the warehouse had discovered the secret of not being too hot or too cold. As for the rest of mankind, they always had difficulty in getting the simplest things right, particularly when they had to live with the perpetual annoyance of being followed.

He stopped in the green pool of lamplight on the corner of Sophia Street, listening to the voices spinning down to talk to him. It was always a problem to know what to say to these voices particularly when they were children's voices; *your* children's voices. *Yes, we will be going to the park this afternoon, if you're good and give your father a nice kiss. No you cannot have a lolly because you had some sweets this morning. I don't care what Mam always said. She's not here any longer so now you do as I say. I am the one who will be taking you to the park.*

He always had to talk to them like that; to make it very clear that their mother had gone away and left them. There was no point in trying to fool them about when their mother might be coming back because he just did not know. A week? A month? Perhaps never. You had to be truthful with children since it always paid in the end. Children only ever really learned to love and trust you when you told them the truth. That's what being a good father was all about.

*I said, I said. I said we were going to the park. Why don't you ever listen to what I say? Eh? Use your ears. They're to be found on the side of your head. But we've got to have something to eat first and, as long as you eat everything, then we will all go together to the park like a proper family.*

He hurried on to escape all their idle chatter, carefully skirting around a pair of grumbling tramps, their legs spread-eagled out of a doorway. Down by the Marl he could just make out the white blobs of a flock of seagulls, all standing motionless on the grass, their beaks all pointing directly into the wind. Yes, even seagulls had their own ways of dealing with the cold.

He was next stopped by a sound which drifted hot and exuberantly out into the still night. A majestic trumpet was duelling with a flirtatious clarinet followed by a lot of shouting. He followed the sound to the closed doors of the Ship and Pilot. Through the thick stained windows, he could make out the backs of lots of people standing on the seats. They were cheering and shouting again, then they all fell quiet and a voice rose moaning above the tinkling din, singing *In the Evening (When the Sun Goes Down). In the evenin' Mama, in the evenin'; in the evenin' when that hot ole sun goes down . . .*

The voice was thick with aching sorrow and regret. The old plantation song spoke profoundly of the disinherited and lost, drawing him closer to the steamy pub windows. He knew that voice all too well, of course; this was his Sophie singing her sad blues to a sad world. He had always loved the sound of singing and to sing himself. Once. He had often found a hymn bursting out of his lips in celebration of some happy mood – and particularly first thing in the morning – but it had been many a long year since that had happened.

The door opened and two women in long dresses, fluffy with ostrich feathers, came clattering out on high heels. They were quarrelling with one another, their voices strident with middle-class money as they crossed the road and climbed into a car. There were lots of other cars parked nearby, he noticed, telling that Sophie was now attracting the attention of the rich and well-to-do outside her world. The door opened again and he scurried into the darkness of a nearby lane where he could still hear her singing surprisingly clearly.

She had often asked him to come down and see them but he never did. These sessions were far too crowded for him; too many people would have recognized him and he just could not have put up with that. They might have asked him a lot of questions about himself also. He had pretended that he just did not like jazz but it was quite good really, he decided. His foot began to tap as Obe's trumpet lead a ferocious onslaught on *Tiger Rag*. Now that he came to listen properly he could also remember the rampant authority of that trumpet; it recalled rather too clearly that musical night of celebration when the Barbadians had first taken up lodgings on the floor of his church.

Ah yes. *His* church. St Mark's had been closed for a few years now and thieves had ripped the lead out of the roof. Weeds were growing everywhere – even out of the walls – and he just could not bear going near it.

Both the music and the voices brought it all back now, stronger than before; those summer days of love before it had all fully and finally come crashing down around his ears. He still wanted Sophie so badly that, even as her plaintive voice made that longing surge again inside him, he was almost sick in that dark lane, captured by the remembered sweetness of her body and the later outstretched hands demanding that he pay for that sweetness and pay in full. Somewhere in the middle of those conflicting demands he had broken himself. He knew all that.

His whole body started trembling now and he wanted to go away; wanted to rejoin that army of men shuffling around the fire; wanted to return to the comforting womb of the windjammer. But he didn't. He just stayed there in the lane, hooked by the melancholy of that loved voice, the tears burning as hot as acid into his cold cheeks. He had to hold his bottle in both hands to steady it sufficiently to get it into his mouth.

*Oh, Sophie girl, we could have found another way out of all this. We could have done it any way but this . . . if only you had been there when I was young . . . if only you had been there on the church outings . . . if only you had married me at the altar . . . if only . . . You would have been mine now and it would have been right – not you in there singing about your heartache and me, here, clutching some old bottle and crying in the dark.*

# CHAPTER SIXTEEN

Inside the pub the band was working up a tremendous head of steam and Sophie was more pleased than she could remember by the way the moods vaulted from tender blues to kick-arse traditional jazz. Somehow Obe had persuaded Errol to return to his banjo, but they were still without a pianist. Yet now Obe was giving all the front men room to move, encouraging the trombonist and clarinettist to grab as many solos as the mood took them. In an odd sort of way this new individual freedom had helped them to come together as a group, making them listen to what one another were doing more carefully. Even in the musical anarchy of jazz you always had to listen to each other.

The members of the audience had taken to turning up with their own instruments. One had a washboard and another bone castanets. They came out with kazoos or blew foghorn noises on their beer bottles. Go-as-you-please seemed to be the new order, with lots of hollering and scatalogical insults, all sprinkled over a driving kinetic music that shouted to be jigged around to.

But it was the blues that Sophie liked to sing the best; those marvellous Bessie Smith rages about desertion at dawn, two-timing lovers and the misery of lusting after another woman's man. Within their sadness she felt happy, giving them every straining fibre of her being. During those songs she became her voice, closing her eyes and calling up something deep down inside her. What came out was what she felt. She was addressing the problems of being a woman when she was singing the blues; it was the only way she knew of grappling with the cruel brutalities of life itself.

She compered the sessions too, often with a bottle of something strong in her hand. She was developing a few mean monologues – working up a few standard jokes and saying something about what a particular song meant to her. 'Well I'd like to thank you from the heart of my bottom for that,' she said after the applause had died down for *Poor Man's Blues*. 'Now we're going to do a little number which I wrote many years ago. It's ah . . . it's ah . . . it's a little story about loss – about being a prisoner an' you just can't work out what the prison is all about. It's *Prisoner of Love*.'

*You came into my life and left it again free*, she growled, closing her eyes and feeling her whole body tense and stiffen. *But what about me, do I stay a prisoner of your love? Do I stay a prisoner of your love?*

Obe stepped forward to beef up the chorus as Sophie smiled and gazed across the crowded, smoky room. Suddenly something curdled thick inside her. Through the smoke and crowded bodies she spotted the balding head of Nathan, standing in the middle of a group near the door. There was virtually no expression on his face as he gazed up at her enraptured. The very sight of him made her unwilling or unable to take up the next verse. Obe frowned, looking at her curiously, but came in with the refrain again as she continued staring at Nathan.

*So where is the key to my cell?* she asked, finding the words in her mouth again but still keeping her eyes on him. *I do not want to stay a prisoner of your love*. Just having him there added a new but familiar dimension to her old hymn of pain. It was with him in mind that she had once written it and now there he was, still bewitching her emotions. It made no sense, of course, but there never had been any sense in love – it was just a wretched and largely incurable illness which gave you, well, the blues. As she continued singing she found both a new sensuality and a new ache in her voice; perhaps this was the first time that she had sung her most famous song with any special feeling – sobbing the lines and choking on some of the words – and the audience were not slow to catch on to her mood, practically willing her to new heights as that bemused, imprisoned misery came spinning right from the heart.

He made no move to leave when the song had finished, she was relieved to see. He even smiled at her and held up his thumb along with the audience's thunderous applause. But he had got to look so old, she decided as she held up her thumb back to him – his dark-featured face so hollow and lean. His eyes had sunk right back into their sockets. There were dark filthy streaks all over the balding dome of his head also. Oh yes, the blues were easy when the man you loved was around – particularly when he was dirty, withdrawn, mad. Yes, love really was as blind as a bat.

Obe had spotted him too, smiling brightly and nudging her in the side. 'C'mon, sister, let's do one for him,' he whispered behind a cupped hand.

'Right, well that was that and now we're going to play us some real jazz,' she announced without taking her eyes off Nathan. 'We've got someone special come to see us tonight so come on now, boys, let's wake this dump up and get that old funk flying.'

With a bugling roar Obe led them off into *I'm Wild About That Thing*, the audience jumping up and down and clapping along with rising enthusiasm. Two be-pearled young girls in diamanté-studded flapper dresses joined in to show off a new form of the Charleston, sometimes grabbing the old man, snapping the bone castanets and whirling him around. A very smart young dude in a black silk suit leaped onto the stage and tapdanced a few solos on steel-tipped heels, with everything getting so tangled and confused that Sophie even forgot what she was singing. They also did *I Can't Give You Anything But Love* and that daft novelty song *Yes, We Have No Bananas*. It was a good rousing session with almost everyone singing themselves hoarse, and Obe rounded off by playing *The Red Flag*. Sophie led the communal singing by conducting with her arms. Even Nathan joined in, singing to the people around him, she was so pleased to see, never realizing that he appreciated anything like this. She could not remember when she had last seen him laughing like that; perhaps this thing called jazz had more going for it than ever she had suspected. She had always enjoyed the way it seemed to bring everyone together; the way in which, during a good hot session, both she and the audience seemed to enter into one mind and spirit.

But as the final chorus faded she saw the bald old bugger edging out of the room towards the door. Oh no, you're not going to get out of it like this, she breathed to herself. 'I'm going after him,' she told Obe. 'I'll see you back home later. Get in a few bottles.'

She all but leaped off the stage, grabbing her coat and flying out after him down the fire stairs. None of the audience had yet left as she skidded out into the cold, empty streets, turning and turning again. Fortunately moonlight was poking through dark, curdling rain clouds and she spotted his hunched figure turning the corner into Bute Street and heading towards the docks. She raced after him, pulling on her coat. She was quite out of breath and still sweating when she caught up with him by the railway station where a coal train was hissing and panting with steam.

He looked at her with curious, questioning eyes but he could still manage a smile as they walked together into the docks. She wondered whether to link her arm in his, waving it around uncertainly before, nervous of rejection, she put both her hands into her pockets. She had always liked just to walk with him and they said nothing for a while, stopping to look up at some of the ships where the dark heads of foreign seamen moved around in the yellow light of the portholes. Rich spicy smells of cooking drifted down to them.

'There's been a lot of Indian ships around here lately,' said Nathan. 'Can't think what they eat. I always think of burning bus tickets.'

'Can't see they've got too many buses on there.'

'No, there is that. Lots of rickshaws perhaps. Did you know that rickshaws are probably the last human-drawn cars in the world? We're all mad about engines now. You don't last long if you are pulling a rickshaw either – seven years at the most. You lose too much energy and don't get enough food. One thing you'll never see is a fat rickshaw driver.'

'Since when were you an expert on rickshaws?' She knew he was nervous of her, just making conversation.

'You get to be expert in lots of exotic things around here. The docks have a faculty in everything; they are a sort of university of the world. Here you can graduate in everything. But you never actually get a degree.'

Shut up, Nathan, she murmured inwardly. Don't talk. She linked her arm in his and he made no move to shake it away as they walked on again. Those who knew her were never slow to point out that her obsession with this down-and-out was quite pointless but perhaps she alone knew how stimulating and interesting he could be in his lucid moments. Most girls fell in love through their eyes but the only way a man had ever moved her was through her ears. Even in the long years of his windjammer exile she had sometimes caught him in expansive, generous moods, able to talk, long and interestingly, about almost anything under the sun. But it had been a long time since that had happened. His condition had deteriorated so much over the last few years that he did not seem to want to talk about anything at all. That sullen rejection was the hardest to take – even if her Effey quite clearly still succeeded where she had failed.

They meandered on again, stopping on a lock gate, water hissing with punctured laughter from the sluices. She looked about her. The very dockscape looked animated and warm with coloured footlights flickering in every corner – the marmalade glow of the East Moors furnaces over on one side, the pale moonlight varnishing the incoming tide at their feet, the stammering ruddiness of the Rowntree warehouse fire in the distance. She took a big sniff on the cold Channel winds. It was a given moment and, inside, she felt as warm as all those dock footlights; the great blues singer about to perform on the very stage of the world.

'So you liked our music then, did you?' she asked.

'Yes, yes I did. It took me by surprise really. I thought there was something strangely replenishing – even redemptive – about it and I'd like to come again.'

'You can come any time you like. You should know that by now.'

'It's good music for the times, a music of extremes – either tremendously happy or tremendously sad. Ballads have extraordinary powers of healing. But you can destroy in a song too. In the old days people rarely lasted long if they were attacked in a song. But another thing: I saw a lot of rich cars around. You may be in danger of becoming very successful.'

'Success is dangerous, is it?'

'It can be. It makes the fall greater.'

'There's always a fall, is there? You're so Welsh sometimes.

So bloody Welsh. There's a punishment for everything. Nothing can be enjoyed unless there's some awful punishment to follow.'

'I can't help what I am, girl. We Welsh are all like that. So where is this jazz thing going to lead?'

'Who can tell? There's been another London agent around today asking us to go up there. We've been offered a week at the Astoria, all found. Do you think we should go?' She was fishing in the light of his sunny mood, she knew, wondering what she could pull out of him.

'Oh, I'm not the one to ask about that, Sophie. I'm just the has-been who never was. If you're ready . . . if that's what you want . . . well, you could give it a try. But you wouldn't be taking Effey, would you?'

Yes, well, you sometimes fished all day and just pulled out a crab. Effey was all he ever seemed to care about. She very nearly became angry but managed to squash it. 'No. I don't suppose I would. London's no place for her. Anyway I don't think Obe wants to go and we couldn't do anything without him. He's got this thing about his people. And we haven't got a pianist either. You can't play a piano by any chance?'

'Me? Play a piano!' He laughed at the very thought.

'What about becoming our hat man then? We've had three now and had to get rid of them all for stealing.'

'What's a hat man?'

'You know, the one who carries the hat around and collects the money while we play. You'd get the same cut as the rest of us.'

He laughed again. 'Sophie, I'm no good at begging.'

'That's not begging. Taking the hat around is not begging.'

'I'd be no good at it. I make a tidy enough living around here. You'd be surprised at what goes on around here at night.'

'No, I wouldn't.'

'But it gets me by and I don't need much. I have almost no needs.'

'I'll tell you what you do need,' she said, not managing to squash her anger this time around. 'You need a good wash. That's what you need. How'd you manage to get so dirty anyway?'

He pulled his fingers down his cheeks, holding out his palms in the moonlight. 'It must be the fire over in that warehouse. I joined them earlier on.'

'And whatever were you doing that for? You look like a smoked haddock. I live in a nice, warm house. You know you can come there any time you like, not walk around that fire with all those bums.'

He began examining both his hands, wriggling his fingers around as if trying to count them. 'I've got to go now. They all come out at night, you know. There's lots of men who chase you around if you don't watch it.'

'Nathan, there's no one. Come back home with me. Just for tonight.'

'There is, there is. They're everywhere, watching you, following you. I've really got to be going. Got to be quick about it. You'd better get on home too.'

'Oh, I can't take . . .' She turned away sharply, her given moment collapsing and dancing off into the cold waters of the dock as she listened to him getting his bad old words back again. Nothing was given for long with him. She swallowed hard and when she turned to look at him again – to plead with him again – he had indeed hurried off towards his wretched ship.

Well, she wasn't having any of this, she decided as she strode after him. A girl can only take so much of this. She bet dear old Bessie Smith had never got mixed up with a man like him. She made no attempt to catch up – keeping a distance of about ten yards – and he seemed unaware that he was being followed, only looking back at her when he was halfway up the gangplank of the windjammer.

'I live *here*,' he shouted inanely, waving his arms around like some scarecrow trying to frighten the birds away. 'You live over in Custom House. I'm tired and I want to go to bed.'

She just stood there, glaring at this mad, waving figure. 'I want to go to bed too and there's been men following *me*,' she shouted evenly, wondering if she had lost as many marbles as him. They always said that blues singing loosens up your brains. 'They're out to get me and, if you send me home, they're going to do me in.'

'Just keep out of the way. Keep in the dark. They can't see you in the dark.'

'But they're everywhere,' she screamed back. 'And they've got guns and knives.'

'Guns? How many guns have they got?'

She had to turn away, biting her lip to stop herself laughing out loud. The fiery eyes of the cats hung in the darkness, all coming out to watch what was going on. 'I don't know,' she called back after a while. 'Lots of guns. There's a whole army of them, all over the place. They're going to shoot me to bits. I can't go home.'

It was his turn to be silent for a while. 'Are you pulling my leg?'

'No-o-o-o-o. I wouldn't joke about this, Nathan. I've seen them coming out of the warehouse. Hundreds of them.'

'Well, get on board here, quick. Lie low 'til they've gone.'

She crossed the deck and followed him into the ward room, standing in the darkness as he muttered to himself and bolted the door before he lit an oil lamp. In an odd sort of way he had become protective and even loving again, clearing some old newspapers out of the way and inviting her to sit down. He seemed to have forgotten about that menacing army of guns too, apologizing for the state of the place and disappearing under a bench where, after a lot of scrabbling about, he emerged again holding up half a bottle of gin.

'Let's have a little nightcap, shall we? I like little nightcaps I do. They always seem to put you away with a little pat on your forehead.'

She took the drink and smiled, raising her glass and wondering if, by accident, she had found the key to the whirling gusts of his personality; that perhaps she could change when he changed; that she could fight fire with fire; madness with madness. Oh she knew all too well what they all said, but when you were obsessed with someone you were obsessed and that was that.

He emptied his glass in one draught, visibly cheering up as he put his feet on the table. 'You look good by the light of an oil lamp. I thought you looked tremendous on the stage tonight too. A singing vision of loveliness. I just felt so proud seeing you standing there.'

Compliments too. This was becoming very interesting, this was. She emptied her glass also, pushing it over to him, even if he did not look terribly interested in re-filling it. Ah well, there were limits to everything, she supposed. She took off her earrings and placed them carefully on the table.

'I was just walking past the pub when I heard the music and your voice. You seem to have a totally different singing voice to your speaking voice. It's so much more throaty when you sing; a bit like you're gargling pebbles. It's a trick I suppose, is it?'

'Oh, I don't know,' she replied, standing up and taking off her coat. 'It's just how it comes out. I open my mouth and it just comes pouring out. No tricks really.'

They talked and drank some more, then she stood up again, pulling her dress up over her head. 'I'm feeling dog tired now, Nathan,' she mumbled inside her dress. 'If you won't come to my place I'm going to sleep right here.'

'No, you're not.'

'Yes I am. Right here. You don't have to sleep with me if you don't want but that's where I'm sleeping.'

She let her dress fall to the deck, turning and facing him, the lamplight shimmering on the one side of her long olive limbs. Her breasts were firm and taut, her neck unbelievably long. The years had taken nothing away from her marvellous, full-boned figure.

'I told you once,' he said. 'You can't stay here.'

'Why not?'

'Why not? Because the neighbours might talk, that's why not.'

'Rubbish. What neighbours have you got around here?'

'You'd be surprised. You'd be very surprised. There'd be complaints and petitions and I couldn't take the scandal.'

'Nathan, I'm just too tired to walk home. All I want is to sleep just there.'

As she climbed into his bed he got up and unbolted the door, making a mock bow and waving her out into the night.

'I can't, Nathan. Just let me sleep for a few hours and then I'll go.'

Sleep was indeed all she had in mind, since she was very drowsy and a little drunk, but no sooner had she stretched out beneath the blankets and closed her eyes than she felt his hand close on her wrist, yanking her out with such a savage force that she landed on the deck with a painful bump on her backside. She sat up, suddenly feeling very awake, and flailed about when, to her horror, she felt his arms around her wrist and she was being propelled out of the open door into that winter night. And with nothing on!

Her ankle banged on something sharp and she was so distracted by the pain she was barely aware that he had already closed the door again, busily throwing the bolts.

'Nathan, I'm going to freeze to death out here,' she shouted, raining blows on the door with the sides of her fists. 'Let me in, will you? Just let me in.'

Through the porthole she could see his hands turning off the oil lamp so she began hammering on the door again. 'Nathan, I'm going to freeze to death. Just give me my clothes at least.'

No reply.

'Nathan, I'm begging you. Please give me my clothes. Give me my bloody clothes.'

Still no reply. She looked around the moonlit dock in desperation, her body goose-pimpling and teeth beginning to chatter in the cold. Clearly this was no time to reason with that mad bugger. She would just have to make a run for it, hoping to work up a good sweat before she got home. Pausing only on the quay to wave her fist at him – and to let loose a volley of choice obscenities – she went sprinting down the dock, her bare feet slapping over the lock gate, when she had to slow down and pick her way gingerly over a gravel path. It was then that she spotted some men wheeling about in the darkness in front of her. She began limping in another direction but another gang of desperados came drifting out of the shadows, cackling with laughter and holding out their arms wide to her. She just could not run on the gravel so she turned and turned again, her hot breath fluming all around her head. She decided to turn back and try to get out of the other side of the dock in Rat Island.

Her feet were bleeding badly and she was just passing the windjammer again when, in desperation and out of breath in this shivering nightmare, she leaped back up the gangplank, hammering again on the ward room door. 'Nathan,' she screamed. 'Open it, will you? They're coming to get me. They're going to get me.'

A group of men was indeed gathering on the quay, muttering to one another as if trying to decide whether to follow her on board. One had actually put his foot on the gangplank when there was an ear-splitting bang together with a spurt of orange and green fire emptying from one of the portholes. Sophie had all but jumped out of her freezing skin at the first bang and very nearly passed out at the second. The men were shouting at one another and running away as she slumped to her knees, hardly able to understand what was going on. The ward room door opened and Nathan threw a blanket over her shoulders, helping her up and taking her inside.

She was still chattering with a mixture of cold and fear when he put her into his bunk. Even piles of blankets failed to quell her manic shivering and neither could she speak, her face hot with tears. She wanted to know if he had shot anyone. She wanted to know where he got the gun. But all that happened was that her jaw kept juddering up and down like that of a voiceless marionette. He seemed to be messing around in the darkness, bolting the door and bumping into the table, then, a few moments later, she felt his naked body move in next to her, enfolding her in his arms, kissing her wet cheeks and smoothing her trembling body, his voice telling her again and again that it was all right. Everything was all right now. They were gone and she was safe.

Her trembling became less violent and she held him tight but she could not stop crying, not even when she felt him enter her, so far and so deep that, for one deliciously painful and dry moment, she thought that he was actually going to break her in two. He went on and on, his hips closing on hers slowly and, with every thrust, she began to feel well again, her fists clenching and unclenching, then she stiffened and several spinning tops of pleasure came whirling up out of her. Every part of her body felt an unfamiliar outbreak of purring happiness as she relaxed on a bed of waving silk but she was careful to keep herself just there as he continued until he, too, came home to her.

In her dishevelled state his act of spontaneous warmth had taken her completely by surprise. It was the first time she had been with a man for many a long year and it was so gracious somehow. Now she was crying with an altogether different kind of ailment which was close to gratitude, holding onto him and kissing his neck, remembering again the full force of that dark and mysterious compulsion which had bound her to him in the first place.

His body had become a complete deadweight but she was careful not to disturb him. Was he going to start performing again? She recollected all too clearly the terrible consequences for everyone after they had last made love. But she was not going to find out just yet since he had fallen fast asleep and was snoring serenely into her hair.

# CHAPTER SEVENTEEN

The rain drizzled and hissed thinly the day they buried Mrs Esme Gurney. It washed over the stone angels and broken pillars that symbolized lives uncompleted. It washed over vases of dead flowers and carved poems of love. The drops gathered along the bare branches of the trees like rows of tears.

It came from everywhere that warm rain, sweeping in over the Garth mountain and down the shale paths of the cemetery. It spattered on the glistening parked cars of the funeral cortege and over the coffin being shouldered up the slope to the family crypt by six pallbearers. Clumps of black-veiled, frock-coated mourners followed the coffin, looking like damp, bedraggled crows in some hopeless search for carrion. The rain dripped off their homburgs and bowlers as they all came to enter into a shared sense of sorrow. You are estimated at a Welsh funeral. You have lived the way you are honoured in your death. The funeral is the final verdict on the way you lived. Mrs Gurney lived well and was duly being honoured well.

The priest was already standing at the open door of the crypt, trying to avoid the thick smell of dead and rotten air which came seeping out of it. Two other coffins were visible on the dark shelves, the gilt handles on one of them still surprisingly shiny. Over on the other side of the path Hamilton was standing alone watching the proceedings. He barely moved as about a hundred mourners gathered around the priest to listen to the Order of the Dead, his eyes studying them all with care.

He knew most of them; knew a lot about their businesses, even if they knew very little about his. He recognized most of the faces of this solemn Mafia of business interests in the city, all come to pay their respects to the widow of the man who had once built up the Oriel Navigation Steamship Company into one of the biggest in the land. They were all here – the champagne openers and the lavish tippers, the genial backslappers and incorrigible Corona-givers, fat on civic corruption and the interest on war loans.

But even the business of corruption never quite stopped at such funerals, he noticed. Long brown envelopes were being passed quietly from hand to hand; the state of the stock market was never from their lips for very long; hands were being shaken on some muttered deal. Only a few of the older women seemed to be crying with real grief; even in the dark shadow of death the men of money had to work hard to keep the business going. Many of the faces there had built up early fortunes in shipping but had cut their losses in the Depression, moving into the newer and more profitable rackets of insurance and estate agency. A few of the bigger crooks had gone into the law. Some had been lucky enough to get onto the council where, they were discovering, it was easier than ever to run a fiddle, particularly in hotel and office development. But these were still tough times, even for the crooked, which is why they had to keep living and breathing their shady deals.

Hamilton nodded at Chief Inspector Watts and Arthur Tatem. He even shook hands with Anthony Elias and Cecil Abraham. They were being carefully respectful to him since he had taken over official title to Oriel. He was one of the few solvent men in an insolvent land and he might be useful to them one day. Any solvent man was worth courting these days, no matter what you might think of him privately. It was the way city business interests had always worked with numerous hands held out to one another in numerous dark corners. Hamilton understood all this and now that his name was on the official crest, so to speak, he had no option but to make himself slightly more visible.

Maddeningly they did not know the exact scale of his wealth nor quite how he had managed to take over Oriel. In the absence of facts, they gossiped ferociously. *Old man Gurney lost most of his stock to him in a card game, I heard. But Gurney never had any stock. He was always a front man for that weird old bastard. They say, you know, that he was having a fling with dear old Esme. That's why he got the lot in the end.*

What they had never done was to ask the man himself. Not even when, a year ago, Hamilton became the declared and registered chairman with sole rights and control of all the Oriel titles. And certainly not now as they gathered for the tribal rites of death in the business family, straining to hear the priest's words muted by the rain: 'We commend unto Thy hands of mercy, most merciful Father, the soul of this our sister, Esme . . .'

Just then Hamilton saw a face which made his throat go dry and his dark eyebrows rise a few fractions. Involuntarily he stepped forward taking his hands out of his pockets. Even his pale, embalmed cheeks flushed. In death there had indeed been a resurrection. Right there, in the centre of a group nearest the door of the crypt, was Edward Gurney.

As the priest continued with the prayers Hamilton quietly circled the rear of a group of mourners until he stood next to Partington, pulling him back a discreet distance by the elbow. 'Do you see who I see?' he asked, softly but urgently.

'I've just spotted him, Mr Hamilton. Those advertisements in *The Times* must have done what we couldn't. I must say I never took Mr Edward to be a *Times* reader.'

Hamilton's manner became more forceful. 'I do not want him vanishing again after this is all over,' he hissed. 'Get hold of Watts as soon as you can and tell him to stick to him, no matter where he goes.'

'What if he doesn't want to come?'

'Tell Watts to bring him to my house, even if he has to break both his legs. I want him there this afternoon.'

Hamilton returned to his spot under the oak tree. As the priest concluded the words of the committal he did not once take his eyes off Edward. For his part Edward was looking alternately at the priest and into the mouth of that crypt where his mother had finally been laid to rest alongside his father. His features were still quite youthful though his complexion was rougher and ruddier. It was certainly not the complexion of a man who had been languishing for a long time in some distant prison. His clothes were not quite so fashionable either, with a certain roughness about their style and cut. Watts moved around the group to stand near him.

So the prodigal had returned. But why? To try and reclaim his lost inheritance? To pay his last respects to his mother? Surely not, Edward never cared about anything outside his own narrow interests. To start trouble? He could get plenty of that. He was still officially wanted by the Cardiff police. To give Hamilton what was his? Edward's eyes strained through the rain and met Hamilton's. There did not seem any hostility in the look and, in fact, he seemed very weary and strained. But that was how you were when you buried your mother, Hamilton guessed.

When the funeral service was over and the mourners were drifting back to their waiting cars Hamilton moved down to stand in Edward's path, pausing to cough into his hand. He looked up at Edward and held his breath. 'It is a great pleasure to see you again,' he said, holding out his other hand and studying the younger man's face for signs. The bulky figure of Chief Inspector Watts loomed behind Edward's shoulders. 'It has been an extremely long time, Edward. A very long time. We have been looking everywhere for you.'

'Yes, a long time,' Edward echoed weakly, taking the proferred hand. 'I've spent some time in Australia.'

'Australia? Oh yes. And how are things in Australia?'

'I wouldn't recommend the place. I had to get out in the end.'

'We need to speak, Edward. We have a lot to talk about.'

'Yes. But not here. We can't talk here.' Edward looked up at Watts and over at Partington. Both stared back at him gravely. He did not look as if he was going to make a run for it. One of the mourners, an old man wearing a bowler, came up and patted Edward on the small of his back. 'Good to see you after so long, Edward,' he exclaimed. 'She was a good woman, your mother. We'll see you later, shall we?'

'Yes, we will all be along later,' Hamilton intervened. 'We will all be along later.' The old man nodded and moved on to catch up with the rest of them. Already two cemetery workmen were labouring to close the door of the crypt. 'You have your family to see first,' Hamilton added. 'They are all going back to Penarth for sherry. But we really do have much to discuss, Edward. You know Chief Inspector Watts? He will drive you to your home and bring you back to mine. Victor, meet Edward Gurney. Take him home to Penarth, Victor, and, when the time is right, bring him back to Howard Close.'

'Am I being taken prisoner at my own mother's funeral?' Edward inquired.

'Absolutely nothing of the kind, Edward,' said Hamilton waving a hand. 'We just want to take certain precautions against another of your premature departures. As I said, we need to speak and there is much to speak about. That is all there is to it.' He motioned them towards the waiting cars.

Later that morning Edward found himself gazing across the crowded room, at the piano, the stag's head on the wall, the gilt candelabra. A youngish woman with mousy looks was eating a sandwich and talking with his Uncle Albert. It was difficult to tell if she had much of a bosom under all that tight black frogging of her twinset but her legs weren't at all bad.

Even at such a time he still could not conjure up any affectionate thoughts for his mother. To him she would always be that unutterable snob who had merely existed in the shadow of his father; who had packed him off to boarding school as soon as it had been conveniently possible. She had been a woman of impossible airs and graces, who had always made him take off his shoes as soon as he had come home – 'We'll have no dirt in here, Edward' – the whining matriarch who would only ever speak to him if she had found fault or wanted to make a sarcastic comment.

The mousy woman was still deep in serious conversation and munching her sandwich. She really did look a bit like a mouse nibbling at some cheese, he decided. He would have just loved to have got those legs of hers tangled around his neck. She wouldn't have felt like nibbling at any cheese by the time he had finished.

He had, in many ways, admired his father. He would have done anything to win his commendation and praise which, when given, rang in his ears for days. But his mother had always been a nothing mother, a mere ornament addicted to fashion and the piano, always dreaming vague dreams about how to become slightly more fashionable, find a better class of friend, play the piano a little bit more elegantly.

Such was the drift of his thoughts as he stood in the drawing room of their Penarth home, watching that sandwich finally finished. He was almost climbing up the wall in his sexual longing. But this was, ah, his mother's funeral reception. The few who remembered him came over and talked. He told them of his journeys around Australia; how he had run a charter boat out of Sydney – even tried sheep-farming in the outback. But he had drifted back to London, picked up with some of his old cronies and read of his mother's death in *The Times*.

The real truth was darker. He had tried sheep-farming but found it horribly boring and hard work. He returned to Sydney and quite by accident latched onto a supply of cocaine coming in from Columbia. The pickings were rich and easy and he had even got away with it for several years until he had come unstuck on a basic and foolish miscalculation. He had amassed a considerable pile of money but had put it on deposit in a bank where it was quietly making interest. The trouble was the bank told the tax people about it – as they were obliged to do. Then the tax people had asked him where he had got it from – as they were obliged to do. When he told them that he had won it gambling they had frozen his account and, when they continued to press him to search his memory for the source of his money, he decided that he had no other option but to pack his bags and do a moonlight flit. He had returned to the London of the charleston and the black bottom, and none of his old cronies seemed to want to know him. So it was something of a relief to read that his mother had died, and he had come down to see what, if anything, he might salvage from the family fortune.

And so here he was, aching with lust, mentally undressing a woman – his cousin? – perplexed, if anything, that he felt so little about the loss of his mother. He had never hated her really, certainly never loved her . . . just nothing at all. His perplexed state was compounded by Chief Inspector Watts who had stayed distressingly close to him throughout his chats with the sherry-sipping old fools and the doddering women who had infested so much of his life. It was probably this domestic atmosphere which had made him bad to the bone. He wondered if there was much left to plunder around here just now. Hamilton had probably taken everything. He might just get the house. But there again he might just be hauled into the pokey as well. The memories of that raid on the castle were still vivid, and doubtless he would have to answer a question or two about it. Hamilton would obviously be keenly interested in the whereabouts of that cup.

The guests thinned out, fond farewells were made and Edward discovered that the mousy woman was *married* to his Uncle Albert. Just where had he acquired her? – a good twenty years younger than the old shoe manufacturer – and, more to the point, what had happened to Albert's first wife, Jean? It clearly wasn't the right moment to ask.

Watts drove Edward down the toll road into Cardiff, not bothering to pay the toll. Nothing much had changed around here, Edward decided, the city was still run by the same gang of crooks who lined one another's pockets and emptied everyone else's. Bute Street was much the same too – the old stone façades flaking with neglect, the same old girls working out of the same old brothels. Watts waved cheerfully at many of them. 'We nick 'em now and then but we stay friends,' he explained with a bovine seriousness. 'Bashed the door down of one the other day and there was this man standing there with the biggest hard on I've ever seen. I told him we were raiding the place and that big hard on just wilted like a lily in a storm.'

Edward remembered his own times in such places and, in an odd sort of way, he felt as if he was coming home; that, through his father's shipping connections, this was about the only home that he had ever had.

'Look at those houses, riddled with bugs and tuberculosis,' Watts continued. 'The bugs have grown worse over the years. They come in on the fo'c'sles of ships which never get properly fumigated. Big bugs and little bugs all breeding away like mad. Summer is the worst. Mothers 'ave to put nets over their prams when they take their babies out. That's 'ow bad it all is.'

If Watts had any plans for locking Edward up he was not revealing them. He just seemed like an old police chief on the take, content to live out his life bending the law a bit here and breaking it a bit there. He clearly enjoyed telling his little stories too. The big man of the Bay. When they pulled into Howard Close he even leaned across Edward and opened the car door for him, ushering him into the house with polite flurries. Hamilton paid handsomely for this kind of service, Edward guessed.

The front door was already open and a Somali woman was on her knees in the hallway, washing the floor. She looked up, her dark eyebrows rising a shade as she recognized the newcomer, quickly lowering her head again and becoming engrossed in her work. He caught that look of recognition but could not place the dark-featured face. He stood still for a moment, gazing down at her, but now Watts's index finger was pointing into the drawing room where Hamilton was standing, staring out of the window.

'Edward, so good of you to come,' he said coming towards him with an outstretched hand. 'You can leave us now, Victor. Mr Gurney and I have much to talk about. Sit here, Edward. I could get you some tea if you want. A small pot of China tea perhaps?'

Edward would have liked something a little stronger than

China tea but decided that he would need to keep a clear head and merely nodded. As Watts left, Hamilton went to the door, asking the cleaning woman to make them some tea. He wanted to ask Hamilton who she was but this was not the right moment. There was, after all, much weightier business to be attended to and he was keen to learn how, if at all, he fitted into Hamilton's plans.

Hamilton returned to the window and lost no time in explaining Edward's situation with Jesuitical care.

'You have been gone a long time, Edward. Much has changed. We made extensive inquiries as to your whereabouts but came up with nothing. We always had this problem with business continuity, you must understand, and finally, with your mother's authority, the Oriel business interests were fully taken over by myself. I had fifty per cent of it anyway – even when your father was alive. It was never publicly acknowledged, but I had it, and there are legal deeds to prove it. So I do not want you to even start entertaining the idea that I took over anything that you should have inherited.'

It all looked very much like theft from Edward's point of view but he managed to contain himself. At this stage in the game he was in no position to demand anything at all. Just now he would have to sit back and see what, if anything, was on offer.

'But just bear with me a moment and . . .'

There was a knock on the door and Sophie came into the room, carrying a tea tray. She placed the tray on the table, shooting another sideways look at Edward before she left.

'But just bear with me a moment and you will see where I am going,' Hamilton continued. 'It matters nothing at all to me where you have been or what you have been doing. I am not even curious. But what I do remember – all too clearly – is that, in the short period you were with us, you did your work well. My instincts tell me that you could do with some work just now. We are entering difficult, dangerous times and I need someone to head up the business here in preparation for some difficult, dangerous moves. I know of no one who could do this work as you could and, particularly with your good family name, you are, in many ways, ideal.'

Hamilton sat down to pour the tea but Edward made no move to touch his. Distant alarm bells were sounding in his mind. Nothing about this talk made any sense. But, there again, it had been a very long time indeed since anyone had described him as being ideal for anything at all. He ordered himself to become cooler; to sit tight and wait to see exactly the strength of the hand about to be laid before him.

'I am not the kind to paper the lighthouse, Edward, and I really do understand the type of man that you are. Please never have any illusions on that score. You plough your own furrow and you have your own code. You work on the basis of your own self-interest and it is to appeal to that strong sense of self-interest that I am making this offer. My own concerns will soon become apparent: Oriel is poised to take on a large munitions contract worth a great deal of money. We are ready to take over another line and it needs a man to get out and meet the people, to arrange the deals, to shade the odds. I am jealous of my privacy – I really do not enjoy meeting people, any people. If you would agree to run Oriel again with Partington's help, if you would be prepared to forget the sins of omission and commission of the past, then I would be prepared to make certain generous dispensations.'

Hamilton made a slight cough and spread his hands apart like a street salesman about to make an irresistible offer. 'If you were prepared to throw your hat in with us and do all that is required I would put you on a good salary, with shares in Oriel. You would be able to live in your Penarth home – perhaps even sell it if you found it too large – and, if our current move works out, I will actually give you, right at this moment, the deeds to the windjammer, *The Solomon*. Yes, we really do still have her; a hulk now, but repairable and safely berthed in the West Bute Dock. Even in its present state it might be worth a great deal of money. We get regular inquiries from prospective purchasers about her but, in a way, I have always regarded that ship as belonging to you.'

He placed the deeds to the ship on the table in front of Edward who looked at the yellowing papers with a mixture of emotions. On the one hand he was quite overwhelmed by the sheer generosity of the offer but, on the other, he was extremely suspicious about what it all might involve. Hamilton had sold him down the river in the past and looked more than capable of doing it again. With this man nothing was ever as it seemed. He really needed more information to find the flaws; more time to see what he was letting himself in for. 'What if I refuse?' he asked.

'If you refuse you refuse. You can go your own way again, just as you have always done in the past.'

'And the police? Are they still interested in me after that castle business?'

'The police are no problem in this city, Edward. They do as they are told. If you join up with us you might even find that they will be of some help in your work.'

'And if I don't join up with you?'

'You can go your own way. They might, of course, make a few inquiries of their own.'

Ah, so that was the direction it was all heading. Pick up the deeds to the windjammer and it would be fine – opt out and there would be inquiries. Hamilton had a way of making irresistible offers – a bit too irresistible really. Edward had the strong sense of this shadowy man cornering him again, blocking out the light. What he really wanted to do was to fight him. But for the moment he was weaponless, wandering around outside his own territory. There were times to fight and times to run. Just now it was time to run or, at the very least, find some ground for himself.

'As you see me now,' he began hesitatingly, 'I am a man without resources. So let's say I'll go with you on this for a while and perhaps we can review it again at a later stage. I really would like to know more about your plans. I've never been afraid of difficulty or danger but I would like to know if they're worth it.'

'That sounds like a reasonable position. Yes.' Hamilton nodded briskly. 'Take the deeds to the ship as a sign of my good faith. But nothing for nothing, Edward. There is one small but important clause in all this.'

'Clause?'

'That night in the castle, Edward. That cup you took away with you. I must have that cup.'

Edward reached for his tea, his mind working very fast indeed. He had foreseen this request and had already thought out his response. 'I can get that cup for you,' he told Hamilton evenly.

Hamilton stood up and walked over to the window, gazing out onto Howard Close. 'You know where it is then, do you?'

'I didn't say that. I said I could get it for you.'

'When?'

'It'll take time.'

'Where is it?'

'At this precise moment I'm not at all sure. But I am very sure that I can get it.'

'You sold it, did you?'

'Yes and no. But just give me some time.'

'Does this mean that you will be vanishing again?'

'No, it's here in this city.' Even as he said it he remembered who that cleaning woman was and where he would be more than happy to start looking for it. First between her thighs. 'Yes, I'll find that cup for you.' He picked up the ship deeds and put them into his inside pocket.

## CHAPTER EIGHTEEN

It had never been a part of Sophie's strategy not to use her ears. When she had overheard as much of Hamilton's conversation with Edward as she dared, she put on her coat and hurried out of the house.

Cold spring breezes sent newspaper tumbling along James Street as she strode along the pavement. She turned the corner and stopped, hands thrust well down into her pockets as she studied the buckles of her shoes. With so many pieces of information colliding together in her mind she was not at all sure what, if anything, she should do. Uppermost in her thoughts was the threat to Nathan's home on the windjammer. What would Edward do now? But then there had been all that talk about the cup in the castle. What cup was that? And precisely what was Edward doing back here? He had come to do something, that was about the only certainty.

She walked on again, passing the Ship and Pilot where draymen were unloading fat wooden barrels of beer into the cellar on ropes. Seagulls wheeled in the wind and a knife-sharpener was working on an axehead, yellow sparks exploding around his gnarled hands as he worked his stone wheel with his bicycle pedals. She stopped again, her back stiffening with further anxieties.

Edward's appearance had produced not so much a turmoil of

the mind as of the emotions. In singular but different ways the men in this as yet incomprehensible drama all meant something to her. People became what they were through a complexity of circumstances but she was not like most people. She was an African who had become what she was – whatever that was – by watching what happened all around her; seeing who was sinking into the bottom of the pile and working out why. She then watched those who were different, those who marked themselves apart; and she attached herself to them, tried to absorb some of their individuality.

Thus it was that she had been attracted to Nathan all those years ago, almost as soon as he opened his mouth. It was not what he was saying out loud but what he was saying to her underneath. He said, *I am my own man, struggling with my own thoughts and beliefs. I am different from the others. What you see before you is unique*. That's what he said to her then and that's why she loved him still because he was unpredictable and unique, a man apart. She understood that this love was probably a barren emotion, but there it was. Oh she had soon seen his weaknesses, that in some ways he was probably never meant to succeed at anything, but that hardly mattered. Even after all his years of failure she still saw the flame of something different burning bright inside him. She had still not despaired of him; still believed with a curious obstinacy that he could yet do something with his life.

By the same token she had also known that she wanted a part of Obadiah Brown's talent almost as soon as she saw and heard him. Here again her instincts were not wrong. It was he, after all, who had first found her singing voice, inspiring her with his own musicality. It was one of the greatest disappointments of her life when he disappeared – first to prison and then into the wretched Valleys – and rarely a day had gone by when she had not thought of him, longed to hear that golden trumpet again. He too had his obvious weaknesses – he was far too political for his own good and she worried, on the basis of no evidence, that he still liked to pinch silly things that did not belong to him. But, nevertheless, she sometimes felt like bursting out with laughter at the sheer pleasure of having him back and actually living with her. She would, if necessary, fight tooth and nail before she let him go again.

She had even, in an odd sort of way, missed Edward from time to time, and she used to ponder about him too. At first she had thought of him as some rich kid, weasly and spoilt, but she had been dead wrong on that. He had emerged as a brave fighter, ready to take risks, determined to take on all comers, no matter what the odds. If he was going to return here and take on a job with Hamilton that meant trouble for someone, probably for Hamilton. But the man seemed more than capable of handling it.

Yes, she had grown strong on the men she had met in her life, trying to absorb their strengths, working out their vulnerability. Yet, in a strange way, it was Hamilton who had exerted the most influence on her; strange because he had rarely even spoken to her and she quite actively disliked him and would have loved to see him fall. Despairing of life as a prostitute she had been referred to Hamilton by Mrs Jacobs, the landlady of the Ship and Pilot. The house needed a cleaner, she had been told and when she went there she had worked hard, taking on responsibilities other than cleaning until, each Friday afternoon, she left with a crisp five-pound note in her pocket. The money, together with any perishable food that she could take home, was more than enough to keep her and Effey in what they needed. She had no current plans for giving it up – even with the singing bringing in a little bit extra.

She found something extremely compelling about Hamilton, particularly his sturdy private independence and mysterious wealth – her Somali mind had always been fascinated by independence and wealth – and, at the same time, she could not decide why he was quite so loathsome. Maddeningly, she could not work out the real source of his wealth either. She saw strange men coming and going and sometimes she was able to eavesdrop on their conversations. But all that she really knew for certain was that Hamilton was about to set up a deal which was going to make Oriel very big in the shipping business.

It was only by happy accident that she had once learned that he needed someone to live on the windjammer, if only to act as a caretaker. She liked having Nathan there since he seemed to enjoy it and she could keep an eye on him. But, now that Edward owned the ship, would he try to kick him off?

A gang of Chinese seamen, quarrelling so loudly it seemed that they were about to start a fight, came out of the dock, and she crossed the railway line to avoid them. A tanker, unfamiliar to her, was moored in the lock waiting for it to fill up. A group of men, belongings at their feet, shouted up at the captain on the bridge, trying to negotiate a Pier Head jump. Such last-minute negotiations were rarely successful but, if a captain was desperately short of men, he might take a chance and let one on board. But the captain would have to be very desperate indeed since those on the Pier Head were always without any kind of papers, often straight out of prison and alarmingly ready to do anything. Only last year one man was hired on the Pier and found to be so useless and troublesome, picking fights in his first few hours on board, that he was actually flung into the sea off Ilfracombe and told to swim for it.

She stopped to listen to the barking shouts. As far as she could make out, the captain did not need any deckhands but he did need a greaser. One of the group was prepared to do that but could not provide any written evidence that he had ever so much as seen the inside of an engine room. He was also unable, offhand, to recall any real details of his previous experience on ships. The tanker began to slip its moorings with nothing resolved, leaving the men standing there, their earlier polite requests for a berth now changing to waving fists and luridly obscene curses.

Sophie smiled as this small pantomime broke up. She carried on down into West Bute Dock where her walk faltered slightly as she approached *The Solomon*. She wondered what mood Nathan would be in today. She knew almost as soon as she saw him, often turning around and walking straight off again if his look was miserable or truculent. There was never any point in trying to deal with him when he was in that state.

But he was in a completely sunny mood, she was relieved to see as she sat down at the ward room table, offering her tea and some salty biscuits. 'They're nothing much, probably only good for axeheads, but that's about all there is. That Father O'Reilly brought them down but you need teeth of granite to make any impression on them.' Her eyes narrowed in new understanding. So the poteen priest had been around. No wonder he was in such a good mood. 'I would guess even those wharf rats would break their teeth on them.'

'So why are you giving them to me then?'

'Curiosity really. I've always thought your teeth would get through anything but I wonder if you'll find your match in them.'

She took a good bite on one and it crunched in her mouth. 'They're all right. Not the greatest, but all right.'

'Yes, I knew it. Those teeth of yours would get through anything at all. How are you feeling?'

She frowned a question mark. 'I'm feeling fine. How are you feeling?'

'I'm fine, just fine. I was wondering, if you want to know . . . I was wondering if you'd like to have a look at my bunk. I've cleaned out one of the rooms in the apprentices' quarter.'

Well, well. She would have to take a closer look at this poteen lark. It had been a very long time since he had come up with a proposition like that. 'What's so special about this bunk then?'

'Nice mattress, good springs, lovely curtains.'

'Mmm,' she said getting up and taking off her coat. 'I feel like a bit of a lie-down come to think of it. Are you sure the springs are all right?'

'None better, girl. None better.'

The apprentices' cabin was large enough for six bunks – three on either side – and had long been given over to the spiders and cockroaches. But somehow he had removed all the beds, except one, clearing and cleaning the cabin; the deck-boards were scrubbed and gleaming, there were even a few flowers in a pop bottle on the table. It all suggested that this had not been the result of some sudden, poteen-soaked mood but something he had long thought out and then worked on.

'It's lovely, Nathan,' she said. 'I call that lovely.'

'Try the bed, girl. The bed.'

She pressed her fingers down on it, finding the mattress soft and yielding.

'Eider duck feathers,' he explained. 'I got hold of some sacks of duck feathers off one of the ships and it started me thinking about a mattress I had as a kid. So I got hold of one of the old palliasses and here we are. It's a funny thing to sleep on. You keep sinking into dips and find it difficult to get out – it's not like an ordinary mattress at all.'

She went over to the porthole, running the tips of her finger around the shining brass. 'You have been hard at work, haven't you? How did you bring that up?'

'Vinegar and soda. Some old swabby told me about that one day. It seems if you give it a rub every day it takes off the salt corrosion. Damn difficult at the start, but as long as you do it once a day, progress is made.'

'And the floors?'

'Just an old-fashioned scrubbing brush and plenty of elbow grease,' he smirked. 'I've been thinking I might get around to the rest of the ship one day. That would be lovely, wouldn't it? We could take on a group of people and just sail away.'

'Yes, that would be lovely.' His new dream chilled her heart a little since she recalled how even now his position on the ship was under threat from Edward; how Nathan had no rights of ownership and could be thrown off at any moment. But, if necessary, she would defend his corner for him; do almost anything to help that special part of him she had once loved rise to the surface again. If he lost the ship now he would certainly lose himself too.

He gave her an uncertain, tremulous kiss and she slipped off her coat and dress, jumping under the blankets and facing the bulkhead, waiting for him to undress himself, free from her inquisitive gaze. In his uncertainty he just took off his shoes and trousers, even leaving his socks on. After they had kissed again she said, 'I never, ever allow anyone to touch me with his socks on,' wriggling down through the sloping banks of duck feathers and stifling a sneeze as she pulled his socks off, staying down there and nibbling the sides of his legs, feeling him rise to full mast as she took him into her mouth.

She had always taken her pleasure in the giving of pleasure and it was so very good feeling his body relax and stiffen in tense, soft waves. She called up a few of her old tricks, feeling him stiffen again, but moved away to another pressure point, wanting this little square dance to last for ever. She heard Bessie Smith's voice in her mind, crying with the pain of it all. But it was not always pain, Bessie – even when you were locked in the exquisite pain of loving a difficult, broken man. Sometimes in the deep, dark caverns of it all you could still find wonderful and unexpected pools of joy; discover something you had long despaired of ever finding again. He had been right about this feather mattress though, her head sinking into some soft dark crater and legs up high as if she was praying on the top of a cliff.

She sneezed again before stretching out on top of him, her legs straddling his thighs. It was the very moment when he broke into her damp tight vagina – the painful violation at the start of the communion – that she always enjoyed the most, feeling him tunnelling deep into her being, making the two of them one and whole. It made her throat go dry and the patterns of her breath change. She lay quite still, feeling the beat of his heart with hers, now hoisting her head up a little and looking down into his eyes – dark, bewildered and streaming with tears. Oh God, he really was such a mess. She licked his salty tears away, her hips moving from him again, happy to feel that he was still deep and hard inside her; that perhaps he was not suffering from that black old guilt again but weeping in some difficult tide of sorrow as she reached out for parts of his old happiness, those things that were once so wonderful.

She *would* put him back together again. She was very sure of that now. And she would fight anyone who attacked him, sensing that, with Edward's return, there was going to be a three-cornered fight in which she would become irrevocably involved. But the prospect of a fight – against both Edward and a man as powerful as Hamilton – daunted her not at all. Everything in her life had meant some sort of fight and she would never accept losing while there was any breath in her body at all; it was her African spirit that helped her to battle again and again for those whom she loved.

Edward would soon come looking for her again; she knew men like Edward – when they got what they wanted they would always come back for more, no matter how many years had gone by. If it helped Nathan at all she would join forces with Edward to beat Hamilton and, by the same token, she would just as happily help Hamilton to beat Edward. She would join any alliance at all to overcome anything which threatened the broken bird now inside her body and lying in her arms – weeping silently in her arms, as she moved slowly up and down along his length.

She just managed to catch another sneeze, wondering if she was getting some sort of head cold. She shifted him over on top of her, letting him rest there for a while then his loins stirred again and he came moving back to her with a sudden and unexpected power, every part of him straining and shivering, then, holding her so very tight, he let it all go and his whole body twitched as if in spasm. He lay quite still, smoothing her hair with his hands and yet still crying.

'Sophie girl, that was about the nicest thing that's ever

happened to me,' he burbled, quite helpless with gratitude. 'A man never really knows how thirsty he is until he goes right to the well of life. There's something deep in your body that's the key to everything; the key to the deepest joy and difficulty.'

She loved him when he spoke like this; that old dark poetry of his mind flowing again – so powerful with the spirit of his generous being. There was so much pure goodness slopping around inside him, so much that had a way of getting lost. It was no accident that, whenever she wrote one of her love songs, she always thought of him – of that which they had both lost.

Even as they lay together holding one another she decided that she would say nothing about the threat to his home. Just for the moment she would look for ways in which she could fight on his behalf and help him find his lost pride. A little sneeze exploded again inside her nose and then she remembered something quite terrible. Some people got hay fever in the summer but she had always had this thing about chickens which, for some curious reason, always set her off sneezing whenever she came near them.

'These eider duck feathers in this mattress,' she said. 'They're difficult to get hold of, aren't they? They wouldn't be chicken feathers, would they?'

'They might. I'm not sure what the difference is.'

'The difference is that chickens always make me sneeze and I'm pretty certain you've stuffed this thing with chicken feathers.'

'Smelly old chicken feathers eh? Well in that case . . . in that case.' He stood up and patted her bottom, indicating that she should stand up too. He then walked over to the porthole and opened it, returned to the bed and picked up the mattress which he proceeded to bung through the hole, punching it again and again until the mattress had flopped into the dock. 'Go and find another ship,' he called after it. 'No room for sneezers here.'

She lay back on the hard horsehair mattress underneath, hands behind her head and smiling at him. That was her Nathan. 'Come here, you daft sod,' she said. 'You're not going to need a mattress while I'm around. I'm going to make you so tired you'll be sleeping on bare boards.'

But it was Sophie who was feeling ready to sleep on bare boards when she reluctantly dragged herself away from the windjammer. She was due to rehearse with the band that night. Her knees were quite wobbly as she made her way along the quayside through the glowing early evening, the phosphorescent flares of the ships' lights glittering all around like a gathering circus.

This was the part of the day that she always liked the best, neither light nor dark, the toil of the day done and the fun of the evening yet to start; today it was counterpointed by her own feelings of drifting serenity. The trouble was that she did not terribly feel like singing the blues while she was in this mood. The very motor power of the blues was misery and pain and yet she could not even remember what they felt like, just now, this night in the slumbering dockland. The sound of music drifted out from one of the ship's radios, a tune oddly familiar which she could hum along to. Nathan's chicken feather mattress was floating on the glassy smooth dock like a collapsed brown porpoise unsure whether to sink or swim. A figure drifted past her disappearing into the shed behind the Norwegian church. Through the shed window she could just about make him out lighting an oil lamp – the sudden burst of yellow-green light swelling and glimmering on a white ivory cross in front of a small altarpiece. So he must be that holy hermit that Nathan was always talking about. This part of the world certainly attracted the oddest of figures and yet there was none odder, she guessed, than her own Nathan.

But with the cold chilling her feet and a rehearsal due this was no time to be hanging about pondering on odd comings and goings. She hurried on through the gloaming, stepping away from the railway line to let a wheezing coal train go spluttering and puffing past. The warm steam blasted at her shins, the rattling wagons loaded high with coal. There had been a number of raids on these coal trains of late – street urchins putting railways sleepers on the line to force the train to stop. Then they would rush out and haul the wagon doors open, letting the coal spill out onto the sides of the tracks. Next thing they were in with buckets and bags, scavenging the coal and selling it off to the local householders.

Obadiah was sitting in the kitchen with his head buried in his hands when she returned home. Effey was sitting at the table studying a picture book and neither of them looked up as she walked in. 'Well, it's so nice to feel so welcome,' she said to no one in particular. 'I might as well go straight back out again. What's the matter with you two then?'

No reply, but Effey did manage to turn over the page of her book.

'Look, we've got a rehearsal tonight, in case you've forgotten. Is anyone going to make a cup of tea for me before we get moving?'

Effey slid off her chair to fill the kettle but Obadiah's head remained well and truly buried in his hands. 'I don't feel like rehearsing tonight, sister,' he said finally. 'It's those West Indians. They're making me ashamed of being black.'

'Oh, not all that again. Honest, Obe, I don't know why you bother at all. Come on then, tell me. What's happened now?'

His words punctuated by frequent sighs and moans, Obe explained that he had called a meeting of the island elders that afternoon in the Institute for Colonial Freedom and seven of them had turned up. He had explained his plan to set up the Sons of Africa group and how he wanted them to go back to their people from their own islands and say that it was time for them to come together and fight for their rights. The trouble was, according to Obe, that no one wanted to get together with anyone and they spent *all bloody afternoon* quarrelling and bickering with one another about the most idiotic points. He had never in all his born days heard such nonsense. There was the one from St Kitts moaning that the problem with Jamaica was that they were all lazy. Jamaica went on about how everyone from St Kitts had trouble working out what a bar of soap was for. Barbados had carved up the domino league and everyone had got most bitter about that. 'I ask you. A game of bloody dominoes and they're all at one another's throats.' Then some man had run off with a Trinidadian wife and everyone was to blame for that. And the more they had abused that woman the more Obe had come to like her and wanted to meet her himself since it turned out that she had slept with almost every black man in South Wales, no matter what island he had come from.

Sophie sighed commiseration, picking up the cup of tea which Effey had put on the table. There was a slab of cake too and she nibbled at that. She really did not understand why he was bothering at all; why he did not accept that there were some people who were just unorganizable. But when you were committed you were committed, she supposed. What she did understand was that a man like Obe would never give up because the African flame of the fighter burned bright in him too. He would hardly extinguish that just because a few old farts could not bring themselves to agree with one another. 'They're old men with daft old ideas, Obe. Nothing always comes from nothing. Why don't you go for the younger ones? They're with us on the jazz band so you've got a start there.'

'I've been thinking of that, sister. I just couldn't deal with those old bastards again.'

'Talking of old bastards,' a cultured voice said from behind them in the living room. 'Here's another one.'

Sophie looked up from her tea at Obe who, in his turn, looked into the living room. A man wearing a light brown hacking jacket with loud check trousers was standing at the far end in the doorway. She knew without turning her head who he was. Edward Gurney had walked back into her home and her life.

'I did knock,' Edward explained. 'But when there was no reply I saw that the door was ajar and just walked in.'

'So I see,' said Sophie, bleakly surveying a part of her past. 'But, as I remember, you never were very much use at knocking, were you, Edward?'

He ignored the jibe. 'We need to talk, Sophie,' he said, taking several steps forward across the living room and offering her a bunch of flowers. 'There is a lot to talk about.'

'We can't talk now, Edward. We're due for a rehearsal.' She made no move to stand up or accept the proffered bunch of flowers, feeling a stiff coldness. 'A few things have changed since you were last around. We've got a band now. Obe, here, is the trumpeter and we're due to meet in a few minutes.'

'It's only a few minutes I want, Sophie,' he said, ignoring Obe and putting the flowers down on the armchair. 'Perhaps we can have a proper chat another time. But just for now, all I want is a few minutes.'

'I don't want to be rude, Edward, but the boys will be waiting for us.'

'Oh, give him a few minutes,' said Obe, with a backward wave of his hand. 'You could give him all night for all I care. We haven't got that much to rehearse anyway. It's always best when it's a shambles.'

'A few minutes and then we're going, Obe. There's only so much shambles I can take.' Sophie stepped into the living room, closing the door behind her. 'I've got this band you see, Edward.

Believe it or not I've become a bit of a singer. If you remember, I also clean down in Howard Close for you-know-who, which has meant that I've been able to give up you-know-what.'

'That's a shame. That's a very great shame since you were the very best at you-know-what.'

'Well, I haven't given it *all* up, if you get my drift.' She stared at him and dropped her eyes flirtatiously – he was, after all, the boss of the windjammer now. 'I just don't take money for it any more. So, tell me, what is this that you want to talk about so urgently?'

'I'm going to work in my father's business with that man. What I need to know from you just at the moment is if, after all these years, you ever came close to finding out who murdered your friend.'

'Why bring all that up again?' She took in a sharp breath of air but shook her head, saying no more.

'You see, Sophie, I have a certain problem that I need to solve. I want to solve it quickly. The night those men attacked me here I had a cup in a shoulder bag. I had stolen the cup out of Cardiff Castle and they stole it from me.'

'A cup's a cup, I would have thought. What's so important about a cup?'

'I really don't know the answer to that one, Sophie. All I know is that it's important to a lot of people: that there's mystery and magic attached to it that no one understands. It is believed that it brings power and benefit to whoever owns it. I don't know. Hamilton will give anything to get his hands on that cup, and if I could get hold of it, I could get my hands on him.'

'You've come back to do him in then, have you, Edward?' she asked evenly.

He looked at her hard, unsure of her loyalties.

'I'm just for myself, Edward,' she said, reading his doubts. 'He's just a man who gives me a cleaning job. I have no feelings about him one way or the other. So you have come to do him in. It'll be tough. Hamilton is a big man in more ways than one.'

'I'm not afraid of him,' he sneered. 'That man has taken what's mine, Sophie, so he must pay. It's that simple. Quite how I'm going to fix him I can't be too sure but I'd like to find a way of letting him slowly bleed to death. Through his business perhaps. Just slowly roast the old bastard.'

Even as he was talking Sophie could hear Obe making impatient noises in the kitchen. She wondered how she might use this information to her advantage. Lever handles were presenting themselves everywhere and, if she pulled the right one, she might well salvage the windjammer for the one that she really cared for. Not that she had any great dislike for Edward, she now remembered. He might be able to roast Hamilton, though somehow she doubted it. All that she needed to do was stay close to whomever won.

'Are you coming or not?' Obe called out.

'Why don't you come down for our rehearsal, Edward? You might find it a bit of fun. The Razzy Dazzy Spasm Jazz Band is getting very popular, you know. You could just sit, have a few drinks and listen to us argue. We argue better than we play.'

'You can say that again, sister,' called Obe. 'Now are you coming or not? Otherwise I'm going straight to bed.'

There was a full tide that night and, with it, came a fast, almost warm wind moaning with vague promises of thunder. Lightning stammered briefly as a derelict sat drinking rough cider in the doorway of one of the ship's chandlers, his old, ripped hands holding the brown flagon as if it was a precious object. Two policemen stopped to look down at him, giving his shoes a few playful kicks before moving on again.

Inside the Salvation Army hostel at the top of Bute Street more than a hundred men were snoring and whiffling in the cold, wood-beamed dormitory. Tattered, dark-stained raincoats hung on the ends of the beds. False teeth dreamed Steradent dreams in jars of water. A man turned over beneath his blue-patterned quilt and groaned as if in the deepest and cruellest nightmare. 'Shurrup, you old goat,' someone called, throwing something metallic which clattered emptily on the floorboards. On the wall was written

> 'Call upon me
> In the time of trouble
> I will deliver thee.'
> *Psalm 50: 15.*

The rehearsal, as Sophie had predicted, was an argumentative affair. Most of the acrimony was generated by a row between

Obe and the pianist. It turned out that the pianist's father had been to the abortive meeting in the Institute that afternoon and it may well have been the pianist's Trinidadian mother who was being serviced by all and sundry. But whatever the bone of contention they were making no progress whatsoever, with Obe repeatedly shouting, 'Right. Let's start it all over again.' Very soon the pianist decided that he did not want to start it all over again and just sat there like a sulking five-year-old, hands on knees and staring at the keys, while the others rattled on as best they could.

In the circumstances Sophie was very glad indeed that Edward had come along since she could spend some time with him chatting, drinking and sharing cigarettes. He told her of how the aborigines in Australia liked to sing a lot and how they sometimes just walked around for days marking out their territories with songs. 'A bit like how a cat goes around pissing out the boundaries of his area.' He also told her of the bars in Sydney where the barmen would be expected to sing ballads, largely to try and calm down the unruly customers who loved nothing better than to have a great fight over nothing. 'Most nights the hill above the port is running with so much blood they actually call it Blood Hill.'

She had always loved those steamy vivacious stories of foreign ports where the men drank and loved and fought in almost equal parts and with equal intensity. She could see that Edward had not escaped his share of injury either, for there were some particularly vicious scars on his neck and hands. He would not elaborate on all of them but did tell her about his epic two-day struggle with one Australian giant who just would not stay down even after being hit with planks, buckets and, at one point, a twelve-foot pole. Edward had finally managed to drive a car at him and hurl him into a dock where, the day after he had been fished out, he came around covered in bandages to Edward's house asking what had happened.

Just like a seaman paid off after a long trip he was full of such stories and she had quite forgotten how personable he could be when he was happy and relaxed, touching her arm a lot as he spoke and even going downstairs several times to buy trays of drinks for the band. But one thing she had picked up quite clearly was that he was hungry for her body too. She did not mind that much either, grateful, at least, that she was with a man who could enthral and amuse her. Nathan had once been able to enthral and amuse her too and her afternoon with him on the windjammer had reminded her all too vividly of the way he had once been – full of life and that old barnstorming poetry. But such moods were rare now and he was no longer any kind of fighter, which was hardest to take of all.

The row between Obe and the pianist was finally resolved when the pianist slammed the lid of his piano shut and walked out. 'We're just trying to make some music, not fight a war,' an upset Obe complained to no one in particular. 'I'm not understanding any of this.'

'He was no use anyway,' Sophie commiserated as the pianist left. 'That one will never play the piano properly as long as he's got a hole in his arse.' She turned to Edward. 'You don't play by any chance?' she asked fluttering her eyelashes.

'Afraid not. Not even when I'm rolling drunk.'

She ran through a few more numbers but there was no great interest or enthusiasm and within half an hour they all decided to call it a day. Obe told her that he was going out with a few of the boys from the proposed Sons of Africa so she walked back alone with Edward through the rumbling streets. 'There's going to be one hell of a storm soon,' he said.

Ever since she had seen that he wanted her she had been trying to decide if she wanted him. It was true that she'd had a wonderful afternoon with Nathan but, while she could manage without it for years, she had always found it interesting that the more good sex you had the more you wanted. Now that she had recovered from the exertions of the afternoon she was practically climbing up that lamp post wanting to start over again. They were also in a sense old lovers – even if the basis had been money rather than any feeling – but given his almost appalling need for it and her rising sap, there seemed no point in any preliminaries or evasions. She took off her coat as soon as they walked into the house and, taking his hand, led him up the stairs, where she stepped out of her skirt. 'Right. Let's have a bit of fun,' she breathed.

He was on her in a flash, dropping his trousers and not even taking off his jacket as he went for her greedily. He did not even give her time to take off her knickers and, in his desperation, he went around the sides of the ripped elastic, fumbling and shoving until, predictably, he finished almost as soon as he had begun.

'Feeling better now?' she asked with mock politeness. 'Well,

I suggest you get your clothes off, have a rest and then we'll try and do it properly. That was no good to me at all.'

'Not had much practice just lately,' he said, rather sheepishly.

Another shiver of thunder rolled over the grey slate roofs of the Bay. In her room in No. 18 Custom House, Madge Williams was lying under her bed, her closed eyes and nose all but buried in small still storms of grey dust. Bed springs pressed down on her backside. Her heart was pounding as if trying to break free. Her hands were shaking even though they were clenched tight. It was as if all that wretched anxiety was going to break her in two at any second since, afraid of no man, she was very afraid of thunder, diving straight under the bed or into the broom cupboard under the stairs almost as soon as it began. She must go and see a doctor about all this one day, she promised herself. Meanwhile all she could really do was to make sure that she remembered to dust under the bed in future so that she did not get so filthy the next time the weather took a rumbling turn for the worse.

Just past the canal bridge there was the Cuban Centre, the Cairo Café, Ghana Club, Coronation Café, the George Cross Maltese Club, Loudoun Hotel . . . all bolted and shuttered just now, their patrons dreaming of distant mountains and steaming dishes, the wine of their fathers and the flesh of their loved ones. Torn posters hung off the canal's stone walls like broken pledges . . . PLAYERS PLEASE . . . JESUS SAVES . . . ROBIN STARCH. There was one for Houdini, the Great Escapologist appearing in the Empire. On one dark wall a chalked inscription declared that, 'Ann Evans luvs Ajmir Singh'. Underneath was written, 'She does not'.

More wind and rain came driving together down Bute Street, shunting against anything and everything as the top of a wooden ladder clattered against the high white wall of the Peel Street Mosque. A man was cussing quietly in the teeth of the rain as he crouched on top of the minareted wall, reaching one arm down to help another man up. Now they both dropped into the courtyard inside, both muttering to themselves as one held up a lamp and the other began trying to jemmy open the door to Rashed's private study. It was painfully slow work since they had to deal with three padlocked bolts on the door and, after making little progress, they decided to take the door off its hinges. It finally groaned open like an old man suffering from terminal arthritis and the two men, already dripping wet from the rain, just both stood there as the beam of their lamp trembled on the gold Islamic lettering of the holy scrolls. One of them had stepped forward, when he was just held there *by a smell*. It was a rich, tawny fragrance like a roasting joint of beef, or else it might have been a light smell of the sea, something and nothing, in one nostril and out the other. But it was there. The other man stepped onto the thick carpeting and he too seemed to be caught but not so much by the smell as by *some music* which, on the other hand, might not have been music at all, rather some melodious trick being played by the rain. Another shiver of lightning lit up their faces as they looked at one another and back at the altar.

When Sophie had been a business lady she may well have had hundreds – thousands? – of men grabbing their needs from between her legs, so it was strange, Sophie thought, how there were a few men who were different; a few men who would always stand out in her mind and heart.

Even when her business had been at its busiest and she had met Nathan, she had found it surprising – even astonishing – how much she had revelled in the deep closeness of his body. It was all to do with emotional bonding, she guessed; an awful lot to do with the fact that she just liked him so much that she wanted to get as close to him as possible. Nothing came closer than the sexual act. She had never been much of a one for the sentimental trappings of love.

Yet here now, this rainy night, with Edward's body moving up and down within her she knew that there was something special and different with him too. She had never much liked him, particularly when he used to abuse her so cruelly and painfully against that warehouse wall, but she had always had a sort of respect for this man apart. Now that he had burned off some more of his immediate excesses he did not seem to have that need to hurt her either, just being warm, grateful and uncharacteristically gentle. He even kissed her a few times which, given her past, was something she had never really quite got used to. Whenever she was kissed she always felt like bursting out into laughter.

But she was not even close to bursting out into laughter just now, enjoying his every move as he rode on in some battle to ease his private terror. He did not seem to want to stop for anything either, his small driving hips bearing down on her insatiably. But she did not mind that. With a hunger like his he could be as insatiable as he wanted.

He stopped for a moment and she wrapped his head in her arms, gazing up at the rain washing against the window. Her eyebrows crouched into a frown when she thought she heard some distant scream but she decided after a minute it must have been a cat.

The two men left the Mosque with the practised movements of circus tumblers, the one making a chair with his hands to throw his partner up onto the courtyard wall. The one left below then threw up a bulky bag before letting the other haul him up by the arm. It was not easy negotiating such a high wall in the driving rain, and not very safe either when, with the sky lit up by thousands of jagged volts, you could be spotted by almost anyone for miles around. With such stage lighting even the police might see you and take you away.

But their confidence and agility seemed unimpaired by the hazardous weather as they both jumped to the ground and ran shoulder to shoulder towards Alice Street, their feet slapping through the puddles in the gutters, laughing brightly and throwing the bag back and forth between them like a rugby ball.

# CHAPTER NINETEEN

As the hour of the meeting approached Obe felt increasingly restless and nervous. He paced up and down the small rostrum of the Institute for Colonial Freedom in Loudoun Square. He was suffering from that familiar fear that everyone has when they call a meeting. Would anyone at all turn up?

So far there were only three people sitting in the middle benches of the corrugated-iron shed, leaving room for around three hundred more. Obe's black face had almost paled with anxiety. For something to do he leaned down between his knees and undid his shoe laces before doing them up again. He sat up. 'Well at least we had a go,' he told his friend Benedict who was carefully studying the backs of his hands. 'At least we had a go. We can't be accused of not trying.'

Few could have tried harder in the last few weeks to set up this meeting, the first ever of the Sons of Africa. They had flyposted every lamp post and telegraph pole throughout the Bay. Posters had gone up in the seamen's lodging houses. Announcements had also been made in the jazz sessions in the Ship and Pilot, with Obe urging everyone with African or West Indian connections to turn up 'before it was too late.' Before what was too late? Just come and find out.

A couple of white students had turned up but Obe had ushered them out. He did not want them there and neither did he want the press since they were already having enough trouble from the Western Mail which had just published the police chief's recent report on the Coloured Problem, going on at such virulent length about the blacks in the city it suggested to Obe that the policeman had missed his true vocation in the Ku Klux Klan.

A few others drifted in followed by a couple more. Sophie had suggested that they took the band along – which would have packed them in easily enough – but Obe had firmly vetoed that idea. He wanted the Sons of Africa to be a serious organization for serious young blacks, not some honky jive with everyone throwing themselves around and having fun. 'Suit yourself,' Sophie sniffed. Obe could be quite the puritan when he wanted to be and she never quite understood how he always played that trumpet of his so sensuously. She often wondered what he did for sex since he seemed to have no interest in that either.

Another largish group from British Guyana came and filled up the front bench. Soon they were fairly streaming through the door. When the meeting was due to start, there might even have been two hundred there. 'I'd like to thank you all for comin' to the first meeting of the Sons of Africa,' he told them, feeling slightly relieved. 'I've called it because we black boys are down on our knees and getting stuffed right and left. We've got our hands tied behind our backs and, what's even worse, we can't even seem to agree among ourselves on the time of day. We have nothing and when you've got nothing you've got nothing to lose. So it's time to face up to all that since we are either going to fight and live together or we are going to die apart.'

Obe was not a natural speaker – having none of the cadences or musical flows of the Welsh *hywl*. He paused now and then to chew on his lip; if anything, his sentences came a little awkwardly. But they were fresh and firm; what he lacked in style he made up for with authority and conviction.

'The real problem for us blacks in this city is that we are caught squarely between two monsters,' he went on, raising a finger and pointing. 'We are caught between that bloated and corrupt council in the City Hall – just about all of them, rotten to the core. And . . .' His finger moved in another direction. '. . . what is an even greater monster – the monster of the old plantation mentality. You know . . . yes, suh, yes, suh, bwana boss. Anythin' you say, suh . . . jus' lemme get down on mah funny black knees an' kiss your sweet white ass. Yes, suh, no suh . . . bwana boss.'

The Uncle Tom imitation, complete with rolling eyes and hands shaking up and down obsequiously, raised a roar of delighted laughter as yet more young blacks came packing into the hall and standing around the back. Already the air was warm and smoky as Obe continued his rant: 'What we need, my brothers and sisters, is the glow of some new fire – a new resolve to come together. We cannot do anything alone. We need to be asking – as one group – just one question. Why? Why do we get less dole payments than white families? Why are there no blacks working on council buses, roads and cemeteries? Why do we have the worst housing in the city and our children suffer from the worst rate of tuberculosis? Why are we living six to a room?'

Some of the younger blacks in the audience were already responding to Obe's angry questions, muttering and repeating: 'Yes. Why?' One was actually standing on a chair, trying to speak, waving an admonitory finger around like a broken twig. Others were trying to get him to sit down again but he would not. In a way the small commotion added to the warmth of the meeting, helping Obe to raise the temperature a little.

'As some of you may know I've just come out of the South Wales valleys where I was working as a miner. The men in those blooming pits have done a wonderful job in getting themselves organized and taking on the government. And how did they manage to do that?' He raised a bunched fist. 'Because the miners are rock solid that's why. They united under the banner of socialism and fought the whole might of the government again and again. They were beaten in the '26 strike but now they're stronger than ever. And that's the challenge before us here tonight. We have to forget all this island tribalism and unite to fight this damned city council. That's what the Sons of Africa can – and must – do. *Together*.'

More foot-stomping and cries of agreement.

'So what I propose we do at the very start is send a deputation to the council to petition for a new black bill of rights. We need to tell them that we want equal dole payments, equal job opportunities and official council support for the Movement for Colonial Freedom. We won't get anything from this gang of Tory crooks, of course, but it's right and proper that we at least set out our demands and then take them from there. In all matters the Sons of Africa must be a lively democratic group who present their arguments with flair and force. They'll listen in the end. They'll *have* to listen in the end. But first of all, we must follow the normal channels and send a deputation with a list of our demands. They won't reply but it will be a start.'

Many present became surprisingly animated by Obe's heady brew of rhetoric and suggestions of revolution. It was clear that he had located a similar vein of anger in many of them. Had he given the word they would have marched on the City Hall there and then.

'We are also going to demand full payment of fares to any blacks who want to be repatriated to Africa or the West Indies. One day the council will recognize all legitimate grievances of the Sons of Africa.'

And so, in a small crowded hut with a corrugated roof on May 16, 1930 the Sons of Africa began their stormy career.

Certain families in certain houses develop their own smells, Edward recalled. There were some smells that he could have identified in any part of the world with his eyes closed, no matter how long he had been away. The home of his old Taunton chum, Bertie Skeffington had a distinct smell verging on a rancid stink. He could have picked up Bertie's stink from half a mile. He had also remembered the peculiar and distinctive smell of the Shipping Exchange in Mountstuart Square and, almost as soon as he had walked into the building, it was as if he had never been away.

The main smell was from the polish on the oak panelling and oak parquet floors. This smoky aroma pervaded the whole building like mustard gas, but there were others too – the rich smell of roasting coffee and frying bacon drifting up from Sculley's restaurant in the basement; the pungent carbolic soap and disinfectant drifting out of the marbled lavatories and the body smells of the brokers themselves – part tawny port, part hair oil and part whiffs of stale, long-smoked cigars. All these drifted together to make something distinctive and unforgettable. As he walked up the steps, he took it all in except that he soon discovered that one key component of the old smell was missing: the wonderful smell of money.

Barely a fraction of the number of brokers of old were now working the Floor. It no longer seemed possible to make a quick fiver let alone a fast £10,000 in a few minutes, buying and selling invisible cargoes in imaginary ships. There simply were no cargoes and even the most imaginative would not find many ships. That week there were barely fifty ships registered in Cardiff, with just nine of them moored in the docks awaiting cargo. Business after business had gone to the wall, with the worth of whole fleets plummeting overnight. A few lines had gone bankrupt and more than a few businessmen had been sent to prison. The clever firms like Oriel had reinvested elsewhere.

Just quietly eavesdropping on a few of the muttering deals he could tell that the old frantic devil-take-the-hindmost approach had gone also. At one point two brokers were discussing the likely profit on a deal and agreeing to split it between them. Even then you could see that there would be very little left to split. The very style of money had gone also. Shoes were scuffed and shirts not properly ironed. A few were even wearing Harris tweeds, which would have won them an outright ban from the Floor just a few years earlier.

Edward put his hand on a pillar and stood with his head

lowered, trying to pick up on another deal which was busy stumbling nowhere. Oh, there were the same grand flourishes and key phrases of old but everything was muted and qualified. Much of it was just talk for the sake of talk. They clearly still liked to bandy figures around and brag about what ship they had where but from where Edward was standing they did not look as if they could raise fifty guineas in cash between the lot of them.

He was still not clear how he could fit into all this, or indeed what he was expected to do. Partington, it seemed, was going to hold his hand for a while. As arranged, there the little man was, busy making notes from Lloyd's List. At least there had been no change in him. He still looked as though he was third-in-charge at a civic funeral.

'Hah, good morning, Mr Edward,' said the dapper clerk, his tongue busy with his customary Mint Imperial. 'Just keeping up a check on some of the lines around here. They're all floundering so we'll have to decide soon which ones to pick off. Most of them have got some movement though it's the Tatem line that we're the most interested in.'

'How many ships has he got just now?' Edward asked, drawing closer to the List and examining it himself.

'Around eight. He's the second largest after us and we're going to need just about all the tonnage he's got – and quite soon too. We could just about take him now but he should get weaker yet.'

'How weak is weak?'

'Four or five ships sitting around without any orders is very weak indeed. We could make a strong and decisive move if he was reduced to that. He's had two moored in San Francisco for three weeks now. You should be able to take him easily, Mr Edward.'

'Me?'

'Oh most certainly, most certainly. Mr Hamilton won't deal with him and I'm too lowly for him to speak business with me. So this is going to be your play, Mr Edward. I'll arm you with all the information you need but you'll be making the play.'

*He'd be making the play*. Why him? Why were these two bringing him back into the shipping business when they were clearly more than capable of handling it themselves? Edward had a distinct feeling that he was being set up again; pushed forward into a position where his defences would be weak, and vulnerable to a quick salient on his flanks. Well he could always rearrange his defences if he could work out where the attack was coming from. Then he could counterattack hard.

'You'll be meeting a representative of the Krupp arms manufacturers in a few days' time, Mr Edward. At the meeting you will be expected to present a complete inventory of all Oriel shipping assets together with the ships' current placements and capabilities. Krupp need to use a shipping line for the distribution of munitions. We are going to be moving large amounts of arms to the Franco Government in Spain but we also have some strong interests in parts of Africa. Krupp are offering an extremely large contract which will build us up very nicely until the world is ready again for war. That's just the way the world is, Mr Edward. There's nothing we can do about it, after all. If the world must go to war then we might as well make money out of it.'

'I couldn't agree more.'

Partington licked his pencil and scribbled down a few more notes before putting his notebook back into his pocket. 'Plotting and scheming is what this shipping business is all about, Mr Edward. That's what you were always so good at and why we were so keen to have you back with us. It's most extraordinarily difficult to find the right person to do this kind of work.' He cleared his throat as if signifying a change of tone, sticking his thumbs into the sides of his waistcoat before pulling them out again. 'I had nothing to do with what happened that night in the castle, Mr Edward. And neither had Mr Hamilton. It all just went wrong. We never knew the police would try and pick you up. I thought I had better say that and now I've said it. All we ever really wanted was that cup. The Germans will probably be asking about it too. You've made no progress in locating it, I take it? It would be very nice to report some progress to Mr Hamilton.'

Edward had already decided that he had better keep the carrot dangling, even if it merely was an illusion. Perhaps it was only the possibility that he would get that cup that was actually keeping him alive. It was, so to speak, his sole life insurance policy.

'I have made some progress,' he ventured, 'but I do not want you saying anything to Hamilton just at this moment. My best information is that a Catholic priest in Newtown has the cup and I might be able to get it off him. If I don't do it by fair means I shall do it by foul. But, just for now, I really don't want you saying anything at all.'

'You're in charge, Mr Edward.'

'But, Partington . . .' Edward looked up and down the corridors of the Exchange before lowering his voice into the softest urgency. 'Partington, just let me ask you one question, which I have asked frequently and have yet to receive a satisfactory reply. Hamilton wants that cup badly. Now you say the Germans will be asking about it. So please tell me one thing. I know there is something very strange about that cup, since I once laid my hands on it. But what is it? What's so special about that cup?'

'I really don't know, Mr Edward,' Partington replied, so unhesitatingly that it suggested he was not lying. 'Neither do I have any theories – fanciful or otherwise. Mr Hamilton has a taste for the mystical. And I just do as I'm told. Thus far, no one at all has explained to me what that cup is about if, indeed, it is about anything at all. But you are near to acquiring it, you say?'

'I'll get it. Don't worry about that. But in the meantime I'm to move against Tatem, am I? When?'

'That's rather for you to decide, Mr Edward. But let's go back to the office and put all our figures together first. We need to have a complete rundown of Mr Tatem's assets and particularly his debts. We need to know exactly how liquid we are and then make our decisions on the basis of that. Perhaps the easiest way to get to Tatem might be through his debts.'

Yes, Partington did not need him at all, this wily old journeyman with his intimate knowledge of the ways of commerce. They must have worked out all the moves against Tatem in advance, so what did they want from Edward unless it was to set him up again? There and then he decided that if he was going to be set up again then Partington's pinstriped bottom was going to be the very first nailed to the wall.

'Do we have the complete list of who Tatem owes money to?'

'We know some. The bookmakers for one. He's won and lost a fortune on the horses – even won the Derby a few years back. There's also a few ship's chandlers, businesses like that. It's all back in the office, Mr Edward. I've been keeping a file on Tatem for years.'

'Yes . . . well. Look, I'll meet you back in the office in half an hour. I just want to go over and have a look at my windjammer.'

'It's in a very big mess, Mr Edward. I remember you loved that ship so much, but be prepared to be heartbroken when you do see it. *The Solomon* is the saddest ship afloat.'

It was a rolling spring morning, dizzy with sunshine, and seagulls gliding on thermal currents as Edward crossed Mount-stuart Square, pausing on the corner of Bute Street and Bute Terrace as a tram went rattling past. This was Windy Corner or Penniless Point, where unshaven men with knotted scarves and flat caps just stood with hands in pockets, looking around them and waiting for the pubs to open. Their eyes had the dull colour of stone. With a slow dip of the shoulder, a few of them moved in the direction of Edward, about to tap him for the traditional price of a cup of tea. But he had seen them coming and walked over to the other side of the road fast.

But even there, other men came jerking out of a side alley to beard him, forcing him to cross back again. Yes, the fall of the Exchange was almost exactly mirrored out in these streets. He remembered Bute Street in particular when it was full of vivacious shunts of people bustling about and making money. But now there was just this. Just what? This!

He was walking towards the dock gate when he heard a strange, hollow human call and saw several seagulls falling down out of the skies, their large wings flapping wildly like aeroplanes in an uncontrollable nosedive. In fact they were attracted by the cry of young Tommy Letton who had taken a load of fresh fish onto his handcart and was just starting his rounds through the Bay. Tommy hated these dive-bombing seagulls and would often stop, picking up the brass dish off his weighing scale and hitting out at them as they hovered just above his cart, their great wings squeaking as their thieving yellow beaks tried to make off with his delicious fresh fish.

Edward had to wait for ten minutes or more before he could cross the lock gate into the West Bute Dock. A sandhopper was due to sail out so he leaned on an iron rail, watching the slow mechanical opera of one gate closing and the sluice gates on the other opening. The sea in the lock itself leaped and boiled like an erupting volcano, the hissing cliffs of water rising to eight or ten feet as all that anxious water rushed together furiously until the different levels evened out again, smooth and placid. The sandhopper moved up into the lock itself, the gates closing behind it again as the skipper stood at the wheel puffing serenely on his pipe before another gate let him out onto the full tide.

There were some five ships, red with rust, lying around the West Bute Dock but, even in her fallen state, Edward recognized immediately the saddest ship afloat. Nothing short of complete demolition would have detracted from the fine, full lines of her hull and the thrilling thrust of her bowsprit. Even with her broken masts and torn, rotten rigging there was still a poetry about her which lifted his soul. In some ways she was the great actress who had lost much with age but had then acquired something else which had made her more mysterious, even more compelling. He wanted her then as much as he had ever wanted her when he had been young. It had always been his most cherished dream that he could sail her one day. Not that it was ever likely now; the hull had gone rotten and she would have to be completely rebuilt.

Something moved at the corner of his eye and he spotted a young boy diving off the funnel of one of the moored ships, chest thrown out and arms apart as he sailed through the air to land in the water with scarcely a ripple. Two others were climbing up the same funnel and calling out to one another before they too made the same death-defying dive.

Edward looked back at *The Solomon* and was very surprised to see his Somali whore stepping off the gangplank. He took a few steps behind a crane as he watched her turn and shout something at a man standing next to the wheelhouse. From this distance – and with the diving children making such a noise nearby – he could not make out what Sophie was shouting about. But from the few odd words that he did pick up, it sounded like nothing so much as an argument.

She was tight-lipped and glaring hard when she walked past Edward who, still hidden from view, waited for her to leave the dock before he walked down to the windjammer. He wanted to know who this man was who was living on his ship. He further wanted to know what this man was doing with his woman. *His* woman? Well, he had to admit that he had never gone back to the same one so regularly and happily. He also had to admit that, even now, there was something green and fiery burning in the very pit of his belly, and this green fire was something very like jealousy. He might even keel-haul that interloper.

But the interloper could not be found as Edward wandered the deck, sticking his head down the hatches. 'Hello there,' he called out over and over again. Now and then he caught the angry flash of a cat's eyes in the dusty darkness, but nothing by way of the man he was looking for. 'Hello there.' He walked into the empty ward room, resisting the temptation to start nosing around in some boxes under the large table. He turned to leave and just behind the door found himself facing the barrel of a gun.

'I'd be very careful indeed with that thing,' Edward said evenly, taking a step backwards, keeping an eye on the gun and not even looking up into Nathan's face. 'Just be very careful indeed.'

'You're trespassing on private property.' Nathan was holding the gun with both hands and waggled its barrel, motioning Edward to leave. 'This gun doesn't shoot straight. There's no telling who'll get shot if you don't leave. Go now and there'll be no accidents.'

Edward was still totally absorbed in the gun, wondering if it even worked. It was an unfamiliar make to him and so antiquated it might even have done service against the Spanish Armada. The bald-headed fool was holding it unsteadily like some ferocious ferret he was trying to strangle. Now, on top of all that, he was saying that he couldn't shoot straight. Nothing about him made any sense. He wasn't Jesse James, that was for sure.

'Just put that thing down there and I'll leave immediately,' Edward said.

'You just leave immediately and *then* I'll put that thing down there.'

Edward shrugged. 'As you wish. I'll leave now.' He saw the gun lower fractionally, took two steps towards the door and, on his third, aimed a kick straight into Nathan's groin. There was a ferocious bang accompanied by a spurt of green and yellow flame. Nathan dropped the gun as if it had become boiling hot and Edward squeezed both of his ears with the hams of his hands before both men looked up at a huge, gaping hole in the deckhead. A thin trickle of dust slithered and tumbled down through a newly-minted shaft of sunlight.

'I told you it didn't shoot straight,' said Nathan. 'Now look what you've gone and done.'

'You're going to kill someone with this,' stammered

Edward. 'Most probably yourself.' His hands trembling, he picked up the gun with thumb and forefinger and took it towards the open porthole, where he dropped it into the dock with a faint plop. Nathan didn't notice the loss of his firearm since he was now busy studying a burn blister on his right hand. 'I've never understood this gun lark,' he wailed to no one in particular. 'That's the second time I've fired it and the second time I've burned myself. You're not supposed to burn yourself when you fire a gun, are you? Those cowboys must have hands like charcoal. Look at this mess. You'd better throw that gun over the side.'

'I've thrown it over the side. You'll need to put your hand in cold water. That'll bring the blister down.'

'Butter helps. Or so I've been told.'

'Not much it doesn't. But you could always prick it with a needle. That'll take away a lot of the pain.'

'I've never been convinced of that one. I'm a bit of a nature man myself. The body finds ways of protecting itself and all that stuff. Nature must have a reason for making a blister. It acts as a sort of shield. Bit like a foreskin. Everyone always goes on about how God made a mistake with the foreskin but it's no mistake at all. Look, there's another blister coming up on this hand.'

'That's not so big. Does it hurt?'

'Not so much as the other one. But it's big enough. Look at it. But tell me. What are you doing on my ship anyway?'

'It's not *your* ship. This is *my* ship.'

'But I always thought this ship was owned by that Alexander Hamilton.'

'It's a long story, but this ship was once owned by my father and now it's owned by me. And I have the deeds to prove it.'

'Oh you're a Gurney, are you? Well, if it's yours, as you say, it certainly does belong to you. I'm only a sort of unpaid watchman. How do you fancy a cup of tea?' He stood up, shaking his hands up and down as if drying them. 'But you're going to have an awful lot of work on your plate if you're going to get her back on the sea again. There's a big hole in the roof here for a start.'

Edward looked up at the shaft of sunlight again. 'You're not much of a watchman, are you?'

'Well, I don't claim to have any special training,' Nathan replied, missing the irony of Edward's remark. 'But you could make this ship seaworthy again you know. There's nothing wrong with the keel at all. I was poking around in the bilges the other day and couldn't find dry rot anywhere. I was reading that those struts were soaked in pitch for up to a month at a time. The men who built this knew their wood all right. Even getting new masts wouldn't be much of a problem. Oh I'd give anything to see this marvellous beautiful thing under sail again.'

'It's certainly . . .'

Edward's reply was cut short by the sound of heavy footsteps on the deck outside. The ward room door swung open and both men looked up to see a large policeman framed in the doorway. His hand moved forward and held up a long feathery object. At first Nathan thought it was some strange bouquet of dead flowers until he looked again and saw that it was a large dead seagull with blood still dripping from its chest.

'Someone has just shot this bird,' the policeman explained. 'And I'm wondering if either of you two gentlemen can throw any light on the subject?'

'I can't move no more
There ain't no place for a poor old girl to go.'

Sophie always loved to sing; it was her way of making sense of the ruin that loomed large all around; her way of drawing all her pleasures and pains through her until they made a sort of sorrowing sense. She knew all about the ruins of love and sang about them until stones formed in her throat. There were times when she thought she could soar on her outstretched arms and butterflying fingers; times when the very centre of her being became like a bird as her lips poured forth all those aching words.

She sang with real feeling that night in the Ship and Pilot. The band was working well together too, no discordant notes or selfish, bragging showboating – just all of them happy to come together to create a soft backing texture for the glory of her voice. They did not even seem to want to change the pace much, content to let Sophie cry on about that which had been lost and would never be found again.

Edward had turned up again. She noticed him in the smoky, still crowd. But she did not mind that too much. At least she knew where she was with him, unlike with Nathan who would fly into the blackest mood about nothing at all. It was his sheer unpredictability which was the most exasperating; the way he would become just downright silly and nothing but argument followed.

Edward, on the other hand, seemed to find life too short to bother with argument. He liked to do things – when did Nathan do anything except feel sorry for himself? – and it was going to be most interesting to see how he would fare in his struggle with Hamilton. She had to admit that there was a large part of her that was relishing the coming conflict; she just hoped that neither she nor Nathan were sucked into it.

When the band took a break Edward brought her a drink and they shared a cigarette. He seemed to be in a relaxed, sunny mood telling her how much he enjoyed her numbers and how he had always liked to listen to the aborigines sing in the outback when the sun went down. Song was very much a part of their life too. She could not quite decide if he was paying her a compliment by comparing her singing to that of aborigines but she let it pass.

Just then one of the tallest black men that Sophie had ever seen interrupted their conversation. He was dressed in a turquoise suit and wore a black silk homburg with a white band. She practically had to peer to see the features of his face – he had a large snub noise and baby-like, almost unformed cheeks. He said that his name was Walter Moken and that if neither she nor the members of the bank had any objection he would like to play a tune or two on the piano. 'Since it looks as if it is getting very lonely just sitting here,' he said, glancing at the makeshift stage.

'Help yourself,' Sophie shrugged, watching his legs and arms go striding and sailing over the stage like some great turquoise tarantula about to eat the piano whole. He opened the lid, stretched and pulled on his hands like he was wringing out a pair of tiny black seals, turned and smiled at Sophie and Edward and began tickling those old ivories in a way that the battered pub piano had never been quite tickled before.

Several phrases of melody drifted over them and Sophie looked at Edward before turning to look at Obe who, a pint in hand, stood up in the group he had been sitting with. Others in the band turned away from their conversations to listen as the cascading runs went chasing one another around and around the room. He seemed to know the charleston and the black bottom but, wonder of wonders, he clearly knew ragtime too and it was not long before the banjoist slipped in behind him, adding some real bounce to the foot-tapping rhythms.

'I think we've gone and found ourselves a real pianist,' Obe told Sophie. 'But just sit tight here and I'll find out what he's really made of.'

The band was hurrying and scurrying around a twinkling Scott Joplin rag when Obe let rip with a blood-boiling blast taking it all in the other direction of Bunk Johnson's *Tiger Rag*. In any session, no matter how improvised, this complete change of pace mid-tune would be an extremely bad-mannered thing to do – even by the very poor standards of bad-mannered jazz musicians – but Obe was just giving Walter a run through to see he ran.

Walter ran very well. His homburg barely moved a fraction of an inch though he rolled his great brown eyeballs upwards as his fingers changed pace and he set up some pounding embroidery to Obe's trumpet. Even though he was going at full blast Obe could hear that Walter was listening and, uncannily, he could hear a few odd echoes of Scott in the pounding of Bunk. Walter was telling him that he was coming along but he wasn't going to be totally diverted from his original design. Obe knew then that they had finally found a pianist of the highest order. He held up his thumb to Sophie. Mr Walter Moken was the final piece to be found for the jigsaw of the Razzy Dazzy Spasm Jazz Band.

Perhaps the new pianist's greatest strength was his strong left hand with which he could manage some thundering barrelhouse rolls, while his right hand was more deliberate, gently restating the melody as the banjo came bouncing in with strong support. Then the clarinet dived in with some hot, eel-like licks followed by a steady chugging trombone.

All that was then left to do was for Obe to lay down the markers and draw together on the same race track, leading them up and over the hill, as thrilling as a cavalry charge, until they all came pounding down at the end of the number in exhilarating victory, bringing everyone to their feet, cheering them on and on.

Sophie stepped back onto the stage and they went everywhere for the next five numbers – from barrelhouse to *Yes, We Have No Bananas* and *You Must Not Get So Nasty 'Cos Your Water's On* – and Walter's piano was inspired, lifting everything he came near, as if he had been rehearsing with them all his life. He even managed to work a few mocking riffs into *The Red Flag*, Sophie was amused to hear. She was getting more than a little fed up with the way Obe always insisted on finishing with that boring hymn to left-wing revolution. She agreed with that writer who likened it to the funeral march of a frying eel and it was good to hear Walter poking some cheerful fun at it. Obe needed a bit more of that.

The whole band crowded around Walter at the end of the session, slapping his back and shaking his hand. 'I'm an extremely busy man but I'll join you tomorrow night,' Walter announced without waiting for an invitation. 'Just pay me in drink and cigars. I drink gin and I like coronas.'

'You'll drink beer and smoke Woodbines like everyone else,' said Sophie. 'Just get here at eight and don't be late.'

It was while Edward was helping her on with her coat that yet another stranger came into her life. He spoke to her in an accent that she could not identify and wore a red silk cravat that she did not like, impaled with a diamond tiepin. He said that his name was Billy Donaldson and that he had come down from London to listen to them after reading about the band in *The Melody Maker*. They were even better than he had read.

He continued that he was part of a management agency with extensive contacts throughout the entertainment industry and that, at the moment, he was looking for a band who might be ready to take up a three-week residency in a London club. Without beating about the bush any further he wondered if they might be interested. They were certainly good enough.

Sophie had always wondered about that ladder to fame; how someone one week could be a nobody and the next be a somebody with her name in lights and splattered on posters. How could such an amazing thing happen to anyone? Well, here was how it went. You were one minute singing in a smoky pub and feeling hungry and more than a little thirsty. For some reason you kept thinking of your daughter and hoping she was tucked up in bed, while you also wanted to eat and drink and then make a little love perhaps. You had a bit of a headache and had a small spot on the side of your nose which was threatening to grow into a big spot. You were full of all these small human worries, looking forward to getting out into the night air when, straight out of the blue, a man wearing a red silk cravat that you did not like, came and offered you three weeks of work in a London club.

So this was what the ladder to fame looked like. Faced with it just standing there, propped against the stage of this London club and waiting for her to climb on the first rung, her mind was a total blank. There were queer pulls of emptiness in her chest and her lips could not seem to frame any words at all. She looked at Edward but he made no comment so she went over to Obe who was still chatting with Walter.

Almost the second she told Obe the news she knew that she would not be climbing any ladder with him onto any stage at all. He immediately become cautious and even hostile, going over to Donaldson and asking if the band would be expected to wear suits in this London club. It would be expected. Would there be free beer for the band? A matter for negotiation but the management did not, as a rule, like performers to drink while they were performing. This was one of the very best clubs in the land. Would it be all right to play *The Red Flag* at the end of each act?

Donaldson's mouth stretched into a grimace but he said nothing, frowning at Sophie for help. But she could not help him at all, rolling her eyeballs up into their sockets before turning and saying to Edward, 'Let's go and eat.' She knew then that there was more chance of Obe getting paid to show his black, left-wing arse at a Buckingham Palace dinner than there was of him ever playing trumpet in that club.

'He's so political he'd go and get himself hung in five minutes flat if we went to London,' she told Edward as they walked past the Gospel Mission Hall in Angelina Street. 'He's looking for some kind of black break-out, and now there's a constant stream of young West Indians coming to and from the house. I'm not sure what he's up to but I'm not all that happy the revolution is starting in my front room. But he's not going to leave the Bay. Not just now anyway.'

'I had the strong feeling that Donaldson was talking to *you*, Sophie.'

'*Me*? What do you mean *me*?'

'It's you he's interested in. Not them. He'll be coming back for you. He doesn't want the band – they're a rabble who'd embarrass everyone who came near. It's you they want – a torch singer they could put in front of a big swing band. That's what's going on in London just now. But what do you want?'

They stopped on the corner of Angelina Street as Sophie looked down at her shoes, wondering what it was that she did want. She looked up and around her. The night was unruly with dock sounds, the streets unusually alive with unsteady drunks, roaming prostitutes and even horses and carts – what were they doing out at this time? – all moving, black on green, through the huge luminous bowls of the street gas lamps. A man fell off his feet and just managed to get back up on them again. Three others came walking towards them, spitting and spluttering with all the drunk talk that was coming out of their mouths. An unbearable wave of sadness broke over Sophie's head.

'I don't know what I want except that I really do want to get out of all this. More than anything I want to get Effey out of all this. Look at it – a slum mobbed by drunks who can't even stand up straight. But there is another man around here, if you want to know. It's not just Effey. There's another man. I'd like to get him out of here too.'

'Ah, the man in the windjammer.'

'How do you know about him?'

'That windjammer belongs to me and I went over there this morning. I saw you leaving. That Nathan is some character. He nearly shot me and ended up shooting a seagull instead.'

'He's got that old gun out again, has he? I keep telling him he's going to kill someone with that the way he's going on.'

'That's what I told him too. I threw it over the side in the end. But he's pleasant enough; a little eccentric but with an amusing tongue. We shared a bottle of something horrible in the end and he told me a lot about the docks that I didn't know.'

'He is different all right but he does try my patience. I've given a lot of myself to him over the years but I am beginning to wonder what it's all about.'

They both stopped off for a meal at the Cairo Café. Sophie was so ravenous she managed to tear apart two meals of chicken curry and rice as she told him of her worries, of her attachments to Obe, Effey and Nathan. She did not say that Nathan had once been a minister but she made it abundantly clear that he had once been a man of considerable standing and that she had long felt responsible for his decline. She could never wash her hands of him now either – she had this Somali thing of abiding loyalty to people, no matter what – and she found it easier to try and be supportive of him during his dog years than actually leaving him. She could never just abandon him – even though she thought of it often enough, particularly after those mad moments when he got abusive about nothing at all. It was just her quiet prayer that his dog days would soon come to an end that kept her going.

Her friendship with Obe had grown to something more than mere friendship too, she explained. It was pathetic but even if she found out that Obe and his boys were planning to kill the Lord Mayor – and that might not be too far from the truth from what she had heard some of them say – she *still* would not kick him out of her house. He was as much a part of her life as Nathan. He had after all introduced her to the wonders of music.

And Effey was her daughter and that was the end of it.

Even Edward had taken his place in the enduring pantheon of Sophie's affections but she did not tell him as much, not even after they had left the café and gone straight home to bed together. They crawled over the endless acres of each other's bodies for almost an hour before they joined together, and she could actually see herself singing in the spotlight of that London club until, quite soon, she saw nothing at all, her limbs stretching and flooding with an exploding happiness which, just for the moment, was more than enough in itself.

Later, in the replete darkness, she could tell by his breathing that he was still awake. 'What are you thinking about?' she asked.

'I was thinking that it would be good if you went to London and I went with you,' he said after a while. 'I was thinking that after I've finished my business with Hamilton we could take Effey to London and get a flat, somewhere in Kensington perhaps. I was thinking we could find a good school for her, even make a lady out of her. Who knows? I could even manage your singing career. I know about things like that.'

'Ah, if only things were as easy to do as they are to say. And when do you think you're going to be finishing your business with Hamilton?'

'That'll be over when I've killed him – one way or another.'

'Be careful, Edward. He's big and strong in more ways than

one. Someone like that would take an awful lot of killing and he might end up killing you. I wouldn't like to lose you just now.'

# CHAPTER TWENTY

A fiery dragon with wings outstretched, its mouth forking fire, reared up on the dome of the City Hall in Cardiff; the destructive and mythic ruler of all it surveyed.

All around, beneath its stone talons, the city was preening herself in huge, slow rolls of warm spring sunshine. The three rivers of the Ely, Rhymney and Taff glowed with glittering shifts of gold and silver as they snaked their way down through the body of the city and into the sea, tossing and heaving around beneath huge blankets of changing light.

On such a day it was hard to be like the dragon and stare directly out over such giant, almost mesmerising artefacts of light. It was harder still to maintain a sense of the proper order of things as strong seductive breezes of perfume came wafting upwards from the serried explosions of pink cherry blossom lining the broad avenues and beds of the surrounding Cathays Park. Massed ranks of closed yellow and red tulips were standing shoulder to shoulder, as formal as drilling guardsmen, before the carved Portland stone cliffs of the City Hall.

This building was perhaps the most triumphant expression of the coal capital of the world. Even today, sixteen years after it had been first built – at a cost of two million pounds and many workmen's lives – people came from all over to marvel at the dragon on its dome, the towering English Renaissance clock tower, its statuary of the veiled ladies of the four winds, and the four great golden dials of the clock itself. All five bells, made from the finest gun metal and tuned to give the hours and Westminster Quarters, were dedicated to God.

But there was far more for the visitor to marvel at inside the building. The air was sepulchre cool, with shivering swords of sunshine slashing across the marble halls and stone staircases. Dark-uniformed men in peaked caps hung around in watchful silence, hoping for someone to have a chat to as they stood guard on the key icons of the city's history . . . here a bronze memorial to Captain Robert Scott who sailed from Cardiff on the *Terra Nova* for his doomed expedition to the South Pole in 1910 . . . there a painting celebrating the one disputed goal by which Cardiff city had won the Football Association Cup at Wembley in 1927. A key goal this, scored by a Scotsman, coming from a mistake by the Arsenal goalkeeper, a Welshman.

A peaked cap came racing out of some shadows in hot pursuit of three children with scuffed shoes and scarred, dirty knees, who had managed to get past the peaked cap on the doorway and were now playing hide-and-seek around the statuary in the Marble Hall. A *very* strong line was taken on having any fun at all within these hallowed walls.

The statuary around which the children were pursued were called the Heroes of Wales, a dozen worthies chipped out of White Serravesa marble, among them St David, the patron saint of Wales; Owain Glyndwr, who last led the Welsh in thrilling rebellion against the English; Bishop Morgan, who translated the Bible from English into Welsh and so saved the language; and the medieval poet, Dafydd ap Gwilym, whose most famous poem celebrated a sexual frolic in church.

And there they all stood, still and for evermore: praying endless prayers with outstretched hands, composing dirty poems in traditional metres, poking the air with accusing forefingers, boring everyone stiff with silent sermons to the multitudes and frozen postures of eternal nobility.

This afternoon, a Wednesday, a full meeting of the council was in progress in the oak-panelled Council Chamber. A bald Tory was on his feet flannelling about the new proposals for the rationalization of the tram service while the Lord Mayor was sitting on his elevated chair, busy cleaning out his ear with a match stick.The rest of the seventy-five members were scattered around the circular seats, some chatting or fanning themselves and more than a few fast asleep. Two men on the press bench were playing noughts and crosses. Occasionally one of the socialists got to his feet and punctuated the Tory's flannelling with some good old-fashioned abuse. Just as occasionally the Lord Mayor pulled out his revolving match stick and examined it closely trying to work out quite what he was managing to dig out of his ear in such vast lumps.

The Tory was making some deeply obscure point about how trams travelled faster in Roath than they did in Adamsdown when something very strange happened. A large rotten cauliflower came sailing out of the spectators' gallery and exploded, with delicious precision, on the top of the luminous billiard ball of the Tory's bald head.

The Tory stopped speaking and the Lord Mayor looked up from the tiny toffee apple of his match stick, when some dozen rotten tomatoes came raining down on the councillors, mingled with some dozen rotten apples and perhaps a dozen rotten bananas – *split, splat, splot, splot, split, splat* – all exploding and ricocheting around the Tory benches who all, as a man, dived beneath their seats in a vain effort to save the fine lines of their expensive suits. *Splot, splat, split.* The members of the press looked up from their games of noughts and crosses, seeing that here, after years of bum-numbing boredom, there was a real story at last.

The Lord Mayor's face jerked up, full of civic thunder. He was appalled to see a poster lowered off the gallery. EQUAL RIGHTS FOR ALL, the poster shouted. END COUNCIL FASCISM. The Lord Mayor – who, as it happened, didn't know the difference between socialism, fascism and rheumatism – was further vexed to see about a dozen men all jumping around in the gallery letting off yet more fusillades of fruit while one of them was trying to make a speech. Far worse than all that *they were all as black as coal.*

Alderman Knott made the grave mistake of lifting his head above his bench and was caught just above the eye by a romping apple. One hurled orange bounced off a crouching Tory backside before smacking against a socialist head. Civic pride took a decided dive downwards when some of the councillors stood up and actually started throwing the rotten fruit back into the gallery. A tomato hit the golden mayoral chains and the Lord Mayor dropped his head into his hands wondering why he had bothered wasting the time and expense to get such a ghastly job. *Splodge, split, splat.*

'We're here serving notice on you all' – *splot, splat, split* – 'that we are not going to put up with all your racial insults any more.' *Split, splat, splosh.* 'We want work. We want proper houses. We are tired of living in slums and seeing our children die.' *Splat, split, splodge.* 'So start thinking about what you're going to do for us.' *Splot, splot, splot.* 'Or we are going to do even more to you.'

By now even those councillors who had tried a counter attack were safely under their benches as Obe hoisted his trumpet to his lips and let out a few jazzed-up riffs from *The Red Flag*.

The bugling bonhomie of the Red anthem went strutting down through the carpeted halls, urging Dewi Sant to give up his preaching to the multitudes; Owain Glyndwr to rise up in revolt against the English again; the other marbled worthies to stop all that boring posturing and dance about on their plinths. It went bouncing down into the Lord Mayor's parlour and over into the rates office, making the clerks look at one another and wonder what the hell was going on. It even went swaggering into the windy lavatories where a few peaked caps were standing around next to a radiator, having a quiet smoke.

But by the time all the peaked caps had been alerted, the Sons of Africa had run out of rotten fruit and threatening speeches, and had left by the side door, dashing past the new law courts, laughing and shouting at one another as they made their way down past the castle and towards the Bay. Their first campaign had been an outrageous success as the furious front-page headline of the *South Wales Echo* – complete with picture of Lord Mayor holding up his tomato-splattered mayoral chain – was soon to prove.

> 'The full meeting of the city council was broken up this afternoon by an astonishing display of anarchy,' the front-page lead for April 10, 1930, began. 'Members were pelted with rotten fruit as a poster was lowered from the gallery calling for an end to "council fascism". Nothing escaped this disgusting storm of fruit, including the mayoral chains of office, the civic mace and even the famous stained-glass window depicting Mother Wales. A coloured man made a largely incomprehensible speech from the gallery about the unemployment problem.
>
> 'As police began conducting their own inquiries into the identity of the attackers – all coloured and who ran away directly after the incident – the Lord Mayor,

Alderman William Rice, described the incident as "an outrageous attack on the very foundations of our democratic way of life" and announced that full charges would be pressed against all of the culprits as soon as they were apprehended.

'The leader of the socialists, R. Peart, claimed that desperate people sometimes resorted to desperate measures to draw attention to their problems. "Everyone knows the way the West Indian community, in particular, is suffering in the docks," he claimed. "Now perhaps at last we will start taking some notice of their very grave and understandable problems."'

The Lord Mayor described Peart's reaction as 'typically self-serving socialist rubbish'. He added that the members' laundry bill was going to be considerable after this outrage and there was nothing understandable about that.

Hamilton strode along Bute Street with such determined intensity that even the wheeling clumps of prostitutes parted to let him through. Normally they would have gathered around any likely client, particularly if he was dressed as well and as fastidiously as Hamilton. But they had seen this queer cove around enough times in the past to be extremely wary of him, believing that he was, perhaps, something to do with the police, or even worse. They just nudged one another with their elbows and stepped out of his way, not even risking their normal cheeky jibes at passing men or indeed saying anything at all.

Even the unemployed men on the corners looking at him with vague curiosity made no moves to try and tap him for the price of a cup of tea as he crossed the canal bridge, pausing to let a tram rattle past before turning into the twilight terraces of Newtown. It was the sheer momentum of his walk that was so unusual, particularly at a time when men ambled around the Bay without purpose or stood around propping up walls, with their hands in their pockets. It was not so much a walk as a drive, back and head unbearably erect, elbows pulled tightly back and into his sides as if the old Warrior Monk was on his way to the fight of his life.

Out on East Moors they were pouring the molten slag into

the sea, making a huge ruddy glow burst out over the darkening sky. This glow gave everything a faintly magical veneer, managing the seemingly impossible task of making the grim, crouching terraces and mean pubs of Newtown seem oddly lovely. Even the sewage spilling over the road – that foul water clock which told of the high tides – seemed to be providing some enchanted setting for a fairy story until, that is, you caught its raw, rotten-egg smell; a more fitting background for a dark horror story.

Hamilton stood on the corner of Needs' Store, his large dark shadow framing itself in one of the moving orange pools of sewage as several bundles of wee children, barely out of the stork's beak, went hurrying past on some obscure childhood mission. Their bare feet broke up Hamilton's shadow and it was still shivering when they disappeared down into Tyndall Street. Then another group of children came wheeling out of the orange-hued darkness in silent pursuit of the first group. Tiny shadows moved in the glittering blackness of Hamilton's eyes. Far away the siren sounded, telling of the end of the afternoon shift in the steelworks.

A couple of staggering drunks were propping one another up and hogging most of the pavement. Hamilton stepped out of their way, pacing down to St Paul's church and catching his breath as he looked up at the windy, pencil-sharp spire. He knocked smartly on the Presbytery door. When there was no reply he knocked again only louder.

'Yes. Yes?' said Father O'Reilly without opening the door. 'It's getting late so it is and I've an awful drowsiness on me.'

'I need to speak to you for a few moments, Father. It is a matter of the gravest urgency.'

A long puzzled silence followed. Hamilton raised a clenched fist, as if about to smash it through one of the panels, but then he heard the door bolts slide back. He found himself face to face with Father O'Reilly in his nightshirt. It was immediately clear from the smell of his breath that the old priest was drowsy not so much through the fatigue of prayer and Christian service as from something more to do with Irish whiskey. The priest moved so that the hall light fell on Hamilton's face.

'I only need a few moments, Father O'Reilly,' Hamilton repeated, putting his hand on the door to make sure that it was not closed again. 'There is just one matter I want to discuss and then I will leave you in peace.'

'Better come in then. I'm just about to be having a little nightcap in my study.'

Hamilton followed the priest down the corridor and into his study where the old rascal had been sitting with a pipe and a friendly bottle. Hamilton refused the offer of a glass with a small dismissive wave of his hand.

'It's been a powerful long day,' Father O'Reilly said, refilling his glass. 'I've been attending a wake all afternoon and the whole family is heart-scalded by it all. Heart-scalded they are. All of them are going about the place with the sound of the grave crying in their ears. Just a little slip of a boy he was too, taken by the croup. One minute he was fine – so strong he could throw a horseshoe around the moon, aye – an' the next he had this terrible crouping cough. Then he was dead. They ask me why, of course, and I try to tell them that in the eyes of the Virgin Mother death is a triumph, but it's awful hard sometimes. Particularly when they are so young an' all. It's these drains I blame. They'll be killing all our little ones before long.'

'Is your parish very short of money?' Hamilton asked.

'Isn't everyone? But somehow we, the dead and dying, manage to keep going.'

'I ask only because I have been told that you have a cup here. I could make a substantial donation to your church if you gave me that cup.'

The priest's eyebrows rose markedly at the very mention of 'substantial donation' and he became wary, even alert. His drink lay untouched.

'This donation might even be big enough to get the drains around here fixed,' Hamilton added tantalizingly. 'It could be as high as that.'

The priest screwed up his blotchy nose into a corroded question mark. 'Exactly who the divil are you?'

Hamilton explained that his name was Alexander Hamilton and that he owned the Oriel shipping line – now the biggest in Cardiff and one of the biggest in Britain. He lived in that large house in Howard Close and was a collector of all kinds of reliquaries. There was a cup, a chalice, which dated back to the Middle Ages and may indeed be earlier than that; some believed that it might even have belonged to the Emperor Nero. It was once in Cardiff Castle until it, ah, went missing. He had heard that the Father now had the cup, and he was prepared to pay whatever price O'Reilly might name to acquire it.

Father O'Reilly believed none of it of course; it all sounded suspiciously like some old sermon done up with a few new jokes – he'd done a bit of that in his time, preparing a year's supply of them during his training and, every year, turning them over and doing them again. No one ever listened to them anyway, no matter what year it was. He had never gone in much for that oratory stuff – no artificial claps of thunder and wrestling with the lectern for him. He just spoke in his normal speaking voice – as you would to a woman you loved or a man you hated. 'You wouldn't know, would you, Mr Hamilton, how I was supposed to come by this cup?'

'No.'

'That's a terrible sad shame because the parish would love to receive your substantial donation. But I fear I just do not have the cup you speak of.'

'In that case . . .' Hamilton half-rose to leave.

'But I'll tell you one thing, Mr Hamilton, because it's a powerful strange thing you're talking about. I had a man sitting right here in that chair once who told me the strangest story that ever got into a priest's ears. It was a confession it was, an' he told me this story how he went into Cardiff Castle with a group of thieves one night, about ten years ago, to lift a cup, and it came alive, he said. It glowed like the very divil, he said. He said that there was this heart in it which was beating and running with blood. They all left fast and most of them were picked up by the police. Most, that is, except my man. He was an old IRA gun, you know, an' he came to tell me all about it.'

'Is this man still living here?'

'He is.'

'Could I speak to him?'

'Impossible. It's the Confessional you see, Mr Hamilton. The priest is always obliged to protect the secrecy of the Confessional. The Confessional and the Catechism – that's all we poor Catholics have got.'

Hamilton stiffened and stared at the old priest with cold aggression. His hand brushed an imaginary cobweb off his cheek. 'There are precedents for breaking the secrecy of the Confessional,' he said flatly.

'None. None at all.'

'There are precedents for breaking the secrecy of the Confessional,' he repeated, his voice becoming harsher and louder. 'That cup, Holy Father, belongs to me. It is my property. The Confessional can be broken if it leads to the recovery of *my* property.'

'That'll win you no prizes for logic, Mr Hamilton.'

'I am not interested in your prizes. But I am interested in my property, and anyone who stands in the way of me and my property will be taken out of the way. You do understand that, do you, Holy Father? Now I am not going to sit around here all night. I am not to be trifled with. Never make the mistake of trifling with me. Now who is that man and where does he live?'

Glanely House,
Penarth.

May 1 1930.

Dear Edward,

I grew up with your father and was very proud to have known him even if we were never exactly friends. For five years we were junior clerks together in the same shipping office. That was where we learned it all, just by watching the others making their expensive mistakes. You learn everything you need to know about shipping when you are a clerk – you learn about it all from the bottom up.

Your father made his move to set up on his own long before me. I never knew quite where he found the capital but the next week he was out buying ships of his own. I had to wait a few more years before I had the idea of pioneering the first type of coal steamer. But, in almost no time at all, we were both the richest and biggest shipowners in Cardiff – within seven years I had a fleet of 150,000 tons deadweight. Although never friends we did share the odd bottle of Canary in the Dowlais, giving one another items of information which helped our causes. That's about all there was to it. There was certainly never animosity between us.

I believe that your father was always an honourable man but have never been at all sure about this

Alexander Hamilton. We always knew that he was around in the background of Oriel but never knew quite in what capacity. We think he may well have been the original source of Oriel's capital and that perhaps he just chose your father as a figurehead. That's not a fact – just what we used to call an Exchange guess. Hamilton only ever appeared on the Floor when it was absolutely necessary. You can see the pain in him when he has to talk to someone, almost anyone. It makes a sort of sense that he's chosen you to become the new figurehead for Oriel. Your father was tremendously successful and it's the Gurney name he wants as much as anything else.

But as there are only a handful of us left in Cardiff who are remotely solvent I was always very keen to get on with Hamilton. Now there's just Oriel, Reardon-Smith, Pantmawr and myself. We're bound to pull out of this wretched depression in the end – all world economic slumps go in cycles – and, apart from munitions, there's going to be a lot of freight in the reorganized steel industry. So why is he moving against me in particular? Or does he just want to eat up everything that's left? Is he going for Reardon-Smith and Pantmawr when he's got me? And for what? A monopoly on South Wales shipping could only make some sort of sense if he was working for a foreign power. You say you will be meeting with the Krupps shortly and there will be an opening in the German munitions export drive. But trade is all that will mean. Germany will never go to war again. War reparations and debts have killed them off for at least two generations. Everyone knows that this new Nazi party is just a joke.

However I am naturally grateful that you have chosen to tell me about Hamilton's planned attack on me in so much detail and I fully understand why you feel that your family business has been stolen off you. You are right that we should never be seen together and, as you say, there are certainly more ways than one to skin a cat. The obvious place is on the stock market and the best method would be through a deal in reversionary shares. This would be difficult but not at all impossible, with you buying my stock at artificially high rates and me bidding for yours at marked-down prices. It's involuntary suicide, sometimes done by business people when they want to bail out and avoid the shame of the bankruptcy court.

Another method would be for you to make a recklessly stupid bid for an impossibly bad piece of property. Almost anything to do with the coal export business would qualify. I know of a couple of idle coal steamers that you could have for, say, three million.

But you must be very careful of this man Hamilton. He is like that panther who, when cornered, can be so very dangerous. You think that you have the noose safely around his neck but then he might well leap and tear out your very throat. Partington is merely his ear trumpet. He carries everything back to his master, so be very careful of what you say and reveal to him.

But I fully understand the nature of revenge and why you want to present Hamilton's head on a platter to someone. That someone might as well be me who, like Salome, will be more than pleased to receive it. Keep in the closest touch.

Yours sincerely,
Arthur Tatem.

A cold drizzle hung over the dock so thickly the cranes actually seemed to disappear into the sky. A stooped figure in a black soutane made his way slowly along the quay. Nathan and Effey were sitting playing chess in the ward room, both of them barely recognizing Father O'Reilly when he came mumbling through the door. He had a blackened eye and one side of his face was crisscrossed with plaster. He had also received some kind of injury to his body, they could tell, the way he sat down so gingerly, making a small pained circle with his lips.

'Been walking into that door again, have we?' Nathan asked finally.

Effey looked up, chin on hand, before studying the board again and moving a pawn.

'That's quite clever, if you're thinking what I think you're thinking,' said Nathan. 'I'd better organize my queen's defences a bit here.'

Father O'Reilly leaned across the chessboard, tapping Effey's bishop with his forefinger. 'That's the one you've got to use, milady. These bishops can do the queerest pulls of things especially if you flash up there with it.'

Effey did not take her chin off her hand nor her eyes off the board.

'Not taking any notice of me wise advice, eh? Suit yourself, but if you don't watch it he'll get you on this side. Just watch it on that side there too.'

'I hate people who talk while you're playing, don't you?' Effey asked no one in particular.

Nathan produced a bottle from a locker and poured a couple of stiff ones. 'So what was it? A door, or have you been going trying your old hands in a boxing booth?'

The old priest held his glass none too steadily and took a large gulp, smacking his lips with great relish before taking another. 'I've been to some odd places you know, Nathan. I've heard things that few men have heard. But I've never been beaten by a mortal man. I've never even *heard* of a priest being beaten by a mortal man. But the other night a man came to see me and, when I didn't tell him what he wanted to know, he just beat me silly. He turned into the wildest sort of animal and beat me.'

'You've been to the police, have you?'

'Foof! They'd be no help an' I'll tell you for why. This man, an Alexander Hamilton . . .'

'Him? The shipowner? Are you sure it was him?'

'As sure as I'm sitting here before you now. That man has the police in his pay. We priests get to know about these things. There's been a long tradition of graft in the police around here. All Lord Bute's original Green Jackets were on the take and that Victor Watts is the biggest divil of them all. All as corrupt as adders, so they are. My people in Newtown have had to work out their own ways of dealing with the problems of law and order. The point is, Nathan, I'm that afraid of telling them anything about this because, you know, laying a hand on a priest is a very serious business, a most serious business. There might even be a spot of murder around an' I wouldn't want any of my flock to get tied up in anything like that.'

Effey picked up her bishop and put it back down again. Nathan refilled both glasses. 'But you'll have to do *something*, Dennis. If he's done it once he can always do it again. You just can't let him get away with it.'

'I've done all I can for the moment. The one little bit of insurance I've taken out is to go and see one of my people – a bit of a roustabout who knows a thing or two about fighting. I've asked him to keep an eye on me 'til I decide what's to be done. This Hamilton is a powerful crazy man, Nathan. All the time he beat me he did so with the blackest smile playing on his lips.'

'What does he want?'

'He wants something that's wild and holy. It's some cup that's around the place and he wants it so bad it's making his heart hurt with the pain of it all. The trouble is that there is something to this cup story. The man he wanted to contact – an old Sinn Feiner, settled here to escape the Brits after some bother in Dublin – knows a thing or two about dynamite and was in on a burglary in Cardiff Castle some years ago.'

Now Effey looked up and stared hard at the priest as he continued speaking, his voice thick with wonder and mystery.

'This old Sinn Feïner was telling me they broke into the castle by going in through the sewers. Then they all had to winch up this statue to get at the cup. And when they winched it up there were lights everywhere, so there were, and there was a moaning of graveyard ghosts in the air. This man saw a real heart in that cup. An' there was blood pouring out of it an' it was still throbbing as if it was still alive, he said.'

'Had he been drinking this stuff?' Nathan indicated the bottle.

'He *says* he wasn't but I'll tell you something now, Nathan. That same man changed after that night. He told me the castle story in the Confession, and became a different man – not drinking, not fornicating, not doing anything. Even when he came to the Confession he could hardly find anything to confess to. There came almost a glow of holiness about him and he started being successful in his little building business too.'

'So what the hell is this cup?'

'A wild and holy cup, Nathan. And, if it's what I think it might be, I want it too.'

# CHAPTER TWENTY-ONE

The next week, on a gusty Tuesday morning when hurrying breezes made shivering catspaws on a still, full sea, some five hundred gathered, as arranged, outside the terracotta clock tower of the Pier Head Building, below its dizzying jumble of hexagonal chimneys, turrets and gargoyles.

This was to be the first public march organized by the Sons of Africa. Even as they greeted one another it became clear that this was going to be the largest protest meeting that the city had ever seen. It was all the more remarkable because, not only were the marchers aged from eight to eighty, but almost all of them were black.

Most of those on the march were West Indians from different islands, but that did not seem to be a consideration at all. For this one breezy morning, at any rate, they had become smelted together in the common fire of the ideals of the Sons of Africa. Sophie, in particular, was proud that Obe had managed the almost impossible mission of uniting the wayward groups, happy to be walking with the other marchers behind him and, in so doing, announcing that she too was getting more than a little tired of this city council which was content to let everyone rot in the docks as long as they caused no trouble.

Obe had picked up a small brass section to head the procession. Almost as soon as they set off he blew a riff provoking a great roar in the marchers. Policemen came and went, telephoning their offices in Cathays Park, uncertain what to do as the procession unwound down the length of Bute Street. There had never been anything like it. They carried placards and posters calling for equal employment regardless of colour. They wanted equal dole payments. They wanted new houses. 'I DO NOT WANT TO DIE OF T.B.', said one child's placard.

Shoppers stopped and stared as the marchers went past the Hayes and the Central Library en route for the City Hall. It had not even dawned on most of the citizenry that any blacks might be suffering from anything remotely resembling a social problem – let alone those who lived under Bute Street bridge where, presumably, with their cauldrons and calypsos, their thousands of bastard children and coal stacked high in their baths, all those darkeys must be all as happy as snails in the rain. But now here they were, placarding their grievances and demanding *rights*, for God's sake. Just who did they think they were?

In many ways they looked like a newly-emergent army from the Zulu Wars; a point not lost on the police who, after the bombardment on the council, had drawn up secret contingency plans in the event of the civic worthies coming under such threat again. Not that there was much they could do at the moment since this march was, to date, peaceful and totally legal – unless the men began taking down their trousers and displaying their enormous private members in public – they'd heard all about them – or else flinging rotten fruit around the council chamber again. No one had been picked up for that attack since, after the spluttering outrage had subsided, it was decided that any further charges would only add to the painful publicity that they had already received.

Sophie was more than a little pleased to be marching behind her lodger even if, come to think of it, he hadn't paid any rent for some time now. As they passed the great department stores of James Howells and David Morgan she felt a high, tight, choking emotion. For a complete triumph this march was – and no mistake – uniting many disparate groups and then getting them out onto the streets to demonstrate with their feet.

She had, at first, been very worried about the attack on the councillors, fearing that Obe was going to end up back in the pokey that he had always hated so much. It wouldn't have taken the police more than two seconds to work out who he was – his photograph playing the trumpet had appeared more than once in the *Echo*, after all – but, mysteriously and despite all the publicity, no boys in blue had come for him. However, it was as a result of that demonstration that Obe had become a sort of black Robin Hood hero, waved at and cheered by the kids in the streets, greeted avidly by the prostitutes on the corners and even courted by the West Indian island elders who sent messages to his home – since they were far too grand to bring their own messages – saying that it really was time to talk and iron out their island differences.

As more and more messages went streaming back and forth it became clear to Sophie what had been clear to Obe for a long time – the West Indians were doing so badly and getting on with one another so appallingly not only because they were without a common leader but also because they had no programme. It was to be Obe's withering marxism, forged in the dark, dripping mines of the Valleys, that provided their revolutionary platform. With that as their yardstick and framework, their real grievances became dramatically highlighted and methods of dealing with them readily suggested.

But as they turned down by the castle, Sophie's mood of triumph turned to one of impending defeat. There, stretched across the road, with Chief Inspector Watts at their flank, was a blue, silver-buttoned line of police, holding riot batons and clearly ready and happy to repel any attempts to inflict further nasty stains on the Portland edifices of their beloved city centre.

If Obe's people were a newly-emergent army in the Zulu Wars then Watts' police force were the Royal Welsh Regiment, just itching to celebrate the most glorious battle in its history by staging a re-run of Rourke's Drift on the manicured tulip lawns of Cathays Park.

Obe looked back at Sophie and frowned. The very last thing he had wanted to do was to make a direct fight of it. They would never win against such disciplined opposition; people would get locked up. Neither did he want everyone just to lose their nerve and make an undignified run for it. His fingers fiddled with his trumpet taps and he thought of his great hero, Aneurin Bevan, the silver-tongued agitator of the South Wales coalfields, who was already giving Winston Churchill and Lloyd George some fine old headaches in the House of Commons. He wondered how old Nye would handle a confrontation like this and decided he would do it with wit and fun; that he would do almost anything to avoid outbreaks of violence or personal injury to any members of his beloved working class.

'Let's all remember the marching wheel,' Obe shouted behind him and, putting his trumpet to his lips, let out a bugling roar before leading the marchers directly towards the police line. A great silence trawled down through the city streets and even the romping breezes fell still. It seemed as if a bloody confrontation was inevitable until Obe lifted his trumpet into the air and pointed it to the left. All the marchers wheeled left behind him, trampling across several civic tulip beds before letting out a loud cheer at the redundant police line and making their way back to the Bay. Their point had been made for the day and doubtless tomorrow they would make it in another way.

There was not one on the march who believed that they had been wasting their time. People had begun talking about them and their legitimate grievances. There had been articles in the local press, asking why they were behaving like this. Left-wing councillors and M.P.s were coming down under the bridge to ask what the trouble was all about. Soon they would be making such a fuss that Right-wingers would be coming down there too. The Tory mind feared civil commotion more than anything.

The very first principle that Obe had drummed into them was that they had to organize some sort of commotion; that, from the very outset, the duty of any revolutionary group was to be controversial and scandalize the pants off everyone. He, in his turn, would be as snaky and sinuous as his master Nye, destructive and peaceful by turns, making fresh points in fresh ways, upsetting all and sundry before beating a swift retreat, and then looking around for new opportunities for new outbreaks of trouble. He had no illusions that such as the police and council would take every opportunity in hurling trouble back in their direction, but their cause was just. They would surely win in the end. The blacks would surely inherit the earth.

Yet the real key to the success of the Sons of Africa was that they also believed in man's inalienable right to have fun. The wildest party seemed to follow every meeting and demonstration, usually at the Colonial Centre in Loudoun Square, where musicians of every musical persuasion rolled up to accompany the singing and dancing, the general noise and music getting louder and yet louder as they bulldozed their way through the afternoon. And so it happened that day.

Trays of sandwiches and the odd cooked chicken seemed to arrive on the trestle tables as if they had just been made in thin air. Barrels of beer came rolling in, pumped from some bountiful source near the Brains brewery in town. Appetites for both food and drink were perked up by the odd reefer.

Walter Moken, as immaculate as ever, was happy to play the piano – no matter what time of the day or night – embroidering all the shouts and laughter of the packed hall with a continual twinkling of his ivories, sometimes breaking into a coherent tune to which everyone could sing along or else pulling out of it and doodling with several different tunes at once.

Even Sophie, who was usually most careful in conserving her vocal energies these days, sang a few numbers, standing next to the piano and banging her fist up and down on it as Walter went dancing around and around her words. She was pleased by the way that Walter kept listening to her as she sang. It was always terrific when she was not actually fighting anyone in the band; when their music was working in your direction. She had always considered it a great privilege to work alongside Obe and she could hardly believe that now she had found someone as good as Walter as well.

But she also saluted the way in which Obe was managing to create a new black culture, free from the old, sterile attitudes of the plantations. Some of the younger ones in particular were behaving as though liberated from some mysterious yoke; a few were now plaiting their hair African-style and wearing bright, gaudy colours. A little by design and a lot by accident, Obe was building something new and vital around the jazz band and the new politics of the Valleys. There were bits of other things in it too . . . a bit of Walter's piano and a bit of African pride and a bit of her own voice too. Bessie Smith would have been proud of all of them – after all Bessie always identified with the poor and dispossessed too. Somehow they had become a sort of new family, all communicating to one another on levels that were not always obvious.

She was sitting next to the piano chatting to Benedict, with Walter playing *If You Were The Only Girl In The World*, when Obe came over to them carrying a copy of that afternoon's *Echo*. Their march had indeed made the front page – complete with picture – and she took the newspaper off him to read the report properly. But her eyes were caught by other headlines, which made her blood run cold:

'DOCKLAND PRIEST
IN MURDER BID

'Angry crowds were gathering outside a Catholic church in Cardiff's Newtown this afternoon following a report that a priest had been attacked there,' the story began.

'Unconfirmed sources said that Father Dennis O'Reilly was found on the altar of his church after being bludgeoned about the head with a large gilt crucifix. He has been taken to Cardiff Royal Infirmary suffering from multiple wounds to the head. Meanwhile the police are anxious to interview anyone who may have had contact with Father O'Reilly over the last few days.

'"It is too early to describe this incident as a murder but it was certainly a base and senseless attack," said Chief Inspector Victor Watts, in charge of the investigation. "We are pursuing a number of inquiries but just now I am appealing for everyone to stay calm." An Infirmary spokesman would make no comment on Father O'Reilly's condition.'

Sophie folded up the newspaper and jammed it into her pocket. Without a thought for the band she flew out of the Colonial Centre and through the trickles of workers shuffling home after another day in the docks. She was unsure why, but she was absolutely brimming over with wild-eyed panic, worrying especially about Nathan and how he was going to react to this attack on his one and only friend.

He was sitting at his huge ward room table, eating toast and studying his chessboard when she put the newspaper in front of him.

'Oh no,' he groaned as he read the report. 'Oh God, no,' he repeated, sweeping the chessboard and newspaper off the table with a backswing of his arm. She tried to comfort him by taking hold of his arm but he shrugged it away, dropping his face into his hands, alternately sighing and sobbing softly. 'The trouble is I know who did it,' he said finally. 'It was that lunatic you work for.'

'The lunatic I work for?' She went quite white with shock, looking down at her shaking fingers. 'Whatever are you talking about?'

'Hamilton did it. He beat the same priest the other night. Now the Satanic bastard has obviously gone back and finished the job.'

'I'm sorry, Nathan. I'm very sorry, but I don't get any of this at all. None of it. Why should a man like Hamilton go around attacking old priests?'

'Why? Because he's totally evil and barking mad, that's why. He has to be stopped, and before I do anything else I have to go straight to the police.'

At this point they both stared in silence at the table as if both their imaginations had been caught by the same misgiving, the very same face perhaps.

'There is just one problem about that course of action,' he said.

'Yes. And I know its name too. Victor Watts. I've seen him back and forth at Howard Close often enough.'

'So what is the point of going to the police?'

'None. None at all.'

He coughed and straightened his back, folding his fingers together, his thumbs circling one another. He looked at her and back at his thumbs. 'So then, Sophie. What are we going to do now? This man clearly has to be stopped, but I'm not at all sure who can stop him.'

'I know someone, Nathan. I know just the man, and you've met him too.'

Edward had met Arthur Tatem in the foyer of the Grand Hotel in the city and the bluff old shipowner had produced a sheaf of documents which contained a revelation of Old Testament proportions.

At first Edward had flicked through the pages, unsure what they meant: so many unfamiliar company names, long lists of assets and holdings. Tatem explained that he had ordered a company search on Oriel and all allied companies just to see exactly what Hamilton's business interests were all about.

The single report on Oriel listed just two directors – Hamilton and Partington – who were also listed as directors of six further companies. Tatem's clerk had done a search on these six and the sixth had lead to another six which, in themselves, amounted to an almost global network of companies based in offices as far away as San Francisco, Singapore, Hong Kong and Tokyo. Many of them were small 'paper' companies with nominal shareholdings, but a lot of them were very rich indeed, with cash assets of up to £500,000.

'You see, Edward, I ordered this search to see where we could get him. But the truth of it is that he has such a wide spread of assets and strong liquidity in all areas we could not usefully get at him anywhere at all. I would go further. I'd say that what we could do would amount to no more than a flea could do to an elephant. This is a cleverly thought-out operation where nothing much depends on anything else. And Oriel, you will see from all this, is just a sideshow.'

'Not to me it isn't. Oriel is mine.'

'Not according to these documents it isn't. Your father isn't even mentioned. But what is really interesting is that Oriel is but the tiniest part of the whole empire. These people in Threadneedle Street would be the accountants. Those are clearly the managers for the Far Eastern operation. They've clearly just registered an office in Durban. So what's going on? What could it all be about? There could well be other principals and shareholders but there is no sign of them. Edward, this man is another Lord Bute. He may even be well on the way to being the richest man in the world. My clerk tells me that there are yet more companies to investigate. Who knows what more we may find?'

Even as Tatem spoke Edward felt the heaviest of weights bearing down on him. For years he had suffered under the shadow of Hamilton, and now it turned out that he had more power and influence than he had ever dared imagine. He controlled the police. He had stolen his father's business. He was threatening to have Edward imprisoned and now it was turning out that he might well be the richest man in the world with control of almost everywhere. There was just no adequate response. He pulled the flat of his palm hard across his forehead.

'Isn't there anything we can do against him?' he asked at length.

'Nothing that would have any effect. He's just too big and strong. Everywhere. Look at it. No detectable weaknesses anywhere and half world trade is on its arse. He could swallow me whole, overnight, in half a dozen ways. I'm surprised that he hasn't taken me out long before now.'

'How would the Germans fit into all this?'

'Who's to know? If they were even thinking of another world war they could do no better than to mount an operation like this. Any country could gain the upper hand with a set-up like this.'

The sky was darkening and black-clothed dummies stood around in the brilliant gold aquaria of the shop windows as Edward walked back to the dockland to meet Sophie. In curious ways the mutinous anger curdling inside him seemed to find an unruly counterpoint in the night. Men were spilling out of the dark streets of Newtown and moving around on corners; you could tell they were trouble in search of trouble. Even the Moslems seemed strangely restless, crowds gathering outside the Mosque as Rashed harangued them heatedly.

Edward stopped again to watch a huge model boat being carried out of the doorway of the Chinese block. Groups of visiting Chinese were stepping out of cars and shaking hands in the hallways. Thick oaty smells of baking moon cakes went drifting over the pavements for this was the night to celebrate the fifth day of the fifth moon, when the Chinese commemorated the suicide of an administrator in the third century B.C. It was the night of the Dragon Boat Festival or the Festival of the Nine Gods.

Edward watched them manhandling the boat along the pavement and he knew that he would never understand the Bay; that perhaps its racial complexities were beyond all human understanding. The place was just an arena into which everyone was pitched, in some vague hope that they might melt into something new. If they didn't they would just keep fighting one another and die. He could hear the Irish abusing the Chinese festival preparations and a bottle came whistling across the road, smashing against some railings next to the laundry. Yes, the place was still full of fighting with no sign of any cooling that he could see.

Sophie was sitting, silent and sullen, in front of a coal fire when he walked into the house. He had barely sat down next to her when there came the strange wail of a conch. They looked at one another.

'The Chinese,' said Edward. 'They're out in the streets celebrating something or other.'

'Lucky Chinese. I couldn't think of much to celebrate just now. Edward, I'm not quite sure how to say this, but there's a mad beast running amok in our lives. It's that man Hamilton. You were right in everything you said about him.'

Edward visibly jumped at the mention of the man who had become his central preoccupation. 'What's he done now?'

'He's gone and killed a priest over in Newtown. Can you believe it? Killed a priest. This priest was Nathan's one close friend and Hamilton went after him over some cup. He died in hospital an hour ago.'

Edward gazed at the flickering fiery chasms of the fire and closed his eyes. He felt the strangest mixture of emotions and not a little guilt for sending Hamilton there in the first place. 'That cup again. Always that cup. He's obsessed by it and it's at the bottom of everything he does. It's the same cup I took out of Cardiff Castle. It's why they murdered your friend.'

'Where is it now?'

'I haven't a clue. But I've found out some more about our Mr Hamilton today. His business empire is absolutely vast. He's well on the way to becoming the richest man in the world, offices almost everywhere. He's almost invincible.'

'No man is invincible, Edward. If he eats and breathes he's not invincible. There's a way of toppling anyone if you prod around far enough.'

'I don't believe . . . I can't . . . Sophie, the only way I can come close to settling my scores with this man is to kill him with my own bare hands.'

The fire spat out a small lump of coal which hit the fender with a sharp crack and spun around on the tiled hearth. Small blue flames of gas spurted across the fiery canyons. Tiny tongues of flames darted and disappeared against the soot-encrusted grate, as mysterious and evanescent as St Elmo's fire in a storm at sea. Sophie could feel the heat of the fire glowing hard and red on her cheeks; it even seemed to burn deep into the very pupils of her brown eyes. She had always had the greatest respect for the purity of fire; the way that it lapped softly around everything, fluttering and beguiling, before burrowing destructively straight into its very heart and reducing it to a pile of soft, cold ashes. Fire was always the great leveller and, just now, it was Edward who needed to take up such a purifying flame against the mad dog in their midst.

'That man doesn't deserve any better,' she said finally, talking slowly and picking her words with the greatest care. 'Our Somali tribe learned a thousand years ago that you always have to fight your own battles; that no one is ever going to struggle for you. If we'd sat around waiting for someone to fight for us we would have been no more than desert sand generations ago. The police are not going to be of any use because he owns the police. You can expect no justice if he owns the courts too. There's only one way out when you think of it. You'll just have to kill him yourself.' She looked directly at him. 'You're not scared of him, are you?'

'Not remotely,' he said, so flatly and spontaneously she knew that he was speaking the truth. 'I've never been scared of anyone. It would give me the greatest of pleasure to kill this Mr Alexander Hamilton. The very greatest pleasure.'

She touched his wrist lightly with her hand, surprised at the clinical coldness of her emotions, particularly in the light of the subject under discussion. 'Do it, Edward. Just do it and let's rid ourselves of him. Nothing is going to grow under his dark tree. Nothing at all.'

Edward seemed to become alive and animated, perching his behind on the edge of his chair and moving his whole face close to the fire as if searching for some secret in its fiery heart. 'Yes, yes. But I need something, Sophie. What I really need is a gun. You wouldn't know where I could get a decent gun, would you? Preferably a repeater since I'm sure it's going to take more than one bullet to stop him.'

'Nathan had a gun. But I don't think it shoots straight.'

'Oh that old blunderbuss. No, I took it off him one afternoon and dropped it over the side. I mean a real gun, not something that shoots sideways. How he never shot himself with that thing I don't know. Isn't there anyone else around here with a gun?'

She smacked her forehead with the side of her fist. 'I've got something better, Edward. It's quieter and far more deadly. I actually stole it from Hamilton's house a long time ago – found it at the bottom of an old chest that I was cleaning out.'

'Found what?'

'It's a crossbow with about six bolts. It looks in good condition but, truth to tell, I've never fired it. You think you could use a crossbow?'

The fire was making a soft lapping noise with a few quiet internal groans and yet more quick darts of St Elmo's fire. Edward pressed his fists into his eyes. 'I *have* used a crossbow in Australia,' he said. 'They really are deadly as long as the balance is right and the sights are level. That's all you need with a crossbow. We used to shoot kangaroos with them in the outback. And what power! Some of those arrow shafts would go right through the kangaroos and they'd just go bounding on as if nothing had happened.'

'Can you keep running like that if an arrow has gone straight through you?'

He ignored the question, staring directly into the fire. 'I'd need at least half an hour to practise on that crossbow. Just to find its balance and check its sights. And we'd have to get him out of that house. Does he ever go out of his house at night?'

'Not that I know of.'

'Well, we'd need him out in the open. Somewhere in the middle of the Close would do. I could pick him off easily enough then.'

'There's a simple way to do that. I know his number and could just telephone a message that we've got that beloved cup of his. He'd come charging out of that door faster than a wounded steer.'

'Yes, oh yes,' Edward said so softly it was almost as if he did not want the fire to hear their conspiracy to murder. 'Yes, I like that very much. But we need to leave it for a while – at least until after the pubs are shut and the people are off the streets. I'll take a little cocaine and you can help me to relax also.'

Outside, light showers of rain spattered over the dark streets of the Bay, when a man went running down the centre of Bute Street with a thirty-foot pole balanced in his jaws. The rain stopped as suddenly as it had begun, and a firework rocket broke into a flaming, multi-coloured puffball in the grey damp sky. Just behind the pole dancer an acrobat was cartwheeling across the road followed by another pole dancer and another and another, all zigzagging across the tramlines of the dusty thoroughfare, while a humming was rising and filling the dock night like a gathering swarm of locusts; softly now and yet louder and louder until such was the hullabaloo of whistles, shouts and drumming the whole street seemed to spring to vibrating life in gaudy streams of musicians, acrobats and the Chinese populace themselves, all moving around a gigantic model of a ship that glinted and hissed with many candles, which guttered and smoked black in the light showers of rain.

Nazeem stood on the corner of James Street, his hands playing with his scarf, when a man with fish hooks hanging off his bare chest went stamping past him in the direction of the docks themselves. Now hundreds of small yellow faces were percolating out of the darkness to join the sacred ritual of the Nine Gods. Another flaming puff-ball whirled over the rooftops. The savage, relentless drumming was battling with the plaintive wailing of conches. The Bay's incredible dream machine had begun again.

The noisy discords had even frightened away the rats who had come up the canal banks to scavenge in the rotten fruit left over in the street markets at one end of Custom House. At the other end of the street, away from the parked, wheeled stalls, a naked Sophie was on her knees on her bed massaging Edward's body with sandalwood oil. She slapped it on generously, working it deep into his muscles, with strong, practised movements of her hands. She had always believed that you could quickly work out what a man was all about by the condition of his body and, even in the pale, hissing light of her bedroom gas-lamp, she could see that Edward was a real fighter, unafraid of anyone or anything. There were cuts on his arms, dark smudges of bruises all over his legs and a whole patchwork of scars on his back. Men with Edward's background and education did not usually go out brawling all over the world. Just where had he got them all from?

Nevertheless it was clear that he was still very tense and even jittery at the prospect of taking on Hamilton. He had spent but ten minutes testing the crossbow in her garden and then had all but dragged her up to bed, trying to take her greedily and hungrily. He failed altogether, coming far too soon, getting angry with himself and, in turn, with her. So she had given him small playful pats on his arms and body, clambering all over him, forcing him to stretch out on the bed, before beginning a long body massage, working her hands around his legs and groin, down the length of his spine and deep into the tensions in the sides of his neck.

She poured more oil over his shoulder blades, using her fingertips to rub it right into those large bones which always, somehow, reminded her of prehistoric weapons. Her battling knight was going to be as fit and well as she could make him. She turned him over, filling up his navel from her phial of oil, now spreading it around and around his tight belly muscles. She found a few more scars there too.

Next she worked the back of her fist around and around his pubic area when his erection came throbbing up again, anxious and more than ready. She lowered herself onto it, baring her teeth a little before smoothing some more oil over his chest. 'You're going to be fine, Edward. You're going to be ready and do it well.'

He put his arm around her waist and drove his thighs up into her. She reached down around him, steadying herself on the bed with splayed-out fingers as she drove back down on top of him. Rain began pattering on the roof with the hollow, repeating sound of dried peas scattering over empty biscuit tins. She closed her eyes as he raised her up again. She would have him ready all right. She knew that now. Soon he would be as ready to kill the mad beast as he would ever be.

Later she was sitting up in bed with his head lying on her belly. He was dozing and she was smoothing his hair reassuringly as he whimpered now and then, sometimes jabbing his elbows around like a boxer loosening up before a key fight. His muscled, oiled body looked strong enough now though; tight and lean, instinctive of danger. She studied some of his scars again, smoothing them with her fingers, wondering what sort of dogfights he had been in to get them. That one there must have been with a knife or razor – grief, it was a good foot long and he must have come very close to bleeding to death with it.

She stared out of her bedroom window over the small back yard walls as another shower began spitting down. She gave a small regal cough which she smothered with the side of her fist. Her breathing was heavy and she stretched her back. She did not think much of her kingdom when it rained. The sunny summer when the air was thick with servicing bees was when she liked her kingdom the best.

'How are you feeling, Edward? I'll go down and make that call when you're ready.'

'I'm ready. But there is something I want you to have. In this envelope there are the deeds to the windjammer. Keep them safe. The ship is now yours.'

Down on the Bristol Channel two ships steamed past one another opposite Penarth beach as the foghorns repeated emptily and drowsily, warning of thick sea mists which were rolling in off the full tide, seeping silently over the mud banks and filtering through the streets of the Bay like disintegrating ghosts. In Howard Close these ghosts had already joined hands to make a small bank of moving mist which seemed to be swelling in the rain. The foghorns droned again, riding over the distant but steady drumming and the conch-wailing of the Nine Gods.

In the mazy darkness of Howard Close, where the green light of the street-lamps refracted in the low rolls of the sea mists, the high, squat face of Hamilton's mansion seemed lonely, set apart, embattled. It just seemed to be sitting there and suffering quietly, defying the intermittent showers of rain which mounted attack after attack on its walls like millions of tiny arrows being shot by thousands of invisible archers. Yet, even so, there was nothing about the mansion that suggested it might be ready to fall. Its thick iron railings and barred windows; the oak door and gabled turrets . . . every feature looked as strong and impregnable as a Norman castle.

Inside, despite the late hour, Hamilton was sitting alone on a chair in his work room, sharpening his six-foot-long iron sword with a whetstone. It was not so much a difficult task as an ungainly one, the hilt of the sword resting on his shoulder and the long blade running down between his knees as he ran the stone in long squealing bursts down the cutting edges of the blade. When he had got as far as he could reach down the blade he had to turn the sword around and let the hilt rest on the floor, taking care that the finely-honed blade did not cut into his neck. The stone on iron made an elongated whine; a little like a howl of animal pain, muted but unmistakably anguished. Now and then he brought the blade close to his cheek and squinted along its length with one eye. He always kept both the cutting edges so sharp you could actually split human hairs on them.

The Knights Templar had always been expected to keep their traditional instruments of justice and revenge in this pristine condition. No territories had ever been conquered with weapons that had been poorly looked after.

He stood up, raising the sword to his forehead, moving his legs slightly apart, ready for combat. His arms were full and strong as he held his great sword aloft. He always felt totally inviolable and invincibly strong with this sword in his hands. This was the very sword that had won a multitude of battles for holy causes. It had never let any man down; never failed if the cause was just. But there were no clear battlegrounds available to him just at the moment. Hamilton's great weapon, sharpened and oiled, would soon be back in its case, ready for the call.

Outside, a puffball of firework flame went shrieking across the sky as Nazeem stood in the darkness of the garage at the entrance to Howard Close, watching the moving shadows of the swordplay on the barred curtains of Hamilton's room. Even as he stood there he could hear the telephone ring inside the mansion; he watched as Hamilton put the sword down and walked away from the window.

As the great Chinese ship was carried into the docks it was followed by a huge, swinging chair held up on poles by four men. This ungovernable, revolving chair swung clear of the width of the road before swooping back again, blessing one home and ignoring the other, giving grace to some in the procession and withdrawing it from others, reducing some of the elderly to fear and trembling as it lurched along the deserted wharves – now on, now back – as if completely driven by an intelligence of its own, independent of the four thin and sweating men who hung onto its poles as they tripped along with the chair's reckless lunges.

Even in the cold shivery night the procession had brought out the strangest crowd of sightseers and fellow-travellers to swell the ranks of those Chinese already on their ritual walk. Many children had been drawn by the fireworks and the noise but there were lots of other nationalities too . . . most noticeably the Sikhs in their turbans, the Moslems in their songkoks and more than a few Irish milling around on the outskirts of the crowd, some still visibly angry at the attack on the spiritual leader of their community, showing the odd glimpse of a shillelagh or uttering a harsh, poteen-soaked curse. Perhaps a thousand or so had gathered around the ship and the careering chair by now, all stunned into silence by the odd rain shower and the continual drumming which, far from competing with the wail of the conches, was now actually beginning to dominate them.

A flood of bright orange light poured out onto the moving banks of mist trapped inside Howard Close as Hamilton opened his mansion door and stepped out into the night, not even pausing to close the door behind him. He was not exactly running but neither was he walking as he crossed the Close, stopping abruptly when Edward moved out in front of his path.

Edward was holding the crossbow against his shoulder, the polished wood of the breech flush against his cheeks as his hands trained the flight directly at Hamilton's heart. From this distance he just could not miss; shattering that heart and setting up so many internal shock waves he would kill the mad beast instantly.

Hamilton stood quite motionless, his black eyes studying Edward's hands carefully since he also knew all about the shock waves from a shattering heart. Even in those moving, gaslit mists he could see that those fingers meant business. He knew that he could not get out of the way of that iron arrowhead. He knew about crossbows. From this distance they were as deadly and accurate as any gun; munitions manufacturers had made no real advance when they had abandoned the crossbow. He had collected them after all but never expected one to be used against him. 'What are you going to do with that?' he asked evenly.

'I'm going to kill you,' Edward explained carefully.

'That would not be a very intelligent thing to do,' Hamilton pointed out, his eyes still on that iron arrowhead.

'I left a white feather on your doorstep years ago, asking you to fight with me.'

'Yes, well, let us fight by all means, Edward. I would like that a lot. I kept that white feather. Perhaps we should have had a real fight years ago.'

'No. No real fights tonight, Mr Alexander Hamilton. Tonight you just die.'

He had squeezed the trigger when he felt a sudden explosion of pain on the back of his head. He fell to his knees, glancing to one side long enough to see Nazeem's painted face appear and then disappear into the mists. A rock had clattered near his feet and almost immediately he could feel a warm downpour of blood over his left ear. Even as he looked back he could just make out Hamilton's shape running into the cover of the mists; the bolt had hit him just above the knee. At least Edward *thought* he had hit him except that it did not seem to have slowed him down at all. Hamilton hurried into the drifting mists, vanishing completely, only to reappear with a malicious smile.

His head throbbing with the blow he had received, Edward rose to his feet, putting another bolt on the crossbow. He ran after Hamilton, moving his weapon around and around but finding nothing but drifting mists to fire at. He trained his sights high up at the castellated roof of the mansion but, apart from the odd javelins of rain, nothing moved up there either.

The sharp noise of running feet came from another mist bank on the other side of the Close and Edward ran straight into it, spotting the shape of a fleeing figure and firing a bolt at it. There was a high-pitched scream, followed by a whimpering cry and Edward rushed over to the stooping figure, holding the crossbow aloft to smash it down on its skull. But he found that he had shot Nazeem, who was down on all fours, barely able to move since his backbone had been split by the deadly arrowhead. His hands fluttered uselessly around the shaft in his back. Edward lowered his crossbow and turned just in time to see a large dark figure go limping in through the yellow light of Hamilton's front door. The warrior king had got back inside his castle. Edward took three or four running steps towards the house and stopped still.

Oddly, Hamilton still had not closed his front door, almost as if he was actually inviting Edward inside. Edward was not falling for that. He loaded another bolt and walked up to the front of the house, standing in the road, framed by the yellow oblongs of the hall light. 'All right, Mr Hamilton,' he shouted. 'Come and make a fight of it.'

There was a small flurry of shadows in the hall itself, and Edward took several steps backwards as something silver came sailing out of the doorway, landing with a metallic clatter just near his feet. He put down his crossbow and picked up the sword, whirling it around and slicing up the air with it.

The showers had stopped just now, with the sea winds picking up and blowing most of the mists away when Hamilton stepped out of his doorway. Edward swallowed hard and even the paralysed Nazeem stopped whimpering to look up in awe at a new kind of fury.

The large dark shape of Hamilton came down the steps. He used both his hands to hold a sword aloft against his temple. Yet this sword was almost twice the size of the one that he had thrown to Edward. Just one accurate swing would have cut his body clean in half. It was a good six feet of glinting murder, Edward decided, made considerably more frightening by the fact that Hamilton was also wearing a protective vest of chain mail. Bizarrely, an arrow shaft was poking out of the side of Hamilton's leg but he still seemed not to notice it as he came lumbering forward for his long-awaited fight.

Edward looked one way and another, as if for a way of escape. There were opponents and opponents, but he did not give much at all for his chances against this man who barely seemed human. This was the promised prophet from hell, a messenger from the dark side of God, seeking blazing expressions in mindless destruction and the bleak impulsiveness of murder. But there was no escape now and, again slicing the air with his sword, Edward took a step forward to meet him.

Red-eyed with a tearful day of drink, Nathan stood at the ward room porthole, gazing across the dock where the Chinese were pushing their boat out onto the still waters of the West Bute Dock. Even so far across the waters he could pick up the sweet smell of the joss sticks, hear the chanted prayers and drumming, see the huge boat bursting into lambent fire as the Chinese threw flaming torches at it.

The flickering flames of the sinking boat made the dockland cranes dance around on the crowded wharf. Even the very warehouses seemed to be on the move as the great ship groaned and tilted to one side, the burning incandescence giving the water all around it an orange and purple sheen. The Chinese were still and silent, watching the boat sink as if they were at the committal of a dearly-beloved member of the tribe.

Nathan began crying again just at the point when the boat seemed to be about to sink. He seemed so very distant from everything as the world sat there before him trapped in a drowning illusion. It was nothing really. It was just that he felt so terribly and scorchingly lonely. He was living alone in a derelict hulk and his one true friend had just been murdered. He had long lost his family and Sophie was interested in another man. Here he was now, with all that aching loneliness reinforced by watching Chinese ritual, all so very far from the one true God – the Father of the Son – whom he had once loved with such a purity of passion and whom he had rejected so finally and disastrously.

Another firework rocket screeched across the night sky as more of the Chinese crowded up to the edge of the wharf, and he turned around, pouring himself another drink with a hand which should by rights have been even less steady considering all the drink he had got through that day. But it was only the drink that stopped him drowning in his grief, he supposed. It was only the drink that helped him to forget those who had died and those who had left him. He raised the glass in a toast to some distant malevolence and saw the flames of the dying ship dancing in it.

Riot and disorder have many faces but no one ever correctly identified the real culprit of the riot that showery night of the Nine Gods. Some said that it was the Irish who wantonly and without provocation attacked the Chinese as they were leaving the dock. Other reports had it that the Chinese attacked the Irish just for the hell of it. The landlord of the Ship and Pilot said that the Irish had nothing to do with it at all and that it was all down to the Arabs.

It even became known as the Arab Riots. But of the seventeen men and three women who were taken to hospital that night, suffering from gashes and multiple fractures, none at all was Arab. Four were Irish and seven were Chinese. And one had died – a Welshman who had been shot in the back.

What was never in dispute was that a racial fight of quite startling viciousness boiled up around the streets adjoining the Pier Head Building just after eleven o'clock that night, raging from corner to corner, smashing shop windows and breaking heads, sending one outfitter's shop up in flames.

The Chinese had never been ones to back off from a fight, particularly where members of their own families were under threat, and fought all comers as more and more people were drawn out onto the streets, ready to defend their own corners with whatever force seemed necessary. Certainly the Arabs played their own part too, later claiming that they were just defending their Mosque. They became involved in a huge brawl on the corner of James Street nevertheless. The only ones conspicuous by their absence were the West Indians, who later said that they had more important things to do than to be out fighting with their own coloured brethren. Throughout the disturbances the police managed to stay on the other side of the bridge claiming that they had not been told about the trouble until it was all but over.

At one point there were four separate fights going on in different parts of Bute Street. Five men had closed in on one young Chinese boy, trapped against the canal wall and gamely trying to defend himself with a small plank. Another Chinese lad had already been forced to jump into the freezing waters of the canal and swim for it to escape his attackers.

In the growing noise and vicious unpredictability of all these wheeling commotions it was not so very remarkable that two men could be seen fighting with swords in Howard Close. In itself almost a natural amphitheatre, the Close seemed to amplify the intermittent clashing of steel on steel, drawing more and more people to watch this gruelling encounter which had now been going on for almost half an hour. Even Sophie had come down to watch it, alternately wincing and averting her gaze as the two duellists thrust and counter-thrust in a combat which could only lead to the death of one of them.

It was not so much a speedy fight as the slow work of the hammer and the anvil. Hamilton, with his large and unwieldy sword, kept circling his opponent, looking for an opening for that final deadly swing while Edward, with his smaller weapon, had to keep nipping any such attacks in the bud by chipping at the larger sword again and again whenever it looked poised to make a huge scythe through the air. If he could not actually hit the sword or make an attack himself he had to keep dancing out of the way as Hamilton came for him; even though this was becoming an increasingly dangerous course of action now he was tiring badly.

His real handicap was that he had no experience of such fighting. He did not understand that this was a fight he could never win since, despite Hamilton's lumbering attack, his large sword also gave him a complete defence. The man who tired first would die and Hamilton showed no sign whatsoever that he was tiring, just grimly moving around and around, not even wincing or blinking when the steel blades clashed. Even more strangely, there was no sign of any blood on his leg from where the husk of the bolt still protruded. He had clearly broken it off with his hands and yet was even now moving without any sign of a limp. Perhaps he really was invincible.

If Edward did not understand that he could never win in this way then Sophie saw it all too clearly, becoming frantic with anxiety as the crowds of spectators grew even thicker. But there was nothing she could do. Looking around her anxiously, she saw that almost every nationality under the sun had drifted into the Close, first drawn out of their homes by the street disorders but now attracted by something even more compelling – two grown men fighting to the death with swords. Yet, despite their diversity and the tensions between the races that night, they all seemed to be oddly subdued by the fight, making no partisan sounds nor indeed any sounds at all as the duel continued on its clashing course. It was almost as if, without having been told, they understood that they were a part of this fight too.

A group of Irishmen started moving around next to Sophie, muttering obscenities in a soft brogue. She heard one of them saying to an elderly man, 'That's him, that's the one.' But who? What? She moved closer to them, wondering whom they were so interested in. 'Are we certain now?' the elderly man was asking. 'Are we that certain?'

More people were pushing around her when she caught a glimpse of something harsh and frightening in the elderly man's hands. It was a Thompson sub-machine-gun which he kept turning around and around away from any prying eyes. Overhearing a little more of their muttered conversations she gathered that they were certainly interested in Hamilton since one of them was fairly certain that he was the murderer of Father O'Reilly. So this was the IRA murder squad she had heard so much gossip about over the years. They had clearly come for revenge. With her heart beating wildly she edged closer to them, putting her hand on one of their shoulders. The man turned to face her with a jump, clearly more scared than she was.

Hamilton came moving forward again, his sword continuing to make slow swings back and forth as Edward valiantly did what he could to stop its deadly arc. Sometimes he had to hit the oncoming swing as many as three times before Hamilton withdrew from the middle ground of the fight to try another tack. By now Edward's arms were but leaden weights. He came dangerously close to not stopping the sword at all, having to leap out of the way before facing yet another slow-rolling attack. Neither time nor strength seemed to be on his side; he was about to make a direct lunge at Hamilton's neck – and to hell with the consequences – when he stumbled and fell awkwardly. He glanced up, knowing that Hamilton was moving in for the kill, his great sword glinting ferociously in the streetlight as it was raised high. Hastily Edward scrambled to his feet.

Just at that moment there was a cry loud enough to clear the sky of all its birds. '*M-u-r-der-eh*. '*M-u-r-der-eh*.'

The crowd began scattering as fast as they could. They had heard the traditional cry of the IRA murder squad and knew immediately what the old man shuffling forward into the arena was carrying in his hands. *Rat-at-at-at-at*. Explosive blasts and tiny yellow flames came darting out of the barrel of the Thompson. *Rat-at-at-at-at*. Each of the stammering yellow flames had a tiny purple heart and the whole gun jumped around as if wired up to a charge of lightning as it fired off yet another round. *Rat-at-at-at-at*. More single shots spat out in darting flames and Edward dropped his sword, his back arching in a shivery pain, the upper part of his torso ripped apart by the murderous bursts.

He spun around slowly as the whole of the Close danced and revolved before his eyes. He saw the screaming, fleeing people, the high dark walls of the mansion and the sub-machine-gun being tossed across the road into the hands of the minder. Even as he continued falling, holding out one hand to break his fall, he could feel the light cold rain on his hot cheeks. 'You silly Irish bastards,' he heard Sophie's voice shouting. 'The other man. I told you. The other man.'

He moved the great, ungainly weight of his body around to try and make himself more comfortable. But, somehow, it was almost as if he had drunk too much. He could not seem to make his arms or legs work at all. He heard Sophie's anguished voice again and wondered about that windjammer and whether they ever really would get it to sail again. But the very last thing he saw before he died was the large, dark figure of Hamilton hurrying in through his front door trailing his sword behind him. The very last thing he heard was the sound of Hamilton throwing the door bolts. Then, with the softest of sighs, he died.

The Close was completely deserted and Sophie was still cradling Edward in her arms when an ambulance arrived. The attendants took one look at him and immediately covered his body and face with a blanket. She did not even travel with him to the Infirmary, just walking away unsteadily into the streets of the Bay rather hoping that she could die herself.

It was only now – when he had gone – that she understood how much she had really cared for her battling knight. And she also understood that she felt so much grief and pain she could not even afford the luxury of tears. What she would never understand was why the wrong ones always died.

The Chinese ship had not quite sunk into the still, cold waters of the West Bute dock. A small part of its prow was poking up out of the surface, charred and smoking like an accusing finger deep in the smouldering forests of hell. It just seemed to be moving around too, almost as if unsure of just whom to accuse. The warehouses? The sky? The very night? God Himself? Finally, in the absence of any identifiable culprit, it just gave up and sank into the water, leaving a tiny armada of blue ashes floating in slow circles directly around the point of the ship's departure.

# CHAPTER TWENTY-TWO

The Arab Riots marked a watershed in the history of the Bay. Spluttering newspaper editorials made renewed demands for the repatriation of all coloureds. The Chief Constable of the Glamorgan Police publicly criticized the coloured communities, saying that these new disturbances 'with swords and guns' underlined that, by and large, these foreigners had disgusting habits, poor health and debased morals. It would clearly be to the advantage of everyone if they were all sent back to their homelands. It was unfortunately not in his power to send these troublemakers home himself but it *was* within his jurisdiction to increase the number of working police in the area. Henceforth there would be eighty men working in threes on permanent patrol in the docks area. Woe betide anyone who so much as dropped an empty cigarette packet in the street.

Even the full council passed a resolution deploring the 'continuing anarchy' there and calling on the community leaders to enter into a 'responsible dialogue' with one another. The message of the civic gospel was that it was time for all the alien ruffians to abandon the hooligan ways of their homelands and start reading a book or two to improve their renegade minds.

What really enraged the Moslem community was that the council's thoughts on the racial problems in their bailiwick were then sent to *them* in a letter care of the Mosque. In all his life Rashed had never even touched a sword let alone seen a sub-machine-gun. Beside himself with rage he led an irate deputation to the City Hall. But none of the councillors would receive them.

Amidst all this public self-righteousness were some quiet and unremarked departures from the area. The police showed a curious reluctance to investigate the machine-gunning of Edward Gurney, still less to make any serious inquiries into a duel that had been witnessed by a few hundred people and had lasted for some three-quarters of an hour. Indeed the main protagonist of the troubles, Mr Alexander Hamilton, was picked up from his home by Chief Inspector Victor Watts the very next morning and driven away, not to be seen for years.

Just after ten o'clock the same morning three furniture vans came to take away all his effects. The job took a dozen men well into the evening and, when the house had been completely emptied, another group of workmen came with planks and nails to board up the doors and windows of the mansion.

Even the Oriel office in Bute Street was closed down. Partington was seen busily loading piles of documents into a wagon before he, too, drove away, never to be seen again. That afternoon the word went out on the Floor of the Exchange that any and all shore assets of Oriel were for sale at a nominal price. Two days later all the line's ships moored in Cardiff sailed for as yet unannounced ports in Africa.

Exactly a week after he had been murdered Edward Gurney was buried in a quiet corner of Whitchurch cemetery. No one came forward to claim his body and the hospital's inquiries could not connect him with anyone, largely because they did not even know his name. The police were informed and they seemed unable to do anything about it either, not even offering his photograph for identification in the newspapers. So the body just sat in the Infirmary's morgue with the hospital administrators becoming increasingly impatient until, without explanation or comment, they received fifty pounds from police funds and instructions to dispose of the body in whatever way they thought appropriate. They then contacted Sophie, the only person who had come to inquire about his body and she suggested that he had a quiet burial somewhere since she too had only met him a couple of times and knew absolutely nothing about him.

So the enigmatic drifter, the black sheep of the family, whom none had ever understood nor even wanted to understand, was finally buried near a yew tree in a cemetery one Wednesday afternoon in May with the sun shining brightly on the surrounding tombstones in mocking irony.

Funerals were the opportunity for relatives and friends to express their final verdict on the deceased. But that sunny day in a Cardiff suburb, it was just left to the priest and the sole mourner to express their own verdict on a man seemingly with no friends, no past, no future and a father whose mysterious life had finally paved the way to his son's destruction. For many he might not even have lived at all. Yet his heroism was still vivid in Sophie's mind and memory. He had become precious to her for raising the standard and daring to be a man. When the priest had finished reading the Order of the Dead, she threw a white lace handkerchief down onto the simple wooden coffin.

She remained standing there in a patch of warm sunlight, even after the priest had left and the gravedigger had begun his mordant work.

'Who was he, this man?' he asked as her white handkerchief was covered by a brown lump of smashed clay.

'I don't know. I never really knew him.'

'Will there be a gravestone, will there, do you know? It'll affect the way I finish off the grave.'

'No. Nothing. Nothing at all.'

It took her more than a misery-stained hour to walk back to the docks, where she found a quiet corner on her own in the Frampton pub. The hospital had given her the balance of some twenty-two pounds, from the fifty sent by the police, so she put that on the table for a sort of informal wake, telling the other customers to help themselves to a drink and bring back the change. It always helped to have other people around when you wanted to get really obliterated.

But it was clearly going to be one of those days when she would not be able to get drunk no matter how hard she tried. Friends and acquaintances drifted in and drifted away again as she sat stonily under the weight of the oppressive reality she was so desperate to escape from. The drink was not making her at all sociable either. Even after a few whiskies she got more and more irritable. Then Obe walked into the pub followed by three of his cronies from the Sons of Africa.

'I can see we're not going to get much singing out of you tonight,' he said, sitting down next to her and nodding at the money and empty glasses on her table.

'I'll sing, don't you worry about that. I'll be singing my little tonsils out. Don't you worry about that at all. You just worry about that trumpet of yours.'

'It doesn't matter, sister. Just get drunk. We can always call it off tonight. We don't want you slurring your words.'

'Have you ever heard me slurring my words?' she asked, with a sharp sideways jab of her elbow. 'You'd have to go a long way to hear me slurring my words – no matter how much I drank. This stuff isn't having any effect on me anyway. Probably watered down. They even water down the lemonade in this place. Here. Do you and your boys want a drink? There's the money there. Help yourself.'

Obe picked up a crumpled pound note and handed it to Benedict, telling him to buy a round.

'Obe, tell me one thing now. Does Benedict kiss your feet if you ask him? And these other boys of yours. Do you put collars and leads around their necks when you take them out for a walk?'

'All right, sister. Calm down now.'

She was silent for a few moments, just sitting there, staring at the table and biting on her lower lip. 'I don't want to sing with that band ever again,' she said finally. 'There's none of them can play a proper note and I'm tired of carrying them. You hear me? Tired of carrying the whole lot of you. I'm going my own way in the future. Going solo.'

Obe kept his drink to his lips as she spoke and, when he was sure that she had finished speaking, he put it back down. He could see that she was in a right old mood but he wasn't going to rise to the bait. He just kept ducking and diving when she got into this mood. 'Well, as it happens, that suits me fine, sister,' he said evenly. 'If that's what you want, it just so happens that it suits me fine.'

'Oh, does it now?'

'Yes, it does. Me and the boys in the Sons of Africa have decided to branch out. We're not making much progress here so we're making contact with our brothers in Liverpool and

Birmingham. The secretary from the Movement for Colonial Freedom is coming down tomorrow and we're talking to him also. We're going to make the Sons of Africa a national organization to fight for black rights everywhere. It will mean a lot of travelling. If you want out I want out too.'

She downed another drink. This wasn't what she was hoping to hear at all. She wanted him to be shocked and outraged. She was rather hoping for him to go down on his knees and beg her to stay with the band. But here he was, as cool as you like, announcing that he was going off to get all those black arses organized in Birmingham – wherever that was. 'You're leaving me then? Oh ain't that just like a black man? You can always rely on a black man to leave you when you're down. It's their real nature after all – black outside and yellow inside.'

'Now hold on a minute, sister,' Obe replied, sitting hard on the simmering volcano of his hurt feelings. '*You* announced that you were going out on your own. I just said that if you were going solo then I would go solo. I can't travel around the country for the Sons of Africa if I'm stuck with the band night after night. I hadn't made up my mind 'til you said you were going. Then that made it up. I'm giving up my music for my beliefs. It's what I prefer.'

She finished yet another whisky in one quick swig, wiping her lips with the back of her hand. 'You know, if there's one thing I've always hated it's treachery,' she said turning on him directly. 'You've been planning this for ages, haven't you? You didn't just think of it, did you? You came to my house and I took you in. You came and heard my band and I took you into that. Everything you've got you've got from me. And for what? Eh? For what? So you can desert me and go off to organize some damned stupid revolution for blacks in Birmingham. Where's Birmingham?'

'You're not making a lot of sense, sister. Why're you saying these things?'

'Why? I'll tell you why,' she began shouting, the tears pouring down her cheeks and forefinger poking him hard in the chest. 'I'll tell you why. Because I'm very upset after burying a very brave man who you couldn't hold a candle to. You understand that, do you? No, you wouldn't, would you. People like you wouldn't. You just want to rush about the country caring for all those black no-hopers you call your brothers. So when you're gone sorting out everyone in Birmingham and Liverpool, what about me? Eh? What about me?'

'You're a big girl now.'

'No, I'm not, Obe. I'm not at all. I'm getting scared of everything. I just can't cope, particularly with my so-called friends stabbing me in the back like this. You'd better go out and wash the blood off your hands. Now.'

It was becoming increasingly hard for Obe to hold onto his simmering feelings and he was going quite white and swallowing a lot. 'I think you'd better have another drink.'

'Why? You want to get me drunk? You want to get your bloody hands into my knickers? Is that it? Find out what's going on between a woman's legs? You don't have to get me drunk for that, Obe. I'll show you any time you like. Yes, it's time you took a lesson in all that. Or do you – you know – prefer the boys? Is that what you really prefer, Obe? Is that why they're always hanging around?'

Obe jumped up as if his back was on fire, his fists bunching. He looked dangerously close to hitting her. There were insults and insults, but she had taken it just too far. The volcano had erupted. 'Sister, I'd like to thank you for taking me into your home and your band,' he said, with the greatest difficulty since he was so angry he could hardly get his words out at all. 'But I am going to walk out of this pub now and I will never speak to you again.' He signalled to his cronies who had been sitting on the next table and listening to the argument with quiet, if appalled, interest, and they stood up and followed Obe out of the door.

'You've forgotten their collars and leads,' she shouted after them. 'Don't forget their collars and leads.'

Now she began crying copiously, her whole body shaking as she stared at the money on the table, the Brains beer mats and her empty glass. She wiped her snivelling nose with her fingers and took in a deep breath of air. Just what was she doing? She was like that child who always kept breaking up his favourite toy. Only one thing was very clear. She really was as drunk as a wheel.

Two days later Bill Huish threw up his hands in mock despair in the Neale and West Fish Wharf as Effey stood her ground and refused point-blank to accept any dogfish.

'You don't understand,' the girl explained patiently. 'The cats don't like dogfish. No one likes dogfish. I know they're little use to you. I'm sorry that you have so many. But the cats need proper fish.'

'It's all very well you demanding proper fish, but where's my proper payment? Have you any idea what it's like running a business when no one has got any money? Have you ever heard of overheads? And wages for the men? Do you know how much it costs me to run a lorry or to pay for oil for the trawler? No? Well you wouldn't, would you?'

'All I know is that the cats just don't like dogfish. That's all. I've tried them with dogfish but even when they're hungry they leave it. They just don't like it.'

'Well, what about some payment then? That Nathan has got some money, hasn't he? He must have some money to live on that ship in the first place.'

'Mr Huish, I'll pay you what I always pay you. I'll be your friend for ever. Isn't that enough?'

Two minutes later Effey went bounding out of the fish wharf with a pile of fresh hake wrapped up in a newspaper under her arm. It was one of those glad-to-be-alive mornings as she raced down past the Norwegian Church and two children playing hopscotch near Beal and Sons' chain-making foundry. Gulls wheeled in the sunshine and, down by the lock gates, the sluice waters roared and foamed as another ship readied itself to leave the Roath Basin.

She quickly and expertly chopped up the fish in *The Solomon*'s galley, carefully putting one of the fatter hake into a locker for Nathan later on. The cats brushed against her legs almost roaring with hunger as she threw the cutlets down with a slap onto the galley floor. They had barely touched the deck when they were snaffled up and carted off to some distant, dark corner of the ship where they could be eaten in peace.

After feeding time had finished she went down to the ward room where she found Nathan sitting alone, staring blankly into the darkness. She pulled back the porthole curtains and he winced as the bright daylight washed over him. He had almost certainly been on the drink, she guessed, as he scuttled over to another part of the bench where he was not so exposed to the light's appalling clarity. He was absolutely filthy and could not have shaved for weeks. His clothes were black and ragged – even worse they stank of stale urine.

But, fortunately, Effey had not yet learned the fastidiousness of adults. She felt no disgust, nor made any comment as she slipped down onto a chair at the table, folding her hands together and waiting for him to say something. Unlike her mother it did not really matter to Effey what state her Uncle Nathan got himself in. There was nothing of the school bully in her. If he liked getting drunk and being as filthy as that, if it made him happy, then that was fine by her.

She smiled at him and he groaned softly, looking away and pressing his forehead against the bulkhead, almost as if he wanted to burrow his way into it and disappear from the deadly accusation of her smiling innocence. 'When you grow up,' he said finally, without looking around, 'you must leave this place and get away as far as possible or you'll end up just like me. Go to Patagonia if you can.'

'What's in Patagonia?'

'Good Welsh people went there to start a colony and keep their culture alive. They went there because they were told that it was the Promised Land; that there were rivers and fields that they could farm anew. But a lot of them died on the journey out there.'

'So why are you telling me to go there? You don't want me to die, do you?'

'No, stupid. That was just the way travel was in the eighteenth century, but a lot of them did make it and that's where they all are now – working out in great farms and entertaining one another in the traditional Welsh way.'

'Sounds all right to me. Why don't we both go and live there? I can work on the farms and you can do a bit of preaching again.'

'Me? Preaching again? A man doesn't preach anything in my state.' His hands smoothed over the oak woodwork as if looking for a secret door. 'A man doesn't do anything in this state and he certainly doesn't go somewhere as precious to the Welsh as Patagonia. I'd just contaminate the lot of them if I went there. The original rotten apple in that barrel I'd be. Something has gone wrong, Effey. I don't know . . . look at these hands . . . these clothes . . .'

'Mam asked me to bring you some new clothes. She's got a pile of them from somewhere.'

'Ah, she won't bring them herself then, will she? What's the matter? Doesn't she want to see me any more now . . . now that other friend of hers has gone?'

'Mam's just having a bad time with everyone right now. She's just staying in bed all the time. She was upset after the accident to Uncle Edward but mostly it's to do with Obe. They had an argument and Obe has just gone and left home.'

'Has he left the jazz band too?'

'Yes, everything. I don't know where he's gone but it must have been a terrible argument since he's left all his belongings behind. All kinds of things there are in his room. I took a look.'

'How long has your mother been in bed then?'

'Uncle Nathan, there's so many things there I'm sure they must have been stolen. But there's this cup there. I've been holding it . . . just, you know, sitting on his bed and holding it in my hands. You remember that day Father O'Reilly was here talking of a wild and holy cup? You remember that he was telling all those stories about a cup at this very table? Well, I think this is the same cup.'

As she spoke Nathan turned slowly away from the bulkhead. He was staring at her curiously, his eyebrows rising a point or so and his insides going quite dry and even hollow. 'The same cup, Effey? But how would you know it was the same cup? The same wild and holy cup?'

'I don't know. I don't understand. I just sit there with it in my hands and I hear things, Uncle Nathan. I hear beautiful things. And I smell things and then I don't.'

'I don't follow.'

'It's just so difficult to explain. I sit there for hours just looking at it and it keeps changing. If you look at it in a certain light it seems to be golden but then you move it into another light and it seems to be . . . well . . . the colour of lead. Even the smells change . . . and there's music . . . just like a Victrola which starts and stops, and then it sounds like that penny organ they play at nights out in Alice Street and then it stops again. I don't know, Uncle Nathan. It's all so very strange but I am sure that this is that wild and holy cup. I'm just sure of it.'

By now Nathan had moved onto the chair next to her. He put his dirty hand on hers. 'So where is this cup now?'

'I put it back where I found it.'

'And the other things there. What things would they be?'

'Watches, bracelets, rings . . . those kind of things.'

'Stolen. What else could they be? Stolen. Effey, I very badly need you to get that cup for me.' He paused and lowered his voice to almost a whisper as he put his arm across her shoulders. 'I've not been too well, as you know, and that cup could make me better. No, no . . . it's not stealing to take it. You can't steal what's been stolen already. Just bring it here to me and it may be a new beginning. We all of us need a new beginning – a chance to become well again. Just get it for me, will you? Bring it here as soon as you can.'

The streets and the very air were sweating that night, with the waders calling out to one another on the mud flats as if they too were afflicted by these stifling nights. To add to the thick and torpid heat the furnaces of the East Moors steelworks were being fired, already starting to stain the bottom of the night a burly orange with faint pink streaks. Very little moved along the cobbled streets around the Exchange except a man pushing a handcart and a sailor carrying a parrot in a wicker cage, its head jerking from side to side as its beady eyes swivelled around trying to work out what was going on.

This sultry stillness was perhaps best captured inside the domed tower of the Greek Orthodox church, just next to the Salvation Army hostel, where a painting of a sad-eyed Christ gazed down from the dome into the dark vestry. Here almost everything seemed to be held in the cupped palms of invisible hands and a visitor, if there had been any visitors, would have been able to feel the centuries of prayer which bound him so deeply to an ancient past and a fretful future.

Soon it would be Grand Week with long, disordered services in Hellenic Greek, dazzling bursts of fireworks, and red-dyed, hard-boiled eggs for all the children. A replica of Christ's tomb would also be carried through the streets, accompanied by lots of jovial hand-clapping and singing.

But, just for now, there was this sweating darkness, thick with the ghosts of drifting prayers, and shadowed corners the colour of old mortar. There were gold religious icons and the smell of old incense. In the distance came the sound of passing cars but, just here, that sense of human continuity which binds the past so tightly to the future.

Even out in the docks themselves there seemed to be no air to breathe this still, almost tropical night, just the cicada-like murmurings of the telegraph wires overhead. Reflections of still ships sat motionless on the shining parallelograms of water and there was not even the drone of the foghorn to relieve this heavy silence as it spread through the empty wharves and yards.

Nathan, his mouth slightly apart and his fingers locked together on his chest, was stretched out asleep on his bunk, much like the tombstone of a Plantaganet king. Sometimes his lips chomped together and, on occasion, a little whimper of pain whined deep in his throat. He was dreaming troubled dreams of parched deserts and vultures circling overhead. It was this lack of water which was the worst, the inside of his mouth crumbling and falling in on itself. Everywhere the sky was a bright, sun-scalded blue with not a sign of a cloud anywhere. He did find some water but it turned into mud as soon as he kneeled down to drink it.

He let out another whimper of pain but it did not carry far through parts of the ship where just the fiery eyes of the cats moved through the dark shadows. There was no sense of human continuity in this old heart of oak any longer – just moth and rust, mildew and damp, defeat and sorrow. Here the past really had parted with the future and the warm suffocating darkness told only of broken connections and the failure of prayer; everything just waiting, perhaps, for the final purification of fire.

He struggled out of the desert now and was back as the great bird plunged her beak into her own chest to give blood to revive her dead young. Even as the beak speared her chest again and again, his hands separated and twisted and he sat up, eyes open wide as he began speaking in tongues. The babble came pouring out of his lips like vomit – '*fatshung, fatashung, scoba, telle, telle, fatshung, fatashung*' – and he held both his hands over his mouth almost as if trying to damn this outpouring but, even when he held both his hands as tightly to his mouth as he could, the words still kept fighting their way out of his mouth like air bubbles furiously rising through deep water.'

'*Shondasin, scupery, shondasin – telle, telle, telle – scoobadordorta, scoobadorta, fatshung, fatshung, fatshung.*' He took his hands away from his mouth and the words came louder. He was wide-awake now, even aware that he had been dreaming of that dying bird again. But just what were these outpourings?

'*Coopa, coppa, sisuhigh – scelpple pellelwall – scootsa fatshung, fushing, stiplle well corrnerie.*' The words – at times a high-pitched jabber and at others a plaintive sorrowing – carried both deep into the vessel and out into the night where, amplified by the warm stillness, they carried along the wharves and through the foundries. Faces appeared at the portholes of the moored ships, wondering what this strange noise could be. The words even carried as far as the Norwegian Church where the hermit was standing at a lectern in his cell, learning of the love and will of God in the Bible. The hermit's whole body gave a shiver when he heard the words and he held up one hand to try and make an ear trumpet, the better to catch the words. They were very faint but he did recognize certain phrases and he paused only to listen to a few more before closing his Bible and stepping out into the docks to follow the sounds.

His stooped body was so slight he might not even have been there at all – a white-shawled wraith perhaps, gliding to the scene of a promising haunting. He stood at the foot of the windjammer's gangplank, his hands moving up and down in a sort of rapture, almost as if he was trying to fly, as the words continued to come babbling out through the darkness.

Nathan was pacing around and around the circular oak table of the ward room, worried now by the stuttering alien babble on his lips, which were working independently of his mind. He had no control at all over them; it could have been any language he was speaking and he certainly had no idea what he was saying if, indeed, he was saying anything meaningful at all. In the middle of the oak table was a solitary object – the cup which Effey had brought to him that day. '*Scalabal, seddle, fanshung – telle, telle, telle – distrung, distang, sceddle.*' The door opened and Nathan looked over at the smiling face of the hermit, his hands still moving up and down. '*Fanshung, spiddle, chatacoogo – skeddle, fashing, spaderooger.*' He too was speaking in tongues and they greeted one another in bursts of strange fresh language, giving Nathan odd feelings of mounting power.

The hermit pointed at the cup and smiled, making an eating sign with his hands before pointing at Nathan and back at himself. He made a drinking sign too, and, still muttering in tongues, Nathan picked up a kettle from the corner of the ward room and filled up the cup with water.

After they had both drunk from the cup they broke bread together, feeding one another and embracing. By now Nathan was possessed by quite dazzling feelings of strength, his inner spirits as lively as flames.

Outside, the fired furnaces of the East Moors steel works glowed like the spirit of the risen princes coming with revolutionary power to reclaim the world for love. Down in the Norwegian Church, a shape, in the form of a black hand, moved around on the altar. Though, given the sultry strangeness of the night, it might not have been a hand at all – an illusion perhaps, or a rat scurrying about its business.

# PART THREE

'The Christian religion not only was at first attended with miracles, but even at this day cannot be believed by any reasonable person without one. Mere reason is insufficient to convince us of its veracity; and whoever is moved by faith to assent to it, is conscious of a continued miracle in his own person, which subverts all the principles of his understanding, and gives him a determination to believe what is most contrary to custom and experience.'

DAVID HUME

# CHAPTER TWENTY-THREE
## 1938

Sophie followed the grey asphalt path down through St James's Park, hunched down into her silver fox fur coat with matching fur hat, until she came to the edge of the lake. It was so cold that, even this late in the afternoon and with the sun shining thinly, there were still patches of frost on the grass. Most of the leaves had fallen from the trees and a workman was sweeping them into brittle, orange piles. When he had finished one pile he moved on to start another.

She watched two children, twins most likely, dressed in identical coats with orange mufflers dangling around their necks, as they fed bread to an agitated swarm of pochard ducks and mallards. A nanny fussed over them ceaselessly, clearly worried that, in their excitement, the children might step into the water. Over in front of them, on the lake itself, was a great laughing fountain. Further on again were the spires of Whitehall. She felt a happiness spread inside her belly as she looked up at those spires. This was her favourite spot in the whole of London; where she always came when she just wanted to nourish her spirit. Those trees and spires always reminded her of a fairy story, even if it had been a very long time indeed since she had heard one of them.

Despite the dim roar of encircling traffic it was always so quiet here; a tiny oasis in a city where she could find the silence to deal with her own thoughts. It was particularly serene this late in autumn, when the leaves had dropped off the knobbly black branches and most people were more than happy to stay indoors in front of their coal fires. Autumn was a good season for sorrow and she was feeling a lot of that. She sniffed and took out a handkerchief, blowing her nose hard and hoping that she was not going to fall for yet another cold. Her singing always went right off the boil when she had the snuffles.

The fingers of her right hand were bedecked with thick gold

rings, some mounted with diamonds and rubies which, at times, glinted ferociously in the sunshine. The hair that fell from her fur hat and was tucked in behind her coat collar was remarkably thick and lustrous too. Even though a little over forty she still had the face of a young woman, with just the tiniest spread of crow's-feet around the corners of her brown eyes which were as sparky as ever, taking everything in and missing nothing, analysing everyone with one sure brown stare. The only real way in which she had changed was that she just *appeared* more elegant and this, in its turn, had made her move in a more gracious manner.

A swan reared up in front of her, his great wings flapping slowly before he collapsed down into the water again. He was displaying, she supposed – telling some other swan that he was ready for a bit of malarkey.

She walked on down towards Buckingham Palace as a few of the other ducks came up out of the water and followed her. It was always the way when it was cold and there were no visitors to feed them. They got so hungry they followed almost everyone that moved, a few of the larger ganders actually poking you in the back with their beaks.

She noticed a man staring at her and automatically jerked her face away from his inquisitive look. She had long learned not to give anyone the slightest encouragement; otherwise they'd pounce on you as if you were the long-lost family cat. Even after all this time she had still not got used to total strangers laying claim to her. They might barely have exchanged two words and she would be invited to their offices, their homes . . . their beds. They offered her presents and bunches of flowers; one day it might be a case of champagne and the next a bunch of car keys. Always there were the requests for autographs. It was all very difficult and she had never quite got the hang of dealing with it all. The price of fame, her husband had always called it. It was all right for him to talk. He had never once paid the price of anything.

She walked on up to Buckingham Palace, staring through the high iron railings at the busbied guards standing around the forecourt and the high grey building itself. Her own problems with fame paled into insignificance compared to the family inside that house, she decided. None of the Royals could lift a finger, let alone shake their middle leg, without it being reported breathlessly to the whole world. She stared up at the bedroom windows where poor old Edward had been bedding his beloved Wallis; trying to reconstruct in her mind the furious rows that must have raged up and down those corridors until he had finally got in front of a BBC microphone and announced that he was packing it all in, 'for the woman I love'.

She remembered the moment well. She had been doing a season in the Kit Kat Club and just sighed and felt very hungry indeed when she heard him. There had been a great cheer that night when she had dedicated her most famous song, *Prisoner of Love*, to the King and Mrs Simpson. He should have defied all the old crabs, she told her audience. Just told them all to go and have sexual relations with themselves, and got on with it. She also told her audience that there was a very great mystery attached to this romance since she had it on good authority that the King's dick was so small you could barely see it, let alone do anything with it. So what did that Mrs Simpson know that no one else knew? The audience always fell about laughing at her dirty little monologues. She was still doing them and if anything they had got dirtier over the years.

The cold began to squeeze her feet and she walked up The Mall, ignoring a man who approached her, beaming brightly, holding out his hand and saying 'Sophie?'

'You've got the wrong woman,' she mumbled, brushing past him and walking on. This kind of thing was very annoying when she was deep inside some private thought,or at a particularly intimate moment. On the very first night of her marriage she was in bed with her new husband who was just moving into second gear, when he was shoved back into neutral by a hotel maid wondering if she could have Sophie's autograph. He had never even so much as managed to get into first gear after that little set-back but, as she soon learned, there were other reasons for that too.

It was extraordinary how wrong she had been about this husband of hers, particularly as she was usually so right about people almost as soon as she first saw them. Perhaps it was because, at that time, she so *wanted* someone she was prepared to settle for anything and to overlook the usual early alarm bells. She was desperate for almost anyone, after being so firmly rejected by that bald-headed bastard Nathan. She might even have come to terms with that if Effey, the ungrateful bitch, had not also turned around and announced that she wanted to stay behind with him. There was the work on the windjammer, her school, her Welsh classes – Welsh! – and she would hate it on the road, she said, just wandering from hotel to hotel. She just couldn't sleep in all those strange beds, this, the same girl she had once found in a box!

Just the very thought of them both being so far away from her burned right down into the pit of her belly. When she got into Trafalgar Square she was ready for a stiff drink, except that the pubs had not yet opened and going back to the hotel would involve talking to her unbelievably wearying husband.

She could see a placard-carrying procession on the other side of the square. They were chanting something: 'Jews Out', or 'Blacks Go Home' – probably Ossie Mosley's Blackshirts on their hateful rampage again. It was all part of the extreme ugliness of the times, she thought – fascism on the rise at home and those Nazi bastards taking over abroad. The rich were getting richer and the poor poorer. Where it would all end she just could not think. All that was left to her was to make jokes about the size of Mosley's dick.

'Or, I wonder, does he actually have a dick at all?' she would ask her audience, hand on hip and one eyebrow raised quizzically. 'I was told only the other day he was in a chemist shop buying some pills for period pains. Now what does that tell us?'

A busker was going about his business amongst the fluttering pigeons next to a Landseer lion when he was grabbed by two policemen and marched away. Yes, that was the way it was now. She often just wished that she could go and live in some backstreet back in Cardiff's Bay. At least the place was pretty much free of the stench of racial hatred these days and any busker could busk his little head off for as long as he wanted.

But it was a redundant wish, she knew. There was no place there for her any longer. She had simply grown out of it. But there was no other place for her either, she feared. Sometimes she spoke of going back to Africa, admittedly only when well into her second bottle.

'Can't see you eating boiled cabbage in a mud hut, darling,' her husband would mock. 'And they don't have caviare out there either, do they?'

'I could live without caviare,' she would protest, refilling her glass with champagne. 'I wouldn't care if I never saw any caviare again. If you really want to know, I'd much prefer laver bread.'

'Why don't you send down for some of that then?'

'You can only eat laver bread when it's fresh. It would be well off by the time it got here. Anyway I like eating what's around. I always eat when I'm miserable and, since I met you, I've been miserable all the time.'

'I've seen you laugh once or twice.'

'Once maybe – never twice.'

Such were the torpid, bored barbs of their married life. She walked up the Strand and into the Savoy Hotel where she stopped next to the reception desk to buy an *Evening Standard*. The hotel's clients were sitting around in the lobby, some of them taking their afternoon tea. She would have nothing to do with any of them – with no exceptions whatsoever. These poor rich things, forever fretting about unprofitable mines and damp mansions; these gentlemen with no occupation and their ladies decked out in ostrich feathers and tulle who developed a fondness for Egyptian cigarettes in long ebony holders, and for dry martinis which made them giggle a lot – when they were not having the afternoon vapours on melancholy chaises longues.

These were the artificial people who were flocking to the artificial entertainments of such as Ginger Rogers, Fred Astaire and Busby Berkeley; who loved nothing more than to wallow in the empty sentiment where there was always moonlight in the tears and crushed gardenias lying in the midnight gutters. The current favourite was the composer Ivor Novello who, she had been intrigued to learn, had also been born in Cardiff. She had later bumped into him in a hotel foyer but thought him conceited and fatuous. He was, as they said in the Bay, all fur coat and no knickers, surpassed only by that other raving woofter Noël Coward.

She winked at one of the bellboys and walked over to the lift as she scanned the headlines. 'What I've always liked about Bognor is its simply marvellous tattiness,' someone said behind her. 'Dahling, everything there is so marvellously tatty.'

Her lips curled into a sardonic smile but she made no comment as she continued reading her newspaper. She saw that there was a quite savage irony in her being trapped in what she disliked so much, but she had her reasons. And they were good reasons. She had never once thought of buying a proper home and had quickly become accustomed to hotel life. She particularly liked being able to pick up the telephone at any time day or night and order any sort of food she fancied. Also, in such places, she was rarely bothered by the other guests – and that counted for a lot. Had anyone in the Savoy asked for her autograph she would have left immediately. There *were* pleasures in being famous – getting the best table in a restaurant for one, never having to queue, always being able to find someone to do your most menial duties.

She fiddled in her pockets for her room key, opening the door with a shove of her shoulder and stepping inside with arms apart. 'Everyone rejoice because I'm back, dahling,' she shouted in the posh Home Counties accent she heard so much around her. 'You can start having fun now, dahling, because we're all going to Bognor which is so marvellously tatty.'

The trouble was there was no one around to hear her invitation to Bognor. When she put her head around one of the bedroom doors, she saw that her dahling was fast asleep on top of his bed, mouth open and gently snoring. He was wearing just a shirt and trousers and, with each snore, his loosened, starched butterfly collar quivered as if in a breeze.

She just stood there looking down at him, almost audibly snorting in disbelief that she had married such a worthless object. All he had ever done properly was arrive in her life just at the time when she was becoming really famous, surrounded by people she could not stand with the ones she cared most about bailing out like mad. It was at this time, when she was taking afternoon tea in a hotel, that this undeniably winsome man came and sat down next to her. She might have got over that except that he then just looked at her and smiled, whereupon she was lost beyond recall. With his finely-chiselled features and twinkling greenish eyes, his luminous smile and black brilliantined hair, he gave off a flash of gorgeousness which turned over the heart of almost any woman who beheld it.

Most women got over it, however, as soon as Richard opened his mouth, prattling on about the ski-slopes of Gstaad or the Golden Arrow to Paris, but she was in the mood for such foolish frivolousness. Almost continually high on champagne, supper followed tea, bed followed supper, breakfast followed that and, in an almost indecent haste in which neither of them had a sober five minutes to reflect on what they were about to do, they were secretly married the next Saturday morning in a registry office in Harrow.

Then they sobered up and there was almost nothing to laugh at after that.

They had been married less than twelve hours – twelve bloody hours! – and they were staying in a hotel in Richmond overlooking the river. Richard suddenly announced that he had no money at all. He had never set foot on the ski-slopes of Gstaad nor so much as seen the Golden Arrow to Paris. Neither did he have a job, nor even the prospect of a job. He just announced all this deadpan – as if reading a list of the war dead – and then, to cap it all, he added that he was also as queer as a bottle of crisps. When he needed money he rented out his arse and, if she wanted him to pack that up, she would have to give him a generous allowance. He was very sorry that he had to tell her all this but it was better that she learned about it now rather than later and, although she might not believe him – how could she do that? – he did mean it when he said that he loved her. *Pfui*!

So what did the most famous torch singer in the world think about all that?

The most famous torch singer in the world was very pissed off by all that and thought of Nathan as she just sat there feeling very cold and ill inside. Something had gone wrong with her somewhere. She had so prided herself on being able to sum up people; on knowing what they were about as soon as she looked at them. But, with Richard, she couldn't have been more wrong. 'Couldn't you have told me all this before?' she asked. 'How could you marry me without telling me all this?'

'There somehow didn't seem to be the time to say anything. It just happened, didn't it?'

'But if you're a fairy how can you still say that you love me? I mean fairies don't do that, do they?'

'Fairies love. Fairies can love too. Anyway, I don't like being called a fairy.'

'Oh, poor poor you.' She said nothing further, putting on her coat and walking down to the river bank where she felt very foolish and just cried. When she had finished crying she returned to the hotel and said that she had decided that it did not matter that he had no money or a job. She would give him both money and a job. But he was no longer her husband. He would be her companion, scuttling around for her as general fixer and minder who, with any luck, would stop her acquiring another husband at such reckless and foolish speed.

What he was not going to do was to continue going around screwing other men, or even less likely, her. They were always going to have separate beds and bedrooms. They were going to be a business partnership out of which they *might* derive a bit of fun. But, above everything, their secret marriage was always going to stay a secret and, should it ever leak, he was out. If he let her down on any of this, she explained with the softest of voices and the gentlest of smiles, she would personally rip his pretty nose straight off his pretty face.

Amazingly, the arrangement had worked better than either of them could have reasonably expected. There was never, she thought, any real substitute for both sides knowing exactly where they were. Richard was all right, just another one on the make really, and she had known more than enough of that type in her life. But she had never come to like him at all. And she was almost always disappointed that, when she saw him lying on a bed sleeping, he was not that bald-headed bastard, Nathan, who loved his windjammer more than her. And to lose her own daughter to that same windjammer had just been too much. Oh she hated ships, particularly windjammers. Yes, that was the real trouble with this famous torch singer's life.

She left Richard's bedroom and walked into the lounge. She picked up the telephone and dialled for room service, ordering a small mountain of chicken and salmon sandwiches together with a bottle of 'that fizzy white stuff'. She then decided that she was very thirsty indeed and went back into Richard's room, pouring herself a glass of his, the bubbles fizzing right inside her nose and coursing happily in her bloodstream as she stared into the mirror wondering what she was going to wear for her performance that night.

Her walk-in wardrobe was packed with every fashionable dress with every fashionable label for every fashionable club. Sometimes she had done the Dominion or the Palladium but she preferred the smaller clubs like the Feldman, Bouillabaisse or the Club Eleven. Tonight she was in the sleazy Kit Kat and, as she was feeling a bit furtive and sorrowful, a bit dirty even, she went for the straight black-silk number with the long fringe of ermine on the hem. Slashed high up the thigh and very low in the front it did not really cover much and there were some who wondered why she bothered to put anything on at all. But the boys always liked it and that was all that really mattered, she supposed.

She could hear Richard stirring in the next room – she never, ever thought of him as her husband – groaning a bit before picking up his telephone and ordering himself another bottle of champagne. So her bill was on the rise again, but she hardly cared and even in some distinctly masochistic way welcomed it. She had developed a dark, destructive streak and often caught herself wondering if he could drink so much he would actually reduce her to penury, forcing her to go back and hustle a living in the Bay. It was extremely unlikely that anyone could drink that much champagne but only a few weeks ago she had been encouraging him to take a large pile of money to dabble in some stocks and shares. She often heard him muttering in mysterious jargon to his stockbroker and wondered how near he was to losing the lot. Not that she would mind at all, so mutter away, Richard dahling.

When she had finished dressing she slapped on the minimum of makeup, taking less than a minute to put on the whole lot before replenishing her glass and walking to the window where she looked out over the Thames, cutting its way down through the city. She always marvelled at this great-gorged sweep of water which coursed along making so little noise. Tonight the river looked particularly lovely, all decked out in the sad and splendid hues of autumn. In places whole armadas of fallen leaves were chasing one another down past the chugging launches and, in others, the city lights trembled on the hurrying waters in broken pillars of fire.

But Sophie found any and all forms of water evocative. They reminded her vividly of her dockland home which, on occasion, she missed with a savage ache. She missed the iron barges on the canals and the hoot of the steamships; she missed those whirling paddles of the paddle steamers and the screaming seagulls diving down to try and steal Tommy Letton's fish. She missed the pubs and shebeens of Bute Street and the heart-breaking beauty of Obe's trumpet. She missed the glittering acres of the docks themselves and those great, towering warehouses. She missed her daughter Effey and most of all she missed her Nathan. It was just so stupid, wasn't it? But there it was.

A police launch went puttering up the river sending out a widening wake of foam which chuckled up against the river bank. Just down there was the strange obelisk of Cleopatra's Needle; over on her right was the ugly Charing Cross Bridge and, further up, the thrilling shape of St Paul's Cathedral riding like a windjammer in full sail over the rooftops of London.

A windjammer, yes. It was no accident that she had thought of that windjammer as she did frequently and obsessively. It had been giving him that windjammer that had finally been her undoing. Nathan just did not want to leave it; he had even begun working on the ship to restore it to its former glories. He converted parts of the hold into cabins, taking on smelly derelicts who pissed in their bunks. Winos stole from him and rough old Woodbiners tried to do quick bits of business on the aft deck. But the worse it all got the more determined he seemed to be to stay there. When she drifted away from the Bay in a miasma of fame and wealth, he hardly seemed to notice.

She could almost have understood it if he had gone off with another woman but instead it was all for a shipful of winos and Woodbiners who pissed themselves. It was that purity of his again. That was really what she found so devastating. But returning to that theme again – when was she ever off it? – it was the allied loss of Effey that stuck right in her throat. Nathan had become the father Effey had never had and it had quite shocked Sophie to find out how strong their bond had become. This young and beautiful girl, with the world at her feet, had gone and thrown it all away. When Sophie did try and get Effey to stay with her in London all the time she had just received the blankest of stares. 'Mam, you'll always find someone to look after you, but who will look after Nathan?'

'He can look after himself.'

'No, he can't. He needs me, and anyway I like it here. I like staying here very much.'

There was always a standing invitation for Sophie to come to the ship but she never went near it. Oh, she admired the ideal well enough, even offered money to help with the work, which was loftily refused since they wanted to do it themselves. But all those smelly tramps were just too much for her. Like it or not, she was now set on quite a different direction. She decided that she would try money and fame to see what it would offer but, as she acquired it, along with a husband who was about as useless as a wet fart in a collander, she often found herself getting angry and upset, marooned in a sea of chinless dahlings and stage-door Johnnies with their horrid double-breasted, box-shouldered suits, extremely jealous of what those two had on that accursed ship. They were always so damned happy and nothing by way of happiness had ever come her way. Nothing.

Oh well, she was no longer ever cold or hungry. She could pig herself day or night and there was always a suite in the Savoy and the fizz of champagne in her nose. But what was that? Now she was getting quite worked up and looked around her impatiently wondering when those sandwiches and the fresh bottle were going to arrive. She was getting very sad and when she got sad she still ate like a horse.

She had never let on to Nathan and Effey about any of this, of course. When she had ever met them, a rare occurrence, she was always the happiest girl that ever lived, enjoying her rising wealth and her retinue of followers. She had never told either of them about her husband, still less even once considered taking him down there. The Bay folk would have just died laughing.

There was a knock on the door and she half turned to watch the maid come in, eyes carefully averted, to put the sandwiches and champagne on the table. Then she heard Richard groaning again before he picked up the telephone to check that the taxi was waiting. He was no husband but wasn't a bad sort of manager, performing such duties as he had conscientiously. She swallowed the sandwiches fast and, within minutes, the pair of them were sweeping silently down the hotel corridor. She never liked to speak before a performance, just letting the crab claws of nerves scrape away at her insides. She hardly drank either, unwilling to let herself off the hook until that terrifying moment when she actually stepped onto the stage in a sea of rippling applause and cheers, half-believing that the audience could see right inside her – at her fear and pain, her disappointment and loss – when she opened her mouth. With her eyes darting around nervously, she was always convinced that no sound would come out and that she had left her voice behind in the hotel.

A sound always did come out, of course, a marvellous husky moan. But tonight, for her first number, she was terribly ragged and snatched at the notes. Not that the audience knew or much cared since they were still too busy clapping and cheering her on. She settled down a bit on her second number, giving them one of her little monologues and, from then on, it was a steady two-fisted fight to get stronger and more powerful. She was the Queen of Breaking Hearts and each performance was a small act of war, a thrilling display of emotional defiance as she fought to break the hearts of her audience. She took the most reckless risks but, even when she failed, she struck back hard, fighting with bloodied bare fists to win all.

Critics had long speculated on the secret of her success; wondered how someone so evidently sad could make so many people so happy. The women adored her, they wrote, because they identified with her, the eternal loser who had lived, loved and wept. The men, on the other hand, fantasized about looking after her, making her whole and happy again. There was something in these theories – even if Sophie knew that there was only one thing men wanted to do with her – but perhaps her chief appeal was that her peformance was totally devoid of artifice. There was not a soul there that night who did not believe that she meant or felt every pained word.

She was that girl who, against all the odds, had struggled out of the Bay. Her songs distilled the bitterness and sorrow of her life. They had taken the jazz out of her voice these days but those old Bessie Smith regrets were still there; the emptiness of loving a man who did not love you; the torture of having him taken off you; the way that, somehow, you still had to carry on.

And as she dug deeper and deeper into herself she took the audience higher and higher, leading them to the final slaughter of *Prisoner of Love* which she still sang with the same depth of feeling that she had brought to it all those years ago. They sang every word with her. They cried with her and died with her as her body tensed and arched, those great arms, with the long tapering fingers, stretching wide. Even as she was singing and dredging the very depths of her spirit her imagination called up all the faces of those she had loved and lost, the hot tears rolling down her cheeks as she invited the world to enter her prolonged torment of frustrated sexuality and confounded dreams.

Every performance was a sacrifice. When she had finished she was nothing, little more than a drained sump, and only Richard was there in her dressing room, feeding her aspirins and champagne to calm her ragged nerves and exhausted body.

A bedlam of excitement surged around the corridors outside and there was the usual crop of messages from the press keen to ask her about the meaning of life, what sort of food she liked or the name of the man she was sleeping with. But she never spoke to them for when she did she got depressed at telling so many appalling lies.

She changed out of her stage dress into something dull and anonymous and, as usual, Richard left with the dress, carefully locking the door behind him. She then lay down for about half an hour, even dozing for a while until there was no one around and she could leave the club unnoticed and slip into the dark streets of London.

These few lonely hours tramping the pavements of the ruined city were the ones she liked best, just walking nowhere in particular through the streetlamps, followed only by the clatter of her own heels. She loved the loneliness of the smog where nothing moved except the odd tramp snoring and jabbing his elbows around inside a box or a patrolling policeman who might flash an inquisitive torch into her face. 'Hello, Sophie. Having trouble sleeping again, are we?' they would ask solicitously.

A van drew up by the arches of Waterloo Station and she stopped, her breath pluming in the cold air, to watch some workers from the Salvation Army handing out bread and soup to the vagrants who came shuffling out of the shadows. There might have been a hundred of them, all queuing up patiently for the warming soup, helping themselves from the tea urn with furrowed concentration as the hot liquid trickled into their cracked mugs. She always liked the way they squeezed the bread before picking it up, testing it to see if it was fresh. Behind them a fire was blazing in one of the arches and all those hunched, shuffling figures reminded her so vividly of that great fire in the Rowntree warehouse in the Bay. Clearly nothing had much changed over the years; the great and small cities playing much the same song. She had been saddened to learn that, a few years back, the 'incombustible' Rowntree warehouse had burned down with the loss of three lives.

One man moved away from the main group, closing his eyes as he held his head to one side, munching contentedly and gratefully on his bread, now and then sipping the soup with shaking, gloved hands. Black, stooped figures carrying bags kept moving through the other side of the arches, coming from nowhere and going nowhere. She turned to leave and jumped when a face came rearing out of the darkness towards her, most of his nose gone and just a dirty crisscross of skin where there was once an eye.

She walked on, thinking now of Obe and the way he always used to get upset by the poor and defeated. She had not seen him for ages, just occasionally reading small paragraphs in the newspapers concerning some rowdy march of the Sons of Africa in some Northern city like Bradford or Liverpool. There might be a small list of names of those arrested and he was usually in there somewhere. Why he should bother with the North so much, particularly now he had a flat in London, she could not imagine; possibly there were lots of his black brethren there. Oh what she wouldn't have given for just a small chat with him – even if it were only about the trends in modern music which had moved squarely away from traditional jazz to the big swing bands. Somehow she could never see Obe playing for one of those huge outfits – all decked up in a glittering tuxedo and dickey bow while moving around in carefully orchestrated dips and swings. Obe was always a soloist. A star.

An hour later she crossed the road near Victoria Station, feeling the rain spattering lightly on her face. She decided on a cup of tea in a late-night café, where amongst the smell of frying bacon a gang of drunks were all involved in some strange game which seemed to consist of pushing one another around and jumping on one another's backs.

She took her tea and sat at a table in the corner with her back to them, lighting a cigarette and staring down at the wisps of steam curling up out of the tea. She really enjoyed these late-night wanderings and found them strangely replenishing. Oh, she understood the glooms that all these memories could bring but, in her lonely, embattled state, they helped her to enter into herself, gave her that continuity with the past that had once been so meaningful while also helping her to face a future so bereft of hope.

She did not look up from her tea when a man came and sat at

her table, a shadowy movement in a soft shuffling of damp raincoat. He gave a quiet cough as if asking for her attention but she still did not look up. Beneath her lowered lashes she caught sight of his hands as they arranged the tea and a buttered scone. He had long delicate fingers with carefully manicured nails and now he rested his hands on either side of his cup with a precise and confident calm. You could tell a lot about a man by his hands, she thought, and in another life and given another opportunity she had always fancied being a palm reader, sitting stroking a crystal ball in a Romany caravan with a huge tabby cat languishing on her lap.

She looked back at her own tea. That man had never done a hard day's work in his life, but he *was* strong – you could tell that by the thickness of his wrists, somehow disproportionate to the slightness of his fingers. She speculated he was somewhere near fifty and terribly self-contained since, even though he must have known she had been staring at his hands, they still remained exactly where he had first placed them. She wanted to look up at his face but did not, stubbing out her cigarette, her eyes watering slightly as the smoke caught in them.

The next moment her eyebrows rose slightly when she felt that his leg was touching hers. But she did not move and continued her close scrutiny of her tea. Then he moved his leg up and down hers while she remained immobile wondering where all this was leading. Now, somehow, for his hands were still in the same place, his trousers had risen somewhat and it was his bare leg against her bare leg, moving around furtively in some strange smudged caress.

And still she studied her tea, every part of her frozen with a certain excitement by this man's most welcome audacity.

'If you don't drink that tea soon it will grow cold,' he said in a soft, educated voice.

'I like my tea cold,' she replied, picking up a teaspoon and stirring it thoroughly. She hoped, prayed, that he had not recognized her. Why didn't he move his hands?

'Do you live around here?' he asked.

'No.'

His leg gave hers another gentle caress. 'I've got a flat just around the corner.'

'Lucky you.'

'I have trouble sleeping. I often come down here in the middle of the night for a cup of tea.'

'It helps you to sleep, does it?'

'Not really. But it helps me to forget whatever it was that was stopping me from sleeping.'

'And what was that?'

'Sex. I can only ever have a good sleep after good sex and there's no good sex around any more.'

She began stirring her tea again, wondering if ever there could have been a cup of tea that had been stirred as well as this. 'Perhaps you haven't looked around hard enough. What do you call good sex?'

'Oh something unexpected.' Mysteriously, he began waving his hand towards the scone. 'Something that you can never foresee – like the weather. What I really like is sudden surprise – you think one thing is going to happen and then it's something else altogether.'

It was most curious, all this. And she rather liked it. Already they might even have been a honeymoon couple exchanging some pillow talk, wondering aloud about a lifetime's campaign on how to make their love life brighter and better. Yet they still had not even looked into one another's eyes. Well, whether he knew it or not, he had found just the right girl to cure his insomnia. She felt in the mood for something unexpected too, so much so that she decided not to look at him at all.

'Finish your tea and just walk out of here,' she said firmly. 'Don't turn around and I'll follow you to your apartment. Don't turn on the light and surprise me. Then I'll surprise you.'

'Are we talking about money in all this?'

The question just dropped like a stone thrown into a pool, and she took a little time to reply, her memories turning over again, returning her to the dark, drunken doorways of the Bay and that procession of drunken and erect worms which she had once squeezed and pulled for a living. And perhaps because she was wondering if she could still turn a trick she said, 'No, no money. But if you're happy when I leave perhaps you can find me a couple of pounds. If you're not happy there'll be no charge.'

'I'm only happy when I come and it's very difficult for me to come.'

'You'll come. Have no worry about that but, if you don't, it'll be on the house.'

'I see. So we have a deal then, do we?'

'We do.'

He left his tea untouched and she followed him at a distance, her insides growling thickly with excitement and even becoming a little wet between the legs. She hoped that, whatever stunts he pulled, they would be good ones. He might go straight for some bodily violence but she could deal with that. There again it might be a bit of bondage or some whipping but she could take all that in her stride too. He was probably going to be very surprised indeed at what she knew but he might just manage something which would take her out of her bored, unhappy self. He was certainly tall and broad-shouldered enough to do *something*. She decided that she did not now want to see his face at all; that, in the circumstances, it was almost bound to be a disappointment.

Wherever he lived it was certainly not just around the corner as he'd said. The smog was thickening ominously when he turned up a lane, pausing only to make sure that she had seen him. She stopped still on the corner of a huge building and he walked down the lane and in through a side door. She followed him up some stairs where the lights were dark and the walls smelled of stale piss. It was certainly not the kind of apartment block that she had envisaged or was hoping for. A door was opened in one of the landings and, in the half-light, she could see that he was standing inside and, disappointingly, still fully dressed. She walked inside, bracing herself for the worst.

He closed the door behind her and her eyes flickered about her with a new kind of fear. *Someone else* was in this apartment and she was not at all certain that she could deal with that. She reached backwards with her right hand for the door handle when two hands grabbed her arm and something cold and metallic snapped onto her left wrist.

'Sorry, lady,' the strange man told her softly. 'This is your real surprise. We're from the vice squad. This is a police station and you are nicked.'

'You rotten bastard,' she screamed and, with a ferocity that surprised even herself, she managed to wheel around hard enough to give him a good punch in the mouth.

'Oh dear,' was about all he said, offering so little resistance that she managed to work in another one before a thick thud crunched through the top of her fur hat. She could actually feel her knees buckling beneath the weight of her body before everything went dark.

When she came to she was in a cell, with an eyeball looking at her through a peephole in the door. It was quite the grimmest cell that she had ever been thrown in: no windows and just a lumpy palliasse and a bucket in the corner. Bolts were pulled and shoved and two policemen stood framed in the doorway. 'Are you ready to answer any questions now?' one asked.

'Sod off,' she replied. 'I want to see my solicitor.'

'We just want some details of your name and address. Then you can see your solicitor.'

'What's the charge?'

'Soliciting and assaulting a police officer. Have you got anything to say?'

'Yes, I've got plenty to say. Bring that bastard back in here an' I'll assault him again. I just hope that I hurt him, that's all.'

'When you're ready to talk properly we'll come back. Just shout.'

She lay back on her palliasse, sitting up suddenly and delicately fingering the lump on her head which had grown to the size of a small conker. Some deep and troubled moaning was coming from the next cell, a little like some animal dying in the bottom of a rubbish bin. That's what they really liked to do though, wasn't it? Lock you up and try and get you to die bit by bit. Well, she wasn't having any of this . . . she wasn't . . . She looked around, her eyesight blurring, and she lost consciousness again.

## CHAPTER TWENTY-FOUR

A flock of seagulls wheeled through a moist, gunmetal dawn above the Exchange, and a Morris Seven car came spluttering down Bute Street. It stopped, it started again and then, twenty yards later, the engine gave a final soft wheeze – a little like an asthmatic fighting for breath – and the car stopped dead, a tiny fountain of steam hissing up out of the bonnet.

The driver banged his hand down on the wheel in despair, opened the door and clambered out to lift up the bonnet only to drop it again quickly when an even bigger fountain of steam hissed and swirled all around him. He stepped back from the car, barely knowing what to do. This was his first car and it had been his first long ride in the thing. No one had told him about jets of angry steam and how they made engines stop.

Even in his despair his eyes were bright and clear with tender youth; his hair sandy and tousled. If anything, his neck was slightly too long for his angular body, which had still to flesh out into the normal curves and stoops of resigned manhood. Even more curiously he had lost several fingers on his left hand.

As he continued peering into the hissing engine, a crowd of children had also gathered around to swell the vigil. They were of sundry colours, and all of them had as little idea as he about what was wrong so said nothing. He looked over the road at an encampment of tinkers who, with their colourful caravans and tethered horses, knew little about these mechanical contraptions either.

Having been to agricultural college the youth knew about horses and was half sorry that he was not on one now since *they* never erupted with steam and just stopped. He looked back at the tinker encampment again, at the horses together with several snarling dogs tied up on long pieces of rope. A few cocks and hens ran around among a small army of children who had scuffed blackened knees and nothing on their feet. Just behind them a long line of clothes was hanging along one of the dock walls.

One of the tinkers walked over the road and asked if he could have a look at the engine. He had black, broken teeth and vast Guinness muscles, taking an age to examine the engine which, at least, had now stopped hissing with steam. 'You'll have to be putting some water in that for definite certain,' he said finally. 'These engines are the very divil for water.'

The youth waved his hand in a sort of gesture of defeat so the tinker returned to his encampment to find a jug of water. There might have been about two hundred children gathered around by the time he returned, all watching with great interest as the tinker slopped water into the radiator and a lot more over the engine. 'I often wish I just had a horse,' the youth said by way of making conversation.

'I'll be exchanging you a horse for this car,' the tinker replied as quick as a flash.

'Ah, perhaps we'd better see if it goes first,' the youth muttered, embarrassed.

'Everyone should have a horse and caravan,' the tinker went on. 'A house is just a payment of rents. It's a chimney to sweep every day and windows to clean. It's neighbours getting on your nerves. Meself I'd sleep on coal before I'd sleep in a house.'

He looked as if he slept on coal, the youth thought but kept his thoughts to himself.

'Right. Try the engine now.'

The youth started the car, surprised that it now worked without clouds of steam. 'So how can I thank you?' he asked nervously, worried that the tinker was going to continue bargaining for his car.

'You can give me a bright smile and wish me the top of the morning,' the tinker laughed cheerily.

'So be it. But, tell me, do you happen to know where *The Solomon* Mission Ship is?'

'I do. Been there meself so I have. There's none better for charity handfuls. Just go right to the end of the road, turn left into the docks and second right. They're all a bit strange in the head on that ship but it's a good crack.'

'Right, fine.' The youth revved the purring engine. 'And the very top of the morning to you, sir.'

'And the top of the morning to you, sir. May the wind always be at your back and the sun high up on your head.'

The car roared off, the youth changing down before turning left into the docks, slowing as he crossed over the first lock gate and gazing out over the forest of cranes and the odd ships. He *was* surprised at how many there were after being told so many stories about the collapse of the dockland traffic after the abdication of King Coal. There were coal steamers, tramp cargoes, one ocean-going liner and myriad sandhoppers and tugs. Bailey's Dry Dock was alive with activity too, welders' sparks dancing and exploding off the hull of a tanker.

He drove on a little further and felt quite sick when he spotted the unmistakable standing rigging of *The Solomon* moored in West Bute Dock. She had been fitted with new masts though not yet with sails. The shrouds and stays made her look like some great bizarre cobweb, black on grey in the damp morning.

He pulled up next to the Neale and West fish wharf, stepping out of the car and locking it before walking towards the ship. He had read enough stories about it and gazed at enough photographs but nothing had quite prepared him for the real thing. It was like love at first sight, his belly sucking blood in on itself as he looked up at this great sailing ship. The history books had once acclaimed windjammers as one of the most powerful instruments of civilization that man had ever invented. It was ships like these, after all, which had first brought the seven seas together and first made world merchandising possible. Ever since he could remember he had read everything about these ships, learning about every aspect of these great canvas cathedrals and always wondering when he might actually see one for himself.

And there she was now, as fatally beautiful and intriguing as he had come to expect. His eyes shone in wonder.

He continued along the quay, stopping again to look and marvel at the tall masts and the crisscrossing yards standing there in high line, like a trio of bare crucifixes. There seemed to be a lot going on below decks with heads moving behind the shining brass portholes and the smell of cooking drifting from up out of the galley. A few cats were sitting outside the galley door, patiently looking up, waiting for any offerings.

By now the youth was so abstracted and lost in the ship's beauty he did not notice a group of men coming up behind him, talking to one another loudly and pointing up at the yards. Nathan was doing most of the talking, almost completely bald now with his hair long at the sides and almost totally silver. But his body was tall and remarkably erect with a real strength in his hands which he waved around with chirpy animation.

'Look, I know what you're saying. I understand all that. I know that we're not going in for another tea race around the Horn but all I am saying is that I want it as it was. Right? So if there was a spanker on the aft deck that's what we want. If we've got to move the mizzen to do that then let's move the mizzen.'

'We wouldn't have to go that far, but it will make a

difference to the positioning of the shrouds. It's not so much the money, you see, Nathan. It's the time and labour.'

Another of the group unrolled a chart as the others continued their discussion. The youth moved near them with the strangest emotions moving and crumbling inside him. His mouth had gone quite dry and his heart was pounding like a fist hammering on a castle door. He listened to the conversation for a few more minutes before he spoke. 'The spanker in ships like these was always discretionary,' he pointed out. 'It was believed that it would give the ship an extra half a knot but no one was ever very sure. In any event you certainly wouldn't have to move the mizzen.'

Nathan turned around and all eyes looked at the youth in silence. Nathan looked him up and down, immediately noticing the lost fingers. 'You look a bit young to know anything about ships like these,' he said. 'Sailed in one, have you?'

'I'm afraid not. Just read about them. I've been to agricultural college but,' he held up his left hand, 'I had to leave. Got my fingers caught in a combine harvester.'

'Never thought much of combine harvesters myself,' said Nathan. 'What happened to the sickle?'

'It went out with the ox and plough. Everything's machinery now. It's the new age.'

'Not on this ship,' Nathan said jerking his thumb sideways. 'We're all old age on this ship, even tell the time with sundials. So what brings you down to these parts?'

'I'm looking for a ship; something that I can sail away on and find a new world.'

'A world free of combine harvesters I suppose?'

The youth smiled but made no reply, shifting his weight uneasily from one leg to the other. Nathan liked him immediately and noticed the car parked nearby. 'Did you drive that car down here? Yours, is it?'

'Just bought it. I decided that I'd learn to drive after my accident.'

'That seems a peculiar thing to do after an accident with machinery. I would have bought a horse myself. Or done nothing.'

'I had to prove that I hadn't become useless; that I could cope with this new world of ours. Either that or I could easily have become a vegetable, sitting around feeling sorry for myself.'

'I don't think you'd ever do anything like that,' said Nathan.

The others in the group were still all standing and staring at the youth, all clearly taken by his winning combination of courage and vulnerability. One of them was Chinese, another a West Indian and the third an odd mixture of races.

'This windjammer is called *The Solomon*,' Nathan explained briskly as if he had just become an official guide, and took a few steps towards the ship. 'We've got about twenty-five on the permanent crew and another twenty or so just living here for a while until they can find somewhere else to live. You name the nationality and we've got it on board. You name the problem and they've got it, or they're in the process of solving it. No one is paid on *The Solomon* and about all you can say for it is that it provides three meals a day which are either good or bad depending on where we've managed to scrounge the food. No alcohol is allowed on board. Just now we are trying to make the ship ready for when we set sail somewhere – destination as yet undecided but fiercely debated.' He paused and gave a small cough. 'Why don't you join us for a while to see if you like us and we like you?'

'You mean you're taking me . . . oh Lord . . . you mean . . .?'

'I mean we're inviting you on for a while. This is Lee, our carpenter. That's Jacko and him there pretending that he can read a chart is Peter. Between the four of us we've been trying to put the ship together and if you've read all those books about sail ships you're going to be worth all the money we're not going to pay you. So how about it?'

'Well . . . I mean . . . don't you want to know anything about me?'

'We're not concerned about things like that. This ship is a sort of Foreign Legion of the waves. Just give us a name we can call you.'

'Bill – call me Bill.'

'Right, Bill. Welcome aboard. Got any kit, have you?'

'A few things. But what about my car?'

'Leave it there for a while. It may come in handy to get a few things but there are no garages on board so you'll have to get rid of it if you decide to sail with us. Just get whatever you want from your car. Jacko will show you your bunk and we have lunch at one. It's now just twelve so you've got an hour to settle yourself in.'

Nathan walked up the gangplank with Lee and Peter, stopping on the deck and patting his mouth with the side of his hand in thought. 'I like that lad a lot,' he said. 'Let's just take it slowly for a while and find out what he really knows. It's odd but I had this really wonderful feeling when I woke up this morning. The pieces of the jigsaw are coming together. We may even have found ourselves a captain.'

Deep within the bowels of the ship there was the tumultuous racket of hammering nails and planing wood as five men were busy fashioning cabins where the cargo hold used to be. You could tell, just by watching them, that none of them was particularly expert. One was hammering a nail gingerly into the shape of a metal question mark and two of the others had thick bandages on their thumbs.

Even with a hatch opening directly onto the deck the inside of the galley was as hot as a steel furnace, with Effey stirring the boiling *cawl*, fishing out a lump of meat and chewing on it to find that it was not yet quite done. Of course it might well have been that the butcher was trying to unload some dud offal on them; that was always the trouble with getting something for nothing. On some days it was wonderful but on others you wouldn't feed it to a dog. They had been lucky with vegetables – two whole sacks of sprouts so fresh it was almost a shame to cook them. Ah well, on some days it was some kind of miracle that they got anything at all, she supposed.

Her hair was thick and black, tied up in a bun, while her pale brown body, poking out of the shrunken boiler suit that she liked to wear on the ship, was full and even muscular, steady with the poise and confidence of a very beautiful young woman.

She went up to the deck to sit on her little stool and, checking that Nathan's disapproving eyes were not around, lit a cigarette. She just loved the exquisite calm that nicotine brought with it, closing her eyes almost in thanksgiving as the drug crowded into her brain. When she opened them again they almost immediately became alert as she watched Jacko and a young man she hadn't seen before walking from a car towards the ship's gangplank. Jacko was doing most of the talking and the young man was smiling a lot. He carried a bag with him, indicating, perhaps, that he was going to stay.

Effey always took a lively interest in any young newcomers – particularly if it looked as if they were going to stay – and her eyes remained locked on the youth intently. It was not so much that he was rather good-looking or even that he had a happy and confident buoyancy about his walk. No, there was something altogether more interesting about him in that he was a clear echo of someone else. Was it something to do with his gait and the rather large size of his nose? More than anything was it his smile? – the way his lips moved back and his head rose slightly. She almost felt ill when she thought of it – though ill with what she could not be quite sure. She had something of her mother's insight into such matters and, unless she was very mistaken, that youth was Nathan's son. But no, it couldn't be . . . could it?

She tossed her cigarette away in some confusion, patting the sides of her hair and hurrying down below where she found Nathan sitting at a table in the ward room, busy berating an old man: 'Gordon, I've told you often enough and I'm going to tell you once more. You stink. Everyone's complaining about it so you're just going to have to start washing and that's the end of it.'

'What if I sleep on the deck?'

'How can you sleep on the deck? What happens if it rains?'

'Perhaps he'll stink less if it rains,' Effey chimed in.

Nathan looked at her and back at Gordon. 'That's a thought. Or we could wash you in your sleep with the deck hose. Look, Gordon, just be a good boy and go and have a wash. And get those clothes changed.'

'Haven't got any other clothes.'

'Gordon, I've told you before. I'll find you some clothes,' Effey offered. 'Give me those and I'll boil them. You'll be right as ninepence in half an hour.'

'He's a good lad,' said Nathan shaking his head sadly as Gordon walked off muttering evilly into his beard. 'Works like a Trojan but just won't wash, and now everyone's complaining about him. Even Ted complained about him this morning and I just didn't have the heart to tell Ted that it was time he had a wash as well.'

'Who's that young man coming on board with Jacko?'

'His name's Bill. He's had a small accident and he's going to stay with us for a while.'

'Where's he from?'

'Where's he from? How should I know where he's from? He wanted a job so I've taken him on for a while. We don't ask questions here, remember? Why all the interest anyhow?'

'Nothing.'

'You seem to be awful curious about nothing. You know him, do you?'

'No. Never seen him before.'

'So why are you getting so fired up?'

'Nathan, you once told me that you had two sons. Two sons that you haven't seen for years.'

He turned slowly to look directly at her. He just *knew* that there was something about that boy. Now it was his turn to feel quite sick, almost as if someone had landed him an explosive punch right in the gut. He dropped his head into his hands.

'Now I may be wrong, Nathan. I may be quite, quite wrong, but he's got your fingerprints all over him. It's the walk and the nose, but mainly it's the smile.'

Nathan lifted his head, his eyes brimming with tears. Unable to speak, he dropped his face back into his hands again. 'This is something I've dreamed of every day for twenty years,' he said finally. 'And when it happened I didn't even know. That's my David. Leave me, Effey. I have to see him alone.'

The newcomer was standing in his cabin, whistling and unpacking his bag on the bunk, when the door opened and he heard a familiar voice behind him saying: 'David, before you start, are you going to give your father a little kiss?'

David did not turn around, quietly putting his shoe brushes next to the pillow. He remembered that his mother had often told him of the regular pantomime they'd had when he was a tiny boy about such big things as little kisses. 'Can't,' he said.

'Why not?'

'My lips have run out of kisses. I was coming home from school and lost them all in the park.'

'Well you'd better get back to that park and find them, hadn't you?'

'They'll be gone by now. Those girls will have found them. They'll have been taken away for a long, long time now.'

'Too long.'

'Yes, too long, Dad. Far too long.'

He had still not turned around as Nathan slipped his arms around him and planted a kiss on the back of his head. David's hand rose uncertainly and caught him by the forearm. 'Thank God,' was all Nathan could say. 'Thank God.'

Sophie kept pacing around her cell with all the restless energy of a panther on heat. The place was so cold and airless, with just that one bucket in the corner which she was going to plonk on some scuffer's head if she had half a chance. They still had not brought her a solicitor, arguing that she needed to give them her name first. They knew it, of course, but she had to confirm it out of her own mouth. And all her own mouth would say was, 'Sod off.'

Even late in the morning after her arrest she was still pacing around, ready to tear apart anyone foolish enough to come near her. It was all so *unfair* and her murderous rage kept raging murderously.

She was aware of the occasional eyeball staring at her through the peep-hole, an intrusion which only served to raise her to new heights of fury, running at the door, screaming obscenities and pounding it so hard that her rings cut into her fingers making them hurt and bleed until she retreated to sit on her bed sucking them and crying bitterly.

She had known other cells – had once even chipped her name on the wall of one in Cardiff police station when she'd had a few free hours as their guests – but she had never really expected to be flung into the jug ever again. Her! The rich and famous Queen of the Breaking Hearts? Huh! It all rather confirmed what she had known all along anyway – that riches and fame were as nothing, particularly when you were locked in a cell with just a rusty bucket to piss in. It would be very difficult indeed to feel famous as you tried to piss into that.

It was odd, though, the way you just longed to be free when you had your freedom taken from you. Most of the time you never even thought about it, until it was lost and then you just thought of it all the time. Many thoughts and images came crowding into her mind but most of them were of the Bay; of those wild and free nights when Obe was bringing them all alive with dazzling cascades of eight-note runs and she was busy strutting her stuff with the Razzy Dazzy Spasm Band. Those were the real nights and she knew now what she had half-expected then – that she would never be happier; that this fame and wealth stuff was just a bitter hoax and fraud. All that really mattered was love. That's all there was when you got down to it and there wasn't much of that around just now.

She thought of her Effey and that made her cry some more. Who would want to be a cook on some sodding ship that was sailing nowhere? She had offered that girl everything but Effey had just flung it all back in her face. 'I've had enough of all this,' she had announced calmly one night. 'I'm going back where I belong.'

Where she belonged! On that ship! With that mad, mad man who was only ever really happy when he was down on his knees praying to his God. It was he who had infected Effey against her, poisoned her mind with all his strange ideas. He was going to end up with a good smack on his bald head, the way he was going. She wasn't going to take all this rejection lying down; the way the two of them always made her feel small, greedy, unworthy. She'd get them in the end. Fix the pair of them good.

Oh dear, it was terrible, she saw all too clearly, when you were obsessed with a man; how his spirit just followed you around, haunting your mind and heart for years on end. Even when he had moved away from the reach of her arms it had just made her worse. Even during that brief ceremony when she had married that wretch of her husband she had wept quietly because all she could think about was that man in the windjammer; of his devastating sweetness and purity. She knew him better than anyone – perhaps even better than he knew himself. Even when he fell into madness she knew that he would recover; that he would rise up again since he was the best. There was only one like Nathan. He was only ever like himself.

She thought of that night when she had been first locked in a cell in Bute Street and had written *Prisoner of Love*, which had become a sort of world-wide anthem of breaking hearts. In many ways it had been her simplest song, certainly the easiest to write and she just wished that she had a paper and pencil with her now. Songs were the one sure way of orchestrating melancholy; of giving pain some sort of meaning.

She found herself humming *Prisoner of Love*, standing up and feeling calmer as the words came softly to her lips, even raising her arms in that posture of crucified pain which the world had come to find so overpoweringly thrilling. Just how would she have managed if Obe had not found that voice inside her mouth? What would she have done? To feel pain and not be able to sing about it would be an unendurable misery.

She pirouetted but stopped singing, suddenly feeling very foolish when she noticed that eyeball back in the peephole.

'Very nice too. We do know who you are, Miss James. But only when you confirm it will we get your solicitor. Only when you confirm it.'

'When I confirm it? *I*? You must be mad.'

For the rest of the afternoon Nathan and David just wandered the docks, at times jabbering almost uncontrollably. David wanted to know all about what his father had been doing, of his dreams and plans, while Nathan was most anxious to know what had happened to his former wife Elizabeth and his other son Stephen. It was one of those disjointed conversations with bits of news from here and bits of thoughts from there, occasionally interrupted when Nathan pointed out some of the more obvious landmarks around – where *The Solomon* had once been moored, the gutted shell of the Rowntree warehouse, the Norwegian Church and the spire of St Mark's church where they had all once lived so briefly and tragically.

'It's a ruin now but I have never once been inside it since. Whenever I look at that spire I'm reminded of the time of my failure. I never knew what happened to us all there. We moved in as a family and then it all went horribly wrong. Now I am looking to the windjammer to succeed where my own church failed. In many ways I see the windjammer as a risen church – a reborn church, if you like – and I can't tell you how thrilled I am you've come back to see me here.'

'Mam married again about six years ago. He was a farmer but Stephen and I never really got on with him. He was always one for orders – clean the bath, don't slam the door, chop the wood – but she seemed to like him well enough. For years she just told us that you had died and it was only about three years ago that, one night, she told us the truth and that you were still alive but she didn't know where. She said that there had been another woman.'

Nathan swallowed hard. 'Your mother knew where I was, all right, because I have never really been out of the area. It's a good place for someone like me because there are so many others here living with their own troubles. Other people's troubles always put your own into perspective, always make them seem smaller somehow.'

'Stephen went into the army finally. He was always a bit like that, you know, very straight and dour. He always sided with Mother – never, ever referred to you by name. As far as he was concerned you really had died – you were the wrong 'un who had deserted us and that was the end of you.'

'Is that what you thought also?'

'I don't know what I thought really. Such memories as I had of you were all good and sometimes Mam let slip a remark which suggested you weren't the crazed ape man that she so often had painted you. It was just bitterness really. She loved you a lot – perhaps still does, I don't know. I thought that I would find out for myself one day. I would never have rested until I had seen you again.'

'You must have been interested in farming yourself if you went to that agricultural college,' said Nathan, changing the subject.

'Not really. It was this new stepfather of mine. I went just to keep the peace in the end and it was almost a relief when I had the accident. One day I read a newspaper article about windjammers. I never realized that there were so many left in the world and, right in the middle of the article, there was your name and a description of the restoration work you were doing on the ship in Cardiff. So I read everything I could on windjammers and then I came looking for you. *Was* there another woman?'

They both stood together looking out over the dock which was capped by the distant mountains of the idle furnaces of East Moors steelworks. A seagull called and a hooter sounded, loud and long, as melancholy as rain on Christmas Day.

'Yes, there was.' Nathan understood that it was not the time for any further lies but was finding the words very painful nonetheless. 'In fact, in some respects, it was far worse than another woman since, at the time, she was little more than a common prostitute.' He noticed David take a step sideways as if trying to create some space between them. But he had started now so he had better finish it. 'But . . . well . . . oh, I want to tell you. I really want to tell you. She . . . she was like no other woman that I had ever met. It was at a time when I knew everything but I knew nothing. I thought I could control it but I was wrong. I just . . . well . . . fell. Not in love . . . but fell from grace, I suppose. But then when I lost you all I couldn't forgive myself, I went around hating myself. I went through this long period of hell, just pain and loss and . . .'

A ship was making slow and stately progress across the dock. One of the seamen saluted Nathan and he waved wanly back. Behind them a train spluttered and hissed along the railway before grinding to a halt in the sidings.

'I tried to get through to your mother. There was one period when I wrote maybe a dozen letters asking if I could just see you two boys. Then, one day, all the letters came back unopened and I knew that all was lost. The divorce papers came soon after that. Desertion, the solicitor called it, but I didn't contest it at all. I just gave in, and signed them. But I never forgot any of you.'

'What happened to the other woman?'

'She stuck by me in my troubles – she was always there, even after I tried to humiliate her, spat in her face, swore at her. She just stayed right there. Oddly enough she is a Somali – yes, coloured too – and, as I now know, they are a bit like pigeons and stick with the same partner for ever. Then an amazing thing happened to her. She stopped being a prostitute and became a singer with a local jazz band. She found that she had the gift of writing songs and was picked up by a London management agency. Then she struck it rich. You may have heard of her. Her name's Sophie James.'

'Her? The famous singer, you mean?'

'The same. The Queen of Breaking Hearts, the newspapers call her, but one thing that the newspapers do not know is that her daughter, Effey, works on *The Solomon* with us.'

'You still see this woman, then?'

'It's a long, complicated story. Nothing could ever be simple with her. Some time ago – when she first came into the limelight – she was still coming down to see us but everything was changing. I was getting stronger and Effey was becoming more my daughter than hers. Sophie was terribly jealous of all this and, when we absolutely refused to join her in London – what could we do in that infernal place? – she did everything she could to get Effey away from me. Effey did spend a few weeks up there but she just became miserable sitting around in hotel rooms and dressing rooms. They also quarrel violently, almost always about nothing. In the end Effey ran away and came back here to work on the ship. There was a short time when we thought that Sophie might even give it all up and join us. I even offered to marry her, to make her feel more secure. But, by that time, she was changing fast, coming down here in huge cars, wrapped in jewellery and furs, wanting us all to stay in some expensive hotel in the city. It just embarrassed us and, seeing that, she just began staying away. One thing about Sophie is that she sees everything in one look. She has a terrible insight, and Effey is a bit like that too. Effey recognized who you were immediately. I suppose that's about the end of the story, though, knowing Sophie as I do, I somehow doubt it. She is the kind of woman who will always be there – she has a shadow bigger than the whole of Wales.'

In a curious but convincing way Nathan felt purged now that he had told his son all. But what he could not work out was how David had taken this confession. He wondered, more tellingly, if his son would give him any absolution. He doubted it; he really did not expect it.

'And what exactly are you doing on that ship?' David asked, after a pause, passing on to other issues.

'We don't exactly know. I suspect that, in my case, it's called atonement. I spent a long time at the bottom of the pit–too long really – but, in some strange way, I discovered God at work inside me again. It was a kind of miracle and I felt myself becoming strong, able to shake off the devastation of sin. I realized that, in the ship, I had found the opportunity and means of expressing my new faith; to redeem myself, if you like. We take in lost people and in return for food and shelter ask them to work on the ship. Eventually we want to take her to sea again, to become a floating mission. A lot come just for a week or so and then leave, finding it doesn't suit them. That's fine but we now have the nucleus of a very good crew who will stay with us and, when we're ready, we'll sail somewhere. Patagonia perhaps.'

'Why Patagonia?'

'Why not? There's a Welsh settlement there, people who left here to find a new way of life, to be at peace with themselves and their chapels. But I did say perhaps. There have been no decisions yet. We still have to get the sails and work out how to sail it.'

'Where does the money come from?'

'I don't really know. It just comes – a bit from here and a bit from there. Most of the time, I believe, it rolls up in answer to straight prayer. Do you ever pray, David?'

'No, never.'

'That's all right. I have a small chapel on the ship but faith is not listed in the signing-on articles. I'll just double my prayer shifts for you. Do you think you *might* join us? Now that you know all.'

David seemed to take an age to reply and Nathan could feel his pulse racing so much that he had to turn away and look at the old warehouses. 'You don't have to give me an answer now. Just stay with us for a while and give us an answer then.'

'There's no need for you to wait, Dad. I'd be really honoured.'

They shook hands and embraced, walking back to the ship the long way around, largely in silence, since both had given the other much to think about. Nathan was very surprised at how completely happy he felt; almost as if something inside him had been rejoined. He even caught himself thinking how wonderful it would be to see Elizabeth again. But no sooner were the pictures framing in his mind than reality returned in the shape of a swaying tramp trying to lift his foot high enough to get on to the gangplank of *The Solomon*.

Nathan ran towards the man, taking him by the arm and leading him up the quay. 'Terry, I've told you often enough. Stop your drinking and you can come back.'

''Aven't 'ad a drink, Nathan. 'Aven't 'ad one.'

'Terry, you can barely stand up. Now get on your way and if you can clean yourself up you can come back.'

David stood next to Nathan as they watched the tramp sway slowly away. 'He's a good lad and we've had him on board a few times now,' Nathan explained sadly. 'But he keeps messing himself up with that cider and then he becomes a danger to the rest of them who, one way and another, have all pulled back from the brink. I can't let one man jeopardize the rest of them and it breaks my heart to send him away but he just keeps coming back. A terrible shame really. He was a doctor once and his skills would be a great help to us if he could find them again . . . if . . . They only ever get cured when *they* want a cure. We provide the conditions but it must come from inside them first.'

They continued standing there, watching the tramp shuffle past David's car and around the back of the Neale and West fish wharf until he had vanished into the thickening twilight. 'I've had my problems with the drink too,' said Nathan. 'I know what it's like to be wandering in that dark wood.'

## CHAPTER TWENTY-FIVE

The cell door opened and the tiny shape of Gregory Fersenstein, podgy of finger and thick of neck, came bouncing in, dressed in a white pinstripe suit and sporting an enormous pink dickey bow. 'Sophie honey,' he exclaimed, his round little face lighting up into an oleaginous smile, hurrying towards her to plant a kiss right in the middle of her forehead. 'I came just as soon as I heard. Are you feeling all right, baby? All this must be simply awful for you. Can I get you anything?'

Now he was jumping around again, opening his briefcase to start shuffling with some papers which he immediately began packing back into the briefcase. Sophie always thought that he had so much bounce in him he should have been a circus tumbler and, every time she saw him, she always took a quick glance over his shoulder as if checking that the rest of the circus was not travelling in his wake. 'Honey darling, it must be simply terrible for you. Terrible.' He began whispering to her, 'But you didn't need the money, did you, honey? I could have loaned you a couple of pounds if that's what you wanted. But that's all past now and I've got a plan.'

She frowned and felt a headache unravelling in her forehead. He was always like this, no matter what time of day it was. Everything was terrific and honey and he always, without fail, had a plan. Everyone said that he was the best solicitor that money could buy. 'Just cut the gush, will you, and get me out of here. I don't want to hear your plans. Just do it.'

He opened his briefcase again, taking out some cigarettes and handing them over to her. 'You'll be out on bail in no time, honey. I'll be talking to the desk sergeant in a minute.'

'He can let me out just like that, can he?'

'Well, yes and no, but they usually go along with what I want. But you'd better tell me what happened first.'

She lit a cigarette and explained what happened; how she was set up and how the policeman went and stuck his eye in the way of her fist. It was no bad injury or anything but then he went and did it again which was just carelessness. The bastard deserved it anyway.

Gregory listened to the whole story, only occasionally getting up to have a little bounce around the cell, which helped him to think, before he asked her another question. When he was satisfied that he knew everything he packed his case again and went off to see the desk sergeant. It was the last she saw of her expensive lawyer – or indeed anyone else, until a good ten hours later, when a policeman came into the cell holding a tin plate which contained one blackened sausage, two rashers of greasy cold bacon and one rubbery fried egg.

'What's that?' she asked.

'That, madame, is your breakfast,' he replied po-faced.

'I wouldn't serve that to a vulture,' she screamed. 'Take it away, will you? All I want is to go home.'

'As you wish, madame,' he said, the sneer thick in his voice as he picked up the breakfast and walked back out with it.

An hour later she was herded into a small transit room along with half a dozen Irish navvies all groaning into the bright brittle sunshine of many hangovers. It was clearly the drunk and disorderly gang. Barely able to believe that this was happening to her, she sat next to one but, on discovering that he stank of beer and vomit, got up and sat next to another one who, if anything, smelled even worse. None of them spoke to her nor indeed to one another, just occasionally groaning pitifully into their black stubble, many of them with cuts on their hands and patches of dried, clotted blood on their hair. They were led out and dealt with one by one until she saw, with growing impatience, that she was going to be last.

When she did walk into the police court there was a huge buzz, almost as if she was walking on to the stage. The spectators' gallery was packed to the gunwales as was the press box where she recognized many old friends, including that nice reporter from *Variety*. Even her husband was sitting on the front bench, next to her lawyer who came bouncing towards her as she was led up the stairs into the dock. 'Just remember now, honey, to say nothing,' he hissed. 'Just pretend you can't speak English. Nothing. Nothing at all.'

She stood stiffly in the dock, looking around her, as the charges were read out in the usual legal jargon which didn't seem to have changed at all over the years. 'Did loiter for the purposes of prostitution in a café in Hope Street contrary to the bylaw of Town and Police Houses Act. Further that she did assault Police Constable Trevor Dan, occasioning him actual bodily harm, contrary to Section 47 of the Offences Against the Person Act of 1851.'

Fersenstein rose to his feet announcing that he was representing the defendant. 'We have a full and complete answer to all the charges, Your Worship. Just for now we are applying for bail to give us a chance to prepare our defence and come back for trial by jury in this court.'

'No chance,' shouted Sophie. 'I want all this settled now.'

Gregory's eyebrows all but vanished before he excused himself to the bench and came tumbling back towards her, one fat forefinger with a thick gold ring raised high in warning. 'We can't settle this now, honey. You've just got to plead not guilty and then we'll get the best barrister in town to represent you.'

'I'm pleading guilty,' she growled back at him. 'I want it over and done with. It'll just be a fine. Gregory, I've never told you but I've been done for soliciting before.'

'You *whaaaat*? Oh honey, don't do this. We'll think of a plan. And there's the matter of the police assault. Don't do this.'

'He wasn't hurt. I just don't want this hanging over me. Better we settle it all now. Who knows what'll come out in a trial?'

All these muttered exchanges were going on behind cupped hands until the magistrate brought his gavel down with a resounding crack, inquiring if the court might be let in on their deliberations.

'Guilty to all charges, Your Worship,' Sophie shouted, turning the court into an uproar and producing another furious gavelling from the magistrate.

'She is *not* guilty, Your Worship,' Fersenstein chimed in,

almost looking as though he was going to burst into tears. 'She is not guilty. She's confused by two nights in her cell. She does not understand the gravity of these charges.'

'Guilty, Your Worship,' Sophie persisted. 'Guilty to all charges.'

The magistrate leaned towards her: 'Miss James, do you – or do you not – understand the gravity of these charges?'

'I do, Your Worship, and I'm entering a plea of guilty to all the charges.'

'Very well. But just to be sure, put the charges to her again.'

The charges were read to her again as Fersenstein sat, shaking his bowed head from side to side. He was so appalled at her folly he could not even bring himself to look at her. Even she was beginning to believe she had not read the situation rightly since the policeman was now standing in the witness box reading out the Statement of the Facts. He made it sound as if she had bodily pulled him off the street. To make matters far worse, he had a swollen jaw and one of the biggest black eyes that she had ever seen.

'Has she any previous convictions?'

'Yes, Your Worship. Six convictions for soliciting' – a huge roar of pure astonishment chased itself around the court –'and all in the city of Cardiff. On the last occasion, in 1929, she was fined five shillings.'

Sophie remembered three, possibly four, but there were two she had clean forgotten about. As the clerk continued reading her record, she realized that she had made a big mistake. A plea of not guilty would have stopped all this coming out but now her secret past was public knowledge and the press was going to have one of its greatest field days ever.

'We understand that you are a woman who enjoys a position of some fame,' the magistrate began gravely, clearly savouring his big moment. 'But these are serious charges, for which you have a long record, and I regard assault on a policeman as one of the most serious charges to be brought before me. Police officers have a difficult job and deserve the protection of the court while you, in your position in the public eye, should set a better example. Therefore we propose to make an example of you, both to deter you from repeating any of these crimes and to warn others that may come before us.'

Make an example of me? What was he talking about? She looked around the court, wanting help, needing help, when her blood ran cold since there, in the front bench of the spectators' gallery was the unmistakable bald head of Nathan. Oh no. Not him. Anyone but him. She turned sharply back to the magistrate, struggling for breath and having almost the physical sensation of sinking into six feet of mud.

'I am taking into account the fact that the other charges for soliciting were almost twenty years ago but I have to weigh that carefully against your assault on Police Constable Trevor Dan.'

She looked back at Nathan who was staring directly at her, giving a slight shake of his head, almost as if, yet again, he was showing his disapproval of the way she was handling her case. Well, she wasn't having any of that. She'd taken her stand and if that bald-headed bastard didn't like it, tough.

The magistrate asked her if she had anything to say.

'No, nothing.'

'Very well. The sentence of this court is that you go to prison for three months and on each offence . . .'

The rest of his words were lost in a great roar of bedlam, Fersenstein shooting up out of his seat as if someone had lit a rocket under his behind while others jeered and shouted from the spectators' gallery. Sophie just stood there blinking, feeling almost distant from all this noise, almost as though this could not be happening to her. Three months. Three months! The penny dropped and she turned back to Nathan when, to her horror, she realized that it was not him at all; that, in her fright, she had just imagined him there; just *wanted* him to be there as he had been when she had got into trouble in the courts in the past. The spectator did indeed have a bald head but now he looked nothing at all like her Nathan.

But as she saw those black prison walls crowding in that did not stop her shouting out his name. 'Nathan! Where are you, Nathan?'

Two policemen had come up behind her, holding her by both arms. She half-twisted in the continuing uproar, seeing that one was trying to put a handcuff on her. 'Nathan! Just get me out of here, will you?'

David soon discovered that his knowledge of ships was purely theoretical; that it had been derived from books, with little relationship to what was going on around him now. Inside the dreams of sails there was the grim reality of a lot of hard work. Everywhere there were lists outlining duties – mess duties, water duties, cleaning duties, watch duties – and, somehow, the whole ship seemed constantly to be throbbing with the sounds of busy work. Everyone in every corner was engaged in some task or another. He wandered about looking and learning.

What he found the most extraordinary fact of all was the unlikely nature of the crew – a veritable hotchpotch of colours, fitness and abilities. And the more he studied them the more he found that, in some ways, there was something not quite right with all of them; a few had surgical boots and others twisted hands; one had a deformed spine and one woman could not move without the help of crutches. More than a couple were trembly and withdrawn, suggesting a continuing battle with the demon drink or even worse. One man had a tin nose and there was one West Indian boy who was all but blind, but who still managed to sing all the day through.

In all this David felt immediately at home, seeing almost for the first time since his accident that he could still be a useful part of the larger family. He quietly marvelled that his father had been able to pull together such an unlikely creation; that he had literally taken the misfits and failures of society, forging them into a working unit and, in so doing, had given them a new home and a new hope, Nathan's Ark.

In the galley he had a chat with Effey for an hour, asking her how long she had known his father and what they all hoped to do with the ship. It was something of a relief to learn that she, along with everyone else, had very little clear idea what they were going to do either; that there were no real plans or timetables. They were just taking it one day at a time since all they really wanted to do just for now was to make the ship seaworthy and then they all would decide where they wanted to go.

David felt immediately drawn to Effey, detecting a lot that was solid and reliable in her. In some ways she almost seemed like a hardened old seaman, wise in the ways of a devious world. Yet, in others, she had an appealing innocence about her – something to do with the vulnerability of her great black eyes, the colour of her pale olive skin and the quick nimble movements of her strong fingers.

Even as she sliced the carrots and they stood together in the galley he became relaxed enough to confide in her that, one day, he wanted to write real, big books about the world. He felt that books were the one positive way in which you could connect with life and indeed yourself. Perhaps he should start by writing about this ship.

Effey smiled at his dreams and continued her work on the vegetables. 'It must be wonderful to write a book,' was her only comment. 'Just to see all your thoughts between two covers.'

He mumbled an excuse and left her soon after that, worried that he had sounded too pretentious; that he had tried too hard and too early to impress her. There was an allied worry too. Even during the course of their brief conversation – which, in truth, was more of a monologue – he had also decided that he fancied her rather a lot and that he would, one day, like to marry her. It was just as simple as that.

He wandered down to the ward room where Nathan was sitting at the dining table talking with a black man. They were clearly fond of one another, chortling a lot and touching one another with their hands. In many ways it was still a bit of a dream for David and, unnoticed, he just stood in the doorway watching his father. Could this really be the man about whom he had heard so many sad stories over the years? How he was a weak and immature dreamer who tried to do everything and achieved nothing? How he had become an adulterer and a drunk, deserting his own children? He had heard a thousand stories about his father and hardly one of them had put him in a good light.

He was still standing there when Nathan spotted him and called him over. 'David, let me introduce you to a very unusual and wonderful man. This is Obadiah Brown, founder of the Sons of Africa, scholar, gentleman and trumpeter extraordinaire. Obe, this is my son David.'

'Pleased to meet you.' David shook hands with the very unusual and wonderful Obadiah Brown, about whom he had also read so much – one of the first coloured-rights activists in Britain, leader of many outrageous assaults on civic halls throughout the country, at permanent loggerheads with the law and claimed by some to be an even greater trumpet player than the wonderful Louis Armstrong. But he looked so much older than his photographs, grey of hair and with lines on his face which were not so much wrinkles as deep furrows. There was still a revolutionary twinkle in his eyes though, David thought; still that rebellious spirit which had attracted the attention and odium of newspapers everywhere.

'Oh, I remember you when you were so high,' Obe said with a bright chortle. 'An' I can just see you chasing around that church now with your brother – Stephen, wasn't it?'

'You've got a good memory, Mr Brown. Do you still play the trumpet?'

'You remember that?' His eyes widened in astonishment. 'You remember those days in St Mark's?'

'No, not really. I've just read that you play a mean trumpet; that, if you had stuck with the trumpet, and left politics to look after itself, you would have been the greatest trumpeter of them all.'

'Stuff and nonsense.' Obe exploded with laughter again. 'That's just *Daily Express* stuff and nonsense. They write rubbish like that to try and get me to give up my real work with the Sons. But Nathan didn't tell me you were on this old tub. How long you been here?'

'Just arrived actually. Came yesterday.'

Nathan studied his son carefully as he spoke to Obe, noting the way that David was standing sideways, almost as if he was trying to conceal his left hand. Even when he sat down he contrived to keep his damaged hand concealed. Nathan bit his lip anxiously. It would clearly take some time for David to come to terms with his disability and wear it openly, without shame. Still, he was in the right place for that. But he was very impressed by his son's curiosity; the way he wanted to learn things.

Under David's polite questioning Obe revealed that his home was in London but he hardly spent much time there, travelling the country a lot, attending branch meetings of the Sons of Africa. Many of his members had gone off to fight in the Spanish Civil War and he would have gone himself except he decided that he was getting a bit too old for all that fighting. But, yes, he did still play the trumpet. In fact he had a little jug band which played in the pubs of Brixton and gave him a small money supply to finance his trips around the country. 'I don't need much. Funny thing but, whenever I get really broke, they throw me into prison and, if nothing else, that means a few more donations from the public. There are more an' more who are getting to understand what it's like to be black an' 'ave the spit of nine men on your tail. We're getting there, David. We are getting there.'

It was smoko time and one by one people were drifting down to the ward room for tea, crowding around the main table and listening to Obe's tales about the latest derring-do of the Sons of Africa. Then Nathan began reminiscing about Obe's early days in the city and how the church members used to smuggle food parcels to him when he was in the local jug.

'They kept me from starving,' Obe confessed.

David felt quite small sitting next to these two big men, seeing how similar they were in many ways, especially in their strong sense of anecdotal humour which could charm and pacify the most hostile ears. He glanced across the room and saw a pale and trembling Effey signalling to him to attract his father's attention.

Even upside down David could read clearly enough the headline in the newspaper Effey was holding:

CARDIFF SINGER IMPRISONED

Sophie James on soliciting
and police assault charge.

Now everyone in the ward room was just standing there staring down at the headline silently, much like a crowd gathered around a body after a traffic accident.

'I thought she had finished with all that,' said Nathan. 'She always said that she hated that part of her life more than anything, but there she is – at it again.'

'Well, when I saw her last she said – she actually said – she never expected to sleep with another man again. "Too old for all that now, Obe," she said. "It's all these old bones of mine." She always has a thing about her old bones. P'raps the police framed her. She hardly needed the money after all. The police would have loved to nail someone like her – black an' all.'

'But it says here she pleaded guilty,' said Nathan, picking up the newspaper and reading it again. 'There was a big fuss, as you would expect with her. But who's this Gregory Fersenstein anyway?'

'A theatrical lawyer.' Obe spoke with obvious distaste. 'Famous. Does deals with Hollywood an' all that. Bet he's never represented anyone for prostitution before. But what can we do? We can't let her rot away in prison for three months.'

'Just give me half an hour,' said Nathan, quite white-faced. David watched him wearily put down the newspaper. He thought again of those words that Nathan had said to him the day before. *She is the kind of woman who will always be there – she has a shadow bigger than the whole of Wales.* 'I'm going to have a chat with the Big Man,' he said at length.

He left the ward room and walked down past some cabins, unlocking a door and descending through a hatch before unlocking yet another door and going into an old locker room which had been converted into a tiny chapel big enough for about six people. He then unlocked another small cupboard on the plain wooden altarpiece, taking out a cup and kissing it before kneeling before it, closing his eyes and trying to clear his thoughts as he entered into communion with the mind and will of God.

On the wall there was a long elaborate scroll which sometimes helped him in his prayers. It was known to the Welsh as *Llythyr dan Garreg* – The Letter Under the Stone – believed to be the only letter ever written by Jesus Christ and found eighteen miles from Iconium, sixty-three years after the Crucifixion.

'Whosoever worketh on the Sabbath day shall be cursed,' the letter began. 'I command you to go to church and keep the Lord's day holy, without doing any manner of work. You shall not idly spend your time bedecking yourselves with superfluities of costly apparel and vain dresses; for I have ordained it a day of rest; I will have the day kept holy, that your sins be forgiven you. You shall not break any commandments but observe and keep them. Write them in your hearts and steadfastly observe that which was written in my own hand and spoken with my own mouth. You shall not only go to church yourself but also send your menservants and maidservants; and observe my word and learn my commandments. You shall finish your labour every Saturday in the afternoon by six o'clock, at which time the preparation for the Sabbath begins. I advise you to fast five Fridays in every year, beginning with Good Friday, and continuing the four Fridays immediately following, in remembrance of the five bloody wounds which I received for all mankind.

'You shall diligently and peacefully labour in your respective callings, wherein it has pleased God to call you. You shall love one another with brotherly love; and cause them that are baptised to come to church and receive the sacrament of the Lord's Supper and be made members of the Church; and, in so doing, I will give you long life and many blessings; your land shall flourish, and your cattle bring forth in abundance; and I will give you many blessings and support in the greatest temptations.'

It took Nathan perhaps two minutes to clear his mind of the sounds and furies of the day, thinking of David and calling attention to the plight of Terry the tramp, calling them both into the family before trying to frame an image of Sophie in his mind, but getting so many – Sophie, the mother; Sophie, the singer; Sophie, the good friend and, ah yes, Sophie the sweet lover. There was always that, wasn't there? There would always be that for him to live and contend with.

The purpose and spirit of his prayer was always to find what would be pleasing to the mind of God; how and in what way he could be helpful to someone else who was suffering. But it was not just *someone else*, was it? It was a woman he had once loved and perhaps loved still. He opened his eyes and gazed at the cup, feeling ineffably tranquil as he waited for glimmerings of ideas, for a suggestion of the right course of action.

'He that doeth the contrary shall be unprofitable,' the letter continued. 'And I will send hardness of heart upon them till I see them, but especially on the impenitent and unbelievers. He that hath given to the poor shall not be unprofitable. He that hath a copy of this letter and keepeth it without publishing it to others, shall not prosper; but he that publisheth it to others shall be blessed of me; and though his sins in number be as the stars in the sky, if he believes in this, they shall be pardoned; but if he believes not this writing and this commandment, I will send many plagues upon him and consume both him, and his children, and his cattle.'

He saw her lying in her prison cell, humming softly as she tossed and turned on her bed, her eyes staring up at the ceiling, lost and mournful . . . and, from somewhere deep within his communion, some ideas began coming together and he closed his eyes again, so still that he could almost be sleeping as he meditated on the first inklings of how and what should be done.

'And whosoever shall have a copy of this letter written with my own hand and keep it in their houses, nothing shall hurt them – neither lightning, pestilence, nor thunder. And if a woman be with child, and in labour, she shall be safely delivered of her birth. You shall not have tidings of me, but by the holy scriptures, until the day of judgements. All goodness, happiness and prosperity shall be in the house where a copy of this letter shall be found.'

He heard the softest of movements and looked down by his side to see that two of the cats had followed him down into the chapel, purring loudly and happily as they brushed themselves up against his side.

# CHAPTER TWENTY-SIX

Whatever thoughts Sophie may have had about having a long rest in her prison cell, writing a few new songs and doing a lot of gazing into space, were almost immediately dispelled when she was flung into the grim, gaunt fortress of Holloway, London's prison for women.

It was the noise and jabber that she was the least prepared for – a more or less continual racket of clanging doors, ringing bells, inquisitive questions and muttered shrieks of madness and pain. In her first days of incarceration, every single minute brought a new sensation of humiliation and nausea, right from the very first moment she opened her eyes in the morning to the sound of the keys rattling in the lock of the cell door and the screw, all silver buttons and indigestion, called, 'Slop out!'

She would carry her bucket along the balcony leading down to the recess, queuing up with the others, gagging on the obnoxious smells. There was no worse way to start the day and, from then on, when you could only expect it to get better it just kept becoming far, far worse.

All around them was the main hall, a towering construction of glass and steel which picked up all the noises, amplifying the sudden obscene shrieks to such a pitch that there were times when you believed that you were suffering from a tremendous hangover until, of course, you remembered that there was nothing to drink in Holloway. The three balconies of the main hall were joined by horizontal bridges, the first floors knitted together by netting to discourage suicide leaps. Even so, Sophie studied it with care to see if there were any real holes.

But particularly for a woman of fame like her quite the worst part of it all was the way the other inmates seemed to need to touch her all the time. She had noticed often enough in the past that another of the considerable penalties of fame was that people were forever wanting to kiss you, hold your hand, brush up against you . . . the women in here managed all of that but some of the grips were quite painful, sometimes sexual and, more often than not, sadistic too. She just did not know how to handle such voracious women, particularly one beefy bull-dyke with tattoos, Martha Smiles, who was always heading straight for her and openly fondling her breasts as she tried to move away. In other circumstances she might have laid dear Martha flat but fighting would not have looked at all good on her already full track record.

After slop-out there was yet another queue, this time for breakfast – always cold and always rubbery, no matter what it was. How could you make cold rubbery porridge? Or put bakelite beans on brittle-burned toast? Then the cell had to be scrubbed and she just felt nauseous with what she had not eaten as millions of technicolour bubbles swelled and popped in whirled banks on the concrete floors. Then another bell rang and they filed down to the work rooms where, yes, they really did sew mailbags. Here the absurd questions continued: 'What's it like being famous?' 'Oh, it's like nothing really. If it's like anything it's like waving your hand around in a warm bath.' 'What's the best man you've ever had? Go on tell us, Sophie.' 'Never had a good man.' The touching continued and almost worse than that, some began drifting over to her workbench asking for her autograph.

A screw might stand near her waving them away, but then the screw would come nearer too, asking her some slightly more original questions like, 'What's it like being famous, Sophie?' *God, did they never think of anything new to ask*? 'Oh it's like nothing at all really. It's like waving your hand around in a warm bath.'

Another queue for lunch was followed by half an hour in the exercise yard where the bull-dyke Martha turned out to be the tobacco baron, dealing in illicit cigarettes in return for money or, well, 'certain favours'.

'Here, have a packet on me, Sophie,' she said one day. 'I won't need paying just for now.'

Sophie brushed past her, ignoring her offer. Yes, she really would be laying her flat if this went on much longer. She was, first and last, a Bay girl, and you don't tangle with them.

After exercise it was yet more mailbags and there was yet more chatter with yet more questions about her fame, money and love life. The evening meal consisted of the warmed-up leftovers of lunch and then they were all banged up in their cells again, relaxing as best they could before lights out.

For the last half hour of daylight Sophie liked to kneel on her bed with her hands on the bars of the cell window looking out over the entrance to the prison and the city beyond. Leafless branches hung off the trees in the prison forecourt as cars and vans chased past one another along the main road. As the daylight died and the night grew cold she watched the streetlamps being turned on, along with the house lights. She liked to imagine what was going on in all those rooms, pictured the little domestic dramas behind all those curtains. At this time the other girls in the cell went quiet too, thinking, perhaps, of their own little domestic dramas, while Sophie alternately hummed or sang one of those sad old Bessie Smith laments about loss.

She had been in here for three days now, refusing point-blank to see any visitors – or such as wanted to see her anyway. She certainly did not want to see her husband, sending a message to him to just go away. He had sent a message back saying that they had a lot of business affairs to discuss, but she didn't want to talk about them either. Perhaps her career was over and perhaps it wasn't but, just for now, she did not care in the least. She really did now hope that Richard had lost all her money on the Stock Market and that, when she came out, she would have to start again, getting rid of him for a start.

The governess, a kindly soul with thick granny glasses and a love of embroidery, called Sophie up to see her, informing her that they had filed notice of appeal with the Inner London Quarter Sessions and it would help her appeal if she saw her solicitor. But she wanted none of that, she said. If they got her out that was fine but she wasn't going to be seen crying for mercy. No one had fought harder than she to get where she was – wherever that may be. She had come from the toughest school and had survived far worse hell than this. She was going to do her time like a good girl.

The newspapers, predictably, gorged themselves on her story, many delving into her past by interviewing those who claimed to have known her in the Bay. Equally predictably their stories were nearly all a pack of lies and she had never heard of most of those who said they knew her so well. One of the local club committee men, a certain Jack Davies, suggested that he had been the first to discover her, in a club audition. That was news to her: she rather remembered that he had paid her off with a shilling, saying that she might make a good pub singer on a bad Saturday night but that was about all.

Oddly enough, though, the tone of the stories was sympathetic rather than hostile. Her rags-to-riches saga was too much of a circulation-spinner to dismiss with hostile jibes. Everyone was trying to get in on the act, particularly Fersenstein who was freely giving interviews to anyone, saying that she had been set up and was going to be freed any minute now. She was relieved to read, however, that no one had yet twigged that she was married. This helped the story too – the mystery woman who had come from nothing, without the help of a man.

By eight o'clock the lights of London were stretching out in great golden crisscrossing necklaces. She was lying on her bunk, still humming her sad songs, when a note was slipped through the hatch in her cell door. One of the girls passed it up and she read it with a frown.

'Sophie, be at your window at nine,' it read. 'It will all start then.'

What was all this? What was going to start then? Surely they weren't trying to spring her? She looked back out over the deserted city streets. There was no chance that she was going to climb down a string of sheets and escape, from all the way up here – that was a racing certainty that was.

She waited with mounting impatience until nine o'clock came, noticing a build-up of people around the lamps of the prison forecourt. When the time came, she heard the sweetest, the most thrilling, the most purely passionate sound that had ever torn at her insides.

It started with a bit of thundering drumming followed by a set of cymbals shivering like a monsoon. Then, as vivid as a punch in the mouth, came the bugling call to rebellion of Obe's trumpet leading a cavalry assault on Tiger Rag. Other musicians were gathered around him as, with shoulders hunched, he roared his troops on – the clarinet dodging and diving as the trombone pooped his way down the melody. More people were gathering around in the lamplight until there were now perhaps two hundred of them, all singing and dancing about the forecourt like life-long sinners who have just been told that there is no hell.

Sophie laughed and cried as, still kneeling, she jigged up and down on her cell bed with her cell-mates crowding around her. 'O-b-e-e-e-e,' she called out when the musicians had torn up the end of Tiger Rag. 'O-b-e-e-e-e.' And with that others in the lines of cells overlooking the street took up the call. 'O-b-e-e-e-e.'

Obe waved and they all began jamming some sturdy barrelhouse. Warders came surging out of the prison gates, standing in line in front of the musicians, uncertain what to do. More lights were flickering on in the surrounding houses with the dark terrapin shapes of people leaning out of the windows. 'O-b-e-e-e-e.' The hot jazz licks seemed to be warming the very heart of that cold night, so that the whole of the prison seemed to be jumping up and down with joy. 'O-b-e-e-e-e.'

Then with a great wail of sorrow Obe led his band into *Prisoner of Love*. Sophie began singing the words, looking around at her cell-mates and blinking at the sheer improbability of it all since they were all singing as well.

> You came into my life alone
> And left it again free
> But what about me?
> Do I stay a prisoner of your love?

She had, of course, first written those words in a prison cell but not only were her own cell-mates now singing it but the *whole* of the prison was now at it, showing, if nothing else, how deeply the lyrics had entered into the collective mind.

This great massed choir could all have been singing their heads off at a rugby international, and as the anthem rose, layer by layer and refrain by refrain, a huge banner was carried out in front of the band.

Oh no, could it be? Yes, it could. At either end of the banner were Nathan and Effey, bouncing it up and down as they sang along with the rest.

> Where is the key to my cell?
> What is this prison with no walls.
> I just do not want to stay
> A prisoner of your love.

Back in Cardiff the coldest of winds scythed and moaned down the city streets. Clouds with moonlight curdling in their bellies swept in slow procession over the castle, the city parks and the hurrying river, disappearing into some distant place where thunder growled softly. The silent black buildings were coated with a veneer of moonlight and, down in the public lavatory on the Taff embankment, four men in overcoats stood motionless around the urinals waiting for their turn.

Hooters droned in the dockland as a woman ran across the road, chasing another, laughing merrily. They both disappeared into a house in James Street. The laughter continued to hang in the silent street like the lingering waft of an extremely cheap perfume. The sound of music difted thinly out of the Quebec pub as a pack of dogs went racing across a patch of wasteland. Amidst the shivering grey squares of the docks themselves Hamilton walked through deep, purple shadows past the huge battleship shape of Spiller's warehouse.

Now and then he stopped to look up at one of the ships or over at the skyline, his ferocious black eyes checking out the ways in which the dockland had changed. But no sooner had he taken a quick, almost military look than he was on his way again, turning around into the darkness behind a line of dockland cranes.

Over the years it was almost as if he had not aged at all. His complexion was unsullied by the slightest wrinkle, his eyes were as clear as a falcon's and there was not a suggestion of grey in his hair. His late-Victorian clothes had not changed either, still the same immaculate top-coat with brass buttons, still the plain black shoes and the silver-topped walking cane.

He still walked with the same purposeful stride of someone with urgent work to attend to.

Once past the Neale and West fish wharf he stopped and stared at *The Solomon*, her lights flaring brightly as she creaked on her moorings. His nose gave a soft derisive snort as he walked towards her, noticing that someone was on watch on the bridge. He also noticed that the gangplank had been pulled up, probably for security.

Careful to retain the cover of the shadows, he walked along the quay, examining the ship as best he could in the poor light. Satisfied that he could not be seen from the bridge he even walked over to her at one point, tapping the wooden deckrail with the silver top of his walking cane, almost like a railway wheel-tapper looking for faults. He reached out with his hands to pull on the shrouds and mainstays, testing their tension and strength. He moved on up to the bowsprit, going down on one knee to examine the ship's huge curved nose and the painted woman on the prow. The sounds of conversation came from the deck so he retreated into the darkness again, pausing just long enough to look through the mess room porthole, noting that they had coloureds on board. There was even a Chinese man sitting there.

With a soft click of his heels he turned back into the dockland night, crossing Bute Street and stopping, briefly, to look up at his old house in Howard Close. He walked down the lane at the side of the house, gazing out over the mud flats where all that could be heard were the sorrowing calls of birds.

Later still he walked down the stairs of the public lavatory on the Taff Embankment, pausing to look around at the men gathered there. They circled one another in heavy silence until one came close to Hamilton, resting his head on the shoulder of his top-coat. There were some scuffling noises in one of the closets, then the thick wooden door opened with a sharp crack.

After the excitement of the impromptu jazz concert outside Holloway – which had even made the headlines – Sophie became even more popular and sought after by the other inmates. The governess had her back into her office again the next morning, saying that she hoped her friends were not planning any more late night concerts since she became very bad-tempered indeed when her sleep was interrupted.

'However,' she went on, 'your notice of appeal has been filed and will be heard tomorrow, Sophie. Have you changed your mind about being there? It might help.'

'I think I'll be better off in here. I'm not very good at court appearances. It's this mouth of mine. Can't seem to keep it shut.'

'Yes, there are a few like that in here. You've no complaints about the treatment in here, I take it? The press will be . . . ah . . . anxious to know all when you do get out.'

'The treatment's all right. I can't say I think much of the building though.'

'Indeed. This place was dilapidated the day it was built but it would be good if you spoke about that when you got out. Strictly between ourselves, I don't think much of it either, and it will only change through publicity.'

If she was looking for a few favours then Sophie decided that the time was right to ask a direct question to which she could never get a direct reply.

'But tell me one thing,' she ventured. 'Why do you allow that Martha Smiles to run the place?'

'Run the place?' She did not seem particularly surprised – or annoyed – by the question. 'How do you mean, Sophie?'

'She seems to do whatever she wants. She openly trades in tobacco, seems to run everyone.'

'Yes, I'm afraid she does. We allow it because it's all part of maintaining prison discipline in a place as potentially explosive as this. In any prison you always have to seek out the keepers of the culture. There might be only three of them but, if you control them, you control the lot. It's as simple and as complicated as that. There are two keepers of the culture in Holloway just now. One of them is keeping very quiet since we are letting her do more or less what she wants – I even let her go to the cinema the other day. And then there is Martha. She likes to take charge so, in return for her behaving herself and getting the others to behave themselves, we let her do so.'

'Oh, it's as easy as that, is it? And what happens if I wanted to take charge?'

'It's very odd, Sophie, but I was thinking along those lines myself. But, in Martha's case, you would have to challenge her for it.'

'Fight her, you mean?'
'Challenge, Sophie. That's all I'm saying. And in circumstances like this, and in the event of a challenge, all official eyes are carefully averted. But, if you're thinking what I think you might be thinking, please remember that your appeal is coming up in the morning.'
Sophie shrugged and pouted, looking over at the window with the misty innocence that she was so good at when she was actually plotting trouble. 'It was just some questions, that's all. Just some questions.'
'Oh, and there's one more thing before you go. I know you've refused to see anyone but there's been a young woman claiming she's your daughter.'
'That's my Effey. She *is* my daughter.'
'Really? There is so much about you that we don't know, isn't there, Sophie? You should write your life story one day.'
'Couldn't. Couldn't live through all that pain again, and there are a lot of things probably best left unsaid.'
Sophie felt uneasy, rather than happy, when she did finally meet Effey, sinking into an inexplicably black mood as she let her daughter kiss her on both cheeks before they both sat down at a trestle table.
'You've not been eating enough,' Sophie said tautly. 'Look at you. There's more meat on a butcher's hook. I hope they're not working you too hard on that damned ship.'
'Oh shut up, Mam. What's the matter with you? Didn't you like our concert last night?'
'It was all right. Too loud if you really want to know. The trouble with Obe is he could never play soft. It always has to be slaughter in the trenches when he blows. As subtle as a car crash.'
'Nathan is outside in the waiting room.'
Sophie looked down at the table top, careful not to show anything of the emotions which rose and groaned inside her. 'What's he doing out there? Why doesn't he come in to see me?'
'He's not on the list. You haven't given them a visitors' list.'
'Didn't want any visitors.'
'Well, that's why he's not in here. It's only relatives unless you're on the list. But he's been very busy. Been to see the solicitor and even arranged to speak in the court on your behalf.'
'That's wonderful,' Sophie snorted. 'They'll double my

sentence, not let me out. What's he going to talk about anyway? How much I used to charge when I was young and inexperienced?'

'Mam, just what's the matter with you? We've come to help you and here you are getting aggressive with everyone in sight.'

'*Are* you still on that damned ship?'

'Oh, now it's my turn, is it? Of course I'm still on that damned ship. Where else do you think I'd be?' She, too, could feel herself getting swept along on the wild horse of her growing bad temper. But, just for now, she decided to pull in the reins. 'Mam, you're not going to believe this but something rather wonderful has happened. Nathan's son, David, turned up the other day. Nathan hadn't seen him for almost twenty years. Now he's staying with us all. Isn't that wonderful?'

'That's wonderful, is it?'

'Of course, stupid. He's a lovely, fine boy too – had an accident on a farm but Nathan says he'll soon find his confidence again. As it happens he drove us up here in his car.'

'You're not telling me you're going to fall for him, are you? I just couldn't take that.'

'What's the matter with you?'

'It was good fun, I suppose, travelling in this car? A good laugh, was it? Stopping at all the pubs and having lots of drinks while I'm rotting away in here.' She put her hand on Effey's arm. 'But whatever you do don't go flashing your tackle with that David, 'cos, if he's anything like his father, it'll just mean a lifetime of misery.'

'Oh I've had enough of all this,' Effey snapped, shaking off her mother's hand, standing up and looking around for a warden. She had long learned not to put up with any nonsense from her mother, understanding that, if you did let her get away with it, she just got a lot worse and that was very bad for her indeed. 'I'll come back tomorrow when you might be in a better mood.'

'Don't go, Effey. Please don't go. I'm just lonely, that's all. Oh I don't know what's the matter with me. I just feel so excluded from you all. Please don't go.'

'Any sense of exclusion has always been of your own making,' Effey observed coldly and stiffly but still not sitting down. 'Every door has been left open. You could still give it all up and join us – always assuming that you've got something to give up after all this business.'

'That'll be no problem. They'll just love me a little more than they already do. But what would you have me do? Peel potatoes and scrub lavatories on that damned ship?'

'Someone has to do them. Scrubbing lavatories is not as bad as some of the things you have to do in here. You might even get to enjoy it.'

'Don't be so soft.' She sniffed at the very thought of it, looking across the room at the other girls sitting at the tables, wondering how many of them had scrubbed lavatories in their time. Quite a few by the look of them.

'Well it's better than prostitution.' Effey looked down at her, living *very* dangerously just now. 'Anything is better than that.'

'Prostitution? You don't believe I did that, do you?'

'You've done it in the past.'

'Go on, get out of here.'

'I'd happily lick out a thousand lavatories with my tongue before I'd sell my body to a man.'

'You think I ever enjoyed doing it, you prissy little cow? I did it to feed you, amongst others. Go on. Get out.'

'Why didn't you just let me starve? I'd have been happier with that. I'd peel a mountain of potatoes before I'd let a man lay a hand on me for money.'

'What man would want to lay a finger on you, you pious little turd. Clear off, go on. Get on out of it.'

'At least I can walk out. At least I can hold my head up.'

'Out, you little slut. Out.'

Now both of them were on their feet, almost nose to nose as they spluttered and spat with angry self-righteousness. It was quite remarkable how similar they actually were in the blood of their bad tempers, their cheeks draining of colour in the same way, their eyes darting back and forth electrically, even framing their fists in the same way and pounding them on the table for added emphasis.

But, although Effey regarded Sophie as her mother and Sophie regarded Effey as her daughter they actually were not related at all – as they both knew all too well. There was a very great mystery here, only partly explained by the fact that they were both natural battlers who had grown out of their own unique circumstances, each unconsciously shaping the other, unafraid of anyone and anything except, perhaps, one another, which was why they quarrelled so repeatedly.

The warders moved closer to them nervously, wondering if it was going to end up in a real fight.

'I want this little tart thrown out of here,' Sophie was shouting, corkscrewing a finger at Effey.

'You don't have to lay a hand on me. I can walk out on my own.'

It was free association time for half an hour, with all the cell doors open, when Sophie paced back to her cell, brushing the other women aside as if she was hurrying to be sick somewhere quiet. The other girls in the cell read her mood immediately, and were careful to stay out of her way as she sat down, stood up and paced around before sitting down again, still white-faced with anger, her nostrils snorting furiously. She thumped her fists down on her knees when a shadow fell over the room and she looked up to see Martha Smiles standing there.

'I heard you had a few problems, Sophie, so I've brought you some things.' She nodded down at a bottle of brandy poking up out of her smock pocket. 'If the other girls would like to leave perhaps we can do a little business.'

Sophie looked up at the other girls and then back at Martha. Everyone knew what doing a little business meant. 'Go on, girls. Give us ten minutes and we'll have a swig of brandy each.'

They filed out slowly, almost reluctantly, past Martha who was still standing in the doorway. Sophie studied her carefully, noticing the strong muscles and thick legs, the broad shoulders and intimidating bosom, laughably exposed by three opened buttons at the top of her smock. It was the kind of bosom you forged horseshoes on. The hair on her upper lip might have been a military moustache too.

But Sophie was well in the mood for her even if her size and strength were real enough. Any real fight was out of the question. Martha stepped inside the cell and pulled the door carefully behind her.

'We'll see how strong your tongue is, shall we, Martha?' said Sophie, dropping her pants and trousers before unpinning her hair and shaking it out. 'You try it first and then you'll see how strong mine is.'

Martha could hardly believe her luck and all but swooned as she came for Sophie, going down on both her knees in front of her and holding her thighs on either side, working her greedy tongue into the fleshy cleft of Sophie's bush, now running her hands up and down her long brown legs.

Sophie wriggled her hips and nuzzled in closer to her. 'Feels all right does it, Martha? Go on, get right in there, Martha baby.' She gave a few small jigs of feigned excitement and, as she did so, leaned forward and plucked the brandy bottle out of Martha's pocket. 'Mmmm. Oh that feels so good, Martha. But tell me now. How does this feel?'

Holding the bottle firmly by the neck she cracked its thick end down on Martha's skull with all the fierce anger of someone doing in a poisonous snake. *Crack*. 'And how does this feel, you lesbian bitch?' *Crack*. 'And this, you old cow?' *Crack*.

Martha almost looked as though she might have got to her feet after the first blow – even managed to look up and get in a bit of glassy-eyed swearing but that was about all, since her knees gave way and, by the third crack, she was out cold. Sophie unscrewed the brandy and took a sizeable gulp, feeling a good deal better, almost grateful that Martha had helped her to exorcise her bad mood.

'That's what you get when you tangle with a Bay girl, Martha,' she added, starting to pour the brandy over her, but then thinking better of it. 'Never forget.'

After straightening her clothes she opened the cell door and dragged Martha out by her feet, leaving her in an untidy heap on the balcony outside. The other girls crowded around, a few applauding and hugging Sophie, pleased that the bull-dyke had met her match.

'That brandy was always bad for her,' Sophie smiled, passing the bottle around. 'I told her to leave it alone. It gives you an awful bad head.'

Any speculation that Sophie might herself become the tobacco baron of Holloway was short-lived since, the next morning, the Recorder of the Inner London Quarter Sessions heard an impressive speech from Mr Nathan Thomas, in which he outlined the tragic circumstances of her past and her work for various charities, particularly in the docklands of Cardiff. He also listened to the arguments of Mr Gregory Fersenstein who said that the prison sentence was 'harsh and inequitable', adding that, in this case, the police had clearly acted as *agents provocateurs*.

Then, after taking an age to rearrange some papers and even peer at something under his bench, he finally spoke. 'Bearing in mind that Miss James has tasted the inside of prison, and the impact that has been felt, I now think that I can reduce the penalty. The sentence was indeed excessive so now I am going to reduce it to seven days.'

'What does that mean?' Nathan asked Fersenstein.

'It means that, with remission for good behaviour, she's out now. We can get a court warrant and get her out this morning. She has been behaving herself, hasn't she?'

'Who knows? If she has it will be the first time.'

## CHAPTER TWENTY-SEVEN

The next three days were amongst the happiest that Sophie could ever remember – an ascending series of perfectly struck musical chords. She was very disappointed when she first came out to learn that Effey and David had already driven back to Cardiff but, to her great surprise and delight, Nathan offered to stay with her for a while. Though not, he quickly added, in her bed and, under no circumstances whatsoever, in the Savoy Hotel.

Every hour came as a new gift. Together and hand in hand, they wandered through the city – still beautiful and sorrowing in the autumn. They managed to give the press and everyone else the slip – she kept the collar of her fur coat well up and wore sunglasses – so few people recognized her and no one at all knew him. She just looked as if she might be someone famous while he was just a well-built balding man who clearly laughed a lot and talked far too much.

They made no plans as such; they just walked and walked until they got somewhere or were too tired to walk any further. Predictably, perhaps, Nathan wanted to explore the

East End around Aldgate, a ghetto which, he had learned, resembled in so many ways their own ghetto in Cardiff.

That's my boy, Sophie thought. Offer him a suite in the Savoy and all he wants is to walk around some slum in the East End.

But it certainly was some slum, she had to concede; much, much larger than the Bay with high, wide streets and narrow lanes teeming with hurrying children and totters' carts. Dribbling drunks accosted them while urchins wheeled around them, watchful for the fat bulge of an unattended wallet.

Just over the road was the towering Victorian edifice of the London Hospital and, right nearby, a stall selling whelks and hot eels.

'These lanes would be where Jack the Ripper did in all those women,' Nathan told Sophie. 'It's a good job you never worked around here then or our Jack would have ripped you from there to there.'

'Not me,' she snorted. 'I'd have ripped something else off if he'd tried any of that on me.'

'He was a very handy lad with the razor, was Jack. You'd have needed more than a good punch to stop him. Some say he learned his surgical skills at the operating table of the London Hospital over there.'

'Oh a doctor, was he? That makes sense I suppose.'

'That shop across the road was where they kept the freak, John Merrick. You know, the Elephant Man. Charlie Chaplin failed miserably when he first appeared in a Jewish theatre down on that corner. Yes, you can feel the whole thrust of the place somehow. Areas like this always produce great men. Dickens drew the world's attention to the terrible poverty here. Marx and Lenin once lived here. Dr Barnardo founded his home for children here. William Booth started the Salvation Army. I've always thought of this place as my spiritual home.'

'How come you know so much about the place? You've never been here before, have you?'

'I told you, it's my spiritual home. You hear a lot from the kind of men I deal with – quite a few actually came here first but then went to Cardiff, hoping for some better luck there. The East End was always the first stop for many – mostly Jews trying to escape persecution in Eastern Europe. A lot of prostitutes came to Cardiff from here too – usually after warnings from the police.'

'You wouldn't be getting at me again, would you?'

'Me, Sophie? Never. But they were all just so poor here. I always remember what one of Jack the Ripper's victims owned when she died. Catherine Eddowes had a bit of string, a white handkerchief, a blunt table knife, a matchbox full of cotton, two clay pipes, a small box of tea and a ball of worsted.'

'That's all right. What's wrong with that? That's more than I had sometimes when I was doing . . . you know, that.'

'But you always did all right, didn't you?'

'Not always. I remember standing around the corners of Custom House with hunger clawing at my belly, hoping some Tom would come along. They didn't always come. It was a lot to do with the weather. If it was too cold they didn't bother, nor when it was pouring with rain come to that. An' I never had any regular customers anyway – I used to take the piss out of them an' they never liked any of that. Sometimes I used to like disgusting them when they'd finished. Told them I 'ad an incurable disease an' all that. Yeah. They couldn't get home to their wives fast enough.'

'It's a wonder you had any customers at all.'

'There were one or two.'

'Did you like any of them?'

'Only one. There was only ever one. He was as bald as a badger's bum and a know-it-all, if you catch what I mean. Always talking like he'd been injected with a gramophone needle. Never paid me neither. Not once. Don't know why I bothered really.'

It came to rain in a sudden, cold shower and they took shelter in a church porch, sharing it with tramps, one a woman. 'Give us the price of a cup of tea, lady,' one said.

Sophie emptied her handbag of all her loose change, distributing it evenly.

'You shouldn't give them so much,' Nathan protested. 'It's never good to give them too much. They only spend it on drink.'

'So what? If I were them I'd be dead drunk all the time. Don't you drink anything at all now, Nathan?'

He looked into her eyes and away at the passing traffic. 'I very occasionally take a glass of wine, but mostly nothing at all. I just – stopped.'

'A little drink never hurt anyone.'

'But it wasn't a little drink, was it? It was a twenty-year-long drink and I was lucky I survived. You see the perils of drink very clearly in a place like this, Sophie. See, they've still got their shebeens and near-beer joints. Those are the ones with the grilles on the fronts. Then there's the mission halls next to them – set up by the religionists to save people from the booze. My life has been one long argument with the booze and whole communities have been built around the same argument. What is more, whole sections of the community have lost the argument and here you see the result – degradation, early death, loss of love. Everywhere there are snuffed-out candles. The only alternative to crying about it is to do something about it.'

She always knew why she had kept loving him, particularly when he spoke like this. It wasn't that dash of purity that was so compelling and unusual; it was more than that. It was his human concern, which so often overrode his own narrow concerns; it was his beautiful idealism which always gave her a lift; gave her hope in a hopeless world. He was also the only person who had made her feel totally worthless. In many ways he had changed but, in others, he had changed hardly at all. He was just an innocent you could forgive anything.

'I wish I could come and work with you on that ship,' she said, putting an arm around him and planting a kiss on the side of his forehead.

'You could, if you wanted,' he said, still staring ahead at the traffic in front of him. 'You'd be as welcome as anyone else on the ship. You've always known that.'

'I wouldn't want to be as welcome as anyone else. I'd want to be more.'

'There are no stars on *The Solomon*, Sophie. We're all the same on board her.'

'I know, I know. I was just joking. You never understood my sense of humour, did you? Are you sure you want to sleep alone tonight? Can't we spend just one night together for old time's sake?'

'Is this another of your jokes?'

'Just one night, Nathan. No one's going to get hurt.'

'No, we cannot.'

'Where's the harm in it? My bed gets so lonely these days,

Nathan. I get so cold. We've been close for so long – you've been my eyes for so long. We're everything but a married couple.'

A totter pushed an overloaded cart through the twilight one way and a weeping woman with a baby in a shawl walked past in the other. A lone policeman stood on a corner superintending a populace too damp and cold to commit any crime in this a crying, lost place which suddenly made Sophie feel very sad.

'So where are we going to stay tonight, then?' she asked. 'There's a Salvation Army hostel over the road. Is that scruffy enough for you?'

'It would suit me fine but they don't allow women in there.'

'What do you care?' she asked with real feeling. 'You'd prefer it that way, wouldn't you?'

'Don't be so silly.'

They found a small hotel around the back of Brick Lane which bordered on a railway line. But it was, at least, clean with two separate singles and a dining room which served a decentish dinner.

'Do you know, I've never come across anyone who polishes off food like you,' said Nathan, marvelling at the way she bisected her steak and just shovelled it in.

'I've always been a great eater, you know that. But it never seems to do anything for my figure. Just stays skinny, no matter what I eat.'

'Your figure's not bad. The newspaper men are always drooling over it.'

'It was all right once. Just a load of old bones now.'

There were four other diners in the room but none of them seemed to recognize Sophie. 'You've no idea what a relief it is to be totally anonymous like this,' she whispered to Nathan.

'You seem to cope quite well. With all the attention you get and everything.'

'I've always coped, haven't I? When you start life on the game you can cope with just about anything they fling at you. Anything at all.' She rubbed her tongue around her teeth before picking up a piece of leftover gristle off her plate and popping it into her mouth. 'The worst part was being in Holloway. There is no escape from anyone in there; no chance of locking a door and just being on your own.'

'Perhaps you should have married me when I asked.'

'Perhaps – but the man I wanted to marry was married already.'

'Who was this then?'

'*You*, you bald fool. Sometimes I just want to give that bald head of yours such a smack. You've been the only one. Oh all right – a few men in a few beds over the years, but no one really except you. It's all right. Don't get embarrassed. No one's listening. I'm not going to do the dirty on you and tell the newspapers or anything. I'm just telling you what you already know. Sleep with me tonight, Nathan. Please. Just for the night. I won't sleep a wink in this hole – those trains will keep me awake.'

'No, Sophie. I just can't.'

'Why not?'

'It's a sin, that's why not. I've been trying so hard to rebuild myself again. My faith means a lot to me now. I can't let myself go again.'

She rolled her eyes upwards. 'He'd have no objection, would he? Where's the sin? Sin means hurting people, doesn't it? No one would get hurt. In fact all that would happen is that I'd feel a lot better. And you might feel better too. What's wrong with that? There's no sin in that. Nathan, I'm getting old. These old bones of mine need to be warmed by your love.'

But her old bones were not warmed by his love that night since he remained adamant that he was going to sleep alone, leaving her awake for most of the night, sitting up and staring at the passing trains. Was there ever, she wondered, anything quite so stupid as love when one just wanted one man. Just one! There were thousands of men – maybe even millions – who would have given anything to be lying in that lumpy bed next to her, feeling her body, and only too happy to sit staring at the passing trains.

Perhaps her kind of love only really flourished on rejection and difficulty; perhaps she would have given up on him years ago if he had just given in to her. Perhaps. But she could not conceive of ever not loving him – no matter what he did or, more to the point, what he didn't do.

Oh this was all so . . . she looked down at the glistening metal rails of the railway tracks before yet another train went past, whistling furiously. This was all so . . . she slipped on her fur coat and padded down the corridor, knocking on his bedroom door. She could even hear him snoring, and tried to open the door only to find that the bald-headed bastard had locked it on the inside.

'I've always liked cemeteries – particularly Victorian cemeteries,' said Nathan as they walked arm in arm down the twisting pathways of Highgate Cemetery. 'You always get the strangest of feelings in them; it's almost a nervousness; a kind of formless panic that you are going to miss the bus yet again. See all those nettles there. They grow well in cemeteries since they thrive on the sulphates of human bones. And somehow you can remember everything in cemeteries. They are the best places I know for listening to remembered laughter.'

They stopped still in the drifting rain mists, looking past some strange gloomy tombs where, in the shadow of one, there was a shy stammering of wild yellow flowers and, further up again, a Celtic cross, rich in mysticism. A robin landed on one of the tombstones and gave a shrill chirp.

'I expect he's hoping we're gravediggers come to dig him some fat worms,' Nathan laughed as they walked on. 'Did you know how they got their red breasts, Sophie? The story goes that the robin was at Calvary on the day Our Lord died. One thorn in the crown of thorns was giving him a lot of pain so the robin pulled it out and Jesus's blood spurted over the bird's chest.'

'Now that's what I call a lovely story. Just lovely that is.' She always loved him in these warm, expansive moods; she was becoming quite drunk on his words and little stories. She loved to be like the child sitting at the feet of the master storyteller, delighted and intrigued by the beautiful emblems of the master storyteller's mind. She doubted that he could say anything boring, even if he worked at it all week.

Further on, they found tombs decorated with sculptures of pianos, violins and slumbering lions. 'A lot of Victorians liked to advertise their products on their tombs – they saw their headstones as extensions of their family businesses,' Nathan explained.

They walked up the Egyptian Avenue of the Dead, staring into the tombs and at the piled-up coffins. 'Elaborate mausoleums like this were once very fashionable. If you could not afford one of your own, you paid to be part of a communal one like that. Look at them all – piled up there dreaming their dead dreams. Charles Kingsley is around here somewhere and so is Karl Marx. Tom Sayers, the last of the bare-fisted fighters, is here somewhere too. Ten thousand turned up to his funeral.'

Sophie walked on feeling the soft damp rain on her cheeks. 'What happens to our love for one another when we die, Nathan?' she asked, turning around and looking at him with real curiosity. 'Does it die also or does it last for ever?'

'That's a tough one. Perhaps it depends on the lovers. Jesus gave his love beyond death and for everyone. Perhaps, in some mysterious way, we pass on his love from one to another. Just the way Jesus did.'

'Oh I don't understand any of this. What about *our* love for one another? What happens to that when we die?'

'It's love, is it?' He seemed faintly surprised and she got faintly annoyed. 'Yes, I suppose it is – something like a well-established marriage. Well it may not be a marriage but it certainly feels like one at times.'

'So, when you die and you are with your God will you then forget me, Nathan? Will you then stop loving me? Is that the way it works?'

'I really don't know. I just suspect that life works on many mysterious levels and the flame of love is passed on in different ways. There is always an overlap. But you cannot *know* these things in any formal sense. They are all just intuitions – sort of poetic insights into the nature of yourself and the world.'

'I don't understand any of this.'

'Well, be comforted, Sophie, my love, that neither do I.'

Autumnal winds came romping in over the Bristol Channel as David and Effey wandered across the parkland next to the River Taff. The winds were blowing the leaves off the trees in great brown storms and thin yellow trickles. The leaves rattled together on the paths and floated out on the river – they seemed to be on the move everywhere.

'What's sadder than autumn?' David asked. 'The leaves like armies in panic and disarray. The shutting up of shop before a long cold winter. The end of a season of life.'

More small storms of leaves blew all around them, many tumbling over the grass like hundreds of acrobats, now pausing for a short rest before the wind lifted them all up again, whipping them into leaping swoops and frenzied little jigs.

Almost ever since the first day that David had stepped on *The Solomon*, he and Effey had been constant companions. She was drawn to his dreaminess and soft poetic insights, enchanted by the ebb and flow of his talk. He was attracted by her practicality and the way she seemed to see all issues clearly. They had been walking the city a lot and talking almost constantly. It was strange, thought those who knew them, how they seemed to be re-creating the relationship of their parents.

'Does a tree lose its strength in the winter, do you think?' Effey asked. 'Does it actually die?'

'No, it couldn't die, could it? Or else it wouldn't come back in the spring in even greater glory. Each spring it comes back with a new crown of blossom, better and greater than the year before. Trees are the very opposite of people. We have a youthful blaze of strength but then progressively waste away and die. The tree gets stronger and better with every year.'

'But trees die in the end. What happens then, would you think? Your father would probably say that trees have immortal souls too but what would *you* say?'

'I'd say that it was all a mystery. It's a bit like the seasons of life. I suppose something is carried on but you can never be very sure of anything. I don't reject God, for example, but neither do I accept Him like my Dad. I *struggle* with Him and hope that, one day, we'll sort it out together.'

'I knew right from the second I saw you that you were Nathan's son. Funny, but you even think like him. I've always thought of Nathan as my real father. He's had the most awful difficulties over the years but he's got so strong now. He won through – just the same way as you are going to win through. He says it's all because of prayer but I think it's something to do with a cup he keeps locked in his chapel on the ship.'

'A cup? What sort of cup would that be?'

'It looks like any old cup. But, David, they say it's a wild and holy cup nevertheless. I got it for him about ten years ago and, from that day, he started to become a great man again. You could almost see him coming alive again, like some tree surging up in the spring. You just wouldn't believe the difference between the way he was and what he has become. My mother has gone daft trying to get him but, somehow, she just seems to mess it up. They've been lovers for years now. Well, sort of lovers. She says he's the only man she ever really loved but they've never quite managed to put it together.'

'But he seems to talk about her as if she's just a wife who's not around much. What about you? Would you want to go with someone for years but never really put it together?'

She stopped walking and looked out over the grass lawns and through the squalling gusts of dead leaves. 'No,' she decided emphatically. 'No, I would not. I certainly wouldn't want to be like those two, who've spent most of their lives fighting with one another. But that's the way my mother always was – she would only ever get interested in someone she could fight with. If she had managed to dominate your father she would have gone in a flash. Perverse, I call it. I don't mind fighting a bit but, most of all, I like peace and warmth. I could never be like her.'

'Do they love one another, do you think?'

'Oh yes,' she said without hesitation. 'Oh most certainly. They just can't face up to it, that's all. They can't accept what it involves. For Mam it would mean her living on a ship and, for Nathan, it would mean him leaving it – I can't see him doing that. Mam just thinks there's something wrong with him and it never crosses her mind that there might be something wrong with her.'

Nathan had been quiet for a lot of the afternoon, not even saying much as they walked around the zoo before strolling on down towards King's Cross. He even agreed to staying in a decent hotel in the Marylebone Road, not exactly the Savoy but not exactly Brick Lane either. He was still keen on single rooms though, she was sorry to learn; not even relenting when she started going on about how she was too tired to do anything even if *he* wanted to try some hanky-panky. Some hope.

But, at dinner that night, he did start living a bit by ordering a glass of wine.

'Thought you'd packed that up.'

'The odd one doesn't do you any harm. The Bible doesn't forbid you to drink; it says you shouldn't drink to excess. Jesus made the finest wine, after all, and, when it ran out, he made some more.'

'Here's to him then,' she smiled, raising her glass to chink with his. She had no particular animosity against his religion – nor even his version of it. As a Bay girl she had come across just about every religion on the face of the earth. There was even a sense in which she was a product of all of them and she really did not mind whom they worshipped as long as they did not bother her. In all the years she had known Nathan he had never once preached to her. She would never have put up with that.

But now he had gone silent again and she was having great difficulty in getting him to speak at all so, when the main course of roast beef and Yorkshire pudding arrived together with tiny steaming hillocks of sprouts and roast potatoes, she picked up her knife and fork and prepared to set about it with her customary relish. But just then he said something so startling that she put down her knife and fork again, her hunger lifting out of her like a hangover under the first kiss of a lot more alcohol.

'Sophie, I've been thinking a lot and I've decided we should get married.'

She swallowed hard, picking up her knife and fork again. She held them upwards on either side of her plate like thin silver guardsmen.

'Don't let me stop you eating,' he interjected almost apologetically.

'I've never felt less like eating in my life. You know what you're saying, do you?'

'It makes a sort of sense when you think about it, Sophie. We needn't live together all the time – not even much of the time. You can carry on with your singing and I'll continue with my work on the ship.'

'If we're not going to continue seeing one another what's the point of getting married?'

'Well, if we did marry, we could at least sleep together when we met. I'd be all right then you see. It's not a sin for a man and wife to sleep together.'

'Isn't it? Well, that *is* a relief. I thought everything was a sin in your book.'

'You know what I mean. But it's not just for that. I love you too. I was thinking in the cemetery this morning that there had never been another woman in my life. Well, there was my wife, but she left me. But there has never been anyone since I met you. And you stayed by me through it all. You kept telling me there's been no one else in your life. Maybe we'll find a few old orange boxes to sit on when we get old – we'll have to stop one day. If it would suit you it would suit me fine. So what do you say?'

She said 'Yes' and smiled mistily but, in her mind, there was the image of another man's face and it was not Nathan's. It was the finely chiselled face of Richard, *her husband*. But there again, she might be able to get rid of that nancy boy as quickly as she had acquired him. Richard would do anything at all provided someone dangled a big enough bundle of money in front of his nose.

'But let's get one thing straight,' she said, becoming serious and stretching forward to tap his arm lightly. 'I'm not going to wait for you to lead me up the aisle before you sleep with me. In fact I really don't want to wait for another hour. It isn't a sin for engaged couples to sleep with one another, is it?'

He shrugged his shoulders. 'Just a tiny bit of a one perhaps.'

'In that case . . .' She picked up the wine and both glasses, leaving her meal completely untouched. 'Let's get moving before it seems bigger.' He stood up and they walked out of the restaurant together. 'But you've got to be gentle with me,' she whispered as they went up the stairs. 'Try to think of me as a virgin on our wedding night.'

'Sophie, if I did that I'd just be laughing myself daft all night. You've got to be pretty serious about love-making, as I remember it.'

'So who did you make love to last? Go on. You can tell me. Who?'

'You. Who else? Apart from my wife there was never anyone at all. No one. And, offhand, I can't even remember what my wife's body was like.'

'Ah, but you do remember this one, don't you?' Sophie said slipping out of her dress almost as soon as they got into the bedroom.

'Yes, I remember it all too well. All too well.'

He made no move to undress and sat on the side of the bed as she poured herself a glass of wine, now standing before him and holding it out in front of her as quietly and politely as if she was just making conversation at a cocktail party. 'I'm glad you are at least taking a drop of wine,' she said as she poured a tiny dribble down her belly.

Nathan felt terrible, resting his chin on his upturned hands as he watched the wine slither and slide, red on olive, down the length of her long body. He had promised to be strong again but hardly knew where any man could find the strength to resist this, this marvellous body on which he had well and truly wrecked himself in the first place. And here he was; falling for the same old trick all over again.

He reached out and ran his fingertip down the path of one of the red rivulets, and she drew in a quick breath of air as she stepped closer to him, her whole body quivering deliciously. Almost every time she looked at him she wondered quite why she found this bald old God-botherer so exciting but, in truth, had no real answer at all. He roused her slumbering emotions, she supposed, and she so much wanted to set him on fire again. Also she remembered all too well what their first night of love had cost him and, in some strange way, that had bound her more deeply to him than perhaps even she would care to admit.

He took hold of both her wrists before pressing his mouth against her belly, licking away the dark smudges of wine. Yes, it was surely all right now. Surely? They had come through too much and travelled together down too many dangerous valleys for him ever to turn his back on her. They should be married; they *would* be married.

It was that precise moment when he entered her, making her cry out in a rapture of pleasure and pain. It was that moment of violation by love that was at the very centre of her life; just this one moment which so expressively justified the emptiness of all the rest of her daily moments. She had longed for this moment again and, when it came, she wondered quite how she had ever managed without it for so long.

She held him tight as he just lay there as if feeding on the very sap between her legs, something deep within him calling out, wild and lost, as he raised his body and drove down into her again, looking deep for that fiery spot where their spirits and souls tangled up together and burned in a common flame.

And when he went down into her again, she opened her eyes and moaned piteously, though not so much from ecstasy now as from real pains of apprehension and terror when she thought of what he was going to do and say when he discovered that she was married already. Oh she was for the high jump all right. She would never get away with it, would she? She couldn't possibly get away with something as difficult and problematic as a divorce without him finding out. Could she?

But then he went shivering down between her legs again and her mind went dark and her blood became bloated with so much raw sex she thought of nothing at all as, tangled and burning, both their souls entered into an iron embrace and went falling towards the same flame.

The night had become unusually warm for the time of year. Black thunderheads were building up over the Bristol Channel; forks of lightning stammered silently on the horizon. Shipping in all areas of the Western Approaches had received severe gale warnings and many were already making for cover. Even the paddle steamers had cancelled their hourly excursions out of Cardiff and over to Weston-super-Mare.

The glassy acres of the docks were deserted, the hurrying siren winds making the normally still surfaces of the water come alive with rippling chuckles. But three men were playing cards on the brilliantly-lit bridge of a sandhopper, shouting and laughing so loudly as they put their cards down they could have been heard in the next dock by the man on watch on *The Solomon*, had he not been asleep in his chair. And had he been alert and not dozing, dead to the world, he would have seen Hamilton moving around in the darkness on the deck, pouring petrol over piles of coiled ropes and old sail bags.

Down in the ward room David was reading *The Wind in the Willows* aloud to Effey. Others were being drawn into Kenneth Grahame's seductive net also. David read with great animation, pausing for effect, poking the air with his finger, his voice rich and good at mimicry. Just like his father, Effey thought, as yet more joined in listening to the ageless stories of Mole, Ratty and Toad.

Outside, the lightning stammered again and there was a bilious grumble of thunder as a match was lit and thrown on the petrol. Even as the flames roared upwards, Hamilton had sprung onto a deck rail and jumped onto the quay, running away into the night. The man on watch was still asleep as the flames roared higher and higher, small sparkling flames flashing one after another up the dark angular cobwebs of the standing rigging.

Effey noticed first the strange patterns of fire reflected on the water through the porthole just behind David's head. It gave him a curious effect – that of a burning angel perhaps – until she realized what it was. 'David!' she shouted. 'There's a fire on the deck!'

'Fire! Fire!' Those dreaded words – particularly feared in those old hearts of oak – were shouted throughout the corridors of the ship as all hands turned to, some just in their underpants as they ran hither and thither, trying to remember the drill. 'Fire! Fire!'

David scrambled up through the deck hatch and had to do a double-take as he looked up and around him. The flames were travelling so fast through the rigging it was as if the very night – the whole of the heavens – had caught fire. He ran towards the burning ropes and sail bags, the smoke ripping at his eyes as he tried to drag them to the side. 'Help me, someone help me,' he cried in desperation.

Others came to help him try to topple the small blazing mountain into the dock but were beaten back by the roaring flames even as David, blindly, recklessly, tried to tackle them from the other side. 'David, give up,' Effey called. 'Just give up.'

Now buckets of water were being thrown over the fire and angry explosions of steam mixed with the staccato sounds of breaking wood. But it was too late. The voracious fire had sidled into another pool of petrol on the deck, exploding into an even huger mountain of flames which danced hungrily and thirstily as their fingers felt around for more wood in which to express their destructive dynamics.

Still the crew kept trying to fight the flames but even the most sanguine among them could now see that they were losing. The flames seemed to be multiplying higher and higher, wider and wider, until now they could be seen for miles around, dancing on the waters of the docks, varnishing the sides of the warehouses a pale orange, even flickering faintly at the end of Bute Street and on the surrounding roofs until it was almost as if the whole of the Bay was on fire.

Sophie stiffened and moaned, clenching her fists as she felt something wet and warm – something long forgotten, something oh so strange and badly missed – hatch deep within her loins. Small spasms of pleasure kept breaking out in every part of her body with everything running richly and quickly when it actually did come – a silent imploding rocket which turned the whole of her insides in upon themselves. She thought she would never breathe again. Just for now, she was magically and wonderfully renewed.

In that moment too he let go, coming in a series of juddering gasps, weeping softly into her hair, which had become tangled in his twitching fingers. In the distant edge of his consciousness he thought he heard a strange and distant scream. 'Marry me,' he whispered. 'Marry me, marry me.' Even after he had come his cock was still bloated and hungry, still anxious to get on with it again, to re-enter and reconnect with the mystery at the centre of their burned, tangled souls.

The fire on the windjammer had attracted seamen from other ships and even people from Bute Street, all drawn by the compulsion of this dark and vivid tragedy. Many were helping to fight the fire, some even lowering buckets on ropes into the dock and throwing what they could onto the leaping flames.

They managed more or less successfully to put out the fire where it had started in the old sail bags but, unnoticed, some sparks had drifted down off the rigging setting fire to the ropes coiled on the aft deck.

Hamilton, lurking by the West Bute dock gates, opened his mouth slightly in a sort of smile as the aft deck burst into flames and David detailed some of the men to run back and fight that. But, just then, there was a huge belch of thunder which startled even Hamilton by its ferocity and closeness. He looked up and saw huge black clouds chasing one another fast across the roof of the sky. He also saw one of the greatest slashes of lightning that he had ever seen, ripping in a shivering blaze at the roof of the Neale and West fish wharf. Another rumbling explosion of thunder followed and then he felt the rain on his face – warm rain, which came down softly at first, before turning into huge torrents, so thick that Hamilton could not now even see the blazing ship. He wiped the rain off his cheek and examined his wet hands, as if in disbelief, before striding away into the weeping thundering darkness.

When the rain started everyone on the ship just stopped, looking at one another in the brief jagged flashes of electricity which were lighting up every corner of the dockland. But it was not the lightning so much as the torrential rain which was coming to their aid, streaming down on the flames and extinguishing them effortlessly and quickly.

David paced around the smouldering deck letting the clean rain of heaven wash all over him, soaking his clothes so much you could see the outlines of his young body. He raised his fist and saluted a smiling Effey who, along with all the others, had remained in the same spot as they had been in when the rain had begun.

# CHAPTER TWENTY-EIGHT

Nathan returned immediately he heard the news of the fire on the ship. His mind for once a blank, he sat in the train gloomily looking out over the damp fields of England as the train sped towards the even damper fields of Wales.

He hardly knew what to make of it all. And, yet again, he could not help asking himself if perhaps this was yet another example of God's punishment for his becoming involved with that woman. One way or another 'that woman' had given him an appalling amount of trouble since they had first met. It continued still, even in their happiness. Just before his departure, she had said that she had a confession to make. Secretly and unwisely, she confided, she had married another man some time ago.

He had taken the news like a sharp slap across the face. Even as she assured him how little Richard meant to her, he could only think she was lying to him again. He wondered if she could ever stop. That tongue of hers had managed to undermine him often enough in the past.

Nevertheless, to the tick of the passing rails, he still tried to pray for her; still looked for the blessing of prayer within which all relationships made a sort of sense. Prayer, he believed, drove out feelings of bitterness and revenge. Prayer handed the matter over to God for Him to deal with. But even so, he thought grimly, he was going to have to work an awful lot of prayer shifts on her behalf. Some needed a lot more than a few quick sentences and that woman was one of them.

He left the railway station and walked down Bute Street, reflecting on how much and how quickly the community had changed since he had first arrived here. It had now become a small, volatile society which was always restless. The Chinese had moved out into the Valleys, introducing the Welsh to the wonders of chop suey; the Indians were settling around their new temple in Ninian Road outside the area. The Italians had moved even further, colonising almost every town in Wales with their ice-cream parlours and snorting espresso coffee machines.

He stood and looked at the deserted ruin of St Mark's church, long since given over to weeds and tramps in search of a place to sleep. The Mosque had been riven by another split too, leaving Rashed with just a small group of his followers based in the Port Said Café in Bute Street. Rashed had become particularly introverted. Nathan had often spotted him down in the docks, sometimes just staring at the windjammer from a distance. Nathan had always found his intensity far too uncomfortable, and avoided him where possible.

He continued walking down Bute Street, trying to work out what kind of society it was now – something which was not quite disorderly but not all that orderly either; a warm, vibrant place in which there had been so much inter-racial marriage you were not at all sure who was what any more. There were brown people with Spanish surnames, black people with Maltese surnames, yellow people with Welsh surnames . . . Almost all of them had become absorbed in one another, except, perhaps, for the hard rump of Rashed's Moslems.

He could still remember seeing, for the first time, the mischievous sparkle in Sophie's eyes when he had first met her outside that church. How different might it have been, he wondered, if he had never met her? Would he have just met another woman and done it all the wrong way with her?

He walked on, feeling quite tired now, nodding at a couple of patrolling policemen. From his knowledge of the area's history over the years – he had become the unofficial historian of the Bay – he recalled how their numbers had changed from the time when the Marquess of Bute had set up the Green Jackets on the docks, who were allowed 'to enter any vessel by night or day to detect or prevent felonies without a warrant'. The Green Jackets had started as a well-disciplined force of twenty-three, paying their constables twopence a week and expecting them to work hard for that. A man had once shown Nathan the Defaulters' Book which had listed the fines for such misdemeanours as gossiping to the dock workers, sleeping on duty, being late, filching the cargo or reading a newspaper on duty. One had a week's pay stopped for going to work in a dirty state and smelling of ale. Another was fined half a day's pay for being caught 'leaning and in a careless position' against the railings of the dry dock. One Alfred Dean was found to be drunk on duty and, when he turned up the next day for his reprimand, he was still drunk.

The Cardiff Railway Company took over the force after the war. Now the constables were paid 26s. a week rising by annual increments of 1s. Sergeants were paid £1 18s. a week and inspectors £2 12s. By 1930 there were 204 men working twenty-four hour shifts, including six constables and three inspectors. But that was the height of their strength and, with the exodus to other parts of Wales and given the more settled nature of the community, the numbers of patrolling policemen had now dropped by more than a third.

Some vital parts of the landscape had stayed the same though. The hermit still lived in his corrugated-iron shed behind the Norwegian Church; Hamilton's mansion in Howard Close was still empty and boarded up (with no news of its former occupant) and the Exchange was still there too, almost empty now and given over to the ghosts of old commercial brokers who met nightly on the Floor to brag about their old shipping deals.

When he did finally see the ship, in the cold light of the afternoon, his heart stopped still as he gazed at the blackened crucifix shapes of the yardarms, the scorched deck rails and piles of charred ropes. It would be all right, he tried to reassure himself with no particular conviction. They would not have to rebuild anew. Everything would be all right.

David took him to look more closely at the damage. It was a little too early to say exactly how much needed replacing but it appeared as if they only needed one new mast and a fair few charred deck planks would have to be replaced. Mercifully the fire had not even started to eat into the keel. David added that he had already sent for a man from the timber yards though, of course, they might well have to go back to the Norwegian dealers to find the right length for the new mast.

Nathan nodded as David spoke, satisfied that he seemed to have taken over the supervision of the work so efficiently. Curiously, he made no comment or suggestions of his own, content that someone seemed to know what to do. Neither did he ask the two obvious questions – who was on watch that night and how had the fire started?

'We think someone set fire to some petrol,' David said later. 'But the real answer is that we don't know.'

Nathan shrugged his shoulders, as if it was a matter of no importance, looking into his son's eyes and over at Effey who was standing next to the bridge watching them. Nathan looked at his son again. That was almost a dart of understanding in his eyes, David thought. It was almost as if, in one quick shrewd look, he had picked up what was going on between them. He knew.

'I think he knows,' said Effey, coming over to David after Nathan had gone below. 'It'll take some time then he'll react – good or bad.'

But over the next few days, nothing did burst out – neither good nor bad – and Effey watched Nathan with growing concern. He was becoming withdrawn and isolated, not speaking much and not even taking any particular interest in the ship repair work. Her main worry was that he was going to retreat deep into himself again; that he was going to lose the tremendous ground that he had made up, and fall back to the wasteful brooding of all those dark dog-years.

She was reasonably sure that her mother was at the root of it all, but no amount of the gentlest inquiries could get Nathan to explain anything about anything.

He did not even seem much interested in the newspaper report on Sophie's first concert after being let out of prison. He just gave a small sniff and dropped the newspaper on the table after reading the first few paragraphs.

'Any doubts hanging over Sophie James's career after her prison sentence for prostitution were swiftly dispelled last night,' the report began. 'She played to a packed house in the Hippodrome who cheered her every song to the echo. Seldom has a performer so completely won over an audience merely by stepping out into the spotlight to sing a repertoire which consistently has the same theme: "I am what I am. I can do no other".

'It is almost as if the trouble and drama of her private life actually enhance her great charisma. She just seems to stand there with her arms raised and the audience know that they are being shown something very special indeed; something almost religious.'

'Well I've never found anything religious about her,' Nathan muttered to no one in particular before going off on one of his long walks around the docks. 'In fact I'd go as far as to say there is not a religious bone in the whole of her body.'

With Nathan refusing to confide, Effey could not find out anything from Sophie either. She sent several notes to her mother but there was no response. Finally she sent a note to Obe asking him, whenever he was next passing through the city on Sons of Africa business, to call in and cheer up Nathan. Alternatively he might contact her mother and find out what had happened. She just might tell Obe.

In the circumstances of the time and place, in the accidents and shadows of their unique young bodies, David and Effey grew together very quickly. It only seemed natural that their closeness should be explored and affirmed in the act of sexual love.

It happened, without forethought or even any discussion, one night after they had been in the city and were walking together back to the ship. They were passing the long curved shape of the Spiller's huge grain warehouse near the Alexandra Dock when David noticed a side door open and, tugging her by the elbow, said, 'Let's take a look in here.'

It was unusual for the place to be left unlocked since, inside, there were small mountains of valuable sacks of grain, rising higher and yet higher in the faint light from the sodium lights outside on the quay. Some of the stacks may have been fifty feet high in places and, as the pair walked around in the half-light, it was almost as if they were roaming the floor of some strange, stepped valley.

Iron hooks hung from thick beams and chains stretched from floor to floor. But even more compelling than the wood and metal geometry of the place was the thick, musty smell, almost as thick and arousing as that of an early morning bakery. This smell surrounded them as intimately as a long scarf and they sat on two grain sacks facing one another in a faint yellow oblong of light.

They both undressed and kept looking at one another anxiously, still unsure of quite how to orchestrate the pandemonium of their hearts, when she took the initiative by getting him to lie down on a bed of bulky grain sacks, giving soft quick snorts and clambering all over him as if trying to find a way inside him. He moved her over and lay on her, their youthful limbs wrapping around one another, crushing against one another tightly, almost bruisingly as the nails of her fingers dug deep into his back. Soon they were both snorting softly together, almost finding it difficult to breathe in the excited dark warmth. He ran the ham of his hand around the bone of her pubic sex, working his fingers into her, finding it warm and slippery, until she held onto his shoulders, hauling her weight up onto him and wrapping her legs around him before she could feel the softest, most exquisite pain of her life as slowly, uncertainly and nervously he entered into her, wondering whether he was hurting her, whether he should stop, whether he *could* stop . . . In the circumstances he just closed his eyes, held her almost vice-like with his good arm and went deeper. She let out an extraordinary cry of pleasure and pain when he did rip through her virginity, bucking crazily but not wanting to let go as he went stabbing up and down into her as if he was in the final stages of extreme panic. He was not going anywhere now and she held onto his body as tightly as her strong arms could, trying to force her legs wider to receive all of him when, at that moment, something collapsed inside her like scaffolding toppling from a wall and she felt such a bright burst of bewildering emptiness she opened her eyes and looked around her, wondering what was going on now.

He, however, had clearly felt no such collapse, continuing his frenzied lunges, until he stiffened, half-thinking he was suffering from cramp in his back, when he let go the stinging spurt of his young manhood which went shooting, hotly and urgently, right down into her. A rat, disturbed by the commotion, went running across the warehouse floor with its fat white tail trailing behind it. The two lovers curled up together, silently and motionlessly, trying to catch their breath as they held one another tight.

Nathan's spirit began picking up a little over the next few days, much to everyone's relief. He took a more lively interest in the ship repairs, even if he was still hanging back in David's shadow because the boy now seemed to be making all the major decisions.

Another foremast had been located in a Scottish shipyard and much of the charred deck had been replanked too. Men were already hard at work on the caulking, running a mixture of melted pitch and rope fibre into the gaps. A lot of the standing rigging had been replaced and Nathan watched with a quiet pride as David climbed the ratlines to inspect and change the positioning of the shrouds, insisting that each of the rope systems be set to the most exact specifications. He seemed to have adapted to life on the ship with amazing speed, Nathan thought, since, on some days, David would be out walking around the high yardarms with all the nonchalance of a man taking a dog for a walk.

He had also noticed that David was drawing a lot of his confidence and strength from Effey and he took a lot of pleasure in that even if, in his eyes, at least, the relationship had a slightly incestuous air. Effey, after all, was almost more of a daughter to him than David had been a son. But at least they were working together well, even if Nathan had to try quite hard to stop the thought of them both making love. But Effey would never do that, he decided. And anyway, where would they do it? There was no privacy on the ship.

David had brought a much-needed impetus to the ship's restoration – particularly after the set-back of the fire – and everyone seemed to share in a rising buzz of excitement, particularly when the huge piles of canvas for the sails were delivered on the quay-side. The crew kept stopping and looking up at the bare yardarms, almost as if trying to imagine what they would look like finally clothed in their great sails.

Even with all the work proceeding apace, Nathan still seemed to have forgotten the secret of the simple smile. But one day, he lit up like the Eddystone Lighthouse when Obe walked onto the ship carrying a suitcase.

As Effey watched the two of them embrace she saw how close they had become over the years; how they had both outfought the most obdurate opponents to become the fine men that they now were. She was very disappointed, however, to see them both slip off on their own, without so much as saying a word to anyone, let alone to her, who had invited Obe in the first place.

When they were alone on a bench on the quarter deck Obe mentioned almost casually that he had spent some time with Sophie recently. Nathan studied the backs of his hands carefully as Obe explained that Sophie was devastated with regret for misleading him in the way she had. 'It had always been a nothing marriage, Nathan,' he said. 'They only slept together once and even then nothing happened.'

Nathan continued studying the backs of his hands.

'She's sent a message through me, asking if she can see you soon. She's, uh, got rid of him – this Richard something – and, oh I don't know, the girl's in a real big fix, Nathan. She'd been stripped out too. That Richard had lost all her money for her. No one has paid bigger for a mistake with a partner.'

'You mean she's lost *everything*? How could she do that?'

'She's lost near enough everything. Some swindle with stocks an' shares Ah think. That Richard was always on the phone selling gilts an' commodities an such. Always said he was going to make a bundle and that's about what he lost.'

'Is she upset about it all?'

'Not really. Very matter-of-fact. You know her and money. An' she's still big enough to make some more money if she can find some new material, always easier said than done. No, she's not worried about that. All she's really worried about is you. No woman ever loved a man like she loves you, Nathan.'

Nathan's eyebrows rose and he looked directly into Obe's rheumy black eyes but said nothing.

'But she just wants to rest up for a while to do some thinking and she was wondering if perhaps she could change her looks a bit – put on a bit of a disguise – and come an' stay here with you.'

'Impossible.'

'She needs you now, Nathan. Do this one thing for her. She wants to be near Effey too. She says she's very sorry about her argument with the girl – it was just the prison getting to her. She's sorry about everything.'

'Obe. Look, Obe. You know what she's like. This ship is not big enough for her, just as the Bay was not big enough for her. We are going to be able to sail soon but having her here would just mean continual disruption. She would attract all kinds of people – it would jeopardize our progress.'

'She helped you once, Nathan. You wouldn't be on this ship today if it wasn't for her. No . . . *she*'s not saying anything about old favours. *I* am. Just let her come down here for a few days. She'll get fed up quickly enough . . .'

'No. She is not coming here under any circumstances.'

'Does that go for me too?'

'What do you mean?'

His black brow furrowed and he looked around, as if to check no one was nearby. 'I'm on the run, Nathan. There's a warrant out for my arrest an', well, I just couldn't face another spell in prison. That's why I've got my suitcase. I want to lay low for a while.'

'Am I allowed to ask what you've done?'

'Better not. It's better that you don't know in case the police do catch up with me. Better not. But it was all political – all of it, political.'

'Serious then?'

'Yup. Very serious.'

'Very well. I'll tell the rest of the crew tonight – not that you are on the run exactly but that you have to keep out of the law's way. There's a few shady characters aboard as it is, but we have always set out to absorb the past; to wipe the slate clean. All we really ask is that those who take up residence on the ship don't do it again – whatever it is – while they are here. But I'm not really asking you to do anything, Obe. You are too old a friend. Just settle down here for a while and make yourself comfortable. How are you at sewing? We've lots of sails to make.'

Obe laughed. 'I'm sort of fair at sewing. Just fair.'

# CHAPTER TWENTY-NINE

When they had first begun the windjammer's refit there had been a six-month wait for the three new masts direct from Norway, so it had seemed scarcely believable that they had traced a ready-made foremast in Scotland which was due to be delivered the following Thursday.

All hands on *The Solomon* turned to for the lifting of the mast off the lorry and its four trailers. There were almost twenty nationalities and, between them and with Nathan at the front, they managed to lift it effortlessly, first laying it down on the quay while David checked the pulley systems they had set up for putting it in place.

The only crew member who had not been at the lifting on the quay was Obe. He was so anxious to stay out of sight that he had more or less volunteered to peel potatoes permanently, sitting in the galley for hour after hour, peeling bucket after bucket of them. He did his duties cheerfully though, humming a lot and even sometimes getting a little song going.

His anxieties about being seen proved to be well-founded. A few days after his arrival the police, in the shape of the red-blotched Chief Inspector Victor Watts and a plainclothes detective, walked up the gangplank. They were greeted by Nathan, politely but coldly. Watts explained that they wanted to interview one Obadiah Brown and that they were checking out his old haunts and known associates.

Nathan said nothing, regarding the inspector with clear distaste. He wondered what sorry story he would come up with if he checked on Watts's old haunts and known associates. He still remembered that day, many years ago now, when he had first seen Watts on Hamilton's doorstep. From what he had heard about both of them over the years, it had been difficult to work out who was the bigger villain.

'There's a warrant out for Brown's arrest. He's needed to help us with our inquiries.'

'Inquiries into what?'

'We are not at liberty to divulge that. These are serious matters which could lead to serious charges. We are here because he has been seen on this ship in the past and he is a known associate of yours. So do you know anything about him now?'

'Nothing at all,' Nathan replied, absurdly crossing his fingers behind his back, which is what he did as a child when he wanted to cancel out a lie. 'In fact I haven't seen him for quite a long while.'

How long is a long while, he asked himself Jesuitically. On the eternally vexed inquiry into the nature of truth couldn't he seriously argue that half an hour was, in fact, a long while, since it was about half an hour since he had last seen Obe sitting on a box in the galley peeling the potatoes.

'When you say "A long while", how long might that be?'

*About half an hour*? 'Can't remember off hand.'

'Just try.'

'Sorry, it could have been a week, a month, it could have been anything.' *Anything like half an hour*.

'Very well. But I must remind you that harbouring a suspected criminal is a very serious offence, as I expect you know all too well. Would you object if I had a look around your ship?'

'Yes, I would. I'm sorry. I couldn't allow that. We've got people on here who are trying to rebuild their lives. We like to think of the ship as enjoying sanctuary; of being a place free of the past and questions from the police.'

'Please, at least remember that it is only the police who guarantee any freedom.'

'There are other ways of looking at it.'

'Yes, there always are, but I don't need to remind you that there is no legal status attached to your comic notion of sanctuary. I could come back with a search warrant and take this ship apart.'

Nathan pulled a face. 'You are very welcome to do that,' he said between gritted teeth. 'But you will still find nothing.'

Watts turned to the plainclothes detective, jerking his head and indicating that they should leave. Nathan watched them both walk out of the dock before going down to see Obe, still sitting on his box and still peeling his potatoes.

'Damn me, I was just getting to enjoy doing these potatoes,' Obe laughed after Nathan had told all, dropping his peeler into the bucket with a plop. 'I'll leave after dark. There's still some safe houses around the Bay.'

'Why are they after you, Obe?'

'It's . . . well . . . it's serious. For once, I'm not totally responsible in the sense that I did not do it. We've got some hotheads in the Sons an' they see violence as the way ahead. There's been some bombing by a few of them and it's my ass 'cos I'm still the chairman, you see. Anything my boys do is seen as rising directly from my orders. They would never believe I was just a victim of a few of my members' recklessness and, in a sense, I am responsible. I am, an' it would give them no end of pleasure to put me away for a long, long time. Nathan, I just can't take any more prison. A lot of my boys are young an' they can do a stretch standing on their heads. I just can't.'

'We'll look after you, Obe. We'll always look after you.'

Obe took Nathan by the arm, gripping it tight. 'I've really enjoyed peeling these potatoes, you know. It's quiet, it's mindless an' I really need all the mindless quiet I can get just now. I'd even like to sail with you.'

'Go to your safe house, Obe. Stay there at least until the police have come back with their warrant and searched the ship. You can still sail with us. You *will* sail out with us, just as, a long time ago, you first sailed in.'

'Where we going, Nathan? I'd just love to see Barbados again.'

'We'll see everything again, Obe, but, just for now, go and make your precious self safe. We may even be able to sail in six weeks. But just hide up for a while, at least until the police are satisfied you're not around this part of the world.'

'They're such beautiful words,' said Sophie, picking up the sheet again. 'I just love the words – they're so strong and yet fragile, so full of sadness and yet there's hope there too.' She eyed the bespectacled youth, wondering why some people were given the key to unlocking the deepest feelings. She knew another man who could unlock the deepest feelings also.

'I know a man who can use words beautifully like this,' she went on, hitting the sheet lightly with the back of her hand. 'In fact I know he'd love this song because he loves nothing more than paradox and mystery. It's all here. Look at them –

every line a winner and every phrase a jewel.' She stopped speaking and eyed him directly. 'You did write all these lines yourself?'

His cheeks flushed and she decided that this one could not tell a lie. Her intelligence usually smoked out lies within seconds. 'I'm glad you liked them,' he said, ignoring the insult of the question. 'Phrases like that seem to just fall out of my pen.'

'Well, you just keep that pen working, you hear? No getting into drugs or dirty women nor nothing like that. So what are you calling this song?'

'*China Dreams*.'

'*China Dreams* eh? A Dream of china? I don't know, sounds a bit porcelain that. Yes, *China Dreams* is all right. How do you see it being performed?'

'Well, that would be up to the performer. I just write the songs, the performer interprets.'

'Never mind all that. How would *you* perform it?'

'Well, very slow, of course. Very operatic, with very slow, precise hand movements. I'd start with a piano quietly picking out the theme, then add layers of sound – some violins, a few horns – very rich and lush until the end of the third verse. A solo here – a trumpet perhaps – then a slow rising final part as the singer takes it all home with a lot of quiet power.'

'If I took it into the recording studios, you'd come in with me, I take it?'

'You mean you're going to do it?'

'Sure. I need a change, need something new. The world needs a change too. I've got a very good feeling about this song and there's a certain trumpeter I want for the middle solo. Yes, this song is the one I've been looking for. It's going to be a Valentine to someone rather precious. But, tell me, I don't even know your name?'

Watts picked up the telephone and dialled a number, chewing on his lower lip as he waited for a reply.

'Mr Hamilton, it's Watts here,' he said at length. 'We went over the ship this afternoon and we're pretty sure we've located what you want. He's built a sort of private chapel in the hold of the ship and there was a cup locked in a cupboard just next to the altar. He didn't want to open it at first so we made him read the search warrant, even threatened to break open the cupboard.'

There was a silence at the other end so he went on: 'But even so I'm not at all sure how we could actually get this cup. The access goes through some crew quarters with many of the bunks out in the open. It would be extremely risky and very difficult for someone to get past there unseen. Even if they managed that it would be extremely unlikely they could break into the chapel without being heard. Sounds carry everywhere on ships like that. They've even doubled their watches after a recent fire.

'Perhaps the only real possibility is to lean on someone in the crew to do the job for us. I didn't recognize too many of the faces but there were certainly a few known to me all too well. I'll explore that avenue, shall I? The other way to him would be through that girl Effey . . . Yes . . . Yes . . . We could do that, yes. Take out the boy and keep the girl somewhere . . . I think they are still in business but I'd have to make a few inquiries in the Midlands. They can be messy but at least it does make it look like some old racial vendetta . . . I agree . . . there's never so much pressure on the police if it looks like some old darkey thing. They'll just say he deserved it for being with a black girl. I'm sure they'll be right too. I'll get in touch with them then and come back to you with the details.'

The next night David and Effey were back on the grain sacks of Spiller's warehouse again, both unclothed and holding one another in an oblong of faint light, both loving and vulnerable in that yellow sacrificial spotlight.

They stopped, they started . . . they touched, they stroked . . . they kissed, they nuzzled . . . all in tight squaredances of fleshy movement, pulled-in elbows and trembling fingers, taut veins and pounding hearts, until those shooting, shivering spasms of rapture brought them to a stop again and the end of another reel. Then they just lay wrapped around one another, catching their breath, their blood venting richly and deliciously in their veins. Then it was time to start another reel again and that sore, blood-gorged organ throbbed upwards again to enter down into that raw, weeping hole in which they fought so hard to essay the first thrilling flushes of their newly-discovered sexuality.

She had become quite drugged and exhausted by the waves of pleasure breaking inside every part of her. Her eyes had become heavy-lidded and all she wanted to do was collapse into deep sleep. But he rose again and came at her, stirring that well-heated cauldron until somehow – and she was not at all sure how – he managed to start bringing her blood to the boil again, edging her back to the edge of that warm coconut shore where it would be quite wonderful to lie with him deep inside her and just die.

But, even in her drugged exhaustion, she did pick up some rustling noises and her eyes caught sight of two men crouching and coming towards them. Both were dressed in white pyjamas, with black songkoks on their heads, but it was the spark of murder in their hands that was so nightmarish. They were wielding *kapak gangs*, small axe heads on rattan sticks, cold couriers of the ritual revenge.

She continued screaming as David pushed her away, turning to face the men but only seeing a blur of threatening shadows as an axe head came scything down on his head, splitting into his skull with a searing crack. The other man joined in the attack too, chopping him on the shoulder. Instinctively, he raised his arm to protect himself but the blows kept raining down on all parts of his body. Icy darts of pain shot into every part of him with warm blood swarming in every direction. 'Run, Effey,' he heard his own voice shouting as he rose to his feet. 'Just make a run for it.'

Another blow cut right into the side of his neck. 'That hurt,' he shouted inanely, feeling his consciousness cloud over as, pathetically and uselessly, he held up his arm to protect himelf again. He just wished he had trousers on or something. It was impossible to fight anyone at all if you were naked. You just felt so, well, silly.

Effey's screams filled up his mind like the furious whistles of a train in a tunnel. But even as he turned to look for her, he realized that he could hardly see anything at all since he had become almost blinded by his own blood as the two men attacked again.

Blindly, even hopefully, he managed to stand up, lowering his shoulder a little and throwing all his weight into it, barging them to one side as he tried to make an escape from the killing cuts. But he hardly made five yards, feeling unbearably sluggish and sticky with all the spurting leaks of his own blood, when the men closed in on him again, measuring and distancing their chops as they made more running impossible by cutting into the tendons of his legs with butcher-like efficiency.

The warehouse roof, the piled-up sacks of grain and the glimmerings of the sodium lamps all moved around him as he sank to the floor, his good hand vainly trying to staunch the bleeding from his many wounds. It moved here, it moved there but, everywhere he touched, there was another gaping, bleeding wound. He could still hear Effey screaming distantly and, with a gentle, warm sigh of regret, he wished that he could hold her just once more when his mind drifted into a peaceful darkness.

Much later that night Sophie was rehearsing *China Dreams* with a band in the Hammersmith Palais in London and not getting it quite right, while Nathan – the object of her thoughts and the centre of the song – was sleeping restlessly in his bunk on *The Solomon,* being revisited by an old and familiar dream.

The dream was of a great bird circling above an ancient blasted tree, calling out her distress to the whole of the surrounding, parched desert. After flying around and around, until she was all but exhausted, the bird glided back down to the tree where all her young were lying dead in the nest. In desperation the mother bird stabbed at her own chest with her beak again and again until huge spurts of blood came gushing down onto her dead babies.

Her dead babies began struggling back to life as soon as the blood began running over them while, at the same time, the mother bird was sinking among them, dying.

Nathan opened his eyes again and just sat up, clearly understanding what the dream meant. The offspring were being reborn in the blood of their mother and this, her greatest gift of life, also meant her death. Even with his eyes open he could still see the elements of the dream all too vividly and it was to remain lodged in his waking consciousness for the rest of the night because, within minutes, he was roused from his cabin by a lot of excited shouting on the deck for him to come up quickly.

He hurried up the stairway and actually felt the beak of the bird strike deep into his chest as he looked on the gashed, naked frame of his beloved son David. He had, somehow, managed to half walk and half crawl back to the ship. Now he was lying on the gangplank, one hand locked on to the rail. Yet more of the crew were coming up onto the deck, all looking at Nathan, uncertain what to do.

'Take him down to my cabin,' said Nathan. 'And someone get back into Bute Street to find a doctor.'

As they carried his son down below Nathan could see how badly he had been injured. There were cuts all over his back and even, in some places, inch-long folds of flesh just hanging off his body. He remembered that Sophie had once had a friend killed after an attack like this; small axe heads which often maimed and mutilated rather than destroyed; a torture of such epic cruelty that death was a welcome release. Poor, poor David. His face was as white as a milk bottle and he was barely drawing any breath at all. It was also a tiny miracle that he had managed to get back to the ship since his eyes were swollen and caked with dried blood.

Weeping silently Nathan rearranged the sheets and blankets to make his son a little more comfortable, lifting his head and plumping the pillow. Where had it happened? What time had it happened? Who was he with when . . . He stiffened. Who else would he have been with but Effey, so what had happened to her?

The mother bird's beak ripped into his chest again. He could feel his own blood running hot and warm down into his child, even began feeling cold himself as if he wanted to die. How long, he wondered, was he going to be able to walk in this nightmare? When was he going to wake up and find that it was all right? Not just yet because now the nightmare became even more nightmarish.

Jack came running down asking Nathan to step outside his cabin, almost as if he did not want David to hear what he had to say. 'We followed his trail of blood an' it took us to Spiller's warehouse. I don't know how to say this, Nathan.'

'Say it, just say it.'

'David must have been there with Effey. We found a pile of both their clothes. She's nowhere to be found. We've no evidence of an attack on her. We just can't find her.'

'Jacko, I have to stay here with David but I want you to raise every man to search the Bay for her. If this was an old-time attack – and it looks as though it might be – start asking around Peel Street. She should still be around somewhere, so do anything at all that you can, anything that seems sensible. Oh yes . . . and most important. Knock on the hermit's door in the cell next to the Norwegian Church. He won't speak to you but just tell him I need him most urgently. Not in the morning. Right now.'

After Jacko had hurried away Nathan went down to his little chapel and unlocked the cupboard next to the altar, not even bothering to lock it again as he took out the cup and returned to his cabin with it. He placed the cup on the table just next to David's head and stood there alone with his fingers interlocked prayerfully as he waited for the hermit. The old man came so silently that Nathan did not see him until he was actually standing at his side. His old hand made the sign of the cross in the air above David.

'Thank you for coming,' said Nathan. 'My son is very ill and we must pray for his recovery.'

'You have brought the cup then,' the hermit said, reaching out and picking it up. 'You are right to do so. The cup has a special place in the history of healing. The cup had always afforded health and protection to those who have owned it. The faith of man becomes strong when he drinks of the blood of the cup.'

The hermit took David's bloodied hand and wrapped his fingers around the stem of the cup. Then he took Nathan's hand and placed it on top of David's, keeping them all in place by his own. They looked a curious conjunction, these hands from some three generations – the young and bloodied, the middle-aged and wrinkled, the very old and fleshless.

'Peace to this ship and all that do dwell in her,' the hermit said in his thin, reedy voice. David's eyes opened a fraction and he blinked once. 'O Lord of all grace and blessing, behold, visit and relieve this thy servant David. Look upon him with the eyes of thy mercy.'

Nathan could feel his own hands trembling quite violently as they held David's cold still fingers. Curiously the hermit's hands were also as cold as stone, almost as if they were dead. 'May it be thy good pleasure to restore him to his former health, that so he may live the rest of his life in thy fear and to thy glory.'

Now David's eyes were neither open nor closed. He might

not even have been breathing at all. Nathan squeezed his hands tighter, raising the cup a few inches as a priest might have held up the holy host. David's bloodless cheeks twitched slightly and he gave a sad little sigh of pain.

'It would be good if we could get him to drink some wine out of the cup,' the hermit said.

Nathan found a bottle of wine and, as they prepared the cup with prayer, the ship creaked long and loud. All its companionways were deserted, now that the crew had gone out to search for Effey, with even those on watch chasing down into all parts of the docks hoping that, if they ran long enough, they might just find her.

Hamilton had been standing next to the Neale and West fish wharf, watching the sudden emptying of the ship with his customary reticence. When it looked as though they had all gone, he made his move, walking straight onto the ship with the coolest audacity. Familiar with the layout of its long corridors and tiered decks – he had once owned the ship after all – he went straight to the chapel, immediately finding the door unlocked and the cupboard next to the altar wide open. He lit a match and felt around inside the cupboard, almost as if unable to believe that the cup had gone.

He lit another match and moved around the chapel, crouching and closely examining the altarpiece and small wooden cross before dropping the smouldering match onto the altar itself. He turned sharply on his heels to walk back off the ship. He was just emerging from the first hatchway when he almost came nose to nose with Obe who was doing up his flies and coming out of the lavatory. Hamilton withdrew quickly into the shadows, waiting for the man to leave before climbing up onto the deck, stepping onto the gangplank and hurrying back into the secrecy of the dockland night.

David was almost unable to drink from the cup so they had to pour the thinnest trickle into his mouth. 'The body of our Lord Jesus Christ, which was given for thee, and his blood which was shed for thee, preserve thy body and soul unto everlasting life. Take this in remembrance that Christ died for thee and feed on him in thy heart by faith with thanksgiving.'

They poured another trickle into his mouth, which was half swallowed and half coughed back up, the red wine making his bloodied face drip and run. 'Lord, they whom thou lovest are sick.'

Nathan and the hermit continued working like a pair of doctors in this long surgery of prayer. They laid on hands and they chanted blessings. They also kept trying to get David to drink the Blood of the Lamb and, as they did so, Nathan thought, yet again, of the dream of the dying bird and the blood she had given to revive her young. He thought how life did indeed renew itself in mysterious ways and prayed fervently that, with the Grace of God, David's would be renewed. 'Lord that I may walk! Lord that I may see! Lord that I may hear!'

Up above them the high black crosses of the yardarms scraped at the violet underbelly of the listening night. Everything was straining its ears just now – the warehouses, the moored ships, the dockland cranes – all putting their ears in the direction of *The Solomon*, all waiting patiently and silently for that little sad sigh of pain to become a joyful cry of renewal and release.

# CHAPTER THIRTY

Sophie had never been much of a one to take time making her records – more than a few of them were recorded at the first take in as long as it took to sing them. But they took a very long time over *China Dreams*. They cut four separate versions of the Robin Constable song but still it wasn't right. Robin came back with the strings completely rescored. Maybe they were taking too long, she was beginning to worry, when, after an hour's rehearsal, they decided on yet another arrangement to record in the Hammersmith Palais.

Much of her earlier music had been ragged – and deliberately so – 'hangover songs' she had called them. But now the songs made her smoother and less rasping. There was still the smell of raw jug 'n' bottle sex in her voice; still that impatient smack on her hip to the beat, as if demanding to know precisely when all the fun was going to start. But she was more poised these days; almost more ruminative in the way she worked into her songs.

But *China Dreams* represented an even greater advance in her development, if only because it was like nothing she had ever done before. The song was serene and almost operatic, with clever internal rhymes. It demanded an almost perfect stillness and even a great deal of thought. And, despite the clear youth of the composer, it had a throbbing maturity; the thoughts of a woman in full flower, reflecting on life itself. *Did it last, did it come true or was it just another china dream*? The fine words explained clearly that there was nothing you could know clearly. *And when you walk through the silence of the twilight did it break like another china dream*? And there she was, taking the final curtain, with her dreams at her feet like shattered china.

The young Constable knew exactly what he wanted and pursued it with a dogged tenacity, once even halting her before she had opened her mouth. 'Now not so hard on the third bar, Sophie. Just a whisper there,' she was told with quiet but firm authority.

She submitted to all this since she still had a very good feeling about the song. Her only real regret was that they could not locate Obe to join them. It was sentimental, she knew, but she would have just loved to have had that beautiful old trumpet right there in the middle of it all. She knew too well how much she had been indebted to that old black rascal, even if only because he had once taught her that, when in doubt, she should always listen for the bass line of the piano.

The trouble was the old black rascal was nowhere to be found. She had sent notes, made telephone calls, even sent messengers to his old addresses with the Sons of Africa – who had more addresses than him? – but it had all been fruitless. Finally the word had come back from the Sons that his black ass was on the run from the law again.

They had got in another trumpeter for the session but, somehow, he did not seem to be pitching it quite right. And she would only know it was right when she heard it. She still wanted Obe there; still believed that the record needed him and that he would find that little bit of brass magic which would set it up well and make it sound good. She particularly needed the song to be good now that her career was poised rather precariously somewhere between nowhere and nowhere.

*Did it last, did it come true or was it just another china dream?* The strange thing about the song was that, even as she brought her mouth close to the microphone, eyes closed and hand to the side of her head, trying to find just that right level of feeling, she could actually see the images of loss building inside her mind. She could see Obe's laughing face basking in the sunshine of good music . . . she saw Effey smiling happily and clapping along with the beat . . . and always there was Nathan turning towards her; this great rumpled man who had made such a permanent stake in her heart.

Within the intense melancholy of her music her loved ones were all there and always, for some reason, just *always* intensely happy. Why should this be so? Hadn't she made miserable everyone she had come near? There it was. She was off again . . . aches, regrets, yet more china dreams . . . She sang the words to the empty dance hall where it was being cut directly onto a disc on the great machine in front of her. Empty dance halls are always so sad, she thought, the corners darkened and the glittering ball still.

Her husband, Richard, never once came into her thoughts, not even with any sense of bitterness after he had managed to lose most of her money. He had been sent to her lawyer's office with the promise that, as soon as the divorce came through – on any grounds that were the quickest – he would receive a handsome pay-off – five thousand pounds had been mentioned. Richard was not a china dream; he was a huge lump of unbreakable clay, a big mistake for which she would always have to pay very dearly indeed.

She sang the chorus again; without her realizing it they had already reached the end of the song. As if in a dream she turned around to see the musicians putting down their instruments. The engineer was looking at her.

'Do you know, Sophie, that's about as good as I think we're going to get it,' she heard him say. 'And in my book that's as good as anything Bessie Smith ever sang.'

With the men at his disposal there was probably no one who could have mounted a more thorough search of the Bay than Nathan but, even so, they made no progress in locating Effey.

He had sent his Indian carpenter to ask the Indians in Ninian Road if they had heard anything; the Spanish deck hand had been sent to check out the Spanish community; the Chinese cook went to learn what was new in the gossip in the Chinese laundry . . . Had they heard anything? Did they know of anyone who might have done something like this? There might even be a rather good reward for any information leading to . . .

Nathan took a firm hand in all this, becoming quite remarkably strong again, making swift decisions and even doubling up on the watches. 'This is now the second time we seem to have been attacked and all we can be sure of is that it won't stop here,' he said when he had finished briefing the crew, giving each their particular area to explore. 'We know now that someone managed to get on the ship last night, even going down into my chapel. If we are to protect what we have we must always be on the alert, always ready to challenge strangers. We have put together something fine on this ship. We are becoming a reborn church and there will always be evil forces in the world that will want to destroy anything fine and reborn. Evil only ever leads to failure and death. So be careful and watchful. Let's just try very hard to find our little girl.'

For his own part there was only one man Nathan wanted to talk to. As soon as the crew meeting was over, he left the ship to find Rashed in the Port Said Café in Bute Street.

The Moslem leader stood up and bowed slightly when Nathan walked in, almost as if he was expecting him. 'Ah, Mr Nathan,' he said, waving his hand at a table and indicating that he should sit down. 'It is a great honour for me to have you visit me here. We have all heard much of your work on that ship. You have done very well with her. Very well indeed.'

The two men sat down facing one another before looking down at the tablecloth, as if waiting for the other to speak first. It was the rich smell of the place that Nathan could not quite get used to – a curious mixture of curry and incense. 'There have been some very strange happenings around the Bay lately,' he said finally. 'Last night my son was attacked most savagely and may not live. Also a girl I have come to regard as my daughter was abducted.'

Rashed made no comment, just leaning forward and picking an imaginary piece of fluff off the tablecloth. When he did look up he raised one eyebrow questioningly.

'These attacks seem to be uncomfortably like Moslem attacks,' Nathan went on, feeling very uncertain himself. 'At least they've involved the use of the *kapak gang*. A long time ago you told me that they were the traditional method of defending the purity of the faith.'

Rashed twisted back his lips in disagreement. 'The *kapak gang* has been used for all kinds of things, never just to defend the purity of the faith,' he snapped. 'It has been used for revenge, extortion, reprisal . . . almost anything at all that involves injuring someone very badly. But we have *never* used it.'

'Can you help us in any of this?'

'Who the attackers are, you mean? No. But, Mr Nathan, I can tell you a few things. I can tell you that these men come from the Kabulukam, a small group of thugs based in Birmingham. But the Kabulukam do not attack people for any religious motives. They do it for money and, providing you have the money, they will attack anyone. They would kill even me for money. Even me. Since I've been here, they have come down and attacked five or six people in this area alone.' He spread out his hands on the table and paused. 'But these killers are merely instruments. They do not really matter. What you have got to find out is who hired them.'

'And who might that be?'

'I couldn't be too sure, but I do have a few ideas.'

'Such as?'

Rashed stopped being coy and became brisk, almost businesslike. 'This girl . . . this girl you call Effey. You say she is almost your daughter, but I tell you that she is almost mine too. And not just almost either. She *is* mine. I am this girl Effey's father. And Sophie is not the mother.'

Nathan's head rocked back as if punched. He opened his mouth and closed it again. His eyes narrowed into dark suspicion. How could he tell lies like this? 'I always believed they were alike,' he said lamely before his thoughts drifted away into confusion.

'Yes they are alike and do you know why? They are alike because Effey's mother was Sophie's sister. I was the father. Sophie's sister died giving birth to the child and it was I who put Effey outside her door in that box. It just seemed that Sophie would be the next best mother.'

'Well I never . . . who could have . . .'

'Effey was always my shame, Mr Nathan. Whenever I saw her I was reminded how bad I was. But I always wanted to know where she was, always looked out for her. Even when I repented and went back to the Mosque I always kept an eye on her, even hoped that, one day, she would become a part of the Mosque, and now it has come to this.'

Nathan swallowed on a very dry mouth and stared at the Moslem hard. 'But why are you telling me this now?'

'I am telling you all this because I must now help you. I knew you would come here and decided that now I must help you, even if only for my daughter's sake. I have already inquired among my people. We think we may know the man who is attacking you like this.'

'Yes?'

He became businesslike again. 'If I help you, if we manage to get Effey back, would you give me that cup which you have on your ship? It was once mine, you see, and I would like it back again.'

Nathan ignored the request. 'Rashed, you say this is your daughter we are talking about. If you know where she is you must help us. This is not a time to be looking for bargains.'

'Might you *consider* giving me that cup?'

'Tell me, Rashed. Who is it?'

Rashed shook his head, seeming to understand that he had blundered his opening gambits. In his eagerness to establish his fatherhood of the girl he had lost her as a pawn in the negotiations for the possible return of the cup. Not that he knew much. He turned and flicked his fingers, calling into the kitchen for some tea.

'It's your old friend Mr Alexander Hamilton,' he said, looking up at Nathan balefully. 'Yes, he's back.'

The name passed over Nathan's mind like an eclipse of the sun. So that strange warrior monk was back in town – creating mayhem again. Just what was it that he wanted?

'My people have seen him around and they say that he has murder in his heart. They tell me that he hired the Kabulukam to commit this atrocity against your son. As a Moslem, I should never have revealed any of this. But in attacking your son, he has also attacked my daughter.' He leaned across the table and dropped his voice, as if about to impart a few state secrets. 'You see, Mr Nathan, we are all of us being drawn into this. We Moslems have always stood apart from the rest, stood outside in the rain, if you like, but we can't stand apart now. We must all join together to defeat this man.'

'Yes, but to defeat a man, you must first know where he is. Do you know where to find him?'

In the thin light of the dockland afternoon they both stood outside the mansion in Howard Close, looking up at the gloomy Gothic pile with its barred windows, high blackened walls and gargoyled drains. With its castellated roof, thick mahogany door and spikey line of ferocious railings it might even have been built to withstand the onslaughts of a medieval army. Certainly it seemed to loom high over them like a giant's clenched fist, strong and invincible, telling the pair of them to bring their flying boulders, their battering rams, their siege machines . . . and still they would not be able to get in.

Rashed walked up the steps and peered through the letter box into the darkness of the hallway. Unopened letters lay scattered over the floor; someone had ripped off the brass bell-push. He stood up and came back to stand with Nathan. 'If he is in that house there is no sign of him at all. Some of my people have been keeping an eye on the place but they have seen nothing. But with this man nothing is as it seems. Come, let us take a look around the back.'

They walked down a narrow lane, where the side walls of the house seemed to be even higher than the front, until they came out onto the mud flats and high grassy banks where seagulls stood around – white sentinels gazing out onto the Bristol Channel. A rat wandered past, stopping to look up at them unconcernedly.

Rashed stretched up and his hands felt around the top of the garden wall but thick shards of glass embedded in cement stopped his being able to haul himself up to have a proper look around. But, even from this distant vantage point, it was the same story of desertion and decay. All the curtains were drawn, a few so rotten they had half fallen off their rings. The windows themselves were grimy with cobwebs and dust while, high up around the chimney tops, horseshoe bats had begun to dart around in the twilight, twisting this way and that as they began their long night's search for food.

'We will only find out if he's in there if we actually break in,' said Rashed dusting his hands together. 'The trouble is that I'm not very good at burglary.'

'Perhaps it would just be better if your people kept a watch on it for a while. But, if we must break in, I've got a few on the ship who could probably manage that easily enough.'

The lamplighter was already doing his rounds as they walked back to the docks, passing a man wheeling a pram piled high with scrap metal. A hooter, sudden and loud, announced the end of the afternoon shift in Chris Bailey's dry dock, the men almost immediately streaming out of the yard gates with purposeful strides, anxious to get into a convivial pub, perhaps, or merely to get home and put their feet up next to the fire.

'I would very much like to come to your ship and see your son,' Rashed said. 'I know he is ill but I would like to see him anyway. I heard that my daughter has found her first love and that she is happy. It is difficult to explain why but that made me happy too.'

'I don't see why you should think that difficult to explain. We all have this blood thing. It runs through us all. All religions affirm the value of the family, don't they? I have always thought that they all more or less teach the same set of values.'

Nathan was almost surprised at how easily he had accepted Rashed's explanation of Effey's parenthood. God knows he had pondered on it for long enough; wondered why, if the girl was a foundling, she looked so like her mother and even at times acted like her. But almost as soon as Rashed explained the mystery he saw that it could only be the truth.

But then, continuing with his thoughts, he began asking himself, if Effey married David, then he would end up as one of Rashed's in-laws. Well, that would have been a fine turn of events. He almost smiled at the very thought: man comes to the Bay as an Anglican minister and sails out again as a brother of the Mosque. Somewhere in all this he supposed that there was the will and wonder of God but he could not, for the life of him, see where.

'We should have spoken to one another before,' said Rashed, as if echoing the path of Nathan's thoughts. 'Who knows what we would have found in common?'

'Yes, well, I suppose there would always have been Sophie,'

Nathan mused, not at all sure that he wanted to discuss his tricky love life with the leader of the Mosque.

'Yes, Sophie. Imagine, Mr Nathan. Think of it. Where once she was just a part of our thoughts she is now a part of the thoughts of millions of men. I still think of her a lot – after her sister died there was no one else. I loved them both.'

'What was her sister like?'

'They both had that same Somali dignity – you know, just so-o-o-o graceful, even when they were being drunk and silly. And neither of them were ever afraid of anything or anyone. If anything Sylvie was quieter and more respectable. All she really wanted was to marry, and Sophie only ever wanted to have a good time. As a Moslem I could have married both of them but they would never have put up with that. But in the end I lost them both. Sylvie died and as I became more involved with the Mosque I had to stay away from bad old Sophie.'

Nathan stopped walking and turned to Rashed, his eyes widening in a questioning innocence.

'But I knew soon enough she had eyes for another. You always knew what Sophie was doing – who she wanted. She always wore her heart on her sleeve, never concealed anything. That's really why she has struck a chord with so many men. I knew from what she was saying about you that I had lost her, but what was worse than that was seeing my own daughter becoming a part of your life as well. But don't worry. I accept the inevitability of life and there is no bitterness in my heart. But there is a desire to right a wrong. I want to help you to get Effey back to your ship. She was very happy there. Yes, I do know a lot.'

Darkness threw her cloak over the waters of the dock as they walked back to the ship in silence. The hermit from the Norwegian Church crossed the railway line and scampered away from them, not even looking up as he went about his hermit business. It was odd, Nathan thought, how, in all the years he had known the hermit, they had only ever exchanged the briefest of words and those had always been formally religious in the sense of being blessings or prayers. He did not have one scrap of information about who the hermit really was or where he had come from. But, knowing the Bay, it might even emerge one day that he was related to the old sage – or, even worse, that he owed him a lot of money. Nothing in the Bay surprised him any more. It certainly had never crossed his mind that Rashed might come near to becoming kith and kin.

Rashed began mumbling something very softly – Islamic prayers, perhaps – as they both stood in front of David's bunk. The boy had lost a lot of blood but there was actually the tiniest flare of colour in the cheeks of his ash-white face. Some of the smaller cuts were already healing. Thick crusty sores covered the larger cuts but he still seemed unable to say anything, his only movement being in his eyes which opened ever so slightly and stared up at the bulkhead above.

Nathan noticed that Rashed was no longer looking at David but at the cup sitting on the small table just at the head of the bunk. He said nothing as Rashed picked up the cup, examining it minutely as he turned it over and over.

Just outside the porthole a rowboat was moving across the dock in the darkness. There was the straining creak of the boat itself as the oars pulled into the water, the long hissing of the water falling back into the dock as the oars were lifted up, and then a brief silence before the oars splashed softly back into the water, starting that straining creak of the boat again. The low black shadow of the boat soon passed out of the windjammer's view, just leaving the glimmering footprints of some giant sculling insect in its wake. But these footprints soon disappeared also, leaving the dock waters as still and even and cold as they had been before.

After Rashed had finished examining the cup he kissed it and put it back where he had found it. 'The boy will become well again, have no fear,' he said. 'I owned this cup for years and nothing ever went wrong until it was stolen from me. Everything was a success for me when I owned that cup. I cannot explain it and there is probably no explanation. It may well be a coincidence but I have always believed that there are the mysteries of ice and flame in that cup. You clearly have found something in it. But do not worry, Mr Nathan, I am not asking for its return just now. I acquired the cup by dubious means and I'm sure that you need it more than me. It will protect you in your struggle with this Hamilton. There will be a struggle, you can be sure of that . . . a very great struggle.'

'Yes, well . . .' Nathan looked down at David, almost crying with compassion. He doubted that he had the strength to engage in any prolonged struggle with Hamilton, but his own son would have been strong enough. His own son would have been able to pick up the flame . . .

Later he took Rashed on a tour of the ship, showing him the crew quarters, the bridge and even the lower galley where, even this late in the day, Obe was ensconced in his box still busy peeling potatoes.

Nathan did not introduce them as such but they clearly knew one another. 'Oh yes, I remember you all right,' said Obe prodding his knife at Rashed. 'Boss man at the Mosque, if I remember right. You still the big cheese over there?'

'Not now. Everything has changed a lot since we knew one another. Are you still playing the trumpet?'

'Sure. I have a blow now and then. But more then than now, if you get me. Too busy peeling potatoes, you see, Rashed, sir. These potatoes are pretty damn important an' they've all got to be peeled right. Every damned one of them. Yup. Every one.'

'Rice,' said Rashed amiably. 'You should get them all on rice. You don't have to peel rice.'

'Ah but you do have to pay for it,' Nathan chimed in. 'And rice is far more expensive than potatoes. Obe, come and join us for a cup of tea up in the mess room.'

As they sat down at the round oak table together Nathan realized that, if Rashed was not what he seemed, he might be learning more about the ship than was good for any of them. Yet, as he knew so much anyway, he probably also knew that Obe was on the run. But, no sooner had such doubts entered his mind, than they sauntered out again. Confronted by the same vision of menace and threat it was almost as if Rashed had become one of them. He had already told Obe that they were sure that Hamilton was the nigger . . . uh, beg your pardon . . . the villain in the woodpile. He was also now wondering what strategies they might pursue, both to defend themselves and ensure Effey's safe return.

Lee brought the tea, sitting down to join them. As they were talking together, Nathan, yet again, had the feeling of entering into some corner of a distant dream. Yet this was not the dream of a bleeding and dying bird but something even stranger and stronger than that; something to do with the sacrament of love which draws all to it and nourishes them in their turn and in the same circle. Jacko came to join them, then two of the ship's carpenters – the most unlikely of bedfellows sitting around and discussing how to tackle the figure of hate who was causing so much havoc amongst them.

And just then his dream of love rolled into yet another scene when an even unlikelier bedfellow came to join them in the form of Sophie, just appearing and walking across the room towards him. She was wearing a fur coat and her throat was thick with chunky jewellery. 'I came just as soon as I heard they got my girl,' she said, holding him by the shoulders and kissing him lightly on the forehead. 'I came as fast as I could.'

Nathan just looked up at her, his face registering neither surprise nor pleasure. Quite simply he did not know what to make of Sophie's reappearance at this moment; he did not know if she would be of any use at this juncture, or if she might instead get in the way of their search for Effey.

## CHAPTER THIRTY-ONE

Sophie read Nathan's uncertainty immediately. It was as if she too was entering one of his strange but familiar dreams. And the next face she turned to was Rashed's – and something deep inside her jumped on its hands.

Her eyes moved on to Obe's silent gaze. It was not like the Great Performer to be stuck for words but although she twisted and pulled her lips nothing came out. She felt she had drifted into a distant moment which was not quite of this life; the first moment of the resurrection that Nathan was always talking about, perhaps; those uncertain weeping moments when you would be reunited with all those you had loved the most and then lost.

And here they all were before her – the three main emotional seams of her life – and the future memory of that distant moment still kept rolling through her heart as she felt lost and helpless, almost having forgotten why she had come. She hoped that her lips would stop twisting about and that she could say something sensible. Her eyes fell on the kettle. 'Is anyone going to offer me a cup of tea, then?' was the best she could manage.

Lee poured her a cup of tea. But even after she sat down, her hands were shaking so much she could not pick the cup up. She sat there, staring wretchedly at the tea and occasionally sneaking a quick look at Rashed, Obe or Nathan, almost as if still unable to believe that they were actually there; still uncertain that she had not gone and got herself completely marooned in that future moment.

Surprisingly, the three men were saying nothing either, as if they could think of nothing appropriate to say. Sophie sniffed and, with her mouth slightly open, lowered her head to find something very interesting on the side of her cup. She was becoming very hungry indeed, wishing that she had at least sent Nathan warning that she was on her way. She might even have managed Nathan on her own, but it was very difficult indeed with the others present. What had they been saying about her? How many lies had they discovered she had told them? Had they been talking about her at all?

She bit her lip hard when she remembered the real purpose of her visit; how she had just been sitting there thinking shallowly of herself. She coughed to clear her throat. 'Is there any news about Effey?' she asked, wrapping both her hands around her warm cup as if needing something to hang on to.

When there was no immediate reply she looked up and caught Nathan sneaking a conspiratorial glance at Rashed. She knew then that she was not going to be told the full story – whatever the full story was. Why did people always need to tell lies when the truth was often just as difficult to cope with?

'Well don't speak all at once. Is there any news?' she repeated.

Nathan lifted his hands. 'Nothing, nothing at all. We have all our men out searching the Bay. Everyone has been told to pass on the message that we are anxious for news of our girl.'

She nodded and swallowed. 'Have you told the police?'

'No. We decided that, under the peculiar circumstances of the Bay, we had better resources of our own. We do not, anyway, put much faith in the police around here.'

'And how is David?'

'He's not at all well, but he may pull through.'

She looked directly at Rashed. 'Yes, those men from the Kabulukam certainly do know how to do their job, don't they?'

Rashed's eyes dropped and he moved around on his chair uncomfortably. 'I hope you are not suggesting . . .'

'But Sophie, how do you know about the Kabulukam?' interrupted Nathan. 'You never told me anything about them.'

'They killed my best friend Betty, you may remember. Over the years I've learned a lot about these gentlemen. I've made it my business to find out all about them since I've never forgotten Betty. Never. And do you know what is the most interesting thing about them? They only ever do it for money. They only ever kill just for money – they would kill you, you and you, if I gave them enough money. Today, as soon as I learned about this, I sent a man to Birmingham to offer them even more money – a lot more money – to kill the man who did this. And do you know what they did? They refused. They even refused to tell me his name. Do we have any idea who this man is?'

'Yes, yes we do.'

Half an hour later they went back, all five of them, and stood silently on the cobblestones of Howard Close looking up at the high walls of the same gloomy Victorian mansion that Rashed and Nathan had been looking up at only a few hours earlier. The bats were darting around in the glowering moonlight, occasionally shooting past their heads with tiny agitated shrieks.

'Just look at it,' said Sophie. 'To think I used to clean that house. The best thing you could do with it now would be to burn it down.'

'I don't suppose there could be anyone home, could there?' asked Obe.

'There were no signs of life when we had a look around earlier,' said Nathan. 'You can see by the dust on the front door that it hasn't been opened for an age. There would have been palm-prints or fingerprints.'

They all stood whispering together behind cupped hands, a group of anarchists trying to decide the best place to fling the bomb.

'We checked the back,' said Rashed. 'There's no way out to the mud flats from there.'

'There's another door on the side,' Sophie suggested. 'He

liked to use that sometimes to avoid the spotlight. Let's have a look at that.'

They huddled together outside the side door in the lane as Nathan took out a torch, lifting its beam up and down the door but finding no telltale prints on that either. Sophie took the torch off him and went down on her knees, shining the beam through the letterbox, but all she could see was the beam of her torch dancing in the cobwebs and dust, motes that flashed and sparkled as the torch beam turned one way and another. There was an old coat hung up on the stand in the hallway – the brass buttons caught the light.

'The best thing we can do is come back in the morning with an axe or something to break it in,' said Nathan as Sophie stood up. 'We're not going to get very far in this dark.'

They had walked out in front of the house again and were standing looking up at it when, from somewhere distant, there came the sounds of footsteps on the cobblestones. Sophie turned and squinted as she saw a dark figure standing in the green lamplight at the entrance to the Close. She thought it might be a patrolling policeman but, when he made no move towards them – or away – she decided that he might be someone else. She nudged Obe. 'I think we've got a visitor.'

They all turned to face the sentinel in the shadows, just the vapour of his warm breath puffing slightly around his lips. The lamplight was not strong enough to reveal any of his features but his size was large and menacing enough. 'It is simple enough,' he called out. 'You give me the cup and I will give you the girl.'

'If that's all you want you can have it,' Nathan called back unhesitatingly. 'Where will we find you?'

'Do not worry. I will find *you*,' the man replied, turning around and hurrying away in the night.

It was Sophie who broke the ranks first, chasing up to the entrance of the Close and finding the surrounding streets as empty and cold as the very night. 'You touch my girl and I'll get you, you great bastard,' she shouted vainly and uselessly down the sleeping terraces. 'You hear me? Touch one hair of her head and I'll fix you for good, you see if I don't.'

Odd windows started going up along the terraces with heads poking out muttering dire threats of 'Shut it!' or 'You'll wake the bleedin' baby!'

Sophie was so beside herself she even began shouting back at them until Nathan put an arm around her. She broke down and began crying inconsolably. 'Come on now, Sophie. At least we now know that he's got our Effey.'

'I am not so sure,' Rashed interrupted. 'Because I am not at all convinced that was Hamilton.'

'No, neither am I,' Sophie sniffed. 'It didn't sound like his voice.'

After they had all returned to the windjammer Nathan went down to check on David, finding him, as usual, just looking upwards. He smoothed his son's forehead before picking up the cup and taking it back up to the mess with him, placing it in the middle of the table. 'This is what all the fuss is about. One small cup made of pewter.'

'For as long as I can remember this cup has been in the middle of something or other,' said Sophie, almost exasperated. 'Why does everything always come back to one sodding cup?'

'Everything comes back to the cup because the cup is where everything started,' said Rashed.

'And what's that supposed to mean?' Sophie asked, glaring at Rashed hard.

'It means that there's more to this cup than any of us can guess,' said Obe, picking it up and holding it aloft in his upturned hands. 'I had this cup once and things went real well. It don't look nothing but . . .' he put it back in the middle of the table, 'it's a blessing of a kind. Certainly that Hamilton has been trying hard enough to get it.'

Nathan gave the top of his bald head a small stroke. 'Which is why I am very reluctant to hand it over – particularly to him.'

'If it was him.'

'If it *was* him.'

Now they were all eyeing the cup in silence and Sophie found herself getting a little impatient with it all, not least because she had never had any time for such hocus-pocus. Always a girl of the firmest basics, she believed a cup was something you drank out of and that was that. If it came to any bargaining she hoped that Nathan would hand over the cup without any fuss. As she made herself ready for bed in Nathan's bunk she could not imagine anything in the world being worth the life of her daughter.

She had a savage dream of the charnel house where all those she loved lay dead or dying, their bodies all piled up on canal barges as she wandered the towpath, looking down on them. What she could not understand was why she was not with them, and why there was this loud hollow knocking on the side of her head. All at once a lot of doors began flying open, whereupon a huge ball of flame came spinning across the sea towards her, making even the dead cry out in fear as Hamilton whirled around and around, dervish-like, at the very centre of the fiery ball, making it grow even bigger and yet more destructive as it came charging towards her, scorching her cheeks, her nose . . . oh dear God, her *eyelashes*!

She came plummeting up out of the nightmare with a fearful cry that stayed trapped within her chest, sweat cutting through her skin, short of breath, as she lay back blinking furiously, listening to an empty bottle which was floating upside down on the waters of the dock outside, its thick base clinking against the ship's hull.

Now she was fully awake and did not even want to get back to sleep, afraid that the nightmare might return. What she really wanted was for Nathan to lower himself between her legs and help her to get rid of all this screaming tension. But the holy bastard had shown no inclination to do that, particularly on his holy ship, nursing his holy cup.

She unbuttoned her fur coat, lifted her dress and shoved both her hands down into her panties, the tips of her fingers still shaking from her nightmare as she felt around the lips of her vagina, carefully parting them, and locating her clitoris, already achingly hard and making her shiver as she touched it, smoothed it, touched it again, rubbed the side of her hand up and down it before clamping both hands on top of one another and pressing up and down rhythmically and quickly until something warm, but not terribly happy, went eddying around and around inside her belly before falling away quickly into dim echoes.

She moved onto her side and back again, feeling even more morose now, wondering why she ever bothered with that. It was very difficult even to start thinking that she was famous when she did that. Dogs did that on the legs of unhappy small boys. She doubted that the dogs got much out of it either. Oh Lord, was there never any release from all this misery? Now all she wanted was a stiff drink of something very strong indeed.

The base of the upturned bottle was still knocking on the ship's hull as she twisted one way and turned the other. She thought of her Effey again – that dear sweet girl who had never done any harm to anyone – and longed to just hold her, to sit around some fire, drink tea and have a good laugh together. She also wondered about David whom, maddeningly, she had not yet seen.

Hamilton's house loomed in another corner of her mind and her hand slid down between her legs again, almost as if to give herself reassurance. She saw the barred windows and the great mahogany door and then, in a series of twinkles, she saw something else. She saw the beam of her torchlight twinkle in the golden buttons of the coat hanging in the side hall. The twinkles came back into her mind, more glitteringly ferocious now and she sat up on her bunk with a spear of insight ripping down inside her so hard it almost made her vomit. Brass buttons had to be cleaned almost weekly to retain their shine. She had cleaned enough of them for him in her time.

Hamilton was almost certainly inside that house.

Obe had fallen asleep on the table in the mess room and, down in his chapel, Nathan was on his knees, fingers interlocked and meditating in front of his cup. Some sturdy snoring was rumbling down the ship's corridors while, up on the bridge, the two men on watch jigged around to keep warm.

All around them a grey dawn was growing, as mordant as an executioner's stare. Seagulls swooped down through the dripping greys and misty blacks as the whole universe took on the fragility of a bubble, neither light nor dark, neither fish nor fowl, just an undecided stillness which half whispered that, just for this morning, the dawn might not break after all and God was finally going to usher in a new Age of Darkness.

All along Bute Street the first trams of the morning were clattering down to the Pier Head, disgorging the early shift workers and office cleaners. This was always the busiest time of day in the docks, with the black shapes of people moving in and out, all engaged in mysterious strategies for survival. The footsteps told of work that had finished and work that was about to start. Some were still trying to bring themselves awake with a good cough and a Woodbine. Others stared red-eyed into evil hangovers, greeting one another with sullen grunts. The merry ping of workmen clocking on shot out into the darkness like scattering money. Just near the entrance of the dock the iron-clad wheels of a handcart made a hell of a noise as they clattered over the silvery slits of the railway lines – a noise even more hellish if you were suffering from last night's drinking.

The quay lights were still on, splashed over the black acres of the docks in orange pools. A few starlings were clearing their throats on top of the Neale and West fish wharf, warming up in readiness for the dawn chorus. Down in the Alexandra dock two prostitutes slipped off a cargo boat, their faces drawn with exhaustion and smudged makeup as they walked over to the other exit from the dock in Portmanmoor Road.

Yet none in that seatown dawn could even have guessed that one of the most famous singers in the country was walking out with the boys from the night-shift. They might have remarked on her fur coat had they noticed it, but, in the dark, it could even have been a donkey jacket. She might have been another prostitute come to the end of *her* nightshift as, with head down and shoulders hunched, she made her way past the policeman on the dock gate and headed back to Howard Close.

It was still dark enough for her to stay well concealed as she worked a piece of wire through the letterbox of the side entrance to Hamilton's house. This simple method had worked well enough when she had been cleaning there and had forgotten her keys and, lo, even all these years later, it worked again. She gave the wire a gentle tug and the door opened with a dull click.

She stepped inside the house, closing the door behind her and keeping her back to it. She stood there, adrenalin-charged, as she took a torch out of her pocket and flashed it all around her. The coats were still there and those brass buttons had, indeed, been cleaned recently. But, that apart, there was no sign of any life at all, just thick layers of dust, and spiders, frightened by the torchlight, hurrying deep into dark holes where they could watch the proceedings in peace.

She followed the corridor until she came into the kitchen,

again just standing inside the door and stroking the walls with her torch beam. Everything had been taken off the shelves and out of the cupboards. There was just the slow dripping of a tap into a stone sink. Underneath the sink her torch spotlighted the thin grinning skeleton of a mouse lying in a trap. Just what was he grinning about?

She walked out into the wood-panelled hallway, turning and turning again as she looked up the stairs which, bizarrely, she saw herself cleaning. She even remembered the smell of the polish. It was how you returned to old scenes . . . who would have thought . . . ? She climbed the stairs to the first landing, turning the knobs on the doors which, despite their thickness, were so perfectly hung they swung open easily and with barely a squeak of the hinges.

But again, except for a couple of wooden boxes the rooms were empty, stripped of all those strange artefacts of war that Hamilton had loved so much. Whatever had happened to the suits of armour . . . and that great sword whose edge she had always liked to touch with her finger to see how sharp it was . . . ? Small avalanches of plaster had fallen off the wall. In one corner some weeds seemed to be growing out of the very floorboards. Light was beginning to stream through the windows now and she no longer needed her torch, which she put back into her pocket, crossing the room and looking down into the Close where a lone black cat was taking an early morning stroll across the cobblestones.

Had she been looking out of the rear of the house she would have seen a sandhopper chugging out onto the Cardiff roads and a Norwegian timber boat making its way down the Bristol Channel. She would also have seen the tide surging in great silvery hoops towards the cliffs of Penarth. Nearer still, she would have seen Hamilton following a path along the mudflats, silver-topped cane in hand and walking so fast he might almost have been running. Birds walked away from him as he surged over ridge after ridge, his face set in the blackest frown. He took no notice of the birds, nor of anything else as he continued his furious walk.

He glanced up at the dull coin of the sun trying, but failing, to break through the thick cloud. The air was so damp the morning might even be getting in the mood for rain. But there was to be no rain, nor indeed any sun for the good folk of the Bay this morning.

As more light came into the rooms Sophie began to relax. It was becoming more and more obvious – brass buttons notwithstanding – that there was no one here at all. She stood on the next landing when there was a sound and she cocked her head to one side to listen to it carefully. It was a sort of quiet fluttering, amplified by the huge emptiness of the stairwell. She stepped over a scattering of rubble and took the stairs to the top floor where she stopped outside the door of Hamilton's old work room, listening to that strange fluttering again. She remembered that the work room had no windows so she took out her torch again, opening the door as quietly as she could and screaming out loud when she saw what was inside. There was a hole in the roof and, next to it, hanging upside down off a rafter, a huge furry pendant of horseshoe bats. With their little heads and eyes poking in all directions, all had been more or less peaceably settling down to sleep together after a night of foraging when they were disturbed by a shaft of alien golden light. Erupting into a panicking swarm of wings, flying one way and another, some went back out of the roof and others hurtled past Sophie, leaving a slipstream of tiny squeals and fluttering wings in their wake.

She dropped her torch, screaming, and covered her face with her hands, turning to one side and shuddering, hoping that none of them would get in her hair, since the story told to her when she was a little girl had it that you had to get scissors and cut your hair off before you could get them out again. Jumping down the stairs two at a time, pausing only to edge carefully past a few of the bats who had come to rest on the stair-rails, she made her way to the door. With their bashed-in noses and staring brown eyes she had no doubt at all that bats were every bit as vicious as they looked and she was not taking any chances.

It really was something of an anticlimax then when she got to the bottom of the stairs and found herself face to face with Hamilton. A bat was leaping around near his feet and he looked down at it before looking up at her again.

'Ah, the famous singer,' he said with the faintest of sneers. 'Have you come to ask for your cleaning job back?'

'No, I've come to find my daughter,' she replied, feeling her body go as stiff as a plank as she put her hands down into her coat pockets.

He again looked down at the bat leaping around on the floor.

'That colony of bats has probably been there for five years. Now that you have disturbed them they will all be out today looking around for a new home. Five years' work – all finished just like that.'

'I'm very sorry about that, I'm sure, but, just for the moment, tell me where my daughter is.'

'What if I told you that I did not know where your daughter was?'

'I'd call you a liar.' She tool a silver Beretta out of her pocket and pointed its compelling snout directly at Hamilton's heart, watching the cane in his hand carefully. 'And just to make sure, I'd shoot a hole straight through you. That's what I'd do.'

Hamilton looked down at her gun and up into her eyes. Then he did something that she had never, ever seen him do before. He *smiled*.

'If you shoot me you will never find out where your daughter is. If you shoot me she will die.'

Even as he announced this shocking news Sophie's thoughts began spilling one way and another, trying to work out quite what he was saying and asking herself if he could possibly mean it.

'Yes, I do mean it. Shoot me and you will also shoot your daughter.'

Her eyes quivered with mounting panic. Even as his words tumbled through her mind, he acted with the speed of a striking cobra, stepping to one side, pulling a sword out of his silver-topped cane and slashing it down on the hand holding the gun. The weapon made an alarming noise as it crashed onto the bare floorboards.

'It is not very nice to threaten me like this,' he muttered, making the air swish as he slashed the sword down again, cutting deep into her dithering wrist with a surgical precision. 'I am not prepared to be threatened like this. I am so very *tired* of being annoyed.'

# CHAPTER THIRTY-TWO

The following morning Nathan did not know what to make of Sophie's disappearance and wondered if she had merely decided that she'd had enough and gone back to London. She was always capable of doing anything at all though his instincts told him that she was not the kind of woman to run away from a difficult situation – particularly when Effey's life was at stake. But where was she?

It had been bad enough worrying about Effey, but now he was starting to feel quite ill worrying about Sophie too. She could be so maddening, often without really trying. But he had to admit that he did care for her; he cared for her infuriatingly and deeply and almost began feeling guilty that he had let her sleep on her own. If he was not such a pious prude, worried about his soul, he could have given her some bodily comfort, he lectured himself. He could, at the very least, have held her for a while.

For most of the morning there seemed to be a constant stream of people running to and from the ship but they all had disappointingly little to report. Finally, in pure frustration, since there seemed to be little else he could do, Nathan asked Obe and Rashed to join him on a tour of the pubs and shebeens of Bute Street, if only to find out if she had simply found a quiet corner of a bar where she was drowning her sorrows.

It was almost the first time for a long while that Nathan had been tempted to drown his own sorrows in a similar manner but, in the event, he managed to resist, while Obe had the odd half-pint, spending a lot of his time keeping his face covered in case he was spotted by the law. They asked the same question in every bar: had anyone seen anything of Sophie James? *Oh yeah, heard she was around. No, haven't seen her. You mean that Sophie James? She's back down here, is she?*

It soon became clear that it was a thoroughly pointless operation since Sophie, had she been around, would have attracted a mob the size of a football crowd, visible from the other side of the Bristol Channel. Women like Sophie were not like the Arabs who simply folded up their tents and disappeared into the sand. Women like Sophie stood out wherever they were. So where was she?

Nathan was surprised, however, at how much comfort he took from the company of Rashed and Obe, if only because they spoke about Sophie with such understanding and insight. Both of them seem to have an endless fund of stories concerning the atrocities she had committed over the years and, at times, all three of them managed to sound like prison officers out looking for their favourite escapee. All of them had a sort of love for her, Nathan supposed, though in Obé's case it was probably as much loyalty as love.

The afternoon light was breaking up when the three of them finally decided to call it a day and return to the windjammer. They were not so jokey now, rather silent and even sullen, walking down through the docks with hands in pockets and giving only an occasional sniff or cough. It was dark with the tawny smell of a wood fire riding on the breeze when they reached the ship, going up onto the bridge to find out if there had been any news.

All their faces turned at the same time when a voice called out from the deep shadows around the warehouses. 'I have got the mother and the daughter. Just give me the cup and you can take them back safely.'

As Hamilton spoke Nathan could actually feel the hairs on his neck standing up and crawling around. He knew who it was and his lips opened and closed as he looked at Rashed and Obe but he just could not think of anything to say.

'Don't give it to him, Dad.' Nathan turned to see that David was clearly feeling well enough to get up out of his bunk. 'Tell him you'll give it to him if you can stuff it straight up his arse.'

The whole group of them were now staring into the mazey phosphorescent darkness around the warehouses, wondering what to do. Wisps of steam drifted past the cranes and there was still that smell of a wood fire. With so many warehouses crowded around it was rather difficult to tell where Hamilton's voice was coming from. Warehouses had ways of playing acoustic tricks; a point which may not have been lost on Hamilton who now repeated his demand.

'So are you going to give me that cup?'

'There's enough of us,' Obe mumbled quietly. 'Let's just rush him an' beat the shit out of him 'til he tells us where the girls are. Me, I'd love to batter the swine.'

Nathan was still trying to frame a proper response when everything was pre-empted by David who picked up a belaying pin and ran down the gangplank, rushing directly at the spot where Hamilton may or may not have been standing. Instinctively Nathan began running after his son, banging his shoulders against Obe who had just beaten Rashed to the gangplank.

At this point everything turned into a panting confusion with the man on the watch ringing the alarm bell and everyone chasing around the docks, this way and that, like headless chickens. Nathan was running directly behind David when he tripped over a mooring rope, plummeting himself forward, gashing his elbow and giving himself a nasty crack on the forehead.

Rashed steamed off in another direction altogether, hoping to cut off any escape route from the rear of the warehouse while Obe went off in the other, frantically looking around for something, anything, which he could use as a weapon. Already others were running off the ship and joining in the hunt.

Nathan shook the slight concussion out of his brain and went running down an alleyway, bringing him out into the next dock where a grain ship was moored and two sailors were leaning on the ship's rail, having a quiet smoke. He ran the length of the warehouse dodging and ducking behind the legs of the great cranes but, not only could he not find Hamilton, he could not find David either. He turned and turned again – the grain ship, the sky and the warehouses, all swirling around him like some monstrous nightmare in which he become irretrievably bogged down. If only he had some kind of torch or something.

Now yet more of the crew were running up and down the quays, pointing in different directions while shouting the most general and meaningless orders to one another. Nathan looked up at the two seamen leaning on the ship's rail, holding his hands apart in a gesture of despair before beginning to walk back. He doubted that they would ever catch a man like Hamilton in the darkness. It was almost as if he came alive in the dark; that, in that region of shadows, he was stronger than all of them. Nathan had no feeling that he was up against anyone human at all. This was spirit that he was grappling with; this man was a fallen archangel who had clambered straight out of hell.

The quays were still full of panic and alarmed shouts when Nathan passed an empty and derelict warehouse. He stepped inside it, looking up and around at the high wooden floors and dark loft spaces, decided that, if Hamilton was concealed there, it would take them all week to search the place. He went further into the warehouse until he stopped next to a set of giant weighing scales. Now he could not even hear the shouts coming from outside, just the stuttering stab of his own frightened heart.

'If you come up against me you will lose all and die.'

It was Hamilton again, but talking so quietly now that it was almost a whisper, his words carrying clearly across the warehouse. Nathan did not look up or around but, even if he had, he could not have seen the ship owner's scowling features concealed in the secrecy of deep darkness.

'Do not put the lives of those women in jeopardy,' Hamilton continued. 'I have just wounded the black trumpeter and do not want to injure anyone else. Everyone wants to be a hero these days but there is nothing heroic or victorious about death. Death is just death. You are a religious man who wants to live more abundantly so just give me the cup and I will return the women. I repeat. Do not go up against me or you will lose. Let there be no extravagant behaviour. I am so very tired of extravagant behaviour. Bring the cup to my house in Howard Close tonight. Then I will return the women. Say nothing of this to anyone. Just nod if you agree. Good.'

Nathan walked slowly out of the warehouse, returning to the ship just in time to see David and Rashed carrying Obe up the gangplank, blood running furiously from his shoulder. Obe just looked at Nathan as if in total despair, if not downright disbelief, in what they were up against. *Just who was this man?* Nathan followed the trail of blood up the gangplank wondering how much more would be spilled before all these issues were finally resolved. But he really did want an end to it all now; he really did want an end to all this.

He looked up at the high crucifix shapes of the yardarms and the crisscrossing netting of the standing rigging. He walked on down towards the bowsprit, feeling explosively edgy as new ideas jostled for his attention until, finally, he just stood there on the ship's prow holding his bruised forehead tight between thumb and forefinger. He thought of that man high up on his own cross and sent up a prayer asking God what he should do now.

He tried to keep his mind clear of everything as he waited for some faint inklings of light which sometimes came with prayer – but often didn't – when, perfectly and vividly, the face of the holy hermit formed in his mind.

Down on the quay his men were drifting back, looking up at him and shaking their heads, telling him that they had been unsuccessful in their hunt for the mad beast who was creating such murderous havoc in their midst. He waved them back on board, as if to reassure them that, just for now, it did not matter; that they would clearly get him another time. But it was all public posture, he knew. He had no conviction at all that he would ever see Sophie and Effey again, let alone beat Hamilton at anything. All he really knew was that he would have to see the holy hermit.

Meanwhile, down on the altar of Hamilton's chapel, in the basement of his house in Howard Close, the Queen of Breaking Hearts decided that she had never experienced such discomfort and pain.

The ropes at least had the effect of acting as a tourniquet, staunching the flow of blood from her badly gashed right wrist. It was being gagged that was the worst of all, making every breath a struggle, particularly as the gag was tight against her nostrils as well. She wondered why he had not killed her and been done with it. She certainly felt very close to death.

Her only small crumb of comfort came from the fact that Effey was lying next to her and, from time to time, they had even been able to look into one another's eyes and have a silent conversation about how they loved one another and how they really should have loved one another more. Indeed, the depth of thoughts and feelings they did manage to convey to one another through their eyes and eyebrows in the half-light was quite extraordinary. In an odd sort of way their love for one another almost made the prospect of death welcome. To die alone and unloved really would have been an unendurable hell,Sophie thought. Hell was where love was impossible. Yes, all of us really were prisoners of love. Nothing else mattered. Nothing.

She sighed and felt bilious again. She had to use all her training as a singer to concentrate hard on breathing properly, feeling so tense that she knew she was in danger of being sick. Her mind swam with terror at the very thought of it. She could not even start thinking what would happen if she was sick while gagged like this.

The hermit received Nathan and David graciously in his cell at the back of the Norwegian Church, inviting them to sit down on a small bench and listening to the full story without making any comment or sound.

The cell was a small, stifling place made of corrugated iron, cold in winter and boiling hot in the summer. There was barely enough room for the hermit to move around and it became impossibly cramped with the three of them. Nathan finished his tale, the hermit nodded understandingly before swivelling around and kneeling at the altar.

Nathan admired the old man's hands; there must have been a good century of prayer in those old hands. The fingers looked so strong and yet so gentle. Those were hands which had reached right into the heart of the mystery of God.

David coughed loudly and theatrically, reminding the hermit that they were still there, but Nathan touched him softly on the knee, telling him to be patient. Good prayer was always a matter of good timing, he believed. It was all a matter of making the right connections; of joining up the right thoughts with the right needs; of seeking out the light which may or may not be shining. Prayer was the oven in which any plan must be carefully cooked and made right. One thing you could never do with prayer was to hurry it.

When the hermit finally spoke he did so in a voice so soft and heavily accented they both had to lean forward and strain their ears to catch what he was saying. 'It is always difficult to deal with the terms of myth,' he began. 'Myth is always a fiction with supernatural characters. But in all this, it has become a reality with the ordinary people of the area. In the way this man is behaving, in his desire for your cup, he is following in the footsteps of myth. This man has become a protagonist of myth. He is acting out a role.'

'So where does this leave us?' Nathan asked. 'Do we, too, become a part of the myth or do we just give him the cup or what?'

'No.' The hermit raised his hand quickly in an animated warning. 'That would be very wrong. If you gave him the cup it would only make him more powerful. That is why he wants it so badly. If he wants to act out a mythic role then you must do so too. The terms of the myth say, quite clearly, that you must take up the lance.'

The lance? Nathan's eyes glanced at David and he began to feel old and weak, certainly not strong enough for any hand-to-hand combat like that. He remembered that, unlike Hamilton, Edward Gurney had been young and strong but he had been defeated nevertheless. He doubted that even his own son would fare any better.

'There are ways you can make yourself strong enough for the lance,' the hermit said, reading Nathan's doubts. 'You can prepare yourself in the terms of the same myth. The knights of old were always dead and blind beneath the weight of their sins. "When the enemy knew the fever of lusts he entered wholly into you and drove out Him who had lodged in you for so long."

'If you want to hold up your head and stalk about like the very lion you must confess all your sins and take on the whole holy armour of God. You must cross yourself and say "Gracious Lord come to the aid of Thy newly-won knight." You must take communion from the cup and you must take his sword and dispose of it in the water. Do all these things and you will become a priest of the sun.'

Nathan rested his hand on David's knee. 'And the lance?'

'I have the lance here. I have kept it beneath the altar of the Norwegian Church for all the years I have been here. People are always prepared in myth and I have been preparing for this in all my years in the dockland. You see it was just for this that I was first sent here. We are all of us moving along strange, wonderful paths and none more wonderful and strange than yours, Nathan, our new priest of the sun.'

It became so very warm for that time of year, that tense, sweating night in the Bay. Thunder rumbled distantly and forks of lightning flickered over the castle. The very air became so stuffy and difficult to breathe that windows were raised a few inches along the terraces. But even that ploy gave the people little release from the night's stuffiness. Many of them stood at their windows in their underwear, looking down into the strangely deserted streets. On occasion a figure hurried across one of the streets or ran around a street corner, the sounds of their footsteps clattering emptily until they disappeared again.

Had anyone been able to cruise these deserted streets – an angel out on patrol perhaps – his main impression would have been of an unreal silence which, in places, was almost mountainous. This silence seemed to hold the Salvation Army hostel in its very arms, moving down past the Greek Orthodox church and over the white dome of the Mosque, brushing up against the doors of the cafés and shebeens of Bute Street before whirling down slowly around the Shipping Exchange.

The only place where there was any movement was on the Glamorganshire Ship Canal. Gas from the sewage had come alight; whole sections of the water were filamenting with the tiny red flames of St Elmo's fire. On other parts of the canal, frothy green circles of fire raced and broke into one another. When the green circles went spinning into the red flames everything erupted into stammering flashes of yellow.

But even this spectacular movement was as quiet as the very grave; a part of the silence of the night, with not so much as a faint hiss or the tiniest crackle.

The silence reigned in Howard Close too. But now all the lights in the mansion had been turned on and, with the front door left open, Hamilton was pacing around from room to room, sometimes coming down to stand in the front porch, hands on hips, his dark frame swathed in brilliant shafts of light as he waited, with mounting impatience, for what he regarded as his. The black beast was on the ramparts, the smell of holy blood in his nostrils.

Over in the towering coke ovens and smelting shops of the East Moors steelworks, on the other side of the dock, molten slag, which had risen to the surface of the iron, was being tapped off into giant ladles on railway trucks. The slag bubbled and spat with a hellish fury as the small locomotive groaned and clanked, an occasional burst of steam hissing from its mechanical underbelly.

The driver, Charles Bethell, shunted the train a few yards further up the line, turning and squinting as yet another of the ladles was filled with the molten slag. On the track on the other side of him were the torpedoes for the refined iron but, for this shift anyway, Bethell was the slag man, about to take it all off to dump into the sea.

By the time the fourth ladle had been filled a crust was already beginning to form on the first and second ladles. It was now time to move before the whole load solidified. With an impatient spinning of the wheels, the steam drove into the pistons and the locomotive began shuffling off down past the blast furnaces and the ingot stripping bays of the steelworks.

Hamilton stood in the porchway and caught his breath when he saw Nathan walking across the cobblestones towards him. Nathan was holding the cup in both hands. Ten yards from the house, he stood stock still.

Hamilton noticed that there seemed to be a lot of people moving around at the entrance to the Close. But if he was worried about them, he did not show it. 'Just put the cup down there,' he called out. 'Put it right down there and leave.'

'I want to see the women first. Show me the women and show me they are safe and I will do as you say.'

Hamilton looked up to see yet more people swarming around the entrance to the Close. 'I am a man of old times trying to find his way into the new times. I am a man of honour. I would never hurt a woman for no good reason. If you want to see them so much, I will show them to you.'

He turned and walked back into the house, disappearing down some stairs in the hallway. With loud cracks the wooden shutters in the basement windows were opened, one by one, and Nathan took a few steps forward to peer down through the railings.

The basement chapel was flooded by a brilliant yellow light. By stooping down slightly, he could just about make out the figures of Effey and Sophie tied up, in a wretched tormented state, on the altar. Just who was this maniac? He wanted to run in and knock him senseless but this was no time to get hot-headed. He put the cup down on the ground, turning and indicating to his people to move forward with a brief wave of his hand.

Huge snooker balls of thunder began cannoning over some distant baulk line in the sky as the Close filled up with people. Hamilton re-emerged at the door. 'Just give me the cup and the women can go free.'

'No,' Nathan replied. 'You are going to have to fight us all for this cup. It belongs to all of us.'

'Do you think that all of you could beat *me*?' He shook his head at the very thought of it, going back into the house before returning and holding his great double-edged sword aloft. 'I could stand on this doorstep and chop a hundred of you down at the legs before you could even get near me.' He sliced the air twice with his sword by way of demonstration. 'The knights of old welcomed enemies. The more there were the happier they became. It was their pleasure to die in a fight – it was all that mattered. But . . . but, be sure that your women will also die.'

'Come and die in a fight with me.'

'*You*? What could you do?'

Nathan turned and took a sword off Rashed, holding it up to his forehead before lowering it slowly, letting its tip rest next to the cup. The people who had moved in close behind Nathan moved away again, making a huge circle about thirty feet in circumference. There were about two hundred of them, faces that were black and yellow, brown and white, swarthy and fair . . . all of them as watchful and thoughtful as people sitting in a dentist's waiting room.

Hamilton stood glaring at them before fixing his eyes on Nathan again. He took two aggressive strides down his front steps to show that he was not in the slightest bit afraid of any one of them. 'Some people just long to get hurt,' he called. 'Some people just want to die. You are one of those men of God, aren't you? As I told you once before, death is only death. There is nothing beyond it, as you are going to find out very soon now.'

He had taken another three steps forward, holding his sword out in front of him, when there came a dart of apprehension on his face. His eyes caught something swishing and spinning in the air over his head. He felt something brushing up against the side of his neck then something else rubbing up against his arm. He raised his sword slightly higher, looking around him and seeing that men were spinning lassoos in the air which were all falling down and around him. More ropes fell over him and he looked down at the cup at Nathan's feet before making a wild hiss of fury and trying to cut the ropes with his sword.

But the more he cut the more lassoos came spinning down around him. One caught his sword and jerked it out of his hands. Now Hamilton was a trussed and maddened bull as more ropes took a purchase on him. Whenever he tried to pull one way the ropes pulled him in another, as if Hamilton were the hub of a whirling compass of men and ropes, all circling around him slowly, checking his every movement. Yet even in all this, Hamilton managed to retain his dignity, sometimes trying one of the ropes to see if it would give but not complaining at all. 'You will pay for this foolishness,' he snarled at Nathan.

'No. It is time for *you* to pay and pay in full. David, give me the lance.'

Once out of the gates of East Moors and past the low spines of slag heaps and mountains of twisted scrap iron, Bethell braked his locomotive to a halt on the foreshore of the sea. Walking behind the wagons, he flicked the levers, which operated the chains, which tipped the mechanisms, which overturned the ladles into the white-capped waves of the Bristol Channel.

Even though shielded by his armour-plated cab Bethell still ducked when the hot slag hit the cold sea. Lumps rocketed this way and that as the inimical elements battled and exploded against one another. There were hideous cracks and furious pillars of steam rising to almost two hundred feet. A screaming wall of heat rushed outwards in search of something to burn. But the greatest and most wonderful glory of it all, and one that never failed to take Bethell's breath away, was the huge explosion of red and orange which began with not a lot more light than a struck match before swelling volcanically and swarming right up the back of the sky until the great East Moors sun had risen in the night yet again, varnishing the whole of the Bay with liquid reds and shivering golds, making every street and building glow as if on fire.

The ruddy night sun glowed in Hamilton's eyes, the romping

reds bouncing off his house and throwing the whole of the Close into red and black relief. David handed the lance to Nathan and, as he held it aloft in the fiery sky, it actually looked as if it was bleeding.

Most of those at the ropes, which were keeping Hamilton rooted to the same spot, were holding on for grim death, as if they were in a tug-of-war which they just had to win. A few moved out of the way slightly to enable Nathan to lower his lance. As he did so, a great silence trawled through the world.

'So you finally understood it all,' said Hamilton, his hands still tugging on the odd rope but finding no give in any of them. 'You finally understood the terms. Well, go on, then. Do what you can – *if* you can.'

It would be easier, perhaps, if there was no light at all, so Hamilton would not be able to see the point of the lance which was going to kill him. But everything was visible in the red light of the East Moors sun . . .

Nathan could see David helping Effey and Sophie out of the house. Sophie was coughing and choking a lot, hardening Nathan's resolve to do what he had come to do. But then, with an almost superhuman burst of strength, Hamilton seemed to have almost pulled himself free. Now, despite the ropes all around him, he was struggling and stumbling back to the door of his house. A terrible wave of fear and loathing swept through Nathan.

He lunged after him, raising the lance with both hands and plunging it straight down between Hamilton's shoulder blades until it shot straight out through his chest. His legs and arms went awry and as he spun around Nathan saw his eyes bulge and a mouthful of blood shoot out onto the cobblestones. The lance had gone through his heart, killing him instantly.

The sea actually boiled and bubbled for a good three minutes after that slag had first gone screaming into the waves. But the overwhelming dark and cold of the water soon took control again. Only the occasional lump of graphite shot upwards now, and soon even these tiny shooting stars stopped. As the pillars of steam drifted away and Bethell drove his locomotive back into the steelworks, to pick up another load, it was as if nothing had happened at all. The waves regained their normal rhythms, rolling in and breaking on the foreshore, ignoring everything including the great bars of red and gold which were still hanging over the sky and glittering incandescently in their rolling curlers of foam. The waves were just waves, rolling in steadily, resolute and endlessly patient in their long-term task of reshaping the world.

The night was still unusually and oppressively warm as Nathan and the rest of them walked back through the streets to the ship. He helped Sophie along with one arm but none of them seemed to have anything whatever to say about anything. It seemed to be neither victory nor defeat; neither requiem nor aria. Or else perhaps it was because they knew that what was killed one night came back the following morning in a new and even more frightening form.

Nathan was thinking that it might be suitable to have some service of thanksgiving when they got back on board. But who among them felt like doing anything? It was this great tiredness which seemed to be besetting them all, even though something heavy had been lifted in their hearts.

They all waited for a train to pass on the dock railway before crossing over to the West Bute dock where Nathan stopped on the edge of the quay, leaning his weight into Sophie to try and hold her up. She still felt faint from the loss of blood. 'We'll soon be back on the ship, girl,' he said softly. 'Everything will be all right then.'

He stared across the water at *The Solomon*, moored in a glittering blaze of lights; this beautiful mythic animal which had become such an important part of his life. Remembering what the hermit had said, he turned and called for Rashed to give him Hamilton's sword.

Obe took hold of the cup and helped support Sophie as Nathan took the sword from the Moslem leader. Standing on the edge of the dock, he used both hands to whirl it around and around him before letting it fly up into the curdling night, every face and every nationality watching its huge silver blade turn and turn again, glittering and spinning in the red-stained night until it arched downwards and a hand reached up out of the dock waters, catching it by the handle and just holding it there, motionless, suspended about a foot above the water.

And the night was drenched with wonder as the crowd moved up to Nathan, all marvelling at this powerful argument for God and the assembly of his people; this token of His desire to seek out and ultimately defeat all evil. Another rumble of thunder and it began picking with rain, the drops falling all around the suspended sword.

Then a cry rolled through the night but not of pain. This was a cry of the most joyful surrender and all eyes looked up at the skies and at each other as the sword slowly disappeared into the water, leaving just the raindrops pattering down on the cold dark waters in tiny glimmering dartboards.

# CHAPTER THIRTY-THREE

*Or was it just another china dream?*

Sophie had always said that she could withstand storm and hurricane, but the events of the previous few days had snapped something deep within her. When she began jibbering inanely in her bed, an alarmed Nathan arranged for her to be put in a private room in the nearby Hamadryad Hospital.

It was a form of breakdown brought on by severe stress, the doctor said. There was nothing seriously wrong but she would have to be sedated and stay quiet and relaxed for up to two weeks. The hospital authorities agreed to do what they could to keep the public and press away from her.

For Sophie the worst part of her confinement was when the effects of the sedatives had worn off and she could recall, all too clearly, those hours of torture and pain in that blighted house. It all seemed such an endless nightmare and, the more she thought about it, the louder she began shouting for another dose of all those lovely sedatives again. She had seen a lot of people in her business take to heroin and cocaine and, although she had managed to avoid them herself, she now understood their dark attractions.

They all came off the ship to see her, bearing fruit and flowers, but Nathan was there almost constantly, even sitting in her room the long night through as her mind wandered in her sedative dreams. It was a great comfort for her to wake up and see him sitting there reading a book. She liked to pretend that she was still asleep, just looking at him with barely-opened eyes as he sat there with his head bowed, his hands occasionally turning over the pages. She liked to look at those clear, bold features, think about what went on in that big brain, study the enormous curve of his nose, the dark stubble on his cheeks . . .

So much had gone on between them – so many quarrels and times apart that, just now, she thought that they had a deeper union than ever; a union which even transcended their long hours of hospital silence.

But they managed to talk a bit too. Nothing too serious, just gossip about the comings and goings on the ship; what they still needed to do with the sails and how they were going to have her first sea trials any day now. She listened to all this with a smiling sadness since she knew that she would never be going anywhere with them. Oh, she made a few ritual noises about how she could travel to odd parts of the world and spend a week or so with them in a harbour but she knew that she was just trading in delusions again. She would never be able to get used to the spartan life on board that ship – not even for a weekend in port – and certainly did not feel like spending even a few weeks of her life seasick in some bunk. The thing even made her feel seasick when it was moored against the quay.

And then her smiling sadness might just get tinged with a paranoid bitterness and she would start thinking that he was only hanging around like this until she was well enough to return to London; that he was then going to disappear onto the high seas and never think of her again. It was no good. This was no way to recover, she decided, swallowing hard and feeling those hot, useless tears well up again.

It was Obe who brought the 'good news' which, if anything, underlined the growing gulf between her and Nathan. *China Dreams* had sold better than any of her previous records, even *Prisoner of Love*. Robin Constable's sheet music was also in demand, and bands all over the country were besieged by requests for 'her' song. The trouble was that no one still knew where she was. There was even talk of an American tour and the record company was going crazy trying to find her – *everyone* wanted to interview her.

She started crying again. Obe could get nothing out of her; it was particularly difficult to explain that there was just this simple sadness in her heart; that her wretched incoherence was simply because she was being forced away from the people she wanted to be with. Even Obe was sailing with them, so who was going to be left?

'I tried everywhere I knew to find you for *China Dreams*. We really needed a bit of your trumpet magic for that. Come on tour with me, Obe. It could be like the old times. Plenty to drink for everyone.'

Obe gave one of his bright, golden chuckles. 'I can't, sister. The police want a word with me which could end up in a long sentence. They've got five of our boys so the Sons are finished an' I've got to get away. I can't face another prison sentence. I just couldn't do it.'

'You're giving up on everything, are you?'

'Giving up what, sister? We never got anywhere. Perhaps we got it all wrong. I dunno, maybe we should have kissed a few more arses – rather than kicked so many.'

'Nonsense. When would you ever kiss anyone's arse?'

'But whatever have we done? What have we done? We've been going for more than ten years an' there's still not a black bus conductor in Cardiff, still not one black working for the council. What progress is that?'

'They're no yardstick.'

'Results, sister. They're the only yardstick. Just going by the results, the Sons of Africa have failed.'

*The Solomon* was almost eighty yards long with a full crew of sixty-two but, even so, it was remarkably quiet that morning when, with Nathan at the wheel and David in charge of the bridge, two tugs took her out into the lock gate where, surrounded just by the pounding waters of the sluice-gates, they made ready to be towed out into the Bristol Channel.

No one had anything at all to say. They just leaned on the deck rails and gazed out on the slow curves of the waves, wondering if the ship could sail at all. The tugs, as planned, kept their ropes on the ship as the crew went swarming up the ratlines to set the sails, all of them now dangling from the yards like little boys watching a football match from a distant tree. The sails were set one after the other – the royals, the halyards, even the spanker – all eighteen of them as the deck became a fever of activity with lines of men pulling on miles of rope and making them fast.

'Two, four . . . heave!' they shouted. 'Two, four . . . heave!'

'Let's 'ave a bit more muscle now.' 'All right now. And another for the King.'

For the newcomers to the ship this spaghetti of buntlines and clew lines were as endless as they were bewildering. They had a few rehearsals, but had never thought it would be quite as complicated as this, with the bosun, striding up and down, ordering them to belay this or put a bit more muscle into that.

It was a sudden billowing miracle when the quiet Channel winds did fill up the great sails and she moved forward with the gentlest of arthritic creaks. Nathan felt as happy and beautiful as a multicoloured parrot fish as he felt the winds ruffle his hair. The winds also began to make the sails boom softly since they were not catching them quite right so he swung the wheel some six degrees. 'They're all right, Michael,' he said. 'They'll do it.'

Just then he ordered the sails all taken up and reefed to the yards again, unwilling to cover any distance at much of a speed just yet. He just wanted the men to get used to the sails; to know what they were doing should they have to tack in a storm or run for shelter from a violent gale.

He had heard what had once happened to *The Solomon* when she had been crewed by the most experienced of men. The storm had literally almost torn her apart and kept her off the sea for close on thirty years. The lesson that everyone had drummed into him was that, in ships like these, there was never any substitute for experience. You should always treat the sea with total respect.

Sophie was telling herself that she was feeling a lot better, when Effey and David brought her some news which made her feel a lot worse. After four more or less successful trials – more or less because they lost the anchor on one and damaged the bowsprit on another – they were now ready to sail, possibly for Patagonia. It was rather for the whole crew to decide.

'Right, well that's it. I'm not staying to see you off. I just couldn't stand it. I've been in touch with my management. We're going to do a short tour of England then a long tour of America. Don't tell Nathan. I'll just leave quietly, just can't face any more emotional scenes. What are you two going to do?'

'What we always planned,' said Effey. 'We're going to sail

too. We thought we might get married on the ship. That would be nice, wouldn't it?'

'Mm. Very nice.' Oh, this was getting worse. She couldn't take any more of this. She was going to leave now, just as soon as these two left the hospital. With the whole of her world sailing away on that ship she was going to end up being very lonely indeed. Inanely she was even wondering if Richard would be around when she got back to London.

That day, a Saturday, small crowds had been drifting back and forth to the West Bute dock to take a last look at *The Solomon* which was due to begin her maiden voyage on the early evening tide. Coloured buntings and flags hung off the yardarms and there was even talk that a brass band was coming down from Tylorstown to see them off.

Nathan called David to his cabin and the youth immediately saw something was up when he noticed that Nathan had packed his bag. 'I am not sure how to say this, David, but I am not coming with you,' he admitted at last.

The look on David's face showed that he was not entirely surprised.

'We've worked hard and the ship is now as ready as she will ever be. I've been feeling for some time that my work is completed when this ship sails; that I have now been released from what I was asked to do. Such adventures are for the young so I am going to hand the ship over to you. The real truth is that I do not want to leave the Bay – these are my people and I am of them. I'm just too old to go wandering away from my home just now.'

'And Sophie? Has she had anything to do with all this?'

'Yes and no. I was more upset than I thought when she left the other day without even saying goodbye. It's also true that . . . I . . . it would be difficult for me to live out the rest of my life and never know if I was going to see her again. Yes, that much is true. But she's such a volatile woman you can never be quite sure what she's going to do next. You certainly could not build any plans around her. No, I shall find a small place somewhere along Bute Street and perhaps she'll visit me now and then.'

'Are you going to tell the crew?'

'No. You tell them after we've sailed. I'm going to stay on until the last hour but I've arranged for Harry the Boat to pick me up on the other side of the pontoon and row me over to the other dock. It's better that way. We don't want any emotional scenes and I'm mostly worried that Obe might not want to stay on board if he learns that I'm leaving. It's most important that he, of all of us, sails away to try and start a new life.'

'I don't know what to say.'

'Say nothing. Just be happy that you are going to a new world and starting a new life. I want you to take over this cup of ours. Keep it safe because it is precious beyond all the wildest dreams of gold and money. Somehow this cup has been central to our success in making the ship the way it has become. Everything prospers in its presence. They say that, if you drink out of it, you can taste the drink of your own homeland; that, if you eat out of it, you can taste the food of your own homeland. I don't know about any of that but I do know you will all be wholly happy and safe while it is in your possession. Let no one take it from you.'

As the sailing time approached the tempo of the ship became more intense. The Tylorstown Brass Band began playing on the quay with yet more people hurrying back and forth with messages or provisions. On the other side of the Pier Head a woman was standing next to the dock traffic signals weeping copiously because her beloved son was sailing away on *The Solomon* to return who knew when.

Most of the crew were also out on the deck of the windjammer, leaning on the rails, staring down at the face of a loved one or sharing a cigarette. Many of them were still unable to believe that they had finally got there and were about to sail away into a new world.

David listened to the weather forecast on the radio and learned that light falls of snow were imminent, together with a storm building up off Lundy. But they could handle that, he was sure. They were a good crew who had learned to work well together. He wrote the times and forecast into the log before looking out onto the deck where Effey was standing talking with Rashed, her father. Her father!

Effey had also taken the news of Nathan's proposed departure with a surprising calm, guessing that he had secretly decided that he wanted to stay with Sophie. But, there again, she had not so much lost an imaginary father as gained a real one. Rashed had decided to sign up as one of the ship's carpenters and sail with them.

It was Nathan who had finally told Effey the whole story. Her relief at learning the truth, at last, had been immense. Ever since she could remember knowing anything she had always known that her relationship with Sophie was a fiction but, there again, she had never been able to decide why they had been, in so many ways, so alike.

Well, now she knew, and it was warming for David to see her spending so much time with her father, asking him about his life and trying to discover a little more about the circumstances of the start of hers, particularly about her real mother. It was a little difficult for Rashed, a formal Moslem after all, to speak about this 'informal' part of his life but he had decided that he would do the best he could. She had to be careful to be as patient as she could be while Rashed struggled, sometimes in clear pain and at others in pure embarrassment, to tell her what she wanted to know.

Fat snowflakes were already swirling and sliding down into the streets of London as a queue of people began forming outside the entrance to the Kit Kat Club in St James's. Already there might have been one hundred and fifty of them, all holding tickets for the show which was going out live on the radio, in support of an appeal for funds for the Hamadryad Hospital.

It was just a small intimate show to launch her British tour. Inside the club Sophie, wearing just a dressing gown, was going through a series of sound checks on the stage. It had been a very long time since she had done a live radio concert *and* they were recording it too. Clearly there was a lot riding on that voice of hers that night. But, oddly enough, she did not feel nervous. The Queen of Breaking Hearts was feeling too sad to be nervous about much; confident, at least, that her melancholy would quickly be perceived in her songs. The people always knew when you were creating an emotion rather than actually feeling it. They just knew when you were really bleeding, hurting, vulnerable.

She stopped singing and started again. She hummed a few bars as the band leader decided on the final flourishes. She just stood there, incongruously, singing a few verses of *Ain't*

*Misbehaving* at full kick while also holding a cup of tea in both hands. But sometimes the band and the engineers seemed to forget about her altogether – as if she was the most insignificant person in the whole club – leaving her to stand there and look vacantly into space, lost in a pleasant day-dream, when she would abruptly be called out of it by a sound engineer's voice asking a very boring question. She always tried very hard to answer such questions and not get too high and mighty about things. It was at moments like these that stars could start to get complacent and she knew that, for someone like her, complacency would be the death of her career. You really needed to live in a permanent cloud of terror.

The snow was still only falling slightly but enough to drive most of the crew off the deck of *The Solomon* as Nathan quietly slipped down a ladder off the aft deck to let Harry the Boat row him to the other side of the dock. He felt a great mixture of emotions as Harry's oars dipped and pulled in the water – a sadness, inevitably; a little anxiety for the future, perhaps but, mostly, a great pride in what they had all achieved with *The Solomon* – how they had given it the gift of new life.

He looked up at the sky and the fine snowflakes dissolved in his eyes like cold tears. Everywhere the sky was darkening with black and purple clouds, making a strange, surreal panorama of rolling mountains of shadow, shot through with shafts of the brightest light. The brass band was still playing as he stood alone on the other side of the dock watching *The Solomon* leave for the last time.

It was both gut-wrenching and thrilling to see the ship finally slip her moorings and be towed out to the lock gates. He was still not absolutely clear in his own mind why he had decided to leave the ship after he, of all people, had put in so much effort to refloat her. Oh, certainly, Sophie had something to do with it. But mostly, he thought, it was the fact that he had simply become too old. It was time to hand on the flame.

Somewhere in the shifting light patterns of that snowing dockland afternoon he could see a great bird flying around and calling out over the parched, cracked desert. But the bird was not calling out in pain or despair. The desert was brimming over with new life and water. Her young were not lying dead in their nest. The bird was calling out in joyful release from pain since the young had become well and been able to fly away and lead a life of their own. The mother bird was joyful that her life's work had become splendid and right and finished.

He could still see *The Solomon* as it was towed out into the light and shadow of the Cardiff roads, her sails being set one after another until the ship was turned into the winds and she began making speed out into the mouth of the Bristol Channel. It was both lovely and beautiful for him to see the sails being filled up by the great winds of God; all the more touching now that a perfect rainbow had formed over the one side of the ship; its huge arc almost like a multicoloured tunnel of truth into which the ship – Nathan's reborn church – was now sailing at last.

He watched *The Solomon* until she had disappeared. But even so he stayed rooted there for some time, looking out into the afternoon until the snow began coming down so thickly he could now barely see the other side of the dock. He picked up his bag and walked out along the wharves of Queen Alexandra dock until he came to the start of Bute Street and the start of another chapter in his life. But what sort of chapter was this going to be? He hardly dared think about it.

Nevertheless he could hardly remember the old thoroughfare looking so pure and lovely as it did in that lowering twilight. Everything was now covered with almost an inch of snow, the green orbs of the street lamps radiating through those magical, falling flakes which were now settling so evenly it was almost a crime to step on them and spoil the perfect white blanket.

Just walking along; with the snow crunching softly under his feet, it was difficult to believe that this very street had watched several generations battle and fight to set out and define their positions with one another. It was even more difficult to believe that here, on this very pavement, groups had fought through hot, bitter nights about the colour of their skins. It was just over there that a shipload of refugee Barbadians had once walked into his church for shelter. And it was in that church that a young family's dreams and aspirations had once been so cruelly shattered.

And they were all here still this magical snowing night on Bute Street – all the ghosts of old failures and gremlins of unexpected successes; the happy cries and the screams of murder; the spirits of dead horses and the exuberant shouts of jazz . . . all mulched into the very fabric of the evening as everything looked beautiful and new, from the Shipping Exchange to the old cafés, the Salvation Army hostel and the Greek Orthodox church. Even the derelict Spiller's warehouse looked great in the snow.

Just then a voice came spinning out of the drifting darkness which told him so well and eloquently of his life. It was the voice of Sophie doing her concert on the wireless and he stopped and smiled as he heard her open up with *Ain't Misbehaving*. But you were always misbehaving, Sophie, he breathed to himself. Even when you were trying to behave you were misbehaving. He moved closer to the house where the wireless was on, enjoying the shouts and applause at the end of the song.

'Some rather special people are sailing on a rather special ship out of Cardiff tonight,' Sophie said. 'This is just for them.'

She was always surprised at how vividly the images of the Bay sprang into her mind when she began singing the first verse of *Prisoner of Love*. Every corner of her mind ran amok with the images of her life; those twisting, screaming streets in which she had grown and loved and lost. She saw the high office buildings around the Exchange and the waves of the Bristol Channel glimmering beneath rolling hoops of sunshine. She saw Nathan smiling at her and Effey teasing her. She saw Rashed when he was young and wild, and right there, in the middle of it all, was Obe lifting his great magical trumpet which just shattered you with its beautiful audacity.

The song had intimate memories for Nathan too. His hand rested against the cold brick wall of the house as she continued into the rest of the verses. He was at perfect peace with himself; in the middle of listening to those much-loved lyrics, he understood it all. He understood why he had been brought to the Bay and how it had not all been for nothing. He understood that he had become a man of the Bay; an indivisible part of the human rainbow; a son of a city which had herself been born in coal, blood, jazz and fire.

But, perhaps most importantly, he understood that man is no more than the sum of his weaknesses which keep undermining him; that there is no great shame in failure but there is a very great shame in not trying again.

And, when he understood these things, he died, that night of March 2, 1939, at eight o'clock, on the corner of James Street. His body just gave up and he could actually feel his hands running down the brick wall as his body slumped to the ground. He lay there for a few seconds and moved around a bit to make himself comfortable as the snow began piling up against him. Then he saw the shoes of a passing stranger who, taking one look at him, hurried on. The next moment he saw nothing at all.

A dog was barking in the distance and a seagull flew along Bute Street towards the high pencil tower of Cardiff Castle, crying with what sounded like a joyful cry of release. Meanwhile, on the radio, Sophie was moving into the final verse of *Prisoner of Love*, singing it with more passion and feeling than she had ever sung it before.

# Daughters
## Consuelo Saah Baehr

*Daughters* is an unforgettable story of courage, love and hope; of two worlds – one ancient, one modern – and of the extraordinary women who bridge them.

Miriam Mishwe is born into a Palestinian Christian family in the last years of the nineteenth century. She marries a man chosen by her family, but centuries-old traditions are on the verge of upheaval.

Nadia is Miriam's daughter. Sent to a local British school, she adopts many modern ideas but is not yet ready to renounce her heritage.

Nijmeh, Nadia's daughter, is the one who will call herself by her English name, Star, and go to live in America. There she will face problems of a new and unknown kind . . .

'A long, richly textured novel filled with wonderful characters and an extraordinary sense of historical detail. Consuelo Saah Baehr has written a blockbuster with a heart.'
Susan Isaacs, author of *Almost Paradise* and *Shining Through*

FONTANA PAPERBACKS

# The Cloning of Joanna May

## Fay Weldon

Joanna May thought herself unique, indivisible – until one day, to her hideous shock, she discovered herself to be five: that though childless she was a mother: that though an only child she was surrounded by sisters young enough to be her daughters – Jane, Julie, Gina and Alice, the clones of Joanna May.

What will it be like for Joanna when she meets the clones? And what about the clones themselves? How are they different and how the same? Will they withstand the shock of first meeting? And what of the avenging Carl, Joanna's former husband and the clones' creator; will he take revenge for his wife's infidelity and destroy her sisters one by one?

In this astonishing novel, Fay Weldon weaves a web of paradox quite awesome in its cunning. Probing into the strange world of genetic engineering, *The Cloning of Joanna May* raises frightening questions about our very identity as individuals – and provides some startling answers. Funny, serious, revolutionary, this is the work of a master storyteller at the height of her powers.

FONTANA PAPERBACKS

# The Sins of Rebeccah Russell

## Arabella Seymour

As a child, Rebeccah Russell discovers that her adored father has two other children: Jamie, jealous and embittered is his only son – and favourite; Alice, Rebeccah's half-sister, has a mother who will stop at nothing to ensure her daughter is generously provided for.

As a young woman, Rebeccah falls prey to the charms of fortune-hunter Rufus Waldo, a dangerous man whose veneer of respectability masks a secret life.

Innocent and vulnerable, unable to trust her husband or family, Rebeccah finds her nightmare only just beginning . . .

FONTANA PAPERBACKS

# Stranger in Savannah
## Eugenia Price

The hearts of three families and the soul of a nation – torn by the passions of the civil war.

*Stranger in Savannah* continues the saga of the Browning, Mackay and Stiles families as they, and their country, are torn by civil war. Here are the turbulence and passion, drama and heartbreak, of a nation struggling within itself. For, as the Civil War shatters the United States, it also brutally tests the strength, love and faith of the Savannah families as they come face-to-face with the conflict that threatens to destroy them – and their way of life – forever.

The Savannah Quartet:

*Savannah*
*To See Your Face Again*
*Before the Darkness Falls*
*Stranger in Savannah*

are all available in Fontana Paperbacks

FONTANA PAPERBACKS